Advance Praise for Claudia Moscovici's *Velvet Totalitarianism*

A deeply felt, deftly rendered novel of the utmost importance to any reader interested in understanding totalitarianism and its terrible human cost. Urgent, evocative, and utterly convincing, *Velvet Totalitarianism* is a book to treasure, and Claudia Moscovici is indeed a writer to watch, now and into the future.

--Travis Holland, author of the critically acclaimed novel, *The Archivist's Story*, a Barnes & Noble *Discover Great New Writers* selection.

Claudia Moscovici's first novel, *Velvet Totalitarianism*, triumphs on several levels: as a taut political thriller, as a meditation on totalitarianism, as an expose of the Ceausescu regime, and as a moving fictionalized memoir of one family's quest for freedom.

--Ken Kalfus, author of the novel *A Disorder Peculiar to the Country* (2006 *National Book Award* nominee), of *The Commissariat of Enlightenment* (2003) and of *PU-239 and Other Russian Fantasies* (1999).

Western intellectuals have often blurred the fundamental differences between the imperfect free world they have been fortunate to enjoy and the totalitarian world of communism they never had the misfortune to endure. Claudia Moscovici's *Velvet Totalitarianism* is a powerful corrective to that ivory tower distortion of reality. Moscovici makes her readers viscerally feel the corrosive psychological demoralization and numbing fear totalitarian regimes impose on those who live under them. At the same time, with style and wit, and informed by her experiences as a child in communist Romania and then as an immigrant in the United States, she tells a story of resilience and hope. *Velvet Totalitarianism* is a novel well worth reading, both for its compelling narrative and for its important message.

--Michael Kort, Professor of Social Science at Boston University and author of the best-selling textbook, *The Soviet Colossus*: *History and Aftermath*

This vivid novel by Claudia Moscovici, historian of ideas and wide-ranging literary critic, traces a family of Jewish-Romanian refugees from the stifling communist dictatorship of their homeland through their settling in the United States during the 1980's. This fascinating and compelling story is at once historically accurate, exciting, sexy and a real page-turner. Ms. Moscovici is as sensitive to the emotions of her characters as to their political entanglements.

--Edward K. Kaplan, Kevy and Hortense Kaiserman Professor in the Humanities at Brandeis University and author of Spiritual *Radical: Abraham Joshua Heschel in America*, 1940-1972, winner of the *National Jewish Book Award*

Moving between extraordinary and ordinary lives, between Romania and the United States, velvet totalitarianism and relative freedom, dire need and consumerism, evoking her Romanian experience in the seventies, the emigration to the U.S. of her family in the eighties, and the 1989 uprising in Timisoara and Bucharest that marked the end of Ceausescu's regime, Claudia Moscovici offers her readers a multifaceted book—*Velvet Totalitarianism*—that is at once a love story, a political novel and a mystery. Love is the last resort left to people in order to counter totalitarianism under Ceausescu's rule. It keeps families united, allowing them to resist indoctrination and hardship and to make sure their children enjoy the carefree beautiful years that are their due. Love gives the protagonist of the novel the strength to overcome cultural differences between Romania and the U.S. and to invent in turn a form of personal happiness in a context that, while far from being as harsh as her initial one, does not lack its own problems.

--Sanda Golopentia, Professor of French, Brown University

Cold historical facts and figures tend to leave us emotionally indifferent. The impact of a nation's tragic events on one single person or family is much better understood and more profoundly felt. This is what makes Claudia Moscovici's book, *Velvet Totalitarianism*, so very special. Her novel is prefaced by a well-researched history of Romania under communism. Depending on one's point of view, Moscovici's work could be considered as the fictionalized story of a real Jewish-Romanian family under communism, based on her own recollections and that of her family and supported by true historical facts; or a brief history supported by the fictionalized story of a real family. It's a book well worth reading. The novel is a page-turner, witty and well written.

--Nicolae Klepper, author of the best-selling book, *Romania: An Illustrated History*.

Velvet Totalitarianism

Post-Stalinist Romania

Claudia Moscovici

University Press of America,® Inc.

Lanham · Boulder · New York · Toronto · Plymouth, UK

Copyright © 2009 by
University Press of America,® Inc.
4501 Forbes Boulevard
Suite 200
Lanham, Maryland 20706
UPA Acquisitions Department (301) 459-3366

Estover Road
Plymouth PL6 7PY
United Kingdom

Library of Congress Control Number: 2009927837
ISBN-13: 978-0-7618-4693-2 (paperback : alk. paper)
ISBN-10: 0-7618-4693-X (paperback : alk. paper)
eISBN-13: 978-0-7618-4694-9
eISBN-10: 0-7618-4694-8

Cover art: "Red Amy," oil on canvas, Edson Campos, 2009

⊖™ The paper used in this publication meets the minimum
requirements of American National Standard for Information
Sciences—Permanence of Paper for Printed Library Materials,
ANSI Z39.48-1992

*With love and gratitude to my parents, Henri and Elvira Moscovici,
whose life stories are the inspiration for this book*

Contents

Acknowledgements

Reincarnations of Love is a novel about a family surviving difficult times under a totalitarian regime due to the strength of their love. This work was made possible by the love I felt from my own family. First of all, I'd like to thank my parents, Henri and Elvira Moscovici, for sharing with me their life experiences and for consistently encouraging my artistic and intellectual endeavors. I'm also very grateful to my grandparents, Gina and Mitica Buzulica and Surica and Avram Moscovici, who helped raise me during my childhood in Romania. Without their patience and devotion, I wouldn't have had such a beautiful childhood in those trying circumstances. Through his unwavering loyalty, friendship and love, my husband, Dan Troyka, has shown me what a real reincarnation of love is all about. I treasure him and the rebirth of our marriage. This book is written above all for our children, Sophie and Alex, so that they discover part of their cultural heritage and come to appreciate even more the rights and freedoms they enjoy here.

Velvet Totalitarianism:
Post-Stalinist Romania

Totalitarianism is a modern phenomenon. It is stronger and more intrusive than dictatorship or autocracy. Totalitarian regimes control not only the state, the military, the judicial system and the press, but also reach into people's minds, to dictate what they should say, think and feel. Hannah Arendt has argued in *The Origins of Totalitarianism* that one of the key features of the totalitarian state is its system of indoctrination, propaganda, isolation, intimidation and brainwashing—instigated and supervised by the Secret Police—which transforms *classes*, or thoughtful individuals able to make relatively sound political decisions, into *masses*, or people who have been so beaten down that they become apathetic and give their unconditional loyalty to the totalitarian regime. Although scholars such as Hannah Arendt, Robert Conquest and Vladimir Tismaneanu have elegantly explained the rise (and fall) of communist governments in Eastern Europe, it's the vivid descriptions we find in the fiction and memoirs of the epoch--George Orwell's *1984*, Arthur Koestler's *Darkness at Noon*, Natalia Ginsburg's *Journey into the Whirlwind* and Lena Constante's *The Silent Escape*—that take readers into the daily horrors, the dramatic Kafkaesque show trials, the physical and psychological torture and the general sense of hopelessness that characterizes life under totalitarian regimes. The writers I have just mentioned tend to focus mostly on the Stalinist period, during which the state governed through arbitrary displays of power and terror, sending millions of people to their deaths in labor and concentration camps. Yet as many who lived under totalitarian rule in Eastern Europe during the post-Stalinist era would claim, the milder, "velvet" form of totalitarianism was depressing and depleting in its own way, killing people's hope and humanity even though it did not physically claim as many lives.

This book introduces students and the general public to the post-Stalinist phase of totalitarianism, focusing on Romania under the Ceausescu dictatorship, through the dual optic of scholarship and fiction. First I provide information about the Ceausescu regime: its feared *Securitate* (or Secret Police); the human rights abuses and outrageous domestic policies which left the Romanian people hungry and demoralized; the dictator's narcissistic personality cult; the infamous orphanages, which were a direct result of the regime's inhumane and irrational birth control policies, and the events that led to the Romanian revolution, first in the Timisoara uprising and then in Bucharest, where the dictator and his wife were deposed, put on their own show trial and executed in December, 1989. To do so, I synthesize information presented by other scholarly works, memoirs and textbooks on the subject, including Vladimir Tismaneanu's *Stalinism for all Seasons* (2003), Peter Cipokowski's *Revolution in Eastern Europe* (1991), Andrei Codrescu's *A Hole in the Flag* (1991) and Ion Pacepa's *Red Horizons* (1987).

Then I translate these events into fiction, to give readers a more palpable sense of what it felt like to live in Romania under the Ceausescu regime. I also attempt to capture the mixture of cynicism and hope that characterized one of the most bloody anti-communist revolutions in Eastern Europe. My novel, *Reincarnations of Love*, depicts the experiences of a family living under the Ceausescu regime whose son gets entangled in a web set up by the *Securitate*. The story then traces the family's difficult process of immigrating to the United States as well as the sometimes comical cultural challenges of adapting to America. The main characters arrive in Eastern Europe on vacation during the period of revolutionary upheavals in both Czechoslovakia and Romania, whose events they witness first-hand.

The parts of the novel that focus specifically on Romania constitute more of a fictionalized autobiography or a memoir in that they're partly based on my family's personal experience of communism. I say "fictionalized" since having left Romania at the age of eleven, my memories are undoubtedly skewed by a childlike perspective as well as by the passage of time. The factual information about the *Securitate*, Ceausescu's policies and the Romanian revolution I depict here, however, is also based on research rather than just on memories and anecdotal accounts. The fiction inspired by real life helps individuate a mass phenomenon. In a post-Cold War era where totalitarian communism has become just another page in history books, fact and fiction are complimentary rather than opposites. Fiction can make what may now seem like a long-gone, dead epoch, and the anonymous suffering of millions of people, seem vivid, significant and real again.

Yet whichever perspective one chooses, fact or fiction, what is being described here is essentially the same reality: conditions in Romania during the so-called "Epoch of Light" were notoriously miserable. People had to wait in long lines for meager supplies of food, clothing and household goods. There was limited heat and hot water. By the late 1970's, the Secret Police had installed microphones in virtually every home and apartment. The whole population lived in fear. As a Romanian citizen said to a French journalist following the fall of the Ceausescu regime, "It was a system that didn't destroy people physically— not many were actually killed; but it was a system that condemned us to a fight for the lowest possible level of physical and spiritual nourishment. Under Ceausescu, some people died violently, but an entire population was dying."

Although this book focuses mostly on Romania, hundreds of millions of Eastern Europeans led similar lives to the ones I describe, struggling daily against poverty, hunger, state indoctrination, surveillance, censorship and oppression in post-Stalinist communist regimes. In actuality, "velvet" totalitarianism was insidious rather than soft and gentle, killing your spirit even when it spared your life.

Romanian Stalinism and Post-Stalinism

Stalinism has at least two different meanings. It can refer to the reign of terror imposed by Stalin himself and by other similar communist dictators during his lifetime throughout Eastern Europe. Or it can mean a totalitarian regime that maintains power through fear and indoctrination in somewhat more subtle ways. In the first sense, Romania was Stalinist during the administration of Gheorghe Gheorghiu-Dej (1948-1965). Gheorghiu-Dej, like his Soviet role model, undertook a program of forced industrialization and elimination of private property. He relied upon public show trials--the most spectacular of which was that of his former Minister of Justice, Lucretiu Patrascanu--to increase his power. He also sent tens of thousands of people to prison and labor camps. Compared to Gheorghiu-Dej's Stalinism, Nicolae Ceausescu's regime (1965-1989) initially showed some promise of becoming post-Stalinist. During the first few years of his leadership, from July, 1965 when he consolidated power to the early 1970's, Ceausescu carried out a thaw of Stalinist communism, which is referred to as the honeymoon period of his rule.

As Vladimir Tismaneanu notes in *Stalinism for all Seasons*, initially the dictator who'd become one of the most despised in Eastern Europe—rivaled perhaps only by Albania's Enver Hoxha—seemed to offer the country renewed hope that communism could include a sense of national autonomy and coexist with (limited) civil rights, (some) freedom of expression and domestic policies that would not economically cripple the country. Of course, in some sense, as Tismaneanu convincingly argues, Romanian communism remained Stalinist. Even the apparent relaxation of totalitarian rule that Ceausescu initially promoted served his Stalinist goal of gradually establishing sole and total control of the state by increasing his popularity, eliminating potential rivals and propagating his all-encompassing personality cult.

By November 1989, it was very clear that the Ceausescu regime had failed to fulfill any of its early promises. The Romanian leader had distinguished himself as one of the worst rulers in Eastern Europe through his dictatorial style, dynastic politics, the country's increasing isolation, the malicious ineffectiveness of his economic policies which created poverty and even famine, the lack of any kind of civil liberties and an ideological dogmatism that served largely personal goals. By the time Ceausescu and his wife Elena were executed on December 25, 1989, the so-called "maverick" of Eastern Europe had become a "dinosaur" among communist leaders, as the revolutionaries called him. I'd like to describe next some of the policies that led Romania along this downward spiral and eventually precipitated the anti-communist revolution.

Nicolae Ceausescu and his Rule (1965-1989)

When Gheorghe-Gheorghiu Dej died in March 1965, Nicolae Ceausescu was only one of his possible successors. Immediately following Gheorghiu-Dej's death, three individuals ruled Romania: Nicolae Ceausescu, the party's first secretary; Chiviu Stoica, the state council president and Ion Gheorghe Maurer, the premier. Like Stalin, who chose the strategic position of state secretary to consolidate power by placing supporters in the government bureaucracy, Ceausescu lost no time in networking and taking control of the country to eliminate his rivals. Due to his maneuverings, Alexandru Draghici lost his post of Minister of Interior in 1965. By the end of 1969, Ceausescu had accumulated a variety of titles, including State Council President and Supreme Military Commander. He also attained control of the Central Committee.

When useful and convenient, Ceausescu followed some of Gheorghiu-Dej's policies. After Stalin's death, Gheorghiu-Dej began to distance himself from the Soviet Union, proposing instead a national communism. He worried that the thaw of totalitarian power initiated by Khrushchev might rub off on Romania and that, as a result, his authoritarian rule might be challenged. Ceausescu also pursued this "Romanization" policy to maintain a degree of autonomy from the Soviet Union. He played upon nationalist feelings by talking about the (long-gone) Nazi threat and by reviving the image of the country's legendary rulers, such as Michael the Brave and Stephen the Great, portraying himself as the apex of this lineage. Propaganda in schools and on the state controlled media, which constantly highlighted the ruler's supposed accomplishments in all areas of life, served to propagate his larger-than-life image. While constantly ranting against the threat of capitalism in his national broadcasts, Ceausescu convincingly presented himself abroad as a "maverick" sympathetic to Western governments and relatively independent of Soviet influence. Such propaganda increased his popularity in the West during the peak of the Cold War.

On the national front, Ceausescu simultaneously distanced himself from Gheorghiu-Dej by portraying himself as a proponent of relative liberalism, to gain trust and popularity. Economic conditions were initially on his side as well. During the late 1960's and early 1970's, he tapped the country's natural resources, labor supply and savings and made good use of Western trade concessions and foreign credits. As a result, Romania enjoyed a period of unprecedented prosperity. This corresponded to a cultural liberalization, where controls upon the media and the intelligentsia were relaxed and some Romanian intellectuals and scientists were allowed to travel abroad for professional conferences. J. F. Brown notes that in the mid 1960's, "Relaxation in the cultural and academic fields became more pronounced, and in June 1965, the new 'socialist' constitution introduced more safeguards for the liberty of the individual... A comprehensive reform program would immeasurably strengthen the popular support the regime had already gained by its nationalist policy." (*The New Eastern Europe*, 71)

As with Stalin, however, it can be argued that for Ceausescu all political moves, including the thaw of totalitarian rule itself, were strategically calculated to consolidate power. At any rate, by the early 1970's, he started to reverse the current of liberalization. In 1971 Ceausescu visited China and was very impressed by Mao Zedong's personality cult. Upon his return, he removed Maurer from office as well as other potential rivals and those associated with the earlier economic reforms. He replaced them with family members and cronies, even going so far as to institute his wife, Elena, as a member of the Politburo in 1974. This set the tone for the rest of his rule, which would be one of "dynastic socialism."

During the late 1970's, the economy faltered. Natural and human resources had been tapped. Ceausescu tightened the economic controls and invested in a few high-risk, expensive ventures, which included restarting work on the Danube Black Sea Canal (or the "Canal of Death," as it was called because it was built through forced labor during Gheorghiu-Dej's administration) and constructing huge steel and petrochemical plants. Overall, these projects proved unsuccessful. Oil production declined; laborers felt they had little incentive to work. In addition, a drought and the earthquake of 1977 also slowed down production. Ceausescu began to be criticized abroad as well, as stories about some of his human rights violations, censorship and the country's dire poverty leaked out to the Western media.

In response, the dictator clamped down tighter on the Iron Curtain. He imposed a program of paying off the foreign debt not only for economic motives, but also to further detach Romania from other countries. During the early 1980's, his foreign policy became one of "national autonomy" and "noninterference," as Ceausescu distanced himself from Western capitalist countries as well as from the rest of the Eastern Block. He openly repudiated the "Brezhnev Doctrine," which postulated that the Soviet Union had the right to intervene in satellite countries if it perceived a threat to communist control.

By the mid 1980's, the country was isolated, its economy bleak and its people demoralized and living in squalor. To add insult to injury, Romanians were constantly bombarded with the ruler's propaganda that they were basking in the "Epoch of Light," supposedly the most flourishing period of the country's history. To maintain this false image, stores were quickly stacked with supplies whenever Ceausescu or other high government officials inspected them while regular people scrounged around for food and consumer goods, awaiting meager supplies in long lines each day. As the Soviet Union began undergoing *perestroika* under Mikhail Gorbachev, or the more liberal "restructuring" of its economy, Romania struggled in the grip of one of its darkest periods, weakened by an economic crisis and under the control of a dictator's whose policies had crossed the line from being simply misguided to being downright insane. By the end of Ceausescu's reign, the dictator's son, Nicu Ceausescu, whose sociopathic tendencies rivaled those of Saddam Hussein's sons, was positioned to be next in command upon his father's death. This led Romanians to suspect that their country was facing an even bleaker future, if that were possible. As Tismaneanu aptly puts it, "By the end of his life, Ceausescu had nothing to offer but his hollow rhetoric and hysterical cries for more repression... By the end of the 1980's the Romanian Communist Party was for all practical purposes already extinct. All that remained of it were a series of ill-concocted legends and huge gatherings of robotlike individuals, mechanically applauding the dictator." (*Stalinism for all Seasons*, 28)

The Secret Police, or Securitate

Neither Stalin nor Gheorghiu-Dej nor Ceausescu himself could have established such total control of society and government without the key instrument of enforcing their power and the main way in which they kept their people living in fear, for their well-being if not actually their lives: the Secret Police. Founded on August 30, 1948, it's no accident that the Romanian Secret Police, colloquially called the *Securitate* and officially called the *State Security Department,* resembled Stalin's notorious NKVD (the *People's Commissariat for Internal Affairs*). The *Securitate* was created with the help of SMERSH, the NKVD unit in charge of replacing local intelligence agencies with a Soviet-style Secret Police in Eastern-Block satellite countries. In proportion to the population of the country, the *Securitate* grew to be one of the largest Secret Police forces in Eastern Europe. It began with 3,549 positions in 1949 and by January 1956 it had acquired 25,468 employees. This figure does not even include the approximately half a million informants, or moles that infiltrated all areas of work, whose job was to spy upon fellow Romanians and take note of any "suspicious" or "unpatriotic" behavior that deviated from the party line.

By 1977 the *Securitate* had installed hidden microphones in every telephone sold in Romania—there was only one model, which came in several colors to give people the illusion of choice. A section of the *Securitate*, called the *General Directorate for Technical Operations*, monitored nearly all of the telephone conversations in the country. They paid special attention to citizens who had any kind of contact with the West or expressed nonconformist political views. Sometimes the plot of sensational movies like the James Bond series are partly based on fact. As Ion Pacepa, the deputy chief of the *Romanian Foreign Intelligence Service* who defected to the U.S. in 1978 documents, hotels, especially the high-end ones frequented by international tourists, were infiltrated with prostitute-agents hired to seduce foreigners and obtain confidential information. Even outside the country, Romanian citizens weren't necessarily safe. The *Securitate* targeted those whom the government considered traitors or disloyal to the regime by hiring special agents (or local thugs) to intimidate, assault and sometimes even assassinate them during their visits abroad. Ceausescu felt a particularly personal rancor against those who spoke out against his regime on *Radio Free Europe and Radio Liberty*, the radio and communications organizations founded by the United States and sponsored by the *CIA* to promote democratic values throughout the world.

Some of the spying was mutual, a kind of tacit agreement between East and West to seek out industrial and political secrets. Ceausescu took such "cooperation" very seriously. As Pacepa explains, "Cooperative and joint ventures with the West became fashionable in the Soviet bloc after they proved their usefulness at providing new technology by both legal and illegal means. The general rule is that all bloc citizens involved in such joint ventures should be intelligence officers. Ceausescu ordered the DIE to make intensive use of every new cooperative venture for infiltrating small armies of intelligence officers in the West." (*Red Horizons*, 336)

The *National Commission for Visas and Passports*, another branch of the *Securitate*, controlled all travel and emigration in and out of Romania. Permission to travel to Western countries was difficult to obtain during the late 1970's and became practically impossible to get by the early 1980's. All Romanians who visited Western countries for either professional or personal reasons—and sometimes their families as well—were automatically considered suspect and placed under stricter government surveillance. Citizens who filed for immigration were usually fired from their jobs and subjected to demoralizing interrogations by *Securitate* agents especially trained in brainwashing and psychological intimidation. The interrogation sessions sought to obtain possibly incriminating information from the subjects as well as to instill self-doubt and weaken their loyalty to family members abroad and their resolve to leave Romania. Like in Orwell's *1984*, family members, colleagues and friends were offered incentives—money, gifts, benefits, promotions or higher salaries—to "cooperate" with the *Securitate* by becoming government informants and making often false or exaggerated allegations to incriminate each other.

The *Directorate for Security Troops* included a paramilitary force made up of 20,000 individuals who were trained to guard the state television and radio stations as well as the communist party buildings. Since Ceausescu feared a coup even more than he worried about an invasion from other countries, these special troops had five times as many officers as the regular troops trained for the country's defense. Security officers were also subject to a more thorough ideological indoctrination. This may explain why during the Romanian revolution some of the members the Security troops remained fiercely loyal to the regime, firing into the civilian crowd upon Ceausescu's orders. Others, however, proved to be more agnostic, turning against the communist government once they sensed its vulnerability.

During the 1980's, when Ceausescu grew increasingly suspicious of secret plots to oust him, the *Securitate* launched a massive campaign designed to instill fear in the population and wipe out any potential dissent. Anything could be used against you to tarnish your "dossier," or *Securitate* file: contact with the West, family members who defected or emigrated, travel abroad, statements that could be construed as critical of the government or any kind of praise of capitalism, democracy and Western values. Firings, denunciations, machinations and frame-ups became commonplace by the late 1980's, as the dictator struggled to maintain control of the country, or "pull in the ranks" as he preferred to call the repression. Whereas during the 1960's Ceausescu had encouraged intellectuals in the arts, social sciences and humanities to recreate a sense of national heritage, by the end of his reign he tended to regard intellectuals with a profound sense of distrust. Even the term "intellectual" itself was used as an insult, often regarded as synonymous with "traitor."

Birth Control Policies and the Romanian Orphanages

From the beginning, Ceausescu made rapid industrialization a cornerstone of his domestic policy. During the 1960's, however, the country approximated zero population growth, which meant, in the long run, a reduced labor force. In response, Ceausescu abolished abortion in 1966, except for cases of rape, incest and danger to the life of the mother or if the mother was over 45 years old and had given birth to at least four children. Later, he introduced more punitive pronatalist measures to offer Romanian citizens further incentives to have more children. The government increased taxes for men and women who remained childless after the age of 25. In 1967 Ceausescu practically abolished divorce. A miniscule quota of maximum 28 divorces was allowed in the whole country that year. The government also offered some positive incentives. Mothers received a monetary reward upon the birth of their third child and the income taxes of couples with three or more children were lowered by 30 percent.

The policy that proved to have disastrous consequences for the country was the abolition of birth control. Contraceptives, which were not manufactured in Romania, were banned, making effective birth control extremely difficult. Initially, the birth rate rose dramatically, but then quickly declined again as women began resorting to dangerous, illegal abortions, which could sometimes be obtained in exchange for a carton of Kent cigarettes. By the early 1980's, the government took more intrusive measures to regulate women's reproductive cycles. Doctors performed mandatory monthly gynecological exams on all women of reproductive age to detect and monitor pregnancies. The government also launched a propaganda campaign praising "patriotic" couples that had several children. These measures, however, failed to achieve the desired results. After decades of repressive policies, birthrates in Romania were only slightly higher than those of nations where abortion was legal. However, these draconian measures did manage to increase the number of *unwanted* children, many of whom were put up for adoption in Romania's infamous orphanages, which began to receive international media attention during the 1980's.

By the end of Ceausescu's dictatorship, there were approximately 100,000 children in Romania's orphanages. Given the regime's pronatalist policies and the country's low standard of living, many families were placed in the impossible position of choosing between food and their newborn babies. Thousands of children were placed in orphanages whose living conditions resembled those of concentration camps. SoRelle notes that even older children were not potty trained and were left to wallow in their own waste. Children slept huddled together on cots or on the floor, covered by the soiled blankets. Many lacked shoes or appropriate clothing for the cold winters. Many were also lice infested because of the unhygienic conditions and lack of proper cleaning supplies. Dunlap observes that orphanages didn't have disinfectant, soap and hot water. Diseases were rampant and medical care insufficient. Instead of playing with toys, the orphans played with dirty needles. Babies lacked proper attention and children were left unattended and uneducated, remaining illiterate into their teens. Even the international attention such a blatant human rights violation received did nothing to change the dictator's pronatalist policies or the appalling conditions of the Romanian orphanages.

The Romanian Revolution of December, 1989

When the regimes of other Eastern Block countries toppled, Ceausescu characteristically refused to see the writing on the wall. Even after the fall of East Germany's Erich Honecker, he continued his hard-lined course, warning Romanians that anti-socialist opposition would not be tolerated in his country. In some sense, the Romanian leader had built himself a buffer. For several years, he had established himself as the absolute leader of the Communist Party and surrounded himself only with family members and cronies. His wife, Elena, and Central Committee Secretary Emil Bobu decided all of the key personnel appointments. Their youngest son, Nicu, had become the head of the party organization in Sibiu and was being prepared to take over the country after his father's death. Although Romania was more autocratic than the surrounding politburo governed communist countries, there were some signs of internal dissent. In early March, 1989 six former top Party officials—which included a foreign minister and three founders of the *Romanian Communist Party*--handed in their resignation in an "open letter" that attacked Ceausescu's personality cult, his dictatorial style, his disastrous economic policies and his violation of the 1975 Helsinki accord on human rights. The regime responded by promptly arresting all six individuals who signed the letter and condemning them to internal exile.

The real triggering event of the Romanian Revolution proved to be a showdown in Timisoara, a Western frontier town where ethnic Romanians,

Hungarians and Germans coexisted and sometimes intermarried. A group of protestors gathered around the house of Reverent Laszlo Tokes, a pastor of the *Reformed Church of Timisoara*, who was placed under house arrest for his outspoken defense of religious freedom. Reverend Tokes appealed to fellow ethnic Hungarians, students and intellectuals for his outspoken criticism of the government's repression of civil rights. He also attracted the attention of the *Securitate*, who began to monitor his movements and intimidate his followers. Four *Securitate* thugs broke into Tokes's home and cut his face with a knife. Tokes, however, courageously continued to preach his beliefs. The *Securitate* responded by sending the minister an eviction notice from his residence. On Sunday, December 10th, Tokes gathered his congregation around his house and told them what was going to happen. When the authorities came to arrest the pastor, his supporters formed a human chain around him to protect him. In response, the *Securitate* troops opened fire on them. The next day more Romanian citizens took to the streets, protesting the state repression and the massacre of innocent civilians. By December 20th, 1989 the city had been seized by the protesters and by a few opportunistic vandals. Most marched peacefully in support of human rights while a few overturned and burned cars, looted stores and threw Molotov cocktails into the Town Hall.

Underestimating the effect this regional uprising would have upon the rest of the country, Ceausescu left for a previously scheduled visit to Iran. When he returned to Bucharest on December 20th, he addressed the nation on television to criticize the Timisoara uprising as started by "a few groups of hooligan elements." He also scheduled a demonstration in support of the government for the following day. As usual, the Communist Party apparatus organized the demonstration, handing out propagandistic banners and planting their members in the audience.

On the day of the rally, Ceausescu stood on the balcony with his wife and other members of the *Political Executive Committee* behind him. From the front rows, pro-government supporters cheered him on. A few minutes into the dictator's speech, someone shook a lamp, which collapsed. A woman screamed. Some of the people around her thought that the *Securitate* had shot her. A momentary panic ensued. Someone shouted, "Timisoara! Timisoara!" Other voices of protest joined in. "Rat!" someone else screamed. "Down with Ceausescu!" shouted others. Not used to such public manifestations of dissent, Ceausescu was caught off guard and didn't know how to react. He waved his arms and said "No, no, hello?" as if he hadn't heard right. Prompted by his wife from behind, he eventually continued his speech, but the damage had already been done. On that day, his vulnerability was exposed on air to the whole country.

The government's downfall happened the very next day. Ceausescu attempted to save face by once again addressing crowds from the balcony of the *Central Committee* building. But this time the protests against the regime were even more vocal: "Down with Ceausescu!" people shouted. Ceausescu ordered the army to fire into the crowd. Apparently the Minister of Defense refused and was shot for his insubordination. Ceausescu and his wife escaped with a *Securitate* helicopter that whisked them away from the roof and landed near Tirgoviste. The dictator and his entourage hid in a seed distribution center, but were shortly found and brought to trial by members of the provisional government. In their cursory show trial, Nicolae and Elena Ceausescu were charged with "serious crimes against the people, which are incompatible with human dignity," as well as with genocide and sabotage of the national economy. The couple remained united and defiant to the end and was executed on December 25, 1989. Romanians followed these events on national television with great excitement and much hope. When the provisional government, which called itself the *Front for National Salvation*, announced the Ceausescus' capture and the collapse of the communist government, most people were euphoric. But as Tismaneanu observes, genuine political and economic reform came much slower and more painfully for a country that had endured decades of totalitarian repression, had a weak tradition for democracy and no capitalist infrastructure.

Writing Politics

It's one thing to read about the institutions and events that characterized life in totalitarian Romania and quite another to have lived through them. For my family and I, the events I describe in this book are real. Like everyone else, we were subject to constant state indoctrination. Like practically everyone else except for the very privileged, we waited in long lines for meager supplies of food and consumer goods. Since my father traveled abroad, our apartment was bugged—we discovered hidden microphones underneath his desk and inside the heating units--and the *Securitate* followed my parents' movements. My father worked at the mathematics institute. His boss was Nicolae Ceausescu's daughter, Zoe Ceausescu, who actually went against some of her father's policies by allowing him to go to scholarly conferences abroad. This rare privilege was essential to a mathematician's—or, for that matter, any intellectual's--career. Nobody can thrive intellectually without a free exchange of information and an awareness of the latest international discoveries in one's field. In spite of Zoe Ceausescu's umbrage, however, my father was accused by the *Securitate* of being an Israeli spy upon his return from a conference in Jerusalem and told that he'd no longer be allowed out of the country.

No doubt this individual decision was not really personal. It coincided with Ceausescu's national policy of closing the Iron Curtain, to further isolate and control the Romanian people. Fortunately, my father obtained permission to attend one last conference, at the *Princeton Institute of Advanced Studies*. He decided to take a chance and defect to the United States. Since my mother and I were still in Romania, my family struggled to reunite in the United States for nearly two years. Although there were precedents for similar immigrations, we lived under the rational fear that we might never see each other again. My mother was subject to demoralizing *Securitate* interrogations similar to the ones I describe in the novel *Reincarnations of Love*. Yet, as I also depict in the novel, we never gave up or lost hope. Several congressmen and human rights organizations intervened on our behalf. When I was a few weeks shy of my twelfth birthday, we finally joined my father in the United States.

"Velvet totalitarianism" is a term that has been used to describe the constraints imposed upon the expression of liberal values in the Canadian and American academia. Just as, conversely, the term "political correctness" has been used to indicate that there's no real freedom of expression of conservative values in the academia. Indeed, whether or not America has turned out to be the country of plentitude and freedom that I dreamed about as a child back in Romania is another story. But what remains clear to me is that the systematic state repression, or what I'm calling the "velvet totalitarianism," we lived through in Romania makes whatever's being criticized in Western institutions today, by both the right and the left, pale by comparison. The United States certainly lacks the absolute freedom that some of its ideologues may rhapsodize about, but what Romanians experienced was an absolute lack of freedom, which is far worse.

In *Velvet Totalitarianism*, I'd like to leave a trace of the scale of comparison, of the difference I experienced between the lack of absolute freedom here and the lack of any freedom there. As the narrator of my novel states at the end, I'm hoping that this description of daily life in Romania under the Ceausescu regime will convey to my children and to my children's children—as well as to American students and all readers interested in this subject--the lost traces of an era in which ordinary people were forced to lead extraordinary lives.

Bibliography

Arato, Andrew. *From Neo-Marxism to Democratic Theory: Essays on the Critical Theory of Soviet-Type Societies.* Armonk, N.Y.: M. E. Sharpe, 1993.

Arendt, Hannah. *The Origins of Totalitarianism.* San Diego: Harcourt, Inc., 1948.

Arendt, Hannah. *Eichmann in Jerusalem: A report on the banality of Evil.* New York: Penguin Classics, 2006.

Ash, Timothy Garton. *The Uses of Adversity: Essays on the Fate of Central Europe.* New York: Random House, 1989.

Bachman, D. Ronald, ed. *Romania: A Country Study.* Washington: GPO for the Library of Congress, 1989.

Brown, J. F. *The New Eastern Europe: The Khrushchev Era and After.* New York: Praeger, 1966.

Brown, J. F. *Eastern Europe and Communist Rule.* Durham, N.C.: Duke University Press, 1988.

Brown, J. F. *Surge to Freedom: The End of Communist Rule in Eastern Europe.* Durham, N. C.: Duke University Press, 1991.

Balas, Egon. *Will to Freedom: A Perilous Journey through Fascism and Communism.* Syracuse, N.Y.: Syracuse University Press, 1988.

Bullock, Alan. *Hitler and Stalin: Parallel Lives.* New York: Vintage Books, 1991.

Cipkowski, Peter. *Revolution in Eastern Europe: Understanding the Collapse of Communism in Poland, Hungary, East Germany, Czechoslovakia, Romania, and the Soviet Union.* New York: John Wiley & Sons, 1991.

Codrescu, Andrei. *A Hole in the Flag: A Romanian Exile's Story of Return and Revolution.* New York: William Morrow, 1991.

Constante, Lena. *The Silent Escape: Three Thousand Days in Romanian Prisons.* Berkeley: University of California Press, 1995.

Conquest, Robert. *Reflections on a Ravaged Century.* New York: Norton, 2000.

Crampton, R. J. *Eastern Europe in the Twentieth Century.* London: Routledge, 1994.

Daniels, Robert V. *The End of the Communist Revolution.* London: Routledge, 1993.

Deletant, Dennis. *Ceausescu and the Securitate: Coersion and Dissent in Romania, 1965-1989.* Armonk, N. Y.: M. E. Sharpe, 1995.

Deletant, Dennis. *Communist Terror in Romania: Gheorghiu-Dej and the Police State.* New York: St. Martin's Press, 1999.

Deletant, Dennis. *Romania under Communist Rule.* Iasi, Romania: The Center for Romanian Studies, 1999.

Fisher-Galati, Stephen. *Twentieth-Century Romania.* New York: Columbia University Press, 1991.

Fitzpatrick, Shiela, ed. *Stalinism: New Directions*, New York: Routledge, 2000.

Gati, Charles. *Hungary and the Soviet Block*. Durham, N.C.: Duke University Press, 1986.

Glenny, Misha. *The Rebirth of History: Eastern Europe in the Age of Democracy*. New York: Penguin Books, 1990.

Havel, Vaclav. *Living in Truth*. London and New York: Faber and Faber, 1987.

Hoffer, Eric. *The True Believer: Thoughts on the Nature of Mass Movements*. New York: Time Inc., 1963.

Holmes, Leslie. *The End of Communist Power: Anti-Corruption Campaigns and Legitimation Crisis*. Cambridge, U. K.: Polity Press, 1993.

Ionescu, Ghita. *Communism in Romania*. London: Oxford University Press, 1964.

Keefe, Eugene. *Area Handbook for Romania*. Washington, D. C.: American University, 1972.

Kessler, Ronald. *Inside the CIA: Revealing the Secrets of the World's Most Powerful Spy Agency*. New York: Pocket Books, 1994.

Klepper, Nicolae. *Romania: An Illustrated History*. New York: Hippocrene Books, Inc.

Kolakowski, Leszek. *Main Currents of Marxism: Its Origins, Growth and Dissolution*. 3 vols. Oxford: Oxford University Press, 1978.

Kort, Michael. *The Handbook of the New Eastern Europe*. New York: Millbrook Press, 2001.

Kort, Michael. *The Soviet Colossus*. New York: M. E. Sharpe, 6 edition, 2006.

Levy, Robert: *Ana Pauker: The Rise and Fall of a Jewish Communist*. Berkeley, University of California Press, 2001.

Manea, Norman. *On Clowns: The Dictator and the Artist*. New York: Grove Weidenfeld, 1992.

Moran, Lindsay. *Blowing my cover: My Life as a CIA Spy*. New York: Penguin, 2005.

McCarthy, Leslie. "Inside a Romanian Orphanage," *Library Weekly*, 2000.

Nelson, Daniel N. *Romanian Politics in the Ceausescu Era*. New York: Gordon & Breach, 1988.

Nyrop, Richard. *Chzechoslovakia, A Country Study*. Washington, D.C.: American University, 1982.

Pacepa, Ion Mihai. *Red Horizons: Chronicles of a Communist Spy-Chief.* Washington, D. C.: Regnery Gateway, 1987.

Rady, Martyn. *Romania in Turmoil*. London: I. B. Tauris & Co., 1992.

Ratesh, Nestor. Romania: *The Entangled Revolution*. Washington, D.C.: The Center for Strategic and International Studies, 1991.

Ratiu, Ion. *Contemporary Romania*. Richmond, England: Foreign Affairs Publishing Co., 1975.

Rupnik, Jacques. *The Other Europe*. London: Weidenfeld & Nicolson, 1988.

SoRelle, Ruth. "Born to be Forgotten," *Houston Chronicle*, 1996.

Sorin, Anthoni and Tismaneanu, Vladimir, eds. *Between Past and Future: The Revolutions of 1989 and Their Aftermath.* Budapest: Central European University Press, 1999.

Tismaneanu, Vladimir. *The Crisis of Marxist Ideology in Eastern Europe: The Poverty of Utopia.* London: Routledge, 1988.

Tismaneanu, Vladimir. *Stalinism for All Seasons: A Political History of Romanian Communism.* Berkeley: University of California Press, 2003.

Westoby, Adam. *The Evolution of Communism.* New York: The Free Press, 1989.

Reincarnations of Love: A novel

by Claudia Moscovici

Part I

Chapter 1

Radu looked at his new Swiss watch—aluminum band, clear dial, red cross emblem, precision timing—which he had bought almost a year before with his first paycheck. It was 5:51 p.m. Time to go home and prepare for his date with Ioana. He should have been happy to have such a beautiful girlfriend. Yet, due to the latest turn of events, Radu was plagued by doubts. Just when his life was starting to improve, he became entangled in a web of contradictions from which he didn't know how to extricate himself. His job and his girlfriend, his main sources of pleasure, had suddenly turned into causes for fear and suspicion. How much his attitude had changed since he came to France last spring, Radu mused. Back then, he was filled to the brim with hope. And who could blame him? At only twenty he got a scholarship to the Sorbonne and managed to defect to France, which, as far as Romanians were concerned, was the second most sophisticated country in the world (the first being Romania, of course). Then, based strictly upon his merit—aided only by a few well-placed connections—he landed a dream job as Assistant Correspondent on Romania at Radio Freedom Europe. RFE! The only station Romanians huddled in front of their illegal shortwave radios in the middle of the night to find out what the CIA said was going on in their country and the rest of the world. Which wasn't all that surprising since, after all, in Romania news consisted solely of propaganda. Time for a little truth and sanity, Radu told himself when he took the part-time job at Radio Freedom Europe. And that's what he did his best to deliver in his political commentaries, with a cracked voice and a beating heart, since his major was chemistry, not politics or journalism. He was still a neophyte, working on a trial basis and anxious to impress everyone at the radio station and move up the ladder, all the way to the sky if possible—say, production manager--although he wasn't thinking that far ahead just yet. At the very least, his boss, Alexei Pavlovich, a Russian dissident, would have to grant him this: the young Romanian spoke with enthusiasm.

After his talk, on the way back to his dorm room, Radu tried to reassure himself that, ethically speaking, he was doing the right thing. But he still felt uneasy about his decision. Maybe he wasn't helping anyone after all. Least of all his family. Nothing seemed clear-cut or simple anymore. At the root of the problem was Ioana, the young woman with whom he had fallen in love.

Radu imagined her as he first saw her, in the Parc Montsouris, a little park next to his dormitory, at the Cité Universitaire. She walked towards him like a beautiful vision, her curvy body wrapped loosely in a long blue dress spotted by the uneven, kaleidoscopic shadows of the trees. Her soft, lean curves undulated underneath that flowing fabric. He was so startled by Ioana's beauty that he stopped in his tracks, and, not exactly tactfully, just stood there and stared at her. As the young woman approached, Radu noticed that she had raven hair, of medium length, frizzed slightly by what might have been an overgrown perm. Far from making her seem unkempt, it gave her a casual, sexy look which he much preferred to a carefully groomed appearance. Although, generally speaking, Radu wasn't particularly observant, he noticed that the young woman wore bright, plum red lipstick. The lip color went well with her olive complexion and deep brown eyes, which were so dark that even when she got quite close he could barely distinguish iris from pupil. Her nose was a little too large for her delicate oval face. Otherwise, he justified in retrospect her minor imperfections, she might have been unapproachably beautiful. It was she who initiated their conversation. "Buna ziua," she greeted him "Hello" in Romanian. "Why is this French woman speaking to me in Romanian?" Radu wondered, at first so caught off guard that he didn't reply. She noticed his surprise and smiled, showing two rows of even white teeth.

"My name is Ioana Marinescu," the young woman graciously extended her hand.

"Nice to meet you," Radu answered. He clasped her slim fingers with an uncertain, nervous touch. By way of contrast, her grip was strong and confident.

"I noticed you at the Cité before," she told him. "I live there too. I'm originally from Iasi. And you?"

"From Bucuresti," Radu answered, with a tinge of disappointment. He would have preferred that Ioana be French. One could never be too careful with fellow Romanians when one worked at Radio Freedom Europe...

"I'm kind of lonely here, so I was glad to hear a fellow Romanian voice," she said.

Touched by her friendliness, Radu felt somewhat embarrassed about his misgivings. They returned, however, after only a moment's consideration. He couldn't figure out how, even before he had spoken, Ioana knew that he was Romanian.

She read his mind, which, given his distrustful expression, must have been quite transparent. "I heard you talking in Romanian to another student in the cafeteria..."

"Who? Diaconescu?"

"I don't know his name," Ioana replied. "Nor yours, for that matter," she added, since Radu hadn't introduced himself yet.

"Sorry. I'm Radu Schwarz."

"Nice to meet you. Did you come here with your family?" Ioana asked, attempting to make polite conversation.

"No, by myself."

"Me too. My parents are still in Iasi."

It occurred to Radu that Ioana didn't have a Moldavian accent, the strongest and most distinctive in Romania, as people from Iasi generally did. He proceeded with caution. "How come you don't have an accent?"

Ioana shrugged. "Mine was never that strong to begin with, and besides, whatever country bumpkin accent I might have had, I lost it in Bucharest during my first year of university studies. I didn't want to seem provincial."

"Do you plan to go back to Romania?" the young man inquired, since if she didn't, perhaps he could trust her a little more.

"We'll see. I'm here on a two-year fellowship. I don't want to make my parents' situation even worse, so I'll probably go back."

"I plan to stay here for good. I mean, I already defected," Radu heard himself declare, to his own surprise.

"How about your family? Do they want to join you here?"

Radu thought about his parents and little sister, eight year old Irina, whom he hoped to bring to France. The young man planned to use his radio show to persuade French officials to apply pressure on the Romanian government to allow his family to immigrate to France. But he couldn't divulge this information to a total stranger. Especially not to a fellow Romanian.

"I don't know," he replied.

They strolled together around the circular path of the Lac Montsouris, discussing other subjects. They commiserated about the Cité Universitaire dorm rooms, which were too small and had dilapidated, straw wallpaper. "They're perfect--if you're a cat!" Ioana quipped. They both approved, however, of the cafeteria food at the Cité. Ioana claimed that since arriving in Paris she had put on five kilos; Radu looked with disbelief at her slim athletic figure, wondering where she was hiding the extra weight. Then they sat down on a bench in front of the lake. Ioana unsnapped the magnetic clasp of her purse and took out a chunk of baguette neatly wrapped in a white napkin. A group of ducks swam rapidly towards her.

"I save my bread for the ducks," she explained, breaking off a little piece of baguette and tossing it towards the smallest of the ducks first, being careful to be fair to all, feeding them one at a time. The birds, however, didn't quite grasp the principle of equality, much less of taking one's turn. They seemed more familiar with the concept of "every duck for himself," as they precipitated all at once towards each crumb. Two ducks, with grayish bodies and green throats, were more aggressive than the rest. They rushed to gobble up the bits of bread no matter how hard the young woman tried to feed their companions.

"Those are the male ones," Radu said with slight embarrassment, as if apologizing for his sex.

"They must be from the Secret Police," Ioana joked. This reference made the young man's face cloud with concern.

"Just kidding! Geesh!" Ioana poked him playfully with her elbow. "I doubt these ducks have microphones hidden under their wings," she continued teasing him. Then, abruptly, she changed her light-hearted attitude: "Actually, I'm usually just as nervous as you are," she whispered, attentively scrutinizing Radu's expression.

"About what?" he asked, still evasive.

"You know…"

"You mean the Secret Police?"

Ioana nodded, looked past Radu, then behind her, to make sure they weren't being observed. "My father, who's an aerospace engineer, refused to sign the papers before going to a conference in Japan," she said in a low, confidential tone.

Radu proceeded with caution: "What papers?"

"You know. The ones for the industry."

"I don't understand," Radu said, even though he did.

The young woman gave him a skeptical and half-reproachful look, as if she wasn't fooled by his professed ignorance. Out of politeness, she offered an explanation nonetheless: "You know Petrescu's policy: any Romanian scientist or diplomat going abroad has to double as an informant or tech spy. Otherwise, it's a waste of the country's resources, right? At least, that's the official party line," she said matter-of-factly, as if she were merely stating the obvious.

Since his father, a scientist at the Atomic Physics Institute of Romania, had also gone through this pleasant experience, Radu understood perfectly well what Ioana was talking about. However, by force of habit, the young man preferred to avoid having such conversations out in the open, even when on safer, Western ground. Now it was his turn to look around, pretending to admire the scenery, to see if anyone might be watching them. The young couple necking on the bench next to theirs and the elderly woman walking her dog seemed innocuous enough.

Unexpectedly, Ioana began to cry. Radu's own mood shifted from suspicion to surprise and then to concern. He didn't know how to respond to this sudden display of emotion. With a mixture of chivalry and compassion, the young man removed a plaid handkerchief from his shirt pocket and graciously offered it to

Ioana. Unfortunately, the handkerchief happened to have already been used during his frequent spells of spring allergies, so she politely refused it.

"Is anything wrong?" he asked, absurdly.

"Yes," Ioana sniffled. "I mean no," she changed her mind and laughed a little, as if embarrassed by her own capriciousness. She put both hands in front of her face, covering the bridge of her nose. She seemed to be considering something, then suddenly decided: "I suppose that I'm taking a leap of faith. But we can trust each other, yes?"

"Of course," Radu agreed, although he wasn't quite sure yet.

"When my father refused to sign the papers he was beaten up by the authorities and thrown in prison. Eventually they let him go, but since then, our lives haven't been the same..."

Radu nodded in sympathy. "I'm afraid this sort of thing could happen to my parents too," he confessed.

Ioana seemed interested: "Why? Did your parents also refuse to sign the documents?"

"My father did," Radu answered, looking at the girl's pretty oval face, encouraging himself to trust her.

"Is your father an engineer too?" she asked.

He shook his head: "A physicist."

"Do you mind if we walked around a little?" Ioana proposed.

"Not at all," Radu responded. After all, spending time with such a nice girl was worth skipping his afternoon classes. They got up and she gently slipped her arm around his elbow, a gesture of intimacy , which took him by surprise. That's how relatives or familiar friends tended to stroll together in Romania, elbows hooked. Feeling somewhat discombobulated by the young woman's proximity and touch, Radu looked down in embarrassment, but that offered no solace, since he became even more flustered once he noticed Ioana's high heeled sandals and her lean, long muscular legs flexing under the flowing dress as she walked. Once again, as during the first moment he saw her, Radu became aware of a feminine magnetism that overpowered him. "So what if she's Romanian? Does every Romanian girl in Paris have to be a spy?" he asked himself, attempting to dispel the state of warranted paranoia cultivated by years of living under a totalitarian dictatorship.

During their tour of the park, they talked about their classes, about books, about their love of French literature, especially Flaubert. Radu adored reading novels; Ioana was a French literature major. As it turns out, their favorite novel was Madame Bovary. Granted, they weren't exactly the first people on Earth to believe that Flaubert had some merit; nevertheless, each point in common helped overcome, little by little, Radu's reservations.

Only hours later, when they were having dinner together in a private corner of a table at the Cité Universitaire cafeteria, did the couple return to the touchy subject of their families and their political situations.

"So why did your dad refuse to sign?" Ioana asked.

Following hours of conversational intimacy, Radu's tongue had loosened up. This time he didn't hesitate to tell her: "He had nothing to spy on. I mean, what's he going to steal? Equations about how the Big Bang got started and how the universe contracts or expands? Petrescu isn't interested in the universe. He only cares about his little fief."

"Does your father work for Silvia Petrescu?" Ioana asked, obviously aware of the fact that the dictator's daughter, herself a physicist, was the Director of the Atomic Physics Institute of Romania.

"Yes," Radu replied. "Actually, they're friends. Otherwise...let's just say ... life would have been a lot harder for my family."

"Why so?" Ioana took a sip of water, keeping her eyes fixed on Radu.

"It's the same story as with your father," he answered. "Except maybe for the fact that we're Jewish--on my father's side--which kind of complicates things. A few years ago my dad got this fellowship to the Hebrew University in Jerusalem. Before he left, he was asked to sign a paper that he'll be a tech spy. He refused, and then, as soon as he returned, the Romanian government accused him of being an Israeli agent. Can you imagine? What twisted logic! If it weren't for Silvia, he might have ended up in prison or some labor camp."

"Did Silvia herself ask him to spy?" Ioana asked.

"I don't think so. I believe the orders came from above," Radu indicated, pointing up with his index finger.

Ioana took a bite of her quiche. She chewed slowly, contemplating Radu's comment. "So what happened when your dad refused?" she asked, after the savory forkful had melted in her mouth.

Radu was trying to find a graceful way to cut the meat off his chicken drumstick, but eventually gave up, held it with his bare hands and took a big bite. "The usual stuff. He was harassed," he answered after having chewed his mouthful. Since coming to France, he was not used to having substantive conversations while he ate, preferring instead to concentrate each ounce of energy on the food, which he was still afraid would somehow disappear from his plate if he didn't promptly wolf it down.

"Phone, car and radiator bugs, being shadowed by the Secret Police, interrogations, debriefings, that sort of thing, right?" Ioana prompted him.

"Yup," Radu answered matter-of-factly, as if these experiences were so commonplace, they were hardly worth mentioning. He eyed with envy Ioana's orange—a rarity in Romania, usually sold only at Craciun, around Christmas.

She noticed his gaze and offered him her orange. "You can have it. I prefer to stick to my diet anyway," she said, attacking the rich créme brûlée. She then added, as an afterthought, "The exact same thing happened to us. So did the harassment eventually stop?"

"Not completely," Radu answered. "In fact, I only made things worse for them."

"How so?"

"Because…"

The girl patiently waited for his response, twirling a spoon in her cup of coffee.

"You see, I work for Radio Freedom Europe," Radu leaned forward and confessed with difficulty in a whisper, feeling like he had just undergone a grueling debriefing session.

Instead of being flattered by his trust, however, Ioana was amused by his reticence. "You're so silly," she said, reaching over across the table and affectionately patting Radu's hand.

"What makes you say that?"

"You treat me as if I were from the Secret Police," she replied, lightly brushing his leg with her bare foot under the table. Not used to such overt flirtation, Radu peeked under the table to see what had tickled him and noticed that the young woman had taken off her right shoe. "Such a silly garçonnet…" Radu didn't know how to react to this unexpected onslaught of sensual affection.

"You and I are in the same boat, Raducu," Ioana kept stroking his foot reassuringly, using the Romanian diminutive of his name. Her knee touched his under the table. "Besides," she smiled at him indulgently, "do you really think the fact you're a speaker on Radio Freedom Europe is such a big secret? I listened to your show already … Isn't that the whole point of international broadcasting? To reach as many people as possible? So why all this secrecy, hmmm, Mr. Bond?"

"So this means…" Radu, still under the young woman's spell, struggled to reach a logical conclusion.

"… that I know perfectly well where you work and what you think about Petrescu's regime," Ioana completed his sentence. "And of course I agree! Who in his right mind wouldn't?"

"Agree with what?"

"With the fact that Nicolae Petrescu is a megalomaniac tyrant who oppresses Romanians and sacrifices the good of the country to his personality cult, what else?" the young woman summarized succinctly the message of Radu's fifteen hours of broadcast to date.

When Radu returned to his dorm room after that first meeting with Ioana, he threw himself on the bed, placing his hands behind his head, his eyes fixed dreamily upon the ceiling. He weighed the pros and cons of their encounter. Undoubtedly, he thought, there was a slight disadvantage to becoming friends with Ioana: she might be a Secret Police agent and kill me. Out of a million attractive French women in Paris, why did I have to fall in love with a fellow Romanian? On the other hand, the pros were at least as compelling: the girl was strikingly beautiful, sweet and charming. Besides, Radu attempted to reassure himself, who said anything about love?

Chapter 2

After their first day spent together, March 12th, 1979 to be exact, Radu and Ioana met regularly at the Parc Montsouris. Despite the young man's initial reticence, they now engaged in open political diatribes and even less inhibited petting sessions generally initiated by Ioana. She'd kiss Radu's curly chestnut hair, lightly and repeatedly right behind the ear, then whisper warmly words he could barely reply to, feeling drawn to her like a fly to honey tape.

Tantalized by her sensuality, the young man strategized late into the night about how to invite himself graciously, casually and unobtrusively into Ioana's dorm room. Smooth overtures such as "Do you need help carrying your books to your room?" or "I've been wondering about what your dorm room looks like. Do you mind if I come in and take a look?" crossed his sharp mind. Despite sufficiently strong incentives, however, he was too shy—and too respectful--to ask her such direct questions. He settled instead for long sessions of public displays of affection on their bench at the Parc Montsouris. With his mouth stuck to hers, his wandering hands exploring whatever they could by valiantly overcoming the flimsy cloth barriers they encountered, his eyes perpetually on the alert, Radu tried in vain to protect the sense of privacy that their circumstances wouldn't permit. When she reciprocated and even exceeded his explorations, anxiety would overcome his desire and he'd manage to say, "Ioana, come on... not in public please..." But her kisses would rapidly silence his half-hearted protests.

"Don't be such a prude!" she'd sometimes retort. "In Paris making out in public's practically mandatory! Didn't you know? Here they deport you for being coy!"

Faced with such irrefutable counterarguments, Radu had no choice but to cast aside common decency and act in Rome as the Romans did. During their occasional breathers, the couple planned Radu's next RFE speeches. Ioana, who called herself half-jokingly an avid fan, faithfully followed Radu's show and, he was obliged to admit, exhibited quite a flair for journalism herself.

"So what's the subject of your talk this week?" she asked him, during one of their meetings in the park.

"I don't know, I was thinking of doing something on Petrescu's obsession with getting the Nobel Peace Prize," Radu said. "You know how he wants to steal the show from Carter and win the Nobel Prize for negotiating peace in the Middle East. My sources tell me he's machinating behind the scenes with his friends in the PLO."

Ioana licked her lips, like a tigress about to pounce upon its prey. "Let's see, how shall we put this?" she asked, rubbing her hands together. "You could begin by announcing, in jest, that Petrescu wins the Nobel Peace Prize for saving the Romanian people from World War III. Then you could say something like, "With his usual benevolence and foresight, Comrade Nicolae Petrescu starved all of his citizens preemptively, before the international cataclysm even took place."

"That's a little morbid, don't you think? Besides, what does that have to do with the Middle East?"

"Everyone knows that's where World War III will start," Ioana retorted.

Radu, however, insisted upon a more topical commentary. She got down to business and came up with part of the text that he later incorporated into his radio show:

"Petrescu has visions of grandeur; he considers himself a maverick in foreign policy and hopes to be rewarded with a Nobel Peace Prize. While the Romanian people are half-starving and without heat and clothes, their beloved and benevolent leader plans to outshine Carter and intercede with the PLO to solve all the problems in the Middle East. What's wrong with this picture? If Comrade Petrescu can't even deal with domestic issues, how does he hope to solve international ones? The answer is clear: the Emperor's lack of clothes should be exposed and the Emperor himself dethroned."

"Do you mind if I expose your lack of clothes?" Radu wanted to know after Ioana had concluded her dictation.

"But I'm dressed," she rebutted.

"Then we must remove your clothes to have something to expose."

"Then I'd already be exposed, wouldn't I?" Ioana pointed out the obvious paradox.

Within a few weeks, Radu had became dependent both physically and emotionally upon the young woman he considered his "special friend." When they parted, after kissing Ioana goodnight in front of her dorm room, he counted the minutes until the next day, when he would see her again. Though ridiculously attracted to her body, which practically enslaved him to his own desires, he was especially moved by her intellect, culture and sharpness. She spoke six languages—Romanian, French, English, Italian, Russian and German—which is to say, two more than him, though he wasn't the kind of man to keep score.

"What are you doing tomorrow night?" Radu asked Ioana one Friday evening, when they were sharing a bottle of sparkling water at Chez Ali, their favorite café near the Cité Universitaire.

"I'm going to an art exhibit. Why do you ask?"

"Just wondering," he said, trying not to look hurt. Like any reasonable man who has been dating a beautiful woman for a few weeks, Radu assumed that Ioana's Saturday evenings were reserved for him. "By yourself?" he asked as nonchalantly as possible. In his own mind, however, he prepared himself for the worst. After all, how could such a gorgeous girl be true to him? She must have dozens of men asking to go out with her--and a few of them actually succeeding.

"Well, no, actually... I was going to ask you to accompany me," Ioana replied after a moment's hesitation. But Radu wasn't convinced.

"This friend of mine's a very famous artist," she continued. "He's giving a show tomorrow at the Centre Pompidou. There's going to be lots of press coverage. You'll see, it will be fun." Since Radu still wasn't taking the bait, she added, to bolster her case: "They're serving free food. Your favorites: pâtisseries."

The young man focused on the only relevant part of her statement: "He?"

"Yes," Ioana confirmed. "His name is Jean-Pierre Renault."

Radu must have winced, since Ioana quickly added, thinking that, for some strange reason, her boyfriend disapproved of bourgeois materialism: "No relation whatsoever to the car manufacturer."

"What kind of art does he do?" Radu inquired, even though, quite frankly, he couldn't care less. Obviously, he was prepared to go to any length for this girl: "Okay, I'll go with you," he answered before Ioana even had a chance to answer his question. He might as well see for himself what was going on between his girlfriend and this Jean-Pierre guy.

"Great!" she exclaimed cheerfully. "You'll absolutely adore his art. It's very sophisticated, avant-garde. Don't roll your eyes at me like that!" she laughed. "Jean-Pierre's one of the most respected contemporary artists in the world! I'm totally serious!"

So they're on a first name basis, Radu silently noted.

Believing that Radu was interested in art despite all evidence to the contrary, Ioana elaborated: "He does these neat installations, with wires, light bulbs, videos... It's hard to explain. Very multimedia. Cutting edge kind of stuff."

"Fascinating..."

"You don't know the half of it!" Ioana pursued. "He's so famous that he's always quoted in *Le Monde*. And, it goes without saying, also in the *Libération*. There must be an article on him in there every other day. He's one of those thinking, feeling artists. A wonderful contact for intellectuals. Especially for you, since you're an aspiring journalist."

"I am?" Radu wasn't aware of being either an intellectual or a journalist. He thought he was an aspiring chemist, but then again, who was he to have a say in his own future profession? At the moment, however, his attention was fully focused on finding out more about the nature of the relationship between Ioana and Jean-Pierre: "Is he... was he... did you..." he stuttered with eloquence.

"Yes?" she looked at him with smiling eyes.

"How old is this guy anyway?" he asked, hoping she'd say a hundred.

"We're just friends, Raducu," she answered his real question.

"Oh, that's not what I meant. I mean, you're free to do what you want," Radu shrugged with consummate nonchalance.

"Am I?" Ioana got close to him once again, her face blurred by their proximity. His mind clouded under the effect of her warmth. They kissed. "So then you wouldn't mind if I did this with him?" she asked after a few seconds, pulling away.

Now that's a strange question. Perhaps, Radu thought, a few details needed to be clarified: "So then... are we dating or not?" he gracefully blurted out.

"Obviously!" she laughed. "Otherwise who's been taking me out to all those movies, restaurants and shows?"

"You tell me," he replied, still dissatisfied. Ioana was about to kiss him once again, but this time he stopped her by placing his hand upon her shoulder. "Come on. Tell me seriously. Are we going steady or not?"

She measured him up and down with her dark eyes: "My, how you've changed, Mr. Bond!"

Although ordinarily Radu enjoyed his girlfriend's flirtatiousness, this time it perturbed him: "Ioana, why are you being so evasive?"

"Is Mr. Bond a little jealous?" she continued her taunting.

"Can you please answer my question?" he heard himself say with the exasperated tone of a desperate man. Either way, he'd have to absolve this overt expression of neediness later on that night in the usual manner, through hours of self-flagellating introspection, followed by resolutions to become either a jaded Don Juan or a Stoic who couldn't care less.

"What was the question?" Ioana asked and Radu felt that his girlfriend was literally laughing in his face.

"Never mind!" he said abruptly. His voice was cold. "When and where do you want to meet tomorrow?"

"How about at a quarter to seven at the Centre Pompidou? Jean-Pierre's presentation starts at seven."

"Do we have time to eat dinner first?"

Ioana looked at him in disbelief: "Didn't you hear me? They're serving free food!"

That afternoon, Radu knew he wouldn't be able to concentrate on his courses. Consequently, purely out of intellectual integrity, he decided to skip his classes and go to a place where he could peacefully contemplate the situation: their bench at the Parc Montsouris. "She's the one who seduced me," Radu told himself. "I'm the one who at first didn't want her to be my girlfriend," he found it necessary to reformulate this apparently crucial point. He then arrived at the inevitable question many men must ask themselves when they deal with sexy, flirtatious and seductive women: "So what the hell happened?"

Chapter 3

Radu attempted to focus upon the blurry symbols of his organic chemistry homework. Every few minutes, he checked his watch. It was already 6:50 p.m. Since he had promised to meet Ioana at the Centre Pompidou at 6:45, he was satisfied that he'd manage to be fashionably late. Let her wait for once, he told himself.

He put on the only outfit he owned that he considered appropriate for a meeting with a famous artist: a pair of black leather pants he bought from a Moroccan street vendor for 20 francs with his first paycheck; an equally dark turtleneck from TATI, a discount store and his nicest pair of black shoes from Romania which he only wore on special occasions (so far, that turned out to be a great-uncle's funeral, the job interview for RFE and this upcoming meeting).

Not wishing to seem peevishly rather than fashionably late, however, Radu ran through the dinner crowds, took a packed metro to the Hôtel de Ville and approached the Dr. Seuss looking building which he instantly recognized as the Centre Pompidou. The exoskeleton of brightly colored pipes and winding external staircases stuck out like a sore thumb in the midst of a traditional Parisian neighborhood populated by somber-looking gray stone buildings.

Once inside, Radu surveyed the place: elegant young women gently guided their children along, explaining the artwork in quiet, "inside voices"; students sought inspiration from the contemporary masters whose works had "made it"; couples impressed one another with their artistic knowledge in the hope that such displays of erudition, plus the fancy dinners that followed, would function as an adequate aphrodisiac and, last but certainly not least, next to the coat room on the ground floor, Radu spotted a few women gathered around a man whom he couldn't quite see. Among them was Ioana.

The first thing he noticed was that she wore high heels, which made her lean over slightly, like the tower of Pisa, in an attempt to keep her balance in a sexy yet sufficiently classic contrapposto position. She wore a gray wool pencil skirt which fell slightly below the knees—but its modesty was negated, Radu thought with some regret, by the fact it hugged her dangerous curves—along with the mandatory black turtleneck, which delighted him since, despite the fact that it was also too tight, it matched his own outfit. Next to her stood an older blond woman dressed in an elegant purple and white suit covered by a bright red shawl that made her resemble a Lichtenstein cartoon. A petite brunette, shorter than Ioana but about the same age, seemed to stick quite closely to the man standing in the center of this group. Suddenly, Ioana burst out in what Radu took to be obviously phony laughter and shifted her weight upon the other five-inch heel. This motion created a break in the curtain of women, giving Radu the chance to catch a glimpse of its shining center: a slight man with salt and pepper hair, round glasses with dark rims and a mysterious, La Gioconda smirk.

Radu approached Ioana and gently tapped her shoulder: "Sorry I'm late," he whispered.

Ioana unpeeled her eyes from the artist and looked at Radu with bewilderment: "Hi. I'm glad you could make it," she said, as if greeting a distant acquaintance. "Radu, this is my friend Jean-Pierre. Jean-Pierre, please meet Radu, the journalist I told you about, who works for Radio Freedom Europe," she proceeded to make the proper introductions in French.

Jean-Pierre's expression, particularly the ironic grin on his face, didn't change; nonetheless, he acknowledged the young man's presence by extending the tips of his fingers in the latter's direction. Radu had made a few cultural adjustments since arriving in Paris: he had learned to shake men's hands instead of kissing them warmly on both cheeks (after all, Western men play it cool); to give women la bise, or three quick pecks on the cheeks in greeting (he had no problem adapting to this tradition), and to never act too friendly or enthusiastic upon meeting anyone who was authentically Parisian (since you didn't want to look like a peasant). However, he had never encountered this particular form of greeting, which, for lack of a better term, he dubbed "the wet noodle handshake"--except perhaps on T.V., when the queen of England was shown shaking hands with the plebeians. Since that was the closest scenario to the present circumstances, Radu answered politely "Enchanté" and leaned forward to shake Jean-Pierre's limp hand.

Radu couldn't help disliking the man, who, for his part, looked at him with the air of an atheist receiving an unexpected visit from the Jehovah's Witnesses. Maybe he thinks I want something from him since these famous artists must receive a lot of solicitations for favors, Radu told himself.

"Mesdames, shall we go?" Jean-Pierre asked turning to Ioana, and the whole bevy of women (plus Radu) followed the artist to the escalator to the fourth floor, where Jean-Pierre's lecture and exhibit were about to take place.

"Where the devil were you? I've been waiting downstairs for thirty minutes for you. Jean-Pierre has to give a talk, you know!" Ioana managed to hiss at Radu in their native tongue when she thought she wouldn't be overheard, then turned with a porcelain smile and flashed both of their tickets in front of the young man waiting by the entrance. They stepped into an exhibit room that was already filled with people seated on foldout chairs brought in especially for the occasion.

The curator of contemporary exhibits, a woman of indeterminate age wearing a gray ensemble and bright red lipstick, stood behind the podium, awaiting impatiently the arrival of the guest of honor. "Ah, le voilà!" she exclaimed throwing up her hands theatrically into the air as soon as she spotted Jean-Pierre, who took a seat in the front row. He looked like the picture of relaxation: his torso was low on the seat; his legs stretched out as far as possible as if he were deliberately trying to trip somebody; his arms crossed; his face devoid of expression, except for the signature smirk.

"Mon ami, Jean-Pierre Renault, needs no introduction," announced the curator, proceeding, just in case, to introduce the guest speaker for about thirty minutes. While spacing out, Radu caught a few key words that were pronounced with special emphasis: "brilliant," "genius," "L'Ecole des Beaux Arts," "avant-garde," "cutting-edge," "latest cry."

To everyone's relief, Jean-Pierre finally took the stage. He grabbed the podium with both hands as if about to wrestle with it and leaned forward to gaze up at the lights for what seemed like a long time to the impatient audience. "These are absolutely awful lights," the artist declared, referring to the spectacular antique crystal chandelier that the museum had recently purchased for several million francs. People laughed, for lack of a better reaction. "Can somebody at least dim them a little?" Jean-Pierre asked in all seriousness. Several women working on the museum staff, whom Renault later anecdotally referred to as "the gaggle of geese" and "the cackling hens," solicitously jumped up from their seats to execute the artist's wishes. M. Renault, however, wasn't that easy to please. "Now they're too dim," he said. The curator took charge of the situation, elevating and lowering the light switch until the fussy artist, though still displeased, got tired of complaining.

"To tell you the truth," Renault went on to say in a very soft voice (which in turn led the audience to lean forward in the effort to hear him) "I don't like to give talks." Some members of the audience found this comment amusing as well.

"In life, there are those who talk and those who do," he kindly explained, "And I prefer to... do neither." Laughter from the audience again.

"Why in the world are we wasting our time here then?" Radu wondered. The shapely leg next to him, which happened to be Ioana's, reminded him of at least one good reason.

"Some artists prepare long, Augustan speeches for intellectuals such as yourselves, but since I dislike both intellectuals and speeches, I basically have nothing to say," M. Renault flattered his audience.

The spectators didn't quite know how to react. A few people looked around to see what the others were doing. Since nobody left, and, furthermore, since a few individuals even chuckled, more people started to laugh. Well, it's either laugh or slap the guy around a little, Radu thought. What does she see in him anyway? What does he have that I don't?

"Isn't he funny?" Ioana whispered in his ear, as if in direct response to his silent questions.

"Hilarious," Radu replied.

"You'll see how brilliant he is once he starts talking about art," she added, still in a whisper.

"I can't wait!"

Ioana took note of her boyfriend's sarcasm and gave him one of her disapproving glances that even a severe nanny couldn't match when the children misbehave.

"Before I talk to you about my art," Renault continued, "I must tell you why it almost didn't make it here in the first place. The installations risked being more minimalist than I had originally intended." Refined chuckles from the audience.

"As it turns out," the artist explained, "My works were shipped by one of my galleries to the wrong address. So we had to hunt down the gallery owner, who, as luck would have it, was away on vacation. After a little research and much effort, we reached his wife, who wasn't especially forthcoming, since he happened to be on vacation with his mistress." More hearty laughter from the audience. "Fortunately, we managed to impress upon the wife the urgency of the matter, got his number and spoke to the mistress in question who was also, unfortunately, his most competent assistant." Laughter again. "She was the one who had mailed my installations to the Musée D'Orsay instead of Le Centre Pompidou. And who can blame her? After all, it's quite easy to mistake postmodern video installations for Impressionist paintings by Renoir, Monet and Sisley, right?" Appreciative laughter from the audience.

"Why are you laughing? You don't believe me?" Renault taunted his audience, now assuming an almost conversational manner. "Do you really think that there's a difference between traditional and postmodern art?" he asked.

During the rest of his talk, which lasted over an hour, Radu could hear over the periodic growls of his own empty stomach the artist's long answer to this short question. As far as he could gather, Renault did, indeed, believe that there was an "unbridgeable gap," "a "giant leap" as well as "an epistemic revolution" between traditional and postmodern art, but even if somebody beat him to a pulp, Radu couldn't summarize what it was. However, once he noticed that everyone was enthusiastically applauding—some had even stood up with a look of wild admiration in their eyes—Radu did grasp that the presentation was, mercifully, over. Now he could spend some quality time with his girlfriend.

"The reception's next," Ioana informed Radu with a wink, mistaking one appetite for another. He shrugged and said, "Alright," not feeling too disappointed to eat first.

The table was filled with all sorts of delicacies, including the pastries with which Ioana had lured him to the art exhibit. Radu heaped six of them on his plate, then followed his girlfriend around hiding behind his little mound of food.

"Could you please at least try to pretend you're civilized?" Ioana whispered to him in Romanian, in the same miffed nanny tone she had used earlier, when he showed up late. Radu was puzzled by his girlfriend's manner, which was usually playful and loving.

"Sure," he agreed, exhibiting a mouth filled with mushroom and cheese filling.

"Make sure you get a chance to speak to Jean-Pierre," she gave him further helpful instructions. "After you've chewed your food, of course," she felt compelled to add.

Radu dutifully swallowed the remains of the food, then asked: "Why?"

"Because of Radio Freedom Europe, why else?"

"What about it?"

Ioana rolled her eyes. "Don't you want publicity for your show?"

"Not that much..."

"But don't you want to get your parents and sister out of Romania?" Ioana reformulated her question.

Radu was obliged to admit that he did, but objected that he didn't see the connection between that fact and meeting a French postmodernist artist whose talk nearly put him to sleep.

"Jean-Pierre isn't just any artist. He's a famous French artist," Ioana emphasized with a meaningful arch of her eyebrows.

"So?"

"Do I need to spell out everything for you? He has connections. He can introduce you to journalists from *Le Monde* and *Libération* and generate enough noise in elite Parisian circles that the Romanian government will have to allow your family to immigrate to France!"

Framed in this manner, Radu began to see the merits of postmodern art. Still protective of his diminishing pile of pastries, he inched towards Jean-Pierre, who was surrounded by several eloquent individuals who were trying very hard to impress him. To Radu's surprise, this time the artist seemed rather pleased to see him, and even grabbed him by the elbow and pulled him aside.

"I've been meaning to talk to you," Jean-Pierre said, placing a fatherly hand upon Radu's shoulder, as if continuing a conversation with an old friend.

"Really?" the young man asked, then corrected himself: "Me too. I wanted to tell you how much I admire your art," he added, thinking that was the appropriate thing to say. Jean-Pierre gave him a look that indicated, who do you think you're fooling, but nevertheless continued addressing him in the same friendly and confidential manner. "Ioana told me that your parents are in trouble."

"They live in Romania," Radu replied.

"Ah! That explains it," Jean-Pierre immediately grasped the gravity of the situation. "Do you want us to apply pressure so they can join you here?"

"Sure," Radu answered, bewildered by this sudden offer. "But... who's 'us'?"

"Ioana has probably already told you that I'm good friends with a few of journalists from the top newspapers in Paris," Jean-Pierre modestly explained.

"Wow!" Radu attempted to sound impressed, which he sort of was.

"Would you like to meet one of them and discuss your family's situation?"

"Okay."

Jean-Pierre raised his index finger, in warning: "But remember: you must act professional. You can't present yourself like a pauper from a Third World country."

Radu hadn't been aware that was the image he currently projected. "Second World," he corrected, with a sense of wounded national pride.

"What I mean is I'll introduce you to my friend as someone important," the artist clarified.

"Really? Who?" Radu asked, wondering whom he was supposed to impersonate.

"Yourself, of course! You're an important journalist at Radio Freedom Europe."

"Oh, okay."

"Talk to him as if you were on equal footing."

"What do you mean?" Radu asked. By now, Jean-Pierre had the exasperated look of a man addressing an imbecile.

"Raducu," Ioana felt obliged to intervene, "What Jean-Pierre means is that you and Claude Bonnefoy, his friend who works for *Le Monde*, will be exchanging information." She gave him a meaningful glance.

Radu's expression, however, remained blank.

"Just think about it," she pursued. "if you were an ordinary Romanian citizen, *Le Monde* wouldn't really care about you and your family. I hate to sound so cynical, but it's true. Since you work for Radio Freedom Europe, however, you're privy to information that *Le Monde* lacks, and therefore have something to offer them in exchange for writing an article on your family. You see how this works?" Two pairs of eyes were expectantly pinned on Radu.

"I see," Radu replied blindly.

"Good," said Jean-Pierre, rubbing his hands together, as if the matter were settled. "I'll arrange the meeting between you and Claude for this Monday."

"Monday?" the young man looked worried. "But I have classes..."

"Monday's fine; we're very grateful for your kindness and generosity, Jean-Pierre," Ioana rushed to say. No matter how clearly Radu indicated that he needed more time to consider the proposal, to his chagrin, Ioana and the artist seemed to regard the interview appointment as final.

As a result of this slight misunderstanding, that evening Radu and Ioana had their first lovers' quarrel.

"Are you completely out of your mind?" he asked his girlfriend once they had reached her door at the Cité Universitaire. "You want me to give out secret information to some French journalist I neither know nor trust?"

"What are you so afraid of? You won't be cited as the source. Everything you share with Claude will be treated as strictly confidential," she reassured him.

"But that's not the issue!" Radu objected emphatically. "Even if I somehow managed to get my hands on those files, which is far from obvious, the letters sent to Radio Freedom Europe are not supposed to be disclosed to anybody other than the staff. We sign confidentiality contracts. People are risking their lives and the lives of their loved ones when they gather up the courage to write anything against the Petrescu regime!"

"Radu: do you care more about total strangers more than you do about your own family?" Ioana asked him pointblank.

"Of course not."

"Then I urge you to consider very seriously Jean-Pierre's proposal."

"Why do you refuse to understand? Even if by some miracle my boss decides to trust me with those misfortunate letters, I have to consider what's right, not just what's good for me and my family," Radu objected.

"Sometimes one needs to sacrifice professional ethics to save those one cares about most in life," Ioana countered. Her tone softened. "All I'm asking is: please think about it, okay?" she said and leaned over towards her boyfriend for their usual goodnight kiss. For the first time in their dating experience, however, his lips were cold and unresponsive. Even more alarmingly, Radu kept his roving hands to himself.

Ioana must have taken note of this disturbing phenomenon, since an hour later she called him on the phone.

"Hi, it's me."

"Hello," Radu answered more formally.

"I wanted to tell you that ... I'm sorry about how I behaved earlier this evening."

Radu didn't reply, patiently awaiting the rest of his girlfriend's heartfelt apology.

"I was a little bossy with you."

"Only a little?"

"The thing is... I truly value Jean-Pierre's advice. I've never once found him to be wrong about anything."

"I'm glad to see you have such independent judgment."

In ordinary circumstances, Ioana would have felt stung by her boyfriend's sarcasm and responded in kind. But this time she let it pass: "Well, obviously you're free to make your own decisions," she emphasized.

"Gee, thanks for the permission! Can I get it in writing to show it to my teacher?"

Ioana let the comment pass. "What I'm trying to say is... I'm really sorry that I pressured you. I feel terrible about it."

"That's alright," Radu began to soften.

Ioana felt encouraged by his response. Her tone became even sweeter: "Please believe me, Raducu, I really want what's best for you and your family..."

"I know."

"What that is, of course, is up to you to decide," she added.

"But there's nothing to decide in this case," Radu's anxiety returned. "Even if I did somehow manage to get my hands on those letters, I couldn't violate every norm of human decency and do something that risks the lives of innocent, trusting people just because that might get my family some media attention which might help my family immigrate. You must understand, Ioana, morally speaking, this decision's is a no-brainer."

"As you wish…" she said meekly, without sounding convinced. "Just, please, don't be so angry with me," she added. "After all, I'm not your enemy, am I?"

"Of course not," he said more gently.

"I'm your best friend…and even… a little bit more than that. Aren't I?"

Her feminine voice tickled his ear. "I'd say a lot more," he answered, his voice getting raspy with reawakened desire.

"Well then… let's act like best buddies, alright?"

"I'd prefer to act like…" Radu began, not finishing his thought.

"…a lot more than that?" Ioana completed his sentence.

"Yup."

"Me too," she concurred. "Whatever you decide about that meeting, Raducu, I'm sure it'll be the right decision. I have a lot of faith in your judgment."

"Thanks," Radu replied, almost believing her.

"And… just so you know: I respect your moral integrity." She punctuated this statement by planting a kiss on the receiver. For a while, Radu's ear remained glued to the phone. Even after they said goodnight and hung up the telephone that evening, he still heard his girlfriend's tender kiss over the dial tone.

Chapter 4

He remembered her the way she was the day he left for Paris: two front teeth missing; eyes glimmering with anticipation of the presents she might receive; a German Barbie doll in her hands with the hair clumping together from being washed too often in the bathtub with cheap glycerin soap. He had already said goodbye to his parents and grandparents, but she clung to him at the door. Little Irina must have been about seven years old. Now she'd be eight. Radu could hardly believe that a year had already passed since he last saw his little sister.

"So what will you get me?" Irina had asked, tugging at his free hand when he was all ready to go, standing in the doorway with his large, boxy suitcase in the other hand.

"It's all about the gifts for you, isn't it, stirbo?" Ever since Irina had lost two of her front teeth, he called her "little toothless one" as a term of endearment.

"By the time you come back, I'll have brand new teeth. Grownup ones," she boasted. "Can you please bring me a new Barbie? A pretty French one. This one's all sticky."

"That's because you play with her in the bathtub. Barbies aren't built to take such abuse."

"I get bored in there all by myself. Besides, the water's so cold. Greta Barbie keeps me warm." In Irina's nomenclature, Barbie was always the doll's last name, but the first name had to represent the country of origin. So far her father had only bought her a German Barbie during his last conference abroad, but Irina hoped to add the whole United Nations to her modest collection of one. "Why are you going to France?" she asked her brother.

"To study at the Sorbonne, a university in Paris."

"So are you going to France or Paris?" Irina was confused.

"To Paris, France. Just like we live in Bucharest, Romania. Paris is the city, France is the country," Radu assumed the didactic tone he used when helping his little sister with her homework.

"That's a nice place, isn't it?"

"Very."

"Then can I please come with you?" the little girl judiciously decided that she preferred a vacation in Paris to a French doll.

"Maybe one day."

"Do dogs really wear bagels on their tails in France?" she asked, as if to confirm an important detail that determined the desirability of the place.

"Pardon?"

"That's what Grandpa Mihai told me," Irina blinked knowingly. To her, Grandpa Mihai, who was the family expert in world history and geography, was an infallible source of information on these subjects.

"I haven't heard anything about that. But, now that you mention it, that's the first thing I'll check out when I get there."

"Promise?"

"Promise!"

Would he fulfill his promise to his little sister? Would he be able to bring her to a place where food and opportunities were plentiful, where she would have a future? And what risks was he willing to take to give his family a chance at the freer life that he was now living?

"May I take your order, Monsieur?" a young brunette waitress stood next to his table, notepad in hand.

"I'm waiting for someone..." Radu answered vaguely, jolted from his recollections.

"Okay. I'll check back on you in a few minutes," the waitress replied and gracefully swayed her hips between the tables to take other orders.

A middle aged man who seemed to be looking for someone crossed Radu's field of vision. He resembled Ioana's description of Claude Bonnefoy: short, with gray steely eyes framed by glasses. "He's a very nice, professional guy. And a brilliant journalist," she had added. "Every man you're friends with seems to be a genius," Radu had commented. "I can't help it if that's the kind of men I attract," Ioana had answered in jest, which, despite the implicit compliment, wasn't exactly reassuring to Radu.

"M. Schwarz?" the journalist asked in a raspy voice.

"Yes."

"Claude Bonnefoy," he shook Radu's hand firmly. "Glad to meet you. Sorry I'm a little late. I hope I haven't kept you waiting for too long."

"No, not at all. I just got here myself only a few minutes ago," Radu answered. Claude's accent was definitely not Parisian, it occurred to him. He had a sing-song voice, like those from the south of France, and rolled his r's more harshly, like Spaniards or Italians. "Are you from Marseille?" he asked him.

"Good guess. I'm from Montpellier," the journalist answered amiably, taking a seat and signaling with his hand to the waitress, with the air of a man with limited time who's used to prompt service.

She came quickly to their table. Claude asked for an espresso; Radu for a Turkish coffee with the grounds still at the bottom of the cup, like the ones his grandmother used to make on special occasions, namely when coffee beans were available. When Claude smiled or even talked, Radu noticed that that some of his back teeth were capped with gold fillings. He found that somewhat unusual, since gold fillings were rare in the West, but quite common, at least for the privileged, in Eastern Europe.

"My good friend Jean-Pierre told me that your family's going through a tough time," Claude delved into the topic at hand.

"Yes... Well.. They've faced some difficulties since I've been gone," Radu replied.

"What kind of difficulties?" Claude removed a little notebook and a pen from the left pocket of his jacket.

"This conversation's confidential, right?" Radu wanted to confirm.

"Of course."

"Well... in Romania... let's just say that those who have family members that defect to Western countries are put on a black list. Actually, what happens is that their dossiers become tainted."

Claude's snow-tipped Montblanc pen lingered in the air. "What do you mean?"

"Communism is in some ways similar to religion, except for the belief in God part."

"That's not exactly a detail," Claude remarked.

"True. Still, basically, in communism, we're all born with a dossier that records not just our own activities but also those of family members and friends as well. Nobody's record is completely spotless, of course, since practically everyone has family members or friends who have sinned."

"Sinned?"

"Yes. By defecting to a Western country or saying something against the government or refusing to do the things the Secret Police have asked them to do, such as spying or becoming an informant," Radu explained. "We're all sinners, so to speak. But the closer the sinners are to you, the more tainted your dossier becomes. And, it goes without saying, the more you and your loved ones suffer as a result. My family's probably being punished as we speak for the sin of my defection."

"How so?"

Radu didn't know what to say. He didn't even have all the information himself; on the phone, his parents could only hint at their problems.

Claude noticed his hesitation: "Look: I can't write an article based on such generalizations. Without personal testimonies, I've got nothing."

Radu raised his eyes towards the waitress, who had arrived with their beverages. She set the coffees down carefully on the table and asked them if they needed anything else. Radu wished he could ask this seemingly kind and indisputably pretty young woman what to say and especially what not to say.

"My parents are being monitored much more by the Secret Police since I left the country and took the Radio Freedom Europe job," he finally answered.

"How can they tell?"

"When my mother was vacuuming one day, she discovered a mike under my father's desk. Then both of my parents searched thoroughly the apartment and found several more microphones hidden behind the heaters. In every room, even the bathroom."

"Isn't that normal? I mean…for Romania?"

"Not really. The government lacks the human resources to monitor twenty million people. Only if you have the honor of making it on their black list do they go through the trouble of observing you and your loved ones more closely."

"Did your parents suffer any harassment at work?" Claude pursued.

Radu didn't want to give him details about his father's job, especially since he worked for the dictator's daughter. "I don't know. They can't really discuss such matters with me over the phone."

"Not even in code?" Claude fixed Radu with his steely gray eyes.

"Well, practically everyone in Romania has some roundabout way of talking about their political situation," Radu answered evasively.

"What's yours?" Claude asked him.

"Mine? I don't have one. I talk about it directly on Radio Freedom Europe," Radu said, in effect changing the subject. But this diversionary tactic only opened a bigger can of worms.

"Which leads me to my next question," Claude said, casting a quick glance at his watch.

"If you're in a hurry, we can continue our conversation some other time..." Radu generously offered.

"No, I'm fine. We have plenty of time. My next appointment's not 'till 3:30."

Radu felt disheartened. He was not psychologically prepared for this interview. The previous night the situation had seemed so clear-cut. He had resolved not to offer to tell the journalist anything that might put anybody else's life at risk. But there was no way to avoid taking risks, since not doing anything to save his family was in itself risky. Having spent the whole night thinking about his family and speculating about what they might be going through because of his defection and radio show, Radu was overcome by doubts and plagued by a sense of guilt. Perhaps Ioana was right. Perhaps he owed his parents and little sister more than he owed total strangers. After all, who was he to turn down what may very well be their only chance to escape from Romania?

Claude grew increasingly irritated by Radu's reticence. "Listen, if you don't wish to talk about this, that's fine with me," the journalist assumed an air of impatience, pushing away from the table with both hands. He has such Latin gestures, Radu couldn't help but notice.

"No. It's just that... I'm in a delicate situation," the young man tried to explain his misgivings.

"I understand," Claude answered, but his voice sounded unsympathetic.

"When one works for Radio Freedom Europe, one can never be too careful," Radu repeated his mantra since he had taken the sensitive job.

"Every journalist is privy to confidential information. Which is why I was hoping we'd be talking journalist to journalist, governed by the same code of professional ethics," Claude replied.

Radu was struck by the similarity between Claude's formulation and Jean-Pierre's, the previous night. In principle, he agreed with them. But in reality human lives were at stake and the whole equation hinged upon an unknown factor: trust of strangers. He wasn't exactly raised with that ethos.

Claude removed from his pocket a pack of cigarettes, then, after lighting one with quick and nervous movements, he asked: "Mind if I smoke?"

"Not at all," Radu answered, after the fact.

Claude blew out smoke to the left while gazing steadily into Radu's eyes. He no longer asked any questions; no longer made any effort to persuade his interlocutor to disclose information.

"What do you plan to write in your article? I mean, what is it supposed to be about?" Radu asked, not so much from genuine curiosity as from the need to break the awkward silence.

"You tell me," Claude replied with a shrug. "So far you haven't given me anything to work with."

Radu looked down and meticulously folded his napkin into a neat, triangular shape. Claude tapped his cigarette on the border of the ashtray.

"Alright," Radu finally decided. "What information do you need from me to write the article on my family?"

To the young man's surprise, Claude didn't seem particularly excited about this step forward in their negotiation. "Basically, what we want…" the journalist began to explain.

"We?" Radu interrupted.

"Sure. We, the editors and readers of *Le Monde*," Claude clarified, "What we need is specific information about what happens to dissident families in Romania. To yours, of course, but also to others. Your family will be our special interest story, to add a personal touch to the piece. But we need information about more than just one family, otherwise your plight might look like an aberration. What interests us is what happens to those who write to Radio Freedom Europe to complain about the Petrescu regime. And we need hard evidence, concrete facts and real names," he tapped the table with his knuckles, "since obviously we're a reputable newspaper and can't publish an article based on hearsay or anecdotal evidence."

"What do you mean 'hard evidence'? You want me to obtain for you the actual names and letters?" Radu asked incredulously, recoiling from the implications of this explicit and, it seemed to him, brutal request, even though he had been considering this very issue for nearly two days.

"Not necessarily. Photocopies will do. Or even photographs of the letters, which we can magnify and decipher."

Radu remained silent.

"Think about our offer and contact me if you're interested," Claude said, then extinguished his cigarette and stood up. Before leaving, the journalist tossed his business card on the table.

Radu picked it up and examined it closely.

Claude Bonnefoy
Redacteur-en-Chef
Nouvelles Internationales
Le Monde
80, bd Auguste Blanqui
75707 Paris Cedex 13

Why in the world didn't he want to interview me at his workplace, like I initially suggested? the young man wondered, tempted to go check out that address.

Chapter 5

All month long, in fact, practically ever since the day they met, Radu saved enough money to invite Ioana out to dinner at a real restaurant, Chez Georges, which was decidedly several stars above their regular cafés and a few constellations above the Cité Universitaire cafeteria. Given what he had just discovered, however, the young man now wavered. Should he still see Ioana? And if so, how should he behave with her? Everything about their relationship had seemed so... genuine. Radu thought about his girlfriend's warm dark eyes, about her affectionate manner. He recalled the way they had written together his pieces for Radio Freedom Europe, their intimate talks, their explorations of Paris, their playful sensuality. Was she faking it all? And if so, how was she implicated in this business? Radu resolved to find out the truth that very evening.

When he got to his dorm room, the young man put on his dating outfit: a blue cotton shirt, slightly wrinkled but with a fashionably pointy collar; flared gray rayon pants; navy blue silk socks, which unfortunately had a few holes in them, but no one would notice, since his feet would be inside the pair of worn-out shoes he wore to both school and work. Though allergic to perfume, Radu even went so far as to spray on some Ralph Lauren cologne. They had agreed to meet directly at the restaurant, on 1 rue du Mail, at 7:00 o'clock sharp. He took the metro, staring out the window in a trance-like state as the scenery rolled by, nursing his suspicions yet at the same time wishing to believe in Ioana's sincerity.

Radu arrived first. He paced up and down the street outside the restaurant, which made the doorman, who was standing stiffly in front of a Citroën Traction Avant waiting to drive guests back to the Ritz, look at him with a hint of disdain.

"Waiting for my date," the young man explained with an awkward smile in his foreign accent.

"Ah! Je comprends parfaitement... Bonne chance!" the doorman declared sympathetically and gave Radu a complicit wink.

When Ioana made her appearance about ten minutes later, the doorman thought he understood perfectly well the source of Radu's agitation. Radu noted how even he, who must have gotten his share of seeing beautiful women come into the fancy Parisian bistro, looked at his girlfriend with undisguised admiration. Ioana was stunning in a low-cut silver top and a black miniskirt which drew attention to her long, lean legs, slim waist and gently curvaceous forms. She smiled and kissed Radu twice on one cheek, once on the other, giving him the typical Parisian "bise."

"Buna," she greeted him "Hi" in Romanian, as usual.

Despite his misgivings, Radu made every effort to make Ioana feel at ease: he pulled up her chair, paid her sincere compliments on her appearance and, although he wasn't exactly the demonstrative type, even went so far as to call her frumusica mea, "my little beautiful one."

The atmosphere at Chez Georges was warm and convivial but not conducive to intimate conversation, as Radu had hoped. The tables were packed closely together; the restaurant was noisy and filled to the brim (he had to make reservations two weeks in advance to even get a table); the waiters were elegant and solicitous, constantly coming by to ask if there was anything else you desired and accept compliments for the elegant presentation and delicious cuisine.

Radu looked at the handwritten menu several times yet he still had no idea what to order, primarily because, although he spoke French fluently, he couldn't understand much of its old-style cursive print. Eager to enjoy a taste of Paris, the couple asked the waiter for suggestions. Both followed his recommendation and ordered the house specialty— a salade frisée composed of curly endive dressed with vinegar and bacon and topped with a poached egg. For the main course, Radu and Ioana said "oui" to whatever the waiter proposed as typically French, though, since the latter spoke very quickly, neither fully understood what they had ordered. Ioana received a spectacular tête de veau sauce gribiche, a veal's head with caper sauce. To her horror, it still included the brains, but she didn't make a fuss, just shifted it around on her plate, pretending that she was so refined that she enjoyed it. Unbeknownst to him, Radu had asked for calf's liver with bacon—although he had avoided liver even when he was half-starving in Romania—so he focused upon the accompanying pommes frites, the part of his meal that he could have gotten for five francs on the street.

"How did your interview go?" Ioana initiated the conversation.

"Pretty good."

"Isn't Claude a fascinating guy?"

"More than I had imagined."

"Did he tell you about how he grew up in a poor working class family and become one of the most important journalists in the country?"

"No, we didn't get that far in our conversation."

"I guess he was being strictly professional with you, huh?"

"It depends upon what profession you're referring to."

"Did you get into the stuff about RFE?"

"Kind of."

"What do you mean?"

"I didn't commit to anything."

"Why not?"

"First of all, because I don't have any information to give. And second of all, I because wasn't sure I could trust him," Radu answered, fixing Ioana with his gaze in a less subtle way than he had planned.

She didn't appear phased, however. "Why not? He's got a stellar reputation. His name's all over the place."

"Not just his name," Radu concurred. "He as well. It's as if he were cloned."

Iona put down her fork. "What in the world are you talking about?"

"I decided to do a little bit of research on this Claude character after our meeting."

"And? Isn't he a well-respected journalist, just like I told you?"

"That he is."

"Then what's the problem?"

Radu had never heard Ioana speak in that nasal, whinny voice. Why was she nervous? What was she hiding? "The problem is that the guy who interviewed me at the café yesterday wasn't Claude Bonnefoy," he stated as calmly as possible.

The young woman appeared genuinely surprised. "I don't understand. Then who was he?"

"That's what I was hoping you'd clarify. I asked to meet Claude at his office, but he suggested that we meet at a particular café instead. And the guy I met, I don't know how to explain it. My intuition told me that there was something fishy about him."

"That's because you're paranoid. You think there's something fishy about everyone you meet," Ioana objected.

"And am I wrong?"

Ioana rolled her eyes in response.

"Be that as it may, this guy I met at the café didn't look or act or even smell French to me. He had a trace of an accent, but at first I couldn't quite place it."

"He was raised near Marseille."

"I know. He told me he was from Montpellier. But his accent wasn't really southern French. Or rather, it was a Midi accent plus a hint of something else. Something closer to... Romanian. He rolled his r's like we do."

Ioana sighed. "Since when are you a linguistics expert? Lots of people roll their r's, you know. Maybe his mother's Spanish, who knows?"

Radu wasn't satisfied with his girlfriend's explanation. "He sounded Eastern European, not Spanish, to me. So I decided to follow my intuition and went to check out his office at *Le Monde*."

"And...?"

Radu paused and examined his girlfriend's expression. She's a pretty good actress, faking ignorance like this, he thought. "...and that's where I met the real Claude Bonnefoy. He had no idea who I was even though you and Jean-Pierre supposedly spoke to him about me. He didn't speak with a Romanian accent.

And he didn't have any plans to write any special interest story whatsoever about Romanian dissidents who write to Radio Freedom Europe to complain about the Petrescu regime. Now how do you figure that?"

Ioana looked perplexed. "I don't know what could have happened..."

"You don't?"

"There must be a logical explanation for this."

"Would you care to share it with me?"

"All I can say is that both Jean-Pierre and I did talk to Claude about your situation and suggested a potential article."

"Which Claude?"

"The real one of course."

"Which one is that?"

"The one you met at *Le Monde*. I think..." But even Ioana didn't seem so sure any more.

"Okay, so, for the sake of argument, we can say that maybe the real Claude had amnesia. Anything's possible," Radu said, his sarcastic tone contradicting that claim. "But then how do you account for the fake Claude I met with at the café?"

Ioana shifted nervously in her seat. "Maybe he's a mole. Someone at Jean-Pierre's party might have overheard your conversation," she suggested.

"Possibly." He allowed for a pause, then added: "I also did a little research on you."

"Are you implying that I had something to do with this?"

"No. I'm stating it directly."

Ioana got up abruptly from her chair. Her cheeks were flushed: "Listen Radu, if you suspect me of being involved with the Secret Police, then I'll have nothing to do with you any more!"

Despite his state of anxiety, Radu managed to find some humor in this absurd situation. "Under the circumstances, shouldn't I be the one breaking up with you?"

Ioana didn't respond.

"What I can say for sure," Radu continued, "is that you're my main contact for Jean-Pierre and Claude, so, whatever you say, you're clearly implicated in this business."

"Jean-Pierre has been a good friend to me. He's helped me a lot," Ioana started to explain.

"Just a friend?" Radu interrupted.

The young woman avoided his glance.

"Ioana, please answer my question. I need to figure out what the hell's going on. My life may be in danger!"

"We made love once," she answered softly, "Shortly after we met at a party. "But we were never girlfriend and boyfriend. He's more like a father figure to me. A mentor. And I truly do love his art."

"Do you think he's connected to the Secret Police?"

Ioana shook her head.

"How about Claude, his buddy?"

"Both are beyond suspicion," Ioana declared with confidence.

"How can you be so sure?"

"Because... think about it... why would they spy for the Romanian Secret Police? Why would they risk their lives when they have nothing to gain from it? They're both French, rich and famous. They have everything they could possibly want. There's absolutely no motive. And, to tell you the truth..."

"For once..."

"...your suspicion really offends me," Ioana completed her sentence. "Why would I ever want to harm you? Don't look at me like that! Are you that blinded by paranoia? Can't you see that... I'm in love with you?

This was the first time Ioana avowed her feelings openly. Under any other circumstances, Radu would have been thrilled. But at the moment, it only made him more apprehensive. "I looked up your family in our Radio Freedom Europe files," he answered softly, deliberately ignoring Ioana's declaration.

She nodded, as if she knew in advance what he had discovered.

"Why didn't you tell me that your dad was such an outspoken dissident?"

"I told you the first time we met that was arrested and imprisoned, remember?"

"Yes, but you never told me that he's known throughout Europe for criticizing the Romanian government!"

"So what? Why does that matter?" Ioana objected.

Radu considered her question. "What I find strange about this whole situation is not that your father is a dissident, but that that the Romanian government allowed you to come to France given your family history," Radu said in a low voice, as if talking to himself. "How did you manage to persuade them to do that?"

"I don't know," Ioana shrugged. "It's not a matter of persuading anybody. You know how it works. The government does what it wants; we have no control over its decisions. It's like in Kafka's Castle."

"Did they ask you to be an informant for them?" Radu looked steadily into her eyes.

"No," Ioana responded. "I just asked to go study French literature for a year at the Sorbonne, and they issued me a student visa, that's all. If I want to return to Romania and see my family again, I have to be careful. So I do my best to steer away from politics."

"Is that why you've chosen to date a guy whose job it is to criticize the Petrescu regime on Radio Freedom Europe?

"I didn't date you for that reason!" Ioana protested.

"Then why did you?"

"Isn't it obvious?"

"No."

"Then your self-esteem must not be that high."

"That much is true. Otherwise I wouldn't have allowed myself to be seduced by you."

"I seduced you?" Ioana asked, incredulously pointing to herself.

"Well, you initiated the whole thing."

"You didn't seem to mind."

"In the beginning I did. I didn't know what to think about you."

"And now?" Her gaze shifted nervously across his features.

"Quite honestly, now I'm more confused than ever."

"Raducu, please trust me." Her voice was sensual, soft. "Don't sabotage our relationship. Give us a chance."

Radu didn't know what to believe anymore.

Ioana moved closer to him. "You must believe me. I don't know what happened with Claude. I don't even know if you met the real Claude or the impostor in that office. I swear that Jean-Pierre and I did mention you to the real journalist. Maybe he forgot about you, since he's so busy and gets literally hundreds of tips and suggestions for articles a week. Maybe someone else, somebody working for the Secret Police, overheard Jean-Pierre set up your appointment with the journalist. Whatever happened, you're right to worry. From now on, you'll have to be extra careful. You're obviously under surveillance." She paused briefly, then reached across the table and placed her hand upon his, adding, "Your job is placing you in danger. Can't you find another one?"

"That's what my parents keep telling me."

Ionana nodded approvingly. "I think you should listen to them. I know this from everything that happened to my father after he spoke out against the government. Consider this brush with the impostor journalist as your first--and last--warning. Stay away from politics."

Radu snickered at her last statement. "If you want me to stay away from politics and care so much about my safety, then why did you pressure me to get involved with Jean-Pierre and Claude in the first place?"

For a moment Ioana looked stumped, but she quickly recovered: "Because I wanted to help you get your family out of Romania. I knew how important that was to you."

"What about your own contact with these men?" Radu pursued.

"What about it? I never discuss with them my life in Romania, much less politics. If Jean-Pierre happens to ask me any personal questions about my family or the Petrescu regime, I change the subject."

"I thought you said you trusted him."

"I do. But, like I said, you never know who else is watching you at these public receptions. Or what others may be able to overhear with hidden microphones. Or even what Jean-Pierre or Claude might tell others, without meaning to be indiscreet or jeopardize your life. Keep in mind, they're Westerners, used to the freedom of expression. They can't understand how life in communism works and all the dangers we face. Raducu, please, I beg you: quit your job."

"We'll see. For now, I like working at RFE. Plus I need the money."

"Is there anything I can do to help you find a safer job?" Ioana asked with a look of visible concern.

"No, but thanks anyway."

Overall, Radu felt somewhat reassured by this conversation with his girlfriend. I never really thought she was an agent, he now told himself. The waiter came by and removed their plates. To compensate for their pickiness with the entrees, the couple unabashedly gorged on the next course—peasant bread and an assortment of tasty cheeses. During this part of their dinner, they hardly talked. All of their attention was focused upon pasting the cubes of blue cheese, brie and camembert to the warm, freshly baked bread. They left the restaurant satiated--Radu with a much lighter wallet--and pleased to have had the experience of the famous cuisine, ambiance, exorbitance and, above all, in their eyes, exoticism of Paris.

Radu walked his girlfriend to her dorm door at the Cité and, as usual, kissed her goodnight. But she didn't leave it at that this time. "Vino cu mine. Come with me," she said. The young man blushed, then felt embarrassed for his inexperience. "Are you sure?" he asked, wishing to treat her with the utmost respect.

"I'm sure," she answered and gave him a long, persuasive kiss. They rushed up the stairs, Ioana leading her boyfriend by the hand. As soon as the door closed behind them, the young woman clung to his body, lavishing him with caresses that simultaneously tantalized and pleased. "Raducu, te iubesc," she whispered "I love you" into his ear. It took them only a few seconds to shed their clothes, each impatiently undressing the other. Being more experienced, Ioana took the lead. She pressed between her lips the lobes of his ears, which curved slightly outward, as if beckoning her touch. She licked them gently, with the tip of her tongue. Her hands paused with instinctive admiration upon the lean muscles around his waist. "What a little Adonis you are!" she said with delight.

"Not really. I just like to work out once in a while," Radu modestly replied. To his own surprise, he assumed the more passive role. He had envisioned the first sexual encounter with Ioana very differently. From the day they met, he had played the scenario over and over in his mind. He thought that the first time he'd be very impatient. That he'd unleash his pent-up desire, his youthful longing, his prolonged virginity and consume her in one fell swoop. He had rehearsed in his mind several variations of this fantasy, in various places, in different positions. But all of them had in common him assuming the lead and taking possession of his delectable girlfriend in one swift motion. In his own mind, Ioana was erotic yet ethereal, her own person yet infinitely pliable to his will, a beautiful doll that could fulfill all of his needs. He recurrently imagined her bent over the desk, her legs spread wide apart, a position he had encountered quite often in soft porn magazines. She wore her high heel sandals and nothing else. Mesmerized by her rounded curves and by the paleness of her skin, he'd aim without mercy at the vulnerable target between her lips and burst inside her all at once.

Now that his dream was finally being realized, however, he felt too moved by the novelty of the erotic experience to rush towards immediate gratification. He delighted at the silky softness of her skin, at the flow of her curves. After hours of petting and kissing, his body ached from the strain of constant sexual arousal. Yet he still hesitated, wishing to explore with his hands, lips and tongue every inch of his girlfriend's taut body before liberating his own instinct for pleasure. He stroked the soft sides of her rounded breasts with the tips of his fingers, like an artist might trace the curves of his sculpture. His lips pursued the sensory trail left by his fingertips. Ioana moaned from his touch and hurriedly lifted his head, covering his lips with her own. She then shivered with impatience, reclined on the bed, pulled him unto her and moved her hips rhythmically. Wave upon wave of pleasure built up inside of him. He closed his eyes, becoming oblivious in that pulsating darkness to all other sensations. In the focused intensity of his desire, he felt an explosion of energy released in several spasms that left him complacent yet drained. He collapsed upon his girlfriend and she protectively wrapped her arms around him, tenderly stroking his back. In turn, he began caressing her, to become reacquainted with her body. Encountering a viscous liquid trickling between her thighs jolted him from his state of tranquility. What if she gets pregnant? it occurred to him to wonder. But he immediately dismissed this idea, feeling certain that Ioana would have been savvy enough to protect herself. She shifted her position, resting her head upon his shoulder. He tenderly stroked her glossy dark hair. Then his hand glided towards the small her back, absentmindedly tracing upon it imaginary circular shapes with a delicate touch.

All of a sudden, a large man dressed in a blue shirt and navy pants burst into the peaceful room. Before the couple had a chance to react, he lunged towards Radu, pulled him roughly by the shoulder and began shouting in French: "Petit con! What the hell do you think you're doing fucking my wife?"

After feeling a sharp pain right below his right eye, Radu pushed the man away with all of his might. "You're married?" he managed to ask Ioana, bewildered and caught off guard.

"No! I've never seen this man in my life," she protested, standing up from the bed and grabbing her dress, which she clutched to her chest. "If you don't leave immediately, I'll call the police," she threatened and picked up the receiver, after having hurriedly dressed.

"Don't bother. They're already waiting for us downstairs," the "wronged husband" announced, nonplussed.

"Who's 'they'?" Radu asked. But instead of answering his question, the intruder pushed Radu against the wall and threw him an unexpected punch into the stomach, making him double over from pain.

"How dare you screw my wife?" The intruder sounded like a bad actor in a farce.

Radu nonetheless tried to reason with him, pretending to play along with the lunatic, if only to calm him down. "Hold on a minute. I didn't even know that Ioana was married."

"Oh yeah? Did you even bother to ask before fucking her?" the man shouted back.

Radu's gaze shifted towards Ioana, who walked towards him and handed him his clothes. She had had a few moments to gather herself and placed herself in front of Radu, facing the stranger: "Listen, I don't know who you are, but the police are on their way, so you better leave," she said quietly yet firmly.

The intruder pushed her aside, like one waves off a fly: "This is between me and him. Don't intervene!" he said, grabbing Radu by the scruff of his neck. He then dragged the dazed young man down the stairs, into the foyer of the dormitory, where two men dressed as policemen were waiting for them.

"This guy raped my wife!" the angry "husband" shouted pointing to Radu, to draw public attention to the scene. Several pairs of curious eyes surveyed Radu and Ioana, both of whom looked like they had hastily dressed after being caught in flagrante delicto.

"I did no such thing," Radu protested, turning to his girlfriend. "Ioana tell them the truth!"

Ioana, who had courageously defended her boyfriend only a few moments earlier, now gazed silently at the two policemen. One of them nodded in her direction—exactly as one nods to a dog when one wants it to obey one's commands. The second policeman looked at her very sternly, which led her to avert her gaze. Meanwhile, as more and more students gathered around the scene, Radu continued to protest that Ioana was his girlfriend and that they had had consensual sex. He even called upon witnesses—the fellow students who were acquainted with them both—to confirm that they were dating. The angry "husband," however, continued to shout obscenities at Radu, while one of the two policemen, a bulky man with a mustache, pretended to calm him down. He spoke French perfectly but with a heavy accent. "We'll clear up this matter at the police station," the officer declared, taking Radu by the arm and leading him out into the street towards an unmarked car. Radu looked around. The angry husband, along with Ioana, had vanished into thin air.

Chapter 6

Eva stood in front of the hallway mirror, nervously passing a worn-out tube of frosty pink lipstick back and forth across her lips.

"After our scare last night, I really don't feel like going to this stupid party," she said, clicking the cap of the lipstick shut, then tossing it back into her black sequin purse, a gift from her mother for her twentieth wedding anniversary.

"There must be a logical explanation for this," Andrei replied. "Besides, we'll ask Silvia about it. Don't forget, that's one of the reasons we're going to her party in the first place," he reminded his wife.

"That, plus the fact that we have no choice," she added.

Given that the dictator's daughter, Silvia Petrescu, had personally invited them to her get-together, Andrei couldn't dispute this claim.

Although in his early forties, Andrei seemed much younger. His slimness, bright blue eyes and glossy black hair, along with a certain awkward coltishness in his gait and gestures--which Eva proudly regarded as a manifestation of his "scientific genius" while her parents saw it as your run-of-the-mill nerdiness— gave him the appearance of a young man.

Andrei put his hands around his wife's rounded shoulders, visible from her strapless gray evening dress which her mother had sown when Eva was seventeen. "It still fits," the husband couldn't help but notice with a sense of satisfaction the way the silky material clung to his wife's hourglass figure. Their glances met in the mirror. That evening, he noticed, Eva's large hazel eyes were surrounded by dark shadows. The signs of sleeplessness and worry couldn't be masked even by the excessive dark-green eye shadow she wore on special occasions.

"It's only been one show, Papusica," Andrei tried to reassure his wife tenderly using her childhood pet name, "little doll," which is how he usually addressed her--unless they were arguing, in which case they ominously called each other by their real first names, Andrei and Eva.

Andrei was not one to panic; nonetheless, he too felt nervous. Each Monday night they listened to their son's broadcast on Radio Freedom Europe. They were proud of Radu's courage, but in their heart of hearts wished that he'd have pursued safer extracurricular activities than denouncing the Petrescu regime on international radio. They had suggested to him joining the chess club, for example. As a result of his son's job, Andrei was beginning to be harassed at work by informants. Eva thought that her boss at the Ministry of Education, where she worked as a school inspector for the National Science Curriculum, had started to become more curt with her. The parents' uppermost worry, however, was not for their own wellbeing but for their son's safety. Petrescu was infamous for having his Secret Police hunt down and eliminate those who criticized him openly. Although Andrei tried to be optimistic and comfort his wife, he sorely wished Radu would call to let them know that he was safe and sound. Having spent the previous night in endless hypothetical discussions about their son's whereabouts and counterfactual mutual blame about which parent was most responsible for his dangerous activities, Andrei and Eva tried to call Radu about half a dozen times that day, but couldn't even get a connection to France.

"Until we hear from Raducu, I won't be able to sleep at night," Eva forewarned her husband, passing a comb through her boyishly short hair. Before meeting her husband, she used to have long, wavy dark hair that reached down almost to her waist. Andrei, however, preferred more subtle versions of femininity—such as women who looked like boys and were pros at math and science. After they began dating, Eva kept her hairstyle short and her look androgynous.

"Panicking won't do anybody any good," Andrei responded philosophically. Nonetheless, his wife's anxiety was contagious. A presentiment of finality passed over him, reinforcing a growing obsession: the thought of flight. "We can't go on living like this," he whispered, mostly to himself. Ironically, the party given by Silvia Petrescu was in his honor. He had recently won a prestigious fellowship in Physics at the Princeton Institute of Advanced Studies, where Albert Einstein had taught. Even the Romanian government couldn't say no to such a rare opportunity for one of its citizens. A few years ago, following his refusal to spy at Hebrew University, Secret Police informants had told Andrei that he'd never be allowed again to travel to conferences abroad. His boss, however, was eager to lead an internationally recognized Physics Institute. Silvia therefore pulled a few strings to make an exception in this general policy. Yet even having the dictator's daughter on his side didn't make life easier for Andrei and his family. Living in constant fear of the Secret Police; foraging for food on a daily basis and, above all, ceaselessly worrying about the safety of their children, outweighed all possible benefits of a decent job and academic honors.

As the couple exited their apartment—a small two-bedroom place in a bloc, or apartment building, constructed with cheap materials in the sixties—they were taken aback by an unpleasant odor in the hallway. The stench of fried onions coming from the family next door and of alcohol emanating from the apartment of the factory worker across the hallway were overpowering. Like her husband, Eva couldn't help but express her thoughts with a sigh, "Ce mizerie! What a miserable existence," she exclaimed as they got into their bright yellow Dacia, the Romanian brand of car that resembled a Citroën. Which wasn't exactly a coincidence, since the prototype for the Dacia was stolen from the French by Romanian tech spies. Of course, the Romanians made several improvements upon the French model. To cite just one significant update Romanian auto engineers made to their version of the Citroën: one couldn't turn the car off by simply removing the key from the ignition; one had to turn on the headlights first. This "unique safety feature" would presumably stump any foreign car thieves living in Romania who were in the market for Dacias—the only caveat being that such thieves didn't actually exist. By instinct, Andrei recalled the date: it was April 15th, which meant it was legal for them to drive that day. Because of overcrowded streets and the scarcity of gas, Romanians living in Bucharest were allowed to drive only every other week, taking turns, even or odd weekends, depending upon their license plate numbers.

Andrei agreed with his wife's pessimistic assessment. The word "misery," particularly given the anxious mood that had overtaken them, captured the mood of their daily existence. Take a typical day in Andrei's life: he woke up at 5:00 a.m., even on Sundays. Milk line, an hour a day, just to find out whether or not one hit the jackpot and got any. Bread line, half an hour a day, which was more productive because usually they had the-day-before-yesterday-leftover bread which was so hard that it could be used as a hammer. For the daily exercise of foraging for food, even more important than infinite patience was having sharp elbows, to defend oneself against the competition, which consisted primarily of little kids who constantly cut in line. Then, Monday through Saturday, Andrei had the pleasure of going to the Institute to teach Theoretical Physics to completely disinterested engineering students who dozed off in their seats. That took five hours a day, not counting the two hour bus commute, which, given that busses were systematically late, few and packed with people who had never heard of deodorant, offered its own delights. Then, at the end of the day, try the milk and the bread lines again, just in case the seller had stashed away some products that hadn't made the cut for small gifts and bribes.

Eva, who came home from the Ministry of Education around 8:00 p.m., two hours later than her husband, was in charge of buying the nearly extinct species of beef, poultry and fish. This was an exceedingly easy job since the occasion presented itself so rarely that it made the local news—by word of mouth, of course, since on the actual news there were always food surpluses. Despite the paucity of meat products, Eva's function was important: she had to inspect the meat, by sight and smell, for traces of bacteria. Since her family was still alive, she was assumed to be an expert in the field, no matter how bad the poultry, pork or beef actually smelled or tasted. At any rate, the odor would be scorched by overcooking or at least masked by plenty of salt and pepper, Eva's usual recipes. Whenever anybody complained about her cuisine, she attributed her culinary talents to fatigue and lack of material to work with. The lack of material was indisputable; as for the fatigue, there Eva also had a point.

Andrei thought: it didn't always used to be like this. Sure, life under communism was hard. But they had managed to have many happy moments together. Eva and Andrei met when they were very young, only eighteen, during their first year of study at the University of Bucharest. There was an instant coup de foudre which, like all lightning, is usually accompanied by torrential rain.

Their parents did their best to persuade them to change their minds. Andrei Schwarz was a Jew from Moldavia; Eva Lörenz was an ethnic Hungarian from

Transylvania. No matter how you shook it, oil and water, their parents claimed, would never mix. The parents were careful to couch their objections in more acceptable non-ethnic terms, however. Since Andrei came from a small village, Tecuci (population 30,000), Eva's parents, who lived in a medium-sized city, Timisoara (population 300,000), claimed that their daughter was too accustomed to "cosmopolitan refinement" to get used to "country bumpkin" life. Country people, they told Eva, are ... how to put it tactfully?... backward peasants. "That's alright, since he's Jewish, which makes him more civilized," their daughter retorted provocatively, knowing the real reason behind her parents' objection. Her parents cringed and Andrei's parents weren't far behind in their reaction.

Despite the social similarity between the two families—they belonged to the minority groups that were most "problematic" in Romania—each found reasons to consider itself superior. Eva's parents came from the elite. Her father had been a navy officer before he retired and her mother was from Hungarian aristocracy (or so she claimed). Andrei's family came from the Chosen People. Even though Jews in Romania seemed to have been chosen mostly for oppression and hardship, the point remained that they were still Chosen. Which is why when the love birds told their parents that they wanted to get married, instead of the usual prenuptial family celebration, they were greeted with the second most common response: disownment. I disown you forever, you are no son/daughter of mine, their parents claimed, but after a couple of hours they changed their minds.

For scientists, Eva and Andrei didn't have such a shabby love story. They met at the university in Physics class. Andrei was the star student; he had even won the Olympiad. Eva was very bright herself, but what truly distinguished her was her gender and beauty. She was pretty much the only woman in her mathematics class who even qualified—without debate or challenge, that is—as female. Furthermore, she was also attractive: she had long dark hair, warm hazel eyes and a sensual mouth that beckoned for kisses (or so the male students thought, but she was so pretty and proud, that nobody dared approach her to test that theory empirically). Andrei was completely obsessed with mathematical formulas, which didn't prevent him, however, from calculating how Eva might fit into the equation. Yet like the other potential suitors, he was too shy to do or say anything.

He preferred to demonstrate his virility by being the fastest prover of theorems in the class. Which impressed all the girls with glasses whose gender was somewhat ambiguous, but it didn't seem to have much of an impact upon Eva. When Andrei was in front of the class, called upon a professor less endowed than him to explain the lesson, Eva didn't pay much attention, confident that she knew as much as—if not more than--the star student. Once, however, she did intervene to correct Mr. Olympiad himself:

"That's not the right answer!" she objected in front of the whole class. Andrei, certain that he found the correct solution to the problem, took advantage of this unique dating opportunity:

"Why don't you show us how to do it right then?" he challenged her, only half-condescendingly. The other half of him was hoping to see Eva swaying her curvy body as she made her way to the blackboard. And, wearing high heels and a tight skirt that looked both demure and sexy on her, Eva obliged. The young woman took the chalk with confidence as all male eyes were upon her. Only Andrei was sufficiently gifted to observe both her physical charms and the errors in her proof. The class voted for Eva's demonstration even though, technically speaking, Andrei's was correct. Hers, they thought, looked better. Andrei had enough mathematical integrity, however, to challenge Eva to a rematch after class. "You got the first part of the proof right. If you wish to join me for coffee and I'll explain to you where you went wrong," he gallantly proposed.

"Alright. That way I can correct your mistakes," Eva said with equal self-confidence. As it turns out, however, the mathematical explanations were brief and inconclusive. Sparks and kisses flew from their very first meeting, which made the wrong and the right formulas pretty much equal.

Chapter 7

"Do you have to smoke even in the car, Andrei?" Eva complained, interrupting her husband's romantic reminiscence.

"It relaxes me," was his usual defense. Kent and, in fact, any American brand of cigarettes was a luxury in Romania, a mark of distinction as well as a handy bribe to get you by in day to day life. Andrei made a mental note to bring back a few cases of Kent and Marlboro cigarettes from his upcoming trip to Princeton.

His wife had a telepathic moment: "Do you still have the list I gave you?" she asked.

"Of course," Andrei replied. "What do you think I am?"

"Don't ask…" Eva answered with a sigh, since whenever he went abroad to professional conferences, Andrei always forgot some crucial elements from her list—lipsticks for relatives and secretaries, for example--and focused instead on impractical details, such as physics. To establish the right priorities, his wife reminded him: "Make sure you don't forget the Max Factor lipsticks, the Kent and Marlboro cigarettes, and this time try to get some nice perfume, not the cheap one that smells like vinegar, like you did last time…"

"What do I know about perfume?" Andrei defended himself.

"All you need to know is to buy the kind they sell at the Shop," Eva emphasized, referring to the duty-free shops at international airports and the tourist stores in Romania, which sold quality products to foreigners visiting the country and to the communist party elite or nomenclatura, as they preferred to be called. By way of contrast, the stores for regular Romanians were for the most part empty, to be stocked plentifully only for show during Petrescu's occasional visits.

Andrei tossed his cigarette out the window and turned a sharp corner, with only one hand on the wheel. The car, not designed for such abuse, screeched in protest. So did his wife: "Raliule!" Eva screamed, her hand flying to her palpitating chest, calling her husband one of the worst insults coming from a Romanian woman to a man: Italian race car driver. Unfortunately, most men took that as a compliment. Her husband was no exception.

"I'm under the speed limit!" Andrei announced falsely but with immunity, since the speedometer wasn't working and the Romanian police had more urgent matters to take care of—such as monitoring private conversations—than wasting their time regulating traffic or protecting lives.

"Andrei! Do I look like an idiot?" Eva asked him. Her husband wisely abstained from answering that question. Eva chose to interpret his silence as a negative. "Alright then. Slow down, for God's sake!"

Silvia Petrescu's mansion was located in the most posh, oldest section of Bucharest—the one that still resembled, despite her father's valiant efforts to "renovate" it in the socialist style, the look of nineteenth-century Paris which it originally attempted to emulate. Her street was packed with cars. Andrei circled the neighborhood a few times, looking for a place to park. He found a small spot between two black Mercedes and parallel parked perfectly—"Not bad for an Italian race car driver, hmmm?" he asked his wife, who didn't respond.

Eva was busy examining the other cars belonging to the guests of Silvia's party: several black Mercedes, a few black BMW's, three real Citroëns in subdued colors, and, last but not least, their bright yellow Dacia, looking like an Easter egg smack in the middle of all those fancy foreign cars. "Now what's wrong with this picture?" she asked her husband.

Oh, oh, here it comes, Andrei thought.

And it did: "How is it that out of all these physicists, who can't hold a candle to you in scientific brilliance, we end up with the crappiest car and living in a dilapidated closet of an apartment?" Eva wanted to know.

"You tell me," Andrei walked more rapidly in front of his wife, hoping that insolence would discourage this line of inquiry.

"Did you know that even that even that nonentity, Ionescu, just bought himself a new Volkswagen?"

Andrei chose to ignore the good news.

"This is simply not fair," his wife pursued. "You get all these fellowships; you're the glory of the Atomic Physics Institute."

Although he usually appreciated his wife's adulation, this time Andrei wasn't particularly thrilled by it.

"We should be in much better shape given your international stature. Why don't you at least ask Silvia for a raise?" she pursued.

This comment proved to be the straw that broke the camel's back. "Eva, when will you ever understand that I'm much more ambitious than that? I don't want the BMW's or a nice house or a lot of money! I want what truly matters: to accomplish something in life," he declared.

"But who's disputing that? Can't you get the BMW's and mansion for your family, so that you'll have a bigger office where you can do your research?" Eva found a reasonable compromise between her ideals and her husband's.

Andrei sighed, since this conversation was painfully familiar: "You don't get it, do you? If I did what it takes to get the mansion and the cars, I wouldn't have any time left over to do physics. "

"I'd get over that tragedy," Eva responded, looking at the spectacular arched glass door of Silvia's villa.

"But I wouldn't. Physics is my life!" Andrei snapped back, just as their hostess was opening the door.

"And that's precisely why we're having this party in your honor, my dear," she said with an amused air, ushering in her guests. Although Silvia Petrescu was certainly beautiful, distinguished would be a better way to describe her. She had very long brownish-red hair, tinted with natural henna. Her eyes were deep brown, like her father's. Her mouth was sensual, without being too large. And she was slim, accentuating her elegant figure at parties by wearing the latest Christian Dior and Prada fashions, many of them gifts from her mother, who was rivaled only by Imelda Marcos in her extravagant taste for a wardrobe composed of thousands of pairs of shoes and designer clothes.

To everyone's surprise and her parents' bitter disappointment, Silvia Petrescu couldn't care less about Marxism. She genuinely loved science, her passion since adolescence, and tried her best to stay out of politics—at least as much as possible for someone in her high position. Petrescu had hoped that his daughter, whose education he entrusted to Mitica Onita, his Deputy Minister of Education and Foreign Affairs, would become something dignified, like an ambassadress. But Onita must have gotten Petrescu's signals mixed up, since instead of encouraging Silvia towards international relations, he made the fatal mistake of cultivating her natural talents and getting her a Master's degree in Physics. By then it was too late for the Petrescus to set their daughter straight. The best her parents could do was protect her from other dangerous influences, especially those of a romantic nature.

To gently guide her in her choice of boyfriends, her parents bugged every corner of her house and even planted a few microphones in her sporty white Mercedes coupe. The men who didn't fit their standards—which was practically all of them—they promptly dispatched on permanent vacations to exotic, faraway places. If the boyfriends were so loyal to Silvia (or so stubborn) that they found their way back to Bucharest, the Petrescus had them eliminated –but only for excellent reasons, such as if they wore blue jeans or chewed American gum. Of the three children—Vladimir, the eldest son who became a biologist; Silvia who disappointed them even more by becoming a physicist, and Matei, the youngest, who fulfilled their wildest dreams by becoming nothing--only Matei showed any political promise. He skipped school and spent all his time partying, drinking and raping young women after having his thugs kidnap them off the streets. Given such indisputable leadership skills, he was clearly marked as the successor of the Petrescu dynasty.

Among the physicists and their wives, Silvia was by far the most elegant. However, she faced some competition from the secretaries of the Atomic Physics Institute, who were selected for their sex appeal and sometimes doubled as tech spies. Of course, this policy didn't take into account the fact that most of the foreign physicists entertained by the secretaries in question didn't have any actual tech secrets to share, nor that, in the rare cases they did, the secretaries who seduced them lacked the scientific training to understand a single equation their lovers might have whispered in the frenzy of passion. Despite this little glitch, however, the system operated quite smoothly. The foreigners who had a weak spot for pretty women were spied upon, which made the government happy. The secretaries got bonuses for the fulfillment of their patriotic duty— not to speak of gifts such as perfume, jewelry and pantyhose from their foreign lovers—which made them happy. And the foreign scientists prone to temptation got what they considered to be fine escort entertainment which some were desperate enough to mistake for love affairs.

Maria, the mistress of the Schwarz's best friend, Gheorghe Opera, the top physicist-informant at the Institute, was the most ravishing among the secretaries. She had straight platinum blond hair and Elizabeth Taylor eyes, a deep blue that bordered on violet. When drunk, she became the life of the party, specializing in self-referential sexual innuendoes. At the moment, she was commenting upon the latest fashion, which hit the streets of Bucharest approximately seven years after Paris, Milan and New York: the mini-mini-skirt. In fact, Maria even happened to be modeling the trend, since she was wearing a very short skirt with a bright geometric print complemented by a tight black turtleneck. Long leather white boots with high heels and a long turquoise necklace completed her sexy yet casual look. "So it took me a few seconds," she was saying to Magda, one of the wives, to realize what he meant when he said, 'Nice belt!'" Someone had apparently complimented her very short skirt. Everyone laughed, especially Gheorghe, who was eying Maria with a hungry glance, his appetite for her constantly reawakened not so much by her humor, which was usually flat, but by her carefree, abandoned laughter, which he took as an invitation for making love.

Not that amused by raunchy jokes and not in the least tempted by alcohol, Eva focused instead on the abundant food, for which Silvia's parties were famous. The buffet was an international tour de force. In a country where most people saw an orange only a few times a year, Silvia's buffet displayed smoked salmon, shrimp, lobster, lamb shipped directly from Athens, and fresh fruit from all over the world. Next to these international specialties, some of which Eva duly sampled, there were a few choice Romanian dishes as well: mititei (little skinless sausages) impaled on wooden toothpicks; chiftele cu varza (or round meatballs with cabbage); plus the traditional, peasant dishes--sarmale cu mamaliga (approximate translation, cabbage leaf dumplings with cornmeal) and mamaliga cu brinza si smintina (the same cornmeal topped with cheese and sour cream) as well as French-inspired selections, such as delicate thin-leafed turnovers filled with either cheese and mushrooms or diced meat.

While Eva sampled the buffet, Andrei was busy talking to Silvia. Being the one who worked with her, he was in charge of broaching the touchy subject of his son's disappearance. Not wishing to interfere with the delicate process of networking, Eva observed the conversation from a distance. She noticed that although Silvia was smiling in a friendly manner and gesticulating in explanation while talking to her husband, something definitely seemed wrong. Andrei's olive complexion was greener than usual and his expression too serious for the news to be good.

Eva moved closer, to hear their conversation. "R-a-d-u," she mouthed soundlessly to her husband when she caught his eye, as if he could have forgotten that little detail.

"I hope you understand, Andrei," Silvia was saying in a low voice. "I've done everything I can for you as a friend."

Andrei didn't respond, just nodded slightly.

Silvia continued trying to persuade him: "You see... I'm placed in an impossible situation," Eva overheard. "I simply can't go against these directives. Besides, it could backfire against you and your family."

"I see," Andrei replied.

"I mean," Silvia pursued, "Rules and laws can be bent. But direct orders..." she shook her head. "That wouldn't be very smart."

When a group of people approached them, Silvia instantly lost her serious demeanor and returned to the role of the beautiful socialite entertaining her guests. But neither Andrei nor Eva could so much as force a smile the rest of the evening, not even when the hostess toasted, in front of everyone, Andrei's prestigious fellowship to the United States.

Chapter 8

"It's already 7:15, Marta. Andrei will be here any minute now," Grandpa Mihai announced, looking with concern at the risky procedure undertaken by his wife only moments before his son-in-law was supposed to pick up their granddaughter and take her to school. "Is this really the best time for a haircut?"

Irina was sitting on a stool in the bathroom holding in her hand a picture of Mireille Mathieu, a French singer who, though a sensation in France since the sixties, peaked in popularity in Romania a mere ten years later. While foreign news was not allowed in the country, the radio stations played European and American pop music, to show the comrades the decadence of the West. The decadence seemed to be contagious, however, as Romanians, from young to old, tried to emulate these slices of what they took to be Western life.

Irina was already dressed in her school uniform: light blue shirt, navy blue skirt and, the most important element of this pioneer outfit, around her neck she wore a red handkerchief patriotically bordered by red, yellow and blue stripes, the colors of the Romanian flag. Like most girls in primary school, she had long hair parted in the middle and put up in two pig tails held together by enormous white silk bows which resembled butterfly wings. The little girl was evidently displeased with something, as the corners of her mouth were slightly down-turned and her eyes still moist from a recent temper tantrum.

Grandma Marta, a dignified lady in her late sixties with bright burgundy tinted hair—the only color of red hair dye available at the time in Romania—stood next to her, one hand to her waist, the other holding a comb: "We've got time, Mihai," she responded to her husband's comment as calmly as possible, but her voice betrayed irritation. "What's wrong with the hairstyle you've got?" she asked her granddaughter. "Since your father took you to the barber when you were five and made you look like a boy, it took us three years to grow out your hair. Why in the world would you want to chop it all off again?"

"Because I hate it," Irina sniffled, then wiped her nose with the sleeve of her freshly washed and starched shirt.

"But why?" the grandmother still couldn't comprehend.

"It looks dumb!" Irina clarified, prepared to cry again if that's what it took to get some cooperation.

"Can't the two of you take care of this matter after school?" Grandpa Mihai reiterated his earlier point, looking impatiently at his watch.

For the second time, however, Grandma Marta vetoed his argument: "Can't you see that the girl is upset, Mihai?" she reproached. "How do you want it?" she turned to her granddaughter.

Her hopes reawakened, Irina held back her tears and showed her grandmother the picture of Mireille Mathieu: "Like this. See? I want a round haircut. All the way around," she pointed with her index finger around her head.

Grandma Marta put on her reading glasses to examine the picture more closely. She wasn't particularly impressed with this new French look: "This looks a little spherical to me. It makes her head look like a pumpkin," she commented.

Irina, however, heatedly defended her new idol: "That's not true! She's the prettiest woman in the world. And I want to look just like her!"

"Alright...if you say so..." Grandma Marta consented with strong reservations, then removed the silk bows and began combing Irina's long brown hair. "Mihai, could you please bring me the fruit bowl from the kitchen? The one where we keep the cucumbers," she specified.

The grandfather looked a bit puzzled, but didn't see any point in arguing with women about hairstyles. He went into the kitchen and returned with the freshly washed bowl, which Grandma Marta carefully placed on top of Irina's head. She then examined her granddaughter's round face and started cutting the hair, beginning with the bangs, then moving all the way around, looking from time to time at Mireille to make sure that she reproduced faithfully the hip style in the picture. When she was done, the borders weren't exactly even, so she removed the bowl and corrected the mistakes.

"A little shorter here," Irina suggested.

"If I cut any more, your bangs will be at the back of your head," Grandma Marta warned. "I'll just trim them a little more and that's all. Enough's enough. Basta!"

Grandpa Mihai assessed the result from a safe distance. "How long does it take for hair to grow out?" he diplomatically inquired.

"It's not important what we think," Grandma Marta pointed out. "What matters is if Irina likes it. Well? Do you?" she asked her granddaughter. "What's wrong? Why are you scowling?"

Irina had gotten up from the stool and was making funny faces in the mirror, trying out different expressions that she assumed to be glamorous and French. "Do I look like Mireille?" she asked for the input of an objective observer.

The grandparents put their reading glasses back on and shifted their glances from the picture to Irina and back to the picture again. Being only eight and not having well-defined feminine features yet, the bowl cut didn't really suit Irina's round face. Their granddaughter struck them more like one of the three stooges than like a sexy French pop star. But how could they break her heart, especially now that the damage was already done? "Very nice," "Spitting image," the grandparents declared in unison.

The sound of the door bell interrupted the beauty session. "It must be Andrei," Grandma Marta hastened to open the door.

"Hi Daddy!" Irina made her smiling appearance in the hallway to greet her father, feeling much better disposed now that she had gotten her way.

Andrei's face froze with dismay as soon as he saw her. "Why are you wearing a wig?" was all he could think to ask.

"Grandma Marta gave me a haircut!" Irina denounced her grandmother in all innocence, while the latter made herself busy in the kitchen preparing the girl's favorite lunch—a sandwich made up of two slices of bread, butter and honey. Grandpa Mihai also unobtrusively vanished into the study to get Irina's backpack, slipping two lemon drops into the outer pocket. But they still didn't escape Andrei, who followed the grandmother into the kitchen: "Could you please explain to me what you did to Irina's hair?"

"She wanted a French hairstyle," Grandma Marta shrugged, disavowing responsibility for the fashion trends of the younger generation.

"So you made her head look like a cabbage?" Andrei inquired.

Without uttering a word, Grandma Marta rushed back into the bathroom and reemerged with the corroborating evidence. "Look," she said, handing Andrei the famous singer's picture, "Don't you find her beautiful and sexy?"

This excellent argument didn't convince Andrei, however: "Irina's eight years old. I don't want her looking beautiful and sexy!" Given the recent haircut, fortunately, this wasn't an imminent danger.

The grandmother felt insulted and taken for granted, especially since she and her husband took care of Irina whenever Andrei and Eva weren't home, meaning every weekday after school. "I have a heart condition," Grandma Marta put her hand to her chest. "This old man can barely can walk any more," she pointed to her husband, who limped just fine. "We take care of your daughter every evening. A modicum of gratitude would be in order," she informed her son-in-law, barely holding back her indignation.

"Don't worry, it will grow out," Grandpa Mihai attempted to diffuse the incendiary situation.

All the while Irina was examining herself in the mirror. She couldn't decide who was right. Did she look like a cabbage, or like a French singer? Both descriptions seemed equally plausible, depending upon how you looked at it, just like in the optical illusion pictures that show a young girl from one perspective and an old witch from another.

"Alright, what's done is done. We're late for school; let's go," Andrei signaled with his hand as he walked out the door.

Before following him, Irina said her goodbyes. She kissed her grandmother's hand, saying *Sarut mina,* a gesture of respect to which women of Marta's generation were accustomed. She also blew a kiss to her grandfather telling him, "See you after school!"

Father and daughter walked past the long, rectangular apartment building, which resembled the four others behind it. Then they cut, as usual, through Parcul Moghioros, a man-made park with a small artificial pond and gorgeous old willows. Andrei may have been slight of stature, but he sure could take giant steps. Even when out on a leisurely promenade with his wife he walked in a hurry, prompting Eva to ask if dogs were chasing him from behind. Irina had to run to keep up with her father's footsteps and, despite her best efforts, he still had to drag her along by the hand to keep pace with him. "When are we going to sing together, Daddy?" she asked, referring to their morning ritual.

"Which song would you like?"

Since it was starting to rain, the weather provided the perfect inspiration: "The raindrops one," Irina proposed.

"Okay. Raindrops are falling on my head

and just like the guy who's feet are too big for his bed,

nothing seems to fit

those raindrops are falling on my head, they keep falling..." Andrei sang falsetto in English, which he had learned in high school along with French and Russian.

"Tra, la la la la la la," Irina piped in with her soft, girlish voice, familiar with the tune, but not the lyrics since, unlike her father, she didn't speak any English.

Andrei dropped off his daughter in front of the main door after they said a quick goodbye to one another since, to her great delight, Irina immediately spotted her best friend.

Chapter 9

"Sofia!" Irina screamed excitedly, running towards her friend, a slim girl with honey colored hair curled in Shirley Temple ringlets all around her face. Their friendship went way back; they met on the first day of elementary school. The two little girls formed an instant bond, since neither beat around the bush. They smiled at one another, then Irina promptly broke the ice, "Hi. My name's Irina. You want to be my friend?" "Sure. My name is Sofia. Want to see my new fountain pen?" Since then the two little girls were inseparable during recess and lunch breaks.

After enthusiastically hugging and kissing each other on both cheeks, as if reuniting after a long and difficult separation (which had lasted since three o'clock on the previous afternoon), Irina wanted to know what her friend thought of her new haircut.

"It's kind of round, but I like it," Sofia answered with an intuitive mixture of tact and honesty.

Irina showed her the picture of the international pop star she was trying to emulate: "She's French. Her name's Mireille Mathieu."

"Oh. She's very pretty..." Sofia admitted.

Then, feeling they had thoroughly exhausted this subject of conversation, the girls switched topics: "During recess, do you want to try the new chewing gum my Dad got me?" Irina asked.

"What's it called?" Sofia opened her eyes wide with interest.

"Menta doubla," Irina whispered confidentially this top-secret information, referring to an old pack of Double Mint gum Andrei found in his suit pocket from a previous trip abroad.

"I'll trade you these marbles for a pack of gum!" Sofia took out of her backpack a few colored glass spheres, eager to cut a deal.

"They're not that shiny," Irina replied, examining carefully the merchandise in question.

"You should see them in the sun…" Sofia countered. "They shine as bright as my Mom's necklace, the one you liked the other day when you came over to my place, remember?"

Before the girls could reach an understanding, however, their haggling was interrupted by less urgent business. Their main teacher for math, science, government and Romanian, Comrade Zapada, had just entered the classroom. They'd study with her for a total of four years, meaning during all of primary school. Since second grade, they also had separate instructors for French, physical education, music, art and history. Ms. Zapada --a fifty year old lady with long jet black hair, dark eyes, bright red lipstick, a robust figure and maternal manner--was still their favorite teacher. She was sometimes strict, but never unfair. She also seemed to care about each and every student, commanding their respect with a gentle indulgence that reassured them. In class she called them, as was customary, by their last names; however, during recess she sometimes dropped such formalities and referred to them as her *bobocei*, or little chicks.

"Buna Ziua Tovarasa Profesoara! Good morning Comrade Professor," the students stood up and shouted in chorus as soon as she entered.

"Good morning class," the teacher replied. "You may sit down," she added, and the students took a seat, clasping their hands behind their backs, as they were supposed to do at all times unless they were writing or had to either ask or answer a question (in which case the protocol was raising the right hand straight up in the air, with only the index and middle fingers elevated, like two perky rabbit ears). Even with the warmest and most maternal of teachers, discipline and order were essential components of a communist education.

The first lesson was math, which Irina discretely tuned out. Ever since she overheard her parents say, back when she was in first grade, that she was destined to follow in their footsteps and go into math and science, she decided, right then and there, that those were her least favorite subjects. The class itself, however, was inoffensive since it provided her with a perfect opportunity to plan out her daily activities. Irina considered such mathematical problems as: after school, would she play with Sofia at her house or with Marinela at home? When Comrade Zapada asked the class "What's 7 times 7?" she heard Diaconescu, the only boy she liked and considered a friend (since, as far as girls were concerned, even in Romania boys between the ages of four and twelve often contracted the international contagious disease called "the cooties") answer "47!" Irina was impressed by Diaconescu's mathematical aptitude. For some reason, however, the teacher was not as pleased with his reply, since she repeated the question. Munteanu, a boy with a nearly shaved blond head and pale blue eyes, answered

"49," which, to Irina's surprise, turned out to be a more satisfactory answer. The multiplication explanations and exercises that followed enabled Irina to zone out once again and think of Sofia's glass marbles. She was sorry when math class was over, since she knew that Madame Codreanu, the French teacher, was much more vigilant than the maternal Comrade Zapada. Daydreaming was lethal in French class.

"Bonjour Madame Comrade Professeur!" the students stood up to greet their French teacher in chorus. Madame Codreanu, a slim woman with washed-out blond hair and cat-rimmed glasses, was best known around the school for her short temper and slide ruler, a very dangerous combination. Since she was young, small and exceedingly thin—from the side, her stomach looked almost as flat as a piece of cardboard--it was mostly the ruler that was feared. Taking a life of its own, it struck the students' palms whenever they got a wrong answer or weren't paying attention.

"La leçon d'aujourd'hui sera le célèbre poème de Vigny, 'La Mort du loup,'" the teacher announced to the puzzled second-graders, who weren't used to the immersion method. But they heard "Vigny" and "La Mort Du Loup" in the same sentence, so they turned to the page of their reader that contained the aforementioned poem. Like during pre-communist days, the French lesson (and, more generally, the teaching of any foreign language) consisted primarily of repetition, translation and memorization exercises.

"Les nuages couraient sur la lune enflamée," recited the teacher in a melodious French distorted only by the excessively pronounced r's of her Romanian accent.

"Be he he be he he be he he be he he," repeated the students almost in unison, not understanding a word of the French but trying their best to mimic the teacher phonetically.

She wasn't impressed: "Non! Ca va pas! We're not speaking sheep here; we're learning French. Répétez: Les- nuages- couraient- sur- la- lune- enflammée," she enunciated more slowly and clearly the first line of the poem.

"Les nage cour sur la lune enfemmee" the students mouthed Vigny's elegant phrase, "The clouds passed over the inflamed moon," managing to say something to the effect of "the swimming courtyard on the womanizer moon," but at least this time they approximated a human language that might have been a distant cousin of French.

Rather than persisting on perfecting their pronunciation, which, at any rate, she considered a hopeless endeavor, the teacher latched on to a much more serious problem: "Codrescu!" she called on a student who was looking dreamily out the window instead of paying attention. "Would you care to translate the phrase for us?" she asked him in Romanian. The red-headed boy with glasses turned pale, despite his usually rosy complexion. "Oui, Madame Professeur," he answered agreeably, not knowing how else to get out this pickle.

"Go right ahead; what's stopping you?" the teacher prodded.

"Traduisez la phrase s'il vous plaît," Petrescu translated in a low voice the teacher's request, which was the only phrase he had heard.

Mistaking the boy's misguided effort to please her for impudence, Madame Codreanu exploded: "So now we're being sarcastic, are we?" She then grabbed the wooden ruler from her desk, which everyone knew wouldn't be used for measuring the decreasing distance between them and marched towards the misfortunate student, who was trying his best to become one with his desk. Trembling with fear, he extended his right palm and closed his eyes, accepting the inevitable. Wishing to dominate students not just with corporal punishment but also with the more subtle element of surprise, however, the teacher abruptly changed tactics. Instead of giving him the usual punishment of ten strikes on the palm, she pulled Petrescu by the ear and took him to the Corner of Shame, right next to the blackboard, holding him as example: "Class, this is what happens to students who don't pay attention," she announced, pointing to the culprit.

Guided by such gentle encouragement, the other students were especially eager to give the right answers. They mimicked their teacher's French as best they could and frantically leafed through their Romanian-French/French-Romanian mini-dictionaries whenever she asked for translations. By the time the bell rang, everyone was exhausted by these rigorous intellectual and linguistic exercises.

The teacher signaled a reversion to more familiar pedagogical methods: "The homework for tomorrow is to translate into Romanian the first verse of the poem," Madame Codreanu announced. "And to memorize it!" she added sternly. Several students couldn't suppress a sigh, since they knew that meant a pop quiz where the teacher selected randomly from her Catalog, or alphabetical list, the names of the victims who would be asked to recite the poem in front of the entire class.

The most challenging part of the day was yet to come: Comrade Ion Stan Popescu's history class was next. Whereas the scariest thing about Madame Codreanu was her ruler, everything about Comrade Popescu inspired fear and respect, like Machiavelli's Prince. He had white hair, cropped very short, like in the army. His bright blue eyes sparkled cleverly beneath bushy white eyebrows. He didn't need to rely upon rulers or corporal punishment to impose discipline; his sharp sense of irony and knowledge of Romanian history more than sufficed. As Comrade Popescu himself proudly announced on the first day of class, he was the only faculty member in the school who was a member of the Communist Party of Romania. He had been there in its early days, when the party was still machinating against King Michael's royalists and, before that, fighting against Ion Antonescu's fascist Iron Guard. This background made him especially suited to teach Romanian history, which was more like a social studies course in that it combined select episodes from the country's past with modern day communist interpretations. Any information that could no longer be stretched to have contemporary relevance—either as a lesson about how terrible and oppressive the days before communism were or, conversely, how the greatest and most courageous Romanian leaders were precursors to the current regime—was omitted from the curriculum.

That day's lesson, which was on Stefan cel Mare (Stephen the Great), one of Romania's most famous kings, would clearly be relevant since Petrescu was also Great. After the exchange of formal greetings with the class, Comrade Popescu began pacing back and forth, his hands clasped behind his back, an indication that he was about to start the lesson.

"Stefan cel Mare," he announced, "is one of the famous leaders in Romanian history. Why so? What did Stephen the Great do?" the teacher asked.

A heroic hand went up: "He helped out the great king Vlad Tepes in the fight against the Ottomans, Comrade Professor!" said Mihai Iliovich, a student who had the tendency to express his eagerness to please the teacher by shouting his answers.

Comrade Popescu nodded approvingly. "Good. Can someone tell us more about this great king?" he asked, looking around the classroom until he spotted Irina with a desperate look upon her face: "Schwarz!" he selected his first victim.

Irina jumped up from her seat, taken by surprise that her silent pleas "Please let him not call on me; please let him not call on me" had no effect whatsoever on Comrade Popescu's iron will.

"Did you happen to stick your nose in the history book last night?" the teacher politely inquired.

"Yes, Comrade Professor," Irina replied.

"What did you find out?"

Irina took a breath, then began reciting the lesson she had practiced several times the previous evening in front of her grandfather:

"Stefan the Great was the prince of Moldova, who reigned between 1457 and 1505. He was known throughout Europe for his noble and heroic resistance against the Ottoman Turks, who had occupied a large part of the Balkans, including our territories. Stefan the Great also defended Moldavia against the Hungarian king Matthias Corvinus, defeating him in the famous Battle of Baia, a resort town where my grandparents on my mother's side of the family go on vacation almost every summer."

"Ah… Now there's a relevant historical detail! I'm glad you didn't forget to mention it," Comrade Popescu remarked.

Not daunted by her teacher's customary sarcasm, Irina boldly continued: "Stefan the Great is also famous for his cultural contributions. No fewer than 44 churches and monuments were built under his reign."

"Whoa, whoa!" the teacher stopped her, evidently pleased at his student's preparation--despite having twitched at the rather unpleasant word "churches"-- but not wishing to show favoritism nor relent on his ever-present irony: "Does your family own a parrot for a pet?" he asked her.

"No…" Irina replied looking confused, not understanding what this question had to do with Stephen the Great.

"Well then, did you bring a tape-recorder to class?" the teacher pursued.

Irina looked at him with bewilderment.

Comrade Popescu smiled at her indulgently: "You seem to have learned the facts, but learning history's not just about memorization. It's what we do with our knowledge of the past that counts," he explained. "Class! Can you tell me why leaders like Mihai the Big and Stephen the Great are so important to the history of our country?"

Diaconescu raised his hand.

"Yes?"

"Because they unified our nation, Comrade Professor," the student answered.

The teacher's eyebrows nearly united to form a frowning unibrow at this mediocre answer. He shook his hand back and forth, like a rocky boat: "Yes and no. It's true that Stephen got together with his cousin, Vlad Tepes, to ward off the Turkish invasion in Moldavia and Wallachia. Together the two voivods united their kingdoms in common interest, but not in fact. Romania wasn't unified as a country until much later, in the nineteenth-century. So can anyone give us a smarter answer?"

Constantinescu, whose parents were also members of the Party, volunteered. The teacher called on him with a rare note of respect in his voice and the student answered in a confident monotone: "We should respect Stefan the Great because he fought for Romania's freedom and independence from other countries. Especially those that invaded our territories. Just like Comrade Nicolae Petrescu is leading an independent and free Romania towards a glorious future."

The teacher was pleased with this comparison: "Did you hear that class? Or does Constantinescu need to repeat it?"

Judging from the students' blank looks, the consensus seemed to be towards repetition, since most of the eight year olds didn't quite grasp abstract concepts such as "freedom" and "independence." Which is also why the repetition technique didn't clarify much, but at least everyone took diligent notes, misspelling the unknown words. Such confusion was usually ignored, since the pedagogical directives insisted upon treating young pioneers as miniature adults who were capable of understanding everything—if only, in Comrade Popescu's own inspiring words, "they weren't lazy slugs, cracked open a book once in a while, paid more attention to their teachers and applied themselves."

"How about Vlad Tepes?" the teacher continued.

Encouraged by the teacher's earlier response to her comments, Irina courageously raised her hand again.

"Let's give Irina's parrot a rest," Comrade Popescu proposed, seeking a new volunteer. "Does anyone else have a memory? Or have you all forgotten even your own names?" Nobody else raised his hand. "Burtica!" the teacher selected a "volunteer."

"Present!" Burtica answered jumping to his feet.

"We can see that. You're not invisible and we're not blind," the teacher replied. "So what's your answer?"

"Comrade Professor, Vlad Tepes was a very bad man," Burtica replied emphatically. Since he was too busy playing soccer with his friends after school, Martin Burtica hadn't had the chance to open the history book that glorified many of Tepes's feats and justified his cruelty. All he remembered was what his grandmother had told him: namely, that the leader, also known as Dracula, impaled people and drank their blood, which neither he nor his grandmother considered very nice.

"So he was bad, hmmm?" the teacher asked, stroking his chin with an air of contemplation.

"Yes, comrade," Burtica stuck to his original story.

"What did he do that was so terrible?"

"He impaled people who stealed and drank their blood," Burtica revealed the extent of his knowledge.

"Did you take grammar lessons from your peasant grandmother?" the teacher wanted to know.

The student looked confused.

"It's 'stole,' not 'stealed'! And you pride yourself on being a pioneer!" Comrade Popescu chastised him, passing, as was his wont with the weaker students, from sarcasm to fury.

"Do you happen to know from your sources—none of which appear to be our history book—whom Vlad Tepes impaled and why?"

"People who were bad, Comrade," Burtica answered, hoping to camouflage his ignorance with vague statements.

"Oh, I see. Did he impale students who came unprepared to history class?" Comrade Popescu asked, and nobody in the classroom except the teacher himself thought he was joking.

Since Burtica's eyes bugged out with trepidation, Comrade Popescu kindly put him out of his misery: "Sit down, you hoodlum, and next time, try reading your history book rather than using it as a soccer ball," he helpfully suggested.

"Has anybody in this class besides Schwarz and Constantinescu done their homework last night?"

Mihai Saveanu, a slight blond little boy with glasses, was, like Irina, a history buff. He raised his hand:

"Saveanu," the teacher called on him, hoping to raise the level of discussion to something higher than folk tales about the cruelty of vampires.

"Vlad Tepes, also known as Vlad the Impaler, was prince of Wallachia, off and on, between 1448-1476. He was born in Sighisoara, Transylvania. He called himself Dracula, or Son of the Dragon Order, and invaded the occupying

Ottoman empire all the way into Bulgaria. Even Sultan Mehmed II, the most powerful Turkish sultan, was impressed by Dracula's bravery."

The teacher seemed satisfied with this recitation, realizing by now that parroting was as good as he was going to get from his students that day. "So, Burtica," he turned back to his former victim who, like a frog dropped by the eagle that had clutched it in its jaws, had experienced a wave of relief at being left in peace. "Was Dracula as bad as your grandmother says he was?" Burtica shrank into his seat, wondering how Comrade Popescu found out about his historical sources. He was starting to believe that his teacher was as omniscient as he claimed to be, and even that he had eyes in the back of his head, as he sometimes warned his students when he wrote on the blackboard.

"There's a small grain of truth in the idiotic things Burtica just said," the teacher added, wishing to encourage young minds. Then he launched into his own narration: "You see, Vlad Tepes was a coin with two sides. He could be brave, noble and fair; but when provoked he could also be ruthless and cruel, some would say, excessively cruel, in his punishments. Both sides of him were historically necessary. Because without the cruelty, it would have been impossible to ward off the enemy. Let me give you two examples. One time, when Sultan Mehmed II sent out an emissary to Vlad Tepes, the emissary refused to remove his turban to show respect for our king, saying it was his custom to keep on his turban. So what did Vlad Tepes do? Did he swallow this mark of disrespect? No . He had the turban nailed to the emissary's head, telling him that in this fashion he was strengthening and honoring the Ottoman custom. Then, when the Mehmed II himself marched with his army to attack Vlad Tepes' castle, the sultan couldn't believe his eyes: Everywhere around the castle there were long stakes with the impaled bodies of Turkish men, women and children. Twenty-thousand of them, a forest of massacred Turks. When the Sultan's army saw this, the soldiers were scared out of their wits. They picked up and ran right back where they came from." Comrade Popescu paused to examine the reaction of the mesmerized class: "Now. What lesson do we draw from this?"

Irina raised her hand. "Comrade Popescu, I don't understand. Why did he have to kill little kids?"

"You tell me," the teacher replied, "What would have been more effective in warding off an enemy invasion: If an army killed only fellow soldiers, in fair and predictable rules of combat in which the Romanians, who were fewer, were bound to lose against the force of a whole empire, or if they surprised and intimidated the enemy into retreat by showing them that nobody who invades our country will be safe from harm, not even their children? Sometimes striking fear is the only way to command respect and get things done," Comrade Popescu generalized a lesson he, himself had learned quite well, both as a Communist general and as a teacher. And with this adage, he concluded the class punctually, like in the army, two seconds before the bell rang.

Next was Irina's most dreaded experience: Physical Education class. Ever since Nadia Comaneci won the gold medal in the 1976 Olympics, physical education in Romanian schools became synonymous with gymnastics. The unanticipated hurdle was that not everyone was born with the flexibility, dexterity and courage of a Nadia Comaneci.

The gym teacher, Comrade Ungurescu, was a muscular, short woman who wore her hair in a ponytail and had been a gymnast herself. She had no sympathy either for roly polies, who couldn't put one foot in front of the other on the balance beam, or for scaredy cats who trembled before the vault. In physical prowess, courage and grace, Irina competed for last place in gym class with Carmen, a blond little girl with frightened blue eyes who was grossly overweight. Although Irina was slim, she combined the courage of a rabbit with the dexterity of an elephant, which didn't exactly make her Olympics material.

The first part of the class both Irina and Carmen passed with flying colors precisely because, assuming all went well, there was comparatively little flying involved in the floor exercises. The students formed a line and each took turns doing rolling drills and cartwheels. Due to the cylindrical shape of her body, Carmen rolled almost gracefully; while Irina rolled quickly and crookedly, dizzy with the desire to get this nightmare over with as quickly as possible.

"How about the cart wheels?" Comrade Ungurescu asked Irina, who had hoped to get away with replacing them with the safer and easier rolling exercises. Irina went back to the front of the line and started doing something that resembled rabbit hops, since her legs didn't make it all the way over her head. Several kids laughed, putting their hands over their mouths as they were taught, to be polite. The teacher had already lost all hope in making a gymnast out of Irina: "That will do. Thanks for demonstrating how not to do a cartwheel."

Next came the parallel bars, where Irina once again helpfully illustrated incorrect form. She hung on for dear life to the taller bar and swung her legs back and forth, like a shirt swept by the wind on a clothes line.

"Let go of the bar!" the teacher commanded, urging Irina to move gracefully from the higher bar to the lower one and vice versa, which apparently was the whole point of the exercise. Irina executed the teacher's orders with precision. She let go of the bar and fell back on her feet on the floor, after which, in emulation of Nadia Comaneci after a perfect landing, she arched her back and victoriously raised both arms high up in the air.

"Pathetic!" was Comrade Ungurescu's assessment. The teacher knew better than to ask either Irina or Carmen to go on the balance beam, since neither had enough limbs to break for the number of times they'd suffer a catastrophic fall. However, Comrade Ungurescu drew the line on the vault, the exercise in which she had excelled as a young gymnast. Every student had to hop over the vault, and this was precisely the challenge that Irina feared most. She stood in line with her heart pounding so loudly that she couldn't even hear the teacher's instructions. Her fists were clenched to the point of turning white, as one enduring stoically the most agonizing suffering. And when her turn finally came, she was so anxious that her knees practically caved in. She ran as fast as she could towards the vault, pushed off with her hands on it, then, refusing to spread her legs over it out of fear of falling, she lunged forward head-first and landed on her hands, after nearly breaking her neck. She observed this suicidal procedure each time she was asked to jump over the vault.

"Schwarz, I told you to spread your legs!" Comrade Ungurescu shouted, making the principal next door wonder what in the world was going on in gym class. Compared to the kamikaze missions in gym, the last two classes of the day, music and science, were a breeze.

Chapter 10

Later that evening, after reading to her daughter a bedtime story, Eva finally had time to run downstairs and get the mail. She sorted rapidly through the envelopes, selecting the most important ones: two bills, a letter from Ester, her best friend who lived in Hungary and... her heart skipped a beat, a typewritten postcard from Radu. On the front, the postcard had a picture of skiers sliding down the slope of a spectacular looking mountain covered with sparkling white snow. Underneath the image was written the greeting, "Bisous des Alpes." Eva impatiently the read the verso:

"Mom and Dad," Radu wrote, "A few words to let you know that I'm doing well. Ioana and I are vacationing in the Alps for a few weeks. It's very beautiful here. Believe it or not, on the highest peaks, there's still snow on the ground even this late in the spring. Give my warm greetings to Irina and tell her that dogs here really do wear bagels on their tails. Love, Radu"

Eva's first reaction was relief; thank goodness, Radu was okay. But something unsettled her about this note. She heard the front door open. Andrei had returned home. The past week he had been preoccupied by his worries about Radu and about what Silvia had told him at the party. Although he had avoided verbalizing his anxieties, his wife could feel them, not least of all in his constant irritability.

"Come take a look at this," Eva extended him the postcard. He glanced briefly at the cover, then read carefully the back. The husband and wife looked at each other sharing the same thought.

"Something's not right about it," Eva was the first to remark. "Why would Raducu go skiing in the middle of the school year? And for a few weeks? Without first calling to let us know about it? He never mentioned taking a long vacation last week when we talked to him..."

Andrei made an effort to examine the evidence dispassionately: "Let's not jump to conclusions. Maybe they're on spring break over there. You know how the French are. Half the year they're on vacation."

Eva took the postcard from her husband's hands and scrutinized it attentively once again, as one examines forensic evidence rather than a loving note from one's son. "I don't know ... When has Radu ever typed a note to us before?"

"He probably bought a typewriter for his essays. You can't expect him to write his university assignments by hand!" her husband countered.

"A postcard's not an essay, Andrei. It's a short, personal note. I can't see Raducu typing letters to us, let alone postcards."

Andrei looked stumped and discouraged. He was increasingly persuaded by his wife's dark intuitions, which were on the back of his mind as well.

"Something else bothers me about this card," Eva continued. "He didn't even mention Grandma Marta and Grandpa Mihai. We've never once received a letter from Raducu where he didn't send his greetings to his grandparents. He's so fond of them; they practically raised him during your trips abroad."

"Now there I think you're exaggerating," Andrei replied with slightly more confidence. "Radu's not a little kid any more, to write to everyone in the family. Besides, he only had this much space," he indicated with his fingers the tiny dimensions of the postcard. "I hope you won't inspect all my letters from America with a magnifying glass like you do his. Stop playing detective, okay? You're making me nervous," Andrei attempted to calm down his wife. But he wasn't that calm himself.

Eva wavered. Her husband's arguments made sense, yet in her heart of hearts she still felt something was fishy about the postcard. However, aside from the fact that it announced an extended vacation in the middle of the school year and that it was typewritten—which could, indeed, be attributed to the fact that Radu was getting used to typing his homework assignments—she had no other objective grounds for suspicion. "And what's this nonsense, about dogs wearing bagels on their tails?" it occurred to her to ask.

"Oh, you know how Radu teases his little sister. It must be one of his jokes."

Eva sat down on a dining room chair and reread several times her son's postcard. Andrei went into the bedroom to brush his teeth and put on his pajamas. "Eva, when are you coming to bed?" he asked.

"In a minute," she responded, then changed her mind and proposed instead: "Andrei, let's try calling Raducu again. Maybe if we call this late, we'll have less competition on the line to France." Andrei agreed. Together the husband and wife went into the study, a room which also served as Irina's bedroom. The little girl was asleep, so the parents had to whisper. Andrei dialed Radu's number and, to his great surprise, he got through on the first try. The phone rang and rang but nobody answered. After letting it ring twelve times, Andrei concluded: "He's not home. Like he said, he's on vacation."

Eva asked: "What time is it in France?"

"8:32 p.m.," Andrei answered.

"Let's try again in half an hour," Eva said.

"Okay," her husband agreed. For days he had been in an apprehensive, dark mood. "The weather's getting worse and worse around here," he said.

"What do you mean? It was so warm and sunny today," Eva disagreed, not realizing that Andrei had switched to the weather forecast code, which they used whenever discussing political matters.

"No, the weather's terrible and our friend told me that it will only get worse," Andrei insisted and this time Eva understood. "Our friend" was their code name for Silvia Petrescu.

"What did she say?"

Andrei shrugged: "Exactly what we expected. After their next voyage, the birds won't be able to migrate to better climates any more." Silvia had told him that Romanian scholars and scientists would face even greater difficulties in going to conferences in Western countries. Petrescu was clamping down the Iron Curtain.

"Will this affect you as well?"

"Of course. It's a national policy."

"But... she's still letting you go this one last time, right?" Eva asked, worried that Andrei would miss the once-in-a-lifetime opportunity to go to Princeton.

"I think so. After all, she announced it in front of everyone at the party."

Eva's eyes glimmered with a mixture of sadness and hope. She looked lovingly at her husband. It was time.

"Then you know what you have to do," she said.

Andrei looked into his wife's eyes and understood. For a long time, before every time he went abroad, he'd hinted at defecting, but Eva had resisted each time because she didn't want to leave her aging parents behind in Romania. Now he knew that he finally had her consent. He felt confident that his argument was sound. The local climate was becoming too severe; birds had to have the courage to find a new land, more hospitable to life than here. Yet they both knew this decision involved great risks. If Andrei defected, the Romanian government might not allow Eva and Irina to emigrate, or, in the best of circumstances, it might take years before they would get permission to immigrate legally and join him in America. The wait and incertitude in themselves would be almost unbearable. What gave them hope and courage, however, was the fact they had seen other families go through this trying process and eventually reunite.

As Eva and Andrei were making this difficult decision, in a government building on the other side of Bucharest, two Secret Police officials were eavesdropping on their conversation. While most Romanian citizens were only monitored about once a month, those with relatives abroad or "high-risk" cases were checked on as frequently as several times a day.

"Do they think we're idiots or what?" one of the Secret Police agents asked.

The other laughed: "They're the idiots! Every nincompoop who wants to defect talks about the weather. How transparent! One would think people who went to the university would invent a smarter code than that."

"You have to admit though, these new DIE bugs are pretty clever," the first Secret Police official said.

"Yeah. Who'd dream even a few years ago that our phone mikes would become so sophisticated as to continue to record conversations after people hung up!" the second official concurred.

If Eva and Andrei didn't think of being more discreet in their conversations, it was in part because they were unaware of the latest developments in DIE technology. The DIE, or the Departamentul de Informatii Externe (the Department of External Information) as it was called, had upgraded the country's phone system. Until 1979, everyone in Romania had phones that contained microphones which recorded private talks only during actual conversations. Once the interlocutors hung up, the phones couldn't pick up what they continued to say in the room. All this changed in 1979, when the government introduced phones whose microphones continued recording for hours the conversations in the room even after the interlocutors hung up. Everyone in the country who owned a phone had to buy this new type, which came in three models and five colors to give citizens the illusion of choice.

"What if they don't let my little chicks migrate too?" Andrei asked, looking tenderly at his wife, appreciating the extent of her sacrifice.

"Don't worry about that," Eva reassured him. "We'll find a way to be together. I promise."

"If I were her, I wouldn't make any promises I can't keep," the first official said to the other.

"They must think they live on Mars," the second agent replied. "That there's no law here, no repercussions for betraying your country!"

"Why don't we tell their friend about this? That should put a damper on their plans," the first agent suggested.

"No, let's be patient and bide our time. Once Silvia makes a decision about one of her physicists, it's final. But believe you me: this is the last time she'll make the mistake of letting one of them go abroad," the second agent replied.

Andrei and Eva called their son several more times throughout the night. As before, the phone rang but nobody answered. Moved as much by her concern about their son's safety as by the weight of her husband's decision to defect, Eva forgot to speak in code: "You know Andrei, the deciding factor for me is not the same one as for you. For me, it's not at about the physics, or the trips abroad, or the conferences or even political freedom." She paused for a moment, to regain her composure, then continued: "No matter what you tell me, I still believe something terrible has happened to our son. If I knew that Raducu was safe and sound, I'd never agree to take such a big risk. But now we have to use every ounce of energy to find out where he is and bring Radu to safety. Our hands are tied here. Maybe in America you'll have more leverage." Her voice became so soft, it seemed to melt: "Just so you know. That's the only reason I agree to let you go and take the risk of never ...." But Eva couldn't finish her thought before dissolving into tears.

Chapter 11

They covered his eyes with a dark scarf, which they tied so tightly with a knot at the back of his head that he saw flashes of red through the blindfold. His body swung first to the left, then to the right, attempting to keep its balance while avoiding contact with the two men disguised as police officers sitting on either side of him. Radu didn't know where they were taking him; all he could tell is that they had been driving for about thirty minutes.

The car came to an abrupt stop. The man on his left pulled Radu out by the elbow. The second officer pushed him from behind; Radu walked forward, then stumbled down three steps and walked a few more feet. The orangey red tint he perceived through the blindfold changed to a darker, burgundy shade and the air around him assumed a moldy smell. When he reached out with his arms to steady himself, his right hand encountered the coldness of a stone wall. They directed him down a set of stairs. Radu ran his hand along a rough wooden rail. The hair on his arms bristled from the abrupt change in temperature; the air in the room was fetid and cool. They ordered him to halt and removed the blindfold. Radu's eyes gradually adjusted to the darkness. After a few moments, he recognized the man with cold gray eyes framed by metal rimmed glasses who was standing before him.

Claude looked at him with a sardonic smile. He shook his head and clicked his tongue, like a parent chastising a mischievous child. "You didn't want to do it the easy way, did you?" he said to him in Romanian. Then he switched to French, for the benefit of his two companions. "We tried to give him the carrot, but he obviously prefers the stick."

The two officers behind Radu laughed, as if Claude had made a joke.

"Refused to do what?" Radu asked him, also in French.

Claude looked past him, still addressing only the officers: "Just listen to him!" he sneered. "He still pretends he doesn't know what we want. Put him away. Let him rot there like the dog that he is."

One of the officers pushed him hard into the wall; Radu exclaimed "Au!" and touched his hurt shoulder. The three men seemed amused by his pain.

"When you're ready to talk, let us know," Claude said.

"What do you want from me?" Radu asked with a sense of desperation.

"When you're hungry and thirsty enough, you'll know exactly what we want," Claude replied and turned around to head up the stairs, followed by the two officers. The door slammed shut behind them with a loud bang.

Radu looked around, acquainting himself with his new surroundings. It appeared that he was in some kind of a cellar. The spacious room was barren except for a metal pot on the floor, presumably intended as a toilet, a wooden chair and a glass window way up high covered by sturdy metal bars, like in a prison.

Radu's first instinct was to pull up the chair underneath the window, climb upon it and rattle the bars to see if there was any way he could escape. There wasn't. He peered outside. All he could see was a large courtyard. No houses, no trees, just a barren, isolated space illuminated by the moonlight. Perhaps they had left the door unlocked, Radu hoped against hope. He climbed down from the chair, ran up the stairs and tried to open the door. Predictably, it was locked. A sense of defeat began to sink in. He was shut up in a dungeon, with no food, no water, nothing but a chair and a chamber pot. He was at their mercy.

Radu tried to piece together the puzzle of his life during the past few weeks. Clearly, as he had originally suspected, Claude was tied in to the *Securitate*. The "wronged husband" must have been an agent too, as were the two pretend police officers who had kidnapped him. But, Radu wondered, why didn't the agent posing as the wronged husband just kill him right there on the spot? It could have passed for a crime de passion, especially in France... Did they want him alive just to pump him for information? They must not have done their research. Didn't they know that he was just a novice radio announcer; that he didn't have access to the dissident files they wanted? Only his boss did. No matter how much they threatened and mistreated him, Radu thought, they wouldn't be able to squeeze any information out of him for the simple reason that he had none to give.

He sat down on floor with his back pressed against the stone wall. One idea in particular began eating at him, snowballing into an obsession: Ioana. What did his girlfriend have to do with his kidnapping? He felt increasingly confident that she was a key agent in his misfortune. He recalled the way she had gazed at the two officers, with a look of recognition and fear in her eyes. It was difficult to avoid the obvious conclusion, even though he wasn't prepared to accept it. Could Ioana have lied to him about... everything?

A wave of anger passed through his weary body. His heart beat faster, his temples pounded. The sense of betrayal hurt more than the fear, more than the hunger, more than the physical pain from the blows he had received. He couldn't fully bring himself to believe that Ioana was capable of harming him this way. Not his soft, affectionate girlfriend. Not the woman with whom he had just made love. Not the woman he loved.

He closed his eyes. In the darkness and dampness that surrounded him he saw quite vividly her beautiful image, her expressions, the now elusive fragments of their former happiness. Her full lips gently parted when she was whispering loving words to him; her full delicious breasts preferring themselves to his touch; her long legs, displayed to advantage in short dresses and miniskirts; the turns of her phrases; the way she would tease him and laugh exposing her pearly white teeth. He could still feel the warmth of her body during their last hours together; the way he seemed to sink into an everlasting source of happiness whenever he held her in his arms. Then the realization came to him: all of this was forever gone. His memories of pleasure abruptly turned into pain. His whole body felt raw, like an open wound.

Radu passed the first few days of his imprisonment oscillating between shock and denial, punctuated by a series of repetitions. Twice a day, in the morning and evening, one of the two officers came down to bring him a glass of murky water and a thin slice of black bread. "You have something to say?" "Ready to talk?" he would pose the same question in various forms. Each time, Radu stubbornly responded "No." "Suit yourself," the officer would shrug and slam the door behind him, leaving the young man trapped in that catacomb. In the afternoon, they would bring him a greenish liquid which they called lentil soup. It tastes like salty pond scum, Radu thought.

On the fourth day, he forced himself to walk, so that at least his muscles wouldn't atrophy. He shuffled back and forth in the hollow room, feeling his way through the semi-darkness. When he got tired, he lay down on the cold floor, which sent shivers down his spine. When he tried to go to sleep, his back would hurt, so he turned on one side, then on the other, then on his back once again. Yet every position was painful; nothing felt comfortable anymore. At night it got very cold. Sometimes he'd sit down and lean up against the wall, pulling his knees up to his chest and wrapping his arms around his legs in the vain attempt to recapture some sense of warmth.

Once Claude himself came down into the cellar carrying a plate of steaming hot soup. Real chicken soup, not the usual pond scum. Radu caught a tantalizing whiff of its delicious fragrance; he could see real bits of chicken, celery, carrots and parsley floating in the yellow liquid specked with clusters of oil.

"Aren't you hungry? Do you really plan to waste away just to protect a few traitors?" Claude asked him in an uncharacteristically gentle voice.

"I have nothing to say," Radu replied.

"Suit yourself," Claude replied and began slurping the soup in front of his captive's eyes. Radu was hungry. Very hungry. The past few days he fantasized about the delicious meals he had had in Paris. The mouthwatering croissants, the fresh bread, the roasted duck, the fish and vegetable soups. He was so desperate that he even recalled the more modest meals he had in Romania. His insides hurt from hunger. His throat was parched from thirst. At times, even his obsession with Ioana's betrayal gave way to an all-pervasive sense of physical discomfort. Day by day, hour by hour, he could feel his body disintegrate.

After Claude's visit, Radu had reached his limit. He began to refuse the water and the bread. Let them kill me. I'd rather die quickly than waste away at their mercy, he resolved. In the dampness of the cellar, within a few hours the bread was covered with mold. He placed the plate with the stale bread and water conspicuously by the stairs, so that they'd be sure to spot it and note his defiance.

During the first few days of their captive's hunger strike, the taller officer bantered about it—"Are you on a diet?"—but on the sixth day, when Radu had become so weak that he could barely open his eyes, Ahmed took the young man by the shoulders and shook him up. "Listen, if you don't cooperate, you'll not be the only one getting hurt!" he said

"What do you mean?" Radu asked.

"We've brought your little girlfriend here. We have no use for her any more anyways," Ahmed responded.

"You can do what you want to her. I don't care. After all, she's the one that got me into this mess," Radu pretended not to care.

"Consider it done! Claude's been waiting for this opportunity," Ahmed barked, turned upon his heels and shut the cellar door.

Only moments later Radu heard loud female shrieks, followed by even more troubling moments of silence, coming from above. With a pounding heart he climbed up the stairs and put his ear to the door, attempting to recognize Ioana's voice. After a few minutes, he felt certain it was her. All of his hatred and resentment melted away the instant he thought he recognized her voice. She may have been responsible for his pain, but he would never be responsible for hers.

"Claude!" he called. "Claude!"

The screaming stopped abruptly and Claude appeared, his delicate, intellectual's face glowing with a sadistic smile. "Yes?"

"I'm ready to cooperate," Radu announced. "Where is Ioana? Did you... Is she alright?"

"We knew you'd come around," Claude patted him on the back. "If you give us a photocopy of those dissident letters we discussed at the café, the world will be your oyster. You and Ioana can marry and live happily ever after pretty much anywhere you wish on this planet. Courtesy of the Romanian government."

"Just what I always dreamed of. A fairytale ending to this nightmare," he couldn't resist the sarcasm.

"What did you say?" Claude asked, his disposition souring again.

"I said I don't want to marry Ioana," Radu reformulated his statement.

"I don't blame you," Claude concurred. "Who'd want to marry such a slut? What matters is that if you do what we ask, you'll regain your freedom and serve your beloved country."

Radu pursed his lips to restrain himself from making any further comments.

Chapter 12

On her way to her meeting with Comrade Stanescu, Eva recalled everything she knew about Secret Police interrogations, mostly from reading books and articles about the *NKVD* and KGB sending millions of people to icy labor camps in Siberia. For extra comfort, there were also the Khrushchev disclosures of horrific sessions of torture interspersed with relentless interrogations in the Lubyanka prison, which Eva could barely imagine, let alone withstand. Although it was safe to assume that Romania under Petrescu wasn't as bad as Stalinist Russia, Eva prepared herself for the worst. She imagined that she'd be questioned by a typical "government thug": a large, brutish man who was used to intimidating, beating and torturing women without even flinching. Eva pictured her interrogator: he'd have beady eyes narrow like slits, high cheekbones and a thin, cruel mouth almost completely hidden by a large square mustache. Come to think of it, this mental image resembled the posters of Stalin she had seen as a young child plastered all over her native town, Timisoara. In those days, during the presidency of Gheorghe-Gheorghiu Dej, Romania was still a satellite state. People had to demonstrate in the streets shouting Stalin si poporul Rus, li-ber-ta-te ne-a adus! ("Stalin and the Russian people, li-ber-ty they brought to us!") to thank the USSR for making Romania almost as advanced in its socialist progress as they were.

On second thought, Eva realized once her lips had nearly turned blue from being pressed together in nervousness, perhaps thinking of The Gulag Archipelago right before the meeting with Comrade Stanescu wasn't the best way to summon one's confidence. By now, however, it was too late. Eva had cold hands and feet; her knees seemed to fold under her as she walked down the sterile corridors that echoed the clicking sound of her own heels. She felt so intimidated that she had practically done the interrogator's job for him, before the interview even begun. By the time she knocked on the door marked 224, the office of Mihai Stanescu, her assigned investigator, Eva was ready to extend her hands for the placement of handcuffs.

"Come in!" she heard a man's voice invite her. She walked into a room that looked nothing like what she had imagined. The office was decorated with realist style paintings of his home town, Iasi, as well as several vases, rugs and wall tapestry with colorful folkloric motifs. Eva felt as if she had just stepped into her mother-in-law's Moldavian house, which, given its kitschy décor, wasn't exactly tasteful, but it was no jail cell or torture chamber either.

"Please sit down," Comrade Stanescu said almost gently, pointing to the comfortable seat in front of his desk. Eva was relieved to see that the Secret Police interrogator didn't resemble Stalin. He was a small, thin man in his late sixties, with short white hair, clean-shaven and silver-rimmed glasses. His dark brown eyes and bushy eyebrows gave him a paternal air that, strangely enough, reminded Eva of her own father.

"I'm not exactly what you expected?" he asked, reading her mind. "Well, I've been doing this job for thirty years now… and it's not an unpleasant one, I must say. Especially if I get to converse with attractive young women like yourself," he complimented her. Eva smiled mechanically. Although she didn't like lingusiri, or empty flattery, she nonetheless said "Thank you," just to be polite.

"Nasty weather, isn't it?" Comrade Stanescu begun making small talk. It happened to be cold and raining outside. Eva wondered if this comment was a double entendre. Perhaps he was alluding to her secret code with Andrei.

"Yes," she answered cautiously.

"I understand you have two kids," the Secret Police agent said matter-of-factly.

"Yes." Is this a threat? Eva wondered, at every step expecting disaster.

"So do I," Comrade Stanescu said affably. He leaned forward and opened the upper right drawer of his desk to take out a picture of a teenage boy with a thin face and red hair and of a girl with blue eyes and blond hair. "Cristian," he said, pointing to the boy, "is already in college. He's studying at the Polytechnic Institute to become an engineer," he declared with an air of fatherly pride, referring to the place where most of the tech spies were trained. "Me, I never liked school. I figure it's up to our kids to become smarter than us, right?" He smiled showing a row of bad teeth, some of them capped with glittering gold crowns. Even the privileged nomenclatura preferred to invest money in glitzy Rolex watches or the stereotypical black Mercedes rather than in trivial matters, like taking care of bad teeth or failing health.

Eva felt a pang of pain as she thought about her own son. She desperately wanted to ask the interrogator what had happened to Radu. But she knew it wouldn't be prudent to bring up this charged subject. Her son's activities would be an even more explosive topic of conversation than her husband's recent defection to the United States, the matter which she had been officially summoned to discuss. Her father's advice—fly below the radar screen and avoid turning on the alarms--was very wise, she thought.

"You must be proud of Radu," Comrade Stanescu said, touching her sore spot.

Eva resisted the urge to respond. The extended silence, rendered more difficult by the agent's invasive gaze, became awkward. To distract herself from her own emotions, Eva attempted to focus on the pictures on the agent's desk. Since the photographs were of his children, however, this made her feel even more ill at ease.

"I assume your son's still in Paris, right?" the interrogator pursued.

"Yes," Eva answered, though what she really wanted to say was "I hope so," or, more frankly, "I don't know where he is," so that the agent would tell her the truth, if he knew it. Eva could tell from the knot in her throat that if she said anything more, she would most likely burst into tears.

For the moment, however, Comrade Stanescu let the matter drop. He picked up the picture of his daughter. "She's beautiful, isn't she?" Eva agreed, even though she found the girl neither beautiful nor ugly. "Spitting image of my wife," the agent explained, as if trying to explain the fact that she didn't resemble him. He sighed. "Eh, a daughter's always the apple of her parents' eyes," he said, remaining keenly attentive to her reaction.

"I know what you mean," Eva tried to establish a better rapport with her interrogator, feeling that, somehow, she was failing the test. "My little girl's name is Irina." But the interrogator already knew that. "We love her very much," she added awkwardly.

"I don't doubt it," Comrade Stanescu answered almost sympathetically. After another extended pause, he put his hand to his mouth, then slowly stroked his chin as if absorbed in deep thought. "So what are we to do about your husband's treason, hmm?" he finally asked the question Eva had anticipated.

She was fully prepared with an answer: "My husband got a good job offer in the United States. He didn't leave Romania for political reasons. My daughter and I would like to join him."

"We'll see what we can do about that," the interrogator replied, appearing to be on her side. "If I may ask: What's your relationship with your husband like?"

"Very good," she answered firmly, expecting this question as well. She wasn't about to let anybody divide and conquer her family. "We love each other deeply and hope to be reunited soon."

"Hmm hm. Based upon our initial observations, that was our impression as well," he placed emphasis upon the past tense. "Until ...we noticed some peculiar incidents."

Eva refused to take the bait.

"For instance," the interrogator continued, "didn't you find it a bit strange that your husband would take the risk of never seeing you and his beloved daughter again just to pursue some... equations? No offense to physics, but shouldn't family count more?"

"My husband didn't consider accepting a job in the United States to be an abandonment of his family," Eva responded heatedly, forgetting her own resolution to remain calm. "He has full faith in our government's humanitarian immigration policies, especially since Romania obtained the most favorite nation status. We assume that the Romanian government has earned it based upon its record of human rights. Not allowing a wife and daughter to join their husband and father would be inhumane. Consequently, we fully expect to be allowed to immigrate to the United States," she concluded her speech.

"Comrade Schwarz, you and your husband are not in the position to make such assumptions on behalf of our country," the agent answered, showing impatience with Eva's obviously rehearsed answers. "Besides, as I'm sure you're aware, humanitarianism has nothing to do with the way governments deal with traitors," he added, pinning her once again with his dark eyes, which flashed irately underneath the bushy eyebrows. He now looked more demonic than paternal, Eva thought.

"My husband's not a traitor!" she protested, struggling to maintain her poise.

In response, Comrade Stanescu picked up and leafed slowly through the contents of a brown leather folder, then proceeded to take out a few sheets of paper covered with typed print. Although before he spoke rather loudly, now he replied so softly that Eva had to strain to hear him: "If I'm not mistaken, our records indicate that your husband spied on behalf of the Israeli government."

"That's not tr..." she began to deny this, but Comrade Stanescu cut her short.

"Please don't interrupt me, Mrs. Schwarz," the interrogator said, raising his voice and calling her "Doamna" or "Mrs.," an old-fashioned non-socialist pronoun often used as a mark of disrespect. "In addition," he continued once again speaking in a deliberately slow and soft manner that gave his words an unpleasant staccato, "As I'm sure you're well aware, defecting ille-gal-ly from this country con-sti-tutes an act of treason under Romanian law. So, though I'm no famous physicist, I can still count and am led to the conclusion that your husband committed treason twice against our country."

Eva realized that it would be pointless to defend Andrei. Everything she'd say would be turned against both her and her husband.

"Either way you slice it, Eva," Comrade Stanescu returned to his friendlier tone of voice, "You need to confront reality: Your husband abandoned you and your daughter. Now," he paused for a moment looking straight into her eyes: "Do you want to know why? Or do you prefer to bury your head in the sand like an ostrich?"

Eva's heart was racing—this time not from nervousness or fear, but from anger. How dare this man suggest that her husband was an unloving father? That he preferred physics to his own daughter? Everything Andrei did, Eva thought with indignation, was in the hope of securing a better future for his family.

"I take it from your silence that you agree with our assessment?" Comrade Stanescu baited her.

"Not at all," she said, growing defiant under repeated provocation.

"What if I told you we have evidence that Mr. Schwarz left you and your family because he's in love with another woman?" Comrade Stanescu asked, removing from the folder three color photographs. He placed them on the table, fanning them out in front of Eva with the deliberate movements with which one reveals a winning hand in poker.

Eva refused to take the photographs into her hands. She gazed at them upside-down contemptuously, thinking that planted evidence wouldn't dissuade her from trusting her husband. The first picture showed Andrei talking to a younger woman. He was gesticulating with his hands, a gesture that Eva recognized as his state of excitement when he was explaining an important theorem. The woman was attractive, that much she noticed. She had long brown hair, glasses and wore pink lipstick. The second and third pictures showed Andrei with the same young woman at a restaurant. They were having coffee and apparently the woman was saying something amusing because Andrei was laughing. All this proves, Eva thought to herself, was that her husband loved physics and had a sense of humor. But she already knew that.

"Well?"

"I don't see how these photographs prove that my husband's having an affair," Eva replied.

Comrade Stanescu shook his head with disbelief and assumed a benevolent, compassionate air: "Eva, Eva... What will it take to open your eyes, hmmm? Your husband leaves you and your daughter in a very... let's just say... precarious position, and that's putting it mildly. Given that both your son and your husband are considered traitors in this country, Mr. Schwarz couldn't possibly have counted on our government giving you and Irina permission to immigrate legally to the United States. In fact, he must have known in advance that he was asking for the impossible."

"Andrei thought that allowing our family to reunite was the only humane course of action."

Comrade Stanescu responded only with an indulgent smirk, as one smiles at an adolescent girl who still believes in the tooth fairy.

"Do you really think our government would allow a known traitor's family to join him abroad? After spying on our top security secrets, we gave him a second chance. And what did he do? He slapped us in the face yet again by defecting."

"My husband will get important people, such as United States senators, to intervene on our behalf," Eva countered, showing her own hand in the game.

Comrade Stanescu chuckled. "That's very amusing. You think American senators give a hoot about you and your little family? Or that our socialist country cares about what capitalist senators do or think?"

"If Romania wants to keep its most favored nation status..." she began to reply.

"Mrs. Schwarz, please! You've already made this irrelevant point before," he interrupted her with impatience. "Politics obviously isn't your strong suit. Forgive me, but you sound a bit... naive." The agent paused and picked up an invisible piece of lint from the sleeve of his impeccably tailored suit. "Do you really think that what happens to one insignificant family," he said, rubbing the lint between his fingers to indicate its microscopic size, "will change the national policies of two countries cooperating bilaterally in the midst of a Cold War? Quite frankly, Mrs. Schwarz, this may come as a surprise to you, but the U.S. and Romanian governments have more important matters to worry about than your family's immigration."

Eva remained silent.

"I'm asking you to reconsider your husband's position," Comrade Stanescu continued. "He hasn't just betrayed his country, a serious enough moral error. Whether you care to admit it or not, he has also abandoned his family. You wouldn't follow his bad example and do the same to your own parents, now would you? After all, even a bourgeoise like you, who's willing to betray her country, still cares about her family. Am I right?"

Eva looked away, to hide her anger, which was welling up in her throat. But she couldn't contain her emotions. Her hands trembled lightly, folded upon her lap. This man, this stranger, had attacked what she and her family held most dear: their love and loyalty to one another. In only half an hour, he tried to undermine her trust in Andrei's fidelity; her belief that he defected to build a better life for her and their children; her hope in their reunion and her gratitude and love for her own parents and brother, whom she had long hesitated to leave behind in Romania.

When Eva stepped out of his office, her only thought was to remain strong in the face of Stanescu's intimidation. Yet, in spite of herself, at night she was haunted by his insinuations. The thought of Andrei cheating on her was so preposterous that even her subconscious could dismiss it. Yet the fear that the government would never allow her and Irina to join him was very real. She also had the opposite worry: of immigrating to America and leaving her brother and aging parents, who had always stood by her side, even more vulnerable to government persecution. Like a Chinese water torturer, Comrade Stanescu harped on these anxieties drop by drop, meeting after meeting, week after week, month after month to persuade Eva to divorce Andrei and stay with their daughter in Romania. He alternated between threats and encouragements. Like a virus, the interrogation sessions attacked everything that was living and healthy in Eva's psyche, eroding her vitality even if it couldn't touch her love.

Chapter 13

"Those good old *NKVD* techniques work like a charm, huh?" Claude said to Ahmed with a wink.

"Well, when it came to torturing people, Yezhov did it best," Ahmed concurred. The two of them were having dinner in the kitchen while Radu was still locked up in the cellar, awaiting his release. Each time they brought him a plate of food, he'd ask them when they would release him, as promised. And each time they answered with an imperative: "Wait!" What had he been doing all these weeks? The young man paced up and down the cellar like a caged animal. He climbed up the stairs and pressed his ear to the door, straining to hear once again Ioana's voice. For a split second, he thought he heard her scream. Were they torturing her again? Even after he had agreed to cooperate? The noise stopped abruptly, as if cut off in mid-sound. In fact, Radu thought, this time the woman's voice didn't even sound natural. Am I starting to hallucinate? he wondered. Given his fatigue, that wasn't entirely out of the question. Yet, unmistakably, a few moments later, he heard it again. The same screams as before.

Downstairs, Claude calmly enjoyed his favorite entree--steak with french fries--which he washed down with a glass of red wine. He wasn't in the mood for making conversation and Ahmed wasn't much of a talker anyways. Between savory bites, Claude amused himself by playing the tape at the moment when the woman screamed the loudest. Then he rewound the tape recorder, took another bite of food and pressed "Play" once again, to relive the moment. He enjoyed hearing the agony in her voice.

Although most women were forgettable to him, he remembered this one. Adriana was her name. She had long red hair and almond shaped green eyes. Her life was a familiar story for prostitute agents, but she refused to follow the script. She had seduced a German engineer, set up house with him in Munich at the Romanian government's expense and was charged with enticing her lover to reveal Volkswagen manufacturing secrets. Once they were married, Adriana abruptly stopped contact with the *Securitate*. When they called her to find out what had happened, she told them in a frightened, weepy voice that she wanted a clean break from the Romanian authorities. She had fallen in love head over heels with her German husband and told him everything. He had forgiven her, she added, by way of explanation. How touching! They promptly dispatched Claude to her house to congratulate her in person. She was alone in the apartment. When she opened the door, she recognized him immediately. He saw the flicker of fear light up her green eyes. It set him on fire.

Claude put a hand over her mouth, pushed her roughly up against the wall, tore down with one hand her underwear and raped her, his hand pressed tightly against her mouth as she tried to scream, to bite him. "Take this, you whore! That'll teach you to betray your country!" he screamed as he repeatedly thrust into her. His own words of insult, her moans of pain, the tears trailing down her cheeks excited him even more. Then it occurred to him to record the experience for posterity. He first tied her up to a chair, then turned on the tape recorder he had brought along. He proceeded to torture her. His favorite method was pulling women's hair, especially if it was silky and long like Adriana's. He passed his fingers over it, almost caressing it. He allowed her long strands to slip gingerly between his fingers and then, abruptly switching from gentleness to violence, tugged hard, bearing a clump of hair in his hand like a trophy. That's when she had made those shrill cries. He saved the tape as a memento, for his personal enjoyment. Soon thereafter, however, he found another use for it. He played it quite frequently to intimidate male prisoners into cooperating with the *Securitate* by telling them that the voices on the tape were those of their daughters, sisters, wives or girlfriends. Feeling himself becoming stimulated by these pleasant recollections, Claude popped the cassette out of the tape recorder. "Too bad Stanescu's protecting that little bitch," he muttered more to himself than to Ahmed, alluding to Ioana. Yet he still had hope. "If she makes another false move, she's ours." His eyes glimmered with predatory anticipation.

Ahmed smiled with complicity, but only out of politeness. "This bastard's a real sadist," he thought to himself. Ahmed liked raping pretty women as much as the next guy working for the Secret Police, but he drew the line at beating and torturing them. Being a gentleman, he reserved that kind of treatment for the men.

"I'm going out tonight. You're in charge," Claude announced after dinner, standing up and patting his stomach. Then he headed out to have some fun at Pigalle, the seediest quarter of Paris. He returned home in a drunken stupor and went straight to bed.

Claude woke up around noon and said to Ahmed: "Stanescu paged me. It's time to go ahead and implement the plan."

The two men went downstairs, into the cellar. They found Radu sitting down, his back against the cold wall. Startled, the young man abruptly stood up.

"No need to stand at attention. We're not in the army here," Claude patted Radu on the shoulder, doing his best to put him at ease. "So are you ready to go back to work after this little vacation?"

"Where's Ioana?" Radu asked.

"For now, your girlfriend's safe and sound," Claude reassured him. "In fact, she's on her way back to Romania as we speak."

"Romania? Why Romania?"

"She has to report back to her boss."

"What's there to report?"

"Her failure to complete her first assignment, I suppose," Claude shrugged.

"I don't believe Ioana's a spy," Radu verbalized the conclusion of his long hours of contemplation. "She must have been somehow lured into this mess without realizing what was going on."

Claude shook his head in disbelief. "Man, for someone who's studying chemistry in Paris, you're not too bright."

"I've gotten to know Ioana quite well," Radu insisted.

"You did, did you?" Claude was beginning to feel irritated by the young man's naiveté. "Alright. Then follow me." The three men went upstairs into the living room. "Let's see what you make of this interesting tidbit," Claude said, looking at Radu straight in the eyes as he slowly removed a cassette from the inner pocket of his jacket. Without losing eye contact, he inserted it into the tape recorder still lying on the coffee table and hit "Play."

"Comrade Stanescu, this is Margarita reporting," Radu heard Ioana's voice, as clear and melodious as ever, only slightly distorted by the static noise on the recording. "The fly has been trapped in the spider's net," she continued. "Schwarz is meeting our contact this afternoon." Click.

"That contact was me," Claude clarified, just in case Radu was as dense as he appeared to be.

The young man stared blankly in front of him, absorbing the impact of this last blow. He felt like someone who has been suffering from a debilitating illness whose doctor has just announced the fatal diagnosis he had feared all along.

"Now are you ready to cooperate?" Claude asked him.

"Like I told you before, all I can do is ask Pavlovich for an assignment that would involve access to the Romanian dissident letters."

"Such as?"

"Such as doing a show on the dissatisfaction of the émigré community with the Petrescu violations of human rights, or something of that nature."

"That's all we're asking for," Claude answered, assuming the tone of a reasonable man. "You don't even need to photocopy the letters. Microdot pictures will work just fine. That way you don't have to remove any documents from the premises."

"What are microdot pictures?"

Claude was happy to exhibit his expertise in the latest spying gadgets: "A microdot photograph can be taken with any decent 35 millimeter camera using the British method."

"I see…" Radu replied.

Claude laughed: "You have no idea what I'm talking about, do you?"

"None whatsoever," Radu admitted.

"You use a high contrast black and white film and take the photograph so that the image of the document fills out the whole frame of the film. Then you process the film and mount the negative in an opening in a piece of black cardboard. When you light it from behind, the text on the negative shows up as white on black. Then presto! All you need to do is cut out the tiny image and you have a microdot picture."

"How exactly is this easier than making a photocopy?" Radu inquired.

"It's not easier, Inspector Clouseau," Claude replied. "It's just safer and less noticeable. That way you're not seen removing documents. You photograph the letters unobtrusively on the spot, then pour the chemicals needed to develop the film right into the camera's stainless-steel body. With this method, you don't even need any other equipment."

"Once I have the letters in my hands, it won't be hard to reproduce them," Radu countered. "The problem is getting such a delicate assignment in the first place. It might take some time…"

"Why?" Claude furrowed his eyebrows.

"Well, put yourself in my boss's shoes. I vanish for a few weeks, which will be tough enough to explain. It would look downright suspicious if right after I return to work, I ask him for confidential information."

Claude once again began to lose his cool: "Is your boss that paranoid? Can't you tell him you got sick and just got back from the hospital? You've lost so much weight and look so pale that this excuse will seem entirely plausible. Besides, what's so strange about a Romanian journalist doing a special on Romanian dissidents?"

"The fact remains that those letters are confidential. They don't trust just anybody with them," Radu clarified.

"You're not just anybody. You've worked for them for a whole year."

"Yes, but I'm still considered a novice. Plus I only work there part-time."

"Just how much do you want to see your little girlfriend again?" Claude narrowed his steely gray eyes.

"All I'm asking for is a little time, that's all," Radu replied.

"You have one week," Claude announced like a man who was not in the mood for further negotiation.

Radu shook his head. "I need at least a month. To get back into the swing of things and regain Pavlovich's trust."

Seeing that Claude was about to protest, Radu hastened to add: "If I rush into this and botch things up, it could compromise the whole RFE infiltration for years to come."

"One month," Claude agreed. "Where do you want to be dropped off?"

"At home," Radu replied.

"Why don't you accompany our friend to the Cité Universitaire?" Claude turned to Ahmed. "Today I might need to take a little siesta. I had a few hot dates last night," he added with a wink.

"Sure thing, Boss!" Ahmed replied and began putting the blindfold on Radu, who objected.

"Why do you need to blindfold me now? I know where we're going."

"Yes, genius. But you don't know where we're coming from," Claude retorted with a snort. "Chemistry major, huh? This guy never ceases to amaze me…"

Ahmed led Radu to the back seat of the car, then drove in the same hectic manner as when he had abducted him and stopped in front of the Cité Universitaire. He got out, untied the knot of Radu's blindfold and smiled pleasantly at him: "One month, or your girlfriend's…" He made a silent gesture with his index finger across his own throat instead of completing the sentence.

Chapter 14

"So!" Pavlovich said, by way of initiating the conversation once he spotted Radu standing in the doorway. He was a rotund, jovial man in his early sixties, with narrow dark eyes shaded by bushy eyebrows and a shiny bald forehead crowned by a strip of gray hair. Back in Russia, he had been a factory worker in charge of agitprop, the communist propaganda machine. Despite the fact that his young Jewish wife had been sent to the gulag in '51 during the anti-Zionist phase of Stalin's paranoia, Pavlovich continued to behave like a model communist until, after nearly thirty years of delivering disingenuous motivational speeches, sitting on numberless ideological committees and inventing figures that showed nonexistent increases in industrial productivity, he saw his chance and made a run for it. During his first visit to an oil refinery near Paris, where he had been sent to obtain secret information, he defected. He gave out enough useful information about the KGB policy of industrial espionage to get both protection and a job from the CIA operatives collaborating with Radio Freedom Europe. In ordinary circumstances, Radu had no difficulty communicating with his outspoken and virulently anti-communist boss. Now that he was entrusted with a *Securitate* mission, however, he found himself nervous and tongue-tied. "You vanted something?" Pavlovich prodded Radu, since he wasn't one to beat around the bush.

"Well, not exactly…" Radu replied.

"Then vhy are you here? Don't just stand there like a corncob, come in!"

Radu shuffled into the office.

"Yes?" Pavlovich arched his bushy eyebrows.

Radu paused for a minute, rehearsing in his mind for the nth time the most diplomatic and natural way in which he could frame his request.

"Vat is it? You vant more money?" Pavlovich asked him.

"No."

"Good! Because ve don't have money to give."

Radu passed his tongue over his dry lips. "I was just thinking, Alexei Pavlovich, about how I really admire the way you coordinate and select the shows on Eastern Europe," he said quickly.

Pavlovich's eyes narrowed with suspicion.

"I mean, it's a big responsibility and you do it so well."

Pavlovich nodded. "I see. You vant my job?"

"No, not at all! I just meant to say… that I respect your judgment."

"I'm glad to hear that. But the more important question is, do I respect yours?" Pavlovich retorted with a sly smile.

"I don't know," Radu answered, discombobulated.

"That is correct! Neither do I. Which is vhy I have to see how you do this year before I give you a promotion."

"But I wasn't asking for one," Radu's wheels were spinning in place.

"Ah, you sly man! You think you are suave?" Pavlovich winked at him.

"No, it's just that... I wanted to see if it was possible to..."

"Of course, of course. It is possible. Everything is possible in life. Ask me again in a year or so," Pavlovich replied, diverting his attention to a pile of papers on his desk.

Radu left his boss' office in a daze. He turned left down the hallway to enter his own office, which was more of an enlarged closet, when, to his surprise, he ran into Jean-Pierre. What is he doing here? Radu wondered. Did Claude send him here to monitor my mission? The sight of the man he now associated with Ioana and the *Securitate* made Radu feel highly uncomfortable. Should he avoid Jean-Pierre's gaze and pretend not to notice him or say hello to him as if nothing were wrong? Before he got the chance to decide, Jean-Pierre greeted him first:

"Radu? Ca va? I haven't seen you for such a long time."

"I know."

"How have you been?"

"Alright."

"You look pale as a ghost."

"Yes."

"How's Ioana?"

"I don't know."

"I thought the two of you were an item."

"We dated for a little while."

"And what happened?" Jean-Pierre probed.

Radu shrugged, trying to appear nonchalant: "Things just didn't work out."

Jean-Pierre approached Radu and looked into his eyes. The young man barely heard him whisper: "If you want news from her, meet me in front of the L'Arc de Triomphe in an hour." He then reverted to a normal, convivial tone: "Well, it was nice seeing you again!"

"You too," Radu mumbled. He went into his office, which looked more like a closet than an office, closed the door and considered Jean-Pierre's strange invitation. What do I care about what happened to her anyways? he asked himself. However bad it may be, it serves her right for what she did to me. Yet the curiosity to discover his girlfriend's fate, and even the trace of a chivalrous desire to save her from whatever misfortunes she may have encountered, proved stronger than his resentment. After all, what do I have to lose? Radu asked himself. I'm already in the clutches of the *Securitate* and haven't even managed to put myself in the position to get the information they want. I'll go! he spontaneously decided.

Chapter 15

Radu took the metro to La Place de L'Etoile, which dropped him off close to L'Arc de Triomphe. He immediately spotted Jean-Pierre, who had changed clothes. Dressed in casual attire only an hour earlier, his dark suit now made him resemble a business man. He signaled to Radu. The young man approached him.

"Are you hungry?" Jean-Pierre asked. It was almost noon, not too early for the déjeuner.

"Not really," Radu replied.

Noticing Radu's reluctance to engage in small-talk, Jean-Pierre launched directly into the subject at hand: "I know about your predicament," he said. The two men started walking around the monument, occasionally interrupting their conversation and pretending to admire it as if they were tourists.

"What predicament?" Radu asked.

"You have a deadline for giving Romanian agents the dissident letters," Jean-Pierre encapsulated the situation.

"You must have talked to Claude," Radu concluded, not at all surprised that Jean-Pierre knew everything.

"Actually, I haven't had much direct contact with Claude lately."

"I thought the two of you were buddies," Radu commented, his voice filled with bitterness.

Jean-Pierre ignored his remark. "You can still escape the tangled web you have gotten yourself into."

"The web I've gotten myself into it?" Radu exploded. "You and Ioana got me into this mess! I wouldn't have gotten entangled into anything; I wouldn't have even met Claude if it weren't for your generous 'help'!"

"Shhh…" Jean-Pierre cautioned, putting his index finger to his lips. "Things aren't as they seem," he whispered.

"You mean to say that I'm not being pressured by the *Securitate* to reveal innocent people's secrets so that they and their loved ones can be harassed, perhaps even killed, by the Romanian authorities?" the young man asked in a whisper that sounded more like a hiss.

"Oh, that you are, indeed. But you're involved in a game that is more complicated than you think. The two sides aren't so clearly delineated," Jean-Pierre answered in a low voice.

"I don't care. I don't want to be involved in any of these political games any more. I just want to be left alone and live my life," Radu declared heatedly.

After a pause, he calmed down enough to ask Claude: "Which side are you on anyway?"

"Mine," Jean-Pierre replied without a moment's hesitation.

"Meaning?"

"Meaning that I understand you. When I was young, I was exactly in your shoes."

"You were loved and betrayed by a woman working for the *Securitate*?" Radu inquired, sarcastically.

To his surprise, Jean-Pierre nodded.

"But why? How?"

"The why is simple. I made it big as an artist when I was still quite young. By the age of twenty-five, I already had international fame. My agent and gallery owners threw parties where they invited fellow artists, important businessmen, politicians, ambassadors."

"What does art have to do with spying?" Radu interrupted.

Jean-Pierre seemed surprised by the naiveté of his question. "Everything. Given all your experience with working for RFE, you ought to know by now. Recruiting agents from NATO countries is one of your government's highest priorities. Now as to the how. At a party before one of my art shows, I met a lovely young woman. Her name was Gratiela Popescu. She reminded me of Grace Kelly in some ways. You know the type: blond, elegant, seemingly glacial, yet at the same time mild and approachable. There was something very special about her demeanor... It's hard to describe... But the point is, I really liked her."

"That's how it all begins..." Radu commented sympathetically.

"...but definitely not how it ends," Jean-Pierre continued. "It was once we got to talking that I became truly fascinated with her and her life."

"Let me guess: she started talking about her problems with the Romanian government?" Radu anticipated.

"Isn't that the technique?" Jean-Pierre replied cynically. "She aroused both my desire and my sympathy. Back then, I didn't know much about the Romanian government except for the fact that it was pretty bad yet trying to appear good. But once she told me about what her family had to endure, it really touched me. She told me about the infamous Canal of Death. Her father, who happened to make an innocuous joke against the regime to one of his colleagues who then informed on him, had been sent there for years. Gratiela made it clear to me that she hated communism and that she wanted to defect. After a few dates, she solicited my help. And that's how I got involved in this whole business of ... Cold War international intrigue, if you wish."

"Those must have been some pretty hot dates!"

"Bien sur! If they hadn't been, I wouldn't have landed into such a big mess."

"Are you out of it now?"

Jean-Pierre shook his head. "Once you get entangled in this web, you can never escape it. The best you can hope for is to find your way around the labyrinth a little better."

"What web are we talking about?" Radu began to feel lost in all the innuendoes.

"The web of espionage," Jean-Pierre replied matter-of-factly, as if he were commenting upon the weather.

The two men stopped walking for a moment. They were right next to the internal wall of the arch. Jean-Pierre leaned against it. "Anyways, to go back to my story, slowly but surely, Gratiela convinced me that she was in love. And during our dates, she worked on me. Pumped me for information."

"What kind of information would an artist have to give? I mean, art is as far removed from politics as possible," Radu once again voiced his skepticism.

"Oh yeah? Have you ever seen Picasso's Guernica? Besides, being recruited as an agent isn't just about getting information from people. It's even more about spreading information through them. Haven't you heard of Operation Horizon? It's principally aimed at propaganda for the West which depicts Petrescu as some kind of Tito. An anti-Soviet maverick."

"I still don't understand. It's not like your art has anything to do with political issues. It's so abstract. I honestly can't tell if it's about anything at all," Radu objected.

"It doesn't matter what you can or cannot tell about my art," Jean-Pierre's tone became defensive, as it got whenever anything remotely negative was said about his work. "What counted for them was the fact that I was a visible cultural figure who gave interviews in prominent newspapers such as *Le Monde* and *Le Figaro*. That I could take positions on political and ideological issues related to the Cold War in general and Romania in particular and that those positions would be visible."

"And did you?"

"For awhile I did. I even spewed off some Marxist rhetoric to sound more in vogue."

"How did that go over with your girlfriend? Wasn't she anti-communist?"

"Ah, yes... But only in the beginning. As it turns out, Gratiela's position was quite versatile. Basically, she explained to me, she was anti-communist, but not anti-Marxist. And once she defected to France with my help, she changed her position. She persuaded me that her family would be persecuted if I didn't say nice things about the Romanian government."

"And you did that? For her?"

"Absolutely. Even gladly. I was such an idiot, huh?" Jean-Pierre asked.

"Well, I wouldn't go that far," Radu replied, not quite prepared to accept that epithet for himself. "Perhaps a little naïve... So then what opened your eyes?"

"Exactly the same blow on the head that opened yours. When I got tired of playing the marionette for Gratiela and was ready to break up with her—actually, I fell in love with one of my models, a gorgeous Swedish girl, but that's a whole other story--she threatened to tell my wife. Did I mention the little detail that when I met Gratiela I was already married? Anyway, that's when I saw her true colors. I ended up breaking up with her and she, in turn, fulfilled her promise. So as a fringe benefit courtesy of the Romanian government, I also got divorced."

Radu was intrigued by the intricacies of Jean-Pierre's life. "Did you love her?"

"Who? The Swedish girl?"

"No. Your wife."

Jean-Pierre reflected for a moment. "Who knows? We got married when we were still kids, barely twenty. When you're that young, who can tell the difference between infatuation and love? Besides, I didn't really give marriage a chance. I cheated on Yvette constantly during the two years we were together. I suppose that fame went to my head."

"But once you broke up with Gratiela and had nothing left to lose with your wife, why did you maintain your ties with the Secret Police?"

"Because I felt exactly like you do right now. Betrayed. My love affair was shattered, my marriage over." Jean-Pierre turned to Radu. His eyes glimmered in the sunlight. "I'm not the kind of man who ca be used without taking vengeance."

"So you got back at Gratiela for betraying you?"

Jean-Pierre shook his head with a look of disgust. "Nah. What would be the point of that? Such women are paid back by life. They're thrown away like used napkins after the government blows its nose in them." He then added in a lower voice: "I wanted to get back at the Secret Police itself. To deceive them in turn. That's how I got involved with Radio Freedom Europe and ...

"And?"

"...I started working for the CIA."

"The CIA? What are you saying? That you became a double agent?" Radu asked incredulously. "Wasn't being a single agent exciting enough?"

"Not when you're double-crossed," Jean-Pierre replied calmly. "Which brings me to the matter I wanted to discuss: you might wish to consider following the same path. Working with the CIA has its advantages."

"Such as?"

"Such as saving your life, for one They'd protect you from the Secret Police. Give you a whole new identity."

"What would be in it for them?"

"Intelligence."

"I've been told I don't have much of that. At least not the practical kind."

Jean-Pierre smiled. "That may be true for now, but you can develop it. Besides, from their point of view, you have the advantage of already working with the Secret Police. "

"Does being locked up in a cellar for a few weeks qualify as job experience?" Radu wanted to know.

This time, however, Jean-Pierre was perfectly serious and without a shred of sarcasm in his tone. "It might. You can lead Claude to believe you're on their side. That's what I've been doing for years."

Radu shook his head. "I'm not as good at lying as you are."

"Merci. Toujours un mot gentil!"

"No, honestly, I meant that as a compliment. With me they'd smell a rat immediately. But I would like to start everything from a blank slate. Could the CIA really help me start a new life?"

"It depends on what you did for them in return."

"What would it take?"

"Nothing short of selling your soul," Jean-Pierre said.

Radu smiled, but that statement seemed to too close to the truth for comfort.

"You'd pretty much have to give up the idea of leading a normal life, with a wife, kids, freedom to do what you want with your time," Jean-Pierre elaborated.

"Well, being pursued by the Secret Police doesn't exactly open up those options either..." Radu mused out loud. He was overcome by a doubt: "Why are you so interested in helping me?"

"I work for the Agency. It's not just the Eastern Block that recruits, you know. We do it too."

"So now I have to choose between East and West?"

"That's one way of putting it. You need to decide in which hands you wish to deliver your freedom."

"What if I wish to keep it for myself?"

"For that, my friend, it's much too late," Jean-Pierre said, assuming an air of paternal indulgence.

Before parting, Radu asked, as a footnote, about the real purpose behind his meeting with Jean-Pierre: "What about Ioana?"

"What about her?"

"Can I see her?"

"Why would you want to?"

Radu hesitated for a moment, considering whether or not to give the real reason. "Because I want her to let her know how much she hurt me."

"I can arrange a meeting," Jean-Pierre agreed. "But only if you intend to hurt her in kind," he added.

"What do you mean?"

"She's already viewed as, shall we say... insufficiently enthusiastic by the Romanian government. If she meets with you and you join the CIA, they would finish her off."

"Then I don't want to see her," Radu promptly changed his mind. "However, if you get a chance, just tell her..."

"... that you still love her?" Jean-Pierre completed his sentence.

"No," Radu replied. "Tell her I pity her."

Chapter 16

Today seemed to be an ordinary day. Dimitrie had returned home from work and was bent over the kitchen table scribbling down an engineering equation that had been on his mind all day long. His grayish hair brushed his forehead and his glasses looked ready to slip from his nose unto the sheet of paper. Roxana was sitting on the sofa scrutinizing at least as carefully the latest bills. Although she was approaching her fifties, with her blond hair cropped short, she retained an air of youthfulness. They heard the noise of a key into the lock; Ioana had returned home with an almost fresh baguette. They were both very worried about their daughter.

Ioana's appearance had changed dramatically during the past few months. She had cut her hair short and dyed it blond, which made her look even paler. Her parents had noticed that she had lost her appetite. Sometimes even the sight of a plate of food made their daughter nauseous and she abruptly excused herself from the table and retreated into the bathroom. She felt like a hunted animal. She was burdened by a secret which would become increasingly difficult to hide. The only person in whom she wanted to confide, she had already betrayed. She longed to start life all over again, from a clean slate. Yet nothing felt clean about her conscience and no change in appearance could alter that fact.

"Were you followed?" her father asked as soon as she stepped into the room.

"Where?" Ioana inquired absentmindedly.

"From the Alimentara (Grocery Store) here, of course!"

"Oh, no, I don't think so..." Ioana answered, her voice trailing off with indecision. She was still shaken by her recent experience. Although she couldn't share its details with her parents, she did tell them that she left Paris because she no longer wanted to be an informant for the Secret Police. Needless to say, this caused her parents a lot of anxiety, since they both knew that one didn't quit such a sensitive job like one leaves a post at the local bakery. When Ioana had returned home unexpectedly from Paris, her father had asked her why she had taken such a risk. "I took that job to save you," Ioana had told him, "and I quit it to save myself." That statement sounded very enigmatic to him. But no matter how many questions he asked her, Ioana wouldn't elaborate.

Dimitrie and Roxana assumed that their daughter was only an informant, like about twenty percent of the Romanian population, not an actual agent working for the Secret Police. Ioana knew that she couldn't tell her parents, or anybody else for that matter, anything about her experience. About the extent of the sacrifice she had made to save her father from prison. About the risk and brutality that her job entailed. About the way she had fallen in love with the man she was hired to ensnare. About the way she had unwittingly contributed to her boyfriend's misfortune. About the guilt and torment she felt since his kidnapping. Radu had been her first "case." She would rather rot in a prison cell or be killed by the Secret Police than have to endure another such "case" ever again.

"Did you look around?" Dimitrie persisted. He hoped that if his daughter remained vigilant and walked only in crowded, public places, the Secret Police wouldn't dare nab her and might even, with God's help, eventually forget about her. After all, they had much more serious problems to deal with than hunting down a frightened, disoriented young girl.

"No, but I would have noticed if someone were following me," Ioana tried to reassure him.

Believing that Ioana wasn't taking their advice seriously, the parents exchanged a look of exasperation. "Please come with me into the bathroom," Roxana said in a grave tone. Her daughter knew that a long and, under the circumstances, futile lecture on caution would follow. "Can't this wait, Mom?" she pleaded for a moment's peace from this unnerving state of constant alert. "Can't we enjoy life together without worrying every single second?" Her question was answered by a loud knock on the door.

Dimitrie opened the door hastily and in stepped an officer, followed by two younger agents behind him. "Sir, you and your wife are under arrest for sedition," the main officer announced.

"But why?" the father asked, although he knew in advance that such questions were pointless. All government decisions were unquestionable and irrevocable.

"You're currently protecting a dangerous criminal. An enemy of the people," the officer informed him, with the same air of routine courtesy.

"Who?" Dimitrie asked, bewildered by this charge.

"Your daughter. We hired her as a prostitute agent and she ended up colluding with the man she was hired to seduce. Her boyfriend is a known traitor who denounced our government on Radio Freedom Europe. We're certain that as dutiful parents and citizens you were aware of your daughter's behavior and therefore consider you accomplices in her acts of treason and conspiracy."

Ioana's parents were stunned. The words "prostitute agent," which the officer had uttered as matter-of-factly as if he had said "secretary" or "doctor," rang in their ears. They were not surprised by the fact that the *Securitate* was looking for Ioana. Nor were they surprised that she had spoken out against the communist government. After all, so had Dimitrie. But they were shocked to find out that their daughter was using her sexuality as a political weapon. Everything they had taught Ioana about feminine virtue, they felt, had been irreversibly corrupted by this rotten government.

Knowing it would be pointless to deny these charges even if they were false, Roxana pleaded for her daughter with tears in her eyes: "I beg you, please don't arrest our daughter. She's so young; she didn't realize what she was doing…"

"Citizens don't tell the government what to do," the officer sharply reprimanded the mother, who was so overwhelmed by shock and sorrow that she seemed ready to collapse.

"The Justice Committee has not yet convened regarding your daughter's case," intervened the second officer in a deep voice. "She needs to supply further information concerning her exchanges with the aforementioned traitor," he explained. "We will take her to the Department of External Information for a debriefing session. As for you and your husband, your case has already been processed by the authorities through the appropriate channels. Please follow me."

Gazing lovingly at their daughter, unspeakably more wounded by her sexual transgression than by any political action she could have possibly taken, trembling with worry about her future rather than their own, Dimitrie and Roxana embraced their only child with tears in their eyes, then followed the officer out the door.

The two officers left, a younger man with a mustache and the older one who seemed to be his boss, now focused their attention on Ioana. Feeling dazed, she looked at the dingy walls of her own apartment as if they were unfamiliar surroundings. The darker streaks of green on the bluish paint formed a secret code which might have provided some answers, if it were not for the fact that she was too disoriented to ask any questions. Unpeeling her glance from the wall with great difficulty, she fixed it upon one of the two men standing calmly before her.

Catching her absentminded stare, the main officer reassured her: "Ioana, you must trust in your state. If you cooperate with us, no harm will come to you and your parents. Their fate rests in your hands."

At the sound of his steady voice, Ioana twitched in her seat, as if awakened from a bad dream. Pain saturated her body, trickling from head to toe, as she realized that she was not recovering from a dream, but returning to a nightmarish reality. A nightmare which seemed to repeat itself over and over, with only slight variations, since she had been through a similar experience with her father's first arrest, and later on, of course, with Radu's kidnapping.

"There's no reason to feel nervous. We won't hurt you" said the younger officer with the mustache, trapping her in an indulgent, even affectionate, gaze. Ioana was taken aback by his unexpected gentleness. She had often heard about *Securitate* interrogations. Rumors of loud shouting, torture, rape and severe beatings circulated everywhere. No one ever mentioned this strange cordiality and calmness. Would the beatings follow the apparent kindness, as in a cruel sadomasochistic ritual? Small, frail and exceedingly sensitive, Ioana knew she would have no tolerance for physical pain. She would say anything they wanted to hear if they lay a single finger on her. Gazing nervously from one man to the other, without realizing it, the young woman was pleading for mercy.

The officer with the mustache approached her. Ioana was sitting on a chair in the middle of the living room, which had been abruptly transformed from a family haven to a seat of terror. The officer then kneeled by the young woman, so that their eyes met almost on the same level. He looked tenderly at her, then reached over and caressed her cheek with the back of his hand, tracing it like an artist, with a smooth, painterly motion.

"You're so lovely," he continued to whisper close to her face. "You'll tell us everything, won't you? We wouldn't want to hurt such a beautiful girl," he grinned provocatively, displaying at least two discolored teeth. Despite his proximity, she could barely hear him, as his soft voice was overpowered by the strong, irregular beat of her own heart. This sickly tenderness was even more disconcerting than brutality. After instinctively recoiling from the man's touch, Ioana remained immobilized, her back pressed tightly upon the grill of the wooden chair.

"Now tell us," the officer continued in a regular, almost mesmerizing tone, "what were you talking about with your boyfriend, for hours, in the Parc Montsouris?" he asked, playing suggestively with the top button of her white shirt collar. His heavy body emitted a pungent odor of alcohol mixed with perspiration.

Although no overtly violent word or gesture had been made, Ioana felt assaulted through all of her senses. The offensive smell, the masculine touch, the deep, hushed voices, the very presence of these men playing with her like a cat with a mouse, made her feel frightened and vulnerable. In her agitation, she even forgot the dangers her parents were facing as she called for their help, silently, with desperation.

"I was attempting to persuade Radu to cooperate with us regarding the Radio Freedom Europe infiltration," she responded. The officer continued to invade her space, touching her body as if searching for hidden weapons. He was reassured by her rapidly beating heart, by the drops of perspiration condensing on her forehead, accumulating where delicate hairs met the paleness of her skin.

"When did you meet Radu?" the first officer pursued. He was now playing the role of the aggressive interrogator, while the man with the mustache was supposedly the nicer one.

"I met him a few months ago when we both resided at the Cité Universitaire. I was only following Comrade Stanescu's directives, as I'm sure you already know," the girl answered.

"What was Radu doing there?"

"Studying chemistry."

"Is that all he was doing?" the officer asked with a knowing smile.

"Of course not. He also had a part-time job at Radio Freedom Europe. That's why you were interested in him in the first place," Ioana replied, surprised by this line of questioning.

"What did he do there?" the officer pursued.

Her boyfriend's speeches were public. Anybody could listen to them. "He discussed some of the practices of the current Romanian regime," Ioana replied, since the interrogators obviously knew that fact as well. She felt confused. Why were they trying to blame her for actions which they, themselves had directed?

"So then your boyfriend was planning out acts of sabotage against the leader of our nation," the officer concluded from her admissions so far.

"No, nothing that extreme. He was trying to point out some things that could be improved in the current conditions in Romania."

The officers exchanged an amused look, as if Ioana had just told them a good joke. "Oh really?" the main interrogator asked. "I guess a traitor knows better what's best for Romania than Comrade Petrescu, his wife and the whole Executive Committee of the Romanian Communist Party, huh?"

Ioana didn't respond, though she certainly agreed with that statement.

"In his speeches, was Mr. Schwarz attempting to incite the Romanian people to overthrow their government?" the officer pursued.

"Not overthrow it. Just bring attention to a few issues related to human rights," Ioana said, adding silently to herself, "or lack thereof."

"There are no human rights abuses in Romania!" the main officer shouted in Ioana's ear and with a swift motion swept the seat from under her. The girl fell on the floor, stunned by his loud voice and rapid maneuver. She then instinctively raised her hand above her face, in a gesture that combined fear and self-protection. The irony of the agent's exclamation only hit her a moment later.

"Did you plan out Radu's inflammatory speeches against our government?" the first officer asked.

"No," Ioana answered, not eager to volunteer self-incriminating information. "In fact, most of our conversations were apolitical."

"Aha. So then you consider your conversation about Petrescu's policies in the Middle East apolitical?" the officer asked, somehow informed about each of Ioana's conversations with Radu.

"We were joking around, being silly," Ioana answered.

"You find it amusing to criticize your country and its General Secretary?"

"I was just playing along," Ioana shrugged.

"How about your discussion of the supposed oppression of your families by our government? Were you playing along then also?" the officer pursued, making several butterflies in the air to indicate Ioana's misuse of words.

"Absolutely. I had been instructed to make Radu feel comfortable enough with me to consider being our mole inside Radio Freedom Europe," Ioana replied and sat back down on her chair.

The mustachioed officer became irritated: "Who gave you permission to sit down?"

"I'm a little tired," the young woman answered quietly.

The mustachioed officer began to push Ioana from the chair, but his boss stopped him with a gesture. Patience, he seemed to indicate.

He then stepped forward in front of Ioana and began talking in a gentler voice. "Ioana, you know as well as we do that you were dragging your feet in the Schwarz case. Instead of being on our side and obtaining the information we needed as quickly and efficiently as possible, you allowed yourself to be duped by a Jewish traitor, a Jidan. And thanks to your supreme incompetence, we were obliged to resort to messier, more complicated procedures."

"I did my best," she retorted.

"So that was your best? I'd hate to see your worst!" the older officer replied, then turned to the other officer: "It looks like she's mocking us. Let's get down to business." He grabbed Ioana by the arm and pulled her up from the chair. The officer with the mustache tied a thick black strip around her eyes. She felt pushed forward from behind, then guided roughly down the set of stairs leading to her parents' apartment, then propelled forward again a few steps. Someone pressed her head down and shoved her into a car, which took off at top speed. Then everything was enveloped in darkness and all she could hear were the noises of the street interrupted by the even louder pounding of her own heart. Whatever happened to Radu will happen to me now, she thought, her fear strangely tempered by a sense of justice.

Chapter 17

Comrade Stanescu picked up the phone. It was line seven, reserved for the prostitute agents trained for covert operations in the West.

"Yes?"

"It's Margarita," an officer said, referring to Ioana.

"Bring her in," Stanescu answered in a neutral tone.

A few moments later, Ioana stepped into his office. With her hair dyed blond, she looked pale, frightened, and exceedingly thin. Nothing like the athletic, raven haired beauty Stanescu himself had hired eleven months earlier.

"Sit down," Stanescu pointed to the chair across from his desk. "I must say ... we're very disappointed in you, Ioana."

The young woman took a seat and meticulously straightened out her skirt on her lap.

Stanescu's usually soft voice now boomed loudly: "How the hell could you fuck up such a simple mission, and then have the gall to try to leave the service? Is this how you express your gratitude for everything we did for you?"

Ioana remained silent.

"Answer me!" Stanescu shouted.

"No," the young woman replied softly, still looking down.

"Then how? How do you express your thanks for the money, the trip to France, the dresses, and the scholarship to the Sorbonne? For all the material goods and opportunities that our country has lavished upon you?"

Ioana didn't respond.

"Are you deaf?" Stanescu persisted.

"I couldn't take that kind of life anymore," Ioana tried to explain. "When I got into the service, I didn't know it would involve acts of violence. I never thought anything bad would happen to Radu. I wanted to persuade him gradually and gently."

Stanescu's eyes twinkled with malice: "Oh really? What do you think we are? A matchmaking service for Romanian couples in exile?" He then raised his voice: "That piece of trash you were trying to persuade so gradually and gently is the son of an Israeli spy and defector who spends his life criticizing the General Secretary of our country! And you didn't think anything would happen to him? What planet are you from?"

"I was told that Radu would be needed to get information about Radio Freedom Europe and the traitors who write against our government."

"And it didn't occur to you that the program announcer himself was such a traitor, worse than all the rest of them put together?"

"I was assured he'd only be used as a source of information," Ioana insisted.

"What idiot told you such a preposterous lie?"

"You did, Comrade."

Stanescu was obliged to change tactics. "So what if I did? Do you think I was about to share with you all my information? Do you believe you're that trustworthy or that important to us?" He scrutinized her closely.

Feeling uncomfortable under his gaze, Ioana averted her glance once again.

"Look at me," the investigator said more softly, as if his fit of anger had passed. "Do you know what you are to us?"

"An agent for the Romanian government," Ioana ventured.

"No, my dear. I'm an agent. You're a whore. You're one of the hundreds of disposable young women we hire to seduce men so we can squeeze valuable information out of them and then eliminate them if they pose a threat to our country. When we're double crossed, we toss away like garbage sluts like you.

You're putty in our hands, Ioana. You're a nobody!" He leaned to the side and spit on the floor to underscore his last statement.

Ioana could hardly believe that the polite, refined gentleman she had met a year earlier had turned into a man who shouted obscenities, called her a whore, and spit on the rug like a peasant. She looked at Stanescu's wrinkled face, his thin mouth distorted by cruelty and felt a sense of liberation, as if a veil had been lifted from her eyes. The glamorous world of secret agents, seduction and spying which had initially enthralled her had turned out to be nothing more than a corrupt bureaucracy run at the top by hoodlums, sycophants and sadists.

Stanescu didn't notice the change in Ioana's attitude, her inner defiance. "So what are we going to do to straighten out the fucking mess you made?" he asked her, deliberately using vulgar language to make her feel small. The interrogator then removed a thick, tan dossier from the numerous files lying on his desk. "See these letters? Your ineptitude has opened up a whole Pandora's box for us. Andrei Schwarz, that skunk, is raising a stink all over the United States about his goddamn family."

Stanescu impatiently flipped through some of the letters. "We got letters from senators, ambassadors, professors. All asking about your darling Raducu and demanding that the whole family be reunited to live happily ever after with their traitor in America. Just look at all this crap," Stanescu ordered, flippantly tossing the pile of letters towards Ioana's side of the desk.

She picked them up and examined each one closely, almost lovingly. Because they were all, at least indirectly, related to Radu. The first typewritten letter was written by Andrei Schwarz himself and addressed to a prominent Human Rights organization in the United States:

```
Dear Ms. Shlosberg,

My name is Andrei Schwarz and I'm a physicist from
Romania. I got my Ph.D. in 1971 and soon afterwards
my scientific work began to attract the attention of
the international physics community. However, during
the course of my career, I was frequently prevented
from traveling abroad to attend many of the
international meetings in my field to which I was
invited.

A few months ago, the Institute for Advanced Study
offered me a visiting position. Perhaps impressed by
the world-wide fame of the Institute, whose first
appointed professor was Albert Einstein, the Romanian
authorities granted me an exit visa for eight months.
I was allowed to leave Romania without my family.
```

Once in the United States, I decided, for political reasons, not to return to my country. I wrote a letter to the Romanian Embassy in the USA in which I expressed my decision. A few days later, my wife Eva Schwarz and our daughter Irina, who live in Bucharest, also applied for emigration from Romania asking to join me.

In addition, our family is very grieved and concerned by the fact that our son, Radu Schwarz, has mysteriously disappeared. Since he denounced the Petrescu regime on the program Radio Freedom Europe, where he had hosted his own show, we can no longer reach him. We have very strong reasons to believe that the Romanian Security Police had something to do with his disappearance and that foul play was involved.

Although, in order to get the most favored nation status and trade credits, Romania has committed itself to respect human rights and the freedom of emigration and has also signed the U.N. Covenant for the Reunification of Families, up to now the Romanian authorities have refused to give us any information they might have regarding our son's disappearance and to take into consideration my family's application for emigration to join me in the United States.

Knowing that HIAS is an immigration and human rights organization of long standing, which has a lot of experience in this respect, I appeal to you to help me find out what happened to my son and to bring my wife and daughter from Romania as soon as possible. I thank you for your attention and appreciate any assistance your organization might be able to offer our family.

Yours sincerely,

Andrei Schwarz

Ioana went on to read similar exchanges between Andrei and members of the United States Congress. Her attention was caught by a letter from a famous scientist to Magdalena Petrescu herself. Its author must not have known that the Romanian president's wife was more cruel and disturbed than her husband. He had written to her in the name of scientific collaboration, since, though completely ignorant and uneducated, Magda was the president of the Romanian Academy of Science:

Dear Dr. Professor Petrescu:

I have recently had scientific contact with the renowned Romanian physicist, Professor Andrei Schwarz. His work on quantum mechanics marks a significant advance in the subject. I was, however, disturbed by a personal conversation I had with him yesterday concerning his family. He informed me that his son is missing under what appear to be suspicious circumstances. In addition, his wife and daughter are still in Romania and are facing considerable obstacles in their immigration request to join him in the United States.

I am a scientist first and foremost. World politics is not my primary concern. However, I am sure you will agree with me, Dr. Professor Petrescu, that it is part of basic human rights to allow families to live together. Family unity is the basis of world existence. In addition, I truly hope that Radu Schwarz has not been harmed and am asking for his release in case he is being held by the Romanian authorities.

The scientific community and I urge you, Dr. Professor Petrescu, to use your good offices to the fullest extent possible to ensure the unification of the entire Schwarz family as quickly as possible. Thank you very much for your most kind assistance in this pressing matter.

Yours sincerely,

Leon Brodsky,

Professor of Physics
Harvard University

To Ioana's delight, several important senators had initiated an inquiry concerning what they called the Schwarz family human rights violations case. If she couldn't find out what had happened to her boyfriend, then hopefully their investigation would offer some promising leads. One senator had even forwarded Andrei Schwarz's file to the Helsinki Commission:

```
Dear Dr. Schwarz,

Thank you very much for your letter. I'm
forwarding it to the US Commission on Security and
Cooperation in Europe, better known as the Helsinki
Commission, which monitors compliance with the
Helsinki Accords. The Commission, on which I serve,
is compiling an up-to-date list of individual cases
to take up with the Romanian authorities. I have
already written to the Romanian ambassador to express
my concern for the suspicious disappearance of your
son and the treatment of your wife and daughter by
the Romanian government.

With all good wishes,

John Radinski,

Member of Congress
```

When she had finished reading through the entire dossier, Ioana looked up at Comrade Stanescu. "I don't know what happened to Radu," she told him. "After Claude met with him at the café, Radu became very suspicious. He checked out the journalist's office, who naturally turned out to be a different person, and confronted me about it. I tried my best to allay his fears. But it wasn't easy. Radu had realized something was fishy and that Claude wasn't who he claimed to be. We went back to my dorm room and you already know what happened there. I never saw him again after that incident. I wish, however, that I knew where he was and that I could say, with a clear conscience, that I had nothing to do with his disappearance and misfortune."

"Ioana, I'll be frank with you," Stanescu leaned back in his chair reassuming his polite, gentleman-like tone again. "Several important officials proposed that you be eliminated for your blunder. The reason you're here, and, more importantly, why you're still alive, is because I pleaded your case."

The interrogator got up and paced slowly around the desk with his hands clasped together behind his back, like a wolf circling its pray. He stopped by Ioana's side and lifted up her chin towards him. She was forced to look directly into his eyes. "One thing you can be sure of: I didn't do it just to save your pretty face," he said in a suggestive tone that seemed to go against the gist of that comment. "I did it so that you can finish the job."

He paused, awaiting her reaction. Since she didn't respond, he continued: "If you do, we'll continue to sponsor you as our agent in Paris and cover all of your living expenses. You can keep your room at the Cité and continue studying at the Sorbonne."

Ioana, however, wasn't even remotely tempted by the offer.

Stanescu mistakenly believed that she was holding out for more compensation. He bent down to whisper in her ear in a confidential tone: "I'll tell you what. How about we sweeten the deal, since you know much RFE sticks like a thorn in the Boss's side. If you find Radu and persuade him to be our mole inside RFE, on top of all the benefits you have enjoyed so far, I have authorization to offer both of you three months' salary plus additional spending money for each document supplied."

She couldn't believe her ears. This man was crass enough to believe that she would willingly sell her boyfriend for some extra spending money.

"Plus a pension after your early retirement," he added, noticing that the young woman still didn't seem impressed. "That's our final offer," he said, smacking the table with his hand.

Since Ioana didn't respond, Stanescu lost patience and once again switched tactics. "Listen to me! You have no choice but to cooperate with us. If you don't accept the deal, we'll be obliged to discontinue your services." He knew from extensive experience that when the carrot didn't work, the stick proved quite effective.

They make me sound like a phone line, Ioana thought.

"Don't get me wrong, it's nothing personal. You just know too much, that's all," Stanescu made it even more clear what the Security Police meant by discontinued. "Of course, because of their contact with you, we have to assume that your parents also know too much as well and punish them accordingly," he added matter-of-factly.

Ioana sensed a real threat in that statement. She struggled to come to grips with this unforeseen turn of events. Before this meeting with Stanescu, she had nearly lost hope that Radu was still alive. She recalled the day her boyfriend was brutally taken away, quite literally, from her arms. She remembered her shock when the man burst into her dorm room and attacked her boyfriend; then her fear when she recognized Ahmed and Claude in the lobby. She felt paralyzed. She couldn't call the French police because then the Romanian Secret Police would eliminate her. She also felt sure at the time that there was nothing she could do to save Radu. If she intervened on his behalf, she would have no effect whatsoever and most likely share his fate. Yet at the same time, she couldn't continue living a life which she now knew to be based on brutality and deceit. The only course of action left, she thought, was to stop colluding with a criminal government. And that's what she did. She exercised a form of passive resistance.

"I thought...I mean... the intruder really hurt him," she managed to say. "There was blood all over his face." Her voice faded.

"That was just a broken nose," Stanescu replied. "Like I told you from the very beginning, we didn't intend to harm the guy. Basically, when we put you on the case, we wanted to plant him as an insider in that wasp's nest of traitors at Radio Freedom Europe. Of course, eventually we lost patience once all your seductive powers accomplished a sum total of zilch. Your incompetence forced us to use more effective means of persuasion."

"What did they do to him?"

The interrogator shrugged. "You know, the usual stuff, but that didn't wear him down fast enough. He only broke down and agreed to cooperate with us when we told him we'd harm you."

Ioana's heart beat faster and her hand twitched upon her lap.

Out of the blue, Stanescu's anger flared up: "Go back to your French lover and see if you can pick up the thread of your Houdini Jewish boyfriend!" he commanded.

This time, Ioana agreed. Perhaps Jean-Pierre could help her. She wanted to find Radu and explain to him everything. To let him know how sorry she was for deceiving him; to tell him that she had never meant to hurt him. If he ever found it in his heart to forgive her, perhaps they could both change identities and run away together to America. "Where should I begin?" she asked, ready to implement her plan right away.

Stanescu snorted: "If I knew where that hoodlum was, you wouldn't be here, now would you? But if I were you, I'd go first to the snakes at Radio Freedom Europe. And this time, try using your head, not just your cunt."

Ioana got up to leave, but Stanescu made a stop sign gesture with his hand.

"One more thing. Be a dear and type up this letter for me so we can mail it to your sweetheart's father in the land of milk and honey." He handed the young woman a handwritten note which said:

"Dear Comrade Schwarz,

We are writing to let you know that the competent Romanian authorities have informed us that your family's request to settle permanently in the United States of America has been denied. Due to this fact, we will not be granting you passports to the country in question.

Sincerely, Ion Georgescu
Embassy of the Socialist Republic of Romania, Washington D.C. "

Ioana stumbled out of Stanescu's office. She felt a sharp pang in the pit of her stomach, which, for a brief moment, she covered protectively with her hand. The feeling of nausea overcame her again. If only she could lay low and avoid the scrutiny of the Secret Police during the next few months, she thought, perhaps there was hope.

Chapter 18

"Radu! Where are you?" Irina heard her mother's apprehensive voice echoing loudly in her ear. She pressed her eyes shut and turned over in her sleep, as if that movement could, like a curtain, block away a bad dream.

"I can barely hear you," Eva was almost shouting. "Are you healthy? Are you safe?"

Irina made an effort to wake up. Suspended between dream and reality, she couldn't erase the image of her brother from her mind. He was pale and, although she was peering at him up-close, his features appeared blurred and distant, as someone who had survived a dangerous storm, maybe a shipwreck. He was lying down on a soft surface--it might have been sand, Irina vaguely imagined. But she saw quite vividly her brother's deep brown eyes, the only lively part of his features, which were now wide open and fixed on some distant point in space above him. Radu was so immobile that she couldn't tell if he was dead or alive. Both she and her mother were bent over him, shaking him, desperately trying to revive him. Eva kept repeating very loudly "What happened to you? Are you alright?"

Even in the semi-coherence of her half-dream, Irina thought that these questions didn't make sense. "Can't you see that he's here and that he's definitely not alright, Mom?" she articulated this logical idea in her own mind and that effort was enough to fully awaken her. She opened her eyes. As her vision gradually adjusted to the darkness, she saw her mother sitting at her father's desk with the phone in her hand. Eva's voice was shaky, just like in the dream, only she didn't seem to shout quite so loudly.

"But why haven't you at least called us to let us know you were alright? We've been worried to death about you," Eva was saying. "What do you mean?"

"Mommy, is that Raducu?" Irina asked, still sleepy.

Eva made an impatient sign with her free hand. "Shhh….. I can barely hear him. There's so much static on the line. But why?" she continued. "Do you realize how worried we've been? Thank God you're alive! Your father even contacted senators to try to find you. We thought…well, we never lost hope… but sometimes we feared…" her voice trailed incoherently.

Irina could overhear that Radu saying something, but she couldn't quite make out the words. Her mother listened intently. "Alright. Can you please come home now?" Another response from Radu.

"Can I talk to him also?" Irina asked.

"Not now," Eva told her. "I mean home to your father, in America," she addressed Radu once again. After listening to her son's response, she abruptly looked at the alarm clock next to Irina's bed. "Why only two minutes?" she asked, with a note of panic in her tone. "Who's trying to track your calls?" Her voice escalated. "Then hang up the phone for God's sake! Wait! When will you call again?" she asked, but Irina could already hear the sound of the dial tone.

For a few minutes, Eva sat stunned, with the telephone still in her right hand. Irina approached and sat down on her knees right next to her mother, not daring to disturb her. Eva was so preoccupied that she didn't seem to notice. She hung up and picked up the phone again, then frantically dialed a phone number.

"Hello?" Irina overheard her father's voice much more clearly than she had Radu's.

"It's me," Eva said, trying to sound composed so as not to worry her husband.

"What's the matter?" Andrei immediately sensed the anxiety in his wife's voice.

"I spoke to Radu a few minutes ago. He called us," she answered.

"Where is he? Is he okay?" Andrei seemed to abstain from breathing.

Eva sighed. "I don't know where he is... but at least he's alive. Thank God he's alive. He's hiding from..." she was about to say the *Securitate*, then changed her mind. "Well, I don't really know from whom. He wouldn't say," she belatedly attempted to fake ignorance for the benefit of the Secret Police monitoring the phone microphones.

"We both know perfectly well from whom," Andrei promptly spoiled that effort.

"The plants are wilted and the sunshine's gone, Andrei," Eva forewarned him. Both husband and wife were so discombobulated by finally receiving news from their son that they were botching up their own secret code.

"Is he healthy? Is he safe?" Andrei returned to the subject that really mattered.

"He sounded very guarded. I could barely hear him; the connection wasn't that good."

"You think they're holding him hostage?" Andrei asked.

"He assured me that he was safe and sound," Eva replied without conviction.

"But did he sound safe and sound?" Andrei insisted.

"Who knows? We barely talked for one, at most two minutes. He said he was afraid they'd track him."

"That's a pretty good sign," Andrei concluded. "If he's afraid they'll track him, it means he's free. At least for now... If only he'd get in touch with me, I would do everything to bring him here, to safety. Next time he calls, tell him to call me, alright? Give him both my work and my home numbers. And don't keep him on the line for too long. Never for more than two minutes at a time. That's very important, Eva," he added gravely.

His wife remained silent for a moment. Then she replied: "Everything happened so fast. Every night since Raducu disappeared I've been praying and waiting at all hours of the day and night for him to call. And now that he finally did ... I was completely unprepared for it. I was so stunned to hear the sound of his voice that I couldn't even be happy about it. And as soon as I realized it was him, I became worried about his safety. I want him to come home to us... I want so much for Raducu to be safely back in my arms."

"Your arms wouldn't be that safe now, Papusica," Andrei replied softly. "I think it's best that he call me so that I can arrange for him to join me in America. Alright?" he asked his wife, to confirm that she had calmed down enough to process this crucial information.

"Yes," she answered, still sounding lost.

"Remain strong, Papusica. There's reason to be optimistic. Even U.S. senators are on our side. You'll see. Soon our family will be reunited in America."

"I hope you're right," Eva replied, with some hesitation. But she wanted to end the conversation on a positive note: "I love you."

"I love you too," Andrei replied. "Celebrate with Irina that Raducu is safe and sound. Remain strong and focus on the positive. Can you promise me that you'll do that?"

"Yes," his wife answered. But after hanging up the phone, charged with contradictory emotions, Eva finally allowed herself the luxury of breaking down in tears. Without saying a word, Irina got up from her knees and wrapped her arms tenderly around her mother.

Chapter 19

To help out their daughter after her husband's defection, Eva's parents sold their modest one bedroom apartment and moved in with her and Irina. Grandma Marta assumed most of her daughter's household responsibilities, taking charge of laundry, cooking and cleaning, thus leaving Eva free to pursue her single-minded, exhausting goal of immigration. Grandpa Mihai walked Irina to and from school, doing his best fill in for Andrei, which wasn't easy since he didn't know any French or American songs. Missing her father and their morning ritual, Irina got into the habit of inventing her own songs on the way to school. Since she was now almost ten years old and behaved, precociously, like a teenager, Irina felt ashamed of being seen by other kids walking to school in the company of her grandfather. "Other kids walk to school by themselves," she would complain to her mother and grandparents in the hope of being granted the same freedom. But Grandma Marta insisted on what Irina considered a gratuitous humiliation. "It's safer with Grandpa," she would invariably respond. "It's just as safe without him," Irina would stubbornly retort. The danger, which her family hid from her, was being kidnapped by the Secret Police, which was a common strategy of intimidating dissident families. In fact, more than once Grandpa Mihai noticed they had been shadowed on their way school by a suspicious looking man.

Fortunately, Irina's best friend, Sofia, lived only two blocks away and also accompanied her to school, which made their elderly chaperone appear less conspicuous. That morning the two girls had composed a new song, which Grandpa Mihai, who was walking—as directed by his granddaughter—a few steps behind the girls, could overhear:

"Si in anul doua mii

Cand nu voi mai fi copii

Si bunicii vor muri.

(And in the year two thousand,

when we're no longer kids

and our grandparents are dead)."

They didn't finish the song, which began with absurd snickering and degenerated into maudlin tears. Having become very attached to her grandparents, Irina felt equally apprehensive about the request being denied and never seeing her father again as she did about their wish being granted and never seeing her grandparents again. Her repertoire generally consisted of songs that expressed these conflicting anxieties.

"Ce prostii! (What foolishness!) Why don't you sing some nice songs for a change?" her grandfather suggested.

"Because we like this one," Irina replied.

"How about those Mireille Mathieu songs you used to like?" Grandpa Mihai asked.

"That was a gazillion years ago, Grandpa!" Irina rolled her eyes at his hopelessly out-of-date musical taste.

"Now we like Nana Mouskouri and ABBA," Irina updated him. "They're sooo much better!"

Grandpa Mihai noticed that his granddaughter no longer wore her hair in a bowl style, like her former pop idol, Mireille Mathieu. She now had it longer and parted in the middle. All she was missing was the dark-rimmed cat eye glasses to look like Nana Mouskouri.

"Well, Mireille Mathieu's songs are much better than whatever drivel you just concocted," Grandpa Mihai retorted, even though, technically speaking, he had never listened to the songs in question. Personally, he preferred the soothing panpipe music of Gheorghe Zamfir. The grandfather picked up the pace to catch up with the two girls.

"Grandpa! People can see us together," Irina reminded him in a whisper, since they had almost reached the school. "You're embarrassing me…"

"Aren't you a little young to act like a teenager?" Grandpa Mihai asked her. "Besides, you should consider yourself lucky to have a grandfather at all. I could be dead by now, like in your song."

"Oh come on…" Irina replied skeptically, though she immediately regretted her harshness. To compensate, she looked around and, after confirming that the coast was clear, gave her doting grandfather a furtive hug and kiss on the cheek.

"I knew you'd come around," Grandpa Mihai beamed, not being hard to please.

"See you after school!" Irina responded in an upbeat tone, having quickly forgotten her sentimentality.

But at 3:30 in the afternoon, when Irina and Sofia waited together by the front entrance of the school as usual, strangely enough, the reliable Grandpa Mihai wasn't there.

"Where could he be?" Sofia wondered, after a few minutes of waiting.

"You know how Grandpa walks so slow," Irina responded, examining carefully the throng of children, teachers, parents and grandparents dispersing around the school. Twenty minutes later, the school yard was nearly empty. The two girls decided to start walking home on their own. When they crossed the empty field between two large apartment buildings close to Sofia's apartment building, they were relieved to see Grandma Marta walking towards them. The grandmother, however, looked even more pale than usual. Her sallow complexion was covered with beads of perspiration, giving her the unhealthy glow of someone recovering from a high fever.

"I'm so glad to see you, Grandma!" Irina ran to give her a hug. "Where's Grandpa?"

"He had to go away," Grandma Marta replied evasively.

"Where?"

"Back to Timisoara," she said, still not looking her granddaughter in the eyes.

"Why?" Irina asked surprised, since her grandparents hadn't lived in that town for the past year and a half.

"To take care of some … urgent matters related to his old job," Grandma Marta hastily explained, incorporating an element of truth into her story.

But Irina still found her grandfather's sudden absence somewhat peculiar: "That's weird… Why didn't Grandpa tell me this morning that he was leaving?"

"We thought you forgot about us," Sofia interjected, only half-joking.

It was difficult for Grandma Marta, who was on principle against any kind of deception, to keep embellishing the lie.

"I wouldn't do that," she responded to Sofia's comment and took her granddaughter's hand into her own to reassure her. Irina immediately withdrew it: "Grandma, I'm too old for this! Geesh, you're almost as bad as Grandpa," she exclaimed, her eyes nervously shifting towards her friend. For a moment she had returned to her old self, the "big girl" who refused her family's cocolosire, or cuddling. But her need for independence, Irina's worries weren't fully dispelled: "When will Grandpa be back?"

"In a few days," Grandma Marta said as calmly as she could under the circumstances, which happened to be that her husband had been arrested only a half an hour before he was supposed to pick up his granddaughter from school. An officer came to their apartment and informed them that Mihai was wanted for questioning at the police station. Marta had the guts to ask: "Questioning about what?" As it turned out, they were accusing her husband of having collaborated with someone who had been arrested as a Soviet spy back in the 1960's. Of course, even if it were true that his friend was a spy, the charge was absurd since Mihai hadn't known anything about it. He was nevertheless "imprisoned for collaboration in espionage."

As soon as her husband was taken away, Grandma Marta called Eva at work to inform her of the newest misfortune that befell their family. "They're going to finish us off," she told her daughter.

"No, they're just trying to scare us," Eva answered defiantly, in case the Secret Police was monitoring their conversation. Although all the phones were tapped around the clock, the Department of External Information still lacked the staff to listen in on every single conversation.

"Well, they've succeeded!" Grandma Marta exclaimed. "What are we going to do now? How are we going to get your father out of jail?" she asked, not at all confident that being completely innocent led to the immediate acquittal and release of the accused.

"I'll have to talk to Stanescu about this matter on Friday," Eva responded with deliberate calmness, having felt for a long time now that she was playing a game of endurance with the Secret Police. "It looks like they're trying out all their weapons against us," she added, "since today I was fired."

Her mother was flabbergasted by the accumulation of so much bad news: "Why? You've always worked so hard…"

Although Eva couldn't disagree with her mother's objective assessment of her professional merit, she did challenge its conclusion: "Mama, don't you understand by now how the system works? There's never a reason why. It's because they want to. Anyways, we can talk about this when I get home," she said, feeling exhausted. After she hung up the phone, she began packing up her office supplies, papers, and ornaments—all the little traces of fifteen years spent at the Ministry of Education.

After enduring weekly interrogations and harassment, Eva had grown accustomed to the government's intimidation tactics and coped with hardship by taking shelter in a hardened shell of apathy. Even the latest blow, the loss of her job, she had expected for a long time. For nearly a year and a half her boss, Anton Georgescu, the Vice-Minister of Education, who was more or less courteous before her husband defected, had become colder and curter with her afterwards.

"He blows with the wind," is how Eva described her boss to her husband long before the winds started to blow against them. Anton Georgescu was a short, stubby man with thick-rimmed glasses and disheveled hair, who combined the flexibility and instinct of self-preservation required for politics with a naturally obsessive and self-righteous personality. More than anything, it was the deep-seated convictions of this state bureaucrat that rendered him potentially dangerous. If you stood out of the way of his principles, he was relatively innocuous. But if you happened to pose a threat to them, he became your ruthless, single-minded enemy. Thus, despite personally liking Eva, he fired her for the good of the state.

That morning Comrade Georgescu was especially curt in his manner: "We need to talk," he told her. Which was never a good sign. "When are you available?" he inquired.

"Right now," Eva answered, wishing to spend as little time as possible engaged in nerve-wracking speculation.

"Please sit down," he pointed to a wooden chair. His office was sparsely furnished but filled to the brim with piles of dusty dossiers and paperwork that seemed to take over the place.

Rather than facing Eva, Comrade Georgescu peered out the window through his thick spectacles: "I'm afraid I don't have very good news for you," he said.

Eva could tell that much. The thought that her boss might know something awful about Radu occurred to her. Or that something terrible had happened to her husband. Her mind wondered down the path of a nearly infinite regress of unpleasant possibilities.

When Comrade Georgescu told her, after a pause, "It looks like we're going to have to let you go," Eva cheered up a bit. This announcement sounded like good news by comparison to what she had envisioned.

Comrade Georgescu drummed his fingers on a folder lying crookedly on his desk. He felt compelled to offer some sort of justification for his decision: "You haven't been performing as well as usual during the past year and a half," he indicated, alluding to the period of time that had elapsed since Andrei's defection.

Eva knew that was bogus—during this period she had worked longer and harder than ever, precisely because she knew that her performance would be under greater scrutiny.

"Don't get me wrong: we don't deny that you're diligent. And the teachers, for the most part, had good things to say about you," he added, referring to Eva's professional evaluations by the science teachers she had inspected, to give the impression that he was taking all relevant factors into consideration and reaching an unbiased conclusion. "Nevertheless, your reports have become perfunctory and, quite frankly, we need someone much more invested in this country's long-term education program for the development of our science curriculum. Your mind is obviously ... elsewhere," he said, alluding to Eva's immigration request.

"You're only saying this because I applied for immigration," she found the courage to say.

Comrade Georgescu looked irritated. The slightest contradiction of his decisions, which he always considered correct, angered him: "Just what exactly do you mean by that, Comrade Schwarz?"

Eva didn't flinch. "I'm saying that you knew that my husband defected and that consequently I applied for immigration to join him. This information colored your evaluation of my performance."

"Comrade Schwarz, I don't let anything but facts color my evaluations!" Georgescu's voice boomed as he repeated part of Eva's sentence with evident sarcasm.

Thinking of the welfare of her family, Eva momentarily put aside her pride and, appearing to accept her boss' conclusions, asked him if there was any course of action she could take to ameliorate her performance and keep her job. She even attempted to appeal to his sympathy by stating that her salary was her family's only source of income.

"Well, you and your husband should have thought about this little problem before he chose to defect. Now, I'm afraid, it's too late. I don't see what you can do at this point," Comrade Georgescu answered, his voice softening and his demeanor simulating a sense of compassion. "I wish I could give you better news..."

You certainly could, Eva thought, since you're the one who decided to fire me in the first place. She abruptly stood up. "Thanks for your time, Comrade Georgescu," she said dryly. Her boss also got up and headed to open the door out of a strangely dated sense of courtesy towards women. By the time he reached it, however, Eva had already walked out.

When she arrived home, her trials and tribulations for the day weren't over. She found her mother crying in the bathroom. The bathtub was filled with water which had turned light blue from the jeans Grandma Marta had just washed with her own hands, which were swollen by arthritis.

"We have a washer and dryer, for God's sake!" her daughter exclaimed, feeling guilty about working so late at her futile job that she burdened her elderly mother with household chores, which Marta persisted in doing the old-fashioned way, placing no faith whatsoever in modern technology.

Grandma Marta held in her hand a ripped up, soggy 100 lei bill, which she had forgotten to remove from Eva's jeans. Although it was barely enough to buy a pack of cigarettes, its loss, apparently, was the straw that broke the camel's back.

"You worked so hard for this money," Marta said, shaking with emotion. Irina tried to calm down her grandmother, gently stroking her back. "That's alright, Grandma. Mama will make even more money. You'll see. Much more. It's only 100 lei."

Under the circumstances, however, this statement didn't prove to be exactly reassuring. The grandmother stood up from the border of the tub and looked at her daughter with pity in her eyes: "How are we going to live now? We can't survive on Grandpa's pension. That's barely enough to buy bread for a month!"

Eva knew she had to remain strong for the sake of her family: "We'll find a way, Mom," she said. "If worst comes to worst, Andrei will send us some money."

"If he sends it by mail, the authorities will steal it," Grandma Marta stated the obvious.

"They'll probably give me my job back," her daughter felt compelled to lie.

"You lost your job?" Irina turned to her mother.

"They're trying to scare us, and they played their last card. But I'm sure Daddy will save us."

"How? He's millions of kilometers away," Irina objected.

"He told me on the phone that he got a very important senator to write on our behalf," Eva replied. "He used to be a famous astronaut, but now he's the senator of Ohio."

"Ohoio?" Irina mispronounced. "I thought Daddy lived in America."

"He does. America's made up of many different states and they all have leaders called senators."

"Then what does the president do?"

"How should I know? I haven't spoken to him lately," Eva grew impatient with this tangential quiz on the ins and outs of American government. "The important thing is that very important people are pulling strings for us. That's why they fired me and took away Grandpa. To retaliate against Daddy's petition to the senator."

"Grandpa was taken away? Where?" Irina asked, her eyes widening with a mixture of despair and disbelief. The news was getting worse and worse.

Eva didn't sugarcoat the truth: "To prison," she replied, surprised that her daughter didn't know this already.

"But... why?"

"To bully us into withdrawing our immigration request. Which we won't do, of course."

"What if they hurt Grandpa?" Irina asked.

"They won't," Eva answered, even though she wasn't as confident of this fact as she sounded. "It would cause too big a scandal. Don't worry, Irinuca," she drew her daughter into her arms. "Daddy will find a way to protect us."

Help works like a lever or pulley in accordance with the principles of physics, Andrei would explain to his wife on the phone, no longer resorting to their useless weather code. If he were still in Romania, he said, he'd have no leverage to help them. But from thousands of kilometers away he could build up the force to lift his family up higher and higher, all the way to the United States of America. The only thing they needed was a lot of confidence and patience, he maintained. Moved by the sound of his distant voice and the familiar analogies to physics, Eva almost believed him. But when he hung up the phone, she often felt discouraged and alone once again.

"We'll manage, Mom," Eva turned to her mother, who was still dazed by the day's misfortunate events. "Please try to rest a little. If you get sick from crying over this stupid money, what will Irina and I do? We need you to be healthy and strong for all of us." It was much easier for Eva to comfort her mother about the lost money than to allay the real sources of Grandma Marta's anxieties—Radu's safety, her husband's sudden arrest, the incertitude of immigration or, in the best case scenario, a possibly lifelong separation from her daughter and granddaughter.

"You're right, I better go lie down. I'm having those terrible palpitations again," Grandma Marta replied softly, walking unsteadily to the sofa, one hand feeling her way around seeking support on the table top and chair, the other held to her chest to monitor her irregular, racing heartbeat.

When Marta lay down on the sofa, Eva was struck by her mother's death-like pallor and immobility. These persecutions will be the end of her, she thought with bitterness. A flash of anxiety passed through her from head to toe. How long will we have to endure this, she wondered, feeling that, despite all of her husband's talk of uplifting levers and the forces of physics, the daily struggles and barriers posed by the Romanian government were pushing her family lower and lower into ground.

Chapter 20

When she stepped out of the Artisanat (Crafts) store where she bought a knitted wool scarf for her daughter, it occurred to Eva that the warm, Latin temperament for which Romanians were known had chilled during the past few years. The saleswoman didn't even bother to look at her clients, let alone smile or be courteous. She hastily rang up the scarf, 156 lei, a small fortune for Eva, who was still unemployed and living on family savings. By mistake, the saleswoman had entered into the cash register 256 lei. Eva politely pointed out the error.

"What?" the saleswoman pretended not to understand. She was young, petite, with black hair and dark eyes which looked lifeless and dull in the midst of her pale oval face.

"If you don't mind, you made a small mistake. You charged me 256 lei instead of 156 lei for the scarf," Eva said as nicely as possible.

The young woman grabbed the scarf from Eva's hands, checked the price tag with an air of disbelief, sighed as if Eva were making an outrageous request, then, still without saying anything, pounded the new price into the cash register, with jerky and obviously irritated movements. "Here!" she handed Eva the new receipt along with the scarf, without placing it in a bag or even wrapping it. Eva paid, took the merchandise and left the store counting her blessings that at least the error had been corrected.

Like most Romanians, she had become accustomed to mistreatment by the "service sector" which, needless to say, had no incentive to serve anyone. In stores, you had to wait in two separate long lines: one to select the merchandize, another to purchase it. The government had made it maximally inconvenient to buy consumer goods in order to discourage people's material desires, which the economy wouldn't be able to satisfy. At restaurants, waiters and waitresses took their time. When they finally showed up, they often brought the wrong order or food that looked and smelled like road kill. Taxi drivers charged whatever price they thought their customers could afford. At the post office, there were invariably long lines and Eva had to resort to bribes to buy international stamps for her letters to Andrei. Food was so scarce that the even the infamously long lines yielded meager results. At the Alimentara, or state-run grocery stores, the vegetables looked wilted, meat was practically nonexistent, fruits were shriveled up. During the cold season, people were compelled to live mostly on rationed portions of milk and bread supplemented by jars of preserves (especially musaca, made from that summer's tomatoes, garlic and green peppers) making the old Romanian saying (borrowed, no doubt, from Lafontaine's fable) that only those who had the foresight to store food in the summer, like the ant and unlike the grasshopper, made it through the winter—seem quite literally true.

While Eva waited for the pietoni (pedestrians/walk) sign to turn green, her eyes couldn't help but focus on the poster of General Secretary Petrescu directly facing her. The dictator's face was frozen into the larger-than-life image he wanted to convey: his hair was still dark, glossy and youthful; his brown eyes sparkled with a reassuring warmth; his sensual mouth smiled with compassion; his aquiline, Roman nose took away some of the face's natural beauty but gave it an air of authority. Eva thought how different this man was, and his benevolent image, from the day-to-day reality facing most Romanians. She turned away her gaze with disgust, yet found no consolation in her immediate surroundings. That winter evening, everything looked gray—the streets, the dingy buildings, the people scurrying about. Even the falling snow couldn't add a glimmer of beauty to the gloomy atmosphere. Disoriented snowflakes fell helplessly onto the ground and disappeared without a trace into the pavement. What a pity, Eva whispered to herself, thinking that during the past few years, Bucharest in the evening had become a depressing sight. The formerly lively capital, filled with dazzling lights, picturesque cobblestone streets, Napoleonic-style buildings and its very own version of L'arc de triomphe (Arcul de Triumf) looked anything but triumphant now.

Eva hurried to take the next bus, which, as usual around 5:00 p.m., was packed with people returning home from work. No matter how much they pushed, shoved and squeezed into each other, many were still left hanging on the stairs, barely holding on to the pole inside like clusters of overripe grapes. In the old days, Eva recalled, men were chivalrous enough make room inside the bus for the elderly, women and children and sometimes even gave up their seats for them. Nowadays, however, people were so miserable and atomized that nobody could count on such gratuitous acts of kindness any more. Eva stood by the door, on the stairs, pressed next to an older man with a briefcase and three tired looking younger men, whom she surmised were students.

She had no choice but to take this overcrowded bus if she wanted to avoid walking home ten blocks in the semi-darkness, as she used to do only a few years ago. More often than not, the city lights were out in the evening due to a national emergency decree to save electricity. Without her husband in the country, it occurred to Eva, at least she was sheltered from the latest humiliation. In order to transform Romania from a dinky Eastern block nation into an international force, Petrescu had banned birth control and abortion. This law aimed to forcibly double the country's population during the next twenty years. Birth control was outlawed for all women under the age of 45 who had fewer than five children. Women were monitored on a monthly basis at the state clinics. Each couple was required to "patriotically produce at least four children for the state." This injunction itself functioned as a means of birth control in lieu of the more effective scientific methods. Monetary incentives were offered to those who complied; those who did not (or could not) were heavily taxed. The law did little to enhance Romania's international prestige, but it did succeed spectacularly well in augmenting its citizens' misery. The number of orphaned children increased dramatically.

Her nose plastered to the transparent bus door covered by fingerprints, Eva looked with compassion at a sadly familiar scene: abandoned children now roamed the streets of Bucharest. Left to fend for themselves without food, shelter or adult protection, they grouped together in gangs of beggars and thieves that stared at passers-by with empty eyes and took whatever they could to barely survive. At night, under the cover of darkness, they were the only ones left to wonder around in the desolate city, despite the fact that the laws against truancy and petty crime were inhumanely strict. There was no way to stop them, and in fact, their numbers grew, since people had less and less money and more and more children in a country with fewer and fewer resources.

Even "regular people," Eva mused still gazing through the transparent bus door, now resembled beggars. During the day, the streets were crowded with weary looking people wearing dingy dark coats and the staple Eastern European fur hats, more often than not partly eaten by moths and worn high above the ears, which turned red when exposed to the bitter cold. Hardly anyone smiled or even greeted each other. People were resigned to a daily existence made up of many hardships and few joys. Covered up by their somber winter attire and immersed in their troubles, even the young seemed ageless.

Eva sighed as the bus rode by a beautiful part of the city currently being destroyed. Demolition trucks had overtaken the historical part of Bucharest. Old buildings, constructed during the nineteenth-century in the French style modeled after Haussmann's Paris, were being torn down to erect the new presidential palace, a building of gigantesque proportions that celebrated the dictator's unlimited power. How ugly this building is, Eva thought, as the bus passed by it. After twenty minutes, the bus finally reached her own part of the city, Cartierul Drumul Taberii (Camp's Way). Eva saw the familiar long food lines at the grocery stores, as people foraged for provisions before going home to feed their hungry families. She instinctively held on to the scarf she had bought for her daughter, grateful that she had managed to find it, since almost all commodities—food, clothes, shoes—had become exceedingly scarce. Whatever goods Romania produced were now earmarked for export, to pay off the large foreign debt accumulated during the 1970's. On the brink of losing the country's "most favored nation" status due to countless human rights violations, Petrescu decided that his best bet was becoming independent from the West, indebted to nobody and free to oppress his citizens as much as he wanted.

Romanians didn't even have foreign T.V. shows and radio programs to look forward to any more, Eva thought with regret, since on Friday evenings the family had enjoyed getting together to watch foreign films. Lately, the media had become exclusively centered on ideological news about the Petrescus. Even Eva's favorite soap opera—Dallas—was cancelled and replaced by Viata Taranului ("The Peasant's Life"), a show which practically nobody watched that celebrated the imaginary fruits of collective farming. Eva thought that the phrase Radu had used on Radio Freedom Europe to criticize the government, "Petrescu's personality cult," was much too weak to capture the oppressiveness of the dictator's power. The more disassociated Petrescu became from the international scene, the more detached from reality was his sense of his own importance. Megalomania now served as a substitute for both national and foreign policies.

Eva was interrupted from these speculations by the whiff of an unpleasant, acrid smell right next to her nose. The tall, older man with the briefcase had raised his arm to hang on to the upper rail to steady his movements in the bumpy ride. Apparently, he hadn't used deodorant or soap. The odor from his underarms overpowered Eva's senses. Squeezed tightly in the crowd and breathing the malodorous air, she felt almost ready to faint. But it wasn't Romanians' fault that hygiene had become a problem, Eva thought. After all, hot water was available only from 3:00 to 4 a.m. and not necessarily every day.

Those who wanted to bathe had to determine if cleanliness was a higher priority than sleep. Based upon the powerful smells emitted from people's bodies, it was safe to assume that many opted for sleep. Even heat was available only off and on—mostly off—such that people were obliged to wear their winter coats and hats even indoors.

Once Eva reached her apartment building, as usual, she immediately rushed to the mailbox to see if she had received any letters from Andrei or Radu. Her heart sunk once she saw that she hadn't. But as she shuffled through a few bills and two postcards from acquaintances, she saw a letter from the Ministry of Internal Affairs. Oh, my God, this is it, she thought, her heartbeat racing wildly with nervous anticipation mixed with a sense of dread. If they denied her application once again, who knows how many more years she and her daughter would be stuck in Romania. Perhaps forever. At any rate, she realized, their case would become dangerously close to hopeless. With trembling hands, she impatiently tore open the envelope and read the letter with great haste. The thin piece of paper announced:

"The Ministry of Internal Affairs is happy to inform you that your immigration request has been approved by the government of the Socialist Republic of Romania."

Not trusting her eyes, Eva read the note a few more times in a row. She was stunned. Incredibly, the Romanian authorities had changed their minds and were letting them go. Eva couldn't understand why; what had made the difference. She rushed to her third floor apartment running up the stairs two steps at a time to let her family know that their tenacity had finally paid off. Now all she needed was the approval of the American side—the visa to the United States-- and their dreams would be fulfilled. Eva's elation was tempered by a nagging doubt: did the Romanian government let her go because they knew in advance that the United States would not accept her and Irina into their country? But the sense of relief conquered her suspicions and for a moment she saw the light at the end of the tunnel. She'd soon be reunited with her husband; her daughter, now almost adolescent, would once again have a father again.

Irina and her parents were eating supper: cartofi prajiti (french fries) and snitele (fried chicken breast) made from the measly supply of meat which, if very fortunate, they found about once a month. Grandpa Mihai had been released from jail long ago: as his daughter had surmised, he had been incarcerated for a few days as an intimidation tactic. When Eva stepped into the kitchen, Irina was negotiating getting permission for a play date later that evening at Sofia's, while Grandma Marta was protesting that it was too close to bedtime to make such plans. "But everybody does it, Grandma," was Irina's objection to just about every denial of her wishes.

Eva couldn't contain her happiness: "We got the papers! They're letting us go to Daddy!" she burst out. Her news was met at first by confused and surprised eyes; then, once the brains registered the information, the whole family rejoiced. "Thank God," Grandma Marta said, while Grandpa Mihai exclaimed "It's about time!" and Irina shouted "Hurray! We're going to Daddy! We're going to America!" After every member of the family examined the letter several times—Grandpa Mihai, who couldn't see very well even with glasses, even took the magnifying glass out to make sure that his eyes weren't deceiving him—the group elation gradually gave way to a state of deflation.

"Of course, we haven't received the American visa yet," Eva voiced the doubt that had been on her mind all along.

"When will we see Grandma and Grandpa again?" Irina asked, seeing the other side of the coin.

"They'll visit us every year," Eva reassured her.

"Only once?" Irina's voice cracked with disappointment.

"Twice a year," her mother said, just to appease Irina.

That turned out to be insufficient as well. Irina began crying and hugged her grandparents, who tried to console her and promised they'd visit her in America at least ten times a year. "Especially once you marry a millionaire, so we can afford it," Grandma Marta added, for the sake of realism.

Irina then focused on a different problem: "What about Sofia? And Marinela? And Stela? And all my other best friends? When will I see them again?"

Since Eva couldn't vouch to function as an international airport and hotel for all of their friends and relatives, she proposed the following pragmatic solution: "We'll visit our relatives and friends in Romania once a year, during the summer. Plus you'll make new, American friends as well."

"I don't want any new friends! I like the ones I have," Irina objected. Then, reconsidering the issue, she added: "Besides, how am I going to make American friends when I don't even speak English?"

"That won't be a problem," Grandma Marta waived her hand dismissively, as if swatting a fly. "Kids learn languages really fast. You'll learn English in no time at all."

"DADDY," "HELLO," "HOW ARE YOU?" "I DON'T SPEAK ENGLISH," Irina proudly recited her whole English repertoire.

"See? You're fluent already!" Grandpa Mihai encouraged her.

That night every member of the family lay awake with nervous excitement. Eva was already focused on how to obtain the American visa. The grandparents discussed in whispers their mixed emotions. They wanted their daughter and granddaughter to be reunited with Andrei but worried that they'd never see them again. And, after the initial wave of excitement, Irina fell asleep wondering if she'd get the bilingual pet parrot who'd teach her to speak English. That was the gift her father had promised her in jest at the airport, on the day he left.

Chapter 21

Obtaining the American visa, which Eva had hoped would be the easy part of emigration, took yet another eighteen months, which is to say, even longer than it took them to get permission to leave from the Romanian authorities. After nearly three years of separation from her father, it was difficult for Irina to believe that they were finally on their way to America, despite the fact that all the evidence pointed logically to that conclusion. Her seatbelt was buckled; her mother, seated next to her, was reduced to a state of raw emotion by the recent separation from her parents; the stewardesses were walking down the aisles checking that everyone was in their seats with the luggage safely stowed away or locked in the overhead compartments. The Tarom plane to Rome was about to take off. Rome rather than New York City, since Eastern European immigrants, much like stray puppies found by the Humane Society, had to spend two weeks in Italy to get their immunization shots and papers in order before being accepted, in a properly disinfected state, to the United States.

Irina held in her hand the last picture of her with Grandma Marta and Grandpa Mihai, taken by her mother six months earlier. In the photo, the girl sat between her grandparents wearing a lilac dress with ruffles, a gift from her father, who had bought it during his conference trip to Germany. She smiled broadly and one could see that two of her front teeth slightly protruded, giving her an impish air. Her grandfather was sitting on her left, with one arm around Irina's shoulders, the other proudly holding a lit Kent cigarette. His dark eyes— "the eyes of a Tasmanian devil," according to his wife, who had never actually encountered such a creature—twinkled with mischief. As usual, Grandpa Mihai was wearing his worn-out gray suit since, having been a former navy captain, he took pride in looking "dignified" even if just on his way to the grocery store. Standing on Irina's right and reaching the same height as her husband (who was sitting), the diminutive Grandma Marta was looking at her granddaughter lovingly, beaming with pride. She had just tied Irina's hair with elephantine white silk bows and was admiring her fashion creation. She must have been impressed with Irina's look, since she seemed ready to spit three times into the air—"Ptiu ptiu ptiu! Sa nu te deochi"—so as not to jinx her granddaughter.

Irina's heart skipped a beat and her stomach sunk as the plane started to take off. She had never been on an airplane before, but thought it felt very much like a roller coaster, which she had taken only once in her life, and that had proved more than enough for both her and her breakfast.

"Mama, I'm nauseous," she told Eva the good news.

Eva looked at her daughter with concern and removed the white paper bag from the pocket of the seat in front of her and handed it to Irina. The girl made a few gagging sounds, but, to the relief of the passengers around her, she was unsuccessful in her efforts. She gracefully handed the empty bag back to her mother.

Eva took not only the bag but also the precious family photo from her daughter's hands, just in case Irina changed her mind. She gazed for a moment at the image of her parents, then closed her eyes to contain her emotions. Tears stubbornly trickled onto her cheeks anyways.

"I miss Grandma Marta and Grandpa Mihai," Irina said, echoing her sentiments.

"We'll see them often," Eva reassured her with tenderness. "The important thing is that we won. In a few days we'll be reunited with Daddy again. Aren't you happy about that?" she looked at Irina with red and puffy eyes, not exactly the picture of jubilation herself.

Thinking pragmatically, Irina came up with a practical solution to the separation problem: "You know what? Once we get to America, we can build a huge house so that Grandpa Marta and Grandma Mihai can move in with us. Then we'll all live together as one big happy family."

"Yes, Irinuca, maybe one day we will ..." Eva replied, as one does to humor the dreams of a child.

For Irina, however, this possibility was entirely within grasp. "You, Daddy, Radu and I will live on the first level; Grandpa and Grandma will live on the top floor, and maybe even Uncle Mircea, Aunt Maria and cousins Gheorghe and Nicu can move in--if they decide that they like America. They could come visit us first," Irina allowed for some contingencies in her plan.

"That sounds good. I only wish that Raducu would join us there also."

"He will, Mama," Irina reassured her. "For now he just likes Paris better than America, that's all."

Eva gazed at her eleven year old daughter with a mixture of love and pity for her immaturity and innocence. Irina's eyes were filled with hope, which her mother didn't have the heart to crush. "At my age, it's not so easy to leave everyone and everything behind and to start life all over again." Eva was only forty-four, but her suffering and struggles during the past few years, especially following her son's disappearance, had taken their toll. She felt prematurely aged and exceedingly weary.

Mother and daughter remained silent for awhile, each focusing on her own immediate plans. Eva was already thinking about how she'd perfect her English (she had been taking private lessons during the past two years) and pass the State Board exam for high school science teachers, to get a job and help support the family.

Simultaneously, Irina was designing the spacious house she had described to her mother. The imaginary lodging looked like a cross between Sleeping Beauty's castle and J.R. Ewing's skyscraper: it was tall, had dark, reflective glass windows, but also sported some nice Kremlin-looking spiraling towers on top, since Irina found skyscrapers a bit too simple for her more refined Eastern European taste. Such a palace, Irina thought, would house all the pets her father had promised her to make immigration seem more appealing. The most important one, needless to say, was the bilingual parrot who'd teach her English, since learning the language was a priority. She had also asked for two fluffy cats who'd sleep on top of her head--without even giving her lice. Since cats are a bit too independent, however, she thought it would be nice to add two dogs to the menagerie: a nice Labrador retriever with warm brown eyes and reddish fur who'd walk her to school and a little cocker spaniel who'd greet her at the door and lick her face when she returned home. Thinking about her future animal kingdom, Irina fell asleep with her head leaning upon her mother's shoulder. Eva looked at her daughter's subconscious smile, and, knowing Irina, surmised its reason: "What will she do when she finds out that Andrei's allergic to animals and hasn't bought her a single pet he promised?" she wondered, naively resolving to buy her daughter a few plush animals in their stead at the first toy store they found in America.

They arrived in Rome's Fiumicino Airport (a.k.a. Leonardo Da Vinci International Airport) around 4:00 a.m. "Imigranti?" a pretty woman in uniform asked Eva and a few other families emerging from the Tarom airplane, which was the Romanian airline modeled, unfortunately, after the Russian Aeroflot and with a similar track record. The greeting procedure in Italy didn't provide much of a culture shock, since the group of Romanian immigrants, soon joined by Russian and Polish newcomers, were welcomed in the West by having to wait in about five different long lines to get their papers in order and their luggage examined several times. The only immediately apparent difference between East and West was that bribes didn't seem to work any more, at least not the kind of trifles—Kent cigarettes and Max Factor lipsticks—that Eva had on hand.

A minibus took the group of immigrants to Pensione Carla, a hostel reserved just for them in a scenic part of town where prostitutes also happened to conduct business. The building looked dilapidated and had graffiti all over the walls and front door. Even its elevator creaked, protesting having to run at such an advanced age, and landed with a loud boom on each level. Eva put down her suitcases and pressed the button to take the elevator up to their room, on the fifth floor. When it finally got there, its door wouldn't open. A middle-aged man who spoke Polish to the woman next to him took out of his pocket a two lire coin with a hole drilled in the middle and hanging by a string. He introduced the coin into the elevator slot, then, before the machine got a chance to grab it, quickly removed it. Tricked, the elevator door finally opened. Poverta, the man said in a language as close to Italian as he could muster, obviously proud of his clever invention. Eva nodded, and replied gratefully "Grazie!" one of the few Italian words she knew. The man handed her the coin on the string, indicating with a gesture towards his pocket that he had backups. Eva was touched and thanked him once again, this time in Russian, Spasiva, since she didn't speak a word of

Polish. Without this act of unexpected generosity, Eva thought, she and Irina wouldn't be able to afford taking the elevator; while carrying the heavy suitcases by hand up five flights of stairs didn't seem like an appealing alternative.

Although Irina hadn't been brought up in a mansion, she was nonetheless dissatisfied with the lodging, which didn't meet her expectations of Western luxury. The room resembled a jail cell, down to the vertical metal bars covering the small, dingy window. Inside, the accommodations were reduced to the bare minimum: a rusty metal chair, a wooden desk, a latrine with a sink and a twin-size bed.

"The bed's too small for us," Irina complained.

"We'll sleep head to toe," Eva proposed the only possible way in which they'd both fit.

Irina crinkled her nose: "These sheets look dirty! I bet they haven't been changed for weeks."

Eva examined the sheets in question as closely as she could in the semi-darkness, since the sole source of light in the room, an unadorned yellow bulb on the ceiling, was very dim. Aside from some stains of unidentifiable origin and a few dark holes made by cigarettes, however, she couldn't find anything wrong with them. She put her nose next to the pillow. "They've been washed recently," she concluded from the detergent smell. Apparently, however, Eva wasn't fully persuaded by the results of her own investigation, since she took out a couple of towels from her suitcase and placed them over the pillows.

"This place is disgusting!" Irina pronounced the final verdict, feeling sleepy, cranky and tired. She took off her shoes and crashed unto the bed fully clothed.

"Please wash your hands and brush your teeth before you go to bed," Eva said.

"I already did!" Irina protested.

"When?"

"Yesterday..." the girl answered more softly, going to do what her mother asked before getting some much needed rest.

The following morning, after a four hour nap, Eva and Irina were on their way to the clinic where they were about to have their first set of immunization shots. Being in a better mood after a few hours of rest, Irina was thoroughly impressed by the Italian sense of fashion.

"What beautiful clothes they have here!" she exclaimed. "Mom, can you please buy me a skirt like that one?" she pointed to one of the prostitutes, who was wearing a very short skirt made up entirely of silver sequins.

Eva didn't know how to respond to this manifestation of questionable taste. Fortunately, Irina's attention was diverted by something even more spectacular: street vendors populated booth after booth selling every kind of fruit one could imagine, including strawberries, oranges, mangos and bananas.

"Can we please buy some bananas?" Irina pleaded, her mouth watering in anticipation of tasting delicious, fresh fruit. Eva had converted enough lei to lire to afford three bananas, which the mother and daughter shared for breakfast.

"Slow down, for God's sake! Chew before you swallow," Eva cautioned, seeing Irina stuff a quarter of a banana into her mouth.

"Mmm… I ammmm!" Irina managed to protest with her mouth full, eyeing with longing the oranges and strawberries they had left behind.

"We'll buy oranges after lunch," her mother said.

For lunch, Eva had a rendezvous with Doina Troiescu, one of her closest friends and Andrei's former colleague at the Institute of Atomic Physics, who had recently immigrated to Italy. Doina was not only a brilliant physicist but also fluent in six languages to boot, including Italian. At the Institute, she and the dictator's daughter had been close friends, being two of the few women physicists and, more importantly, both having a penchant for elegant clothes, heavy drinking and lavish parties. Eva and Irina didn't know their way around Rome, so they agreed in advance to meet Doina at noon at the Colosseum, the most popular tourist attraction in town.

Since the amphitheater wasn't within walking distance from their hostel, Eva bought a city map to figure out which bus or subway would take them there. Following a long and careful examination of the map, a supplemental questioning of the locals in Romanian and listening to their directions in Italian (in turn accompanied by their repertoire of gestures that even the conductor of a brass band would have envied), Eva finally figured out which bus they were supposed to take. Like in Romania, there was no room to sit down—although, fortunately, here people didn't cluster on the stairs.

As they made their way towards the back of the bus, Eva was startled by someone pinching her behind. Having gotten her attention in this chivalrous manner, a young man winked at her and said something in Italian that sounded friendly enough. He was politely asking how much she costs. By instinct, Eva decided that since they had entered the bus at the station where prostitutes usually wondered, it would be best to remain silent and ignore him.

Her daughter, however, saw things differently. "Ce impertinenta! How rude," she exclaimed in Romanian at the offender and walked decisively towards him with the express intention of pinching his butt in return, to see how he liked it. The young man laughed good-naturedly at Irina's spunk, and, since she was nearly adolescent, even rewarded her with an invitation to a possible three-some. Being in no mood for provocation, however, Eva prudently yanked her protofeminist daughter by the back of the collar towards the end of the bus, with the cautionary gesture with which a tigress protects her cub. "Irina, stop it. What were you thinking? We're in Italy now. There are lots of perverts here and we have to be very careful," she whispered in her daughter's ear.

Once they stepped out of the bus, even the simple act of crossing the street to the Colosseum proved to be quite a challenge. There appeared to be a tacit agreement between Italian pedestrians and motorists that neither should mind the traffic signs, as long as everyone got to shout loud insults at one another. The pedestrians crossed the street whenever they could, especially when might made right and they united in large numbers against their four-wheeled rivals. The drivers rarely bothered to stop on red and acted like they were about to run over the pedestrians, hitting the breaks at the last minute with loud screeching sounds of wheels desperately clutching the pavement. This, in turn, started a chain reaction of sudden stops in the bumper-to-bumper line of traffic as well as provoking a chorus of mutual insults—"Imbecile!" "Pazzo!"—which sounded close enough to the Romanian equivalents to make Eva and Irina feel right at home. "That's exactly how your father drives," Eva commented.

When they finally made it to the Colosseum, Eva and Irina were taken aback by its magnificence. Even in ruins, Eva thought, the former majesty of the ancient amphitheater was still apparent in its monumental size, circumferential arcades and congruous combination of different architectural styles. From the smattering of art history she had studied in high school, Eva recognized Doric columns on the first level, Ionic on the second and Corinthian on the third.

Meanwhile, her daughter was equally impressed by the large number of compatriots that had gathered in the area. Dozens of little Romanian gypsy children, mostly girls walking barefoot and clothed in long, colorful skirts, were begging the tourists for money. Irina asked her mother for a little change, which she placed in the hands of a little girl with beautiful large brown eyes. "Multumesc frumos," ("Thank you kindly") the little gypsy girl said to her in Romanian, having noticed that Irina's negotiations with her mother took place in her (second) native tongue. Very soon, the little girl's sisters and brothers also gathered around their benefactress, which led Eva, who had very little money left, to take her daughter by the hand and walk as quickly as possible towards Doina, whom she had just spotted in the crowd.

Chapter 22

Doina Troiescu had the double advantage of being a world-class physicist and a striking beauty, much like her good friend Silvia Petrescu, who had been her boss and friend at the Atomic Physics Institute. She had long red hair, beautiful green eyes and a curvaceous body, exactly to the taste of Italian men. The qualities that stood out most about Doina, however, were her resourcefulness and generosity. "Too bad she married an alcoholic," Eva couldn't help thinking with regret, feeling that her friend's beauty, brilliance and character were wasted on a mediocre husband, who was almost always drunk and frequently unemployed. "One day he'll be the end of her," she mused, suspecting that the main quality that united this odd couple was their love of drinking and parties.

"Eva, buna! It's so good to see you!" Doina said warmly and embraced her friend, kissing her and leaving red lipstick stains on both cheeks. Irina hid behind her mother's back to escape being stamped with the same colorful greeting. "Irina, my, how you have grown!" Doina exclaimed, spotting her. "Eva, dear, you never told me your daughter's so pretty; she'll break men's hearts in America!" Doina flattered her friend, in accordance to the time-honored Romanian custom.

"We're so fortunate you're here! We don't speak a word of Italian, and would be completely lost in this big city without you," Eva returned the compliment.

As hostess, Doina took matters into her own hands: "Nonsense! Italian's just like Romanian. You'd get along just fine without me. So girls! What would you like to do first? Have lunch or do a little tour of the city?"

"Since we're already here, how about we tour the Coliseum?" Eva proposed about the same time that her daughter shouted: "Eat. I'm starving!"

"Then lunch it is," Doina laughed, "Followed by a nice promenade through the Colosseum and everything else you might want to see while you're here."

"There's so much to see, we don't even know where to begin," Eva replied.

"How about right here?" Doina pointed to a restaurant, Nerone all Collie Oppio, which was located right across the amphitheater and had patio seating from which you could admire the ancient ruins. "If we eat outside, we can see also the Colosseum, to kill two birds with one stone."

"Sounds perfect," Eva approved.

When they entered the restaurant, Doina said something very fast in what sounded to her companions like perfect Italian. The friendly waiter, a brown-haired young man, nodded and asked them to follow him outside. As they passed through the restaurant to get to the patio, Irina's eyes lingered on the antipasto table laden with vegetables and tasty side dishes. "I want that and that and that and that," she pointed with her finger to pretty much everything in sight.

"Now that great food's available everywhere, you'll have to start watching your figure," Doina said.

"Good thing we can't afford it," Eva answered.

"Don't worry about that. Today's my treat!" Doina announced. "Absolutely not," Eva protested; "No! I insist!" Doina objected; "We simply can't abuse your generosity," Eva retorted; "It's nothing at all," Doina rebutted; "I won't hear of it," Eva replied; "I'm on my home turf. When I come to America, you'll treat me, okay?" Doina delivered the final argument, winning the bid. Irina looked with bewilderment from one woman to the other, following their debate like a ping-pong match. She found the whole discussion very counterintuitive.

She would have understood better debating about who would get stuck with the bill than vice-versa.

When the waiter asked for their order, Doina engaged in a series of rapid translations between Italian and Romanian. Being a cheese lover, Eva ordered a lasagna classico, filled with mouth-watering layers of pasta, meat sauce and mozzarella, ricotta, parmesan and romano cheese. Irina requested a linguine alla marinara since the fresh, ripe tomatoes reminded her of her grandmother's musaca. Doina, a carnivore by taste, sampled sausage and peppers rustica—a tasty blend of sausage, bell peppers and mozzarella simmering in a bold marinara sauce.

Needless to say, for the girl the most interesting part of the meal was the dessert. The waiter came by holding a large silver tray that displayed the vast selection of house specialties: lemon cream cake, which was a delicate white cake with lemon filling and vanilla crumb topping; an irresistible chocolate lasagna with butter cream icing; tiramisu, a creamy custard set atop espresso-soaked ladyfingers; white chocolate raspberry cheesecake filled with rosy swirls of fresh fruit and black tie mousse cake consisting of rich layers of chocolate cake, interspersed with layers of dark chocolate cheesecake and creamy custard mousse. Everything looked so delicious, it was nearly impossible to choose.

"I've gained five kilos just looking at these desserts," Eva declared.

"Tell me about it! I've been on a diet ever since coming to Italy, and all I've done is gain weight," Doina replied.

"I can't resist the mousse cake!" Eva caved. The waiter nodded that he understood and complimented her selection. Doina selected the tiramisu. To everyone's surprise, Irina, who was crazy about desserts, refused all of them.

"Are you feeling okay?" her mother asked, placing her hand on her daughter's forehead.

Fever didn't turn out to be the problem, however. "I want what she's got!" Irina pointed to an adjacent table. She had spotted a little girl, who was probably no more than five years old, eating a gigantic double banana split gelato that was so big that it didn't even fit on a normal plate; it took up an entire bowl. The little girl kept digging with her spoon into the mountain of creamy layers of chocolate and vanilla ice cream topped by two large bananas and whipped cream smothered in a thick, swirling layer of chocolate fudge. Irina, used to measly popsicles in Romania, had never seen such a gigantic ice cream in her entire life. The little girl's mouth was covered by a Charlie Chaplin mustache of chocolate sauce and she kept licking her lips and the spoon in an effort to get every last drop.

"That's called a banana boat," Doina explained the heavenly concoction.

"You can't eat that much ice cream; you'll get sick," Eva immediately objected. So she ordered for Irina a smaller chocolate ice cream with whipped cream and a cherry on top which came in an elegant crystal cup. The girl, however, refused to touch it.

"What's wrong now?" Eva asked her.

"My ice cream's too small," Irina replied, looking with disappointment at the modest cupful in front of her. Tears of indignation were trickling down her cheeks, falling unto the whipped cream as the ice cream began melting quietly underneath.

"Are you nuts?" her mother wondered.

"The banana boat's much bigger," Irina accurately pointed out.

"Your behind will be as big as a boat if you eat that much ice cream," Doina chimed in good-naturedly.

"I don't care," Irina said defiantly.

"Alright, then let's get her the boat!" Doina proposed. "Her eyes are bigger than her stomach. I doubt she can finish it anyway."

Eva, however, stood her ground: "Absolutely not. She's acting like a spoiled brat. Besides, I wouldn't put it past her to eat the whole thing and get really sick. I'm sorry, but this city's much too beautiful to be seen from a hospital room, where Irina will be getting her stomach pumped."

"Then I won't touch the ice cream," Irina replied.

"Good," her mother held firm.

While Irina focused on the grave injustice she had just suffered and sniffled into her melting gelato, Eva and Doina tried to enjoy their desserts while catching up on each other's lives.

"So how's Costin doing?" Eva inquired.

Doina didn't answer the question immediately. Her eyes glimmered with life as she took another sip of her fourth glass of red wine. "Why don't you live a little?" she filled Eva's glass to the brim, but the latter pushed it away with a smile.

"You know me, if I sip two millimeters of wine, I'll start singing."

"I'd like to see that!" Doina laughed. "Costin's fine," she answered. "Looking for a job; drinking too much—life as usual."

Eva wondered if it would be apropos to tell Doina her friendly and unbiased opinion that she should have stuck with her first husband rather than divorced him. "How about Liviu?" she expressed this idea indirectly.

Doina didn't harbor any ill feelings towards her ex: "He recently married a German woman. You already know that he moved to Stuttgard about two years ago, right?"

"Andrei told me," Eva answered. "I'm glad to hear he's doing well. What an excellent man!" She wanted to ask Doina, do you regret leaving him, but asked instead a more metaphysical question: "Are you happier now?"

Doina twirled a bit of the fresh bread between her thumb and forefinger, feeling well disposed and dreamily contemplating the question. "I suppose so. I think I'm more compatible with Costin."

"Why so?" Eva asked, sounding a bit too surprised.

Doina's eyes glimmered. "He's so much fun," she said. She then stole a glance at Irina, who was watching with unspeakable envy the little girl conquering her mountain of ice cream. "Plus he's great in bed," Doina leaned forward and whispered in Eva's ear.

"Our bed at the hostel is too small," Irina put in her two cents' worth, having overheard the word "bed."

"Why don't you sleep over at our place?" Doina graciously proposed.

"Out of the question!" Eva answered at the same time that Irina declared excitedly "Great idea! Do you have a bathtub?"

"Absolutely. And three cats!" Doina enticed her.

Eva, however, drew the line: "We're already taking up your time and money for lunch. Enough's enough. Our room's just fine."

"Easy for you to say," Irina replied morosely.

"Don't take that tone with me, young lady!" Eva warned.

"Well then don't take that tone with me either!" Irina replied, foreshadowing the pleasant teenage years to come.

"Do you want to be grounded?" Eva asked, looking at her daughter sternly. "Because that can be arranged."

"Where would you ground me? In that stupid jail cell?" Irina challenged her.

"That's right. If you continue in this vein, you and I will spend the rest of the week in our room instead of touring this beautiful city."

"Fine with me. I don't care," Irina shrugged. "I hate stupid Rome anyways."

Wishing to nip this friendly mother-daughter conversation in the bud, Doina changed the subject to more serious matters. "Eva, have you had any news from Radu lately?"

At the very mention of her son's name, Eva felt a nervous tightening in the pit of her stomach. "He called me a few times. But something was very strange about those conversations... He didn't sound like himself."

"Did he sound ill?"

"No... Just very vague and...extremely cautious. He wouldn't tell me where he was, what he was doing or when he was coming home. Basically, he didn't answer any of my questions."

"What did he say?" Doina asked.

"That he was safe and healthy. But I wonder about that..."

"Do you think he might be held hostage?"

Eva's eyes clouded with anxiety: "Well, that possibility has occurred to me... and I still haven't ruled it out. But Andrei doesn't think that's likely since Radu's always afraid that his phone calls will be traced."

"When was the last time he called you?"

"About two months ago," Eva answered. "I lie awake almost every night worrying about him and waiting for him to call again... The worst of it is not knowing where he is or what's happening to him. It's excruciating to live with such constant fear and doubt. Sometimes not knowing much is worse than knowing everything. Because when you don't know, your imagination runs wild."

"I know what you mean," Doina sympathized. "Besides, what you imagine may not be far from the truth. Silvia Petrescu once told me that her parents have…let's just say certain methods of getting rid of troublesome dissidents." Eva didn't look particularly comforted by this fact, but that didn't stop her friend from elaborating: "She was telling me about what they did to some of her boyfriends, whom her parents disapproved of. They harassed them, staged car accidents and even hired hoodlums to beat them up until they finally got the picture and chose exile to some far away country in the Middle East or Asia."

"It's a good thing that Radu never dated Silvia," Eva commented, attempting to avoid the implications of her friend's statement.

"My point is," Doina pursued undaunted, "that the same logic applies to other people whom the Petrescus regard as a threat. Especially those who work for Radio Freedom Europe." Doina's voice lowered to a whisper and she looked at her friend confidentially: "Silvia even told me that her father always keeps the report on the Radio Freedom Europe broadcasts on top of his desk. Right underneath the Department of External Information reports and the folder containing embassy telegrams selected by the minister of foreign affairs. That's how much of a priority targeting RFE has become for him. It's like a thorn in his side."

Even Irina's attention was diverted away from her melting ice cream and riveted by the conversation between Doina and her mother. Her eyes opened wide with a mixture of concern and morbid curiosity: "What does he do to them?"

"To whom?" Doina asked.

"To the people who talk against the government."

"You're too young to worry about these sorts of things," her mother interjected, wishing she could have had this discussion with her friend in private.

But Doina, not used to treating children that differently from adults, answered in all honesty: "When the offender lives abroad, the Secret Police often hires foreign gangsters that won't be traced back to the Romanian government to shake up and sometimes even kill the person who spoke against him or his regime."

"I've heard about that," Eva replied softly, her heart sinking when considering even worse possibilities than those she had envisioned so far.

"But that's not likely to have happened to Radu," Doina added.

"Why not?" Eva's hopes rose again.

"Because you said he called you not that long ago and he was fine. Besides, why would they kill him now that international attention is focused on his case? That makes no sense. What's more likely is that the *Securitate* is trying to convert him into an agent for the Romanian government."

"Radu would never agree to that," Eva replied.

"You never know. They have pretty effective methods of persuasion. Just a few years ago there was an international scandal about that sort of thing. Did you hear about the Diaconescu case?"

Eva directed her friend an incredulous look. "How could I have? You know very well we don't hear about anything in Romania."

"I thought the information might have leaked back into the country by word of mouth, as it sometimes does," Doina replied. She then leaned forward towards Eva and added confidentially, almost in a whisper: "A few years ago the *Securitate* co-opted the secretary of the Romanian program manager at Radio Freedom Europe in Munich. Both she and her husband made quite a good living out of copying dissident letters and handing them over to the *Securitate*. They got paid for each document delivered and even got a pension from the Romanian government. When they got caught by the German authorities they almost ready to retire. As it turns out, the Diaconescu woman, Elena I believe was her name, had been working at RFE since 1952."

"You don't say...." Eva was intrigued, but at the same time this wealth of information aroused her suspicion. She studied closely Doina's face. Could her good friend have been an informant back in Romania? Everyone knew that the country crawled with them. "How did you hear about all of this?" she asked her.

Doina shrugged matter-of-factly. "I read about it in the Washington Post. It was front page news at the time I was at a math conference in Nashville, Tennessee of all places," she said.

Eva felt somewhat reassured. Doina didn't have the personality of an informant, she told herself. She was too honest, spoke too much. There's no way she would have been able to hold her tongue about state secrets. She could hardly keep a lid on her own affairs. "Quite frankly, I hope that they're trying to get Radu to spy for them. That's better than killing him," Eva commented out loud. Upon further consideration, however, she found even this scenario implausible: "But wouldn't they have let him continue to work at Radio Free Europe if he was their mole? He hasn't worked for them in years. The station manager himself told me so."

Doina herself seemed perplexed by this information. "Quite honestly, I don't know what to tell you. What's obvious is that you need to rely upon someone *sur place*," she said. Then her face suddenly brightened, as if she had just had a revelation: "Listen, I'm good friends with a French artist I dated a long time ago, when I spent time in Paris. He's quite well-known; his name is Jean-Pierre Renault."

"You mean the French *amant* you told me about?"

"I know what the word 'amant' means, Mom!" Irina announced proudly, to her mother's displeasure.

"I meant to say *ami*," Doina attempted to correct her faux pas. "We've remained on pretty good terms ever since. He comes by to see me whenever he's in Rome and I go visit him in Paris practically every summer. I know for a fact that he is, or at least was at the time, involved with Radio Freedom Europe. Perhaps he'll be in a better position to talk to the station managers and see if they'd be willing to give him any additional information about Radu."

Eva wasn't ecstatic about this proposition. "I don't see how this would help. As I said, the people at RFE have no idea where Radu is. I talked to them myself."

"Or at least they claim that they don't," Doina replied.

"What are you saying? That RFE is in on this too?"

"No, I wouldn't go that far. But, given their affiliation with the CIA, you can well imagine that they have their own secrets to protect. At any rate, their top priority isn't finding your son. That's your top priority."

Eva's eyes flickered as she confessed her main hope: "Radu's only a small fish. He was only a program assistant. Maybe if he lays low for awhile, they'll give up looking for him."

Doina, however, didn't share her friend's ostrich policy. "That's not very likely," she countered. "The *Securitate* generally prefers to work with small fish since they can do covert operations without being noticed and be eliminated without creating an international scandal. Besides, the dissident letters are too important to Petrescu for him to give up his prey. Without dissident criticism, he believes he'd be bigger than Stephen the Great. Tss... He's completely delusional!"

"But there are so many people who complain about him abroad," Eva objected.

"Yes, but most do so in the privacy of their homes and only to people they know and trust," Doina pointed out. "Those who complain publicly, like Radu, are generally top targets."

Eva's earlier suspicion returned. "Did Silvia tell you all this?"

Doina seemed taken aback by her friend's question. "No... why do you ask? This is all common knowledge. Plus I've heard so many personal stories from friends..."

Eva's eyes opened wide with curiosity: "Like who?"

Doina once again lowered her voice: "Do you know Crina Laftarescu? Emil Laftarescu's wife?"

"Vaguely. I met her once at an Institute party. Wasn't she an editor for the physics journal?"

"That's right. She's small of stature, brunette, with lively blue eyes," Doina specified.

"...and looks a bit mousy?" Eva completed the picture. "I remember her. She acted like she was very important, assumed these affected manners with me. She hardly gave me the time of day at that party."

"Well, she can be a bit reserved, but overall she's a nice person," Doina defended her acquaintance. "Well, to make a long story short, Crina defected to

West Germany a few years ago, in '73 as I recall, and I ran into her at conferences a couple of times since. You wouldn't believe the story she told me about what happened to her husband...," Doina said, clicking her tongue for emphasis.

"Wasn't he a famous literature professor in Romania? Also kind of snobby?" Eva reverted to her original prejudice about the couple.

"They were always very nice to me," Doina replied, once again discouraging criticism. "Anyways, once they defected to West Germany, Emil became the supervisory program editor in the Romanian Department of Radio Freedom Europe. Like Radu, he was very outspoken about Petrescu's human rights abuses. That man must have seven lives, otherwise he'd have never survived what they did to him..."

"What?"

"First they tried to frame him for bribes. They disseminated these cockamamie stories that he received illegal money from Romanian émigrés."

"And did he?" Eva inquired.

"Of course not! It was all a bunch of lies. When that didn't work, and he continued criticizing the Romanian government on the air, they tried to frame him for something more serious. They spread rumors in the media that he had been a Nazi, an important member of the Iron Guard. But even that didn't stick and Emil continued his criticisms."

"So did they try to kill him?" Eva asked, her eyes glued with curiosity to her friend.

"Absolutely. You don't play around with the Secret Police. They hired a bunch of thugs, a team of French drug smugglers working for the DIE, to stage a car accident and shake him up. The hoodlums later confessed that they were supposed to beat him to the point of seriously maiming him after the accident, but they didn't get the chance to finish the job since the police showed up."

"So then did Laftarescu decide to give up sticking his nose in politics?"

Doina shook her head. "You don't know Laftarescu! He's a very stubborn man. That's probably why he and his wife got a divorce..."

"They divorced? I thought they were perfect for each other," Eva commented.

"Perfect or not, Crina couldn't take the constant state of anxiety, since Emil refused to give up attacking the Petrescu regime. After the last incident, she gave up."

"What happened?"

"They hired another group of thugs to beat him up, and this time they broke his spine. He was in the hospital recovering for six months afterwards, that's how serious it was. But he still didn't learn his lesson."

"I hope Radu won't be as stubborn as that... I wish I could at least see him in person and persuade him to give up all this political hocus pocus. It's not worth risking your life for it. "

"Once they're after you, you may not have a choice in the matter," Doina commented. "If you wish, as soon as you arrive in America, I can put you in touch with Jean-Pierre, and you can take it from there," she reiterated her earlier suggestion. "At any rate, what do you have to lose?"

Eva remained silent for a moment. Even during her most despondent moments, she had never lost hope that her son would at some point find a way to escape whatever terrible situation he may be in and rejoin his family safe and sound in America. Could it be that this stranger, this French artist who didn't even know Radu, would be able to find out more about their son's whereabouts than his own loving parents? Eva was skeptical, but felt compelled to try everything. Even pursuing improbable leads would be better than accepting defeat. "Okay," she said. "We'll give your French friend a try."

Chapter 23

After being tied up in New York City for three days due to a bureaucratic mix-up regarding their entrance visa, Eva and Irina were about to take a plane and meet Andrei in San Francisco. The brunette at the PanAm counter asked Eva very sweetly: "Hi, how are you?

Not accustomed to friendly service, Eva was caught off guard. "Does this girl know me?" she wondered. "Why in the world does she care about how I'm doing?" Since the young woman smiled in an amiable enough manner, however, she decided to give her the benefit of the doubt and answered her question in earnest: "I very tired—we have long flight. Come from Italia. Have not seen her father," she pointed to Irina, "for near three years. We are from Romania. Imigranti," she emphasized, in case there was any doubt.

Upon hearing this rather unconventional answer in broken English, the girl's affable smile was replaced by a glazed-over, disinterested gaze, and from then on she was all business: "That's nice. May I see your passports please?"

Eva handed them to her.

The girl looked from the photos to Eva and Irina, then asked: "Are you checking any luggage?"

Eva had made some progress on her English, but not enough to fully understand the question: "Yes. Go ahead!" she threw up her arms.

The girl at the counter looked puzzled.

"Our luggage is been checked three times. Already done! We have nothing undeclared inside. Nothing! You can see if you vant…," Eva invited the girl to rummage through her luggage, as the security guards had done at customs.

"No, I mean do you want to check it on the plane?" the girl clarified, speaking louder for the benefit of her foreign client, who had perfectly good hearing, just poor English comprehension.

Eva still couldn't fully understand what was going on, but for the sake of expediency and the benefit of the people waiting in line behind her, she acted like she did: "Okay," she replied. For the next few months, this was to become her stock answer whenever she didn't understand something in English, since people tended to react better to it than when she said with her heavy accent "I don't speak English."

"Here are your tickets for Flight 340 departing for San Francisco from gate 23A," the girl at the counter handed Eva the plane tickets. She then turned to the next customer in line, reassuming her former friendly persona: "Hello, sir. How are you? Checking any luggage?"

The gentleman in question, an American, already knew the lesson Eva had just learned: "I'm fine, thanks," he answered flatly, without getting into the details of his personal life. He then said that he had one suitcase to check and showed her his driver's license.

Eva whispered to her daughter in Romanian: "Strange country, this America... They ask you how you're doing yet they couldn't care less about your answer."

Once they got on the plane, Eva's mind was fully occupied by her imminent reunion with her husband. She felt butterflies in her stomach. What would Andrei think of her after nearly three years of separation? Would he still love her as much as before? Would they adjust to being a couple once again? And how would he behave with Irina, who had changed from a little girl to a young woman?

For Irina, the idea of finally seeing her father again still felt like an abstraction; an implausible event that blurred the line between dream and reality. Since for her three years of separation was practically an eternity, she remembered only traces of her father, not his whole personality: the way they'd sing together on the way to school; his bright blue, intelligent eyes; the way he always seemed to be in a hurry; his insistence that she do correctly her math and science homework (a task which she always vehemently resisted); his awkward gestures of affection (stroking her head as if she were a puppy); his congruous mixture of indulgence and severity.

Mother and daughter arrived at the San Francisco International Airport around 1:00 a.m. Andrei was supposed to greet them at the gate, but he was nowhere in sight. Rather than going to get their luggage, Eva and Irina waited for him, scrutinizing every thin man with dark hair and blue eyes.

"This is so typical of your father! He's been in this country for almost three years, and he still can't manage to find our gate," Eva said to her daughter, after a nerve racking twenty minute wait and in answer to the latter's repeated questions, all variations upon the same theme: "Do you see him yet?" "Is he here?" "Is that him?" "What's taking him so long?" Despite her unsentimental words, Eva's heart was racing with excitement. In a few moments, the indefinitely postponed future would become an immediate, palpable present.

Suddenly, she thought she spotted her husband: a slight man with a lost gaze, who, at that moment, was looking precisely in the wrong direction. Andrei seemed thinner than ever and his dark hair had turned salt and pepper, but Eva recognized the confused expression he assumed whenever he attempted anything practical.

"Timpitelule! Little Dumdum! We're here!" she shouted affectionately in Romanian, waving to her husband and feeling relieved that, in spite of his cluelessness, at least he was lost in the right area.

Andrei moved so fast towards his daughter and wife that his face became a blur as he hugged and kissed them on both cheeks, several times, as if not quite trusting his senses, reassuring himself through these repeated embraces that after all these years, they were finally reunited as a family.

"Gogosica mea, my little dumpling," he said to Irina, his voice cracking with emotion. But the terms of endearment that had worked magic when his daughter was eight no longer had the same effect on her at nearly twelve: "Daddy, I'm not fat! I just ate a few ice creams," his daughter felt compelled to justify her food frenzy in Italy. She immediately regretted saying that, however, since she had imagined the first words out of her mouth to her father as being slightly more sentimental.

"We ate like pigs in Rome," Eva excused herself as well for the extra pounds she had put on lately, which, she thought, her husband was bound to notice.

Andrei finally got a chance to look at his wife, who had filled out slightly and looked understandably tired. Nonetheless, to him, she was the most beautiful woman in the world: "You look perfect," he said and kissed her tenderly on the mouth this time.

"Yuck!" their daughter interrupted this otherwise romantic reunion.

"I hope you haven't spoiled her in my absence..." Andrei said, looking at Irina with mock sternness.

"If you only knew... You have your work cut out for you," Eva replied, while Irina tugged at her sleeve looking at her mother with an expression of disapproval.

"What do you mean you? Where do you plan to go?" Andrei asked his wife.

"Who knows? I may also need a three year break from parenting," Eva replied.

Andrei couldn't resist the urge to hug his wife once again: "No more breaks for us, Papusica. No more separations. Ever again."

Eva looked into her husband's eyes, finally allowing herself the luxury of feeling emotion: "For so long, all I've dreamt about was being reunited as a family. With both of our children. With Raducu also."

Andrei nodded gravely: "I've made some progress on that...."

"Did he contact you?" Eva asked.

"No. I would have told you. But I got in touch with that French artist, Jean-Pierre, as soon as you told me about him. I pulled a few strings at the university and found a way of inviting him to give a talk at our Institute for the Humanities. That way we can meet him in person and see how much he may know. But you need to be careful, okay? Don't spill your beans to him immediately."

"Oh, I don't have any beans left to spill, Andreias," Eva sighed, looking discouraged and weary, as she always did whenever the subject of Radu came up.

"Where's your luggage?" Andrei changed the subject, recalling they still needed to take care of practical matters.

"I don't know," Eva shrugged. "They talk so fast that I couldn't understand which baggage claim we're supposed to go to."

Uncharacteristically, Andrei took charge of the situation. He looked up their baggage claim number and, once they retrieved the luggage, chivalrously insisted on carrying it all by himself. His slight form looked like an ant struggling with giant bread crumbs.

"I have a new car which I think you'll like," he told Irina as they made their way through the crowd to the parking lot.

Irina gazed with undisguised admiration at all the large sedans they passed by. Her father stopped in front of a tiny, European-looking vehicle: a 1980 metallic blue Horizon. Despite its unimpressive size, Irina's eyes sparkled with delight. The car was her favorite color, the kind she had only dreamt of: light blue with silver sparkles which shimmered like diamonds under the parking lot lights. Irina felt confident that even her doll, Greta Barbie, would like it.

"I love it!" she declared, sitting down in the back and bouncing up and down on the cushy seats, touching with open hands their soft, velvety covers.

"What luxury!" Eva said, equally in awe of the modest, economy-size vehicle. Having prepared in advance an explanation why he couldn't yet afford a Mercedes, Andrei felt relieved that his family was so easy to please. Maybe they'd also overlook the bullet hole in the door of the cheap apartment he had rented for the summer in Berkeley.

"I didn't quite understand your explanation on the phone. How come we're not going directly to Ann Arbor?" Eva asked.

"This spring quarter I'm Visiting Associate Professor at an even better university. It's called the University of California at Berkeley," Andrei declared with pride.

"Berkelei?" Eva repeated, unimpressed. Back in Romania, she had only heard of Harvard.

"That's right."

"If this Berkelei's so smart, then how come they didn't hire you permanently?"

"I suppose I haven't made an important enough breakthrough in physics. I was too busy struggling to get you and Irina out of Romania," her husband responded with an affectionate smile. He felt elated. After all these years, his spunky, pragmatic wife hadn't changed one bit.

"You mean you're blaming us for your failures again?" Eva wanted to know.

"My biggest success is reuniting with my family," Andrei replied with an uncharacteristic sentimentality which, his wife surmised, would wear off in a couple of days.

In spite of her sharp tongue, Eva's eyes twinkled with warmth. She placed her hand on top of his, which was holding, by force of habit, the automatic gear shift.

Andrei drove fast, as usual. Eva scolded him, calling him an Italian race car driver, and warned him that he'd be pulled over by the police if he didn't slow down, also as usual. Irina looked out the window, mesmerized. The Golden Gate Bridge shimmered with its bright yellow lights, like a garland illuminating the darkness of the night. The skyline of San Francisco flashed before her eyes, looking exactly like the girl had envisioned--extrapolating from the American movies she had seen—only even more shinny, beautiful and inviting. Colorful billboards displayed alluring women in sexy positions lying next to what looked like bottles of tuika (vodka). These Americans must drink even more than we do, Irina speculated. Her parents kept on talking excitedly in Romanian. Irina basked in their familiar presence, as the distant past folded almost seamlessly unto the present, leaving only the faint scars of long years of separation, which neither the present nor the future could erase.

Chapter 24

"Andrei, why is there a bullet hole in our front door?" Eva inquired, examining in the light of day their one bedroom summer apartment in Berkeley, which her husband had described to her on the phone as "spacious" and "luxurious."

"It was already there when I got here," Andrei exculpated himself.

Eva looked at him askance: "I didn't think you had suddenly turned into John Wayne. But why in the world did you rent an apartment in a place where people have gunfights?"

Andrei assumed the air of an expert on all things American, since he had almost three years of seniority of living in the country compared to his wife, whose only cultural exposure was the soap opera Dallas. "What are you talking about? Here everyone owns guns and shoots each other!" he explained.

Eva, however, remained skeptical about her husband's expertise: "Did you bother to research the neighborhood before you picked out an apartment for us?"

"Of course," Andrei assured her. To save his time and energy for physics, the aforementioned research consisted of taking the first apartment he ran across in the section of the local newspaper marked "Apartments for rent, $200 a month or less."

"If this is the result of research, I'm definitely taking charge of finding us a place in Ann Arbor," his wife resolved.

"Only if you'll also be in charge of earning our income as well, since I only make 20,000 dollars a year," Andrei considered it apropos to inform her at this point.

Eva was stunned: "That's all they pay a professor at University of Michigan?"

"Associate Professor," her husband corrected.

"You made more money in Romania," Eva said, which was not entirely correct. Andrei made 20,000 lei a year, which translated into an annual income of about 2,000 dollars.

Meanwhile Irina, who had just finished her first bowl of American cereal—Cheerios—whose taste, she speculated, resembled what ground-up straw must taste like, was closely inspecting the bullet hole. Unlike her mother, she was intrigued by what might have taken place in that apartment.

"Daddy, did you know the people who lived here before us?" her eyes sparkled with curiosity.

"No. I rented it from a realtor. But what does it matter? Why are you making such a big deal out of nothing?" he shrugged, looking at Eva. "We're only staying here for three more weeks. Our real home will be in Ann Arbor."

"Can you please show us Berkeley? And San Francisco?" his daughter was eager to learn everything there was to know about California.

"Okay," Andrei said. "But tomorrow I have to return to work," he announced, not one to waste time on frivolous vacations. "I'm collaborating with someone from this department," he tried to place the blame of his obsessive workaholism on someone else.

His wife didn't buy the excuse. "A few days of vacation with your family won't destroy your career. We just got here after a three–year separation, for God's sake! You haven't changed a bit," Eva concluded, at that moment not appearing enthusiastic about this fact.

"Daddy, what are you going to show us first?" Irina asked.

Andrei was obliged to admit that he didn't know much about Berkeley, the town where he had lived during the past two months, nor San Francisco, the gorgeous city which was only an hour away. However, he was fully prepared for the task at hand, having purchased in advance an informative guidebook. He looked at the index, then flipped to page 76, which announced: "Berkeley, California is a thriving and creative college town, home to the prestigious

University of California, Berkeley..." Since by spending every day, including weekends, at his office Andrei considered himself to be very knowledgeable about campus life, he skipped down a few lines to get to the more interesting section on "Berkeley Attractions": "Stop by and admire the Tuning Fork Sculpture on Shattuck Avenue," the book urged, "or take a leisurely stroll along the picturesque Telegraph Avenue, the center of hippie activity during the 1960's and 70's, where 'old timers' still reminisce about the old days."

"What are hippies?" Irina wanted to know, since her father hadn't translated in Romanian that particular word.

"That's something which can't be described," Andrei answered philosophically. "You'll have to see for yourself."

The first thing Irina noticed on the picturesque Telegraph Avenue, was that people were waiting for something in a long line. "What are these people waiting for?" she asked with a tinge of disappointment since, according to highly reliable sources (i.e., her grandparents), such things weren't supposed to happen in America.

"They're getting money from the bank. That's called an ATM machine," her father explained.

Irina was impressed. "Free money? Then what are we waiting for? Let's get in line before all the money's all gone!"

"They're taking their own money from the bank," Andrei clarified.

This turned out to be less impressive: "How unfair! You have to wait in a long line just to get your own money? Then it's not so different here than in Romania," Irina commented.

These similarities notwithstanding, when observing more closely a group of people walking by, Irina and Eva were obliged to admit that there were some cultural differences between the two countries after all.

"American women wear their hair so long," Eva noted with admiration.

"Those are probably men," Andrei surmised.

Eva and Irina did a double take. Indeed, one of the women whose long hair Eva had admired even had a mustache.

"They're the hippies you asked about earlier," Andrei explained.

"Are they like gypsies?" Irina asked, seeking a familiar frame of reference.

"No, they're more political. Basically...they're communists."

"You mean they're involved with the Secret Police?" Eva asked, alarmed.

"No, just the opposite. Here the leftwing is under suspicion by the CIA, which is the American Secret Police."

"I thought we didn't have to worry about all that political stuff any more," Eva said, longing for some peace and quiet.

"We don't. Unless we're planning to join the Communist Party," her husband quipped.

"God forbid!" Eva said, instinctively crossing herself in the Romanian Orthodox tradition, despite her agnosticism.

A short visit to Aquarium Bay in San Francisco, where they walked through three hundred feet of tunnels filled with fascinating sea creatures, was enough to convince Irina that this was, indeed, the country of her dreams. Her favorite part of the visit was a spectacular show that included sea lions trained to do various tricks and jump high up in the air.

"Can we get one for a pet?" she asked her parents.

"Sure, we can keep it in the bathtub," Andrei joked.

But Pandora's box had been opened: "What happened to my parrot, dogs and cats?" Irina inquired.

Her father looked puzzled.

"The ones you promised if I came to America?" his daughter jogged his memory.

"You mean I have to bribe you? Reuniting with your father wasn't enough of a reason to come to America?" Andrei asked, feeling slightly wounded.

Irina rolled her eyes. "Of course it was, Daddy! But the pets are the fun reason why I wanted to come here."

Eva and Andrei promptly made a short stop at the aquarium gift store, from which their daughter emerged triumphant, holding in her arms a plush whale, dolphin, sea lion, shark and swordfish.

Since Irina and Eva fully believed that Andrei was capable of concentrating three weeks of vacation into one day, they religiously followed the guidebook's suggestions. After the aquarium visit they took a trolley ride down "the Byzantine serpentines of the incomparable Lombard Street." Irina was amazed by its exciting, roller-coaster curves, while Eva eyed with envy the Russian Hill neighborhood, with its stately mansions, condos and townhouses.

"Those damn Russians are always smarter than us Romanians. Couldn't you have chosen an apartment in this location?" she chided her husband.

"Sure, if you had about two thousand dollars a month to spare. I certainly don't," Andrei retorted.

This didn't prevent his wife from enjoying the free gorgeous scenery. The entire street, filled with yellow, pink, white and red roses in bloom, vibrated with color. "If only Grandma Marta were here to see this..." Eva said in a soft voice, recalling that the yellow rose was her mother's favorite flower.

To prove to his wife his generosity, for dinner Andrei decided to splurge and offer his family an expensive treat. They went to Huston Restaurant, a place that had opened a year ago in the old section of town which, the guidebook indicated, was famous for its steak and seafood specialties. The Schwarzes ordered a three-course meal. They started with appetizers consisting of house-cured smoked salmon, capers and dill cream cheese artistically decorated with crisp toast points. For the main course, Eva tasted for the first time in her life roast filet mignon cooked to perfection in a wild mushrooms and pinot noir sauce. Andrei, who had become health conscious once food was finally available to him in America, half-starved himself on a vegetarian and fish diet.

He therefore ordered the poached Atlantic salmon without butter. Irina, who was holding on tightly to her five species of plush fish, declared that "Fish are our friends," and sampled a mesquite-grilled steak (since, presumably, cows were less amiable) with a side of scalloped potatoes. She also thoroughly enjoyed the desert, an old-fashioned chocolate cake with white chocolate anglaise. Eva went all out and had a glass of Merlot, which put her in an excellent mood. Her eyes sparkled with delight as she kept stealing glances at her husband, still not trusting her senses, not fully believing in his presence. From time to time she touched his hand, brushed his knee with her knee and even stroked the table leg a couple of times mistaking it for his foot, just to confirm that he was real. The adoring look he gave her in response offered adequate proof of his existence.

Chapter 25

"My dearest Sofia,

How are you? I miss you very much. I haven't received a letter from you yet, so I hope you'll write me soon. There's not a day gone by when I don't think about you and miss all the fun things we did together. America's a very exciting country, and so is Ann Arbor, the interesting city we moved to. It's much smaller than Bucharest, but my dad calls it a very cultured town. We already got a nice apartment here which is called a 'condo.' It looks just like a regular apartment building, the only difference being that it's much prettier—it even has a courtyard with lots of flowers—and quieter-- you can't play outside or make a lot of noise inside since the neighbors complain. Back in Romania, they didn't worry about how much noise we made. Remember how we used to run around in the apartment when we were kids? I really miss that.

You must be wondering how I like school here. Well, school's great! I can almost understand English and am learning how to speak it in a special program for the smartest students which they call 'Remedial Education.'

I made lots of new friends. But none of them will ever replace the dear friends I had in Romania, especially you, my closest and best friend. I can't wait to hear about how you're doing and how you like 7th grade. Which teachers do you have? Did you get Comrade Popescu in history again? I promise to visit you this summer and wish we were together now.

Affectionately, your friend, Irina"

Having written this letter to her best friend, Irina went into the spic and span bathroom of their new condo. She locked the door, placed down the lid and sat on the toilet, putting her face into her hands and allowing herself to cry so hard that she was hiccupping and hyperventilating. When she reemerged from the bathroom, she was ready to compose another letter, this time to her grandparents, to whom she wrote at least once a week:

"My dear Grandpa Mihai and Grandma Marta,

If you only knew how much I miss you! I cry every day from the pain of our separation and wish so much you could take me to school and that we could be together every single day and do homework together, as before. Mama and Daddy don't have much time for me. Daddy's very busy with Physics—are you surprised?—and Mama is studying for the TOEFL exam so she can become a high school science teacher. The TOEFL is the English language exam, and from what our Russian friends tell us, it's very difficult. After that, Mama plans to take an equivalency exam and then she'll look for a teaching job, since we need the money. We're hoping that to teach science in this country you don't really need to speak English because, at least for me and Mama, this language is not that easy to learn. It's much harder than French. Anyway, the fact that there are quite a few professors in Daddy's Physics department who don't speak English (but they speak Russian and Chinese fluently) is somewhat encouraging.

I'm a little sad since even when my parents are less busy, they worry a lot about Raducu and don't care that much about me. I feel terrible about the fact that my brother may be in danger. Please believe me, I'm not as selfish as I seem. But I wish so much that they could pay attention to me the way you always did. Grandpa Mihai, remember how you used to walk me back and forth to school every day? And how much I was trying to get rid of you so that I'd seem all grown-up in front of my friends? Now I would rip out my heart out to get you back (and, please believe me, I'm not being dramatic or exaggerating at all).

Here nobody walks me to school. I take the bus to what is called Junior High School, which means sixth, seventh and eighth grades. The school bus is yellow and almost always late, but if you happen to be late, it doesn't wait for you. By the way, remember all those pets Daddy promised me so that I would go voluntarily to America? Well, he lied about them. He's allergic to fur and I can't even get a gerbil.

Grandma Marta, I bet you're curious about the food here. In the Aprovisionat—which is called in English 'Kroger'—there's so much food you can go crazy just looking at it. But we can't afford most of it. Mama cuts out these little tickets with pictures on them called "coupons" so we can get reduced prices called "savings." She cooks pretty much the same thing every day—

chicken and vegetables—not that I'm criticizing her or anything, since I know she has so little time because of her worries and English lessons.

I just wrote Sofia a nice letter and kind of lied in it. Grandpa, remember how you used to tell me when I fibbed that my nose would grow long like Pinocchio's? Well, it's pretty long right now. I told Sofia that I love school and made lots of new friends here because I didn't want her to feel sorry for me. After all, I have my pride! Besides, by the time I visit Romania this summer, all of what I told her will hopefully be true.

I wish so much I could close my eyes and get over this hard bump in life. If I could magically absorb this impossible language by slipping a dictionary under my pillow at night and wake up in the morning fitting in at school without even trying, that would make my life so much easier. Daddy says that I don't make enough progress with English because I'm stubborn and don't apply myself. But you already know that he's almost always wrong... Mama says I'm too sentimental and nostalgic. Whenever I'm sad, she tells me that I need to learn how to live in the present, not the past. But who is she to give me lessons about that when she cries herself to sleep every night because she misses you so much? To tell you the truth, she doesn't like America either. Only Daddy does. He loses patience with both of us—calls us his 'weeping willows'-- but that's only because he doesn't understand how hard it is for us to adapt.

I mean, how would he like it if he were called 'Draculetta' at school? It turns out that the only thing American kids know about Romania is that Vlad Tepes was a vampire from Transylvania and that we're communists (which they call "commies"). So now I'm a commie and a vampire! The fact that my two front teeth stick out a little doesn't help, so I've begged my parents for braces, but they're too expensive (the same as our rent for half a year). Now I'm afraid to even smile—fortunately, I'm so sad here that don't feel like smiling any more, so it's not that big a deal.

In conclusion, (in my English class we're learning how to write essays with a beginning, body and conclusion), I HATE America and want to go back home as soon as possible. I don't want to sound too negative, but you're the only ones I can still talk to about these things. America has so many things—toys, color T.V., skyscrapers and lots of food—but I can't enjoy any of them without feeling the love that I felt with you and my friends back in Romania. I prefer to live in poverty and without much food—though your dishes were always so delicious, Grandma—than to live in this country, an outsider to everyone and everything, including my own parents.

With infinite love, your granddaughter, Irina

P.S.: I'll try to cheer you up more in my next letter, promise! Your loving granddaughter, Irina"

After finishing her letter, Irina took a deep breath, opened the window of her little room, visually inspected the brand new white furniture with green flowers around the borders, and, all things considered, felt a little better. She then unzipped her backpack and tackled the most unpleasant task of the day: her English homework. The assigned reading was a chapter from Salinger's *The Catcher in the Rye*. Irina worked at it for an hour, looking up almost every word in the English-Romanian dictionary. She wished she could talk to Holden Caulfield in some kind of sign language, to make him understand that she wanted to find out what was happening to him. Although Irina didn't quite grasp all the details of the plot, she understood enough to realize that Holden was also unhappy and felt out of place at school.

Her mother knocked gently on the door: "Supper's ready!"

Irina looked back at her mother's face and was struck by the mirror effect which was displaced only by their age difference. Eva's eyes were swollen and her cheeks flushed; which meant, Irina inferred, that her mother had also been crying.

"Your Daddy's so impatient with me," Eva explained. "He expects me to speak perfect English in three months. He can't understand that the tutoring in Romania didn't help that much. It's terrible to depend on a man..."

"Then let's go back to Romania," the girl attempted to offer a constructive solution to this problem.

"Don't say such crazy things!" Eva answered, jolted out of her self-pity. "We just need to be more positive, just like Daddy says. To give this country a chance."

"What's for dinner?" Andrei asked, once mother and daughter arrived downstairs. He was, all things considered, much more cheerful—or at least less suicidal--than the female members of his family.

"Chicken," Eva announced to no one's surprise.

Irina felt like saying, "Again? I'm not hungry," but didn't want to hurt her mother's feelings. She moved around the baked chicken on the plate and even swallowed a few bites. Her cloud of emotions wouldn't leave her, however. She felt a constriction in her heart knowing that tomorrow, once again, she wouldn't understand much of what went on in her classes and that during recess she'd be teased as usual by some mean foreign kids. Thinking about how she was treated at school made her throat constrict from emotion. She needed some fresh air. She was about to go out for a walk when she realized that her parents would want to know where and why she was going out. Basically, she thought, they treat me like a little girl and never let me have any freedom.

Feeling that she lacked the psychological strength to face yet another parental lecture on safety, Irina went upstairs to pick up the two letters she had written in order to have an alibi. "Mom, I'm going to mail these letters," she announced and ran out the door, shutting it behind her. "Be careful! It's already getting dark outside ..." she heard Eva's warning.

Before going to the mailboxes, she stopped at the playground and, dropping the two letters on the ground, got on a swing. As she pumped with her feet to rise higher and higher into the air, her emotions vacillated along with the back and forth movements of the swing. She recalled how when she was a young child, her grandfather would push her on the swing and a fresh wave of pain overcame her. To escape it, she hopped off and picked up the two letters which were by now covered with dust. She attempted to wipe clean the one to her grandparents, but only succeeded in smudging its address. Should I go back home and put the letter in a clean envelope? she asked herself. Eh, what does it matter anyway? she thought. These are just words. I can't see them for almost a year; I can barely talk to them on the phone a few minutes a week. I wish I could go back home. I wish I were this letter and could mail myself right back to my grandparents.

Once she reached the street corner, she gazed with some confusion upon two nearly identical boxes. One was green; the other blue. Which one is the mailbox? Irina wondered. So far, only her mother had mailed their letters to Romania. One of the boxes had some writing in English on it, which Irina couldn't understand. To her relief, however, she noticed on the blue box three sets of numbers, 10:00 a.m., 1:00 p.m., and 3:00 p.m., which she assumed indicated the times when the mail got picked up.

She dropped the letter to Sofia into the blue mailbox, but couldn't quite let go of the one to her grandparents. Somehow, she felt that she needed their actual presence, not just these exchanges of words on a page. Which is what all of their promises, and all of her parents' promises to her had been. Meaningless, empty words, just like my letter to Sofia, Irina thought, feeling her nostalgia turn into resentment. Her parents had reassured her that in order to join her father in America, she wouldn't have to forgo everyone and everything she loved in Romania. And that was precisely the deception that got me here in the first place, Irina now thought. She came to America under false assumptions. "Ce mincuini! What lies!" she whispered to herself. With a slow and deliberate motion, she placed the letter to her grandparents into the green box, marked "TRASH." She then turned sharply upon her heels and ran as fast as she could back to her apartment, suspecting that her parents would be worried by now.

When she got home, to avoid any questions from her parents, she immediately retreated into the bathroom, her sanctuary. She looked at herself in the mirror. Everything that had seemed right about her look in Romania felt wrong here, she observed. For one thing, her pigtails in white ribbons were too young for this country, where girls her age wore their hair long and in wavy layers or, better yet, "feathered" like Farrah Fawcett. Irina slowly removed the silky white ribbons and combed out her long, straight hair. How was she ever going to look normal when there was not a single feather in her hair? Then there was the whole wardrobe issue, which consisted of the fact they couldn't afford normal clothes. Eva still dressed her daughter in the pleated navy skirts and white shirts with round collars they had brought over from Romania. But Irina could see in other girls' eyes--the way they looked her up and down with little crooked, malicious smiles--that her clothes were what is called in English "dorky." She wanted to wear tight Jordache jeans and Polo shirts, like every other teenager in the new fashion center of her world, Saline Junior High School. Instead, she thought with regret, she went to school still dressed like a "commie" with crooked, "Draculetta" front teeth.

"Look forward, not backward," her mother's advice rang in her ear. Her new sense of resolve felt as soothing as a prayer. If she could only become a miniature Farrah Fawcett overnight, speak fluent English, and forget everything about her previous existence—her childhood, family, language and culture—she'd do it in an instant. Irina's top goal now was becoming American.

Chapter 26

"Maria's plump breasts heaved under José's rough, manly hands. She tried to push him away, but lacked the strength. A force more powerful than her will, the blind surge of sexual desire, overcame her womanly modesty, pushing her towards him in a torrent of passion. Unable to contain himself, José tore her corset and the globes of her golden breasts were suddenly freed from bondage. He covered them with sweet kisses, sucking slowly, meticulously, with infinite patience, the aureoles of her dark nipples. She cried out with joy as his lips grazed her navel, then went lower, much lower, into the inner depths of her being. Feelings she had never felt before overcame her senses in waves of unalloyed pleasure."

"This sounds kind of nice," Irina thought, her eyes nearly popping out of her head as they went over this scene twice. "Your Mom lets you read this kind of stuff?" she managed to unpeel her glance from the page to ask Alice, her best friend since eighth grade. She closed the book, feeling "flushed with desire"— an expression she had picked up from the romance novel, which didn't hesitate to use it at least a dozen times and that's only in the parts she had read (granted, she had skipped forward to all the juicy love scenes, since who cares about the rest).

The book cover featured a picture of a bosom brunette who seemed to have nearly fainted with pleasure in the arms of a handsome, muscular tanned man. He was holding her waist, her head leaned back, her eyes closed—presumably in ecstasy, Irina conjectured, based upon the frequent use of this word—leaving her heavy breasts exposed and popping out of a revealing corset. "Man, it sure helps to have American parents!" Irina couldn't help but say out loud. "All I get to read is *The Brothers Karamazov*. You know, stuff with no love scenes," she lamented.

Alice, a plump brunette who was already filled out at the age of fifteen, responded: "Are you kidding me? My Mom doesn't know I read Harlequins! I buy them secretly, out of my allowance."

"Really?" Irina asked with undisguised admiration. "Cool!" she approved, using the lingo she considered most appropriate for the occasion. She was intrigued by the "slumber party," a time-honored American tradition where, as far as she could tell, girls spent the day and most of the night talking, giggling, putting on make-up, painting their nails, piercing holes in places where they didn't exist naturally, dying their hair with wild, washable colors (preferably pink or purple, for shock value) and--the best part--doing forbidden, naughty things thinly disguised as innocuous childhood fun.

Barbara, a slim blond with light blue eyes reminiscent of the Barbie dolls she still secretly collected, assumed an air of superiority:

"That's nothing! They barely get to the good stuff in these silly women's novels," she said with disdain, removing from her backpack a more anatomically correct journal.

Irina peered furtively at the picture of the man on the cover, whom she assumed was a cowboy, since he was wearing nothing but a Western hat, hung very well as if on a hook, upon his incontrovertibly well-endowed member.

"*Playgirl*? Wow! "Irina exclaimed. "Do they show everything in here?"

"Why? Have you never seen a naked man before?" Barbara taunted her.

"Of course I have! I once walked in on my brother by mistake when he was going to the bathroom," Irina responded, not wishing to seem more naïve than the next girl.

"I mean a real man, not family members," Barbara clarified her standards, even using a double entendre—which her friends didn't get, however.

Irina had to think fast on her feet. "Everybody's seen naked people. We, Europeans, are very open-minded about that sort of thing," she generalized assuming an air of cultural superiority, hoping this would discourage further specific inquiries into her personal sexual experience, which so far, knock on wood (as her mother would say), was nonexistent.

It didn't: "You mean in Romania people walk around naked on the beach, like at the French Riviera?" Barbara asked.

No matter how much she wanted to impress her friends, Irina couldn't stretch the truth quite that far: "No, but we do get bitten on the butt by jellyfish at the Black Sea!" she cheerfully pointed out the advantages of Romanian beaches at Constanta over the resort towns of the French Mediterranean.

Alice burst out laughing—"She cracks me up!"—but Barbara, who had a mean-streak and was already on her third older boyfriend, wouldn't let Irina off the hook quite so easily.

"Did you ever have sex? Or are you still a viiirgin?" she whispered tauntingly into Irina's ear.

Alice overheard the question and, still being a virgin herself, vehemently defended her friend: "Stop teasing her! Can't you see she's foreign?"

Irina, however, was determined to stand her ground as an American resident, with a perfectly legitimate Green Card: "For your information," she announced, "It just so happens that I already have a boyfriend."

Alice, who spent every recess and lunch break with Irina, raised her eyebrows in disbelief while Barbara smirked. "Who?" her friends asked practically in unison.

"Misha Petrov!" Irina declared triumphantly, coming up on the spot with the name of the only other Eastern European immigrant in her class--and consequently, despite her love for American culture and general open-mindedness, the only boy she considered a possible candidate for a potential marriage maybe someday if she ever fell in love and chose to get married. She had already given the matter serious consideration.

"You poor soul," Barbara said.

"You mean the guy who hid all your books in the tree during lunch last week?" Alice asked.

"My mom told me that was just his way of showing that he has a crush on me," Irina explained teenage, immature male psychology to her friends. She was perfectly used to it from hanging out during her childhood with her father's colleagues, all adult physicists.

"It's more likely a way of showing he's a dork..." Barbara offered an alternative interpretation. "At any rate, for future reference, hanging your books up on trees is not to be confused with having sex." She tossed the issue of *Playgirl* unto Irina's lap. "Here! It looks like you need this more than I do."

Irina was obliged to change tactics: "In my country, a young lady saves herself until marriage." She never thought she'd see the day when she'd resort to her mother's moralizing.

"Why in the world would anyone do a stupid thing like that?" Barbara asked.

"Because! My Mom said she'd put a dagger through her heart if I lost my virginity before the wedding night!" Irina calmly explained.

"Did she mean that literally?" Alice asked. She was sufficiently acquainted with Irina's family to believe there was a strong possibility the expression wasn't being employed purely metaphorically.

"I'd rather not find out," Irina responded in all honesty. She had a sudden flashback to the first time her mother brought up this delicate subject, about two years ago. She was almost fourteen years old. One morning, she discovered a much-awaited spot on her panties and made the mistake of telling her mother about it.

Eva immediately seized the opportunity to inform her daughter of the facts of life. She didn't use, however, the figurative approach about the birds and the bees generally preferred by American parents. She relied upon the Romanian method instead.

"Do you know what this means?" she asked her daughter in a grave voice.

"Sure, Mom. Lots of my friends already got their periods last year. Mostly the boys," Irina hazarded a joke.

But Eva was in no mood for comedy, at least not when addressing such a serious moral issue.

"You have to be extremely careful from now on," she said.

"Okay," Irina shrugged.

"A young woman's virginity is her greatest jewel," Eva pursued.

"Yes, I know," Irina said, optimistically thinking that instant agreement would be the best way to bypass further discussion.

"If you don't protect your honor with young men, they'll take advantage of you," Eva continued in the same vein. "And then you'll not only lose your honor, but also disgrace your whole family," she added.

Irina looked at her mother with what must have been a frightened gaze, since Eva felt compelled to reassure her: "Well, I don't mean to scare you, of course. I just wanted to let you know that being a woman is a big responsibility. And to congratulate you for becoming one!"

"Thanks, Mom," Irina responded, promising herself to avoid such mother-daughter conversations in the future.

As Irina was struggling to banish this rather troubling recollection from her mind, Barbara took the opportunity to snatch the *Playgirl* from her hands: "Well then you won't be needing this after all! We wouldn't want you to get any ideas before your wedding night, now would we?"

Irina was startled enough by what she had barely glimpsed at, which didn't seem particularly beautiful or appealing, not to wish to delve any further into the mysteries of male sexuality.

"So are you going to ask Misha out to the Valentine's Day dance?" Alice asked.

Irina hadn't considered the possibility. "Yeah, probably. Since I already asked him out to the library," she boasted.

Noticing Alice's perplexed look and Barbara's blank stare, she bolstered her argument: "It was very romantic. We read Dostoievsky and Tolstoy together."

"Never heard of those playwrights," Alice declared. She was an active member of the drama club and considered herself an authority on Shakespeare.

"Those are novelists, silly! Duhhh!" the more savvy Barb corrected her.

Irina was saved from further inquiries about Misha and Russian fiction by Alice's mother knocked on the door and entered the room before Alice had the chance to say "Come in!" The girls barely had time to hide the contraband reading material under the throw pillows.

"Mooom! Can't you knock on the door first, like I told you zillions of times already?"Alice complained.

"Sorry," Mrs. Benetti said. "Irina's father's on the phone. He's coming to pick her up in ten minutes."

"But it's barely nine p.m.! Why does she have to leave so soon?" Alice protested.

"It's his daughter, his rules," her mother exculpated herself.

Irina's eyes opened wide with outrage. Why was this happening to her? What did she ever do to deserve such embarrassment? Then a streak of paranoia overtook her: Could her father have known what she and her friends were doing? At almost sixteen, Irina thought, it was an indignity not to be allowed to spend the night at a totally harmless slumber party with her best friends. They weren't even planning to crash Todd Bernstein's coed party—since he had changed it to next week anyway. Irina hastily gathered up her overnight bag, preparing however to defend her basic human rights tooth and nail.

"Let's go!" Andrei said as soon as he arrived, with the typical wave of the hand that, to her chagrin, reminded Irina of the days he picked her up from kindergarten in Romania. "When will he finally get it that I'm all grown up now?" Irina wondered, seething with irritation.

"Daddy, you said I could spend the night with my friends!" she objected.

"No, Mama gave you permission, but I don't agree."

"Why not?"

"Irina, no debate please!" Since she had joined the Saline High School Debate Team the previous year, everything Irina said in protest or disagreement was called in her household a "debate," a word that assumed the negative connotations of "rebellion" or "insurgency" against parental authority, which, whenever she lost an argument, Irina referred to as "the party rule".

Having the advantage of being surrounded by sympathetic witnesses, Irina nevertheless presented what she considered to be her strongest argument: "But Daddy, everybody does it in America."

Andrei's unflagging lack of tact didn't fail him now: "And that's why American teenagers take drugs, have premarital sex and end up in rehab or prison by the age of eighteen."

Mrs. Benetti, a practicing Catholic who was born and raised in the United States, took issue with this description: "Well... not necessarily...Not all American kids are raised like that."

"I didn't mean Alice, of course," Andrei awkwardly attempted to save face.

"Then why can't I stay?" Irina spotted a loophole. "The party's at Alice's house. Her Mom's here, watching us, aren't you Mrs. Benetti?"

"Of course," Mrs. Benetti confirmed.

"Mr. Schwarz, we're not doing anything wrong… Just reading novels and scientific journals together," Barb, with her precociously cynical sense of humor, intervened.

Irina and Alison simultaneously gave her a warning look.

"Can't I stay, Daddy? Pleeeease… ?" Irina relied upon her favorite method, begging, since such persistence usually paid off with her mother.

Andrei, however, was less flexible: "Irina, please don't argue with me. Your curfew is 10:00 p.m. and you know it. Those are our family rules. As long as you live in our house, you must abide by our rules. Period."

"At least let me stay 'till midnight! " Irina latched on to one last hope. "American girls have a later curfews in junior high than I have in high school. That's just not fair!" her eyes welled up with tears of indignation.

"Well, you're not an American girl!" Andrei delivered his final verdict a bit too proudly, causing Mrs. Benetti to feel that her own chauvinism against recent immigrants was warranted. Irina felt so embarrassed that she couldn't even say goodbye to her friends. She followed her father to the car in sullen silence.

"We have some news about Radu," Andrei announced.

Irina felt that her parents behavior was very unfair. After all, it was Radu who was missing and they were subjugating her instead.

"We can't find our son and we're not going to lose our only daughter as well," Andrei confirmed her hypothesis. Since coming to the United States, Irina felt like an overprotected, confined—practically imprisoned—teenager who was, furthermore, a poor substitute for her brother. How she wished she could have normal, American parents, like Alice and Barbara did—well, sort of, since Barb's parents were divorced and no longer on speaking terms. She resolved not to say another word to her father and go on a hunger strike—meaning no food, other than the three slices of pizza and two Twinkies she had had at Alice's, until tomorrow—in protest of the public humiliation she had suffered.

When she got home, a man she had never seen before was seated at the dinner table. Her mother appeared more cheerful than usual, revolving around the mystery guest with pots filled with steamy Romanian dishes.

"More sarmale?" she asked, placing five little grape leaf dumplings upon the man's already overflowing plate before he even opened his mouth to defend himself.

The guest, a thin man with graying hair and round glasses, patted his stomach with an apologetic air. He spoke perfect English with a slight French accent: "Your sarmale are wonderful, Mrs. Schwarz, but I'm afraid I can't take another bite. I've already gained five kilos just from your delicious dinner."

Eva mistook his graceful refusal for a compliment and, out of an exaggerated sense of hospitality, plopped a ladle-full of mamaliga--or corn meal--on his plate. Irina felt momentary solidarity with the guest. Nobody's wishes are ever respected in this household, she thought.

"Jean-Pierre, this is my daughter, Irina," Andrei presented her. "Hi," Irina said unenthusiastically. So this was the famous Jean-Pierre, Irina thought. They had expected his visit ever since Doina first mentioned him to her mother in Italy almost four years ago, but it was delayed for various reasons—or was it pretexts?--each time.

"Jean-Pierre tells us he's been in touch with Radu many times since his disappearance," Eva briefed her daughter.

Irina remained skeptical. "Oh yeah?" she answered, insolently popping a bubble of chewing gum she had put in her mouth in the car, knowing that got on her father's nerves. Was this guy trying to get money from her parents? If so, given they survived on her father's small salary and still bought food on coupons, he was definitely barking up the wrong tree.

Eva, on the other hand, was bursting with hope: "Jean-Pierre confirms that Raducu's safe! He can't tell us the details of Radu's current whereabouts, but he's told us that the CIA saved him from the clutches of the Secret Police." She leaned towards Irina and whispered in her ear: "But don't tell anybody about this, it's top secret information, you understand? Only the immediate family can know about this. We told everyone else that Radu is a diplomat. Don't even tell Grandma Marta and Grandpa Mihai the real truth, since their phone is bugged. And certainly don't mention anything to *the vultures*," Eva added with empahsis, referring to the tiny yet tightly-knit Romanian community in Ann Arbor, which met regularly mainly to exchange ideas about the degradation of American culture, the superiority of Eastern European education and--the highlight of their get-togethers--gossip about the improper sexual activities of each other's teenage daughters.

"I'm not stupid, Mom," Irina objected.

Despite the inherent delicacy of the subject, Eva and Andrei wanted to know more. When could they see their son? They miss him so much. Given that he's still hunted by the *Securitate*, it would be too dangerous to set up a meeting at this point, Jean-Pierre replied.

Upon hearing that, a look of sadness shadowed Eva's face. "We haven't seen our only son for so many years now…" she pleaded.

"But doesn't he call you regularly?" Jean-Pierre asked, obviously already aware of that fact.

"Every once in awhile. But you understand… that's not the same as seeing him, as spending time with him. We miss Radu, in flesh and blood. Please help us set up a meeting with him," Eva insisted.

"I'll see what I can do," Jean-Pierre replied. "As I'm sure Radu explained to you over the phone, since the Secret Police was after him even abroad, we went through a lot of trouble to give him a new identity. All that would come to naught if somehow they identified him while he was with you."

Eva nodded, without seeming convinced. "You think the *Securitate* is following us even here?" she asked.

"Quite possibly. At any rate, why would you want to the risk?"

"Because we want to see our son," Andrei reinforced his wife's message.

"Have you heard about the most recent incident?" Jean-Pierre appeared to change the subject.

"What incident?" Eva asked.

"A few months ago a Political Science professor at the University of Illinois was killed in his office, after hours, by a janitor. It turns out that the janitor was a fellow Romanian, a *Securitate* agent, and the reason for the crime was the fact that the professor had spoken against the Petrescu regime in his classes and at conferences. As you well know, Radu has done a lot worse than that and they have even more of an incentive to track him down," Jean-Pierre told the already exceedingly worried parents.

"So that means we'll never see Radu again?" Eva inquired, with a sense of desperation.

"Not necessarily," Jean-Pierre answered, not wishing to sound too discouraging. "But a face-to-face meeting has to be planned very carefully, so as not to place Radu or the organization he works for in jeopardy."

Eva and Andrei were visibly disappointed with this noncommittal response.

Jean-Pierre calmly removed an envelope from the inner pocket of his jacket. "The important thing is that your son is alive and well and in good hands now. He has asked me to give you this letter," he extended the envelope to Eva.

Chapter 27

Irina noticed her mother's hands tremble as Eva ripped open the envelope and took out Radu's letter.

"My dearest parents and sister, by the time you read this letter you have already met Jean-Pierre, the artist and friend who saved my life," Eva began reading in Romanian.

"It's his handwriting, Andrei!" she exclaimed. "I'd recognize it among a million! He still writes with these rounded letters, like a little boy."

"What does he say?" Irina asked impatiently. She looked at Jean-Pierre, beginning to feel intrigued. So he was a real spy? She scrutinized the artist's face so intently that he noticed and smiled at her. She looked away with embarrassment. In spite of his spectacles and slight frame, which hadn't impressed her initially, Irina now thought she saw a definite resemblance between Jean-Pierre and Roger Moore.

"My dear parents and sister," Eva retraced her steps, "by the time you read this letter you have probably already met Jean-Pierre, the artist and friend who saved my life and introduced me to the Agency. Mom, I can almost hear you sigh and say 'I warned him not to get involved in politics!' True, if I had followed your advice and stuck to studying chemistry in Paris, my life would have been a lot less complicated. And yes, I could have chosen more judiciously my girlfriend. Next time I fall in love—if there's even going to be a next time—I'll be sure to avoid Romanian women. They're nothing but trouble."

"How can he joke about what happened to him?" Eva couldn't resist making the editorial remark. She then continued reading out loud:

"Still, I must say, I have the same philosophy as Frank Sinatra—as I recall, one of your favorites, Dad—that, no matter how much trouble I may get myself into, at least I can honestly say that 'I did it my way.' Even though, technically speaking, my life is still pretty much directed by others. But at least that's the result of my own choices. Ever since leaving Romania, I've dreamt of being able to at least try to make a difference in our country. That's why the Radio Freedom Europe job appealed to me. The fact that the Secret Police thugs roughed me up was quite motivational as well. I'm very grateful to the Agency for having saved my life and want to do my best to make them—and you-- proud.

Of course, this life of a spy isn't like in the novels and, unfortunately, even less so like in the movies. Most of what I do is pretty boring, and what sounds exciting—people promising you the earth and sky in exchange for money or other benefits-- usually turns out to be false leads. As you used to tell me, Dad, if something sounds too good to be true, it probably is.

I already told you about how well the Romanian Secret Police treated me. Given the choice between the carrot and the stick, they sure don't hesitate to opt for the stick. The CIA usually dangles the carrot first. Yet, strangely enough—or maybe I was naïve getting into this—they're driven by a similar logic. Recruit as many "scalps" as possible—which means get as many foreigners as you can to risk their lives and sell out their native countries. Identify people's top vulnerabilities, and give them whatever it takes—bribes, sex, money—to get them to work on behalf of America. It's a very patriotic job!"

Eva looked up from the letter. "Good thing he's writing us in Romanian. Because what he says about the CIA isn't exactly flattering," she commented in her native tongue, looking first at her husband and then furtively at Jean-Pierre, as if fearing he might understand Romanian. She then continued reading:

"Almost every time we talk on the phone, Dad, you ask me how I ended up switching careers from chemistry to foreign intelligence."

"You rebelled against us, that's how!" Andrei interjected.

"I never really answered your question," Eva read on. "In the beginning, I felt that this job was a natural continuation of my work at Radio Freedom Europe. After all, it's based upon similar premises: criticizing communism and the Petrescu regime and praising democratic principles. This was not a tough thing to do—except, of course, for the risk to life and limb-- since it entailed saying exactly what I believed.

Once I became a foreign agent working for the CIA, however, things didn't prove quite so easy. First of all, because most of my missions were back in Romania, where as we well know, the Secret Police was quite literally out to get me. Second, because I had no real protection. I was only an agent on a limited budget hired for specific missions, not a CIA officer with a steady income, extra money and a fancy car at my disposal. So the next logical step I took was to try out for a promotion—by applying to become a real CIA officer, with all the prestige, stability (in this business, it's a relative term...) and perks that come with such a job. "

Andrei seemed puzzled. "I didn't know there was a difference... In my mind, a spy's a spy."

"And it boils down to the same dangerous life, which I wish he'd have stayed away from," Eva completed her husband's thought.

By now, Radu would have probably concurred with his mother. But two and a half years earlier he was more innocent—or at least more desperate. Fearing that the *Securitate* would eventually catch up with him in Europe, Radu decided to follow Jean-Pierre's advice--that a deeper commitment to the Agency would result in greater protection—and sent in his formal application to the CIA. The application turned out to be almost as thick as *War and Peace*, only harder to get through. Radu hesitated in his answers, not knowing how much to reveal. He wondered: Will they be impressed by my dealings with Ioana, or would they completely write me off as a result? Ultimately he decided to skip that episode, telling himself that he wasn't really lying by omission since they already knew about it anyway. After filling out the 35 page document, however, he no longer felt as confident about being a shoo-in.

To his surprise, Radu was invited to an interview and informational meeting in Washington D.C. He was put up at the Sheraton in McLean, Virginia and was told to report to the CIA building the following morning. The first order of business at the orientation was viewing a welcome video which informed the applicants that,

"There's hardly any more diverse, complex and truly worldwide organization than the CIA. As our name indicates, our primary concern is intelligence, that is, information that helps protect the security interests of the United States. The scope of this intelligence includes virtually every kind of information from all parts of the world—economic, political, military, scientific information about people, places, and events. Events that have happened and might happen. Wars, coups, terrorist acts, crop failures, elections, famine, drug trafficking, and natural disasters. All of these events and many more worldwide are of concern to the CIA."

The word "coup" in particular caught Radu's attention. He didn't know if he could do much for famines but, last time he checked, the term "election" was still understood as "one-party rule" or "choosing among one candidate" in Romania. Thus the idea of a "coup" sounded quite appealing.

Theoretically speaking, Radu was ready for the next part of the orientation—a complete physical, which included a drug test, followed by the infamous psychological exam. He passed the physical with flying colors, but got stumped on the True/False part of the psychological exam which was filled with ambiguously phrased questions such as "I rarely torture small animals." Maybe they assume that, in moderation, torture is okay, Radu postulated, confidently marking "True."

He felt especially nervous about how to respond to comments such as "I was never involved with a person detrimental to U.S. interests" and "Neither I nor my family were members of the Communist Party." What choice did we have in Romania? he thought. The polygrapher, Sherry, a woman in her mid-fifties with short hair who apparently couldn't even fake a smile, however, wasn't all that sympathetic to Radu's special circumstances. "Just answer: Yes or No, True or False?" she insisted. After a brief hesitation the young man blurted out "No!" The polygraph machine must have experienced a sudden spasm, since the next day Radu was cordially invited to the psychiatrist's office. Dr. Schule was an elderly gentleman who wore dark-rimmed glasses and had the aura of a distinguished German scholar. As a matter of fact, Radu could have sworn that the doctor was related to Freud himself.

"Congratulations! You passed with flying colors," Dr. Schule announced. Before Radu could celebrate the good news, however, the psychiatrist added, "except, unfortunately, for the poly ... There you evinced psychological reactions."

"Of what kind?" Radu didn't want to say anything incriminating unless it was absolutely necessary.

"Of the non-truthful variety," Dr. Schule clarified.

Radu looked like the picture of innocence. "It says I lied? About what?"

"You tell me," Dr. Schule answered calmly, leaning against the edge of his desk.

The young man felt compelled to tell him about Ioana. He also explained that since the dictator's daughter was the head of the science institute where his father had worked, his parents were obliged to join the communist party—at least if they wanted to keep their jobs.

"Why didn't you disclose this information on the exam?" Dr. Schule asked.

"Because I wanted to get the CIA job," Radu replied. To his surprise, the doctor seemed sympathetic to this justification. He even saw a way in which Radu's communist contacts might come in handy—"You might be a perfect fit for the FRD," he informed him.

"What's that?"

"The Foreign Resources Division—a branch of the new Domestic Resources Division."

"Oh, that one!" This was the first time Radu had heard about either of them.

"They're the branches of the DO which recruit people to spy for our government," Dr. Schule elaborated. "The officers affiliated with the FRD operate under commercial cover, pretending to work for private companies. Each CIA officer has three aliases —one as businessman, one as ordinary government employee and one as CIA officer."

"Fantastic! That means I'll get three salaries," Radu declared cheerfully.

"I'm afraid not, since two of the jobs are covers. You'd get paid only for being a CIA officer."

"But why do you consider this kind of job particularly right for me?" the young man asked.

"Because the Foreign Resources Division targets Soviet block countries and the Chinese. You could visit and recruit some of your former communist party friends. You know, rely upon your parents' connections."

Radu thought that he'd have to respectfully decline this gracious offer. He knew full well that many of his family's "communist party friends" were actually informants, who might get a Rolex or, if lucky, even a Mercedes for his head.

"I prefer to work under cover," he prudently declared.

"The Agency decides how you work, where you work and when you work," the psychiatrist responded.

This turned out to be an understatement, Radu later realized.

"Only once I actually started working for the Agency full-time," Eva continued reading her son's letter, "did I come to see how difficult it was to lead such a secretive life. I got a new identity, so that the *Securitate* wouldn't be able to trace my whereabouts. Pretty much everything I do is considered classified information. If I don't report to my superior every eight hours, I set off an emergency situation. On the positive side though, life as an agent is a lot like living in Romania under the Petrescu regime, so at least I'm used to the system."

"Good thing we went through all that trouble to escape communism so our children could live in freedom," Andrei remarked to his wife, who let out a sigh and finished reading her son's letter:

"I'm writing to let you know that I'm doing well and not to worry, since I have every intention to stay alive. I miss and love you all very much. By the way, Irina, a word of brotherly advice: continue your studies, and whatever you decide to do in college, please stay away from the CIA recruitment booth.

Yours,
Radu

PS: Irina, this time I'm *not* kidding!"

While her parents exchanged a worried look, Irina's eyes shone with excitement. She stole furtive glances at Jean-Pierre. Perhaps it would not be such a bad idea to keep in touch with him, she thought. Who knows? Maybe one day he'll help me lead an interesting and exciting life, like Radu's. As her curiosity about her brother's secret life expanded, her opinion of her own safe existence diminished. All of a sudden, a normal teenage life in provincial American suburbia seemed much too small and insignificant to Irina.

Part II

Chapter 1

On March 1st 1987, the last gust of a winter storm, now depleted of snow but still hitting otherwise cozy Collins College with unusual Arctic, ten below zero temperatures, sunk its teeth into Paul's defenseless back, propelling him forward unto the Department of Art History's sidewalk like a Mary Poppins minus the children, self-confidence and umbrella. In his haste that morning, Paul had grabbed his fall coat by mistake—a navy blue windbreaker that he had bought almost ten years ago. His philosophy was: if it still fits, why toss it? Besides, on this chilly afternoon, he had more important matters than coats on his mind.

"Those damn technocrats.That's it! I'm moving to Thailand," the young professor muttered under his breath, walking as fast as he could while carrying a large box full of office supplies in his arms. That box carried the precious contents of his academic career: brand new art history textbooks (free instructor's copies); coffee table books with worn-out covers; slides, pencils and pens; department letterhead (just in case they changed their minds), and dozens of ragged-looking articles worn out by age, dust and neglect. Walking behind all this volume, Paul couldn't see that well ahead and was obliged to turn his body a little sideways, which made him limp a little more than usual as most of his weight shifted upon his bad leg. Well, "bad" relatively speaking, since the good leg wasn't doing too well either. Although on principle Paul parked two miles off campus (Europeans walk instead of driving, that's why they're not obese), he wasn't exactly what you might call in top shape. For one thing, he had congenitally poor circulation, which made it painful for him to stand or even sit down for an extended period of time. When teaching, he constantly shifted his weight from one leg to the other to ease the pain, as one might toss a hot potato from one hand to the other to cool it off.

Despite this minor circulation problem, however, at thirty-five, from afar (say, about 30 feet away), Paul still resembled an adolescent boy. Slight in stature, his dark wavy hair usually uncombed (why voluntarily pull out your hair? at least let genetics do the job), dressed in bright, preferably yellow colored Izod T-shirts and jeans he wore nearly every day for a year (his motto was, if the crotch is still intact, don't replace them), Paul was, if not actually youthful, then at the very least ageless. Eager to escape the embarrassment he had just suffered at the hands of his peers and encouraged by the strong wind moving in his direction, he walked so fast that he didn't even have time to contemplate with sufficient attention the bundled up coed speeding past him in boots with stiletto heels. Geesh! That was almost a head-on collision, Paul thought, protecting his precious box. Then a sad truth dawned on him: there's no escape from temptation ... Even though he couldn't see the girl's face or body, for someone who knew a thing or two about Freudian fetish theory, those stilettos looked pretty suggestive...

And that was the root of the problem, though, to his chagrin, everyone kept blaming it on him. How is a hot-blooded man supposed to resist all these barely legal, hardly clad coeds wearing even in the dead of winter skin-tight jeans, low cut blouses that exposed well-developed chests along with bellybuttons flashing something that resembled nose rings in the midst of flat, little stomachs with navels that just beckoned for kisses? (Not that Paul paid attention to any of that) Nevertheless, his principled argument remained: how could the Sexual Harassment Special Committee fail to take into account all this irresistible provocation and place the blame so squarely upon the sloping shoulders of an innocent man? Had he not always struggled as hard as humanly possible to abide by the rules in the face of constant, unrelenting temptation? After all, he was teaching in an all-girls school, which should have at the very least been considered "attenuating circumstances."

Paul was appalled by the injustice of the American system of higher education and what he called, for once agreeing with the Republicans, "political correctness." Never mind that he, himself had written a few articles on feminist readings of "Renoir's Phallocentric Gaze" in the days preceding tenure. For as everyone knows, pre-tenure is pre-tending while post-tenure is...well, somewhat closer to truth. Besides, theory's one thing and practice's quite another. It's not like Marx, a bourgeois himself, would have been thrilled to be killed by the scruffy proletariat in an actual communist revolution. Let the future generation of middle-class men suffer; in practice, Marx and Paul both shared pretty much the same philosophy as Louis XIV, the Sun King: "Après moi, le deluge." Following this natural course, the older Paul got, the more sympathetic he became to the male gaze. If even looking at girls is forbidden, one might as well be blind or imprisoned in Siberia. That's not, Paul pursued a rebuttal in his own head, how the truly civilized societies where he had traveled—Thailand, Japan, Brazil, Italy and France--dealt with normal, heterosexual male desire. Thailand, Paul thought, was particularly progressive in its treatment of young women.

Besides, what exactly were they accusing him of? Harassment? How absurd! Female students always seduced him. It's true that during the past few years he had sexual relations with two students while they were still taking his class, "Desire, the Male Gaze and Modernism," a departmental requirement. But he was, as in the Muslim tradition, quite honorable about it: at least he had married one of them. Since his first marriage was going down the tubes, he might have married the second one as well had she not filed a sexual harassment suit against him. Obviously, Paul felt, he showed more heart than the male members of the Sexual Harassment Committee, who, he suspected, waited to have affairs after the course was over, then dumped the poor girls. At least he became emotionally attached to them. Which was precisely the cause of his tragic downfall. What hypocrisy governs this world. What injustice! Take Dan Rothstein, for instance, the scrawny-looking guy who was most preachy about Paul's measly infraction during the sexual harassment hearings.

Paul could swear on any stack of Bibles—though he didn't have any at his disposal since he was Catholic only philosophically-- that Rothstein had had flings with at least three of his grad students. One could see it from the way, a few years ago, as soon as he got tenure, Dan insisted on becoming Graduate Student Advisor in the Department of Art History's Masters Program, even though that had been, by all rights, Paul's domain. At first Paul felt somewhat territorial about this particularly pleasant department function, but then, when he found out that he was going to become Undergraduate Student Advisor, he suddenly became generous: "He can have it! I get along better with the undergrads anyways," he consoled himself.

And that's how Paul took on this administrative responsibility for which he was particularly well suited but which, unfortunately, landed him into a whole heap of trouble. He had always felt grad students were too old and jaded for him. They talked the right jargon, acted strategically—in a way intended to maximize chances of navigating department egos and actually obtaining a degree—and frankly, they just didn't look all that young anymore, at least not in the eyes of a man whose second favorite novel was *Lolita*. Besides, he felt that the gothic uniform of dyed black hair, rouge and heavy eyeliner that was quite the rage in art history departments for the past hundred years or so didn't do the female sex justice. Skin like a peach and you spoil it with make up, Stendhal, a writer who knew a thing or two about feminine beauty, wrote in his discourse *On Love*.

Paul liked to quote him—at least mentally—every time he noticed a young woman wearing heavy makeup and, by way of contrast, took positive note of all the little undergrads who subscribed to his preferred beauty regime: no makeup, short plaid skirts, cute and lovely and readily described in terms of nineteenth-century metaphors (preferably angels, porcelain dolls or flower buds). Paul liked Romanticism so much that, after obtaining tenure, he courageously specialized in two much-neglected and unjustly debased artists that used to reign supreme in nineteenth-century French Academic art before the less competent Impressionists took over: Cabanel and Bouguereau. What technique! Polished, smooth pictures of young women, erotic yet angelic; a nudity you could almost touch, especially after putting it on a diet (since, as far as weight was concerned, Paul preferred modern conceptions of beauty, preferably those modeled after anorexia nervosa victims and the model Twiggy).

Despite its inexplicable plumpness fetish, Paul had to give nineteenth-century Academic art its due: what fascinating essays on the male gaze could be written about it! A whole career of scholarship could turn upon Bouguereau's "The Young Shepardess" (1885), a masterpiece filled with adolescent yearnings and, better yet, "The Broken Pitcher" (1891) where the virginity symbolism was even more fertile. In those days, Paul lamented, adolescent girls still had pitchers to be broken; now you'd have to take a damn pottery class just to find one intact cereal bowl.

To express a challenge to the current academic system which frowned upon real art, a year ago Paul put up on his office door a poster of Bouguereau's "Nymphaeum" (1878). This famous painting featured thirteen young women, all about college age, engaging in normal middleclass women's activities which must have been quite common during the Victorian era: such as posing naked in various uncomfortable positions that exhibited for public display the erotic parts of their bodies. This revival of sensuality and beauty in the Collins Art History Department lasted about two hours, as it was immediately squelched by Judith Harrison, the Assistant Chair, who was in charge of enforcing affirmative action and sexual harassment policies. At first, Paul stood his ground:

"What about the freedom of speech?" he inquired.

"This is a painting. It doesn't speak," Judith retorted.

"I realize that. But it's expressive. It states: long live beauty, loveliness and art!"

"I don't quite see that. To me it says: Stop drooling over girls and get a life."

Used to her colleague's predilections for pretty students and consistently inappropriate remarks during faculty meetings—to the tune of "the prettiest girl gets the highest grade; after all, I've got my standards"--Judith added: "If you prefer, during parents' weekend, you could wear a sign on your back saying 'Your daughters are in good hands with me,' and they'll get pretty much the same picture as from your Bouguereau poster." But Paul couldn't disagree more. How could this painting possibly be construed as offensive to adolescent female students and their parents, he wondered, looking tenderly at the plump young bodies of those poor innocent nymphs that would be forced to go back into storage.

"I thought harems and moral relativism were back in fashion," he protested, showing that he knew a thing or two about the latest trends in Cultural Studies. The Assistant Chair's answer—inspired by the highly respected Marxist theorist Louis Althusser, who had just strangled his wife--came swift as a veto: "Not for hegemonic white men!" I can't believe they actually say such absurdities out loud, Paul muttered to himself. Annoyed by the pointless argument which she thought she had won from the beginning of Bouguereau's dated apparition upon Paul's door, Judith pirouetted back into her office.

Come to think of it, her door was adorned in a much more acceptable fashion. She proudly displayed a poster of a Cindy Sherman imitator that posed ambiguously gendered inflatable naked dolls. Underneath the artists had collectively signed the masterpiece "Art Sluts," to show that the era of phallocentric individualism was long gone. "Like this will put parents at ease," Paul thought to himself, but didn't say anything, especially since the next office over, Keith Dunkin's, the department's specialist on contemporary art, proudly displayed a none-too-ambiguous Mapplethorpe image involving a fist. And so Paul's soft porn Bouguereau poster was replaced by a stark, non-representational Rothko--horizontal tan, red and black unevenly painted stripes—whose artistic value nobody would dare challenge.

To think that this is the woman who represented my promotion case, Paul thought, feeling betrayed by Judith in more ways than one and regretting that he had ever considered her an ally and friend. A mental image of his colleague only fed his disgust: ageless timeworn face, small dark eyes that flashed with anger or impatience, dyed brown hair that, left to its own devices, would have preferred to turn white to match her nearly forty years of premature old maidhood. This was the very same Judith with whom Paul had volunteered to share an office eight years ago, when he was still clueless and naïve. How she had fooled him... In all fairness to his judgment, however, when Judith was untenured and needed Paul's support, she spoke in a softer, more feminine voice, agreed with most of what he said, and even cracked a smile or two once in awhile. The post-tenure Judith, however, was almost unrecognizable. Her first move was to demand her own office, then become Assistant Chair, schedule meetings over every burp in the department and filibuster about every point until the other faculty members, who preferred to make it home by midnight, pretended to agree with her. To think this former friend was the woman that had proved to be his undoing! She was the one Linda had contacted first; the one who brought the case to the attention of the Collins College Sexual Harassment Committee.

Paul's brief fling with nymphs on his office door was what you might call... foreshadowing. It was a manifestation of the very intellectual and artistic integrity that cost him his promotion to full professor in the first place three years ago. Had he continued to work on Impressionism and modernism like everyone else, he would have received the well-deserved raise. But now, we can safely say that the point was moot, since Paul was indefinitely suspended from teaching at Collins College.

All in all, Paul's professional path could be described as meteoric—only instead of the usual, run-of-the-mill rise, he had a meteoric fall, a much more apt use of the metaphor since meteors usually fall on Earth anyways. Paul was a promising grad student from Princeton, trained with rigor in nineteenth-century art. His dissertation, "(De)centering (re)presentations of modern visuality," was one of the first few hundred or so to demonstrate that the Impressionists were truly postmodern—subversive, decentered and deconstructive—though, poor souls, they didn't know it, which made all the art history scholars, by implication, much smarter than them. Having published a ground-breaking article on "Impressionism and Visuality" in graduate school, Paul proceeded to get four job offers: Harvard, Yale, Columbia and Collins College.

As the message from its president still indicates, Collins College is an all-girl school in cosmopolitan Roanoke, Virginia where "friendships thrive, minds catch fire, careers begin, and hearts open to a world of possibility." How could any heterosexual man in his right mind resist the invitation of being surrounded by pretty young girls, with open hearts to a world of possibilities to boot? Based strictly upon academic considerations, Paul selected Collins College, a decision he would have never regretted had it not been for the school's arbitrary gender policies.

"Now where the heck did I park?" he wondered, looking for the usual spot where he left his car for the past ten years. "Here it is!" he sighed with relief recognizing the little pale blue Toyota Camry, frozen at the seams yet so familiar and enchanting, that he simply couldn't bear to let her go. Which was fortunate since now he'd have no money to part from her anyways. At first he couldn't open the door--the key was frozen in the bolt-- then he jiggled it nervously until it relented, threw the overflowing big box of art history stuff on the passenger seat, and, after a few wheezing tries, started the ignition. Well, at least he had lived life to the fullest and had no regrets, Paul told himself, without finding his own Edith Piaf "Non, je ne regrette rien" attitude entirely convincing. Come to think of it, what had he lived through? Let's see: a failed marriage, a disastrous extramarital affair and an academic career which was going down the drain. Nothing to write home about, he concluded.

Paul honked the horn, stopped abruptly and muttered shit! in polite French at several jaywalking students. Collins students tended to cross the street in much the same fashion as geese, without following pointless signs such as walk and don't walk. Drivers had adapted to this practice: when students crossed the street it meant stop and when students weren't crossing, which usually occurred between 2:00 a.m. and 8:00 a.m. –except for weekends-- then they could go.

By instinct—a kind of backwards one which he seemed to follow quite often (despite solid evidence that it never worked in his favor)—Paul headed straight for Lloyd Residence Hall, which is where Linda Dubrovsky resided. As usual when he visited Linda, he drove around waiting for someone to vacate a parking place in a convenient location close to Lloyd, then parallel parked in a half hour parking space, since it hardly ever took longer than that.

Although seeing Linda might elevate the charge of harassment to stalking, Paul was willing to take that chance. He considered it his moral duty to get to the bottom of things. Frankly, he couldn't understand why the girl who had breathed I love you in his ear only three weeks ago had turned him in to his nemesis, Judith Harrison. What did he ever do to her? Didn't she end up getting an A- in his class? Paul wanted to talk to Linda directly, not in the presence of all those accusatory strangers, to at least understand why she was hell bent on destroying his life.

He thrust his hands in his thin, foil-like pockets, since his fall coat was not much more than a windbreaker and his gloves were safe at home, nestling in his winter coat. Although his fingers didn't find any solace from the biting cold, they did get scratched by a ruffled piece of paper he had carried around with him during the past week. It was the college's Sexual Harassment Policy. He peered at it in disbelief, as if the paper itself, like a bad lawyer, had betrayed him. He read the Code for the nth time, though by now he could recite it backwards and forwards, interjecting at the appropriate places his own irrefutable defense.

"Sexual harassment is a form of sex discrimination that violates Title VII of the Civil Rights Act of 1964." So this is when the insanity started… "Sexual harassment is defined as unwelcome sexual requests for sexual favors and other verbal or lewd physical conduct of a sexual nature" What are they talking about? We had consensual sex; there never was any lewd physical conduct! Paul's annoyed gaze surveyed further the crumpled paper.

"a) The conduct is made as a term or condition of an individual's employment, education, living environment or participation in a University community." So now they say one can't date one's own students? That's outrageous! Who in the world is a heterosexual man supposed to date at an all–girl college in a small town in the middle of Nowhere-ke, Virginia? Have they even bothered to take a look at the female faculty? Of course, this line of defense was somewhat weakened by the fact that Paul was already married. But the bottom line is, Paul had protested, that legally speaking harassment consists of unwelcome overtures, whereas in this case, Linda had welcomed him with open arms (not to mention legs) and even wanted a serious relationship, which kind of spoiled the whole fling (he omitted the latter part of the statement from his actual defense).

"b) The acceptance or refusal of such conduct is used as the basis or a factor in decisions affecting an individual's employment, education, living environment, or participation in a University community." What exactly is she complaining about? I never threatened anything and even gave her a solid A-, despite the fact she couldn't even spell her own name, let alone Van Gogh's.

"c) The conduct unreasonably impacts an individual's employment or academic performance or creates an intimidating, hostile or offensive environment, or participation in a University community." Now that's the clause that applies least of all to me, Paul thought. I was never hostile or offensive. I just told her we had to break up since she was, after all, my student and I was going through serious marital problems.

They always blame the victim, Paul concluded, recalling how it all began. For one thing, Linda came voluntarily to his office hours to discuss future careers in art history. As the official Undergraduate Student Advisor, Paul was the obvious expert on the subject. On that fateful day, Linda, a student in his theory of art class, knocked briefly on his door, then proceeded to enter his office before he even got the chance to say "Come in."

"Hi," she greeted him and he instantly recognized the only B- in the class. Since grade inflation was rampant at Collins (in respectful emulation of the Ivy Leagues), Paul felt it would be unfair to his students—and even more so to his own student evaluations—to give anything lower than B range grades. "I pretend to teach; they pretend to learn," was his pedagogical philosophy. For once, his practice was on the same wavelength as that of his colleagues—though they would never admit it-- since at Collins College a B- was really a D. You had to work hard to obtain such a rare distinction. Quite reasonably, Paul initially thought that Linda had come to complain about her grade, so he immediately preempted her: "Congratulations on your last essay. It wasn't half-bad!" So what if it wasn't half-good either?

"Thanks. My folks were proud that I finally managed to get a B. I worked hard on that essay!" Linda responded with a friendly smile. Paul couldn't help but notice that her teeth were a little crooked but dazzling white; she had these amazing almond-shape green eyes and her blond hair was so frizzy that it stuck out like rays of sunshine.

"So then you're not here to talk about your grade?" he wanted to make sure he was, indeed, completely off the hook.

"Why would I? I'm pretty happy with it," Linda reassured him.

"Then please, sit down," he pointed to a chair two feet away from his.

Linda dropped into the seat, one leg folded underneath her crotch in a semi-yoga position.

"So. What did you want to talk about?" Paul looked at Linda regaining complete composure while stealing glances at her unusual skin-tight jeans which had long zippers running down both sides, from waistline to ankle. He couldn't help but wonder, in a purely hypothetical fashion that spoke strictly to his mechanical curiosity, if one could unpeel those jeans from her body by a simple tug of the zipper. Linda must have noticed his subtle stare, since she addressed that very issue:

"Cool, huh? These are my rock concert jeans. But they're good for school too. Very easy to get in and out of," she explained.

Paul heroically attempted to change the subject and get back on track: "Is there anything you wanted to… clarify about today's lecture?"

"What lecture?" Linda slipped, since she hadn't gone to class. The alarm clock didn't ring, most likely for the usual reason, namely, that it hadn't been set.

"You know, the one on Pulvey, visuality and the male gaze,"

"Sorry, I must of missed that one," she coyly confessed. "But you know," her face brightened, "I don't really need any lecturing on the male gaze. I handle that stuff all the time." She's so pretty when she's modest, Paul thought, interjecting a little irony into his admiration of the student's unvarnished beauty, just to cool himself off a little. She was petite yet curvy, with the compact little body of an athlete.

"Do you play any sports?" he wondered out loud.

"I used to do gymnastics," Linda responded.

That's always nice to know, Paul thought.

"But I'm too busy with school now, so I dropped it," she added.

"That's too bad..." Paul said with genuine regret, envisioning all the plasticity of a youthful female body trained by gymnastics.

"Well... I may pick it back up. It's just that school's hard enough, and gymnastics takes a lot of discipline. At least three hours of practice a day."

"I imagine so..."

"Actually, the reason I came here was... I was wondering if you could advise me ... you know, on what I can do with a major in art. My Dad thinks I should go into something more practical, like business. He says—no offense—that art history's a waste of money. But there's probably lots of things I could do if I major in art, right?"

"I'm not a career counselor," Paul began with his usual disclaimer, "But I can tell you from experience that the world is your oyster with a degree in Art History."

"Really?" Linda sounded very surprised. "Well, I want to do something ... wild and interesting," she specified her academic requirements.

"Well, for one thing, you could become an art history professor," Paul indicated what he considered to be the most desirable career choice in the world. He failed to mention, however, the little detail that about one in one thousand graduates actually landed a good job.

Linda didn't seem too impressed. Her easy-going attitude faded, but she tried to remain diplomatic: "I meant... nothing boring or anything," she replied, then corrected herself: "Not that teaching's boring, of course. But I was just hoping to, you know, live a little, travel, meet people. Do things," she emphasized.

Paul felt a little stung: "Why don't you become a stewardess or waitress then?" he suggested, not meaning to sound condescending, but thinking that it involved traveling and wearing tight clothes, which seemed to be Linda's strong suits.

"But... how does that relate to a degree in Art History?" she wanted to know. "I mean, I could do that kind of stuff right out of high school. My dad invested lots of money in my education. So I want to do something that relates directly to art. French art specifically," she added and this time Paul felt flattered.

"Let's see... You could work in a museum," he proposed.

Linda dismissed the idea with a casual wave of the hand: "Nah, I wouldn't like that. You have to memorize all this stuff ... when everyone lived, when they died, what they did, their names, the titles of their paintings.... I can't handle so much information. You might have noticed, memorization's not my thing. That's why I flunked the introduction to art history the first time I took it, you know, with Professor Harrison. Thank God you passed me the second time around or else my Dad would have freaked!" Linda shifted uncomfortably in her seat and started flipping nervously her left zipper. Paul's eyes fixated on that dangling piece of metal, that lucky dog, lying so close to Linda's hip.

"Well, if art history's not your thing," he repeated part of her phrase, "then why are you majoring in it?"

Linda looked up, contemplating his question. "I don't know... It sounded kind of interesting," she finally came up with the precise reason, the same one that had impressed her father so much that it got him wondering why he was wasting his money on college tuition in the first place.

Paul felt they were grasping at straws, but didn't mind Linda's company. "Is there something about French culture in particular that strikes your fancy?" he asked, searching for another angle.

"Yeah," Linda's face brightened. "They have, you know, what did you call it in class? Jouissance?"

Paul worried for a moment that Linda must have read his mind. It occurred to him, however, that she might be confusing the word "orgasm" for another term: "You mean joie de vivre?" he asked, rolling the rr's, proud of his perfect pronunciation of French.

"That's right!" Linda said. "They like to have fun. So, aside from the fact that they're a bit snooty and hate Americans, the French are kind of cool."

"Maybe you could take a few language courses and work in France," Paul suggested, since he had studied both literature and art history in Paris—Jussieu, Paris VII to be exact-- and had become bilingual and, even more exceptionally for an American, one hundred percent Francophile.

"Nooo...." Linda turned down the suggestion, opening her mouth into an oval. "Spanish was more than enough for me, thank you very much! Foreign languages are not my thing either. We're going back to the original problem of memorization, you see."

"Ah, yes," Paul replied, running out of ideas.

Linda stood up with her natural flexibility and ease, arched her back like gymnasts springing from a summersault—though they probably wouldn't expose a bellybutton ring as cute as hers—and declared: "Well, gotta go now, but... maybe we can talk about this later, you know, over coffee."

"Was I just asked out on a date?" Paul wondered, not believing his good fortune. "Sure!" he answered enthusiastically, since he wasn't one to play hard to get. But then he felt that, from closed-minded people's perspective, there might be something inappropriate about going out with his own student, so he

          Reincarnations of Love

added: "We'll make another appointment for undergraduate advising," to cover his bases.

Linda picked up her neon green back pack which she had dropped on the floor next to his chair, then fluttered a friendly bye-bye before she closed the door behind her. When the student was gone, Paul basked in her energy and thought she was exactly what he needed. Lovely arms, lean, flexible, muscular gymnast's legs wrapped around his body, soothing his desires and absorbing his anxieties. His marriage might be in shambles, his wife might be a hysterical nutcase, but he was not alone. As long as there were pretty girls in this wretched world, by God, he was not alone!

Chapter 2

Paul slipped his university ID card through the security detector and entered Linda's residence hall. He had some misgivings—what if she'll charge me with stalking or something vaguely occurred to him—but since he'd never been in jail and couldn't fully imagine the unpleasantness of the experience, he took his chances. Squeezing his way past two girls chatting on the stairway, he climbed up to the second floor, Room 205 to be exact, two steps at a time, thinking to himself, "As long as I climb like this, I'm still a spring chicken." Which is pretty much how he had viewed the whole affair with Linda. Seeing how his marriage wasn't working out, he sought a little consolation in something light, youthful and ephemeral.

After their initial meeting, the courtship with Linda didn't take long to bloom. They had tea together. Linda talked about her family, while Paul listened and drank her with his eyes, as the French say. She told him that her father was a successful businessman working for a car manufacturer. Her Mom had been a housewife who became a legal secretary after the divorce.

"Interesting..." Paul mused while Linda was flavoring a cup of hot water with a raspberry tea bag, absentmindedly placing the bag in and out, in and out, mesmerizing him with that rhythmic motion.

"You see, it's kind of like he wants me to be exactly like him," she was saying.

"Hmm hmm...How's that?"

"I don't know... driven. That's all he wants from life. Success."

Paul promptly identified an erroneous assumption in that statement: "But where's the problem? Can't you be successful doing art history?"

Linda gave him an incredulous look: "Come on! He means real success. You know, money, power, fame. That sort of thing."

"Yes, I'm familiar with the concept. And I take it," Paul extrapolated from Linda's grades, "that you don't want to be successful?"

Linda seemed ambivalent: "I do, but you see, I'd rather marry into it. I don't feel like living my father's life. I mean, what kind of life is that? He gets up at five in the morning, goes to work, comes home at nine at night. Sometimes even later."

"How about on weekends?" Paul ventured.

"What weekends?" Linda got riled up. "He works then too. Golf, dinner parties. Calls it networking. The thing is, he never had any time for us. That's why Mom left him. But that's another story..."

"I'd like to hear it," Paul answered, since he was always curious to discover a new woman. That was part of the thrill. Discovering not just another body, but also another being, a soul.

"I don't really want to get into it right now," Linda frowned, stirring a packet of Sweet and Low into her tea with a plastic spoon. "Maybe another time."

"When did your parents divorce?"

"Oh... when I was young."

Paul was enticed by this answer, which the very young tend to give. "And how old are you now?"

"Twenty. So," Linda calculated, "that means they split up almost ten years ago. Gosh, has it been that long?"

"Did you ever get over it?"

"They couldn't decide on custody, so the judge left it up to me. But how can a ten year old chose between her Mom and her Dad? I mean... there's no right decision." Linda's eyes welled up with tears which she wiped on her oversized sleeve. Paul felt so much sympathy for the poor girl.

"I'm sorry," he whispered sincerely.

Linda smiled through her tears then asked, to Paul's surprise: "Do you want to come to my place?"

"Pardon?"

"I don't really feel like drinking tea," Linda said by way of explanation.

"Sure, I'm up for coffee," Paul framed the invitation more properly, in case some of his colleagues or students might have been spying on him in the coffee shop.

"What? I don't even own a coffee pot," Linda said. "I just really want your company right now."

Paul looked around: "Why don't you make a public announcement?"

This comment made Linda smile: "I'm saving that for class on Monday." Which didn't exactly allay Paul's worries. But horniness, curiosity and the desire to prolong his youth proved stronger than his caution. So he followed Linda to her dorm room like a string led around by a free-flowing kite. It must have been fate.

"Do you have a roommate?" he asked upon entering the Lloyd Residence Hall with the stealthy movements of a burglar.

"No, I'm in a single. You're walking kind of funny," she observed.

"I want to be discreet," he whispered.

"You're only drawing attention to yourself. You look like that guy from *The Pink Panther*."

"Shhh.... I'm known around here!" Paul put an index finger to his mouth.

"Don't be so modest, just admit it: you're downright famous!" the student assumed a maternal tone with her nervous little professor. "You think that walking on tippy toes and looking around like a mouse makes you seem less obvious? Just act natural. Be yourself, " she urged.

"I am myself! Do I have any choice in the matter?" Paul protested.

"Alright, then pretend you're someone else. Someone normal..."

Everything was turning out exactly as Paul had wished for in his wildest fantasies, except for the confusing part that he always desired contradictory things. He wanted to stay together with his wife, but couldn't take their constant fighting and her hysteria. He wanted Linda, but not as she was--his student, somewhat needy, an underachiever, spoiled, sweet and easy to love--in other words, not in the present circumstances and with her particular characteristics. That's because Paul had a peculiar personality trait. He was driven by strong desires, yet as soon as he fulfilled any of them, he immediately began focusing on their downside. "I'm a pessimist," he used to tell his wife whenever she stumbled upon the psychological barriers he constantly set in their path and accused him of "sabotaging" their relationship. "If only you were so simple," Mary would sigh, since even the word "pessimist" didn't quite capture Paul's quirkiness. "They broke the mold when they created you," she'd tell him whenever he objected that he was just a regular guy who enjoyed sports and pretty women.

It's true that Paul could be thrilled by the slightest smile of a cute girl, by the beauty of art, by the feel of the spring breeze, by reading a good novel or watching an interesting movie as much as anybody on the most ecstasy inducing drugs. As long as everything was "in his head," as he put it, life was great. But once this mental pleasure got mixed up with the inconveniences of reality or, worse yet, real emotions, everything became more complicated, even burdensome. Then Paul would hop around trying to avoid one potential disaster after another. Which turned out to be the best strategy for making them happen. And that's precisely what occurred with Linda. From the moment she stepped into his office, he wanted her and feared his own desires. Every touch, every kiss, every tender word was mixed up with a sense of dread—oh, oh, the shit will hit the fan any minute now—which had the slight disadvantage of putting a damper on their budding romance. "Geesh... Stop being so nervous! What do you think I am?" Linda would protest when in the middle of a kiss Paul would somehow manage to whisper: "Don't breathe a word to anyone about this, you promise?"

His first reaction when stepping into Linda's room—right after Boy, this is really messy—was Wow, I'm in a room all by myself with a pretty girl. Piles of books, laundry, and scattered shoes were lying around all over the place. Yet, despite being an obsessive-compulsive neatness freak, Paul didn't seem to care. All he saw were Linda's almond shaped green eyes. The agile, graceful gestures with which she removed her clothes in a natural strip-tease mesmerized him and took his mind off, even if all too briefly, his innumerable anxieties. Her small breasts with unusually rosy nipples practically hypnotized him. He couldn't believe his good fortune and was almost afraid to touch this young woman with the body of a little gymnast--lithe, lean, flexible and indisputably made for tender kisses and embraces--for fear that she might vanish into thin air.

"I certainly have a type," he'd periodically remind his wife, who knew more about his taste in women than she cared to find out. "See that girl? The one with the curly black hair on the left?" "I'm not really interested in the details," Mary would try to preempt. "She's my type!" Paul would nonetheless declare triumphantly, as if he were announcing he had just won the Nobel Prize. "Yeah, and your point is?" his wife would try to deflate him. "And my point is... that I like small, petite, cute women. That's all I ask from life. I don't need gorgeous, *Playboy* types. I prefer cute to beautiful," he'd elaborate in a completely superfluous manner. "How many times have you told me that?" Mary would reply with impatience, not particularly fond of Paul's favorite subject. "How many times have you said 'hello' or 'Here's the grocery list?'" Paul mistakenly thought that he had an excellent rebuttal.

Well, Mary would certainly have something to be jealous about now, Paul thought, since Linda was very cute. Her diminutive figure kept boyish by gymnastics played upon all of his fetishes and even created some new ones. The delicate lace underwear that showed a peak of curly brown hair through the white lace took care of whatever was left of his scruples. Without having even touched her, he was ready for anything.

"Do you want to kiss me?" she asked, since he was just staring at her, mesmerized, without making a move and with a blank, zoned-out expression on his face which he assumed whenever he was aroused.

"If you insist," he replied.

Linda wasn't used to this particular variation of seduction: "Why do I have to insist?"

She didn't. Paul approached her, then placed his hands upon her hips, letting them glide into her barely-there panties while his tongue was already exploring the moistness of her mouth. Linda's lips tasted like raspberry tea; her body felt like a flower that gently, sweetly devoured his fingers.

"Are you on the pill?" it suddenly occurred to him to ask when they were tumbling around naked on the messy bed.

"No, I do the rhythm thing."

At this news, Paul instantly went limp. "Don't you think you should use something… that works?"

"Are you saying that you don't trust me?" Linda recoiled.

"No, I'm just saying I would trust you even more if you were on some kind of birth control."

"Well, I've always done the rhythm method and, knock on wood, never once got pregnant."

"Just how many times was there a risk?" Paul was curious to know.

"Why do you ask? Did you think I was still a virgin?" Linda's tone sounded downright sarcastic.

"No, of course not," Paul conceded, though he had actually very much hoped that were the case. Virginity went so much better with the whole innocent nymph, Bouguereau motif. "But, I was just wondering, how many boyfriends have you had?"

"Only two."

"Oh, okay." Paul felt relieved.

"The rest of them were, you know, just hook-ups."

"Maybe we should use a condom," Paul proposed.

Linda moved away from him, offended: "I told you to trust me. I know my body. Now do you wanna make love or play pharmacist?"

At the mention of the word play, Paul's good humor returned: "How about I play gynecologist instead?"

"Isn't that a bit naughty for a professor?" she flirted.

"Not if I grade you. Besides, you're long due for a thorough examination," Paul said gliding down to her mound, kissing it, parting her lips with the tip of his tongue.

Linda shifted her position, pushing her body towards his mouth. She felt caught on the border between pleasure and ticklishness. "Stop, stop!" she cried, when sensitivity got the best of her. "Oh my God, that feels so good…" she giggled. He then glided up on top of her. In the rhythm of their pleasure, his anxieties disappeared, flowing into her, absorbed, practically annihilated by her delicious little body.

A few minutes later, they were both lying on their backs, on top of the pile of hypothetically clean but, from the smell of it, most likely unwashed laundry that lay sprawled on her bed.

"He's pretty hot-- for a professor," Linda thought. "Maybe I'll get finally get an A at this freaking school."

What have I done? Jesus! I just screwed my own student. Have I completely lost my mind? was the romantic afterthought that occurred to Paul once his pressing needs were satisfied. Both were silent. Linda got up to dress; Paul went to the bathroom to clean himself. With their clothes back on, the new lovers felt more awkward than when they had been naked. They had to say something, anything, to break the silence.

"I love you," Linda went first.

"Me too," Paul answered, not to be left behind.

Something about these declarations rang almost true. They were compelled by the same loneliness to find relief and solace in one another. Six times to be exact. Before Paul, with his usual talent, ruined everything.

After a few clandestine meetings in Linda's room, Paul became increasingly nervous. What if she calls my wife? What if she talks to other students? What if we break up and she tells someone in my department? How can I trust her to be discreet? These questions obsessed him during the day, but they really simmered in his brain at night, stewing along with other thoughts, which weren't exactly conducive to a passionate affair: How can I get Mary back? he wondered, not yet prepared to give up resuscitating his comatose marriage. By the time the sixth encounter with Linda rolled around, Paul had reached a boiling point of anxiety. He arrived at her door wishing to break up before their relationship became really dangerous, yet not really sure about how to extricate himself amicably from the whole situation. He was afraid of her reaction and, to make matters worse, had grown genuinely fond of her.

Linda opened the door walking on her heels, since she was in the process of painting her toenails. Passion red, she pointed proudly with already lacquered fingers to her toes, which were glistening with bright nail polish and separated by little cotton balls.

"Great!" Paul exclaimed. "That's the last thing we need right now."

"What's that supposed to mean?" Linda asked, instinctively going on the defensive.

"Listen, we need to talk."

"Oh, oh, I've heard that line before. Right before my parents divorced, that's exactly what they said to me."

Paul felt terrible. He didn't want to hurt any woman he cared about, let alone this abandoned kid. Nevertheless, he felt he had to say something before the situation got out of control: "I'm a little concerned about the fact that... you're my student," he finally blurted out.

"Did you just find this out?" Linda raised an imperious eyebrow.

"No. But it's really starting to bother me."

"Why now?" Linda asked.

"You see, people have a sixth sense. It's impossible to hide this sort of stuff for long," Paul tried to explain.

"I'm not going to blabber to my friends about it if that's what you're implying!"

"I know."

"Then what are you so afraid of?" Linda plopped down on the edge of the bed and fanned her toes with the student paper. Paul caught a glimpse of the first-page headline—Famous artist visits Collins—and his eyes slowly replaced that title with a slightly different one—Infamous art history professor has affair with Collins student. He felt torn between Linda's sexy little painted toenails and that imaginary headline which had been obsessing him ever since the affair began.

"Let me tell you something that happened in my department last year," Paul thought of a roundabout way to explain his thinking. "Last year there were two professors in the art history department who fell in love and started dating."

Linda nodded in acknowledgement: "You mean Bob Steward and Mindy Cracken?"

Paul's eyes widened in disbelief. He knew gossip traveled fast, but was surprised to see how widely it had spread: "That's right. Well, he was tenured and she was a new Assistant Professor. They tried to keep the nature of their relationship secret, acting like friends around the department. But in a matter of days everyone knew about it. The secretary discovered them kissing in the hallway late one afternoon and told a few people, who then told a few others. By the end of the week the whole department found out. Now in their case, the situation was delicate since Bob will have input into Mindy's tenure case. But still, it wasn't that big a deal. Our situation, however, is a whole different story. If anyone found out about us, it would be a total disaster. You see what I mean?"

"So what do you propose we do about it?" Linda asked in a flat voice, resisting the implications of Paul's anecdote.

"We can stay friends, you know, platonic, until you finish my course. We've only got a month and a half or so to go."

She raised her eyes to him: "And then?"

Paul felt uncomfortable: "I don't know… We'll play it by ear."

"Play it by ear?" Linda raised her voice. "What do you think I am? A song?"

"It's just a figure of speech," Paul defended himself. He sat down on Linda's bed and tried to put his arm around her, but she pushed him away.

"Please leave!" she commanded, as firmly as she had ever said anything to him.

"Why are you behaving like this?" Paul asked, astonished by her anger. "I told you I'd stay your friend. I'm very loyal. All I'm saying is: let's wait until the semester's over, alright?" But the girl wasn't placated at all. She turned away to hide her tears.

Paul did his best to comfort her: "Linda, listen to me: in two months, we'll be free to do anything we want. Well, not exactly free since I'm married," he qualified, "but still, much freer than we are now. You understand? I can get fired for this."

Linda didn't respond or even look at him.

"I didn't make up these stupid rules," Paul said by way of apology. "Believe me, this hurts me as much as it does you," he added, but this statement rang false.

"Oh yeah? Then you shouldn't have fucked me in the first place if you thought it was wrong!" Linda exploded.

"Linda, for Christ's sake, please lower your voice! The neighbors will hear you," Paul hissed, becoming alarmed and straightening out his hair nervously, like a rooster who had just been pecked and wished to put his feathers back into place.

"It would serve you right!" Linda said.

Paul made a last desperate attempt to calm her down: "I swear I didn't mean to hurt you."

"I know. You only meant to use me."

"Not at all. I was just..." Paul started to convey his idea he was the victim in the whole affair since, after all, she had seduced him.

But Linda didn't give him the opportunity. "I asked you to get out," she repeated, in a voice so fierce that he almost didn't recognize it. Linda looked disheveled and her nail polish had smeared all over her toes. More like "blood red" than "passion red" was Paul's last impression of his young mistress as she walked over on her heels, the cotton balls still separating her toes, and unceremoniously shoved him out of her room, slamming the door in his face.

Let's hope this is not dejà-vu all over again as Yogi Berra used to say, Paul thought, bracing himself for confronting his ex-girlfriend once again. "Expect the worst and you won't be disappointed," was the motto that had saved him from many moments of untainted pleasure and hope in life. Unfortunately, this pessimist philosophy did little to diminish his many disappointments. Because, ultimately, Paul wanted to be on good terms with all the women who had left him. "When you're intimate with a woman," he once tactfully explained to his wife alluding to his ex-girlfriend, a French girl who, to his dismay, never answered his postcards after they broke up, "she becomes a part of you. Breaking up doesn't change any of that. Throwing away your memories is like throwing away your life."

Wishing to avoid such emotional waste, Paul knocked softly on Linda's door, but got no answer. He heard the hum of the blow dryer coming from her bathroom and deduced she was in. He knocked louder.

"Yeees? Who is it?" Linda answered back in a melodious voice which he recognized as "the old Linda," meaning before ruining life.

"It's me."

"Who?"

"Paul, " he answered in a voice that indicated he wasn't too proud of that fact, but there was nothing he could do to change it.

Linda cracked open the door but didn't let him in.

"What are you doing here?" she asked, looking surprised and a little concerned.

"I just want to know, why did you tell Judith about us?"

Linda avoided his glance. "I didn't. She noticed my grades were slipping and wanted to know the reason why."

"Your grades weren't exactly high to begin with, " Paul tactfully pointed out.

"Yeah, but because of you, they dropped even lower."

At this point Paul wanted to interject that he had given her the highest grade of her entire academic career, but held his tongue thinking it might not leave a favorable impression.

"Anyways," Linda continued, "She noticed I was depressed; I told her why and that's all," she said very quickly, to get the interrogation over with.

"May I come in?" Paul asked, preferring to discuss the matter in private.

"No."

"Linda, please... We have to talk about this."

"Alright," the young woman relented and opened the door. She had a big, pink towel wrapped around her body and Paul's first thought, in spite of everything, was how much he wanted to remove it.

As soon as they shut the door, he got straight to the point: "Listen Linda, I know what happened. You went to Judith. She didn't ask you anything. You told her the whole story on your own. What I want to know is: why? Why would you want to ruin my career like this?"

Linda felt uncomfortable. "I'm sorry," she answered. "I don't know what to say. I wanted to hurt you, but not..."

"...Destroy my life?" Paul completed her sentence. Linda's chin started quivering with emotion: "I'm really sorry, alright? I honestly didn't know you'd get into so much trouble. All I wanted was for Professor Harrison to say something to you. I didn't mean to get you fired."

Paul tried to understand better the girl's motives: "So you only wanted me to get into a little bit of trouble, is that it? Like receive a reprimand from my department?"

Linda nodded, looking like a child caught with her hand in the cookie jar. Paul gently stroked her cheek. "Well, it doesn't work like that. Because of you, I lost my job and may never be hired again by another university. There's a permanent stain on my academic record." He thought for a moment and couldn't resist adding, "Quite literally."

Linda looked positively miserable. "I'm so sorry... I really am,." she murmured.

He almost believed her. To demonstrate his magnanimity and ability to forgive and (especially) forget, he gently raised her chin with his hand and kissed her softly on the mouth. The towel fell on the floor of its own accord. When he made love to Linda that afternoon, he realized how interlinked tenderness and resentment could be. "You little bitch," he kept saying to himself as he thrust into her. She moaned softly, with desire, with relief. She never noticed the anger. She only noticed the love.

Chapter 3

At night, Paul played over and over in his mind a popular commercial about Walgreen drive-through pharmacies. It featured first a drive-through dentist, then a drive-through lawyer, followed by a drive-through psychiatrist, and at the end of this parade reeled in the drive-through pharmacist, who was the only real and plausible one of the bunch. The deep male voice in the commercial asked: Don't you wish everything could be drive-through? Except for one or two things, Paul did, indeed. In fact, what he desired most was to combine the drive-through pharmacy with the drive-through psychiatrist because he urgently needed refills on Prozac and Anafranil. He took the latter for his Obsessive Compulsive Disorder and the former for the mood swings that resulted from the latter. Add to that the insomnia he suffered from practically every night due to anxiety attacks and you get the idea why refills were a matter of urgency.

The problem was that Paul believed in prescription drugs, but not in the psychiatric consultations he had to endure to get them. Which is why, despite his principled opinions against big-business advertising, this particular commercial appealed to him. Why not shoot two birds with one stone without having to endure the humiliation of conversing with a stranger about his most intimate problems? Nonetheless, since he had run out of the prescription drugs that barely kept him on the edge of sanity, and, furthermore, since he hadn't been able to get a decent night's sleep for weeks despite the heavy daily doses of Sominex, Paul decided to bite the bullet and make another appointment with his psychiatrist. "His," in a manner of speaking, because Dr. Elizabeta Bogdanovich was really his wife's therapist. Mary had been seeing her for almost a year before she persuaded Paul, when their relationship was precipitously moving from bad to worse, to undergo some marriage counseling.

As luck would have it, Paul and Mary successfully completed one couples' counseling session, after which they promptly divorced. Paul remembered very well that fateful day. They stepped into the well-decorated office of Dr. Bogdanovich, the only Jewish Serbian in the area, and probably, at least since World War II, on Earth. Expensive looking vases filled with exotic, phallic looking orchids were perched up on glass counters. Paul was pleasantly surprised to notice that Dr. Bogdanovich was young and pretty, for a psychiatrist that is, since for obvious reasons his expectations were lower with respect to professional and intellectual women. She was tall, thin, with short wavy brown hair and elegantly dressed in what looked like an updated Channel two-piece pencil skirt suit that revealed just enough leg and figure to be both sexy and professional.

"Please sit down," the doctor pointed to a chaise longue with her beautifully manicured fingertips. She had a trace of a foreign accent, but one couldn't detect its country of origin. "May I offer you some coffee or tea?"

"No thanks," "I'm fine," the couple concurred (for once). Dr. Bogdanovich was silent, which made Paul feel slightly uncomfortable, not least of all because they were paying her two hundred bucks an hour.

"I appreciate you joining us in our sessions, Paul," she finally said. "Most of the issues Mary and I discussed this past year concern both of you," she smiled encouragingly. "I think coming here together is a bold, courageous step in the right direction." The doctor's manner and accent were quite elegant, Paul noticed. He responded in the flustered manner he usually adopted with attractive women: "What? Oh... Yes... I'll do my best." Since Paul said this in every problematic situation he encountered, Mary promised that if she was to outlive him, she'd engrave He did his best on his tombstone.

"Good will's all we're asking for," Dr. Bogdanovich replied. "So, Mary, since you and I already know each other quite well, would you like to begin?

Mary felt somewhat embarrassed, given all the bad things she had said to her psychiatrist about her husband behind his back. This initial reticence, however, didn't stop her from saying: "Well, like I told you in our last few sessions Doctor, I'm very worried about our marriage. In fact, it's the main cause of my depression," she tacked on the conclusion that she and her psychiatrist had reached following a year of weekly analyses funded by the husband in question.

"Yes...please go on," Dr. Bogdanovich nodded, prodding Mary on, while Paul assumed the expression of the guest of honor in one of Stalin's show trials. "What are some of the things worrying you in particular?"

Once she got started, Mary welcomed the opportunity to unburden herself: "For starters, he's not interested in me anymore."

Paul had expected to be called an unromantic, inattentive or inexpressive husband--all common misdemeanors, really--but he was taken aback by this emasculating accusation. "What are you talking about? That's the last thing in the world you can charge me with! I'm always the one putting the moves on you and you're always telling me that you're too tired or not in the mood."

Which was more or less accurate, but that didn't prevent Mary from identifying her husband as the source of the problem: "That's only because all you want from me is Wham, bam, thank you ma'am! You don't take me out to dinner or talk to me or buy me flowers or act romantic any more. You just want sex on Saturday nights." She then added, after a pregnant pause: "Preferably in two minutes or less."

Paul looked around, as if seeking the support of imaginary impartial witnesses: "Mary, how can you say that? You're the one who closes her eyes and wants it to be over as soon as we get started. Making love to you is like resuscitating a corpse!"

"Given your bizarre sexual tastes, you would know..." his wife sharply retorted.

Dr. Bogdanovich turned her beautiful head from husband to wife, like a spectator following a tennis match. The ball's in my court, Paul told himself, thinking that Freud's theories about castration complex might actually apply in this case. He decided it was time to assert himself and prove to the doctor that he was the mature one in the family.

"Mary, you act like a teenager sometimes," he said, assuming a paternal tone. "You expect marriage to be like in one of your novels. Well, real life's not like that. I mean, people start out being romantic, but after a few dates, you know, once the newness is gone, reality sinks in."

"Excuse me? When were you ever romantic?" Mary protested. "Don't you remember? I seduced you?"

"Yes, but that's only because of our difficult circumstances," Paul said, alluding to the fact that Mary had been his student.

"Paul, your whole life's nothing but a series of difficult circumstances," Mary countered.

At this point the doctor intervened: "Very good. Mary has expressed some of her needs, and Paul, it's understandable that you feel you're not the only one responsible for satisfying them. Perhaps the two of you can meet half-way. For example, did you ever consider having a date night on Saturdays? Many couples set aside a special evening for one another. That way they can hold on to some of the romance Mary was alluding to. Without trying to fulfill an impossible romantic ideal, as you, yourself, objected. "

"Saturday night's my fantasy football league," Paul announced.

"Well, it doesn't matter which day you set aside. It could be Thursday or Monday night," the doctor patiently suggested.

"On Monday nights I watch football," Paul ruled out another possibility.

"You see what I mean?" Mary exchanged meaningful glances with her increasingly sympathetic psychiatrist. The husband felt besieged by demanding women. Perhaps they should all get together and form an anti-Paul coalition, it occurred to him. But the doctor didn't want to take sides. She stuck to her mediating function, clinging to some notion of scientific objectivity.

"I understand you have your habits, Paul," she replied, and before she could finish her thought, Paul nodded: "Yes, I'm completely a creature of habits," which got the psychiatrist's attention and even provoked an interested look of raised eyebrows.

After asking him a few probing questions, the psychiatrist determined that Paul was a more interesting case than she had originally suspected. The way Mary had described him, he was just a typical guy who preferred pretty young women and sports to his own wife. Boring, run of the mill kind of stuff, at least from a clinical perspective. Now there seemed to be a glimmer of hope: this man might be genuinely disturbed. The more Paul elaborated on his habits—his compulsion of confirming at least three times that he locked the doors before he went anywhere; washing his hands constantly; the recurrent insomnia caused by obsessive focus upon a combination of real worries and imaginary maladies— the more the doctor focused her energies on Paul rather than the mundane issue she was paid to address, such as his marriage falling apart. Clearly, the doctor hypothesized, he was at the very least suffering from Obsessive Compulsive Disorder. Noticing that the discussion had strayed too far from her main concern, however, Mary interjected:

"He's obsessed with his female students."

"You could hardly object since you were one yourself," Paul rebutted.

"Only now he prefers eighteen year olds to me," Mary continued still addressing only the psychiatrist. "I'm already an old maid, seeing how I'm almost twenty-four."

The doctor, who like all good scientists enjoyed a challenge, perked up at this good news as well: "Paul, is that true?" she turned her statuesque head in his direction.

"Of course not!" Paul vehemently denied the false accusation. After all, Linda was twenty. But since, for some reason, this denial didn't fully exonerate him, he continued: "What can I say? I find young girls beautiful. Is that such a crime?"

"As a matter of fact, in this country it is," the doctor replied.

"Well what man doesn't?"

"So then you admit you have a special predilection for younger women?" Dr. Bogdanovich confirmed.

"Maybe a little bit," Paul admitted.

"Hello? More like a huge one!" Mary set the record straight.

"I find young women aesthetically pleasing. That doesn't mean I want to sleep with them," Paul rebutted.

"True," Mary conceded. "He only sleeps with them if they're taking his classes."

Dr. Bogdanovich maintained her cool throughout this exchange. "Let's pause for a second," she moderated. "There's nothing wrong with finding eighteen-year old girls--or even sixteen year old girls, for that matter--attractive. Paul, you're right to claim that many men do, although research shows most prefer slightly older women, between the age of 21 and 30, shall we say. Nevertheless, I'd like to ask you a question—and please, don't feel defensive, since nobody's charging you with anything," Dr. Bogdanovich reassured him, attempting to raise the discussion unto a higher plane.

"...Except for the fact that he's a pedophile," Mary interjected, frustrating that effort.

"Mary, please! The two of you are here to understand your behavior and talk things out, not insult one another," Dr. Bogdanovich extended her hand into a stop sign motion, palm facing outwards, trying to prevent the spouses from transforming her sophisticated therapy session into a circus.

"She doesn't know what she's talking about," Paul answered, addressing only the doctor. "First of all, a pedophile is attracted to children, which I'm most certainly not. Second, like I said, my interest in young women is purely aesthetic, not sexual."

"Paul, I understand. However, it seems to me that you don't just gaze at young women the way people do at beautiful paintings, at a museum," the doctor gently suggested.

Paul was prepared to concede some mild ambiguity, but Mary's comment— "Then your eyes must be located on a lower part of your anatomy and have some serious feelers!" -- put him once again on the defensive.

"The fact remains," he replied, "that I've never had sexual relations with any woman under eighteen. And I don't have the slightest desire to do so. Sure, I may be attracted to young women, but that's all. Look but don't touch is my policy."

To which Mary replied very casually: "He's having an affair with one of his students as we speak."

Paul felt like one of Jupiter's thunderbolt just landed on his head. Had his wife hired a private investigator?

"Is this true?" Dr. Bogdanovich asked, adopting the tone of a mother who must decide which one of her children is lying.

Paul still refused to answer, playing over and over in his head all the ways in which Mary might have found out.

"Your friend Linda called about a week ago," Mary solved the mystery. "She sounded very upset."

"What did she say?" Paul asked, not prepared to give out more information than absolutely necessary.

"Nothing," Mary answered with a triumphant smirk on her face. "She didn't have to. I recognized her situation as mine a few years ago. Poor girl..."

The doctor promptly intervened: "Paul, I feel that we need to set up some separate sessions together. It seems to me that a large part of your marital problems stems from your compulsion to have sex with much younger women."

"It's not a compulsion," Paul objected. "It's just run of the mill, garden variety male sexuality. Actually, the women always run after me," he added. "What am I supposed to do?"

"Perhaps exercise good judgment and will power?" the doctor suggested one remote possibility. "Think of your marriage? Think of the young women you're involved with?" she threw out a few other, equally unpalatable options.

Mary felt vindicated by this discussion while Paul felt pressured to experience guilt about something he didn't even consider wrong. How can liking young women be considered a sin, or a psychological disorder—or whatever else they chose to call it—when it was something completely natural that occurred routinely in medieval Europe and even some contemporary tribal societies? After all, what was the harm of enjoying the beauty, pleasure and freshness of life? But Paul knew he couldn't verbalize such thoughts out loud without inculpating himself even further. Geesh! Next they'd be calling him a sociopath for feeling no remorse...

Paul left the couples' session silent and dejected. A few weeks later, his wife left him. She packed up her things and vanished. For days he looked for her, calling her family and friends to find out where she might have gone. But nobody knew, or at least so they claimed. Then Paul started looking around for her car in the Roanoke area. Finally he found it parked in front of a small apartment building near the campus. She had moved in with her ex-boyfriend, who was still a delivery boy at a local pizzeria.

"This is only temporary," she explained apologetically, feeling more awkward about moving in with her unambitious ex than about leaving her husband.

In a peculiar reversal of positions, Mary was more or less calm about their situation while Paul was the one who felt distraught. "Mary, please come back home," he implored. "I promise to see Dr. Bogdanovich as often as you wish."

Since Mary didn't seem particularly reassured by this proposition, he added: "We can work out our problems. I'm not seeing Linda any more," he informed his wife of his selfless sacrifice for the sake of their marriage, failing to mention that his student had, by then, already filed and won a sexual harassment suit against him.

Despite her husband's generous concessions, Mary shook her head, resolute in her decision: "I want a divorce."

He looked straight into her eyes, to see if she was serious about this. Apparently, she was: "I mailed you the divorce papers yesterday," she announced. Having delivered this unilateral blow, however, she tried to be nice about it: "Please, Paul... Don't raise a stink about this, okay? Just sign them. Let's part on good terms and move on with our lives."

This, however, wasn't an option for Paul just yet: "Can't we at least give it another try?"

"No."

"Why not?" Paul's eyes widened with despair. He may have taken his wife for granted, but he never expected to lose her as a result.

"Because I don't love you anymore," Mary answered. Which was the only response Paul felt wasn't within his power to change.

Chapter 4

Once rejected by Mary, Paul finally fell in love with his wife, with all the anguish, turbulence and other fringe benefits afforded by unrequited passion. After ignoring her almost to the point of oblivion during the two years they were married, in the weeks following the divorce, he compensated by spending night after night concocting belated solutions to their previous problems. To his surprise, nothing seemed to work. The messages on the answering machine were ignored. The letters came back to him "Return to sender," with an accusatory finger on the rubber stamp pointing straight to him and making him feel guilty for the marital catastrophe.

Paul's life was spinning out of control. He blamed himself--and the affair with Linda--for the loss of his job and the break-up of his marriage. However, in all fairness, Mary's hot temper had also played a significant role. Paul recalled that even when they were dating, she dropped—or rather, hurled in his direction--a few hints. For instance, whenever she disagreed with him, she would scream hysterically and fling objects—glasses, pots, pretty much anything she could lay her hands on--full force at the wall. Their apartment was acupunctured by marks of their daily struggles. Paul nonetheless clung to the hope that his wife would grow out of this phase. Much as a mother patiently awaits the end of her child's "terrible twos," so Paul told himself, after all, she's only twenty-two, still young and immature. I need to have a little more patience with her. Unfortunately, during the years they were together, their marriage stagnated in the terrible twos. Until, that is, an even worse phase overlapped and took over—Mary's depression—which did nothing to improve their relationship.

A year or so into their marriage, Paul recalled, Mary became increasingly withdrawn, practically inert. When they first moved in together, she'd spend hours styling her strawberry-blond hair until he'd say, "What are you doing in there? Preparing for the Ms. Universe pageant? I have to use the bathroom too! It's urgent."

Mary, however, didn't let such mundane considerations interrupt her toilette. She'd first comb her hair to remove the tangles, then use a round brush, wrap the hair around it and blow-dry it at length to straighten out the natural waves. The make-up procedure, as Paul called it, was even more involved, providing an illuminating Mary Kay lesson all unto itself. After washing her face, she'd apply toner, day cream, sun screen, foundation, powder, blush, lipstick, eyeliner, eye shadow, mascara and nail polish in that order—a full armor of cosmetics—even if she only went to the grocery store. "What's the mask for?" Paul would tactfully inquire, preferring women au naturel in all senses of the term. "I just want to look pretty, that's all!" she'd respond. "But you are pretty!" he insisted. "Make-up just spoils a woman's natural good looks," he'd put forth his Stendhalian philosophy, which evidently his wife and the entire cosmetics industry didn't share.

"It's not like you notice me anyways," Mary replied. But that was an unfair accusation. Paul did notice her; he just didn't like to show it. He was drawn to his wife's strawberry-blond hair, which matched her softly rounded face, delicate features and light blue eyes. He absolutely adored her straight body, small breasts and those narrow hips to which he clung for dear life when they made love. He even liked the strawberry patch between her legs that matched the color of her hair, a sure sign that she wasn't one of those fake blonds.

Once her apathy period began, however, Mary underwent a complete personality change and hardly even bothered taking a bath, let alone applying make-up. The cosmetic armor disappeared, not only from her face, but also from the bathroom drawer. This, her husband immediately realized, was sufficient reason to be on suicide watch.

"Why don't you anoint yourself any more?" he asked, concerned.

"I thought you didn't like it," she replied.

"That never stopped you before. Where's all your make-up?"

"I threw it away," Mary replied. "Who needs it? It's not like anybody's going to notice me anyway." A recurring theme, repetition in a minor.

By then Mary had been seeing Dr. Bogdanovich for a few months and the psychiatrist had managed to convince her that all of her known problems (as well as several that hadn't occurred to her before) stemmed from low self-esteem. Which, the doctor went on to explain, developed because Mary had never discovered who she was as an individual. Basically, she was first her father's little girl, then her older husband's wife. She never got a chance to mature as an independent woman, to know herself, as Socrates would have urged if he were still alive. Although Dr. Bogdanovich never spelled out the logical conclusion to this chain of observations, to Mary it soon became transparently clear: she had to separate from Paul in order to "find herself." Whenever her husband asked her what was wrong, Mary answered, simply, "I'm depressed."

Depression is a crisis of energy, Paul had read in Ann Landers' advice column before. And that was certainly true in Mary's case. She had never cooked—"I burn water," she'd proudly declare. Nevertheless, like Paul, Mary was something of a neatness freak, so she vacuumed and cleaned the house at least twice a day. After a year or so of marriage, however, about the same time that the make-up arsenal disappeared, the apartment began resembling a fraternity house following a decadent party (minus the fun, girls, beer kegs and wild sex). She let dirt accumulate; allowed crumbs to take over the counter tops, floors and kitchen table; adopted dust bunnies as pets.

"Don't you think it's getting a little messy around here?" Paul gently prodded his wife to return to her duties, given that she was, technically speaking, a "housewife" since she didn't work outside the home.

"I'm not your servant, if that's what you're getting at!" Mary answered defiantly.

"I realize that," the husband foolishly persisted. "But since you don't work, or rather, since you supposedly work at home, don't you think it behooves you to clean the house once in a while?"

Paul thought that he was making a reasonable request, not realizing that Mary had become a woman of the postfeminist era and thus was perfectly capable of refuting such Neanderthal arguments.

"Listen," Mary's eyes flashed with self-righteous indignation, "The fact that I'm currently seeking employment doesn't make me your personal servant. So clean your own fucking mess!" she concluded and, to underscore her point, threw the remote control that she had just used to flip to of Knots Landing full force past her husband's head.

Paul was horrified. He couldn't even tell if his wife had meant to decapitate him or miss, and felt helpless in the face of her tornado-like tantrums—brief, focused and irreversibly damaging. Although he wouldn't even admit it to himself, Paul feared his own hundred-and-ten pounds wife. So he did nothing, except bury his head in the sand, dream of attractive female students and continue hoping that this phase would soon be over. He didn't want to give up on their marriage, however, no matter how unhappy it was. Marriage is not meant to be taken lightly, his widowed mother had taught him, and he clung to that principle—without the cumbersome fidelity part --more tightly than to love itself.

After Mary had gone through a year of counseling, the marriage pursued its natural downward course. However, thanks to her psychiatrist's help, she became more articulate about her negative feelings: "Paul," she'd say, "I'm not happy with you any more. It's not your fault; you see, I'm not blaming you," she would qualify, feeling generous and setting the stage for an easygoing "irreconcilable differences" divorce. "We're incompatible, that's all."

Paul felt stung, but couldn't object since he had little or no evidence to the contrary. "What can I do to make you happier?" he'd ask.

"Nothing. Just give me my freedom," his wife would respond in a Rousseauistic vein. Paul was puzzled by this comment. He wasn't aware that Mary, who came and went as she pleased, never cleaned or cooked any more and dropped from her agenda even minimal sexual duties, was "everywhere in chains."

Seeking sound advice, he began leafing through his wife's Cosmopolitan magazines. He didn't pay much attention to the articles since he was distracted by the pictures of barely clad women, who bore a striking resemblance in both looks and poses to those in his *Playboy* magazines. So women are into this sort of thing too, Paul concluded. Personally, he couldn't blame them. I mean, what would any reasonable person rather touch: a soft and curvy female body or a hairy, rough male one? These deep speculations about the nature of human desire, however, were tangential to the more daunting task of understanding his own wife. Paul did find some helpful tips in the ads; unfortunately, none of them worked on Mary. He'd buy her candy; she'd complain he's only trying to fatten her up so as to make her unattractive to other men. He'd give her a romantic card or perfume; she considered such gestures insincere and commonplace.

One night, when they were both reading in bed, Mary proposed: "I think we should start seeing other people. You know, have an open marriage." Paul had a flashback to the seventies and didn't know how to respond. He couldn't outright reject his wife's offer, given he had a chip on his shoulder due to the fling with Linda. Furthermore, being a fair and open-minded man, he was perfectly willing to have an open marriage only on his side. But since his wife was proposing this idea for both of them, he was somewhat less enthusiastic: "Why are you asking about this now?" he asked, getting suspicious.

"Two guys expressed interest," Mary replied with a shrug.

"What? Are you in love with either of them?" Paul fixed her with his glare.

Mary looked at her husband as if he were hopelessly old-fashioned: "What does that have to do with anything?"

"Then why in the world would you want to have an affair?" he asked, since in the Ann Landers column normal heterosexual women didn't have sex without being in love. Paul obviously hadn't read any of the articles in the *Playboy*s he had purchased for the past ten years nor those in his wife's Cosmo articles he occasionally peeked at, since he was obviously unaware that these magazines had proven beyond all reasonable doubt that most attractive women under the age of forty were borderline nymphomaniacs.

"Because I feel like it, that's why," Mary confirmed this well-documented scientific conclusion. "Do men need any other reason to fuck?" she politely inquired.

"Mary! Why are you being so crude?" her husband flinched.

"Well, do you?" she persisted.

Paul considered the question for a moment, then replied: "Unfortunately, I get attached. But I suppose, for most men, mild attraction's more than enough."

"Well there you have it," Mary yawned, put down her book—*Therese Raquin*, a reassuring Zola novel about a wife who got her lover to kill her husband--and turned off the lamp on her side of the bed.

"Hold on..." Paul didn't feel particularly satisfied with these closing arguments. "I still don't get it. Why exactly do you want to have an affair?" He turned off his own lamp and started stroking his wife's lower back, with a circular motion. "Aren't you happy with our sex life?"

Mary chuckled. "What sex life? It's more like miniature golf."

"Well, if that's how you feel, then good night," he answered coldly, turning away wounded from his wife.

"Whatever..." she responded like an overgrown teenager.

After Mary left him and he got fired thanks to his mistress' discreteness, Paul decided that he needed some heavy-duty doses of Prozac. He didn't have much faith in Dr. Bogdanovich since his marriage ended right after their couples' session with her, a fact that Paul didn't consider a cosmic coincidence. However, seeing how Ann Landers didn't provide adequate solutions to all of his problems, Paul didn't know where else to turn.

Dr. Bogadonvich opened the door and greeted him with her usual mixture of professionalism and warmth: "Paul! I'm glad you're back."

Paul instinctively wondered if the doctor might be interested in something more than conversation, but in a rare flash of lucidity he decided against the likelihood of that happening: "Thanks," he smiled awkwardly.

"Please sit down," she pointed to a Freudian lounge chair.

"Do you mind if I sit here instead?" he asked, identifying an upholstered, more conventional looking chair across from the psychiatrist's desk. You could at least still keep your head on your shoulders sitting there.

"Whatever makes you feel most comfortable," the doctor answered obligingly.

"Are you still seeing Mary?" Paul asked in a tone generally reserved for jealous lovers.

"I'm sorry, but I can't disclose such confidential information."

"I see," he answered, concluding, So that means yes. "Then... what would you like to talk about?" he asked as if he were doing the doctor a big favor in paying her a visit.

"Do you mind if we begin by discussing some of the issues related to your childhood?"

What issues? he wondered. I have no issues. "Like what?" he asked.

"For starters, I'm curious to know a little more about your family life. Did you have any brothers and sisters?"

"Two brothers. Unfortunately."

"Why unfortunately?"

"Because I like girls better."

This time, even the unflappable doctor seemed a bit concerned. "I'm well aware of that, however... we're discussing siblings here..."

"Oh, I didn't mean sexually, of course. I just meant girls are nicer, gentler, softer and more fun. My brothers were really rough."

"In what way?"

"I don't know. To tell you the truth, I don't remember much about my childhood. Adolescence was more interesting."

Dr. Bogdanovich, however, preferred to take it one step at a time: "Do you think hypnosis might facilitate childhood recollection?" she inquired.

"Actually, now that you mention it, I think I just remembered a few things," Paul decided to cooperate, feeling somewhat apprehensive about the information he might unwittingly disclose during hypnosis. "Our childhood can be summarized by two words: hard times."

Dr. Bogdanovich smiled: "Sounds like the title of a novel I once read."

"Well, unfortunately hard times were more exciting in Dickens' novel than in our lives. You see, my Mom raised us practically all by herself. My father died when I was six."

"I see. Could you please describe your relationship with him?" Dr. Bogdanovich scrutinized her patient's face.

"I don't remember it too well," Paul started to say in all honesty, then recalled the threat of hypnosis and added, using choppy sentences like someone recounting a dream sequence: "He was kind of strict. Stern, even. He used to do a lot of handyman kind of work around the house. I have several memories of him on a ladder. He liked to drink quite a bit in the evenings, which was pretty much the only time he was cheerful. Unless he drank too much. Then he had a hot temper and screamed at us, especially at my mother. He got very loud. I remember fearing him. To this day, I still can't stand the smell of wine. It fills me with a sense of dread of his authority. I drink beer instead," Paul concluded. "Guinness," he added, to prove the veracity of his claims by offering irrelevant corroborating details, as they do in court.

Dr. Bogdanovich seemed pleased. She was busily jotting down notes on a legal pad. "What was your father's occupation?" she looked up from her notebook.

"He was a welder. As working class as it gets. Mom used to tell me that when my father was alive, we were poor, but we managed. But once he died, we became downright indigent. His social security check could barely feed the dog, let alone an unemployed widow with three boys."

"Do you remember how your father passed away?"

Paul nodded. "One day he didn't come home for dinner. I remember Mom, who almost never cried, being in tears. She told us that her sister would come to baby-sit; that she had to go somewhere. I found out later that she went to the hospital to visit my father, who had been having very painful headaches for the past two months. They thought it was stress-related migraines. As it turns out, he had a malignant brain tumor. The doctor told mother that it was just a matter of weeks before he was gone. They couldn't operate on that part of the brain and chemotherapy wouldn't work. But they pumped him full of drugs, just in case."

"How did you feel about your father's death?" the doctor pursued.

"I didn't fully take it in because I was so young. But I remember my mother's swollen eyes. Her her negativity. And… I felt bad for her."

"Her negativity? You mean her sorrow?"

"No. I mean her constant pessimism. I don't really remember how she was before my dad died, but I know that afterwards she almost never had anything positive to say about life. If we were excited about Christmas, she talked about the commercialism of the holiday and how sad it was for us, since we were poor. Even Santa couldn't afford to buy us presents. If I got good grades in school, she would complain about my brothers' bad grades and make them feel inferior, which only increased their hostility towards me. But she didn't mean any harm. That's just how she was. She couldn't help it."

"So you don't blame her?"

"Not at all. It's difficult to imagine anybody being happy or upbeat about such a difficult life."

"Do you think she loved your father?"

"In her own way...."

"And what way was that?" Dr. Bogdanovich wanted to know.

"I suppose... as a duty. She saw her place in life as a mother and wife. Without either choosing or questioning that identity."

"Do you have any happy moments from your childhood?"

"When I was asleep," Paul joked.

"Come on! There must have been a few bright spots..." Dr. Bogdanovich insisted.

Paul shifted in his seat, trying to recall any event that might fit the bill. "I had an uncle from my mother's side who was an English teacher. We didn't see much of him since he only visited us once in a while on holidays. But he was very nice. He'd always bring us books for every occasion—birthdays, Christmas, Easter. It was always books. My brothers complained about that. They would have preferred cars, trains. For them, books were work; toys were fun. But for me it was the other way around. So I really looked forward to his visits."

"What kind of books did you read?"

"At first, books that were for kids, but also for adults in some way. Like Alice in Wonderland. Later, when we got older, he sent us the classics. Got us started in high school on Flaubert, Proust, Nabokov. Well, me at any rate, since my brothers didn't like reading."

"*Lolita*?" Dr. Bogdanovich's face brightened at this much-anticipated revelation. "Your favorite novel I presume?"

To her surprise, Paul shook his head: "No. I like *Ada* better. It's a more developed love story."

"Still by Nabokov?"

"Well, he's the greatest American writer, hands down."

"If you love novels so much, then how come you went into art history rather than literature?"

"I studied both. I went to France to study French literature, but also got interested in the art."

"Aside from books, what else did you like?"

Paul shrugged. "Girls of course."

"That goes without saying," the doctor smiled again. "Did you date a lot?"

"Not really. I was what you might call... a late bloomer. I only started dating in college."

"So then..." Dr. Bogdanovich wondered out loud.

"Books and girls sort of fit together," Paul clarified.

"You mean to say that you preferred love stories?"

"Not necessarily. It's just that both were an escape from reality to some far away place filled with beauty and excitement."

"How did girls function as an escape? I can see how novels or movies might have. But since you didn't date..."

"Love's all in the head," Paul declared.

"What do you mean by that?"

"Well, it's just like Proust says. Being in love's mostly psychological."

"Given my occupation, I'm the first to acknowledge that; however, this still doesn't explain..."

"What I mean is, it's so much easier to escape to another world with women who are part of your dreams than with those who are part of your actual life. At least that proved to be the case in my marriage."

"So you prefer fantasy girls to real women?" Dr. Bogdanovich asked.

"Well, at first, it's not like I had a choice. After all, I went to an all-boys Catholic school..."

"And afterwards?"

"Even once I started dating in college, I kept the dreams alive. I was what you might call an introverted Don Juan."

"Meaning...?"

"I fell in love every other day, usually with women who weren't even remotely interested in me. And I seduced none of them."

"I see. You're sort of a Don Juan manqué, right?"

"You could say that," Paul confirmed.

"Did you prefer younger girls?" Dr. Bogdanovich returned to her patient's Achilles' heel.

"Usually."

"Do you know why?"

"Sure. The reasons are obvious. Adolescent girls are young, beautiful and innocent. They're the closest thing to angels on earth."

"And how do you feel about grown women?" the psychiatrist pursued.

"I like them too."

"But not as much?"

"Maybe not," Paul conceded.

"Why not?" Dr. Bogdanovich fixed him with her eyes, as if trying to drill through directly to his inner essence.

Paul hesitated. "I don't know... Perhaps I find grown women a little intimidating," he answered softly.

"Whereas you prefer to be the one in charge?" Dr. Bogdanovich completed his thought.

"Not at all. I'm usually pretty passive. In all my relationships, it's the women who make all the moves."

"Then I don't understand."

"Maybe younger women make me feel more in control. At any rate, they seem more pliable. And sweet. And beautiful. Like I told you earlier, for me, it's all about aesthetics. I think the beauty of women peaks at sixteen. After that it's all downhill."

Dr. Bogdanovich, who incidentally was pushing forty, didn't respond to Paul's tactful remark. She focused instead on the psychological implications of his statement: "So what you're saying is that you prefer to be in a paternal role in a relationship?"

"I suppose. I hadn't thought of it that way."

"Do you know why you might have this preference?"

"Not really. Maybe it's because I never had any sisters and went to an all-boys school. Girls were a mystery for me."

"I suspect there's more to it than that," the doctor said. She took a breath and spoke in a pleasant, sing-song voice, as one narrates a story to a young child: "From what have told me, much of your childhood was out of your control. Your father's death. Your mother's pessimism and sadness. Your brothers' rougher masculinity. There was so little you could do about your circumstances. You couldn't bring your father back to life, or make your mother happy, or bond with your brothers on your own terms. So you escaped from reality. A permissible escape, not into insanity, but into culture, desire and fantasy. You found pleasure in reading novels and in fantasizing about beautiful, sweet and innocent girls. That was your way of coping with a difficult childhood without losing your mind."

Paul was pleasantly surprised by this revelation: "So then... you're saying I'm normal?"

Dr. Bogdanovich shook her head, "No. I'm just speculating that if you had not found these escapes, you'd be in even worse shape. But what I'd like to understand better, with your help, is why still rely upon your adolescent fantasies to cope with your adult life. What frightens you so much about adult reality and real women that you feel the need to revert back to your adolescent world? Could you please think about this question for next time?"

Next time? There's going to be a next time? Paul wondered, somewhat alarmed. Despite his instinctive resistance to psychotherapy, however, he left the doctor's office a little less resistant to counseling than he had entered it. Proof was that he forgot to ask Dr. Bogdanovich for the Prozac and Anafranil prescriptions which had been the original purpose for his visit.

Chapter 5

Paul didn't get the opportunity to make much progress on Dr. Bogdanovich's psychology homework. Only a few months later, he moved to New Jersey. Although by the late eighties, male instructors found guilty of sexual harassment wouldn't be among the most solicited by other colleges or universities (how things had changed since the sixties and seventies...), thanks to the open-mindedness of some of his former professors, Paul was offered a Visiting Associate Professorship at Princeton University, his graduate school alma mater. Of course, it didn't hurt that the Art History Department was made up of a nearly all-male faculty that was growing wary of the newfangled feminism and indulged in quite a bit of "male gazing," Paul's scholarly specialty, themselves. Since he moved to Princeton, Paul's best friend, a sculptor named Ricardo, did his best to dispel his lingering depression over the recent divorce.

That afternoon, Paul went by his friend's studio. Instead of Rico's suntanned, angular face, he was greeted by a more pleasant apparition: a young woman with a lovely oval face framed by rich, long brown hair. She wore bright red lipstick and her cheeks had a peachy tint, which gave her beauty an artificial quality. With instinctive modesty, which usually melted upon the slightest intimacy, Irina averted her glance when she noticed Paul looking at her. "She looks like a porcelain doll," Paul thought, wondering why he, who preferred untainted natural beauty, was so struck by this girl's painted prettiness. In fact, the young woman's whole appearance had the look of a doll. Not of a Barbie, with its grown up, stereotypical beauty--large chest, narrow waist, long legs--but the kind of doll you'd give to a younger child to prolong her innocence by avoiding hints of sexuality. Irina wore a delicate light blue top with a rounded collar, buttoned all the way up to the neck, similar to the ones that were fashionable during the nineteen-fifties. Her pleated, navy A-line skirt, which reached slightly below the knees, simultaneously hid her figure and emphasized her narrow waist. Like a vintage school girl, an odd yet congruous mixture of child, doll and woman, she still wore knee-high socks and Mary Jane shoes.

"He looks so... French," the young woman thought, in one split second taking in the delicacy of Paul's features and the slightness of his frame; his burning coal-like eyes illuminating the paleness of his face; his narrow yet expressive mouth and the minimal roundness of his cheeks, which suggested the limits of thinness, before the face loses its plasticity and youthfulness.

Rico had his back turned to this touching encounter. Rico wasn't much into playing the role of the gracious host. "Hey!" he said without turning to his guest, but knowing who it was. "What do you think of this one?" he asked, pointing to the clay figurine he was in the process of molding into a lovely, nude girl standing in a pose akin to one of Degas' ballerinas, hands clasped behind her arched back.

"She's lovely," Paul whispered, following the model with his eyes as she made her way out the door and down the stairs. "What's her name?"

"Dancer," Rico answered.

"No, I mean the girl's."

"That's Irina, my new model," Rico answered in a tone Paul found way too matter-of-fact to do the young woman justice.

He examined the sculpture, taking in its delicate limbs and airy feel with a voracious gaze, the way a starving man might look at a still life of an appetizing bowl of fresh fruit. "Well...I don't envy you," Paul informed his friend.

"Why not?" Rico asked absentmindedly, absorbed in shaping the knee of the figurine, which still had an exaggerated bump at the joints that detracted from the sculpture's grace and movement.

"Because if I had your job, I'd either be in jail or hospitalized for priapism."

"What's priapism?" Rico asked, not familiar with one of the most useful words in the English language.

"It's when you have an erection for a few hours."

"Sounds like heaven," Rico laughed.

"It kind of is, since you can actually die from it."

"Well, if you have to go, it might as well be that way."

"So how come you're not dead yet?" Paul wondered.

Rico looked up from his sculpture: "Pardon?"

"You look at gorgeous nude models all day long.... Is there something you haven't told me ...?"

Since Rico considered himself a macho Latin lover, he was stung by the implications of his friend's question. "These girls aren't my type," he answered.

Paul's mouth hung open in disbelief: "Are you kidding me? They're everyone's type!"

"I prefer women to girls," Rico stated, alluding to his wife and mistress, both of whom were slightly older than him and over forty.

"Well, nobody's perfect," Paul shrugged. "Speaking of women, are you still seeing... what's her name...?"

The sculptor wiped his hands on his shirt, which was already covered with excess clay. His tone was slightly reproachful: "Diana. You always pretend to forget her name. Do you have it in for her or something?"

"Not at all! I honestly forget. How do you expect me to keep track of all your women?"

Rico turned and looked at his friend with incredulity: "Did they hold you up in preschool? I've had only two for the past seven years: my wife and my mistress."

"That's one too many."

"You're not exactly in the position to give me lessons on fidelity," Rico pointed out.

"I most certainly am," Paul protested. "You can look at me as a living example of what happens to men who cheat on their wives. What does Sally think about all this?"

Rico looked around nervously, then whispered: "Shh! She might be listening at the door. Hold on!" He walked stealthily to the door and placed his ear flat on the freshly painted wood. As Rico removed his tanned face, Paul noticed a white blotch, plastered upon the sculptor's cheek, looking like a modern version of the Scarlet Letter.

Paul was amused by his friend, whose warranted paranoia nearly matched his own imaginary anxieties. "So I take it that you haven't told her yet?"

"She already knows. How could I keep such a thing a secret when I've spent most of my weekends and vacations with Diana for the past seven years?"

"When are the three of you moving to Utah? I heard bigamy's still legal there."

"Well, you heard wrong. Which is unfortunate, since at least bigamy's better than divorce. I don't want to hurt the kids, you know."

"I imagine when they grow up they'll be thrilled to discover that their dad has a mistress."

"Actually, it's Sally I'm most worried about."

"I don't blame you," Paul comforted his friend. "I can't imagine a wife who would tolerate such an arrangement," he said, thinking of his first wife's reaction to his brief affair.

Rico was displeased with the turn the conversation had taken: "Can we please talk about something else?" he lifted one eyebrow.

"Okay," Paul agreed. "Just one thing though: Don't you find it a bit weird that Sally puts up with all this?"

"That's exactly the same subject," Rico pointed out.

"Do you think she's taken a lover?"

Rico's tanned face turned a shade lighter: "I hadn't thought of it, but thanks for planting the idea in my head."

"And what does Diana think?"

"About what?"

"The affair."

This time, Rico beamed: "She's absolutely crazy about me!"

"Then why doesn't she marry you?"

"Because of the little detail that we're already married to other people!" Rico answered rather loudly, momentarily forgetting his prudence.

"But if you love each other, don't you want to live together?" Paul persevered.

Rico sat down on a chair near a wooden work table filled with clay, wires and the beginnings of several sculptures. He started twirling nervously a piece of clay between his fingers: "Why rock the boat?" he asked, looking as if he were trying to convince himself in the process. "I mean, we already see one another whenever we feel like it. Besides, she's got two kids; I've got two also. You do the math. Somehow, we're not ready to become the Brady Bunch, you know what I mean? We prefer to keep things simple."

"I'm glad to hear you consider listening at the door to see if your wife's spying on you simple," Paul retorted, as usual looking at the bright side of life.

"I told you that's not a problem, man! Sally lets me see Diane," Rico said, though not very convincingly.

"I can imagine how thrilled she is about it," Paul stated, knowing full well that Sally, a traditional Irish Catholic, must have raised one or two objections to this arrangement.

"Well, when she first found out about it she didn't take it too well," Rico was obliged to admit.

"I'm not surprised. What did she say?"

"Nothing. I mean, she freaked out. Screamed, cried, threatened divorce, the whole spiel. For a while there, I thought she was suicidal. I had to put her under psychiatric care. But now she got used to it and now she's feeling a lot better."

"Last time I saw her she seemed heavily sedated," Paul observed.

"That's what I mean. She feels better because of the drugs."

"Well, at least you're not losing any sleep over this."

Despite his bantering tone, Paul felt genuinely sorry for Sally. He had been Rico's best man eight years ago, when he and Sally got married. She seemed so normal and happy back then. Granted, Paul never considered her the kind of woman who would appeal to an artist specializing in female nudes. She was short, dark-haired like Rico, stocky, with a plain face. Even back then she looked much older than she was. But she was solid, reliable and nice. Before the wedding, she told Paul that her dreams were coming true. All she ever wanted was to have a family of her own. Rico was Catholic, just like her, so even though he was Mexican American and she American Irish, at least they'd share the same religion and moral principles. In fact, that was precisely the sales pitch Sally made to her conservative parents, who had initially objected to what they considered "an interracial marriage." So much for the common moral principles argument, Paul thought, with 20/20 hindsight. The root of the problem was that Rico was an artist, with everything that calling implied. Even during their honeymoon Sally complained about neglect and began swallowing antidepressants. But she refused to take the birth control pills, even though Rico went with her to the gynecologist for a prescription. Sally never got it filled. She put the prescription in her nightstand drawer, right next to the Bible. Why intervene with God's will, she thought. Besides, early in the marriage she feared losing Rico to one of his models and hoped that having a family together might hold him in place.

Usually cheerful, self-absorbed and a workaholic, for his part, Rico refused to shoulder the blame for his wife's negative disposition. He suspected that Sally had some sort of undiagnosed manic depression. Her moods oscillated like a pendulum clock, and he, for one, had neither the time nor energy to cope with he psychological issues. "You don't even try," Paul sometimes reproached him, defending Sally. As for Diana, she put up with Rico's artistic temperament in part because she didn't have to live with it. As an art dealer, she also understood that for Rico everything was art and art was everything. Sculpting was not a choice; it was an extension of his identity: a necessity, an obsession. Which is why Rico preferred nontraditional, artistic women with sturdy personalities who could handle heavy doses of neglect. Aesthetically, except for his sculptures, he didn't go for conventional forms of beauty. Diana was tall, blond, with a bony appearance both in her chiseled face and her lanky body. Her one striking feature, Paul thought, was her unusually blue eyes with heavy eyelashes, which were warm and youthful compared to the severity of her features. As luck would have it, Rico found the perfect woman a few months after he took the wedding vows with Sally. He met his mistress through a mutual artist friend who told him he found a dealer interested in classically inspired modern sculptures. Diana, however, became more interested in the sculptor than in his work. Rico's art was not modern and edgy enough for her taste, but she was instantly drawn to his intense and independent personality.

Even Diana's name struck Paul, a priori, as a good match for his friend. Diana, Artemis, the goddess of the hunt, who loved without needing anyone— and who had slightly bisexual tendencies, Paul surmised, though this hypothesis remained to be confirmed. Whereas poor Sally was a milder, less vengeful version of Juno: constantly jealous of her husband's open affair, tolerating everything for the sake of family unity, while finding some solace in setting the children against their father and wallowing in a self-pity relieved only by occasional bouts of apathy.

"It would be better if you divorced," Paul had advised his friend the first time the marital problems related to his affair began to surface. "Before it's too late."

"It's too late," Rico had replied.

"Why?"

"Because Sally's pregnant." And that was that, since after all, they were both practicing Catholics. Which is how their first daughter, little Ellen whom Paul adopted as his godchild, was born in the midst of this unhappy, mismatched marriage.

Diana's family situation was somewhat simpler. With two grown daughters, one sixteen, the other eighteen, both of whom were her husband's children from an earlier marriage, she could have divorced immediately. Nonetheless, for her, such measures didn't prove necessary. Her husband, John, a marketing executive at Borders, had been having the proverbial affair with his secretary for several years. Diana didn't mind it too much since she had grown tired of her sexual duties and led an independent professional existence as an art dealer. In fact, at the beginning of their marriage, her husband had half-seriously encouraged her to follow suit and take a lover. What he didn't know was that occasional flings proved more than sufficient for his wife—until she met Rico. After which, John did mind quite a bit being displaced by another man, especially since by then he had grown bored with his mistress. Morally speaking, however, he didn't have a toe to stand on, which is why he didn't make too much of a fuss when his wife went to see Rico. He just became even more distant and cold, an attitude which Diana actually welcomed. As far as she was concerned, the more freedom she had, the better. For all practical purposes, their marriage was long over.

Paul, who hadn't dated since his divorce nearly a year ago, found all these amorous complications confusing and even sadly comical. But Rico didn't put up with his friend's unsolicited advice and criticism without dishing out some of his own.

"How about you? How's your love life going since your wife left you, Don Juan?" Rico turned the tables on his involuntarily monastic friend.

"Very well," Paul answered with naïve enthusiasm.

"Oh yeah? Whom are you seeing? Your own mug in the mirror?"

A smile lit up Paul's face: "I'm head over heals in love with this gorgeous Greek girl."

"What's her name?"

"Eleni."

"Have you said 'hi' to her yet?"

"Of course. I've even said, 'May I please have a decaf with cream but no sugar,'" Paul declared, proud of the degree of intimacy he had achieved with the young waitress in the brief span of only four months.

"Oh, yeah, now I remember .... So you're still dreaming about that little waitress... When are you going to take the plunge and try a more conventional approach to dating? Like asking her out?"

Paul smiled with sadness, moved by his own tragic fate: "I can't."

"Why the hell not? Too shy? Man, if you want, I'll do it for you!"

"It's not that. She's married."

Rico, however, didn't see that particular detail as a necessary barrier to dating: "So?"

"Her husband's a policeman," Paul clarified.

Rico began to understand the gravity of the situation. "Is he bigger than me?" he asked.

Paul looked his short and slight friend over: "Are you kidding? He's bigger than both of us put together! He'd pulverize us in a second."

"Maybe if we caught him off guard..." Rico proposed courageously.

"That's alright. I'm fine with the way things are," Paul said quietly.

"And that's precisely your problem!" Rico exclaimed. He couldn't understand how fantasizing about married, inaccessible waitresses could possibly qualify as a satisfying love life for a single man in his mid-thirties.

"You're a sculptor; I'm a scholar," Paul proceeded to explain the difference between them. "You need to see and touch while I'm perfectly content with thinking and dreaming."

"Great! Maybe together we can make a whole person. How about Isabelle? Is she still in the picture?" Rico touched upon a delicate, and still painful, subject. Isabelle had been Paul's first serious girlfriend, while he was still in graduate school at Princeton. She was an undergraduate exchange student from Paris, four years Paul's junior. For almost a year, she and Paul lived together in his studio apartment on campus, which saved her six thousand dollars' worth of rent and was a source of endless wonder for him. When the academic year was over, she even persuaded Paul to follow her to France.

Well, not technically, since the convincing went something like this: Isabelle told Paul that she had a boyfriend back in Paris with whom she had forgotten to break up during her sejour aux Etats-Unis. Paul exploded about the fact that she had failed to mention the boyfriend in question during the whole year they had dated. Isabelle indicated that, at least in her own mind and according to the superior norms of French culture, the relationship with Paul wasn't necessarily exclusive or serious. That turned out to be news to Paul. He felt angry and betrayed, but as soon as she left, he missed her terribly. So after a few months of unbearable separation, he called his ex-girlfriend to ask if he could visit her during the following summer. She said yes. At least, to Paul's ears, that's what it sounded like: consent. To an outside observer, however, her reply sounded something like this: "Oui, tu peux venir bien sûr, rien ne t'en empêche, mais je te previens que j'habite toujours avec mon copain Philippe." Which means, in plain English, come at your own risk and don't complain about sleeping on the sofa while I sleep with my boyfriend Philippe. Paul felt so attached to his former girlfriend that he endured this additional humiliation. But he felt heartbroken. He knew that Philippe would be there, unfortunately, but wasn't prepared for Isabelle's reserved demeanor towards him and their lack of chemistry. It was as if she weren't the same woman with whom he had fallen in love. So he returned to Princeton feeling completely defeated by his romantic rival, even if, following this setback, he loved France and all things French more than ever. After all, the women were very pretty and he couldn't have any of them. What more could a neurotic pessimist want from life? Paris was a haven of temptation and rejection.

"It sounds to me like you're in dire need of a new girlfriend," Rico diagnosed. "Do you want me to set you up with one of my models?"

Paul was, in his own way, open to the idea: "Are you nuts? Why would any of these gorgeous girls want to go out with me?"

"Now there's an attitude that will get you far in life! How many girlfriends have you had as a result? Almost three? Come on! How about I hook you up with Irina?"

Paul was torn between feeling outraged and being dizzy with hope: "You mean the angel that just floated past me?"

Rico smiled. "You'll discover that all chicks are made of flesh and blood."

"I don't like the word chicks," Paul disapproved.

"What do you want me to call them? Doves?"

"That's better. Doves. Doves of peace and doves of hope..." Paul rhapsodized.

"Right on! Don't worry about a thing, man. I'll take care of it," Rico patted his friend reassuringly on the back, before returning to his sculpture.

Chapter 6

That evening a momentous national event was about to take place: the Yankees were playing the Red Sox. Being an avid baseball fan, Paul prepared to give the match his undivided attention. Before the game, he drank two glasses of water and ate the five almonds usually reserved for the evening to aid the digestive process. He also took his shower early, shampooing and drying his hair very gently, by patting it softly with a towel, so as not to lose any more hair than nature intended. He then scribbled in his journal the most exciting activities of the day, as was his habit since adolescence: "Today I got up at 8:30 a.m. Listened to sports radio half an hour. Ate breakfast: glass of orange juice, bowl of cornflakes and five almonds. Went to the Eureka Café to see Eleni. Ordered coffee with salt instead of sugar, just to see her smile. She wore a miniskirt. Returned home ecstatic. Tended to boring administrative stuff. Read Gombrich. Ate two boiled eggs and toast for lunch. Taught The Modern Vision again. Class in vegetative state except for Monica Levin (too bad she's not my type). Went to the library. Read *Le Monde* and Libération to keep up with real news. Tonight, big baseball game: Yankees versus Red Sox. Can't wait!"

With the possible exception of the baseball game, Paul could have simply copied the journal entry from the day before verbatim, or the day before that for that matter, since his activities were ritualized. He never missed a single chance of writing in his journal, however, firmly adhering to the principle "A day not recorded is a day not lived." To make himself more comfortable, Paul took off his jeans and stretched out on the sofa in his paisley boxer shorts, which enabled him to concentrate more comfortably on each move of the game. He shouted, screamed, made loud commentaries, gave advice and applauded just like a regular fan at the stadium--minus the dress code. Around 8:00 p.m., the doorbell rang. "Geesh! I hope it's not one of those salesmen," Paul thought and went reluctantly to open the door.

He blinked twice, to make sure that he was not imagining things. "May I help you?" he asked the young woman who was waiting by the door. With her long brown hair and expressive eyes, she seemed very familiar, but Paul couldn't quite place her. Was she one of his students? An ex-student perhaps. But since she was a pretty girl, wouldn't he have remembered her? After all, he wasn't senile yet.

"I hope I'm not disturbing you," Irina said looking at Paul, who, clad in his boxer shorts, didn't seem exactly prepared for her visit.

"Not at all," Paul lied, feeling too flustered to invite his guest inside.

"If this is a bad time, we can set up another meeting," Irina noticed Paul's reticence.

"Meeting? No, that's okay. Please come in," he said, flustered.

Irina walked in and took a seat on the edge of the sofa. She was surprised by the fact Paul had no French accent.

"Aren't you French?" she asked, as if continuing a previous conversation.

At first he was surprised by her question, but then it occurred to him that the girl must be mistaking him for someone else: "What, me? No. Sorry. I think you must have the wrong apartment."

"But I recognize you. For some reason though, when we first met, I thought you were French," Irina replied.

"Well, as a matter of fact, I do speak French. I studied French art and my first girlfriend was Parisian," Paul didn't want to disappoint his guest.

Irina nodded, as if Paul's answer confirmed her initial conjecture: "That's what I thought. You seem... very... continental."

Paul was glad that the young woman approved of his cultural heritage, but still didn't know who she was or why she showed up at his apartment. "Would you like something to drink? Juice or a glass of water?" he offered, out of an instinct of politeness.

"No thanks. I don't drink before work," Irina replied. "I'd rather not have to go to the bathroom right in the middle of it," she added with a smile.

It? What was "it"? Paul was puzzled yet intrigued. "Do you usually work in the evenings?" he fished for more information.

"Sometimes. It all depends, " she answered unhelpfully.

"So you have a flexible schedule?" he probed further.

"Yes. As long as I can work around my classes, it's not a problem. Except for weekends, of course."

"What happens on weekends?"

"I travel," Irina answered.

"Where?"

"To New York City."

"I see," Paul replied, even though he didn't.

Irina looked around, wondering where Paul held his canvases and paintings. He must have placed them in another room, she speculated, since his living room didn't look like your typical studio. First of all, it was unusually neat and clean. The light oak furniture was just dusted. The kitchen was spotless. The light tan carpet was freshly vacuumed, and there were no paint stains on it.

Paul noticed Irina's surveillance of his place: "Sorry about the mess," he apologized, regretting that he hadn't dusted and vacuumed since that morning.

"Not at all!" Irina exclaimed. "I was just thinking how spick and span everything looks... it made me wonder... where do you do your work?"

"At the university," Paul answered.

"Are you a grad. student?"

"No I teach. I'm a visiting professor."

"Oh really? Where are you visiting from?"

"At the moment? Nowhere."

The young woman looked confused, so Paul felt obliged to clarify: "I'm originally from Collins College. It's an all-girl's school," he boasted, as if that were the highest mark of academic distinction. He preferred to avoid mentioning the part about getting fired for sexual harassment, however, since only a few of his buddies were impressed by that fact.

"That's a nice school," Irina said, not wishing to appear ignorant, though this was the first time she had heard of the place. "Are you traditional or modern?" she asked after a brief pause, to make conversation.

"Pardon?"

"In your painting style."

"Oh. Traditional, I guess," Paul answered, thinking of Bouguereau and the Impressionists he analyzed in his scholarly articles. "Well, actually, a little bit of both," he corrected himself, since it would be unfair to call his work on the Impressionists purely traditional. After all, they had been avant-garde.

"Kind of like Rico?"

"Yes!" Paul exclaimed, happy to finally recall where he had met his uninvited guest. She was the porcelain doll, Rico's new model. "Though it's difficult to compare painting to sculpture," he added more calmly, since she had a puzzled look on her face when he had shouted "yes" so enthusiastically.

"I suppose so," Irina agreed.

"You're Katrina, right?" Paul wanted to confirm.

"Irina," she corrected him. "It's a Romanian name, but my parents thought it sounded kind of international."

"I've never heard the name before," Paul commented.

Irina wasn't used to such lengthy preliminary small talk, since with Rico she got to work right away. In fact, that's how it usually went in the business, since Irina charged a hundred dollars an hour and artists didn't have a lot of money to waste. To save Paul unnecessary expenses, she decided to go ahead and prepare for the job.

"Do you mind if I use your bathroom?" she asked, thinking it would be most appropriate to change in private the first time.

"Not at all. First door on your left," he pointed Irina in the right direction, though there was no danger of getting lost in his tiny, one-bedroom apartment.

"Thanks," she smiled and headed for the bathroom. Once again, she was struck by its cleanliness. The toilet, with its lid down, was shiny and white. The sink was also impeccable. Not even a hair could be found in it. A toothbrush and a tube of organic spearmint toothpaste shared a clear plastic cup. The towels were all white, like at a hotel, neatly folded in two upon their racks. He must either have a maid or be one, Irina concluded.

In the meantime, Paul was still trying to figure out why Irina had paid him a visit. Not that he had any objections to it, though he did wish she had chosen a more propitious moment for it. He suspected that Rico must have had something to do with her visit, and intended to ask Irina about that. But the question froze upon his lips once Irina emerged from the bathroom with one of his large white towels wrapped around her naked body, her hair done up in a ballerina bun.

"Did you just take a shower?" Paul asked with bewilderment, since she had only been in there for about two minutes. He must have had a funny expression, since she laughed.

"No. I just didn't want to undress before you the first time, you know. Before we got to know one another a little better," she explained.

"Oh, okay."

"Where do you want me?" Irina asked.

"Pardon?"

"On the sofa or on the floor?" she specified, surveying the area.

"On the sofa, I guess," Paul answered, feeling a spell of excitement mixed with a serious dose of confusion.

"In what position?" Irina asked, very business-like.

"Excuse me?" What the hell is going on here? Paul wondered. Did Rico ask this girl to play a practical joke on me? "Not that I mind or anything, but can you please tell me, why did you take your clothes off?" Paul finally asked her in a very sweet, polite manner.

"I'm sorry," Irina said, blushing and regretting that she hadn't called to confirm their meeting in advance. "I guess I better leave," she added, turning to go back into the bathroom and dress.

"No, wait!" Paul stopped her. "I didn't mean to sound rude. It's just that I honestly don't understand why you're here."

"Didn't Rico tell you?"

"Tell me what?"

"About our appointment. He said that you're a painter friend of his who's looking for a good figure model. He said you'd be expecting me this evening at your place around 7:30 p.m."

Paul smiled, finally realizing that Rico had attempted to play matchmaker in his own crude and ineffectual fashion: "He must have misunderstood. I said I'm looking for a model with a good figure," he showed his cleverness with jeux de mots.

But Irina did not seem impressed.

"Look, I think Rico made a misguided attempt to set us up, " Paul explained.

Irina blinked, dismayed that the sculptor could have behaved so unprofessionally. "What do you mean?" she asked, trying to give Rico the benefit of the doubt.

"I'm not an artist," Paul said.

"Then what are you?" she asked, drawing up her towel more tightly around her body.

"An art history professor, like I said. I work on French Realism and Impressionism."

"Oh. Do you also paint?"

"Not really. My best drawings look like stick figures."

"Miro, Surrealism?" she gave Paul a last chance to be a real artist.

"No, they're just plain bad," Paul disappointed her once again.

"Then why in the world did Rico ask me to pose for you this evening?"

"I think it's because… I told him that I found you attractive."

"So you guys played a joke at my expense?"

"Yes. I mean no. No! Of course not. Like I said, I didn't even know you were coming here this evening."

Irina looked at him with distrust.

"I swear to God!" Paul defended himself. "This was all Rico's doing."

"Well then I'll never model for him again," Irina resolved. Although she enjoyed a good joke, she didn't tolerate lack of professionalism.

"Listen, I've known Rico for many years now and can assure you that he didn't mean any harm. He was just trying to do us a favor, that's all."

"Shouldn't he have consulted with us first?" Irina inquired.

"He did. I mean, he mentioned something to me about it."

"You were in on this also?" Irina fixed him with her gaze.

"Not at all! When Rico asked me if I'd like to go out with you, I said no."

Irina grew increasingly outraged by this apparently infinite regress of offensive remarks: "Excuse me? You said no? Who said that I'd want to go out with you?"

"That's exactly what I told him. I said, why would such a pretty woman want to go out with me? So he took it upon himself to set us up on a blind date."

"I'm going to put on my clothes now," Irina said softly and walked into the bathroom with as much dignity as she could muster, this time locking the door behind her.

Paul sat down on the sofa. He felt like he had completely blown this golden opportunity at a first potential date with the kind of girl he usually dreamed about. The worst part of this whole misunderstanding was, he didn't even get to see her naked. How stupid of him to deny being an artist right away! He could have at least waited for the towel to come off. Would it be too late to ask her out, he momentarily wondered, then decided that it was a lost cause. Which kind of took the pressure off the whole situation. Now that a date was out of the question, he felt free to desire Irina without too much anxiety. As far as Paul was concerned, the young woman was safely back where she belonged, in the realm of fantasy.

Chapter 7

Radu went to see her again at their little Parc Montsouris. More out of duty than out of genuine desire. He wavered between bitterness and nostalgia. After all these years, he was going to face his first love and his worst enemy, Ioana. He was early, as usual. Their bench was free, so he took a seat. When is it the optimal time to face once again the woman who broke your heart? he wondered. If you see her too soon, it hurts too much. But after awhile indifference washes away both the happy memories and the pain, and all you're left with is regret.

For the past two years he had been free to see Ioana but he had chosen not to. He was afraid it might reopen old wounds. Now, with the feelings of love only a distant memory and the wound nothing more than a scar, he didn't know what he could say to her. There was nothing left between them, he told himself. Not even the beauty of their past, since she had destroyed it through her actions.

Jean-Pierre persuaded him to agree to this meeting. "She has suffered so much. More than you can imagine," he told Radu. The young man felt like replying, "It serves her right." But that's not quite how he felt. No matter how much pain Ioana may have caused him, he never wanted to hurt her in turn. He was bitter without being vengeful.

In a matter of minutes, they would meet again. An anti-climax, Radu felt, a toy car offered as a Christmas gift to a child who has already grown up. He was so preoccupied with his own introspection that he hardly noticed a young woman slipping quietly next to him on the bench.

"You're as handsome as ever!" she uttered softly.

Radu turned around. Who was this skinny blond girl? was his initial reaction. "Ioana?" he couldn't repress his incredulity.

Her smile looked sad. "I know, I've changed quite a bit. You can't even recognize me." She noticed that he too had changed. His hair was much darker, an Espresso brown, like hers used to be. He now wore green contact lenses. And he was heavier, more muscular. No longer the slight young man in need of protection that she had dated many years ago. Yet she still recognized his delicate features and his sensual mouth, with its slightly curled lower lip.

Radu didn't know what to say. In the first few years after their break-up, he had imagined that when he'd see Ioana again his anger would resurface; that he'd finally give vent to it, like a volcano that had been dormant for too long. Yet now, confronted with her reality, he looked at the young woman's pale face and felt only concern. "Jean-Pierre told me that you're going through a tough time," he said.

She nodded. "I did. But I'm alright. He's our knight in shining armor, isn't he?" she smiled again, awkwardly. "He even helped both of us find jobs."

"Are you working for the Agency too?" Radu asked.

"You could say that. I do some translations for them from Romanian to English. But it's not much of a job; it barely covers rent."

Radu nodded. He knew exactly what kind of job she was talking about. "So you work for the FBIS?" The Foreign Broadcast Information Service was the branch of the Directorate that monitored and translated foreign media and clandestine radio stations abroad.

Ioana nodded in response.

"So what did you want to speak to me about?" Radu asked her.

"As you probably know, Jean-Pierre helped me more than I could ever thank him for. But I still have family in Romania. I'm very worried about ... one person in particular."

"Unfortunately he can't get our entire families out of the country," Radu answered reasonably. He recalled that Ioana had been particularly close to her father, who had been incarcerated as a political prisoner. "But I can understand why you might be worried about your dad. The Petrescu government notoriously retaliates against those who are left behind."

Ioana looked intently into his eyes, as if to decide whether or not to tell him everything. Was he ready for such news? Would he be sympathetic? Would he help her? Or would the news alienate him even more? she wondered. She felt torn. At that moment, Radu felt her emotional energy and a trace of his former feelings reignited.

"Why did you hurt me, Ioana? Why did you deliver me to those brutes?" he voiced the question he had wanted to ask her for so long.

"I had no choice," she answered in a low voice, almost a whisper. "They forced me."

"You could have left the organization."

"Yes, but only in a body bag."

"You could have not joined it in the first place."

"I didn't know what I was getting myself into."

Radu seemed skeptical.

"It's true!" Ioana protested, noticing his glance. "I swear. I didn't know about the violence."

"Oh, come on! Don't even pretend. Everyone knows that the Secret Police is violent. You could have not pretended that you were in love with me!" Radu heard himself say more loudly.

To this reproach, Ioana had no reply.

"Why did you fake love for me?" Radu insisted. "That's what really bothered me. Not that you used me for your own political ends. But leading me to believe that you cared about me... that was so low, Ioana, so low."

"I didn't lead you on."

"Right. And black is white and white is black."

"But I did love you," Ioana replied.

"Well, you had a funny way of showing it. You used me, made me believe that you loved me, turned me in to the butchers working for the *Securitate*, and then left me in their hands for dead. If that's your idea of love, I'm afraid to see your hate!"

"Raducu..." Ioana placed her hand gently upon his shoulder.

"Please don't touch me and don't call me Raducu! We're not lovers any more."

She removed her hand quickly, as if she had touched fire. "We weren't supposed to fall in love. And I didn't mean to betray you. Things just got out of hand," she tried to explain.

"So now you take no responsibility for your choices," Radu interjected.

"We didn't come here to fight," Ioana tried to pacify him.

"We didn't come here to be friends either," he replied coldly. "We can't be lovers because you betrayed me. We can't be friends, because friends trust and care about each other. Ioana, if I didn't want to see you the past few years since you came to the United States it's because... everything between us is dead."

The young woman's eyes filled with tears. "No. Not everything. A part of us, a very important part of our love, still lives on." In spite of her words of hope, Ioana felt profoundly discouraged. She was moved by Radu's pain yet defeated by his bitterness. Whenever the optimal moment to tell him what she needed to say might have been, she understood now that it was gone.

Chapter 8

Since it was already 10:00 p.m. on a Saturday night, Irina suspected that Lori, her roommate, would have returned by now from the art history library and may already be asleep. They had experienced quite a bit of tension lately due to the fact that, unbeknownst to Irina, Lori had switched from a mild case of Buddhism to hardcore Evangelical Christianity during the previous summer. Armed with a reborn moral consciousness, she now objected to Irina's extracurricular activities. Irina wished she had been informed about Lori's conversion before becoming her roommate. The previous year, she recalled, Lori had been a nerdy but nonetheless gregarious freshman. Aside from spending most of her days and pre-exam nights in the glass cubicle of the art history library, during mealtimes--the only moments Lori could spare for socializing--she also engaged in normal sophomoric activities such as gossip, giggling and discussing her secret crushes on guys who weren't aware of her existence. Since her spiritual rebirth, however, the two roommates began to experience some tension. Of course, Lori didn't know for sure what went on between Irina and Jean-Pierre, and, furthermore, she considered it none of her business. However, since Irina posed nude for strange men and dated a much older Frenchman with dubious morals every weekend, her roommate assumed that her friend's soul was in great peril.

To avoid stirring up discussions, Irina proceeded with caution. She slipped the key into the lock noiselessly, then felt her way into the living room without turning on the lights. In her painstaking effort not to wake up her roommate, she stumbled over a backpack, leaned on a little table to catch her balance and knocked off a lamp. An inquisitive light appeared underneath the bedroom door.

"Irina, is that you?" came an apprehensive voice from the bedroom.

"Yes. Sorry about that! I was trying not to wake you up!" Irina announced as she entered the small bedroom, furnished sparsely with two desks, two chairs and two bunk beds. Lori was perched on the upper bunk since Irina was scared of heights. She was dressed in a Hello Kitty pink nightgown. "Worked like a charm. But that's okay, since I wasn't sleeping anyway. I get worried knowing you're wondering around at night."

"Lori, normal college kids go out partying on Friday nights," Irina informed her roommate.

"My parents didn't pay 30,000 dollars a year for my college education so that I can waste my time on parties," Lori retorted.

"Precisely. That's why kids don't generally tell their parents about what they do in college," Irina concurred.

"Excuse me, but I'm not into dishonesty."

"To each his own," Irina replied with a shrug.

"So how did it go?"

"What?"

"The meeting with the artist."

"Okay...I guess."

"Is he good?"

"I didn't really get to find out."

"How come?"

Lori avoided her roommate's glance.

"Did he hit on you?" Lori asked, adopting the tone of someone whose worst suspicions are confirmed.

"No, nothing like that."

"Did he sketch you?"

"No."

"Sculpt you?"

"No."

"Then what in the world did he do?"

"Nothing. As it turns out, the whole thing was based on a misunderstanding. He's not really a painter. Nor a sculptor for that matter. He's an art history professor."

"At least he's got the word "art" in his title… What's his name? I may know him."

"Paul Smith."

"He teaches Impressionism, right?"

"Yes. Did you take a class with him?"

"Not yet, but I've seen him around the department. He has a pretty good reputation."

A few rapid knocks on the door interrupted their conversation. Irina went to the door and peered carefully through the peephole. She was surprised to see Christine, her freshman year roommate. The two of them got along okay, given that they were polar opposites. Christine was the perfect sorority girl: athletic (a member of both the rowing and the swimming teams), popular, and exceedingly social. She was as disciplined about going out to parties at the eating clubs on Thursday through Sunday nights (to which, to her credit, she was invited by junior and senior men) as she was about waking up bright and early at 5:00 a.m. to do three hours of rowing or swimming practice. The two roommates would have gotten along even better if it weren't for Christine's quick metabolism: she had such good circulation compared to Irina's catatonic pulse that she slept with the windows wide open even in the dead of winter. Which made Irina feel like an experiment in cryogenics despite swaddling herself in the five exotic, camel wool blankets shipped express (by ship) by her grandmother directly from Romania.

Under more propitious circumstances, the girls might have become closer, since Christine wasn't your typical vacuous party girl. Although she did look the part --long blond hair with fringed bangs brushed to the side; light blue eye shadow that matched the color of her eyes; heavy mascara, and glittery pink lip gloss—in private conversation she was able to say quite a bit more than "cool" and "what's up?" Her parents lived in Switzerland most of the year and had a second home in their native Hartford, Connecticut. Christine had been educated in some of the best boarding schools and was fluent in English, French and German. With Irina she would discuss Brecht and Marquez, yet, unlike her less socially adept former roommate, she didn't let culture stand in the way of her social life.

"Hi!" Irina said, her eyes wide with surprise.

Christine brushed her fringy bangs from her forehead. "Hey. I just dropped by to see if you guys wanted to go out to a club," she said very casually.

Irina instinctively looked behind her, to check if there were any other guys in the room. "Us?"

"Yeah. This junior I hooked up with last week gave me free passes to Ivy," Christine explained.

"And you're inviting me and Lori to... Ivy?"

"That's right, " Christine confirmed the good news, however implausible it may have sounded.

Something was fishy about this whole scenario, Irina suspected. If it had been an invitation to Quadrangle, the dining club for which both Lori and Irina had signed up she might have understood. But Ivy? The most prestigious and selective of Princeton's eleven eating clubs? Ivy was so posh that even F. Scott Fitzgerald wrote about it in This Side of Paradise. Its importance to undergraduate life couldn't be overestimated. In fact, the eating clubs in general were the center of the universe for Princeton upperclassmen. It's there that they ate, hosted parties, listened to bands, got wasted, watched movies and—most importantly--hooked up, usually in the aftermath of a drunken stupor and right before, or sometimes even during, the bathroom barfing sessions.

Some of the clubs, like Quadrangle and Terrace (the artsy ones) and Colonial Club (which future doctors and lawyers tended to join) were non-selective. Which essentially meant that you entered your name in a lottery, listing your top three choices in order of preference, and automatically got into one of them. Independently of one another, Lori and Irina had both selected Quad, since it was comfortably literary and artistic without being pretentious. Unlike Terrace members, Quadies didn't have a mandatory non-conformist uniform of all black attire (preferably dingy and in shreds) complemented by a wide variety of ripped fishnet stockings, black leather boots, and, if you were cool enough to pull it off, an optional bdsm dog collar. Irina's number two choice, Colonial, was the nice, clean-cut professional club. Her third choice was, by default, Terrace, which is where the Studio Art crowd generally hung out. Terrace should have been Irina's most logical first choice, given her interest in art. However, generally speaking, she preferred to read about decadence rather than practice it.

By way of contrast to these open admission clubs, Ivy was selective—in fact, the most selective eating club on campus. To get accepted, you had to bicker—meaning be chosen by its members after passing a series of interviews and challenges—and, above all, be one of the beautiful people. For women, beauty was a quality you were born with, confirmed by a rigorous hazing ritual that tested your social abilities, especially the most useful ones such as how sexy you looked in high heels and a tight and appropriately exorbitant evening gown; how well you handled eating a six course meal using three forks; and, last but not least, how well you tolerated near-lethal doses of alcohol while still maintaining your poise and conversational skills in at least three languages (though, in all fairness, all three of them could be slurred dialects of English).

"Thanks, but we've already signed up for Quad," Lori responded curtly. Irina, who had a hankering for adventure, however, was interested in finding out more: "Why us?" she asked Christine.

"What do you mean?"

"Well... you must admit, we're not exactly Ivy types...."

Christine feigned disagreement: "Of course you are!" she declared, looking at Lori, who, in her Hello Kitty pajamas and wide-rimmed pink glasses, must have looked like a scene from Revenge of the Nerds II with a female cast.

"I'm going to bed!" Lori announced and promptly withdrew into her bedroom like a turtle retreating into its shell.

"Are you bickering?" Irina peered straight into Christine's cool blue eyes.

"Yes," the latter was obliged to admit.

"So then, Lori and I are your challenge?"

"All I have to do is train a novice in the art of hooking up," Christine cheerfully declared.

"What's hooking up?" Irina asked, clearly qualifying both as a novice and as a challenge.

When discussing such matters, Christine naturally slipped into her best imitation of a Valley girl accent: "Well, you like get together with this guy you don't really know, but you sort of know him. Like a friend of a friend. Or the cute guy in your orgo class you were hoping would ask you out. There's no point waiting by the phone. We're liberated women of the eighties, after all." Since Irina's liberated face still looked puzzled, Christine added: "Anyways, you'll love it. It'll be fun."

Irina was not entirely convinced: "In order to hook up, do you have to sleep with the guy?"

"Not necessarily. If you don't like him, you can just make out or something."

"Now that's a relief!"

"But for it to be technically a hook-up you've got to do stuff that, you know, you can't really do in public. At least second base, preferably third," Christine elaborated.

"I already have a boyfriend," Irina announced, hoping this would dissuade Christine from pursuing the matter any further.

"You mean that old dude you were dating last year? Your French grandfather? Sorry, but he doesn't count. You need to be with someone your own age. Or at least your father's age," Christine took a seat next to Irina on the sofa. "Alright," she said slapping both hands on her knees to indicate that she was ready to get down to business.

"First step in a hook up: dress the part."

Irina looked down at her knee-length pleated skirt, blue knee socks, Mary Jane shoes and fifties shirt buttoned all the way up to the collarbone. She was pretty pleased with herself: "Done!"

Christine begged to differ: "Are you kidding me? You couldn't even go to a funeral dressed in this outfit!"

"But I like my clothes," Irina objected. "They're from Petite Sophisticate. Look: I even match, see?" she pointed with her forefinger to her light blue shirt and navy skirt ensemble.

"Irina, your clothes might be okay if you were postmenopausal. But you'll never get a guy dressed like this. Unless of course he's postmenopausal," she added, alluding once again to poor Jean-Pierre.

"I don't see anything wrong with my outfit," Irina held her ground.

"Gosh! Where should I begin? For one thing, you don't wear blue knee socks after graduating from grade school. Second, your skirt may have been popular in the fifties, but now it's totally out..."

"The fifties are making a come-back," Irina wanted to show that she too read Vogue and knew a thing or two about style.

"Not in this country," Christine cut short that Eurofashion trend, and started picking on another: "How about your lipstick?"

Irina pressed and rubbed together her bright red lips: "What about it?"

"We're not in the red light district of Amsterdam. Here," Christine opened her slim Gucci bag, unzipped an inner pocket, and took out a glittery lip-gloss with sparkles: "This one's more subtle."

"If you're a Christmas tree perhaps," Irina mumbled.

"Listen, if you don't want to look hip, that's your problem," Christine zipped up her purse to indicate that without cooperation, the pre-hookup mentoring was over.

Irina looked at her companion to understand better what it meant to look hip and ascertain if she herself could have such high aspirations. Christine wore a tight, stretchy white tube top through which you could see the areolas of her nipples. The shirt was so tiny that it exposed, to her advantage, other parts of her anatomy as well, such as her bellybutton. The bottom was as fashionably undressed as the top: she wore a low-rise blue miniskirt with ruffles, which barely covered her behind. If Christine dropped something on the floor and had to bend over to pick it up, she could spare several lucky voyeurs the cost of buying a *Playboy*. Her hair was bleached platinum blond and her fringed bangs fell in a sweep upon her eyes, obliging her to periodically toss her head with confidence. Unconsciously, Irina imitated that motion, though perhaps slightly less gracefully than her companion.

"What's the matter? A fly landed on your head?" Christine inquired.

Irina gave her a dirty look, but Christine continued her constructive criticism: "No wonder. Just look at your hair. It's a mess. You're in desperate need of a haircut."

"I prefer my hair long," Irina said.

"Then you need to do something with it."

"Like what?"

"I don't know. Comb it?"

Given the turn the conversation had taken, Irina became even less enthusiastic about being selected as Christine's hazing subject. "I don't know about this hook up, make-over thing. Maybe it's just not for me," she tried to back out of the whole operation.

But it was too late. "Nonsense!" Christine said. "After I get through with you, you'll look sensational. I guarantee it. The guys will stick to you like flies," she reassured her, spraying a generous dose of Polo for Women on her former roommate.

"I'm not exactly the femme fatale type," Irina pointed out.

"Well... I can't argue with that," Christine acknowledged the great challenge she was facing. But becoming a member of Ivy and partying hard every weekend with la crème de la crème of Princeton undergraduate society made the hardship and pain well worth it. With a renewed sense of resolution, Christine got up from the sofa, walked into the bathroom and came back with moist towel in her hands.

"First things first. We've got to get rid of this dreadful make-up," she said, alluding to Irina's bright red lipstick and orange blush, which the latter thought went beautifully with her long dark hair, giving her the glossy look of a painted doll that was still in vogue in some corners of Eastern Europe (at least for the older, babushka generation).

"What brand of make-up do you use?" Christine inquired.

"I don't know. Whatever they sell at Wal-Mart," Irina responded. That, apparently, was not the correct answer.

"L'Oreal? Max Factor?" Christine jogged her friend's memory.

"No way! That stuff's expensive. I use the one dollar kind."

"Grody," Christine scowled. Once she wiped Irina's face clean of the cheap discount paint, she reopened her purse and exhibited each of its wonders, one by one, patiently explaining to Irina their purpose: "Try using Estée Lauder. It's good stuff, plus affordable. You can find it at Macy's, Filene's, Sack's Fifth Avenue, you know, all the discount stores," she said, concluding the beauty session.

"You call those stores discount?"

"Yes. What do you call them?"

"Expensive."

"Well, you know what they say. You get what you pay for," Christine expressed her philosophy of life and started patting foundation with the tips of her fingers upon Irina's face. She stepped back to take a look at her canvas, after which she approached again, took out a little brush made out of fine pony hair, gently dipped it in a palate of Delectable Peach blush and began applying it with little strokes along Irina's cheekbones. "Better," she concluded, taking once again a step back to examine her masterpiece. Then she took out the Magic Pink gloss and rubbed it on Irina's lips. "Go like this," she instructed, pressing and moving her own lips together in example. Irina complied. "What an improvement!" Christine congratulated herself. "Let's move on to the hair. What do you call that bird's nest on top of your head?"

"My bun?" Irina wondered.

"So that's what it is! Buns are for grannies and cinnamon places," Christine informed her.

Irina would not accept criticism of her hairstyle as easily as the other comments: "For your information, elegant French women wear chignons."

"But since you're neither elegant nor French..." Christine allowed Irina to draw her own conclusions. She then undid her companion's hair, which fell down in gentle, long brown waves. "What a lot of hair! Now what should we do with it..." Christine pondered. A solution occurred to her. She took out a slim, brown comb from her magic purse and parted Irina's hair straight in the middle, except for the straight bangs, which Irina preferred because they camouflaged imperfections during a certain critical time of the month. "Do you want spiral curls?" Christine asked.

"I guess."

"Okay, then hand me your curling iron."

"I don't have one."

Christine's eyes widened in disbelief. "Are you kidding me? You're a sophomore in college and you don't even own a curling iron?"

"I have books," Irina thought this bit of information might compensate for her deficiency in the styling department. Her comment was duly ignored. One had to admit, however, that with parted, smooth long hair, mascara, pink lip gloss and a more subtle shade of peach blush than the usual bright orange, Irina looked almost sophisticated. Christine now felt prepared to confront the even more daunting wardrobe challenge.

"Could you please remove your knee socks?" she asked politely yet unequivocally.

"Why? I like my socks!"

"Irina, you're not in grade school any more. In college, you—and by you, I mean a normal woman, of course--wear pantyhose with closed-toe shoes, or bare legs with open-toed sandals. That's the rule."

"Alright," Irina reluctantly removed her Mary Janes and blue knee-highs.

"Do you have any air freshener?" Christine inquired, crinkling her nose once this procedure was over. She bent down to spray some Polo for women on Irina's feet. "Oh, my Gosh!" she screamed in utter shock, her hand flying to her chest.

"What happened?" Irina asked, startled.

"Are you planning to join the East German women's swim team?"

"What are you talking about?"

"Have you ever heard of shaving?"

"Why? I don't have a beard," Irina protested.

"I mean your legs! They're horrid!"

"But I do shave my legs! Once a week."

"Clearly that's not enough..." Christine ran her fingers past the stubble. "You should wax."

"I should what?" Irina asked, confused about what cleaning floors had to do with personal grooming.

"Wax. They apply these strips of wax and pull your hair away everywhere it's necessary: legs, bikini line, underarms," Christine explained. "It hurts a little at first but in the end it's well worth it. Irina, you're in desperate need of a spa treatment. Look at your toenails! We can't be seen in public like this. When was your last pedicure?"

Irina didn't have to think hard: "Never. I didn't think I needed one."

"Of course you do! Every self-respecting woman needs one. What a mess! But we don't have time to fix all this right now. You'll just have to wear tights with a mini and pray that whoever has the misfortune to hook up with you won't turn on the light. Or touch your legs. Oh, hell, let's just hope he'll be drunk out of his mind."

"Who said I want to hook up with anyone, let alone a drunk?"

Since this was Christine's main challenge in the hazing process, it was the one point she refused to concede: "Do you have much tolerance for alcohol?"

"I drink half a glass of champagne on New Year's Eve," Irina informed her.

"Good," Christine pronounced. "A few shots of tequila and you'll be good to go."

She examined Irina up and down. The pleated long skirt still didn't pass the minimum standard. "Do you have a nice short skirt? And this time... please, something that's not borrowed from your grandmother's closet."

"I've got jeans," Irina proposed the next best thing.

"Alright. But at least wear them with a tube top!"

"How about this shirt?" Irina showed her a pink top.

Christine shook her head: "Too prosaic. Unless, of course, they'll have a wet t-shirt contest tonight." Then she looked at Irina's modest sized chest and had a change of heart: "Or maybe not ..."

Irina went into her bedroom, rummaged frantically through her closet, and came out dressed in a white extra-small white t-shirt, tight Levis jeans and blue flats.

"Change those clods to high heels," Christine commanded with the poise of a general. Irina reemerged like a brave solider—or guinea pig—wearing high-heeled shoes: "So how do I look?"

"Like you're going out for an ice-cream in the afternoon with a former boyfriend you're no longer in love with," Christine pronounced the fashion verdict and the two girls finally headed out to Ivy Club.

Chapter 9

Irina and Christine made their way down Prospect Street, the main artery of Princeton's pulsating social life, where all the eating clubs were located.

"Walk like a girl," Christine advised her companion.

"I am!" Irina protested, looking around. As far as she could tell in the darkness, clusters of young women and men were walking in a more or less serpentine, uneven manner, leaning upon one another, talking loudly and laughing. "What's the point of learning how to walk sexy if once you leave the clubs, you're so drunk that you can barely put one foot in front of the other?" she asked.

"Don't you make your bed in the morning?" Christine inquired.

"Yeah, so?"

"Since you're going to mess it up anyway, why bother?"

Although impressed by her friend's Socratic reasoning, Irina resisted its conclusion: "Walking is the most convenient way of getting from point A to point B. I learned how to do it when I was two," she retorted.

"And that's precisely your problem. You're a case of arrested development. Take longer steps. Stand up straighter and swing your hips. Like this," Christine demonstrated a sinuous walk, something between the model's catwalk and the prostitute's catcall. Irina tried to mimic the movement, swaying her hips and teetering on her high heels.

"Let's just stick to the toddler walk, okay?" Christine proposed, after silently observing her.

Since the girls were about to enter Ivy Club, Christine flashed an artificial smile that remained glued to her face for most of the evening. The club was dark, crowded and noisy. Everyone strived to talk a few decibels above the blaring pop music. The popular song Shake it, shake it real good set the romantic tone of the evening. Every room was redolent with the aroma of beer mixed with expensive cologne and perfume that were punctuated by a hint of vomit.

Christine apparently knew her way around the place pretty well. "Hey. How's it going?" she greeted a few acquaintances, then pulled Irina by the sleeve into a corner, to give her a few more pointers. "You're in luck tonight," she announced.

"Why?" Irina asked in all sincerity, since she was intimidated by crowds, was attracted to older men rather boys her own age, didn't drink except for New

Year's Eve and preferred French songs of the sixties and seventies to American pop music.

"Since this is hazing week, there are a few men in your league here tonight. It shouldn't be that difficult to hook up," Christine delivered the good news. "See that tall guy with the little hat and glasses on the left? The one standing next to the gorgeous blond?" she discretely pointed with her pinky in their direction.

Irina looked to the left. "That's not a hat, it's a yarmulke," she instantly recognized Ben, the lanky boy with a twin brother from the Hillel Club. They had engaged in a brief conversation a few weeks ago, following an inspiring lecture on the future of Zionism. Irina went to Hillel from time to time to get back in touch with her Jewish roots.

"I'm kind of into the blond guy myself," Christine staked her claim.

"Do you know him?"

"Yeah," Christine affirmed. "His name is Josh. We've never actually spoken, but I see him all the time at the Arch Sings. He's so unbelievably cute, don't you think? He's a Footnote." She didn't need to say more, since everyone from Princeton knew that being a member of The Footnotes, the oldest all male a capella group on campus, represented the epitome of coolness. The Footnotes were all gorgeous and sang with beautiful, well harmonized voices, wooing the female members of the audience with their boy band charm: head cocked to the side, hand to the heart, looking straight into the longing eyes of the prettiest girls in the crowd while singing timeless love songs. Even Irina was obliged to admit that Josh was a hottie: blond hair cropped short, sparkling blue eyes, tall, the built of an Adonis, white Polo shirt and jeans with strategic holes in them which cost extra.

"What if I prefer Josh to Ben?" Irina wondered out loud.

Christine gave her a look that clearly indicated such a violation of the girl code would most certainly not be kosher. "I thought you were Jewish," she said.

"Only on my father's side. Which doesn't really count. Except when it comes to persecution and pogroms," Irina explained her ethnic status.

"That's too bad..." Christine replied, thinking about how the two of them could double score with the guys. "Let's go say hi to them, okay?" she proposed a logical first line of attack.

Josh smiled charmingly at Christine as soon as they made eye contact. "Hey. What's up?" he struck a smooth conversation.

"Nothing much, just hanging out," Christine eloquently replied.

"I saw you at the Arch Sing the other day," Irina informed Josh.

"I know, I was there," Josh laughed, attempting to impress the girls with his wit. Christine laughed obligingly, but Irina just found the comment a bit rude, so she turned to his companion.

"Hi Ben. Do you remember me?"

Ben drew a blank.

"From the Hillel lecture? On Zionism?" Irina refreshed his memory.

"Trina, right?" Ben replied.

"Irina."

"Oh, yeah. Now I remember. You're Russian," Ben informed her.

"Romanian. Same difference!"

"Do you girls want something to drink?" Josh asked.

"What do they have? I'm in the mood for a Cosmo," Christine replied.

"We've got Miller light, Bud and Guinness. On tap."

"I guess I'll have a beer then," Christine said, amused by the variety of options.

"And what would you like?" Josh graciously turned to Irina.

"I'd like a Perrier with a lime twist, please," Irina named her favorite beverage. She felt a sharp elbow poke in the ribs—on the side closest to Christine-- and abruptly changed her mind, "I'll have a beer too. Thanks."

"Be right back, ladies," Josh answered gallantly and headed for the bar. Which left Ben on his own with the two girls. "Do you go to Israel often?" he asked Irina, preferring to start on familiar ground.

"Once a year, to see my grandmother," she replied.

"Where does she live?"

"In Carmiel. Do you know where that is?"

"Sure. Near Haifa."

"That's right!" Irina exclaimed, surprised to see that someone else had heard of Carmiel. "Is that where your family lives too?"

"I've got a few relatives in Haifa and Tel Aviv," Ben said.

"Do you visit them often?" Irina asked.

"About once a year. I spend my summers either with relatives or at a kibbutz. But I plan to move to Israel permanently once I finish college."

Christine was beginning to feel left out, so Ben attempted to include her in the conversation:

"Are you Jewish too?" he turned to her.

"No. German on my mother's side; Swiss on my Dad's, protestant on both," she replied.

Ben considered her genealogy for a moment. "Was your grandfather a Nazi?" he pursued tactfully.

"I beg your pardon?"

"Nothing."

Christine's face brightened when her knight in shinning armor returned with two beers to save the damsels in distress.

"Thanks," the girls said in unison when Josh offered them their drinks.

"So, you're trying out for Ivy?" Josh asked Christine.

"Does your grandmother like Carmiel?" Ben asked Irina.

"Sure, why not?" Christine shrugged. "It seems fun."

"Actually, it's a very sad story," answered Irina. "My grandfather died a few years ago. My grandmother Sara is only seventy-four, which is not that old, but she's very ill. She has Alzheimer's' or something very similar to it. The doctors aren't sure, since the symptoms of her illness resemble the advanced stages of senility. Basically, she's losing her memory. It fades in and out. Last summer, there were times when she didn't even recognize me. It's terrible to see someone you love deteriorate like that."

"I can't complain. Life's a blast," Josh cheerfully told Christine.

"I know what you mean," Ben answered sympathetically.

"If the rumors are true, you guys sure know how to party..." Christine replied.

"That's not the worst of it," Irina said. "She has these weird hallucinations that people are coming to steal her clothes. She once ran out naked into the street. Can you imagine? At her age?"

"Whew! Man, is it getting hot in here or is it just me?" Josh asked, shaking his shirt, which clung to his moist skin.

"Gee, that's a serious problem," Ben responded.

"I'm getting hot too," Christine answered and took a sip of her cold beer, looking seductively into Josh's eyes.

"Is there something you guys can do about it?" Ben asked Irina.

Josh was already thinking ahead, about where he might be able to carry on a more private conversation with Christine later on that night. "What do you like to do for fun?" he asked her.

"Unfortunately, not much," Irina replied. "I mean, from thousands of miles away what can one do, right? After that incident, we hired someone to take care of her. She definitely can't live on her own any more."

"I try to live life to the fullest," Christine answered. "I do a little bit of everything: swimming, dancing, rowing, skiing, hanging out at parties...I even learned how to surf last summer. Though I grew up in Switzerland, I love hot weather and the beach."

"So why don't you move to Israel then?" Ben suggested. "It would be so much easier to take care of your grandmother if you're actually there."

"No kidding!" Josh said, intrigued by Christine's athletic abilities. "I'm from Colorado, but I'd love to learn how to surf. Maybe you can teach me some day."

"I can't," Irina answered with certitude. "It would be too complicated. My family's settled here. My parents have jobs in Ann Arbor; we bought a house; I'm going to college here. As for Israel, to tell you the truth, my sentimental ties are to my family, not the country. Generally speaking, I love people, not places. You know what I mean?"

"Sure," Christine answered breathlessly. "If we ever happen to visit California together," she added.

"No," Ben firmly responded. Irina's answer hadn't scored any bonus points with him. "How can you say that Israel's just a place? It's our home. The only place the Jewish people have left on Earth. Aren't you Jewish? Don't you care?"

"Maybe one day," Josh answered. "I also love to swim and play tennis. In high school I was Varsity on both teams. Do you play tennis?"

"Of course I do," Irina responded. "But one can be Jewish without living in Israel. Don't Jews live all over the world?"

"Yes, but not that well," Christine replied.

"And that's precisely the problem," Ben said. "Without a nation of their own, Jews are at the mercy of the world."

"Don't sweat it," Josh calmly replied. "We can practice together this weekend if you want," he proposed.

"Now wait a minute: I think you're going a bit overboard," Irina replied. "The Jewish people can survive without all moving to Israel. Besides, it's a sliver of a country. Where would we all fit?"

"I'll see if I can squeeze you in," Christine smiled playfully at Josh. "Who knows? I may surprise you. Maybe I'll beat you at your own game..." she teased.

"How stupidly optimistic! That's called sticking your head in the sand like an ostrich," Ben declared.

"Oh yeah? We'll see about that..." Josh answered cheerfully. "So do you have a roommate? Or do you live all by your lonesome self?" he charmingly segued to his more immediate concern.

"Now how can you talk to me this way? For God's sake, you don't even know me!" Irina protested. "Don't you think you're being a bit narrow-minded to judge me?" she narrowed her eyes at Ben.

"Yes," Christine replied. "I have a single in Joline Hall. It's small but cozy," she added, toying with one of Josh's shirt buttons.

"What you need is to marry a good Jew and have a dozen kids," Ben suggested.

By then, Josh had his hands all over Christine's behind and his tongue was attempting to tie the knot with hers.

"A woman's duty is making babies," Ben pursued, showing how enlightened orthodoxy could be even when it lagged a few hundred years behind the times and adopted nineteenth-century Pale of Settlement ghettos as its cultural ideal.

Christine and Josh seemed prepared to practice what Ben preached.

"Excuse me, but I want to be an artist, not some man's baby machine," Irina said.

Josh felt in his pant pocket to check if he still had that extra condom.

"Women are no good at art," Ben declared.

Josh, however, considered Christine pretty adept at the art of love.

"Oh yeah? Have you ever heard of Berthe Morrisot? Or Mary Cassatt? How about Georgia O'Keeffe?" Irina countered.

"Man, if I make out with this hot chick," Josh vowed, feeling particularly romantic that starry night, "tomorrow I'm buying her flowers."

"Big deal! Babies and flowers. Who cares about that stuff anyways?" Ben retorted.

Apparently Josh did. He cared about flowers that resembled female genitalia and definitely liked female genitalia that resembled flowers. "Do you wanna go over to my place?" he whispered hotly in Christine's ear.

"I thought you liked babies and wanted to have twelve of your own," Irina said to Ben.

"How about we go to my place instead?" Christine proposed, preferring to be on familiar turf with an unfamiliar man.

"I think women should make babies, not paint them," Ben replied.

Josh and Christine more or less concurred with this plan--at least with the process, if not exactly the end result. "Irina, Josh and I are going to go hang out together," Christine announced. "We'll talk tomorrow, alright?"

"Okay." Irina found an entirely unnecessary excuse to part company with Ben and return promptly to her dorm room, feeling that if "hooking up" is what dating entailed in America, she'd give serious consideration to her grandmother's idea of an arranged marriage.

Chapter 10

Later that night, Irina stayed awake for hours thinking about her conversation—if one could call it that—with Ben. At the party, she found his comments sexist, irrational and chauvinistic. But now she thought there might be a grain of truth in them. At any rate, they made her think about her family's past in Romania. She thought of her Jewish grandparents on her father's side of the family, Grandma Sara and Grandpa Abram, with whom she spent every summer in the little Moldavian village of Tecuci. She recalled moments that had seemed to her akin to magic: her grandfather taking her to the synagogue one summer evening when she was four years old. Irina was the only little girl among a group of pious men. She dropped the Torah on the floor by mistake; her grandfather picked it up and kissed it with unspeakable reverence. At home, her grandmother had prepared the Shabbat dinner. Before they ate, she prayed, in a sing-song, lamenting yet beautiful voice, speaking in another tongue, her eyes closed, her hands moving circularly above the Sabbath candles like at a séance. Her grandmother's thinning curly white hair was covered by a basma, the handkerchief used to protect feminine modesty. Being raised in a communist regime, Irina had never learned the meaning of these rituals; in her eyes, they belonged to the otherworldly realm of fairy tales and magic rather than religion. Nonetheless, they left a lasting impression that was also this worldly. Jewish rituals filled her with a sense of family tradition, of belonging to something greater than the individual, and of a spiritual intimacy that she would long for later in life.

She also learned, however, about the flip side of being Jewish, which was very different from these nostalgic childhood recollections. When she was eleven years old, a year before leaving for America, she asked Grandma Sara whether Grandpa Abram had fought in WWII, since she was learning about that in history class. Her grandmother answered, "No he hadn't, because he was Jewish." Which seemed like a nonsequitor. Irina couldn't understand what being Jewish had to do with the issue of fighting for your country. After all, wasn't Grandpa Abram Romanian also? That evening, her grandmother told her about their lives in Romania, before either she or even her father were born. They had survived terrible times. In August of 1940—"I remember the exact day," her grandmother said, "when the Iron Guard and the Legionarii, the Romanian fascist movements under the leadership of Marshal Ion Antonescu, took power from King Carol."

"Why did the king allow that?" Irina pursued.

"I don't know. He was in on it too, I guess," Grandma Sara answered vaguely, alluding to the king's high tolerance for anti-Semitism. "He was no better than the rest of them," she shrugged.

But actually, after King Carol's abdication, things got much worse for Romanian Jews. Grandma Sara's recollection of historical events wasn't perfect; years later, Irina complemented it by reading books on the subject. She learned that after the Nazi-Soviet pact, the Russians wanted to occupy a large portion of Romania, which included Bessarabia and Bukovina. Since Germany depended upon Romanian oil, however, the Nazis were anxious to minimize tension in the area. So they put pressure on King Carol to allow the Russians to take nearly a third of his country's territory. After doing that, King Carol felt so politically impotent and humiliated that he abdicated. That's how Marshall Ion Antonescu, an avid admirer of Hitler, and his Legionarii and Iron Guard fascist movements took over the country.

"And then the Iron Guard started killing Jews?" Irina asked.

"Yes. Many, many Jews," her grandmother answered. "They wanted to eradicate all the Jewish people from the face of the Earth."

"But why?"

"I don't know," Grandma Sara shook her head with sadness. "It's better not to talk about such things. Maybe when you're a little older...."

"How did they kill them?" Irina, whose curiosity had been aroused, didn't relent.

"You're too young to know about so much suffering," her grandmother repeated.

Years later, in America, Irina sought the answer, once again, in historical accounts. She found out that as soon as the Antonescu's regime took power, it instigated a series of brutal pogroms, which claimed the lives of more than half of Romania's 750,000 Jews. Some people were shot. Others were skinned alive and placed on hooks in Jewish butcher shops, with the sign "kosher meat" attached to their corpses. Many were forced at gunpoint to dig their own graves, remove their clothes and set them aside for the fascists to take. They were subsequently shot in the back of the head to fall into the mass graves that they, themselves, had dug.

But for the time being Irina had to content herself with what her grandmother could, or wanted to, tell her. "Were any of our relatives killed by... what was their name again? The Iron Fist?" she asked.

"The Iron Guard," Grandma Sara clarified. A faraway look shadowed her features. "My youngest sister, Lucia, died back then. She was a flower of a girl. Only sixteen. And Grandpa's older brother was taken by those butchers too. We barely escaped the pogrom ourselves. Most of the killings took place right here in Moldavia."

"What's a pogrom?" Irina wanted to know.

"You're too young to learn about these terrible things," the grandmother stuck to her original argument.

"Please tell me. I'll do my best to understand," Irina pleaded.

"I know you will. But these are adult subjects. They're too sad for kids."

"I'm not a kid any more. I'm already eleven!" Irina objected.

"You're not a little kid, but you're still a kid," the grandmother stroked Irina's hair.

"But, Grandma, since this happened to our own family...I have the right to know," Irina insisted with the stubbornness of a child.

"I think it's best that you ask your father about this."

"He's in America, remember? I barely talk to him on the phone a few minutes a week."

Grandma Sara gave in and told Irina, as far as she could recall, an abbreviated version of her family history. "What do you want me to say? We went from a rock to a hard place, as they say. My family's originally from the Ukraine, a country next to Romania that was part of the Russian empire. Ironically, the reason we came to Romania is because we were running away from the pogroms there."

"You still haven't told me what that word means," Irina reminded her.

"That's what I'm about to explain," the grandmother answered. "At the time, Jews weren't allowed in Russia itself; they had to live only in this area called the Pale of Settlement, which was part in Poland, part in the Ukraine. Like I said, our family lived in the Ukrainian part. And from time to time, when the tsar or hordes from neighboring villages were looking for someone to blame for their problems, they attacked Jewish villages, stole property, and killed tens of thousands of innocent people."

"Even children?" Irina wanted to know, recalling her history lesson on Vlad Tepes.

"Yes. Women and children also."

"But how can people be so mean?"

"The more downtrodden you are, the more you're mistreated," was all Grandma Sara could say. "That's why when you go to America, you should marry a powerful millionaire."

Irina couldn't see how becoming rich would solve the problem of anti-Semitism, but she knew better than to challenge that point, since it was her grandmother's solution to everything. Having lived a life of hardship and poverty, all of her idealism concentrated in dreaming of a better future for her children and grandchildren.

From histories of the Holocaust, Irina later learned the details that her grandmother wouldn't tell her, or didn't know, or perhaps wanted to forget. The Romanian holocaust began in Bucharest and Moldavia; then, once Romania became allied with Germany, took monstrous proportions in the provinces of Bessarabia, Bucovina and Northern Transylvania. Some Jews were shot in mass, but most lost their lives in "death trains" and concentration camps. Thousands of human beings were packed together like cattle in closed, windowless train compartments. Left for days on end without fresh air, water, food or latrines, they died of suffocation, dehydration or illnesses as the train wondered aimlessly around the countryside. Well, not aimlessly. Because by the end of its journey, the objective had been reached. All of its passengers were dead.

"How did you and Grandpa manage to escape the pogrom?"

That question was easier to answer. "We bought our lives," Grandma Sara replied. She explained that sometime in 1942, Antonescu abruptly changed policies. Instead of killing Jews, he declared that he wanted to get rid of them by exporting them abroad for large sums of money, mostly to Palestine. Several hundred thousand Romanian Jews found their way to what later became the state of Israel, including all of her grandparents' surviving siblings. In fact, Irina found out from her grandmother, out of her Jewish side of the family, her grandparents were the only ones who didn't leave Romania. By the time the war was over, after the pogroms and the exportations had ended, a country that had included three quarters of a million Jews was left with fewer than 30,000.

"Why did you and Zeida decide to stay behind?" Irina wondered. "Why didn't you move to Israel like the rest of our family?"

Her grandmother shrugged: "Romania's the only place we knew. We were born here; this was our home." She tried to explain: how could they pick up and go to such a faraway land, when she and Abram didn't even speak the Hebrew language? They were afraid to face the unknown.

"Even if it meant dying?" Irina asked incredulously.

Grandma Sara sighed: "One always has hope. Besides, what you don't know is often scarier than what you do know and things can always get worse," she said, and Irina understood her, since, no matter how bad life in Romania was under the Petrescu regime, she too felt nervous about leaving everything and everyone she knew behind to face the unknown in America.

Chapter 11

At 9:00 a.m. on Saturday morning, Irina waited at Princeton Junction. She was about to make the usual weekend trip to New York to see Jean-Pierre Renault, who had moved to the city a little over a year ago. Although a sophomore in college, Irina hardly ever socialized with her peers. Most of her free time was spent with Jean-Pierre, who was thirty years her senior, and networking with his artist friends. There was one redeeming feature about this whole arrangement, Irina focused on the positive: at least my parents don't have a clue about it. Besides, she sometimes justified herself in rare moments of guilt, it was her parents who had introduced Jean-Pierre to her in the first place, when they invited him to their house almost four years ago, to get news about Radu.

The two of them bonded during a key turning point at the end of his ten day visit to Ann Arbor. Irina had left to go shopping at a mall close to their home without telling her parents where she went. She was gone for five hours, lost in the Juniors section of Macy's, trying out as many outfits that she couldn't afford as possible. By the time she returned home, her parents were on the verge of a nervous breakdown. They had contacted all of her friends, who said they had no idea where she was, and were about to alert the police. Irina didn't have to check the weather forecast to predict a storm.

"Moash-ta pe ghiata!" her father initiated dialogue in polite Romanian. "Where the hell have you been? We've been looking for hours for you! Your mother"—Andrei pointed to the victim in question—"almost had a heart attack because of you!"

"I just went shopping at the mall and kind of lost track of time," Irina defended herself without much confidence.

"Couldn't she have told us that, Andrei?" Eva stayed in the background, playing second fiddle to the main tune of her husband's anger.

"Just look at your mother! Do you want to kill us both? Tell me honestly! Because you almost succeeded. I was just about to call the police; none of your friends knew where you were!" he reiterated his grievance, approaching Irina, who retreated slowly backwards, towards the safe haven provided by the living room curtains.

"We're in a foreign country now, Irina. It's not like in Romania, where only Petrescu's thugs killed people. Here everyone does it, " Eva seconded Andrei's wind, in a calm but grave manner. "There are so many weirdos in this country. Rapists. Serial murderers. Don't you watch the news?"

At this crucial point of juncture, Jean-Pierre, who had been watching this heart-warming family scene with the look of a man who finds himself in the wrong place at the wrong time, intervened. He saved her like a deus-ex-machina apparition, Irina later thought, exactly like in the Greek tragedies she was reading in Ms. Bernstein's World Lit. class.

He cleared his throat, like a man about to make an important announcement: "If I may say something, Mr. Schwarz."

"Please, call me Andrei."

"Andrei, actually, Irina told me that she was going to the mall and asked me to let you and Mrs. Schwarz … I mean Eva… know about it. I'm truly sorry, but it slipped my mind."

"Even when you saw us worried to death, screaming at each other at the top of our lungs and running around the house like headless chicken looking for her?" Eva asked somewhat skeptically.

"Well, you have to admit, that's awfully close to your normal behavior," Jean-Pierre pointed out. "Besides, you were speaking in Romanian," he bolstered his argument.

Both parents looked expectantly at Irina.

"I did tell Jean-Pierre," she said. "But I should also have told you guys. Sorry I made you worry like that. It won't happen again." Would this lame excuse actually work? Irina wondered.

After a few seconds of silent, telepathic consultation with his wife, Andrei announced the parental verdict: "Alright…But if you pull another stunt like this, you'll be grounded for a month!" he declared. Since it would have been impolite to accuse his guest of lying, he had no choice but to pretend to believe this dubious scenario. For one split second, Irina and Jean-Pierre's glances met. He saw gratitude in the girl's eyes; she noticed tenderness and compassion in his. He was her savior.

After Jean-Pierre returned to Paris, they kept up a regular correspondence via letters and postcards, at first about American culture and her brother—whom he couldn't tell her that much about--then about art, Irina's growing interest. Once Jean-Pierre moved to New York, they met at one of his art exhibits, which had really impressed her. The artist suggested that she become his figure model—and she later posed for him in his studio—which was enough to get the whole thing started. What would it take for it to end? Irina now wondered.

Apparently many students had the same idea as her since the Dinky, as the train to New York City was affectionately nicknamed by Princeton undergrads, was always packed on Saturday mornings. Irina's attention was caught by one young couple in particular. You'd have to be blind not to notice them, since they were engaged in some heavy duty petting which ventured slightly beyond the PG13 rating. Irina tried to act like she was minding her own business, looking to the left for the train, while periodically sneaking a few peaks at the enamored lovers. The young man had longish brown hair. His lean body was camouflaged in ragged jeans and an oversized T-shirt with the Princeton University logo, the standard student uniform. The girl had blond bobbed hair with long bangs which fell in a sweep over her face, hiding the couple's kisses. She was casually but fashionably dressed in a tight, low-cut shirt that emphasized the perfect, firm pears of her breasts, which seemed to preoccupy the young man. Occasionally, the couple took a breather from their kisses to whisper and break out in bursts of laughter, deeper in tone from him, bell-like giggles from her. Irina eyed them again, with renewed curiosity, wondering what they had found so amusing. The boy's roving hands were now gently stroking the girl's rounded behind, with a circular motion which made the girl coo something to the effect of "Stoooop it!" Her half-hearted objection got lost in another long, smoldering kiss, while the boy continued busily with the task at hand.

"Talk about P.D.A!" Irina said to herself, but truly, she thought the young couple had found a rather pleasant pastime. The train arrived. It occurred to her that Jean-Pierre never played around like that, though she would have certainly enjoyed it. He took himself too seriously, Irina decided, as she hopped on the train, deliberately choosing an entrance far away from the young lovers, so as not to get any more ideas. Am I jealous of what they have? Irina wondered. I mean, why should I waste my time with pimply adolescents when I can be with one of the greatest contemporary artists in the world? Put this way, the question was purely rhetorical. Yet Irina couldn't help but wonder if she was missing out on something pimply adolescents might have to offer. Speaking of which, a young man with a Princeton backpack, gelled hair and a face spotted with a crop of fresh acne plopped down right next to her.

"Is this seat taken?" he inquired.

"No," Irina replied. She would have preferred to sit by herself and ponder her increasingly cumbersome relationship to Jean-Pierre, but since the train was packed, solitude was not an option. From the boy's looks, she had every reason to believe that he'd be one of those shy, nerdy types who wouldn't bug her. She had apparently misjudged him.

"You go to Princeton?" he asked.

"Yeah," Irina replied in the most laconic and uninviting manner she could muster.

"Me too," the young man smiled, pointing to the logo on his shirt and backpack.

"Great!" And that's the end of that, Irina hoped.

"So where are you going?" he asked, though it was clear that the Dinky was heading for New York City.

"To New York," Irina looked him up and down questioningly, to indicate his pick up lines needed work.

"Me too."

"What a phenomenal coincidence," Irina allowed herself to express sarcasm, since the situation called for it.

"Well, you could have been going to Trenton..." he remarked.

"Who goes to Trenton?" Irina objected.

"I don't know. Some people may have family there...." After a moment of silence, the young man pursued: "So what are you doing in New York?"

Irina stared ahead, hesitating between telling him the truth and telling him buzz off, this information is personal. She compromised on a middle-ground: "I'm visiting someone."

"Really? Who?"

Irina decided that the subtle approach didn't work too well with her companion, so she turned to him and said: "I consider that a personal question."

The young man was visibly offended: "Well, excuuuuse me. People tell me that kind of stuff all the time on the train."

Irina begged to differ: "For your information, I haven't even told my own parents that I'm seeing a man who's thirty years older than I am!"

The blond boy suddenly laughed out loud and held out his hand like a stop sign: "Too much information!" Despite this denial of interest, however, Irina's disclosure evidently aroused his curiosity: "So why are you dating an old dude?"

"He's not old! Besides, he helped save my brother's life and he is a very famous artist," Irina defended Jean-Pierre.

The smirk didn't leave the blond boy's face, who, now that Irina had exposed herself, assumed an air of ironic distance: "Famous, huh? So what's his name? Do I know him?"

"I seriously doubt it."

"Why? You don't think I'm cuuuultured?"

"Let's just say that you don't exactly strike me as the artistic type..."

"Now that's not nice!" the boy protested, even though before this conversation he would have considered being called "artistic" to be an insult of the same order of magnitude as being called a "sissy" or a "mama's boy."

Irina paused, looking at his washed-out blue eyes with a pimple right between his bushy eyebrows. She felt responsible for the bad turn their conversation had taken. After all, it wasn't this boy's fault that she was put off about having to visit Jean-Pierre. "Listen, let's forget about it, alright?" she said by way of apology. "I'm really preoccupied with something. I wish I weren't going to New York, but since I have no choice in the matter..."

Her companion seemed appeased. "What do you mean? Your boyfriend's forcing you to visit him?"

Irina flinched at the word "boyfriend." "He's not my boyfriend!"

"Then what is he?"

Good question. Irina searched for the right word to describe their relationship. "Boyfriend" was out of the question, since Jean-Pierre had several so-called girlfriends. More of a harem, really, if it were not for the fact that being highly protective of his freedom, he wouldn't marry any of them. "Friend" didn't work either, since their relationship was sexual and most certainly asymmetrical. Jean-Pierre gave her advice and guided her art, yet he never accepted any advice or support from her. The age difference had something to do with this imbalance, but not as much as one might think. Irina felt that it was mostly Jean-Pierre's ego that got in the way of any reciprocal dealings with anybody. "Mentor" seemed like a more apt characterization, except that Jean-Pierre was too busy to spend much time on educating anyone. He was more of an artistic prophet, articulating pithy aphorisms like Nietzsche's Zarathustra for anyone who was smart enough to listen and actually comprehend what he was saying.

"He's ... kind of a friend," Irina finally settled on the least inaccurate term.

"But why is he making you go see him?" the blond boy still wanted to know.

Irina thought about this question. "He's not forcing me. Part of me wishes to see him, part of me doesn't. I can't make up my mind," she answered.

Suddenly, Irina missed the way she used to look forward to meeting Jean-Pierre. The sense of excitement, the anticipation of seeing this glamorous stranger she knew mostly through his brief but eloquent hand-written letters. Unfortunately, seeing one another in person kind of spoiled their relationship. From afar, Jean-Pierre had attracted her with the magnetism of art, talent, fame, connections, galleries, interviews, articles. The world was at his fingertips and, when she communicated with him, it seemed to be within her reach as well. But, Irina had been wondering lately, was basking in the aura of a famous artist the same thing as being in love?

"So why are you going to New York?" she asked her companion, to point the conversation away from herself.

"I'm going back home to break up with my ex-girlfriend."

Irina looked puzzled: "If she's your ex, then why do you need to break up with her?"

"It's kind of complicated."

What isn't! Irina thought.

"You see, I dated this girl for three years back in high school, and we sort of broke up when I went to college, but it wasn't all that clear," the young man explained.

"To you or to her?" Irina inquired.

"To her. We sort of said we'd see other people."

"You or her?"

"Both of us. But I'm the one who wanted it."

"I see."

"The thing is, we still kind of get together when I visit my folks in the City."

That's it! Irina found the most eloquent and accurate way of describing the nuances and complexities of her own relationship to Jean-Pierre: "kind of get together."

"But why are you breaking up with her? If it's clear that it's not clear, I mean?"

"Because I sort of have a new girlfriend."

"Are you going out with the new girl or not?" Irina asked.

"We just started to. But I'm really into her. So I don't want to blow it, you know what I mean?" he quizzed her with his pale eyes.

Irina nodded. "How about your ex? Were you ever in love with her?"

"Maybe a little bit… in the beginning. It's hard to say. I was only fifteen when we started going out. I guess we were what you might call…high school sweethearts."

"If you dated for several years in high school, is there any doubt?"

"If you're not really into someone, there always is."

"Then why did you go out with her in the first place?"

"I don't know. It seemed like the thing to do. Besides, I had no clue back then. I had never been with anybody else."

Which got Irina thinking about Jean-Pierre again. He was the first man she had been with and, quite honestly, she wasn't sure that she had been fully there when it happened. Her heart was never really into it. But thinking like this made her feel somewhat guilty: maybe she was just feeling out of sorts and being too harsh. After all, Jean-Pierre wasn't treating her any differently from the way he treated everyone else. By his own admission, he had no energy left for anything other than his art and, she would add, his mysterious networking.

She recalled a telling incident from the previous spring. When she was wavering between majoring in Comparative Literature and Studio Art, Jean-Pierre advised her to make a choice: "Your average person wastes his energy on a dozen activities," he said. "I focus mine primarily on one thing: art. Everything else is sacrificed to it—love, family, friends. Even myself." That was the truest thing he had ever said, Irina thought.

"So are you dating this dude just because he's famous?" her companion asked.

"Of course not!" Irina protested. That would be cheap and mercenary. Then she remembered that Jean-Pierre promised to introduce her to Sven Wilson, a well-regarded New York art critic and Anton Pondinsky, a powerful art collector, and she cheered up a bit. Somehow, it made the whole New York trip worth it.

Chapter 12

Irina was late (for the third time in a row) to Jean-Pierre's exhibit. Only a few months ago she used to feel so excited about being with the man whom she enthusiastically described to her acquaintances as a superfamous Frenchie. But now all she felt was... a growing need to date someone closer to her in age. To "get a life," as her high school friend Alice used to advise, way before she, herself, actually had one. She glanced at Jean-Pierre's installations, centrally exhibited at the MoMa, with the bored air of looking at an old, familiar sofa. Even if this exhibit featured the artist's new work, it was in a style that Irina had come to know all too well.

Irina paused in front of one particular ready-made which a prominent New York Times art critic hailed as "the fresh highlight of an all-around spectacular exhibit." It was called, touchingly, "Homage to a friend." One of Jean-Pierre's childhood friends had died a few months ago. In Irina's recollection, Jean-Pierre hadn't been particularly shaken by the loss. He nevertheless spoke to journalists about it and commemorated it through a work of art. The latter consisted of two long wires intertwined through a maze-like structure culminating in two light bulbs which turned on and off randomly, but—and this was significant--not at the same time. That same New York Times art critic eloquently described this concoction as "a moving symbol of our mortality; the randomness of human life, flickering in and out of existence, beyond our control and powers of consolation." Couldn't a decent electrician have fixed this little problem? Irina wondered. And couldn't Jean-Pierre have come up with a better metaphor for human mortality than these poorly wired Christmas lights?

What's come over me? she immediately chastised herself, wishing to shake off her bad mood. Why am I being so bitter towards poor Jean-Pierre? Only because of the little detail that I'm not in love with him, another part of her brain answered back for about the nth time that day. In all fairness, however, there was nothing really binding them together. Didn't Jean-Pierre himself emphasize that they were free? Even on the very first day she came to his studio to model for him he had said so—in such a poetic and complicated way that she could barely understand him.

She had climbed up the wooden steps of his New York studio and rang the bell. He opened the door and she stepped into the obstacle course of a hazardously messy room filled with wires, bits of newspaper, discarded video screens, even pieces of faux fur scattered all over the floor. "That's for the fetishism ready-mades," he explained. "I combine them with video clips."

"That's what I thought," Irina responded, not wishing to appear ignorant about contemporary art.

He was very direct, a characteristic which she later noticed in other artists as well. "You can take your clothes off now," he unceremoniously informed her.

"Excuse me?"

"You offered to model for me, right?"

"Yes, of course," Irina blushed. "I just didn't think that there was any actual... nudity involved. I thought that perhaps you wanted to do a portrait or something." Then it dawned on her: what a ridiculous suggestion that was! What normal, heterosexual man ever focuses on a woman's face?

"I'd like to see if your body corresponds to my mental picture of it, " the artist said gravely, contemplating her.

Now it was Irina's turn to smile with infinite feminine wisdom, honed by several years of experience with speculating about men: "Well, if women took off their clothes every time a man wants to see if they look the same as they imagined them, heck, then we'd never wear any clothes!"

"And would that be such a tragedy?" Jean-Pierre retorted with a crooked smile. "I thought you said you were a figure model. Did you ever do this before?"

"Sort of."

"Who did you model for?"

"Nobody famous," Irina hedged.

"I may know him anyway."

"I seriously doubt it."

"I'm very well connected in the States also," Jean-Pierre modestly declared.

"Yes, I know. But I don't think you met the guy at the Sears' Portrait Studio who did my senior picture. That's... the artist... I posed for."

"I see." For a moment, even the usually eloquent Jean-Pierre was speechless. But he quickly recovered: "Don't put that on your resumé." Upon further reflection, he added: "That's okay. A figure model doesn't have to have a lot of experience to be really good. She just needs to be very flexible."

"Then I should warn you in advance that I failed gymnastics in Romania."

"I meant flexible in following the artist's instructions," Jean-Pierre clarified. He approached her slowly and, piece by piece, removed all of her clothing. Irina felt more embarrassed than during a gynecological examination—especially since at least her physician was female. Yet, strangely enough, she didn't feel threatened. Once she was nude, Jean-Pierre backed away and began studying her. The studio was bathed in a dim light, on the edge of shadow. The artist was tense with concentration. His eyes didn't leave the model for a second. Irina stood awkwardly in the middle of the studio, not really knowing what to do with herself, periodically shifting her weight from one foot to the other to regain circulation. The silence was so complete that she could hear each beat of the clock on the wall.

"Aren't you going to sketch me?" she finally asked, after fifteen minutes of this cathartic aesthetic experience.

"I only sketch from memory, to maximize creativity," Jean-Pierre announced.

Irina nodded, once again to indicate that she had full comprehension of the artistic process. Then, for lack of anything better to do, she smiled and waved to him.

"It's amazing how much your body resembles my initial mental image of it, back when we first met in Ann Arbor," Jean-Pierre observed, not waving back.

If my mother only knew this guy was having mental images of me naked when I was fifteen, she wouldn't have given him all those sarmale for supper, Irina thought.

"That will do. I know exactly how I'll sketch you starting tomorrow," Jean-Pierre announced a few minutes later.

Irina sighed with relief: "Thank goodness! I don't know how much longer I could have lasted. I was getting that annoying sensation of prickly ants all over my legs from standing too long in one position. Plus I'm a little cold."

"If you want to be an artist's model, you need to learn how to master your body and forget about your physical needs. Try to focus on something else, step outside of yourself, as it were. Posing for an artist—and even more so, being an artist--is a process akin to meditation. It takes intense concentration and infinite patience."

"Shucks. Those are precisely the qualities I lack," Irina informed him.

"You'll have to cultivate them. Didn't you write in your letters that you wanted to be an artist? Do you still want that?"

"More than anything else in the world!" the young woman's eyes shone with passion.

Jean-Pierre mesmerized her with his steady glance and calm, soothing voice. "I can help you reach that goal. But you have to do your part."

"How?"

"Being an artist takes thought and practice. Tumble in your head an idea of what you want to do—the subject of a painting, for instance, or the media, the colors, the composition, the fresh angle you wish to bring to a work of art— until, before you even put charcoal to sketchpad, it's already polished like a glossy, sparkling rock tossed by the ocean waves. Do it over and over until it's exactly as you want it: perfect."

At the time, Irina liked what she heard. If Jean-Pierre had tried to touch her, or if he had made any (highly implausible) declaration of love, he would have scared her. But he had followed his own advice. He had been slow and patient. Each time they met she posed for him and he'd help her define her own goals until they seemed more attainable.

She often painted in his studio. To her surprise, he'd never tell her what to do or not to do. He only commented on her work in general terms, such as, "In a painting, give people some of what they expect and something new and surprising as well. Make the familiar be unfamiliar to them." Or: "If a composition has too much symmetry, it tires the eyes. Each work of art needs an element of asymmetry. And a sense of movement that continuously engages both the glance and the mind. Real art is, above all, cerebral."

Months later, when they finally made cerebral love, the artist was remarkably gentle. He covered her with kisses and caresses. His touch was as soft and tingly as a paintbrush. In the egoism of her youth and inexperience, Irina had barely moved. She let him do all the work and was nearly as still as a canvas. By then, she had mastered some of the figure model's patience, only this time she used it not to step out of herself towards higher contemplation, but to get lost in the pleasures of her own body. She let herself go, became pure sensation—a concentration of titillated feelings and feverish spasms. Until he eased into her. That's the only time he lost control of his own impulses and made frantic movements and animal-like sounds, in a raspy, throaty voice that made Irina feel helpless in his arms, at his mercy.

When it was all over, he cradled her and kissed her tenderly on the cheek. She felt once again reassured by his gentleness. "This moment is our true beginning," he whispered in her ear. "We can't tell in advance how long we'll be happy together. Everything exists in a limited quantity—especially happiness. Let's do our best to draw out our pleasure together for as long as possible and not a minute longer."

Irina, who had never dated philosophers before—or even grown men, for that matter—did her best to decipher Jean-Pierre's profound postcoital discourse. She had read in both Cosmo and Vogue that, in their heart of hearts, men feel like leaving women right after having sex, while at the same time realizing that they need to justify this act in nobler terms. Was this what Jean-Pierre was doing? Since she was in his apartment, however, Irina was obliged to revise slightly the theory advanced by the leading women's magazines: "Are you telling me to go home?" she asked him.

"No." Jean-Pierre seemed puzzled by her question. "What makes you say that?"

Irina, who before dating Jean-Pierre had considered herself an intellectual, felt embarrassed by her misinterpretation. Still, in her own defense, she thought, after men get what they want, which is generally quite simple, their behavior tends to become more complex and difficult to decipher.

"Do you like poetry?" Jean-Pierre tried another tack.

"Yes, I love it. Especially by Mihail Eminescu," she named Romania's greatest Romantic poet.

"Alright. Then allow me express my ideas metaphorically. What I meant to say is... Love is like a butterfly's wings. If you want them to keep their sheen— that is, if you want the butterfly have the strength to continue flying--you can't wear them out by too much contact. Love is the most fragile, delicate aspect of human existence."

When she left Jean-Pierre's studio that afternoon, Irina felt that she had lived through something very important. Being only eighteen, she knew that she couldn't fully absorb its significance. But she felt privileged to have lost some of her butterfly's sheen to an older, wiser man who seemed to know so much about art, love and life in general. However often--or rarely--he wanted to see her, that would be just fine with her. She promised herself that she wouldn't abuse his generous friendship or try to monopolize his time. This noble, other-regarding attitude was greatly facilitated by the fact that, no matter how hard she tried to focus upon Jean-Pierre's numerous admirable qualities, she never really managed to fall in love with him.

And now, a year into their relationship, she thought that the butterfly in question should try to pollinate other, preferably younger, flowers. Above all, she no longer wanted as a partner a prophet or mentor who occasionally made love to her. She wanted an equal: a lover, not a father.

After the exhibit and reception were over, when they returned to his studio, Irina realized that she didn't quite know how to break up with a man.

"I've got something to tell you," she announced in a timid voice.

"So do I," Jean-Pierre replied.

"You go first," Irina said.

"No, that's alright. My news requires a little more explanation. What did you want to tell me?"

Irina thought for a moment of the most diplomatic way of putting it: "Do you remember what you told me last year about the butterfly's wings?" she began.

His glance was cool: "Yes?"

"Well... my wings, I mean, the particles on them, you know, the sheen... Geesh! I'm so much less poetic than you are... The thing is, I would like to fly off a bit. On my own," she blurted out.

The artist seemed surprised, but shrugged with an air of exaggerated indifference: "You're perfectly free to buzz off wherever you want and with whomever you want."

Irina tried to smile, which didn't quite work: "I know. But I still want us to remain good friends."

"Are you saying you don't want to be my *maitresse* any more?"

Irina knew she couldn't hesitate now, or everything would return back to the point de départ. "Yes."

"Why? Did you find yourself a little boyfriend?" Jean-Pierre pronounced the word *petit ami* with evident sarcasm.

"I did," Irina heard herself reply, to her own surprise.

"Who is it? Is the other guy you pose for? What's his name... Rico?"

"No, it's definitely not him," Irina answered, still put off by Rico's behavior. Then, by association, she had an epiphany: "His name is Paul," she announced with conviction. After all, she thought, dating Paul was a distinct possibility.

"That's so typical of you! You think only of yourself," Jean-Pierre's ostensible cool visibly melted in the heat of his anger.

"I'm really sorry," Irina tried to soothe him. "It's just that I haven't dated that much before—except for a little bit in high school, when I went to the opera and symphony with the geeks my father approved of—and, you, of course, which has been a truly wonderful experience. But I'd like to see what it's like to date someone closer to me in age." Since he, himself only dated much younger women, he was sure to sympathize with her reasons.

Jean-Pierre, however, didn't seem particularly reassured by Irina's tactful explanation: "So you want someone younger, huh? I turned you into a good model, and, more importantly, into an artist in your own right. I introduced you to important people. And this is how you choose to thank me?"

Although she felt quite confident of the correctness of her decision, Irina couldn't even look Jean-Pierre in the eyes. She contemplated in contrite silence the dark stain on his Oriental rug which she had made by accident when she had brought him coffee a few weeks ago.

"Well, " Jean-Pierre pursued, assuming his prophetic tone, "I have only one thing to say to you, and mark my words, since I've never told you something that didn't turn out to come true: Paul, or whoever the guy you're replacing me with is, will have all of my faults and none of my virtues. You're exchanging an extraordinary man with flaws for an ordinary man with flaws. And an ordinary man will never make you happy or help you fulfill your dreams."

Jean-Pierre then took a few resolute steps towards his desk and removed from its upper drawer the Montblanc pen Irina had given him for Christmas. "Here. I'll no longer be using this," he announced, returning it to her.

That's it! Irina thought, her Latin pride coming back to her in a surge of indignation. This charade has gone far enough. After all, Jean-Pierre wasn't her husband, dated several other women, was old enough to be her grandfather (at least in some countries, where they start early) and, the bottom line was, she had the right to have a life of her own. "And I'll no longer be using this," she retorted, taking off her watch, which had been his Christmas gift to her. They looked at each other for a moment considering the absurdity of the situation and even cracked a smile. The tension diminished, although they didn't exactly radiate with mutual warmth.

"I guess I better go," Irina attempted to extricate herself.

"Before you do, there's something else I have to tell you."

"Yes?" Irina expected another prophetic statement.

"Would you like to go out for coffee? Jean-Pierre asked.

Now that's out of the blue, Irina thought. "Why?" she asked him.

Jean-Pierre made a few silent gestures pointing to his ears, then to the phone. "I don't know, I just feel like having coffee," he said out loud, still gesticulating in the same strange manner. Great! He's acting just like my parents, Irina thought. Next he'll be telling me his that his studio is bugged by the Secret Police or something totally lame like that. She nevertheless agreed. Before leaving the apartment, Jean-Pierre went to his desk drawer and removed a tan manila envelope, which he folded and stuck in the inner pocket of his coat.

"Let's go!"

Once they got into his little red sports car, Jean-Pierre proceeded to drive aimlessly around the town—which was more like an obstacle course since this was, after all, New York City. Irina started having serious doubts that she was being kidnapped.

"I think it might have been simpler to walk to Starbuck's," she remarked.

"No, it's too public," Jean-Pierre responded, repeatedly looking over his shoulder as he was driving.

"We want public. Public is good," Irina underscored. Would it be safer to open the car door and hurl herself out? she wondered.

"Not in this case," Jean-Pierre replied. He turned to her with a serious and earnest glance: "Please Irina. You'll have to trust me. This is important."

Irina gauged the speed of the car, which she surmised must have been going at least 55 miles an hour, and decided to remain in the vehicle. It looked like they had reached the outskirts of town and were somewhere in the suburbs. At least we're not in the woods, she focused on the bright side.

"Forgive my curiosity, but where are you taking me?" she asked.

"To a friend's house."

Her eyes shifted nervously. "Couldn't you have put me out of my misery back at your studio?" she only half-quipped.

"I want to introduce you to someone," Jean-Pierre replied with a strange smile upon his lips.

Chapter 13

Jean-Pierre pulled into the driveway of a nondescript suburban house—ranch style, dark roof, evergreen bushes planted in the front yard. He removed a pair of keys from his coat pocket and unlocked the front door.

"Do your friends know that we're paying them a visit?" Irina asked.

"As a matter of fact, yes. This house actually belongs to the parents of one of my friends. He gave us permission to come here while his parents are away in Florida."

"I'm sure they'd be thrilled to hear that we're h..." Her words, however, froze upon her lips. In front of her stood a blond young woman with very short hair, blue eyes and delicate features. In her gray pencil skirt and white shirt, she was so slim that she appeared to be tall. She looked at Irina with a warm, familiar gaze, as if they already knew each other. Without making the customary introductions, Jean-Pierre withdrew to an adjacent room, leaving the two women alone.

"Have we met somewhere before?" Irina broke the ice, feeling awkward as soon as the words came out of her mouth for having used the same line men use when they're trying to pick up a woman.

"No, but somehow I feel like I've known you for years," the young woman answered.

Irina thought that was a strange thing to say, at least coming from someone who wasn't using it as a pick-up line.

"Your brother talked a lot about you when we were in France," the young woman explained.

"Oh, you're a friend of Radu's?"

"Unfortunately, I don't think that your brother considers me a friend any more."

In that instant, Irina understood. "Ioana?"

Ioana advanced and extended her hand: "Nice to finally meet you."

Irina, however, didn't reciprocate the friendly gesture. She looked nervously around for Jean-Pierre, not understanding why he had played such a dirty trick on her. Was it because she had broken up with him? But how could he have known in advance that she would do so? Whatever his intentions may have been, she wasn't pleased to meet Ioana. She recalled snippets of conversation between her parents which had given her a distinct impression of Ioana as an evil woman, the curva as her mother politely put it, who seduced her brother and almost caused his death. Later, when Irina wanted to find out more about what had happened to Radu, Jean-Pierre explained to her a little about the sad lot of prostitute agents in Eastern block nations, hoping to generate some sympathy towards Ioana. After hearing the details, however, Irina became even more disgusted by such women and their lifestyle. "Don't get me wrong, it's not because they're prostitutes. I think women should be able to do whatever they want with their bodies," she attempted to explain her continental open-mindedness to Jean-Pierre. "What I object to is the fact that they use sex as a weapon to destroy other people's lives," she clarified. "Don't we all?" Jean-Pierre retorted, with characteristic cynicism.

Sensing resistance, Ioana withdrew her hand and said in a low, apologetic voice: "I understand why you're not too happy to meet me."

Irina stared at her in silence.

"I wouldn't have asked Jean-Pierre to bring you here if I didn't have something very important to show you," Ioana said gravely. She unzipped her black purse, dug around in it and took out a wallet, which she opened and exhibited to Irina.

Irina bent over it to look at the picture underneath the plastic cover. In the photograph a little boy, who looked no older than three or four, was smiling crookedly. He had large dark brown eyes, long, feminine eyelashes and very short light brown hair.

"Your son?" Irina inquired.

Ioana nodded. "His name is Lucian."

Irina's eyes shifted back and forth from the photograph to Ioana. He doesn't resemble his mother, she concluded.

"I used to have dark eyes and long brown hair," Ioana explained and instinctively touched her short hair, as if sensing Irina's judgment. "What I wanted to tell you is... Lucian is our son," she added.

"Whose?"

"Mine and Radu's," the young woman announced, looking straight into Irina's eyes.

Irina examined once more the picture, this time attempting to find dissimilar features between the little boy and her memory of her brother. Although the boy's features were rounder and more delicate and his hair lighter than Radu's, Irina was obliged to concede that there might have been some similarity between them. Nonetheless, she answered neutrally: "Your son's very cute."

Ioana gazed affectionately at the photograph. "Thanks. In this picture he was three and a half years old. Now he'd be almost ten."

The use of the conditional tense puzzled Irina: "What do you mean 'would be'?"

"They took him away from me when he was four years old."

"Who did?"

"The *Securitate*."

Ioana explained that one Monday morning she dropped Lucian at the state run preschool, as usual, and went to work at her new job as Assistant Editor of a scientific journal. She recalled that the little boy was particularly restless that day. Initially, she didn't think much of it. It was quite common for Lucian to throw temper tantrums before school in the hopes of getting the chance to stay home with his mother. Sometimes he'd complain that he didn't like his breakfast, at others that his shoes were too tight. That morning he had told his mother that he wasn't feeling well. She checked the little boy's forehead for fever, and it wasn't hot. Then she asked him to stick out his tongue, which also looked healthy. Ioana tried to reassure him that once he got there he'd play with his best friends, Dimitrie and Georgica, and everything would be just fine. Little Lucian, however, wasn't persuaded. He continued his temper tantrum. In protest, he refused to take his morning bath or brush his teeth. Ioana patiently hugged him, kissed his tear-stained cheeks and read him his favorite bedtime story, Mica Murdarica, "The little dirty one". It was a tale about a little girl who doesn't wash her hands or brush her teeth and, as a result, becomes unpopular at school and loses all her friends, who plug up their noses whenever she passes by or approaches them (which never failed to make the little boy laugh). Once she cleans up, however, everyone likes her again. After Ioana read him this story, the little boy relented and took his morning bath. Yet, his mother thought in retrospect, he still seemed out of sorts.

After dropping off her son at the preschool, Ioana had a sinking feeling, which she later interpreted as a premonition of disaster. All day long she felt on edge at work, but tried convince herself that she couldn't start a pattern of missing work for no good reason, just because her son had separation anxiety. She nevertheless left the office earlier than usual that afternoon and went to pick up Lucian from preschool at 3:15 p.m. As soon as she stepped into the classroom, she knew that something was wrong. Lucian wasn't in the room playing with the other kids and the teacher, Comrade Popescu, looked pale. "His uncle has already picked him up," she announced.

"Who did?" Ioana asked with a racing heart.

"His uncle," the teacher repeated. "He said you had to work late tonight and asked him to pick you son up."

"What uncle? Lucian doesn't have an uncle. I'm an only child. What did the man look like? Did he show you any identification?" the mother asked breathlessly.

"No, nothing," Comrade Popescu replied, averting her glance.

By now Ioana had reached a state of panic. "Please," she implored the teacher. "If you have any sympathy for a mother's pain, please tell me who took away my son."

"It was Comrade Stancu," the teacher leaned over and said in a whisper, then looked nervously around her. "He told me to tell you the story about the uncle and not to describe him. Please don't tell anybody I said anything."

Ioana turned pale. She instantly recognized the name of the *Securitate* informant working for the school district where she lived and realized that she had fallen right back into the spider's web.

"Since that day, I never saw my son again," Ioana concluded her story, staring blankly ahead of her, like a woman in a trance.

"But why would the *Securitate* do a thing like that? What would they want with a little boy?" Irina asked, naively.

"The official reason they gave me was that I was a traitor. They accused me of deliberately 'sabotaging' their missions. But what I really believe is that, once they retired me, they took Lucian to get me to keep quiet about everything I knew about the organization and its inner workings. That was their form of blackmail."

"But once they kidnapped your son, didn't you agree to do everything they asked, just to get him back?"

"Of course."

"And?"

"And I was unsuccessful. I went through the whole chain of command, all the way up to Stanescu, my former senior boss. But no mater how much I begged and promised them anything they wanted, they wouldn't change their minds. After several years of trying to no avail, I decided to rely upon my contact with Jean-Pierre and leave the country. I had nothing left to lose. They took away my child and persecuted my parents. I was hoping to get more help for them abroad."

Irina nodded. "That's what my parents thought when Radu went missing," she said, then felt awkward about sympathizing with the woman responsible for her brother's plight. "Why is it that you wanted to meet me?" it occurred to her to ask.

"I wanted to see if you could do me a little favor."

Irina didn't exactly feel like jumping at the opportunity.

"I realize that I'm probably the last person on Earth you and your family would like to help," Ioana preempted her response. "But I'm not asking for my sake. I'm asking for his sake," she pointed to the photograph of the little boy. "Ever since I arrived in the States, I've asked the Agency's help in finding my son. They claim they have looked, to no avail. But I'm convinced that they really tried. There are 100,000 children in *Securitate* orphanages in Romania. Why should they care about the fate of one little boy? After all, Lucian's not their child. As Jean-Pierre says, this is a personal matter."

"Then why haven't you tried to find your child on your own, without their help? From the States, I mean."

"Believe me, I have!" Ioana's calm and weary voice was now tinged with desperation. "Before I left Romania, I spent two whole years going from orphanage to orphanage. I've made literally hundreds of phone calls. I begged the directors of the orphanages and the assistant directors and their secretaries to help me find my son. I've asked all of my former contacts from the *Securitate* for their assistance. But my search proved fruitless. Most of the time, they don't even keep records. Or at least, you can't get to them. And even in the rare cases where they do show you some documents, the information has already been altered so that you can't separate truth from fiction. In some cases, they make up phony genealogies to hide the children's real identities."

"Couldn't you recognize your own child, if you saw him again in person?"

"I believe I could, even though he's probably changed dramatically. The problem is, they don't let you see the children unless you have some kind of permit, which is almost impossible to obtain," Ioana explained. "Through some of my more sympathetic connections and many, many bribes, I did manage to go inside a few of the orphanages, and what I saw was... well, there are no words to describe it." Ioana leaned forward and covered her face with her hands, attempting to compose herself.

"What makes you think that my brother can find your little boy if you haven't been able to find him after so many years of searching?" Irina inquired.

Ioana looked up. "I'm not a CIA officer," she answered calmly. "I just do a few translations for them and was given protection by the Agency thanks to my ties to Jean-Pierre, that's all. But I have no idea how to conduct an actual investigation. Your brother, on the other hand, works for them. And unlike other CIA operators, he will care. He has to." Ioana sounded like she was trying to convince herself.

"But even if he's willing to try," Irina answered, "why did you want to meet with me? How could I possibly be of use to you?"

"You are the one who can start the whole process in motion."

"How? I'm not a spy."

"That's not the kind of help I need from you, Irina. Jean-Pierre has told me that you have a good heart..."

"He's probably changed his mind by now," Irina interjected, alluding to their recent break-up.

"No, I assure you. He's told me only positive things about you."

"I appreciate that, but I still don't see how I can help."

"Please tell your brother about his son," Ioana stated directly.

Irina didn't feel that it would be tactful to express her doubts about Lucian's paternity. She tried to avail herself of the responsibility nonetheless: "But I don't understand. Why you can't contact Radu yourself?"

Ioana seemed discouraged by her response. "I have already gotten in touch with your brother. We met in person and talked ... My impression was... well, I don't think Radu was ready to receive the news from me. Had I told him, he wouldn't have believed me. He would have thought I was trying to trap him again. If you could only talk to him, try to convince him."

Irina looked perplexed: "If the supposed father of your child doesn't believe you, what makes you think that I do?" she blurted out.

Ioana wasn't offended by her directness. "Because you don't have the same reasons to hate me," she answered simply.

"I love my brother and hate what you have done to him," Irina countered.

Ioana opened her wallet once again and leaned forward towards Irina, once again exhibiting the image of the smiling child to her. "Whatever you may think of me, this little boy is not an abstraction. He's real and he needs our help. He needs his parents. Please think about it. If we act now, we may still be able to save him." She paused and her gaze seemed to darken. "If it's not too late..."

Chapter 14

"Hello, Mom? It's me."

"Buna."

"What's the matter?"

"Nothing..."

"You sound sad. Are you crying?"

"No. Everything's fine."

"Okay, now I'm really getting worried. You only say that when something's seriously wrong."

"I wanted to tell you in person, not like this, over the phone…"

"Tell me what?"

"Grandma Marta passed away."

"When? How did it happen?"

"She had a heart attack last night. Grandpa Mihai said she expired very fast, without much suffering…"

"I'm so sorry," Irina said, feeling overcome by the rapid oscillations between denial and despair one feels under the fresh impact of tragic news. She then immediately thought of her dependent grandfather. "What's Grandpa Mihai going to do now?" she asked.

"They already have a woman in mind whom they'll hire to do his cooking, groceries and laundry. Of course, emotionally speaking, what can anybody do? He's devastated. You know how close they were…"

Irina felt helpless when she heard her mother break down sobbing. She attempted to say something soothing but couldn't find the right words. The news had sunk into her consciousness with a wave of pain and regret that brought tears to her eyes as well.

"What did you want to tell me?" Eva asked in a strained tone, after a pause.

"What?" Irina asked, in a daze.

"You called to tell me something."

"Oh… this isn't the best time to talk about it."

"Did something bad happen?"

"Not really."

"Then what?" Eva insisted.

"It's nothing. I just saw Jean-Pierre, who had an exhibit in New York City this weekend. You knew I've been in touch with him, right?"

"Yes, via letters."

"Well, as I said, he's in the City right now doing a few art shows."

"Does he have news from Radu?"

"No, but he has news from Ioana."

Silence at the other end of the line.

"She says that…"

"Please don't tell me anything about that *curva!*" Eva sharply interrupted. "I don't want to know anything about her; I don't care. Don't even mention her name!"

"Mom, I have to tell you about this. It's kind of important."

"I told you not to…"

"Listen to me, she says she has a child with Radu," Irina blurted out.

Her mother didn't respond.

"Did you hear me?"

"I don't believe it. She's trying to trap Radu again," Eva replied.

"Jean-Pierre seems to think that she's telling the truth."

"Of course. Just like she told the truth last time. Radu barely saw that woman before she handed him over to the vultures."

"They dated for a whole month," Ioana reminded her mother.

"So what? That doesn't mean anything. We raised Raducu right. He wouldn't jump into bed with a woman after only a month. He'd wait until the wedding night, like your father and I did."

Realizing that debate on the subject of premarital chastity would prove fruitless, Irina tried a different approach. "I met her in person."

"How did you meet her?" Eva asked, surprised.

"Jean-Pierre took me to see her at a secret location. She's been living in the United States for the past two years. The Agency helped her escape, like they did Radu."

"That's what she claims. She's probably lured Jean-Pierre as well with her sex."

Irina once again veered away from that touchy subject. "She told me that Radu's son has been in a *Securitate* orphanage for years. His name is Lucian and she showed me a photograph of him right before he was kidnapped. She's asking for our help to save him."

"Even if that were true, which I seriously doubt, what could we do to help?"

"She says that Radu might be able to do something to save his son. With Jean-Pierre's support, of course."

"Are you that out of touch with reality? If Radu returns to Romania they'll kill him!"

"Mom, you know as well as I do whom Radu works for. You can deduce for yourself that he hasn't exactly kept away from that area of the world..."

"I don't believe anything that woman has to say and I'm totally against getting Radu entangled in her life ever again," Eva held her ground.

"Okay, but if she's telling the truth, please remember that little Lucian is your grandson too. He's almost ten years old now. Don't you want to see the child of your child?"

"Even if this child exists, he's her child, not Radu's. And why are we even arguing about this? It's absurd! I'm sure she's lying."

Irina began to lose patience. "If you don't want to tell Radu, then at least give me his number. I'll talk to him myself."

"Out of the question! I'm not supposed to give out his number to anyone. Only your father and I know it."

"Mom, obviously I can't know for sure that Ioana's telling the truth. But if she is, are you willing to take the chance of having your grandson waste away in some orphanage? What would you say if Grandma Marta hadn't cared about me?" Irina asked.

"Don't make such inappropriate comparisons, Irina! Not at a time like this... Leave your grandparents out of this sordid tale."

"It's not the little boy's fault that his mother worked for the *Securitate!*"

"Why didn't that woman contact Radu directly?"

"She said she tried."

"Well, why didn't she succeed?"

"I don't know. Probably because they don't get along any more. But she hasn't worked for the *Securitate* in years."

"And you believe her because she told you so, right? Genius!"

"Mom, I'm not defending her, okay? I barely knew of this woman's existence before we met, and what I heard about her from you and dad didn't exactly leave a favorable impression. But Jean-Pierre confirms her information and I tend to trust him on these matters."

"Then why doesn't he tell Radu? He's in touch with him much more than any of us are."

"He says it's a family matter."

Eva sighed. "I can't give you Radu's number, Irina. If Jean-Pierre wanted you to speak to your brother, he would have given you his number himself."

"Then will you tell Radu?" Irina insisted.

This time there was slight hesitation in her mother's voice. "I'll have to consult with your father first. But I don't think Andrei will approve either."

"All I'm asking you is to allow Radu to make his own decision," Irina repeated. "He's not a child any more."

"Unfortunately, he hasn't been our child for so long…"

Irina didn't know how to best comfort her mother. "I'm really sorry that this bad news is hitting you all at once. If you think it might help, I'll call Grandpa right away to console him."

"Some losses are impossible to console," Eva responded, her voice breaking once again under the impact of a fresh wave of pain. Even after immigrating to America, she remained extremely close to her parents. Her life revolved around the focal points of her parents and her own nuclear family. She called herself "an ellipse," an analogy which appealed to her scientifically minded husband.

"I'll write Grandpa a nice letter," Irina said.

"It would help if you actually went to visit him this winter break. You haven't been to Romania since we emigrated. With his failing health, who knows how much longer he'll hold on. Especially now that she's gone… He'd be so happy to see you again."

"I will, Mom, I promise. Is there anything I can do to help?"

Eva sighed. "Nothing. Just stay safe. As they say, bad news always travels in pairs."

"What do you mean?"

"Losing my mother and my son both on the same day."

"But you haven't lost Radu."

"Knowing him, he'll probably throw caution to the wind and decide to look into this bizarre story. He's turned our lives into a roller-coaster ride. First feared for his life. Then we feared for his safety. Now he's flirting with death again. And there's nothing we can do about it. He's never listened to us; he's always done only what he wanted," Eva said, with a sense of resignation before inevitable misfortune.

After Irina hung up the phone, she sat down at her desk, contemplating a letter to her grandfather. She couldn't think of anything to say that could alleviate his pain. She remembered how close and inseparable her grandparents had been. They complemented each other perfectly—Grandma Marta was practical and had what she, herself, called a "spicy" personality; Grandpa Mihai was mild and, let's face it, utterly helpless without her. They were constantly engaged in discussions, disagreements and debates. Yet even as a child, Irina sensed that her grandparents weren't actually fighting. Bickering was their way of flirting with one another; of keeping the flicker of passion alive psychologically even when their physical desire had diminished with age. Her mother was right, she thought. Some losses are impossible to console. Because there's no positive side to losing forever someone you need and love.

Nevertheless, Irina wanted to write her grandfather a note that would make him feel less alone in his pain. Maybe her love, nurtured by all the beautiful memories he had created during her childhood, would uplift and support him in these difficult moments.

She searched in her desk drawer for her old fountain pen that she had used in Romania and taken with her to America only as a keepsake. As she filled the pen with fresh ink, memories of her grandparents flooded her with bittersweet images. She began to write in Romanian, naturally retaining some of the terms of endearment and affectionate expressions she had used with her grandparents as a child:

"September 25, 1989

My dearest Grandfather,

I ask you from the bottom of my heart to stay strong. I miss you and Grandma Marta very much and hope to be able to see you as soon as possible (I'll try to come to Romania during my winter break). How can I console you, or Mom, or myself, when the pain of losing someone we love is inconsolable? I can't. All I can say is that I'm feeling so much pain, so much regret because I didn't come to see while Grandma was still alive. You were the best grandparents I can imagine. Without you I wouldn't have had the pleasant childhood I had, and in fact, since Dad defected, I wouldn't have had any childhood. I would have been the one to wait in long lines for milk and bread in the early morning, or to cook and do the laundry to help out Mama, who was carrying such heavy burdens upon her shoulders. With your caring love, you sacrificed your peace to preserve my childhood and Mama's youth.

Thanks to you, I think so often, so fondly, about my childhood. I remember our history lessons; our daily walks in the park; going sliding on the hill at Park Moghioros in the winter; the visits to the circus on Sundays; the delicious pastries that Grandma made, and the honey drops you'd sneak to me when nobody was looking, bought out of your small pension.

I truly regret that I didn't write you as often as I should have during the past few years. I tried so hard to close my eyes to everything I had lived in Romania and maybe even to those I loved most, so that I could adapt to America more easily and with less pain. The only thing I can say in my defense is that I never stopped loving you or thinking about you. I hope so much that you felt that in my letters and in the drawings and sketches I sent you.

I want to be once again the good granddaughter that a caring grandfather like you deserves. This winter, when I visit you in Romania, we can play chess together and talk about history, like in the old days. So please don't despair and save your energy, so that we can recapture some of the friendship and fun that we had before. In the meantime, dear grandfather, let's write to one another frequently and raise each other's spirits once again, okay? My new address at Princeton is:

Irina Schwarz
262 Joline Hall
Mathey College
Princeton University
Princeton NJ 08544
USA

Your loving granddaughter,
Irina"

In her wallet, Irina carried an old picture of her with her grandparents, the one she had taken with her when she left Romania. This photograph was very special to her. In it, all three of them were smiling. Her grandfather held a Kent cigarette in his hand. Grandma Martha also looked happy and proud, standing next to her granddaughter, whom she had primped up with the classic elephantine white bows in her hair and a frilly lilac dress. Irina's "Draculetta" teeth protruded slightly as she smiled.

As usual, Irina thought the best way to express her affection—and, more importantly under the circumstances, to comfort her grandfather—was through art. She used this photograph, now torn at the edges and faded, as inspiration for a new, vibrant painting. After hours of effort, she produced a composition filled with warm tones—shades of yellow, brown, red, burgundy and orange—in which the pieces of the painting fit together like a puzzle. A flowing, sinuous, embracing version of cubism, where the parts of their faces, their bodies, the room itself, were broken up into a kaleidoscope of colorful curves rather than sharp angles. Through art, Irina hoped to make her family whole again—if only in feeling, since it was no longer possible to do so in fact.

Chapter 15

"So where would you like to eat?" Paul asked Irina. Prompted by a series of recurring fantasies about her after their providential meeting in his apartment, he had obtained her number from Rico and mustered the courage to call and ask her out on a date. He justified this momentous decision by saying to himself that although she was a student, at least she was not technically his student, so probably dating her wouldn't get him fired.

"I don't know. Somewhere not too expensive," Irina answered. She disliked fancy restaurants where she was confused about which fork to use and where the sauce exceeded in volume the food on the plate.

"How about Le lapin blanc?" Paul proposed, thinking Irina was just being polite.

She wasn't: "Isn't the food there like a hundred dollars a plate?" she asked, puzzled.

"Oui! But that's not a problem," Paul responded, showing his immense generosity, which generally dissipated by the second or third date.

Irina, however, was not one to take advantage of it. "I was thinking of somewhere more along the lines of Taco Bell," she replied in earnest. To say that she had simple taste would be an overstatement. She had absolutely no taste; any food, no matter how cheap, was delicious by comparison to the deprivation she had suffered during her childhood.

"Ha, ha!" Paul laughed, not taking the comment seriously.

"Okay, then how about TGI Friday's?" Irina compromised. That was about as fancy as she could tolerate.

"Sounds good. When do you want me to pick you up?"

"Does seven o'clock sound alright?"

"Sure."

"Okay. I look forward to seeing you soon!"

"Me too," Paul said.

As an afterthought, before hanging up, it occurred to Irina to ask: "Hold on. Do you know where I live?"

"No. Where?"

"In Joline Hall. Right next to the Mathey cafeteria and across from the Blair Arch. I'll wait for you on the bench outside the dorm, okay?"

"I'll be there."

Excited about the prospect of seeing Irina again, Paul took all of two minutes to prepare for his date. He looked at himself in the mirror, arranged a few unruly tufts of hair by licking his fingers and pressing the rebellious curls against his temples (deciding that, after all, the situation didn't warrant the more extreme measure of actually passing a comb through his hair), then put on his tan winter shoes. His outfit, consisting of a colorful striped shirt he had worn for three days in a row and a pair of old jeans, struck him as suitable for this informal occasion. After the quick grooming session, he was ready to go, which left him with about two hours to relax and read the newspaper before his date.

Back in her dorm room, Irina was equally excited by the prospect of a date with an older man who was nevertheless younger than her father. Ever since she had falsely announced to Jean-Pierre that she was dating Paul, his image kept popping up in her head. In all honesty, she found him kind of cute. So now the inevitable and exceedingly difficult question presented itself: "What should I wear?"

Irina examined her closet with a look of disappointment: she had only ten skirts, twelve pairs of pants and jeans, about fifteen blouses and nine pairs of shoes in there. How in the world was she going to find something suitable for a date? Most of the skirts, she thought, were too long (below the knee, to please her parents) and totally outdated (ditto). Two of them, the ones she had bought in secret with her friend Alice back in high school, were too short, which wouldn't have been a problem if it weren't for the fact that she thought they made her behind look big. The blouses were too goody-two-shoes, especially since she wanted to convey a sexier image as of late. After trying on and removing, in rapid succession, various matrix combinations involving four pairs of pants, three blouses and five skirts, she settled on one of the miniskirts, deciding that, after all, men prefer to see curves. To complement this minimalist look, she chose her only tight shirt and a faded jean jacket. In the shoe department, she didn't even have to think about it: high heels were practically obligatory with such an outfit.

On the make-up front, Irina was armed with a new arsenal of weapons: the shimmery pink lipstick that Christine had suggested, a pale blue eye shadow and a subtle peachy blush (as opposed to her former bright orange one). Although she was not entirely satisfied with her outfit—what self-respecting woman ever is?—she thought it was presentable enough to head to the bench at 7:07p.m., only seven minutes later than agreed. That would definitely fall into the rubric of fashionably late, she thought, satisfied with how quickly she had gotten ready for her date given the serious wardrobe constraints. Due to her haste, she didn't have time to straighten out her closet which was now filled with discarded clothes, looking like a physics lesson on the effects of entropy.

Paul was calmly waiting on the bench next to Joline Hall, enjoying the scenery. His head followed back and forth, like at a tennis match played back in slow motion, the young women who went in and out of the girls' dorm. One of the girls he followed admiringly with his eyes turned out to be, much to his surprise and satisfaction, his own date, Irina. He instinctively scoped out her legs and seemed delighted with the miniskirt. Irina noticed his positive reaction and silently congratulated herself on her excellent choice of outfit.

"Where did you park?" she asked him after they exchanged polite greetings.

"On Prospect Street," Paul answered with a shrug, naming the busiest street in a wealthy town filled with ten minute parking slots closely monitored by vigilant—and exceedingly bored—parking cops.

"Let's run! Your car's probably already towed by now!" Irina exclaimed.

Fortunately, Paul's car was still there and hadn't even gotten a ticket. Of course, "barely there" would be a more accurate characterization, since after the divorce, Mary had taken his good car and left him with a beat-up, rusty-looking '72 Chevy that he had purchased for five hundred dollars four years ago. If he was lucky, he might be able to give it away for free.

"You think we'll have to push it to the restaurant?" Irina inquired, as Paul gallantly struggled to open the clenched door on her side.

"I doubt it," he reassured his date. "So far, that's only happened to me a couple of times before."

"I'm relieved to hear that."

At the restaurant, a blond waitress with exaggerated affability greeted them.

"Hi! Welcome to TGI Friday's. My name's Cindy and I'll be your waitress. What can I do for you this evening?" she chirped the rehearsed introduction in a high-pitched, girlish voice that instantly got on Irina's nerves. Not so in Paul's case, however.

"Do you really want to know?" he asked in his typically inappropriate manner. The waitress smiled and his date smirked. Was this guy going to turn out to be a weirdo? Irina wondered. She ordered a Diet Coke while Paul splurged on a glass of water. He followed the waitress with his eyes assuming a look of longing that reminded Irina of a puppy whose master has just abandoned him forever. Geesh! It's like he's never seen a waitress before. How pitiful men are... The only thing missing is the panting, tail wagging and tongue hanging out, Irina thought.

But Paul didn't stop there. He felt compelled by some strange and obviously self-destructive instinct to push the envelope even further by also making editorial comments: "Wow! I'm in love. Did you see that little waitress? She's adorable. And so nice. I'd marry her in an instant," he announced his wedding plans to his date once the waitress had turned the corner.

Irina could hardly believe his gall. Paul's remarks raised a few red flags in her mind, to say the least. How old is this guy anyway? she wondered. She looked at the thirty-five year old man facing her and thought, "He acts like a twelve year old." Plus, quite frankly, she didn't consider the waitress that cute or nice. Riled up by Paul's hyperbolic and way out of line praise of the waitress, Irina's feminine competitive instinct kicked into gear. After all, Cindy was a bit overweight and chipper in a superficial kind of way, just to get an extra big tip, Irina sharply evaluated her rival.

"So you're from Romania, right?" Paul expressed some interest in his own date—for a change.

"Yes. We came here when I was twelve."

"Do you miss your country?"

"No, not really. I miss my family, but not Romania. I was extremely close to my grandparents." Here Irina paused, feeling sad again. "My grandmother recently passed away. I hope so much to get the opportunity to see my grandfather before… it's too late. I haven't been to Romania since we left the country."

"But how come you didn't visit your family during the summers at least?" Paul wanted to know.

"Partly because we feared the government. But also because I wanted to adapt quicker to this country, you know, become Americanized."

"Why?" Paul, who aspired to be European, asked with genuine puzzlement.

Irina shrugged. "Because I live here. I even got my citizenship last year. Basically, I'm an American now."

"Well, nobody's perfect," Paul remarked.

"The main thing is that I was afraid that if I went back, I'd become too attached to everyone and everything all over again. I had a pretty tough time adapting to America when I first got here. I didn't want to go through that kind of pain ever again—not if I could help it."

"I don't understand. Once you already adapted to America, it's not like visiting Romania would make you unadapt, right?" Paul asked, then looked up and smiled at the friendly waitress who had arrived with their drinks.

"Are you guys ready to order?" Cindy chirped.

Paul became distracted from the conversation with Irina. Aside from his female students, he was extremely fond of waitresses. They embodied pretty much everything men liked about women: youthfulness, friendliness, obsequious servility and conversation strictly limited to how to please them.

"Sure," he nodded with a smile that, Irina noted, resembled the Cheshire cat grin. "I'd like a vegetarian burrito. Chicken are my cousins," he turned to Irina, eloquently justifying the ethical basis for his vegetarianism.

"Then that explains your behavior," she replied. The waitress was the only one to appreciate the joke—even though Irina was being serious.

"I'd like to start out with the house salad and then I'll have the grilled salmon," Irina informed her.

"What kind of dressing would you like on your salad?" Cindy asked.

"Italian."

"I'll be right back with your order! Let me know if there's anything else I can do for you," the ever cheerful waitress announced.

When she was gone, Paul couldn't resist saying under his breath: "I can think of a couple of things..." and rolling his eyes suggestively.

Irina finally decided to comment upon this egregious lack of tact: "Listen, if you'd rather go out on a date with her rather than me, I'll get out of the way and leave the two of you alone."

"What?" Paul was genuinely surprised by her reaction. He thought he was just being a normal guy, perhaps a little more sincere and expressive than most, but he perceived that as a good thing. Don't women say they like openness and honesty in a relationship? He figured he'd start on the right foot with Irina.

She, on the other hand, looked just about ready to use her right foot to kick his behind: "Well, from your comments about the waitress, it doesn't look like you need me here. I feel superfluous."

"I was just saying that she's cute and sweet. What's so offensive about that? I love waitresses, that's all," Paul defended himself with the air of a reasonable man.

But Irina didn't find his argument particularly compelling. She wasn't going to put up with being a third wheel on her own date. Enough was enough. She stood up: "Enjoy your date with Cindy and be sure to send me a wedding invitation. Goodbye!" she said and grabbed her purse, ready to go and hitchhike a ride back to campus if she had to.

"Hold on! I'm sorry. I didn't mean to insult you. Geesh... You're so sensitive."

"Is that what you call an apology?" Irina asked, placing one hand to her waist, a position which, for a Romanian woman, practically expressed a declaration of war.

"Actually... I've been thinking about you ever since we met. You know, in my studio, with your towel," Paul blurted out, regretting that he was messing up a date to which he had looked forward for quite awhile.

Somewhat placated, Irina sat back down. "Do you understand why your behavior upset me?" she asked him calmly.

"No, not really. But I truly am sorry," he said sincerely, looking at her pretty oval face and wounded eyes. He never wanted to hurt anyone, let alone a pretty woman he was dating. It's just that he had this habit of voicing nearly everything that crossed his mind, especially if he considered it to be positive.

"All you've done so far on our date is talk about how much you like another woman!" Irina said exasperated that she even had to explain such an obvious faux-pas. Was Paul mentally challenged? she wondered. As if to confirm this doubt, he made the mistake of continuing his self-defense:

"You don't understand. All men look at pretty women. That's our favorite pastime in life. You take that away from us and all we've got left is sports," he explained to Irina, judging that her overreaction must be due to ignorance about male psychology.

"I realize that. But it's considered impolite to do it so obviously, and then make comments on top of it, when you're out on a date!" Irina gave him a few pointers.

"Why?" Paul recklessly pursued the debate. "There's no point in censoring your behavior. That's the same as lying. Do you want me to lie? Don't you want me to be myself?" he reasoned with her.

"Of course not! What, you're going to burp in my face next, while we're at it?" Irina replied, appalled by the prospect of skipping over all the nice and fun parts of dating to get straight to the boring and honest ones. "That's what marriage is for.Don't you get it? We're on our first date. You're supposed to be polite, nice and on your best behavior with me. You know, *romantic*," she emphasized.

"Oh, sorry. I forgot," Paul smiled. As irritated as she was with him, Irina felt amused by the absurdity of the situation as well as, strangely enough, by Paul's utter cluelessness. No doubt, she would have to teach him a thing or two about love, the expert nineteen year old who had dated semi-seriously only one man told herself.

When Cindy came back with Irina's salad, Paul looked down at his glass of water, deliberately restraining himself from making eye contact with the problematic waitress. But once she left, he slipped again: "I hope she returns soon!" he said.

Irina looked at him in utter disbelief. What had she just explained to him?

"Because I'm very hungry," Paul hastened to add, noting Irina's marked disapproval. "She doesn't matter at all to me," he attempted to exculpate himself further, sounding strangely similar to a man explaining his mistress to his wife.

Irina's jaw almost dropped to the floor following these further manifestations of highly unusual dating behavior. She shook her head: "You know, I must say, you're certainly unique…"

Paul nodded with a sense of satisfaction: "Every woman I'm with tells me that."

"Well, they can't all be wrong," Irina confirmed. "Just out of curiosity: do you ever get any second dates?"

"We'll see," Paul smiled and, in spite of her better judgment, Irina once again felt alarmingly charmed by his boyish…dorkiness.

By the time their meals arrived, Paul had made some progress on discovering the root of Irina's emotional inhibitions. "So then, as a teenager, you didn't want to visit your family in Romania because you felt too attached to them?"

"The real reason I never went back was that my father didn't want my mother and I to return there. His greatest fear was that, after all those years of struggling to immigrate, we'd disappear behind the Iron Curtain never to reemerge again. But in my heart of hearts, I also didn't want to go back because I thought that I'd suffer the pain of separation all over again," Irina answered.

"But it wasn't a conscious decision, you know. I only realized this had been my self-defense mechanism a few days ago, when I was writing to my grandfather trying to console him about my grandmother's death. After we lost her, I felt so guilty for my behavior the past few years. My grandparents practically raised me once my dad defected to America."

"Did you stop communicating with them altogether?" Paul asked, taking a bite of his burrito, whose contents began to spill out the other side.

"No, nothing like that. I just didn't call or write them as frequently as I should have," Irina explained. She was distracted by the sauce trickling down Paul's chin. At least I don't have to stand on ceremony with him when I eat, she thought with some relief, polishing off very quickly the defenseless salmon and wiping the plate spotlessly clean with bits of French bread.

"Eat slower! You'll get a stomach ache!" Paul warned his date as one does a child. He reminded Irina of her father in some ways; in other respects, however, he was more immature than she was.

"Half of your burrito's in your lap," she retorted with dignity, to let him know how much she appreciated his friendly advice.

"I felt something hot there, but I thought it was because of you," he quipped.

"You mean because of the waitress…"

"Her too…"

"So anyways," Irina returned to the original subject, "What I've decided to do is to go back to Romania in a few months."

"Great idea!" Paul wholeheartedly approved what he thought was Irina's decision to return permanently to a totalitarian dictatorship. "This country's a total mess. You're better off living under the Petrescu regime."

Irina looked at her date intently, trying very hard to ascertain what planet he was from. "Excuse me?"

"At least everybody knows that Petrescu's a criminal. Unfortunately, people are foolish enough to give our president the benefit of the doubt."

"What's there not to give?" Irina replied, being a firm defender of American democracy. "He doesn't put people in labor camps or torture them for their political views. And he doesn't leave his whole country without heat, electricity and even food."

"Oh yeah? Ask the parents of the children who died as a result of his policies…"

"What are you talking about?"

"The embargo on Cuba…"

"How can you compare a Stalinist dictator with a democratic president?" Irina fired back.

"It doesn't matter what you're called. What matters is what you do. Since WWII, U.S. foreign policy has been criminal! Cri-mi-nal! With all the useless wars and invasions, its support for reactionary dictatorships in South America, the embargo against Cuba, the coup d'états planned by the CIA..." Paul raised his voice enough for the occupants of several tables to look at him with curiosity.

"Are you sure you're not French?" Irina asked, recalling having similar discussions with some of her father's French friends.

"No, but I do have a continental education," Paul boasted.

"I wouldn't brag about it," Irina clipped his wings. She was afraid that he might get a second wind on the political debate, so she smoothly changed the subject: "Anyway, what movie do you want to see?"

Paul was fully prepared for this question. "I have a few videos at home. One of my favorite movies is *Walkabout*. It's about this beautiful, proper young woman who gets lost in the Australian desert with her little brother and meets an aborigine who falls in love with her. The girl is gorgeous and the scenery spectacular. Do you want to see it?" he asked eagerly.

"Okay," Irina gave in to his childlike enthusiasm.

The couple went back to Paul's studio and cuddled next to one another on the couch. Irina enjoyed the feel of Paul's warmth and fragility next to her. They were so close that she could feel the tickle of his hair upon her cheek. The movie, however, turned out to be about as exciting to Irina as the proverbial act of watching paint dry. As Paul had forewarned, the whole thing consisted of a camera following a teenage girl in a miniskirt over the Australian desert for two excruciatingly long hours. To Paul's delight, there were a few brief scenes of nudity showing the girl swimming underwater as she was, presumably, becoming one with nature. Paul followed that episode with special interest and Irina even thought she saw his glasses fog up.

"I can see why you like this movie," she commented once the ordeal was over.

"It's amazing... "

"Yup. Two hours of following around a girl who does nothing. I haven't seen anything like it in my entire life."

"You mean you didn't like it?" Paul asked, feeling surprised and even a little wounded. He assumed that any sensitive being with good taste would enjoy the same movies that he did.

"Hey, what can I say? I'm a heterosexual woman. Girls in miniskirts just don't do it for me. Sorry to disappoint you!" Irina replied.

"You think I liked the movie only because of the gorgeous girl in school girl clothes?"

"Given your earlier comments about the waitress, the thought did cross my mind."

"Absolutely not! Everything about this movie is spectacular—the superb Australian scenery, the plot, the love story."

"What love story?"

"Didn't you watch the movie? The young man committed suicide because he fell in love with the girl and she rejected him."

"I must have dozed off during that part. But seriously, that wasn't love. You can't fall in love just like that, unilaterally. Love's mutual and takes time," Irina shared with Paul the fruits of her wisdom, honed by many years of inexperience.

"Of course love doesn't have to be mutual! In fact, it's much more interesting when it's not shared; when you long for someone or something you can't have..." Paul explained his own philosophy, relying upon his many years of experience with failed relationships.

"I'll try to remember that," Irina replied.

The occasion presented itself soon enough, since Paul was delighted to rediscover that Irina wore a miniskirt, was slim and had long brown hair, just like the young actress in Walkabout. "You kind of remind me of the girl in the movie..." he hinted, looking at Irina with a sparkle in his eyes.

"Really?"

"You have her hair, her figure, her legs..." Paul indicated, brushing his hand lightly along the features he listed--strictly for illustrative purposes, of course.

Irina retreated flirtatiously to the other end of the couch. "Too bad you can't get near any of that."

"Why not?"

"Didn't you just tell me that it's much more interesting to want what you can't have?"

"Oh, I was referring to fiction and movies, not real life," Paul was prepared to violate his own principles under the circumstances.

"I don't think so," Irina retorted. "I think you were talking about life. And, in fact, you said... " But before she could finish her argument, his lips were on top of hers, offering a rather eloquent rebuttal. He kissed her softly, with little pecks which became more fervent, deeper. His tongue probed the inner recesses of her mouth and his hands seemed to take on a life—and itinerary—of their own, exploring her curves and even checking if she was wearing panties. She gently pushed his hand away, following the advice he now sincerely regretted offering.

In her own bed alone that night Irina had trouble falling asleep. Her desires were ignited, her body a bundle of nervous energy. There was something about this irritating little man with unconventional manners and ultra-leftist leanings, she told herself (not without a degree of surprise and serious objections from the rational side of her brain) there was something about him that, to her own surprise, she found ... how to put it?... strangely irresistible.

Chapter 16

During the rest of September and the beginning of October, Irina relieved her roommate of her company. Feeling instantly comfortable with Paul—despite, or perhaps because of their constant little squabbles and sparks--she practically moved in with him after only a few dates and undertook the daunting project of teaching him how to behave properly with a girlfriend. In her estimation, all a man had to do was follow a few basic rules: don't talk about other women (and if you must, at least have the decency to stick to unflattering terms); don't stare too obviously at them (though staring a little is unfortunately normal); don't flirt too much with others (i.e., preferably much less than your girlfriend does with other men); don't talk about previous girlfriends during sex (because that's anticlimactic).

That pretty much covered it, except that training Paul, who was extraordinarily attached to his bad habits, was not that easy. For instance, it took Irina several fits of public hysteria just to persuade him to control his waitress habit. And, generally speaking, whenever Paul saw a pretty woman, he stared at her with puppy eyes, made a few ecstatic exclamations cut short by Irina's gestures of severe disapproval, then turned to his girlfriend and said "Oups! Sorry!" which of course only aggravated the matter. Obviously, he had a ways to go in becoming a suitable boyfriend, but Irina was cautiously optimistic--not so much about Paul's pliability, which was comparable to that of a block of wood, as about her own perseverance. She didn't undergo years of ideological indoctrination in Romania for nothing.

Despite these challenges, from the first week, Irina and Paul became glued to each other. They did everything together: ate lunch and dinner at Irina's cafeteria (where Paul could unobtrusively mingle with the co-eds); shopped together; saw movies together, and even went to the library together, right before dinner, meeting in the lobby of Firestone Library at 5:30 p.m. sharp. Paul would read international newspapers to get what he called "the real news"—particularly from *Le Monde* and *Libération*—while Irina would browse through *Scinteia,* the Romanian Communist Party's official paper, to get what she called "appalling propaganda," just for old times' sake. Even now, seven years after having left her country, she become inflamed when reading headlines to the effect of "Our beloved leader paves the way for Romania's progress," next to photos showing poor, haggard looking people forced to hail the Führer at one of the mandatory rallies convened by the Secret Police. How long will this tragic farce go on? Irina wondered. Sometimes she felt so outraged by an article, that she'd even forget that Paul didn't speak Romanian, and would read to him a particularly offensive passage. "Thanks for sharing this with me," he'd reply, not understanding a word. "I find your comment very perceptive."

No matter how distressing the treatment of the Romanian people might have been, that didn't seem to bother Paul half as much as whatever the French news said about the actions of the American government. He'd get all red in the face and state "I can't even read this any more, it makes me so mad! This country's an embarrassment." But invariably he'd return the following day to the library, his eyes seeking precisely the international section of *Le Monde* to find further European grievances against the United States.

One Friday evening Irina put her new boyfriend's loyalty and endurance to the test. She took Paul shopping in preparation for her upcoming trip to Romania, since she figured that if a beginning relationship survives an intensive shopping spree for a Second World country, it can live through anything.

They decided to go to Quaker Bridge Mall, the biggest shopping center in the Princeton area.

"So what do you need to get?" Paul asked, wishing to be efficient and especially brief about the whole trip.

Irina thought for a moment. "Well… it's tough to say since I don't know where to find any of the things my relatives actually asked for."

"Then why don't we just stay home and do a little hanky panky?" Paul selflessly suggested.

Irina ignored the comment. "You don't understand. They're asking for the impossible."

"Like what?"

"Well, like my great-uncle on my mother's side of the family wants a new hip."

"A what?"

"He can't find a prosthetic hip in Romania, so they want me to get one here. How in the world am I supposed to do that? I'm not a doctor. How would I know where to buy it or what size to get? I mean, don't hips come in different sizes? They think you can just walk into Kmart and buy someone a new hip."

Paul nodded: "At least we can safely cross that gift off your shopping list. What else do they want?"

"My second cousin wants braces because her front teeth stick out."

"They must have some kind of medical fetish in your country," Paul remarked.

Once they reached the mall, Irina proposed: "Let's start with T.J. Maxx. It's got everything." At the entrance, she grabbed a large shopping cart.

Paul was taken aback: "Why in the world do you need a grocery cart? You're only getting a couple of hips."

Irina shook her head: "You're so inexperienced."

"I've been married and shopped with a woman before," Paul countered.

"Yes, but not with an Eastern European woman. You have so much to learn! Let's get going since the store will close in four hours."

Her boyfriend looked alarmed: "Four hours?"

"Don't worry. If we can't find everything today, we can always come back tomorrow," his girlfriend reassured him.

"Didn't you say you can't buy anything your family asked for? We should be out of here in two seconds. I don't see any hips. Except possibly for that cute girl over there," he indicated a curvy teenager.

"Don't even start with me on that!" Irina warned him. "I can't buy anything my relatives want, but I can certainly get them what they need."

"Such as?"

"Underwear!" Irina declared joyfully and headed straight for the lingerie department. To Paul's regret, however, she didn't go into the sexy nightie and teddy section, but went for the cheap packaged cotton underwear aisle instead.

"Why would you get them these ugly things?" Paul asked. "What did they ever do to you?"

"They lack basic necessities in Romania. Do you know what happens to my mother's friend when she goes back there every summer?"

"No, but I have a feeling you'll tell me."

"Her underwear gets stolen at the Romanian customs, that's what!"

"She must have some sexy underwear."

"Not at all. She wears granny panties like these ones. See?" Irina lifted a hermetically sealed bag of cotton underwear with a pink flower design.

"That's more information than I need to know about your mother's friend," Paul said, then quickly changed his mind: "Is she pretty?"

Irina placed her hand upon her hip: "You never learn do you? My whole point is that they need useful presents in Romania, not sexy nightgowns."

Having explained how the system worked to her boyfriend, Irina began pitching bag after bag of underwear into her shopping cart.

"Take it easy! Show some restraint," Paul suggested an approach to shopping that Irina hadn't considered yet. "How many pairs of underwear does your family need?"

"They change them every day, unlike some people."

"Even so. You must have a hundred pairs in there."

"They're also for bribes."

"What do you mean 'bribes'? Don't people generally prefer money in those situations?"

"Not in Romania. Because even if you have the money, you still can't find the underwear."

"If you say so... Personally, I think taking underwear off, rather than putting granny underwear on, would be a much more effective bribe. "

"You always think taking one's clothes off is the solution to everything," Irina retorted.

"Not really. Only if you're a pretty woman. Okay! I never thought I'd say this, but shopping for women's underwear is really boring. What else do we need to get?"

"Cosmetics. L'Oreal and Max Factor are Romanian favorites."

"That's for bribes also?

"Of course. Plus all the women in my family like them as well." Irina started to open a jar of L'Oreal face cream.

Paul rushed to stop her: "What are you doing? Are you out of your mind? They'll arrest you for shoplifting!"

"Why? I'm not stealing anything," Irina replied calmly.

"In this country, you're not allowed to open a product before buying it. That's the same as stealing."

"Then how are you supposed to know that you're not purchasing an expired cream, hmmm?"

"The civilized way. By checking the date on the bottom," Paul indicated, closing the jar and turning it upside down to read the stamp on it.

"That method's unreliable," Irina objected. She took another jar off the shelf, checked the date, opened it, examined its color, sniffed it, then placed the evidence under her boyfriend's nose. "See this cream? Take a whiff. It's slightly yellow when it's supposed to be white and it smells funny. That's because it's been under these hot lights for too long and the chemicals are starting to disintegrate. It's already gone bad, even though the date indicates that it should be fine. If I gave cream like this to my relatives, they might develop some sort of rash and never forgive me for the rest of my life. Do you really want me to have their skin disease on my conscience?"

Why do women even bother with these stinky face creams anyway? Paul asked himself.

"You have to be very careful about the gifts you take to Romania. I learned about all of this from my mother's best friend, Sanda. She goes there every year," Irina added to bolster her argument.

Paul didn't seem too impressed. He also couldn't understand why Irina was examining and piling up ten jars of cream into the shopping cart. "Are you a millionaire?" he asked her.

"That's another thing you don't know. You can't go to Eastern Europe unprepared. It takes some of my mom's friends a whole year to stock up. All we've got is four measly hours."

"You keep threatening me with that. I hope that in about fifteen minutes we'll be out of here."

"Such a novice..." Irina said with a sigh, pushing the cart towards the make-up section.

In the shopping frenzy, somehow her barrette, which held her hair in a neat chignon whenever she wanted to be all business, broke. Paul looked at her, with her hair down and slightly disheveled: "Actually, you look very sexy like this. I think you should wear your hair down more often."

"But I really liked that barrette," Irina said with regret.

While his girlfriend was tossing a few more items into her cart, Paul wondered around the hair product aisle to find her another barrette. Almost immediately he spotted one that he was almost certain she'd like: it glimmered golden bonze with dark brown animal print stripes. He bought it and presented it to Irina with pride: "So what do you think?"

"Paul, this is perfect. I definitely want to get it," she reached to place the barrette into the shopping cart.

"No, this one's my gift," he said. "I already bought it for you, since I thought you might like it."

"That's so nice of you!" Irina was touched.

"May I?" he asked, wishing to place it in her hair.

"I think you'll need a little help," she said, turning around and twisting her long hair in a bun while he fixed it into place with the shinny new golden brown barrette. "Thank you so much," she said, punctuating her statement with a kiss.

The couple emerged triumphant from the store with about five large bags filled with tons of make-up, bags of underwear, face creams, pantyhose (a very rare commodity in Romania), jewelry that could be sold on the black market, Tylenol (for Paul, who had a headache) and slippers.

"I'm glad that's over with," he declared when they got back to his apartment. He looked at Irina mischievously: "What do I get in reward for my patience?"

"Hold on. I'm taking inventory," she announced, sorting with great care through her merchandise, which she had spilled on the floor and divided into neat piles, vicariously experiencing the pleasure her relatives would get from all those cheap commodities.

"Can't you do this later? When are you going to Romania anyway?"

Irina looked at her boyfriend with a dazed, distracted look, still contemplating her loot. "I don't know. Probably as early as November."

"November? But the semester won't be over until the mid-December!"

"Actually, that's something I wanted to discuss with you," she announced. "This friend of mine is offering me two free tickets to Prague. The problem is that they're for mid-November, meaning in just a few weeks."

"Why is this guy giving you free tickets? Does he want to sleep with you?" Paul asked, not above jealousy himself.

"He already did. He's the kind-of-ex-boyfriend I told you about earlier. Jean-Pierre. Remember him?"

"You never told me you slept with him! What's the return policy on virgins?"

"The same as for the face creams. Once you use them, they're non-refundable. Seriously, though!"

"I am serious!"

"Paul, this is a once-in-a-lifetime opportunity. I mean, how often does one get free tickets to Prague, right? Plus that way I can go to Romania by train right afterwards, to see my grandfather, which I was planning to do in December anyway. I'll just go a little earlier and stay a bit longer in Eastern Europe, that's all."

"You seem to forget one little detail. It's called your studies."

Irina gave her boyfriend the beseeching look of a little girl asking for her father's permission to go to a party: "Pretty please... I can always take the finals right after the winter break and get incompletes. But I may never get a chance to visit Prague or my grandfather again. At least not for free. I really want to go, Paul."

"You do what you want," he shrugged. "But I find this behavior highly irresponsible and, to be honest, quite pointless. Why can't you see your grandfather at Christmas, like you originally planned?"

"You're missing the whole point," Irina gesticulated with her hands, as she always did when she was very excited. "This way I get to travel to Europe for free. And we get to visit Prague, one of your favorite cities, on top of it."

"Just a minute. What do you mean we?"

"Didn't I just tell you that Jean-Pierre's giving me two tickets? Who else would I take with me?"

"Don't I have a say in the matter?"

"Of course you do!" Irina exclaimed, getting more and more excited about the idea. "But why wouldn't you want to go to Prague for free? You have no excuse. This semester you're on sabbatical. All you have to do is give a couple of presentations. Plus think of all the pretty girls in Czechoslovakia..."

"Okay," Paul was more or less persuaded by the second, irrefutable argument.

"...that you won't be able to touch," Irina completed her sentence.

Paul approached her with a smile: "Oh really? Says who?"

"Says your girlfriend," Irina responded.

"And what will happen if I touch?"

"You don't want to find out," Irina answered, looking steadily into Paul's eyes and moving closer to him.

"I'm not intimidated by a little college sophomore," he taunted her.

"You will be once I get through with you," Irina responded, unbuttoning her shirt. He pulled up her bra and began kissing her breasts, then suckled gently her little nipples. She moaned with pleasure, placing her hands on his head, stroking his hair.

"Can I do it on my knees?" she whispered.

"Do what?"

"You know... Do I need to draw a diagram?"

Paul stood up while Irina rubbed her face against him. "Mmmm... You smell kind of nice," she mumbled.

"I'll remember not to take a shower tomorrow too," Paul replied with his incomparable talent for setting the mood.

Irina began licking him circularly, like a delicious ice cream cone, then with slow vertical motions from base to tip. After about two minutes he announced, with a sense of urgency: "Okay, I'm ready for phase two."

Irina took him into her mouth, while he pushed her head back and forth. She had the feeling of absorbing life, a raw energy fueled by youthful desire.

"Let's get on the bed," he proposed breathlessly.

She was about to remove her skirt, but he stopped her. "Keep it on this time." She got on her hands and knees on the bed and he lifted her skirt, pulling down her panties and pantyhose to mid-thigh. He then began gently stroking her, enjoying her warmth and moistness, excited by the view of her rounded bottom. He glided in with no resistance, rocking gently at first, then more and more frantically, until they both made sounds of pleasure in an incoherent, ecstatic harmony.

Chapter 17

The horizontal blinds let through a few slim, refracted rays of light. Irina turned over and checked the green neon light of the alarm clock. It was 7:00 a.m. on a Saturday, which meant Paul would probably stay in bed until at least 9:00 o'clock. She turned over slowly, trying not to disturb her companion and examined his thin face, the eyes covered up by the black, Zorro mask she had given him. It came as a free gift with one of the make-up kits she had purchased for her family. Paul was a very light sleeper, sensitive to light and noise, so he had to wear an eye mask and ear plugs if he wanted to get any rest. She saw the orange tips of the earplugs stick out of his ears, surrounded by curly locks of dark hair. His lips were thin yet delectably soft, reminding Irina of the velvety moistness of his kisses. She was an early-riser; Paul a late-sleeper. They had learned to adapt to these seesaw biological rhythms. As Irina went to bed at 10 p.m., Paul read a chapter of a novel to the dim lamp light and scribbled in his little black book the occurrences of the day until he finally fell asleep around 11:00 p.m. She would wake up early but remain in bed as still as she could, enjoying his proximity and the softness of the bed until she felt his slight body shift restlessly, about to awaken. Responding to his movements, she turned and cupped in a fetal position into the hollow of his stomach, which is how they preferred to sleep, each protecting the other from the stresses of the day. In the morning, she usually felt something poking her and responded by caressing him gently.

"Good morning," Paul mumbled, not fully awake. She turned to him bright eyed and bushy tailed, eager to start the day: "So what should we do today?"

"What?" he asked, pulling off his eye mask and squinting at her, his eyes gradually adjusting to the light. With the exception of his morning desire, he was still somnolent. She, however, was filled with anticipation: "I was thinking maybe we could go for a walk in that little park, you know, the one with the swings. Since it looks like a nice, sunny day."

"It's freezing outside," Paul objected.

"Cold yet refreshing!" Irina countered, jumping out of bed. "Do you want some coffee?"

"Sure, thanks."

Irina went into the adjacent kitchen—Paul's studio was really all one room--filled the coffee pot with water, placed a Maxwell's bag into the cylinder and started the machine gurgling.

"It will be ready in a few minutes," she announced in a sing-song voice, snuggling up next to her boyfriend in the cozy bed.

"Ouch! Your feet are so cold! Why don't you wear slippers? You bought about a dozen pairs."

"For Romania! Besides, it takes too long to find them."

"You should put them right next to the bed, parallel, as I do mine. That way they're always there when you need them."

Irina caressed his legs with the soles of her cold feet: "Why do I need slippers when I have you to warm me up?"

"Precisely because of that," Paul answered, but allowed his girlfriend to rub herself unto him like a kitten.

He began stroking her body: the shoulders first, then her back, her behind, which he focused on especially with slow, circular caresses. "The park idea sounds okay. Especially after I've had some coffee."

"First things first," Irina whispered. His fingers touched her with a few tentative strokes: "Geesh!" he feigned protest. "When are you not mushy?" he asked. The word "mushy" was their code word for "aroused."

"When I'm not with you," Irina cooed in all sincerity.

"You don't give me much of a break, do you? You should pick on someone your own age," he said, growing more and more mushy himself despite his usual disclaimers. He stroked her absentmindedly with his member, then slipped in easily from behind, his hands cupping her breasts. He planted affectionate, tender kisses on the back of her neck, her long hair, her shoulders, sending shivers of pleasure throughout her body. After a few minutes, the percolator began protesting loudly.

"What perfect timing! The coffee's ready," Irina announced.

She went into the kitchen, filled two cups of coffee to the brim, pouring four packets of Sweet and Low into her own cup, nothing into his.

"You're going to die of cancer before the age of thirty!" he forewarned to no avail every time she used artificial sweetener.

"At least I'll have lived to the max," Irina responded with a wink.

Paul made a sour face as soon as he sipped the first drops of coffee: "This American coffee's so watery. I need a cup of Espresso to really wake up."

"We can stop by Starbucks if you want," Irina suggested.

"No, theirs is not authentic either."

"Okay, then let's take a trip to Italy together."

In the shower, they took turns washing each other. Like in everything, they had developed a ritual. He sung oldies songs—Ben E. King's Stand by me was one of their favorites—while she washed his arms, his chest, then got on her knees and lathered up with special solicitude his privates, prompting him to declare—"There are other parts of my body, you know"—a comment which invariably made her laugh. She washed his legs with long vertical strokes, then twirled him around and this time began with the back of the legs and moved up, washing his bottom as thoroughly as she had his front.

Then it was her turn. She closed her eyes with delight as she felt his soft hands pass all over her body, caressing it with the fragrant, foamy soap, planting an affectionate kiss here and there as he went along.

"I don't think I could ever go back to showering alone," she said as he rinsed the shampoo out of his hair, head tipped back into the abundant flow of water, eyes pressed shut.

By the time they stepped out and enveloped each other in towels, Paul was fully awake.

"Here's what I propose," he suggested methodically, since for him everything had to have an order and a place. "We dress, have breakfast at the House of Pancakes before the whole herd of students gets there, then we go to the park, then to the library to read the newspaper and maybe you can do some of your homework--for a change--then we'll go have lunch somewhere. And this evening we can see a movie. How does that sound?"

"Sounds good, mon cher professeur," Irina smiled, since his systematic attitude to everything reminded her of her French teacher. Though not exactly easy going by nature, with Paul, Irina was surprisingly easy to please. It felt nice to like someone for whom he was and enjoy every little thing with him. Strange, but nice, she told herself. In the back of her mind, however, she divined the reason behind her unusual attitude towards her new boyfriend: I'm finally in love, she told herself. She hesitated to inform him of this exciting discovery until the right moment, when she could spring the good news upon him naturally and spontaneously.

The pancake restaurant turned out to be packed with about a hundred students and their families waiting outside in a long line. A few pancakes with a side order of eggs weren't worth freezing their buns, they decided, stepping into the bagel place next door.

After breakfast, they made their way via the back roads to a little park, which belonged to a grade school. Since it was a very cold fall day, the playground was empty. They took parallel swings and pumped vigorously with their legs to fly high, singing off-key oldies love songs, since nobody was around to complain.

Then Irina had the idea of swinging together on the same swing, which, dressed to their teeth as they were, proved more easily said than done. "Hold on, move over a little to the right," Paul said, trying to shift her position when she plopped unto his lap. "I don't think I'll be ready for round two tonight," he announced, given the part of his anatomy that had suffered the brunt of her weight. She had had a fantasy about this position the other night, Irina explained to Paul to persuade him that it was a good omen that dictated it. He sat on the swing facing forward, while she wrapped her legs around him and faced him.

"What do you think of this?" she asked grinning with childish joy, as he pumped both of them higher and higher.

"I think this activity should be rated R," he answered, "and that if any parents bring their kids here, they'll call the police and we'll be promptly arrested."

He may have complained out loud, but Paul's thirty-five year old heartbeat with excitement, like an adolescent boy's enjoying his first love. Irina opened him up to a fresh taste of life, filled with a flavor and energy that he'd almost forgotten.

"What did you say?" he asked, since at the apex of the swing's arch she had screamed with joy, leaned forward, then whispered something in his ear.

"I said 'I love you,'" she repeated, looking straight into his eyes. "Te iubesc," she translated in Romanian.

"I love you too," he answered, not even thinking about it, sharing her elation. But a few seconds later he stopped pumping and allowed the swing to come to a gradual stop.

"What is it?" she asked.

"I think we should talk about this," he said.

"About what?"

"About what we just said to each other."

Irina couldn't understand her boyfriend's attitude. What did they say? Only the obvious. Weren't they spending all of their time together, making love, having fun, discussing everything, being so close? Weren't they about to take a trip to Eastern Europe together? What was there to discuss?

Paul looked serious: "You're nineteen; I'm thirty-five."

"My name's Irina, yours is Paul. Nice to meet you. What's your point?" she asked, anticipating his next argument.

"My point is that I've had this problem before, with my first wife. Like you, she was younger than me. And she thought she was in love with me, I with her, we married and it ended up a total disaster."

"And what makes you think we're bound to follow the same course?"

"Because. It's inevitable. Don't you see?"

"No."

"In ten years I'll be forty-five, you only twenty-nine," he predicted.

"Wow! You've got excellent mathematical skills on top of your other qualities."

"Irina, please. Let's be serious for a moment," Paul insisted. "I've been through a divorce and am more experienced than you are. Believe me, I know what I'm talking about."

"Good. Then explain it to me, cause I sure don't understand you."

"I'm saying that we don't have a future together."

Irina was stunned by the harshness of this comment. "Just because of the stupid age difference?"

"No, not just because of that. Because of everything that goes along with it. You're so inexperienced and I'm so jaded."

"Yeah. I could tell from the pleasure you took in swinging like a little kid," Irina retorted.

Paul paused, looking at her warm almond-shaped eyes, blushing cheeks, the oval face of the little doll he was becoming dangerously attached to. "I wish we hadn't fallen in love," he finally said with a sigh.

Irina's eyes glimmered with delight. "What? Are you saying that you're in love with me too?" she asked, obliged to see the positive side of things with him, since he seemed compelled to point out the negative.

"Of course. I wouldn't be so worried if I weren't."

"In your own weird way, you're so romantic, little Paul," she said, touched by his awkward declaration of love.

"Aren't you even a little worried that we're heading straight for disaster?" he asked her.

"No. What's the worst that can happen?" she objected.

"We could marry and divorce and hate each other's guts for the rest of our lives. To offer a purely hypothetical example."

"Just because it happened to you and Mary it doesn't mean that it will happen to us. There are such things as happy marriages, you know. And happy couples. You can't go through life always expecting the worst," Irina countered.

"I've managed just fine with this philosophy."

"That's right. Maybe this attitude even led to your divorce. Like a self-fulfilling prophecy. Come on … Can't you try a little optimism and hope for a change? You might like it. What are you so afraid of?"

But Paul wasn't one to be easily dissuaded from his opinions: "I told you what I'm afraid of. That we're jumping into a serious relationship before you're ready, before you've even tasted love with other men. Men your own age, I mean. Jean-Pierre doesn't count. He's in worse shape than I am."

"But I want to taste life with you, Paul," Irina whispered softly. Her lips touched his ear. "I'm so ready to experience love with you."

He pushed off the ground with his feet, setting the swing in motion once again. They swayed together on the swing, breathing in the fresh air, the cold breeze rejuvenating their senses. Her sincerity and youthful beauty moved him. He leaned forward and kissed her, feeling reassured by her words, her tone, her emotions. "You're so nice. And I believe you're sincere," he added.

But his doubts weren't laid to rest. In the middle of a long, absorbing kiss which brought to Paul's mind their powerful physical attraction, with his perfect sense of timing, he came up with a brilliant objection: "I think you're in lust with me. You just like me for the sex," he announced, ungluing his lips from hers.

"This sounds more like something a woman might say to a man," Irina observed, amused. "But it can't be true in our case," she added more soberly.

"Thanks a lot!" Paul felt a little offended by such a quick dismissal of his sex appeal. "Why not?"

"As you pointed out so kindly, I'm no expert. But rumor has it that lots of men have your equipment. I seem to be drawn to yours in particular. Now how do you explain that?"

"Simple. I'm the one in whose apartment you stumbled by accident," Paul retorted.

"So what?"

"So we crossed paths and you got it into your head that you're in love with me."

Irina scrutinized his thin, pale face with round hazel eyes that shifted around nervously: "Are you a little insecure?" she asked him.

"Not at all. I just don't understand what you see in me, that's all. I'm a divorced, balding, mediocre man approaching middle age. One day you'll wake up, realize what I am and wonder, what did I ever see in this guy?"

"Well, at least I'm glad to hear that you're not insecure!" Irina responded. She stepped off the swing, pulled her boyfriend gently by the hand and they walked together side by side in silence. She considered his earlier question for a few moments.

Suddenly, she turned to him feeling confident of her answer: "You want to know why I love you? I'll tell you why. I love you because you're so youthful and immature. Because you're caring and you always listen to me. Because you're unbelievably sensual and affectionate in your gestures, in the way you touch me and hold me. Because you want to make love to me all the time and, I must say, because you do it so well and so lovingly. Because you're so stubborn and quirky and irritating that you get under my skin. Because we disagree and debate about everything. Because you have all these weird, unconventional political opinions and voice them so vehemently..."

"...yeah, well, so did Hitler," Paul interrupted.

But his girlfriend pursued undaunted: "...and because you have this absurd, dorky sense of humor that makes me feel like I'm living in a Woody Allen comedy. No offense, but sometimes even when we fight I feel like bursting out laughing. In sum, I love you because you're... you. Any more questions?"

Paul didn't have any at the moment. He did, however, make a comment: "You're either infatuated with me or you have very strange taste in men."

Chapter 18

How should she break the news to Paul without making him feel even more anxious than he already was by nature? Irina wondered. His feet sought hers under the table, as it was their habit to play footsie whenever they sat across from each other. That evening he had generously given in to what he called her "plebeian taste" and they were having a nice, romantic dinner at Taco Bell.

"My Dad's a well-known physicist, you know," Irina attempted to broach the subject indirectly.

"Yes, I know," Paul replied. "You told me that several times already." He sniffed his vegetarian burrito, suspecting that it might have a trace of meat in it. "What do they put in these things anyway? I bet they cook the vegetables on the same grill as the chicken and the beef," he complained loudly enough for the staff to hear. Nobody seemed alarmed by the allegation, however.

"Probably," Irina nodded sympathetically, then returned to the subject at hand. "It looks like you might get the opportunity to hear my Dad's presentation in person."

"What presentation?" Paul asked absentmindedly, still preoccupied with his burrito.

"He's been invited by the Institute of Advanced Studies to give a talk here right in a few weeks. In fact," Irina said in a chipper voice, "both of my parents are coming to visit me at Princeton."

"That's nice," Paul answered, not grasping the implications of this momentous news.

Irina took a bite of her burrito, contemplating how to make them more obvious.

"I was thinking, since you're going to meet them..."

"I am?"

"Yes, of course. It might be a good idea to prepare you in advance for their visit. So that everyone feels more comfortable with each other."

"What's there to be uncomfortable about?"

"You'll see. For now, just take my word for it. You need a little coaching on how to behave with my family."

In protest, Paul withdrew his feet to his side of the table. The footsie session was officially over. "Irina, I'm thirty-five years old. Almost thirty-six. I think I know how to behave socially by now, okay?"

"Yes, but not very well," Irina answered with an indulgent smile.

"What are you talking about?"

"No offense, but you tend to come across as a little... eccentric," Irina tried to put it as diplomatically as possible.

"Speak for yourself!"

"Hey, I'm the first to admit that I'm weird also. The difference is that my parents are already well aware of that fact and they love me anyway. In your case, however, let's just try to hide your eccentricity from them for as long as possible, okay?" Irina thought she was making a reasonable request.

Paul disagreed. "Why should they care if I'm weird or not? It's not like I'm their child. It's none of their business."

"You say that only because you don't understand my situation. Everything about my life is my parents' business for as long as they're alive. Plus, I plan to tell them that we're dating, which raises the stakes that much higher."

"What stakes? There are no stakes here. I dated several bizarre women in my life and that never bothered my mother. In fact, I never even told her about them, except for Mary, since we got married."

"That may very well be, but our circumstances are different. I never told my parents about the nature of my friendship with Jean-Pierre. So as far as they're concerned, you're my first real boyfriend. You can imagine how big a deal that is for my entire family."

Paul made a sour face: "I'm relieved to hear that there's no pressure."

Irina looked at him pleadingly: "Paul, all I ask is that you fake normalcy for a few days. Can't you do me this one little favor?"

Paul chewed carefully his burrito, ruminating over what Irina might mean by "normal." He came up empty, given that all his life he had been under the assumption that he was already normal. "So how do you want me to act?" he finally asked.

Irina was prepared in advance with several pointers. "First of all, try not to mention your leftist political views."

"Why not?"

"My parents feel they've suffered enough persecution in Romania."

"But I'm always on the side of justice and the oppressed."

"I know that's how you feel, Robin Hood. But they'd still mistake you for a commie."

"Are your parents the kind of people who escape from communism and become right-wing zealots?" Paul asked scornfully.

Irina was impressed by her boyfriend's perspicacity: "Yes."

"I can't stand people like that," he declared.

"And they can't stand the views of people like you... Which is precisely why I'm coaching you."

"I can't wait to meet your parents!"

"That's not all."

"I don't like censorship," Paul defended his freedom of speech.

"I'm just offering a few helpful suggestions, that's all. For instance, I don't think you should mention your predilection for much younger women either. Despite what you may think, it doesn't make the best impression on people."

"Geesh! What's there left to talk about?" Paul wondered.

"And another thing," Irina pursued, "please don't make a fuss over your vegetarianism. You tend to get all preachy about it. These people half-starved most of their lives. My mom really doesn't want to hear why she can't eat some chicken, alright?"

"Now hold on. I don't agree with this logic at all. Your parents aren't starving in this country. There are plenty of things they could eat now, without contributing to the yearly slaughter of hundreds of millions of innocent animals."

"Well, at least you seem to have a pretty good grasp on what not to say."

"And you complain about how you guys lived under constant censorship! How about me? Everything's off-limits."

"Actually, I'm not done yet. About your profession…"

"What about it?"

"That's another touchy subject."

"Irina, I'm a professor. What's in the world is wrong with that?"

"Nothing except that my Dad's under the assumption that if a field's not scientific, then it's automatically bogus. We have to do our best to explain to him how scientific and objective art truly is."

"Good luck with that!"

"Well, that's where your bullshitting skills will be put to the test. As for religion," Irina moved on to the next order of business, "my Dad's adamant about me dating only Jewish men."

"Is he totally out of his mind?"

"No. He's just normal Jewish. What religion are you?"

"I already told you. I was brought up Catholic. But actually, by faith, I'm a little Hindu."

"How can you be a little Hindu?"

"I believe in reincarnation. You see, there's this scientist, Professor Peterson, who works at the University of Minnesota and does research on the subject. There's actually a lot of scientific evidence in support of reincarnation. In fact, it's probably the only religious belief in the world that has been substantiated by scientific data."

"What you say is all very interesting, Paul, but please don't mention this quack to my father, alright?"

"Dr. Peterson's not a quack!" Paul heatedly protested. "He's a highly respected scientist. Besides, if we can grant that Jesus walked on water and that Moses parted the Red Sea, we can certainly accept the idea of reincarnation. There are literally tens of thousands of people on earth who have had recollections of previous lives that can't be explained in any other way."

Irina didn't even know how to begin addressing this topic. "At least you're eclectic, I'll give you that much," she said, not quite prepared to get into a theological debate with her boyfriend.

"What religion are you?" Paul asked, launching straight into the discussion Irina had hoped to avoid.

"You know very well what I am: Jewish on my Dad's side, Catholic on my mother's and agnostic on both. But my father's the dominant one in the family, so I guess that makes me Jewish."

"That doesn't make you Jewish!" Paul protested. "What you believe makes you one religion or another. Not what your father wants you to be. What matters is: what do you want to be?"

Irina considered the question. "I honestly don't know," she answered. "I suppose that having been raised in a communist country with very little exposure to religion, I have no particular faith."

Paul shook his head disapprovingly: "It's really sad not to believe in anything greater than yourself."

"That's not quite right," Irina corrected him. "I believe there might be beings smarter than us on other planets."

"Big deal! Belief that extraterrestrials might exist is not the same as believing in a perfect God who actually cares about you. It's certainly not the same as being spiritual. How about the afterlife? Do you believe in that? Or do you think that this wretched existence is our one and only shot at it?"

"I can't say for sure, but I suspect that this life's our only shot, so we better make the most of it. Besides, I don't see how being reincarnated as a pig remedies the situation," Irina answered.

Paul got excited: "Because that shows there's an ethical framework guiding our lives. That there's a higher justice," he explained with his hands. "Look: if you become reincarnated as a pig it's only because you behaved like a swine in life. You get what you deserve, see what I mean?"

"What I don't understand is, how can you believe in both a Christian God and in the Hindu gods and reincarnation?" Irina objected.

"Lots of people believe that reincarnation is not incompatible with Christianity," Paul answered. "Jesus says that a man 'must be born again' to enter the Kingdom of God."

"I seriously doubt that Jesus was referring to being born again as a chicken."

"Well, it's true that the Christian church interprets 'born again' as baptism, but I'm not a prisoner of dogmas," Paul retorted. "I don't think that any one religion has a monopoly on truth and that the others are all wrong. As long as you believe in God. Because I still maintain that it's difficult to have a moral foundation in life without belief in God and the afterlife," he concluded his argument.

Paul's last theological point reminded Irina of an even weightier ethical matter: "Speaking of moral foundations, my parents tried to instill one in me. So whatever you do, please don't say anything to them about the nature of our relationship. Because if you do, quite honestly, I doubt we'll ever get a chance to test your reincarnation theory. They'll be nothing left of us but a handful of dust."

Paul latched on to one particularly ominous-sounding term and shifted around nervously in his seat. "What nature are you talking about? We don't have any nature yet. We've barely been dating for a few months."

"Our relationship is, you know, sexual," Irina leaned forward and informed her boyfriend in a whisper, in case he wasn't already aware of that fact.

Paul felt relieved, seeing how Irina hadn't mentioned the more ominous words "engagement" or "marriage." "Is there anything I can discuss with your parents?" he asked.

"Why don't you talk about physics with my father?" Irina proposed. "Especially quantum theory. He really likes that. It's his specialty."

"For the simple reason that I haven't taken physics since high school."

"Do you remember any of it?"

"Of course not. Besides, I doubt we even studied quantum physics." Paul paused to reflect, then suggested: "How about sports? Does your father like baseball or football?"

"No. He considers sports a waste of time." She reflected for a moment, then came up with another constructive suggestion: "Perhaps you can discuss your travels to European countries. You could talk about how much better their cultures are compared to America. How Europeans are more refined, more intellectual. My parents will eat that stuff up. But whatever you do, all I ask is that you make a good impression."

"Don't I always?" Paul asked sweetly.

Irina rolled her eyes, considering that a verbal reply was not necessary.

That evening, she undertook a similar, but more challenging procedure on the phone with her mother. It would be more difficult to prepare her parents for the upcoming meeting with Paul since she hadn't mentioned to them yet that she had a serious boyfriend and since a priori, without a lot of finessing, there was no way they'd approve of her current selection. But if she caught her parents in a good mood, Irina hoped, perhaps there was a chance that everything might go smoothly.

"Alo?" Eva answered the phone.

"Hi Mom," Irina said cheerfully upon hearing her mother's voice.

"I'm glad you called since your father's been driving me crazy. He's getting really anxious about the upcoming Princeton visit," Eva complained right off the bat. "He says he doesn't have enough time to prepare."

"Well, I'm excited that we'll see each other very soon," Irina attempted to establish a positive tone.

It didn't quite work: "Your father's very worried about his presentation," Eva elaborated. "He hasn't figured out his whole hypothesis yet, or theorem or whatever he's supposed to talk about. He's working on it day and night. You can imagine after this kind of pressure what kind of mood he's going to be in..."

"I don't have to imagine. I remember." Irina recalled that if the proof of a theorem wasn't going smoothly, her father would become exceedingly cranky and short-tempered. "Can't he just focus on the fact we'll all be together?"

"That's what I keep telling him! Any normal person would. But your father, of course, is not normal. You know how obsessed he is with his work, and how it always has to be perfect."

Seeing that beating around the bush wasn't getting her anywhere, Irina attempted a more direct approach. "Listen, Mom, I called to tell you some really good news."

"You switched majors?" Eva asked excitedly. She and Andrei considered their daughter's major in art too impractical and unserious.

"No, it's not that." Irina breathed out the words very quickly: "I have a boyfriend."

Her mother hadn't fully abandoned her previous train of thought: "What's his major?"

"Art," Irina gave the most accurate answer she could think of.

"Oh."

"That means we have something in common," Irina pointed out.

"What? Future unemployment?"

This statement, however, provided the perfect cue for Irina's next bit of good news: "Actually, he's already employed. He's a professor at Princeton," she announced proudly.

She could almost see her mother's eyes stricken with panic in the tone of her voice: "Just how old is this gentleman?" Eva asked.

Irina wished to dispel her mother's doubts: "Believe me, Mom, Paul's not a gentleman," she assured Eva. "Besides, he's very young. An Associate Professor. Not even that, in fact. He's visiting faculty," she added, to bolster her case.

"So he's much older than you and has no job stability," Eva concluded. "Is he by any chance also married?"

"Mooom..."

"I don't know where you find them."

"What them? He's the only one I'm dating."

"How old is he?" Eva insisted.

"35."

"So he's ten years younger than your father," Eva calculated.

"That's nothing! I dated..." Irina stopped her confession about Jean-Pierre in the nick of time.

"What?"

"Nothing. I've seen happy couples with much greater age differences. In a few years, it won't even be noticeable." She was going to add half-jokingly that in a few years she'd probably be too old for Paul, but withheld that bit of information, deciding it might not make the best impression.

"Let's just hope that's because in a few years you'll be happily married to someone your own age," Eva replied.

Irina chose not to tackle that point.

Then her mother raised the much dreaded issue: "Is he Jewish?"

"No. He's Catholic. Just like you," Irina answered.

The guilt trip was not long in coming. "Your father will be devastated. You know how much he dreams about having Jewish grandchildren."

"Mom, he doesn't even have Jewish children," Irina pointed out. "In case you forgot, Radu and I are half-Jewish on the father's side of the family, which doesn't count in the Jewish religion."

"But it counts in your father's heart! And that's what matters," Eva came to her husband's defense.

"Let's not open that can of worms. I don't even know yet if I want to have children. Can't I just date someone I like?"

"Sure you can. Who's stopping you? God forbid that your father and I should ever interfere in your life. But can't you like someone your own age, Jewish, Eastern European and a physicist?"

"Only if you had managed to clone Dad. And, to be perfectly honest, I'm not sure I want to date my own father."

"What's wrong with your father?" Eva jumped to her husband's defense.

Irina began to lose hope in recruiting her mother to her side: "Come on, Mom, haven't you read Freud? It's called the Electra complex. I don't want it. Don't I have enough complexes already?"

Eva couldn't dispute her daughter's last statement, but refuted the first one: "Well, from what you tell me, if you're dating someone sixteen years older than you, you already have that complex. I certainly can't mention this bad news to your father before he finishes his presentation."

"I'm glad to see that at least you're taking it so well," Irina said. In truth, she thought, the conversation could have gone a lot worse.

"Irina, please be careful. I'm really worried about you. This older gentleman wants to take advantage of you. He'll return to his wife or girlfriend wherever he's visiting from, and leave you with nothing but shame and a ruined reputation."

"I appreciate your concern, Mom, I really do," Irina replied as diplomatically as possible, since she needed her mother as an ally. "But once you meet Paul, you'll see that he's not a monster. In fact, he's a very nice guy."

"Whatever you do, please don't have sex with him," Eva cautioned. "Save yourself for the wedding night with the right man, okay?"

"Yes...sure... " Irina replied more faintly.

"We didn't come to this country to be dishonored by our only daughter," Eva reiterated her pro-virginity argument, in case it hadn't been sufficiently clear to her daughter. This conversation left Irina with a growing anxiety about the upcoming clash of the titans.

Chapter 19

Irina crashed on the sofa, feeling drained of energy. She had nothing to look forward to that day. No early kisses with sleepy morning breath. No lunch meeting with her boyfriend. No walk together hand in hand through campus. No making love in the afternoon on his sofa, right after her last class. Paul was away at a conference for a few days. Was she that hooked on that quirky little man? Irina asked herself. She knew that was a purely rhetorical question. Her loneliness that afternoon told her so. What could she do to cheer up a little? She didn't feel like studying. Nor like watching T.V. Nor like taking a walk all by her lonesome self. Nor like shopping without his expert opinion, which usually advised not to buy anything. The shrill sound of the phone ringing jolted her out of her lethargy.

Ordinarily, she didn't pick up the phone and let the call go straight to the answering machine, but this time she hoped it might be Paul. She stretched to pick up the receiver. "Hello?"

"May I please speak with Ms. Irina Swartz?" a foreign sounding male voice requested politely.

"Speaking. Who is this please?" Irina asked, not recognizing the voice.

"It's me. Your brother Radu."

Irina was too stunned to reply.

"Irina, listen to me, I only have two minutes on this line. I'll call you from another payphone within an hour. Jean-Pierre told me that you have something important to tell me. Whatever you do, please don't tell anybody I called you other than our parents, okay?" This time, Radu's voice had a sense of urgency rather than formality.

"Raducu! Wow... I'm so shocked to hear from you... I can't believe it...It's so weird to hear your voice after all these years," Irina managed to answer.

"Irina, did you hear what I said? Don't tell anybody I called," her brother repeated.

"Yes, of course, I promise," his sister reassured him.

"What did you want to tell me? We don't have much time..."

Irina was in a daze. How do you tell your brother, whom you haven't seen or talked to in years, that he has a missing son with the woman who betrayed him? Irina hesitated. "Did you talk to Mom recently?"

"Yes. I was so sorry to hear about the sad news," Radu replied.

"So then you believe Ioana?"

"Ioana? What does she have to do with Grandma Marta's death?"

"Nothing. Do you remember how loving and patient she was to us?"

"Yes," Radu said, with sadness in his voice. "Mom sounded absolutely devastated. And I can't even imagine how Grandpa Mihai will cope with the loss."

"I'll try to visit him in a few weeks," Irina announced.

"Now may not be the best time to visit Romania," Radu replied after a moment's hesitation.

"Why not?"

"Irina, I've got to go. I'll call you shortly from another pay phone."

"Okay," Irina agreed. After she hung up, she tried to recall what her brother looked like in person, but all that came to mind were the photographs of him she had seen displayed in practically every room of her parents' house.

About twenty minutes later, the phone rang again. She grabbed impatiently the receiver.

"Hello? It's me again," she heard her brother's voice.

"What did you try to tell me about visiting Romania?" she asked him.

"Nothing in particular," Radu replied. "It's just that there's a lot going on in Eastern Europe right now."

"Like what?"

"Well, you know, a lot of political unrest. Perhaps you can visit France instead."

"Grandpa Mihai doesn't live in France," Irina reminded him.

Her brother didn't reply to this comment. "You said Mom wanted to tell me something about Ioana? I only have two minutes tops again."

"I asked Mom to tell you that I met Ioana in person," Irina answered.

"Why in the world would you do a thing like that? Did Jean-Pierre put you up to it?" Radu didn't sound too pleased with the news.

Irina felt awkward having to blurt out delicate information in a race against the clock. "Can we talk about this in person?"

"Not yet," Radu replied.

"Then when?"

"When it's a little safer."

"But that may never happen!" Irina objected.

"I think it will."

"When?" Irina insisted, reminding her brother of her persistence as a child.

"Soon enough," Radu replied with confidence. "I have about one minute left," he announced.

Under pressure, Irina let it all out: "This probably sounds totally crazy, but Ioana told me that you have a son together who has been kidnapped by the *Securitate* and put away in an orphanage in Romania. She looked for him for several years and couldn't find him, so now she's asking for your help. Since you're the father, after all."

No reply at the other end.

"Radu?" Irina verified if her brother was still on the phone.

"You're right," he answered in a distant voice. "This does sound totally crazy."

"I also thought so too at first. But Jean-Pierre seems to believe her. Plus she showed me this photograph of the little boy when he was three, a few months before they kidnapped him. His name is Lucian. He's very cute and kind of looks like you. I don't know what to believe... given what I know about her. But she seemed sincere enough."

After a few moments of silence, Radu replied: "Irina, I've got to go. I don't want the call to be traced."

"Will you call me again? Should I wait by the phone?" Irina asked.

"No. I'll get in touch directly with Jean-Pierre, to find out what's going on," Radu answered, sounding like he was about to hang up the phone, then, as an afterthought, added in a warmer tone: "Irina, I miss you so much."

"I miss you too," Irina replied. As she hung up the phone, she thought these words were undoubtedly true yet at the same time rang hollow. Like so many family members she had loved and, with the passage of time, nearly forgotten, her brother had faded into the distant past, becoming little more than a treasured memory of childhood.

Chapter 20

Going against his own habit of sitting in the back row at conferences, in this instance, Paul made an exception and sat in the front row so as to better observe the current speaker. She was talking about possible Hindu and Buddhist influences upon Gustave Moreau's Symbolist art, which was well known for its hybrid mysticism. Under the circumstances, Paul felt free to ogle. Irina had asked him if she could come with him to Los Angeles, to his annual art history conference. However, since he had already bought a ticket and made the hotel reservations months in advance, before they had even met, and, furthermore, since she was going to miss a lot of school during their upcoming trip to Eastern Europe, Paul persuaded his girlfriend not to accompany him this time. He now wondered if part of his motivation wasn't to enjoy his last taste of freedom, since the relationship with Irina was so quickly becoming serious.

Since Mary hadn't really loved him and wasn't the jealous type (these two facts were probably related), Paul was used to indulging in what he called "life's little free pleasures": the freedom to stare at pretty women unmolested and, if all went well, to go so far as to flirt with them. It's not as if we're engaged or anything, Paul told himself, listening intently to the speaker's melodious mixture of Indian and British accents while contemplating with admiration her unusual slimness. Sushma—for that was the young woman's name, Paul ascertained by looking at the conference program—was not traditionally beautiful. Nor was she very cute like Irina. Yet, with her long black hair braided in one single thick strand, dark, in-set eyes, aquiline nose and delicate features, she had a feminine fragility that instantly attracted him.

The young woman wore a loose-fitting colorful blouse with autumnal colors—brown, burgundy, rusty red and yellow--with a pair of dark brown slacks. Although this wasn't exactly a sexy outfit, Paul's gaze was drawn to the narrowness of her hips. She's as thin as a reef, he contemplated with admiration, without paying much attention to the content of Shushma's presentation. He did, however, feel enchanted by the musicality of her voice, as she spoke very quickly, letting the words roll off her tongue; by the liveliness of her eyes; by the movement of her eyebrows when she was emphasizing a point, and by the way she smiled revealing perfectly straight, glistening white teeth when she said something humorous or ironic. Despite her affability, Sushma's cultural otherness gave her an aura of mystery. I should definitely try to speak to her after her talk, he resolved.

Yet something was different about his gazing as of late, Paul thought, and he could even put his finger on it: Irina. Ever since they began dating, he felt somewhat guilty about his behavior. Well, perhaps guilty was too strong a word. He felt more aware of it, let's just say, having been partially conditioned by his girlfriend's invariably negative reactions to his ogling and unsolicited editorial remarks about other women. Whenever he was too friendly with a student, for example, the question "What would Irina say about this?" popped up completely uninvited in his mind. And, unfortunately, the answer was never that positive, since Irina was, as he called her, "more Latin than the Latins" and her jealousy was easily aroused.

Fortunately, Paul had ways to tune out Irina's voice. He told himself that until they became serious, like engaged for example, he was more or less free as a bird, at least in his own mind. Plus he thought that he had learned his lesson from the double fiasco with Mary and Linda and therefore wouldn't be even remotely tempted to repeat the same mistake again. Feeling confident in his powers of restraint, he lunged forward to be the first in line to talk to Shushma once all the other talks as well as the question and answer period were over.

"Hi, my name's Paul," he pointed to his conference name tag, which had the line Princeton University underneath his name. Shushma seemed impressed. "I really enjoyed your talk," he smiled amiably at her, then immediately regretted using the most standard conference pick-up line in the book.

"Thanks," the young woman responded in her melodious voice. "Are you interested in Hinduism?" she asked, since that was the interpretation of Moreau's art she had offered.

As a matter of fact, he was. And his interest was growing by the second. Paul briefly explained his fascination with Peterson's theories of reincarnation, which to his surprise Shushma hadn't heard of, and, seeing how two other scholars were waiting to talk to her, asked if she was interested in continuing their conversation over dinner. As it turns out, however, Shushma had already made dinner plans with a few graduate school friends from Harvard. They could perhaps meet up for a drink afterwards, however, she suggested.

"Great!" Paul answered, his heart fluttering with excitement. "What time do you want to meet?" he asked quickly, wishing to seal the deal before Sushma changed her mind.

"How about in the hotel lobby at 10:00 p.m.?" she proposed. "My friends and I are having dinner around seven, so that should give us plenty of time. I hope that's not too late for you."

"Not at all. On the contrary!" Since that statement sounded somewhat ambiguous, Paul clarified: "I go to bed late anyway."

After having dinner with a few conference acquaintances, Paul made sure that he called his girlfriend before meeting with Sushma, while he still had a relatively clear conscience. Nevertheless, their conversation left him feeling a little off. Irina was so loving and sweet to him that, under the circumstances, it was almost unbearable. Furthermore, she asked several probing questions, such as "Whom did you see at the conference?"

"Oh, just the same old acquaintances," Paul answered for the most part truthfully.

"Did you meet anyone interesting?" his girlfriend was curious to know.

"Not really. Scholars tend to be so predictable. They always talk about their research and promotions," Paul replied, omitting to say, however, that he found one person quite interesting.

"Who did you have dinner with?"

Why is she drilling me like this? Is she suspicious? Paul wondered. "I ate with a few of my old conference friends. You don't know them," he said. He did not volunteer any information about the after dinner drink with Shushma, seeing how Irina hadn't asked about it.

"It's so lonely around here without you," Irina said wistfully. "I can't even take a shower without feeling sad, since I'm not used to washing by myself any more. I miss our duets. And our mushiness. And above all, I miss you, cute little Paul."

"Did anything exciting happen?" Paul attempted to switch the conversation from emotions to actions.

Irina recalled her brother's phone call. "Kind of. I had an interesting conversation with someone I hadn't talked to in a long time, but I promised him not to tell anyone about it."

"Should I be jealous?" Paul asked.

"No. I'm not into incest."

"What do you mean?"

"It's about my family. I'll tell you about it when you return. I don't want to discuss it over the phone," Irina said, embarrassed by her indiscretion towards her brother, then went back to telling her boyfriend how much she missed him and how lonely she felt in his absence.

Alright, it's time to end this conversation before she dissolves into tears, Paul decided, since he too began missing his girlfriend and her emotions were contagious, which defeated the whole point of enjoying a bit of freedom.

"I miss you too, " Paul answered. "But don't worry. I'll be back at 9:35 p.m. tomorrow."

"You're coming on Northwest flight 2678, right?"

"You memorized it?" Paul asked.

"Of course not. You know I barely recall my own name. I wrote it down on a note by the phone. I'll pick you up tomorrow evening at the airport."

"But you don't even have a car," Paul pointed out.

"You left me the keys to yours, remember?" Irina reminded him.

"Are you sure you want to drive that late? I could take a taxi," Paul volunteered.

"Are you kidding me? I can't wait to hold you in my arms again! I miss you so much," Irina reiterated, her voice cracking with the genuine, childlike emotion of a young woman in love.

"Me too," Paul said sincerely.

"I love you..."

"I love you too."

When he hung up the phone, Paul felt that his light-hearted mood had been somewhat spoiled. He went into the bathroom and washed his hands compulsively a few times, preoccupied by his plans. All he wanted to do was talk and enjoy himself a little, he told himself. He wouldn't step over any boundaries and he would remain faithful to Irina. Yet after talking to his girlfriend he still felt a little guilty about the prospect of having a private conversation at night with another woman who attracted him. Who knows what can happen under the right circumstances. Maybe he should have brought Irina along to the conference as his chaperone after all, he thought.

A few minutes before 10:00 p.m., Paul went to the lobby and staked out a chair somewhat hidden from view, where he could observe people without being seen by his conference acquaintances and having to engage in small talk. He saw Shushma exit the elevator, look towards the lobby, spot him, and walk towards him with long, elegant strides. Observant only when it came to attractive women, Paul instantly noticed that she had put her hair up in an intricate bun and she wore the same colorful blouse but had changed her more formal conference pants for a pair of blue jeans which further emphasized her waiflike figure.

"Hi!" he got up and, not knowing exactly how to greet her, awkwardly extended his arm for a handshake. She flashed her bright, white smile and shook his hand.

"So where do you want to go for a drink?" he asked.

"Here's fine," Shushma shrugged nonchalantly. "That way we don't have to walk very far in the dark."

Shushma took a seat in one of the lounge chairs and Paul sat across from her. A glass table separated them.

"So where are you from?" Paul broke the ice.

"Originally, New Delhi."

"The big city!"

"Yes."

"Does your family still live there?"

"I have family there and visit them about once a year. But most of us are scattered all over the world. My parents live in Boston; my younger sister is studying at Oxford; two of my brothers are engineers, one in New York, the other in Paris.

"You're very international!" Paul declared with admiration. "How come your family didn't want to stay in India?"

"I suppose my parents wanted to offer us the best opportunities for a good education."

"Are you a Brahman?" it occurred to Paul that, given the emphasis Shushma's family placed upon education, they were probably members of India's elite.

"No. We're from the Kshatriya caste, the second of the four groups. Historically, that was the royal and warrior caste, but nowadays it's made up mostly of professionals and administrators. My father, for instance, is a civil engineer."

"And what does your name, Shushma, mean? It sounds so beautiful..." Paul gazed at the young woman tenderly. When no strings were attached, he could really let himself go emotionally.

"It has at least two meanings. It can mean 'dusk' or 'natural beauty,'" Shushma informed him.

"In your case, it definitely means 'natural beauty'," Paul instantly settled the linguistic debate without speaking a word of the language. "So Shushma, tell me, what made you go into art history?"

The young scholar replied with a smile: "I like looking at beautiful paintings. How about you?"

"Me? I like looking at beautiful women," Paul replied without hesitation.

Shushma laughed, mistakenly believing that her companion was joking. "Actually, my parents disapprove of my job," she added as an afterthought.

"How can they disapprove of their daughter becoming a prestigious professor?" Paul objected. "Where do you teach?"

"West Virginia University," Shushma answered, sounding somewhat disappointed.

"I've been there! It's amazing we didn't cross paths. I was at an art history conference there four years ago," Paul announced, excited to have so much in common with the girl.

"Well, it's not exactly what you'd call a prestigious university..."

"Maybe not, but Morgantown's great," Paul said. "Apparently it's got an excellent party scene."

"That wasn't exactly my top academic standard when I went on the job market. In fact, that's part of the problem," Shushma complained. "My students are much more into partying than studying."

"And who can blame them?" Paul shrugged. "I mean, they're young, they might as well enjoy themselves."

"I suppose..." Shushma replied. There was a pause in the conversation, where neither of them knew what else to say. "You wanted to ask me something about reincarnation?" Shushma reminded Paul after a few moments, to break the silence.

"Yes. Do you believe in it?"

"I do. I'm Hindu," Shushma replied. "As the Bhagavad Gita says," she added, "Just as a man discards worn out clothes and puts on new clothes, the soul discards worn out bodies and wears new ones."

Impure thoughts occurred to Paul as Shushma mentioned the discarding of clothes. He was rather curious to see the extent of her thinness, as his eyes followed the slight curve of her hip. Even when she was just sitting there with a gentle smile upon her lips, this young woman was mesmerizing. Her whole demeanor suggested calmness, balance. Her movements were graceful, sinuous and slow; in many ways, it occurred to Paul, Shushma was the opposite of Irina. "Do you have any recollections of your previous lives?" he asked her.

"I sometimes get these flashbacks in my dreams of a beautiful, gilded, very elaborate palace. It's rich and sumptuous," Shushma looked off into the distance. "Of course, that might be just from reading Indian fairy tales."

"I don't think so," Paul disagreed. "There's this professor at the University of Minnesota..."

"Peterson? The one you mentioned right after my talk?"

"Yes. He's done studies on thousands of individuals of various ages and has collected all sorts of scientific data that proves reincarnation."

"Well, nothing can really prove faith in anything," Shushma responded cautiously, then looked up at the waiter who asked what they wanted to order. "I'd like a glass of red wine, please." Shushma's voice sounded like a silver bell to Paul's ears.

"Is Merlot fine?" the waiter inquired.

"Yes."

"And I'd like a Guinness," Paul said when the young man turned to him. Once the waiter left, Paul continued his argument: "Well, I agree that nothing can prove conclusively any religious faith. But there's so much evidence for reincarnation. People have birthmarks that can't be explained in any other way. Like when a child has exactly the same birthmark as a deceased person who is genetically unrelated to him. And thousands of people have recollections of previous lives with an astonishing degree of precision. There are people who can reveal under hypnosis all the details of their previous lives. They can tell you where they lived, who their friends were during those lives, what they did, even which shops they went to. And all that information is later confirmed by historical research. Isn't that remarkable?"

Shushma nodded. "You know, these kinds of things happened to members of my own family. Some of my relatives remember their previous lives in even greater detail than I do."

"Really?" Paul was thrilled to have a sympathetic ear listen to his eclectic mixture of religious beliefs and scientific hypotheses.

"What appeals to me most about the Hindu religion," Shushma elaborated, "is not so much what science can confirm about it, however. It's the hope that comes with the idea of reincarnation. Each time we're reborn we have the chance of improving ourselves, of living better lives. But at the same time, during some life cycles, we may make huge mistakes, which may taint rather than purify us. It all depends. Reincarnation offers hope without easy moral solutions. There's no linear progress for humanity. And if we make serious errors, it's not because we're inherently evil. It's mostly because we're imperfect and ignorant."

The waiter returned with their drinks. Shushma leaned forward and picked up her glass of wine. Her bangles twinkled brightly upon her delicate wrist; a gleam of gold also surrounded her long neck. She's so refined, rich, beautiful, spiritual and educated, Paul observed. She must be married or have a serious boyfriend, he surmised, examining her hands in search for a wedding ring. He was pleased to note that Shushma wore several rings, some of which resembled little vines spotted by golden beads of dew, but none of them looked like a wedding band. "Why did you say that your parents disapproved of your profession?" Paul returned to an earlier subject of conversation after this momentary distraction.

"I suppose that no matter how cosmopolitan my parents may be, they're still extremely conservative by Western standards. Which, quite frankly, are my standards as well since I did my studies in this country. My parents wanted me to be well educated, but only in the hope that would make my future husband happy."

"You're married?" Paul asked, with a tinge of disappointment.

"No, but I'm dating someone I really care about. He's American. If my parents would have had their way, I would have been married by now in India to a boy I never met. But I refused to accept an arranged marriage. I suppose I'm too Western to think that such a thing is likely to work out or could ever make me happy. I believe in true love," she said with an ironic smile.

"Then both believe in reincarnation and love!" Paul remarked with a sense of wonder, as if the chances of such an agreement were astronomically small.

He and Shushma continued to speak for several hours about their families, their beliefs, their upbringing, their lives. Paul told her about his first marriage. As before, Shushma was a good listener and sympathetic. They didn't even notice the time fly by and the hours passed like minutes. They said goodnight around 4:00 a.m., hugging like old conference friends. Paul watched Shushma's slim form retreat, then disappear into the elevator with a final friendly wave goodbye, the tinkle of her bangles and her signature bright smile.

Paul left the conference with a vague sense of longing mixed with regret, as if this were his last opportunity to experience a light and free form of happiness which he feared that, once tied down in a serious relationship, he'd never taste again. At least, not in the same way. Even if Shushma came back next year to the art history conference, he'd never meet her for the first time nor would they feel the excitement of discovering each other as they did that day.

On the plane ride home, Paul shut his eyes and pretended to be asleep so that the stewardess wouldn't interrupt his nostalgic reflections by offering him peanuts. He was left with two powerful impressions: the melody of Shushma's voice and her incredible slimness; that feminine fragility which never failed to touch him and which he wished he could have explored and protected with the warmth of his hands.

Chapter 21

Paul didn't have to look hard to spot his girlfriend at the airport: with her braids, girlishness and boundless enthusiasm, Irina came back into his consciousness like a tidal wave of warmth and familiarity. Without saying a word, she jumped to embrace him, her arms around his neck, her lips avidly seeking his. Although they often kissed in public, this time he gently pushed her away.

"What's the matter?" she asked, her eyes round with surprise.

"Nothing, I'm just a little tired, that's all. I don't get much sleep at conferences," he replied without looking at her.

"Why not?" Irina had to ask.

"It's just difficult for me to get any rest in unfamiliar places," he said, half-truthfully.

This answer seemed to cheer her up: "Well, tonight you'll be back in your own cozy nest with your little love bird," she cooed, leaning forward for another kiss. This time he reciprocated, but the moistness of her lips made him feel ill at ease. Had he crossed over a line by fostering intimacy with another woman? he wondered. Did the fact that he was drawn to Shushma mean that he wasn't sufficiently in love with Irina? Looking at his girlfriend right now--small, vivacious, happy and adorable--his heart was melting with love. But within that emotion, he felt the unsettling movements of guilt.

Once they got ready for bed, Irina tried to nibble on his ear; her youthful body hungry for his affection.

He pulled back.

"Is something wrong?" she asked. She was disturbed by her boyfriend's unusual behavior, since, despite his strange ways, he was usually very tender with her.

"No. It's just that I'm really tired," Paul replied. "And I have a bit of a stomach ache."

"Did you have dinner yet?"

"Yes, at the airport."

"What did you eat? Maybe that's what made you sick."

"A vegetarian wrap, as usual. It's possible there was some weird sauce in it. Or maybe I'm just a little airsick."

Irina examined Paul's face closely and found him a little pale. "Would you like me to make you some chamomile tea?" she asked. "My grandmother used to give me that whenever I had an upset stomach and it made me feel a lot better."

Paul forced a smile: "You're so sweet. But no thanks. I think I'll feel better if I get some rest tonight," he reiterated.

"Okay," she replied, then put her palm on his forehead, to check for fever. He didn't have any.

"I'm fine little Irina, I promise." Paul reassured her. "Let's just go to bed."

"I'm so glad to be with you again," she said, leaning over to give him another welcome kiss, this time a chaste one on the cheek, since he was ill. "I'll do everything I can to make you feel better. If you need anything, just wake me up, okay?"

His girlfriend's unvarnished kindness, however, made Paul feel even worse: "I'm sorry that I'm not in form tonight," he apologized.

"I love whatever form you're in," Irina replied. "Especially this one," she touched him with the tips of her fingers.

But Paul wasn't in the mood that evening. Instead of sleeping peacefully with Irina in his arms as usual, he shifted around in bed and couldn't get any rest. He didn't understand himself any more. Retrospectively, he excused himself for cheating on his wife. They didn't get along and besides, it had been clear almost from the very beginning that Mary didn't really love him. The fling with Linda only accelerated the divorce; it didn't actually cause it. But with Irina, things were different. He loved her body and soul; he liked everything about her. Even the parts of her personality that irked him at times, like her emotionalism and jealousy, somehow he preferred her with them rather than without them. How could he be so much in love with a woman and then turn around and almost completely put her out of his mind once he met another woman who attracted him? What kind of a man was he anyway?

No matter how much he tried to dismiss these nagging doubts, to tell himself that men are generally attracted to an almost infinite number of women, he remained troubled by the emotions that went along with his desire for Shushma. It's normal to be physically drawn to many women, Paul told himself. But there was still something strange about the way he became so quickly attached to another woman while being so deeply in love with his girlfriend. He felt oppressed not so much by guilt, since he knew that he hadn't done anything morally wrong, as by the unsettling awareness of an emotional instability, for which, this time, he couldn't find any rational justification. Should he mention his attraction to Shushma to his girlfriend, or let it evaporate on its own? he wondered. Maybe, being so obsessive compulsive, he was blowing the whole thing out of proportion.

In the morning, Irina woke up bright and affectionate, as usual, while Paul was just as queasy and somber as the previous evening. Fortunately, it was Monday and Irina had a class at 9:00 a.m., so they wouldn't have the opportunity to talk. Paul usually worked on his Monet presentation in the mornings, but that day he was not in the mood for scholarship. Needing some friendly advice, he called Rico as soon as his girlfriend left the apartment. The two men set up a meeting at Starbuck's for coffee.

"I need to talk to you about something," Paul said as soon as they sat down.

"Fire away. If it's about love, you've come to the right person," Rico joked.

"Well, you managed to keep both a wife and a serious girlfriend for several years now, so you must be doing something right," Paul concurred.

"Except for the fact that my wife's currently in the loony bin," Rico qualified. "She had another nervous break-down."

"Why?"

"If I knew why, I wouldn't need to pay for round-the-clock psychiatric care for her. So tell me, what's bothering you?" Rico asked, taking a sip of his coffee.

Paul couldn't even touch his espresso and toasted bagel. He had no appetite for anything until this issue was resolved. "I'm afraid that I'm a superficial rogue," he declared.

"We already knew that," Rico quipped. "Is there trouble in paradise?" Rico asked.

"No, that's just it. Everything's going really well with Irina."

"Congratulations."

Paul hesitated. "The problem is that this weekend I went to a conference and might have fallen in love with another woman. She's of Indian origin. Her name is Shushma and we talked practically all night, until 4:00 a.m., about reincarnation," Paul blurted out.

Rico didn't seem particularly disturbed by this confession: "You mean you were attracted to another chick, right?" he translated.

"Yes, and the problem is, the attraction wasn't just physical. I was really touched by her personality also," Paul explained.

His friend stared at him with an air of incredulity: "So that's your big confession? Your discovered that more than one woman on this Earth can have a nice pair of tits and a nice personality to boot? Geesh! You're such a nut job. I'm thinking you need to join my wife in the asylum."

"Rico, how can you take this matter so lightly?" Paul jumped to his own defense. "Irina and I are really getting serious. To cheat on a woman in spirit and emotion is even worse than to cheat on her in body."

"Did you sleep with this other chick or not?" Rico wanted to clarify, confused by Paul's description of the incident.

"No. But I really wanted to. Shushma told me she had a serious boyfriend and I talked about Irina. But who knows what might have happened had she been available or tried to seduce me," Paul explained his moral predicament.

"Big freaking deal! Even married men want to sleep with other women dozens times a day. What matters is whether or not you actually do it. You can't be charged with thought crimes. But if this issue's really bugging you, then why don't you discuss it with your girlfriend? That's better than acting all weird and losing sleep over a little trifle like this," Rico proposed pragmatically. "She'll probably laugh at you for being such a woos."

Despite the insults, that was just the kind of advice Paul needed to hear: "So you think I should mention this episode to Irina?" he wanted confirmation of his own inclination.

"Sure, why not?" Rico replied, without wasting too much thought on the matter. "If it will make you feel better."

Paul hesitated: "But you see, Irina tends to get really jealous when I talk about other women," Paul pointed out the downside of such a discussion.

"How unusual!"

"If I also mention how much I liked Shushma's personality, she might really freak out," Paul continued playing devil's advocate.

"Then you should frame it positively. Emphasize how noble and righteous you were to resist temptation," Rico advised.

Paul shook his head: "I don't think 'noble' is the right word. Scared maybe. Confused. Plus as I told you, I'm not so sure I would have resisted temptation had the opportunity really presented itself."

"If you want to know the truth," Rico said, "I don't believe you're in love with this other woman. You may be attracted to her, infatuated with her, whatever. But I think this little infatuation has made you scared of your commitment to Irina. Things are really getting serious between the two of you, huh?"

"Yes," Paul admitted.

"And how do you feel about that?" Rico asked.

Paul shrugged. "I feel good. I mean, I love Irina."

"But?"

"But... it's true that I'm also afraid that we're rushing into something serious too fast. The real problem is that Irina is a lot younger than me, and has so little experience with men. I really don't want to go through what I went through with Mary again."

"Are you talking about marriage?" Rico asked.

"No, not yet."

"Then stop making a big deal out of nothing. I don't believe you're really freaking out about your little chat with Shushma. Even you're not that weird," Rico said. "What you're really worried about is a reincarnation of your relationship with Mary."

Paul contemplated his friend's insight. There seemed to be a grain of truth in Rico's analysis, he was obliged to admit.

The sculptor hurriedly finished his coffee. "Listen, I have an appointment with an art dealer at eleven," he excused himself. "Talk to Irina about your self-flagellation and you'll see that, if she doesn't determine that you've completely lost your marbles, everything will be just fine," he said as he got up to leave.

Chapter 22

On Monday, Paul and Irina didn't meet for lunch in the cafeteria as usual since Irina had to study for an art history exam. She was supposed to drop by Paul's apartment right after the test, around 4:30 p.m. She'll be back any minute now, Paul thought, looking at his watch. It was already 4:25. He had decided to tell her about Shushma, but hadn't quite figured out the best way to bring up the delicate subject. Should he do it nonchalantly, at dinner? Or should he emphasize how commendable and faithful he had been in resisting temptation, as his friend had suggested? And what did he expect to get from this confession anyway? he wondered. His only answer was: peace of mind. He would be disburdening himself. Yet, at the same time, he still had some misgivings. Knowing Irina, he was afraid the conversation might open a huge can of worms.

As he busily tidied up his apartment--for the third time that day--Paul's attention was caught by a large oil painting of Irina and himself. His girlfriend had given it to him a few weeks ago. She began working on it as soon as they started dating. At first, she had asked him to pose for it, but since he had the tendency to shift nervously his position every few seconds, she was obliged to work from photographs. Panicked about the mess she was making on the floor, he placed newspapers everywhere where she might spill a drop of paint. He recalled a bit more fondly how cute Irina looked with her shirt sleeves drawn up to her elbows, her hands smeared with paint, as she assiduously concentrated on her work.

The painting represented them looking lovingly at each other. Their bodies were slightly turned towards the viewer in the artificially contorted position of Egyptian papyrus drawings, which sought to capture the essence, not the nature of their subjects. The manner in which their arms curved around one another, the warmth of their gaze and the flow of the brushstrokes all reminded Paul of how they slept protectively enveloping each another. Their features were realistically drawn, only more sinuous and elongated, calling to mind the pensive, sensual expressions of Modigliani paintings. Paul was fond of this painting, partly because it was Irina's first gift to him, partly because Modigliani was one of his favorite artists. However, as emerged during their subsequent discussion on the subject, Paul also felt that its style was too derivative. He wanted to encourage Irina to push her talent further; to take the best characteristics of her favorite artists and transform them into something entirely her own. Part of him, however, also desired to tone down her enthusiasm for art; to give it a more pragmatic perspective. He knew how few of those majoring in art actually made a living as artists. No matter how much he tried to be supportive of his girlfriend's desire to be an artist, it was impossible for him to be enthusiastic about such impractical aspirations.

One of their most heated conversations on this subject occurred when Irina had just finished the Modigliani style painting and offered it to him.

"Thanks. That's so nice of you," he said politely, as if she had just given him a bouquet of flowers for Valentine's Day.

Irina immediately sensed the subterfuge. "So what do you think of it?" she asked.

"I like it," Paul answered.

"Do you think it captures us?" she probed further.

"Yes." What else could he say? "But I'm not sure that should be your goal," he added.

"What do you mean?" Irina asked, her eyes pinned on him while she took a sip of her bottled water.

"I mean your goal should be to create something original, not necessarily something that resembles us."

"I don't mean physical resemblance, silly," she countered. "I wanted to paint something that captures our inner essence."

"I understand what you mean. I teach art history, remember? But I'm not so sure that our essence will be that interesting to others," Paul reformulated his critique.

Irina felt more like a little student around her boyfriend than she had felt around the much older and really famous artist, Jean-Pierre. At least the latter left her to her own devices, and even went so far as to encourage her with vague aphorisms once in a while.

"I think every human being and every relationship can be interesting if you know how to show them right," she declared, recalling something Jean-Pierre had told her a few months earlier.

"Which is precisely the issue."

"What issue?"

"You have to show it right."

"Are you suggesting that I'm not talented enough to do that?" Irina asked, getting defensive.

"No, I'm just saying that you're still at the very beginning of your artistic career. Besides, talent's not enough. It takes so much luck, connections, the right market, the auspicious moment, all sort of things outside of one's control to make it as an artist. Art's not really a profession. That's why I think you should minor in something else. Something practical, like business."

"Why not physics, while we're at it?"

"Pardon?"

Irina sighed. "Why do you have to sound exactly like my father? The whole point is that I really want to do art. That's been my dream ever since I was a little girl. I've always loved to draw and paint."

Paul lost his patience. "What do you want me to say? Oh, your art's so great. Oh, you'll be rich and famous?"

"I don't need flattery!" Irina objected. "My best professors in studio art offer a lot of constructive criticism. They're very demanding. Still, none of them advise us not to become artists."

"Of course not. They're not that stupid. Without students, they'd be out of a job and they'd have to earn their living only through their art. Which, as everyone knows, is virtually impossible."

"It's not because of that, Mr. Cynic. They really do their best to teach us how to become good artists."

"Good for them. Then why are you asking for my input?" Paul inquired.

"Because I care about you and I care about what you think!" Irina had replied.

In retrospect, Paul felt that he had done his best to encourage his girlfriend's aspirations. Even though he was afraid she would end up in the unemployment line, he wanted her to flourish as a woman and an artist. Looking at her painting again, he decided it represented the essence of their relationship when they were both asleep. Especially as far as Irina was concerned, since he had never seen his girlfriend look so peaceful and sedate when awake.

He heard Irina unlock the front door. She came by so often, that he had made for her a duplicate key to his apartment.

"So how did it go?" he asked as soon as she entered the room.

Irina didn't seem to be in the best of moods. "Okay, I guess."

"Was the test hard?"

"I don't care," she responded, dropping the backpack on the floor and flopping unto the sofa, hands behind her head, eyes staring at the ceiling. Paul recognized this as her brooding position.

Perhaps this isn't the best time to mention Shushma, it occurred to him. "Was it that bad?"

"I hate exams," Irina declared. "Memorization about what year a painting or sculpture was made doesn't prove you know anything about art. Of course, I thought I did best on the essays, since they require some thinking, but apparently my instructor didn't think so. We got back our last essays."

"What grade did you get?" Paul asked, concerned. Could she have failed? Maybe they were spending too much time together and Irina wasn't devoting enough time to her studies. He certainly didn't want to have her grades on his conscience on top of everything else.

"He gave me a stupid B+!" Irina answered, outraged. "I've never gotten below an A- in my whole life! Not even in Romania—except for gym."

Paul sighed with relief. "Geesh, a B+ is an excellent grade! When I was in Catholic school that was as high as you could get. Anything in the A range was considered God's grade."

Irina looked at him from the corner of her eyes: "Yeah, well, welcome to grade inflation. You know as well as I do that today a B+ is really a C-. I'd almost be okay with it if it was in a useless subject like calculus or physics. But it's in art history, which really matters!"

Paul sat on the sofa and took Irina's shoes off, placing them parallel on the floor. He then gently massaged the soles of her feet, attempting to comfort her.

Despite her disappointment, Irina smiled and wiggled her toes: "Hey! You're tickling me," she protested.

So the diversionary tactics worked, Paul concluded. His fingers crawled up to her waist. Being extremely sensitive, Irina pushed his hand away, "Stop it! I mean it! I'm too ticklish!"

He stopped. "You told me already, but I forgot: who's your instructor? Do you want me to have a talk with him? Or her?" he asked in all seriousness.

Irina got up abruptly from her reclining position: "Are you kidding me? You're acting exactly like my dad did when I was in eighth grade. I didn't do so hot on the math Olympiad, which he forced me to enter in the first place. When I got a low score by comparison to the math geeks, he went to complain to the judges that his daughter was evaluated unfairly. As it turns out, it was all my fault since I was no good at math, as I had been trying to convince him all along. I had written down only the positive numbers of the square roots, which left him feeling like a fool. Let's not repeat the same scenario again. I can handle this problem on my own."

"Okay, but just remind me who is your instructor. After all, I teach in the department. I'm curious to know who's been mistreating my girlfriend," Paul insisted.

"He's not even a professor. He's a grad student instructor," Irina said disdainfully. "His name's John Kazak. He doesn't have a clue about how to teach undergrads. Nobody understands a word he says since he uses too much mumbo-jumbo. The whole class hates him."

Paul nodded: "I know exactly whom you're talking about. I'm not teaching this year, but next fall, if he's in my graduate seminar, I'll flunk him," he joked.

"Good! He deserves it," Irina took him at his word.

"Let me take a look at your essay, to see why this grad student dared mark down your grade," Paul proposed.

Irina reluctantly walked over to her back pack, threw it on the sofa, unzipped it and took out the offensive essay, her eyes flashing with renewed indignation as soon as she saw the disgraceful B+ advertised in red ink on the front page. "Here!" she tossed the essay unto her boyfriend's lap.

Paul adjusted his bifocals and began reading it carefully. "Well, it looks like John's right here. Manet's not really an Impressionist painter, though he's often classified that way."

"Yeah, well, look him up in every encyclopedia of art and you'll see he's grouped together with the Impressionists. The guy's just nitpicking," Irina countered.

"And you say here that the work of the Impressionists was always rejected by the official Salon. That's not true either. Sometimes it was, sometimes it wasn't. Renoir's, for instance, was accepted quite often," Paul continued, his eyes zigzagging across the page, attempting to match Irina's writing with the instructor's comments on the margins.

"Details," Irina protested. "The point I was trying to make is that their work was put into the reject salon at first and the critics made fun of it. Then they became even more famous than the old fart artists, like Cabanel and Bouguereau, who were initially popular in the Salon."

"Hey, I happen to love those old farts! Soon I'll even be one," Paul objected. "You have plenty of spelling and grammatical errors in this essay," he noted, reading on. "You even misspelled the word 'painting' here. And you write 'peace of art' instead of 'piece of art,' which, incidentally, sounds awkward anyway. The correct expression is "work of art." Come on, Irina! You can do better than this."

"So what are you saying? Are you defending this guy? Are you telling me that I deserve a B+?"

"More like a B-," he answered, trying to be objective.

"Thanks a lot!"

"It looks like we need to spend less time making love and more time working on your assignments," Paul concluded, having finished perusing Irina's essay.

Paradoxically, Irina felt a little better after her boyfriend's assessment. At least the grade wasn't a total injustice. Maybe it did have a tiny little bit to do with the miniscule insignificant errors she had made. "Well, since I don't have any exams tomorrow, how about celebrating your return from the conference?" she proposed.

"Aren't you too upset about your grade to get all mushy right now?" Paul hoped.

"You made me feel better," she answered.

"By giving you a lower grade than your teacher did? It doesn't take you much! I'm afraid to imagine your ecstasy if I had said you deserved an F."

"You don't have to imagine. I'll show you exactly how ecstatic I can get," Irina said playfully.

Returning back to their normal flirtation, however, made Paul feel ill at ease once again. He had been more comfortable a few minutes earlier, when Irina was distraught and he could comfort her in a paternal manner. He watched her walk to the mirror attached to his nightstand and take off the bronze, animal print barrette he had bought her during their shopping trip. She used almost every day to put up her hair in a chignon. Her long brown hair cascaded freely down her shoulders. Their eyes met in the mirror. Hers twinkled with mischief. He had to stop to this whole process right away, before it was too late. "Irina, hold on a minute. I'd like to talk to you about something first."

She turned around. There was an intuitive hint of suspicion in her eyes.

Paul's words only confirmed it: "At the conference this weekend, I spent a lot of time with this Indian woman. Her name is Shushma.'

"Did you sleep with her?" Irina's voice cracked with emotion.

"No. We just spent the night together talking, that's all. Until 4:00 in the morning."

Irina's expression wavered between incredulity and outrage: "You expect me to believe that you spent the whole night with another woman and nothing happened? I wasn't born yesterday, you know…"

"That's true. Only the day before yesterday," Paul tried to lighten up the conversation. But Irina wasn't amused.

"I swear I'm telling the truth," he continued to explain. "All we did is talk about reincarnation, our lives, India and our families. I even mentioned you."

"Gee, thanks! How considerate of you!" Irina's voice was almost unrecognizable. Under the impact of distress, it momentarily lost its childlike softness, sounding husky, as if she were a heavy smoker.

"Come on…" Paul approached and tried to stroke his girlfriend's shoulder reassuringly.

Irina recoiled. "Please don't touch me! Why are you telling me about this woman? If all you did was talk, then why are you feeling so bad about it?"

Paul did his best to answer as honestly as possible: "Because I really did want to sleep with her and probably would have had she tried to seduce me. Even on the plane, I couldn't stop thinking about her. It was almost painful, this awareness that we may never see each other again."

"Are you telling me that you've fallen in love with another woman?" Irina asked, looking straight into his eyes.

"I'm probably just infatuated," Paul replied softly.

"Then you can have her!" Irina declared. She moved swiftly across Paul's studio, like a miniature tornado, gathering up everything that belonged to her: her backpack, coat, extra change of clothes, toothbrush and even the Modigliani-style painting she had given him as a gift.

"What are you doing?" Paul asked bewildered.

Irina didn't answer his question. Paul caught up with her and attempted to take some of her belongings from her hands.

"Don't!" she said unequivocally.

"Irina, please calm down. Can't we discuss this? The reason I told you about this incident in the first place was so we could work it through together. I didn't mean to make you upset."

This statement didn't seem to improve Irina's disposition, however: "It's not the fact that you told me about this woman that bothers me. It's how you feel about her."

"But I didn't do anything," Paul maintained his innocence.

Irina hastily stuffed her toothbrush and clothes into her backpack. When she looked up at her boyfriend, he could see tears glimmering in her eyes. At least she was returning back to normal, he thought with relief. There'll be an explosion, I'll calm her down, we'll make love and that will be the end of the discussion, he optimistically predicted.

But Irina didn't explode. "I can't trust you anymore," she said dryly. "You fall in love at the drop of a hat; you spent a whole night talking to another woman. I should have seen it coming from your behavior on our first date. I was such a fool to believe that you ever loved me. Or that you're even capable of deeper feelings. You may be older than me, but emotionally, you're just a superficial little boy."

Paul didn't consider his attraction to Shushma merely superficial, however: "Shushma believes in reincarnation. That's most of what we talked about. You never like to talk about things like that. I was just excited to find someone who believed in the same things I do, that's all. I didn't say I fell deeply in love with her or that I care about her the way I do about you," he tried to explain, to show that he understood perfectly well the difference between being attracted to and loving a woman.

But Irina refused to listen to him. She had heard enough. Before leaving, she looked straight into his eyes and said: "There are eight hundred million Indians who believe in reincarnation. I was the only idiot who believed in you!"

Chapter 23

As agreed upon, Jean-Pierre was waiting for him at a table in the far right corner of Café La France. Radu immediately recognized his friend's slim silhouette, hand to the mouth holding a cigarette, head lifted slightly to the side and blowing off the smoke with an insolent air.

Radu took a seat across from him at the table: "Don't you see it says non-smoking here?" he pointed to a sign. "You Frenchmen have no manners!"

"Au contraire!" Jean-Pierre retorted. "It's precisely because we have such good manners that we give people the freedom to smoke wherever they damn well please."

"Oh oh, here it comes ..." Radu thought, since he must have heard Jean-Pierre make that argument about half a dozen times. But, apparently, his friend was in no mood for preaching that day.

Jean-Pierre seemed preoccupied. He squeezed his unfinished cigarette into the ashtray with impatience. "I got the order to set Operation Spark in motion."

"Is it 'critic'?" Radu's heart skipped a beat, since he knew that kind of information required immediate action.

"No. It's 'immediate'," Jean-Pierre replied. This meant, Radu estimated, that the operation would be set into motion within a few months. The most urgent CIA plans were labeled "critic," followed by "flash," which would be implemented within a few weeks, followed by "immediate" which might take up to a few months, followed by "priority," which wouldn't be prioritized, and last and certainly least, "routine," which generally led to no action at all.

"Do we have a definite timeline?" Radu asked his companion.

"They want us to agitate right before Christmas. They think Petrescu might be distracted at that time by his visit to Iran."

"What internal sources are we relying upon?"

"The Brutus Force," Jean-Pierre stated, alluding to the six former top Romanian Communist Party officials who had sent Petrescu an open letter attacking his domestic policies. They had accused him of violating the Helsinki accords on human rights; of destroying Romania's consumer economy and agriculture by exporting almost all of the goods in exchange for industrial technology and arms, and of indulging in what they called "harebrained schemes" to modernize the country, including demolishing dozens of villages. The six politicians, two of whom were members of the Politburo and one of whom was Romania's Foreign Minister, were warmly thanked for their helpful suggestions by being promptly arrested and placed in internal exile. The CIA communicated with them via family members who had agreed to take the risk to cooperate with the American government in the hope of saving their loved ones' lives.

"I meant whom are we relying upon who's not in jail or otherwise incapacitated?" Radu reformulated his question.

"We're still courting Maneanu," Jean-Pierre answered, referring to the official Commander-in-Chief of the Romanian Army—even though, for all practical purposes, Petrescu assumed that role as well as the commander of all of the country's military and security forces. Since the entire Brutus Force was currently incarcerated, and thus rendered ineffectual until the potential coup would be in full swing, the Foreign Resources Branch of the CIA maintained contact with Maneanu in order to persuade him to part ways with the dictator.

"Any progress?"

Jean-Pierre rocked his hand back and forth. "Comme ci, comme ca. He's still sitting on the fence."

"Well, I can't say I blame him," Radu replied. "I suppose he's well aware of the risk. If the agitation fails to instigate a coup, he and the whole military leadership will be promptly executed. Petrescu has taken notes from Stalin."

Jean-Pierre drummed the table with his fingers. The calmness of his voice contradicted the nervousness of his gestures. "We're doing what we can to get Maneanu over to our side," he said softly, as if thinking out loud. "Because we definitely need his cooperation. Given the strength of the *Securitate* forces, without the help of the army, nothing will happen in Romania. At least not for awhile. And that would be a such a pity, since the times are so ripe for change."

Radu agreed with Jean-Pierre's assessment. All that the CIA could do is start a spark, stir things up a bit, but the Romanian people had to gather the courage to instigate their own coup or revolution. Which, in a country so fully controlled by the Secret Police, would be no simple matter. Even if the CIA had internal political support, which they believed they did, and even if they had popular support, which they were even more confident they did, without the support of the army, their schemes would come to naught. The *Securitate* forces were simply too strong. Established by Petrescu in the 1950's and modeled after Stalin's *NKVD* forces, they rivaled in strength and exceeded in resources the traditional Romanian army, navy and air force combined. In addition to deploying scores of informants throughout the country, they had an intangible yet essential asset: sheer will power. The *Securitate* troops were fiercely loyal to the Petrescu regime. They were given the latest and best equipment and weapons, high salaries, government apartments and cars and all sorts of other perks. Within their ranks, the members of the Special Brigade were the most indoctrinated group of people in Romania. They obeyed Petrescu's orders without question and followed the dictator everywhere. They were in Bucharest when the dictator was there; at Baneasa when Petrescu was at his villa, and at Constanta, the Black Sea resort, when he was on vacation at the beach. Their allegiance was to their leader, not the country. "The *Securitate* are going to be a force to contend with..." Radu voiced his conclusion out loud. "How are we courting Maneanu?"

"We've tried various tactics," Jean-Pierre replied. "Money didn't work that well since he seems to be quite well off."

"All the members of the nomenclatura are," Radu interjected.

"Yes, but some are greedy and want more. Unfortunately, that's not the case with him. He also seems to be pretty immune to blackmail," Jean-Pierre pursued. "There's a sordid story about his daughter having been raped by an important member of the Petrescu regime and being locked up in a sanatorium once she accused him of the act—but we didn't get anywhere with that incident. We prefer not to stoop so low anyway."

Radu couldn't help but smile at that comment, since he knew that the Agency wasn't above using blackmail.

"The one thing which seems to work with Maneanu is pushing the patriotism button," Jean-Pierre continued. "He appears to be genuinely concerned about Romania's fate and believe that Petrescu isn't acting in the best interest of the country."

"Wow, what a genius! How did he develop such strong powers of observation?" Radu couldn't resist the sarcasm.

"Well, for someone as high up in the hierarchy as he is, he seems to be surprisingly lucid. But from being slightly critical of the government to taking the lead role in staging a coup is a giant leap," Jean-Pierre moved his hands wide apart, to indicate the great distance between these two points.

"So then the negotiations have reached a stalemate?" Radu concluded.

"Not exactly a stalemate, but a moment of undecidabilty, shall we say. We believe that he's predisposed to going our way, but aren't sure yet. And there isn't much more we can do to convince him, other than finding the right opportunity to shake things up a bit."

"Easier said than done."

"Let's hope not, since that'll be your job."

Radu hoped he hadn't heard right. "You want me to stage a coup? Only that? You underestimate me! Why not a revolution?" he asked. Humor was generally his best defense against Jean-Pierre.

"You read my mind," Jean-Pierre replied. "We'd like you to participate in a counter-agitation of sorts."

"Could you be more specific?" Radu asked nervously.

"Petrescu has been planning his next large communist rally right after his visit to Iran, in mid-December. As you know, the first three rows of people at these rallies are all *Securitate* agitators, who hold up banners and rile up the crowds."

"Yes, and behind them are all the poor sops like my parents who are forced to go to the rallies and praise the great dictator," Radu completed the picture.

"Exactly. This time we'd like to plant our own counter-agitators in the crowd, to show the military they have popular support. If we manage to get Maneanu on our side, who knows, maybe something can happen."

"And if not, then the counter-agitators get shot," Radu added.

"It depends on what they do and how subtle they are," Jean-Pierre replied.

"How can one be a subtle agitator? That's a contradiction in terms. Basically, if anyone says anything against Petrescu at a rally, they're lucky to escape with life in prison. Most of the time, they're executed on the spot."

"Not if they manage to generate enough confusion," Jean-Pierre countered.

Radu looked skeptical. "So far the Agency has given me only peanuts. Why are you trusting me with such an important mission?"

Jean-Pierre shrugged. "You've earned it."

"I'm not exactly the heroic type."

"I noticed. Fortunately for you, this agitation will take some courage, but no heroism."

"Is there a difference?"

"Sure. It's all about timing and intuition. Feeling out the crowd psychology, if you will. If you sense that the moment's right and you take the appropriate action, then something may come of it. If you feel it's not, you do nothing. You just shout 'Long live Petrescu!' along with everyone else and you leave," Jean-Pierre elaborated.

"I think it will boil down mostly to whether or not we can get Maneanu to switch camps. Riling up the crowd won't be enough. And for that, luck has to be on our side," Radu pointed out.

"No doubt. Everything good in life depends on luck. How do you think I made it as an artist? Or, a better question yet, why do you think you're still alive?"

By now, Radu had moved on to considering a more modest and less philosophical problem: "How are we getting into Romania?"

"Under our usual cover," Jean-Pierre replied.

For the past two years, Jean-Pierre and Radu had gone under cover working as part-time foreign consultants at a Dacia plant in Ploiesti, one of the most industrialized cities in Romania. Since launching operation Horizon, aimed at industrial and technological espionage, Petrescu became open to collaborations with the West. Both sides were happy with such cooperative ventures. Petrescu used the partnerships as opportunities to plant his spies and steal the blueprints for Western technologies, while Western countries, particularly the United States, relied upon their own agents to infiltrate the country and cull military and political secrets from behind the Iron Curtain.

"D'accord," Radu said, looking at his watch.

"Are you in a hurry?" Jean-Pierre asked. The note of regret in his tone indicated that he would have preferred to continue the conversation.

"No, but I thought our meetings couldn't be too long," Radu alluded to Agency protocol.

"Sometimes we need to bend the rules a little, don't we? Perhaps we can shoot two birds with one stone," Jean-Pierre said with a mysterious smile.

"What birds?" Radu asked, confused.

"The personal and the political ones," Jean-Pierre said.

Radu still seemed puzzled.

"Oh come on! Don't pretend that you don't know what I'm talking about. I've been nagging you about this for a while!"

"Oh, is this about Ioana again?" Radu asked, not too pleased about that prospect. He wished people would stop intervening into his already nearly nonexistent private life.

Jean-Pierre looked him straight in the eyes, to indicate that he was being entirely serious. "There's no time to waste on this matter, Radu. I propose that we use our entrance into Romania to take care of personal business. That way we can rely upon Agency covers and resources. But we have to move fast. I'm afraid even now it might be too late."

"Move fast to do what?" Radu asked. He was well aware of the fact that Jean-Pierre was referring to Ioana's child. But he was far from convinced such a child even existed, and even more skeptical that it was his child.

"To rescue Lucian, of course," Jean-Pierre replied.

"Are you even sure that the boy exists?" Radu raised his eyebrow.

"Absolutely," Jean-Pierre nodded with confidence.

"How?"

"From one of my internal sources."

"What sources?"

"Never mind about that."

"Then how do you expect me to believe you?"

"Because I'll give you enough details to convince you. I just can't disclose my sources. Come on, you know better than to ask me about such things!" Jean-Pierre lit up another cigarette. "We have evidence that a little boy, three and a half years old, fitting exactly the description given by Ioana, was registered in an orphanage on the outskirts of Bucharest on the precise date that Lucian was kidnapped."

"But couldn't it have been another little boy? There were thousands of kids given up by their parents each day during that period of Petrescu's madness," Radu objected.

Jean-Pierre shook his head. "No. It had to be him. My source told me that this little boy cried for his mother for months. When asked who she was, he gave Ioana's name and surname. He insisted that his mommy loved him and that she would return. He kept waiting and waiting for Ioana to retrieve him."

"How come she couldn't find him? Didn't she look?"

"Of course she did. But what do you think, that they waited for her with open arms? They gave her the bureaucratic run-around. They let her speak to orphans from other orphanages, but they didn't let her see the one where her son was hidden. Apparently, they had orders from above not to let her near that place. But since she was so persistent and kept snooping around, just to be safe, they moved him elsewhere. My source told me that one morning, about two months after Lucian's arrival, she was asked to pack up his things and they whisked him away to a different location."

"Does your source know where?"

"Things would be much simpler for us if she did, wouldn't they? I suspect that he was placed in another orphanage near Bucharest."

"What leads you to believe that? There are so many orphanages dispersed throughout the country."

"True, but my sources have told me that kidnapped children, especially kidnapped boys, were especially monitored by the *Securitate*."

"Why?"

"For training and possible recruitment in the Special Brigade."

"But what leads you to believe that Lucian is still alive?" Radu objected. "The conditions in Romanian orphanages are notoriously bad. Most of the kids are left to fend for themselves. One woman watches fifty to a hundred kids, so you can imagine how much personal attention they get."

"That's just it. We don't know if Lucian has survived. But I'm hoping that he was given special treatment. Kidnapped children are special cases as far as the *Securitate* is concerned. They usually have a political motive for taking them away from their parents and they tend to monitor them more closely. That's why we believe that they're generally placed in orphanages near Bucharest, close to the DIE headquarters."

Radu paused for a moment, allowing this information to sink in. He had been so engaged in assimilating the sociological details of the situation, that he hadn't even had the chance to absorb the emotional impact of the news. So he had a son, a little boy with Ioana. And his name was Lucian. He would be almost ten years old, and he may not even have survived. But if he was alive, it was up to him to save him, Radu repeated in his own mind the narrative he had been given by Ioana and Jean-Pierre. To his own surprise, he was starting to believe Jean-Pierre's story. "How do you propose that we look for him? Under our usual industry covers?" he asked.

"No, that won't work," Jean-Pierre shook his head. "Why would foreign auto manufacturing advisors be allowed into Romanian orphanages? We're going to have to change identities for that mission. The only people who are allowed to visit the orphanages aside from the personnel who takes care of the kids—well… in a manner of speaking--are inspectors and *Securitate* officers in charge of Petrescu's Special Brigade."

"Wait, I don't understand. What does the Special Brigade have to do with orphaned kids?" Radu wondered out loud. He knew that the Brigade was the special guard forces that defended Petrescu, his cohorts and his immediate family. They were the most militant branch of the Romanian secret service. But he didn't see the connection between the secret forces and abandoned or kidnapped children.

"The Brigade recruits young boys from the orphanages," Jean-Pierre informed him. "They figure that neglected children will be more susceptible to indoctrination and more tempted to follow instructions blindly than normal youth."

"So you think they're training Lucian for that?" Radu asked.

Jean-Pierre shrugged. "Who knows? All I know is that if your son survived, which is far from certain, given that he's the child of a political case, he'd probably be kept in an orphanage close to the *Securitate* headquarters. At any rate, that's where we need to look first."

"Are our covers for the mission already prepared?"

"Yes, I took care of everything," Jean-Pierre replied. "A few weeks ago a *Securitate* agent was caught at the Romanian Embassy in Washington. Rather than be put on trial and spill his beans, he committed suicide. You'll be using his identity."

"Does he even look like me?"

Jean-Pierre cocked his head to the side, with irony: "He's the spitting image of you. What are the odds of that? We'll do what we usually do. Substitute your photo for his."

"How come I can't pose as an inspector? It would be easier."

"Because the inspectors are already known by the personnel of the orphanages. Whereas in many cases they don't know the *Securitate* agents who come to recruit."

Radu was surprised by the level of detailed planning that Jean-Pierre had already put into this mission. "Why are you so invested in this business?" He recalled that Ioana had admitted having been Jean-Pierre's girlfriend. It occurred to him that it wasn't out of the question that the two of them had been involved since.

Jean-Pierre immediately guessed the young man's suspicion and laughed out loud. "Lucian's not my son, if that's what you're thinking!"

"Then why are you so eager to help Ioana?" Radu asked. His eyes narrowed: "Are you still in love with her?"

"Who says that I ever was?" Jean-Pierre deflected the question.

Radu gazed into his friend's eyes, attempting to discern the truth in their expression. "Then, to be honest, I don't understand your motive ..."

"Does there always have to be one?" Jean-Pierre asked.

"For this level of involvement, absolutely."

"Alright. The truth is that all these years... Ioana and I have been together. Off and on."

"So then you are in love with her," Radu reiterated his hypothesis.

"I don't believe in love, only in lust. You, on the other hand, are an incorrigible romantic."

"Me? On the contrary!" Radu objected. Since Ioana turned him into the *Securitate*, he considered himself the most cynical man in the world.

"Where there's smoke there's fire," Jean-Pierre replied laconically.

"What's that supposed to mean?"

"If you're not still in love with Ioana, then why did you get jealous when you suspected that I might be the father of her child?"

Radu became defensive: "It wasn't out of jealousy at all. If anything, I was appalled by the fact that she's attributing this child to me, when she was sleeping around with other men."

Jean-Pierre felt uncomfortable with the mounting tension between them and decided it was time to switch to the less incendiary topic of the spark for the revolution. "I see. Well then, I'm glad to hear that you have no emotional investment in this matter, since you'll have to be as dispassionate as possible in your new role," he replied, meticulously removing from his wallet a computer image of a stern-looking man with dark hair wearing a gray suit. "As mentioned, you'll be assuming the identity of Comrade Mihail Troiescu."

"Won't they know he's deceased?" it occurred to Radu to ask.

"The *Securitate* knows, of course. But the personnel of the orphanages weren't in direct contact with him. They have no idea who he was or what he looked like."

Radu thought of another potential glitch. "How will we be able to identify Lucian even if we do manage to locate the right orphanage? I'm sure he's changed beyond recognition. Especially in those horrible conditions."

Jean-Pierre smiled again. "We'll be obliged to leave that matter up to his mother. If anyone has a chance of recognizing Lucian, it's Ioana. That's why she'll be coming with us."

Radu pushed himself away from the table with both hands. "Out of the question! I refuse to work with that woman." He looked at Jean-Pierre as one measures up a rival. Were they once again lovers? "Why must you get her involved in CIA business?" he protested.

"Only because of the little detail that she's the boy's mother," Jean-Pierre replied.

"I don't want her coming with us," Radu insisted.

"Suit yourself," Jean-Pierre shrugged. "But without her being able to identify the boy, we won't be able to tell Lucian from Adam."

"Can't she give us a photograph and a description of his unique features, like his birthmarks for example?"

"Sure she can. But in your sharp investigative judgment, what do you think is more likely to work: a picture and narrative description of the child or a mother's eyes, being right there to recognize her own son?"

Radu saw Jean-Pierre's reasonable comment only as a rationalization. So he needs to be with her all the time, he concluded. His competitive instinct kicked into gear. This situation might prove interesting. Although he no longer wanted Ioana, he didn't want Jean-Pierre to have her either. "Alright, but after this mission, I want nothing more to do with her," he declared.

"You obviously haven't experienced divorce," Jean-Pierre replied. "If Lucian really is your son, you'll be doing quite a bit of cooperating with his mother. Not to speak of the fact that she'll be working with you on Operation Spark as well."

"Great! Just what I needed. Under what cover might I ask?" Radu asked, with a healthy dose of skepticism.

"As your wife," Jean-Pierre calmly replied.

Radu was outraged. "What? There's no way I'm marrying Ioana! Not even in a fake marriage. If she comes along, I'll ignore her."

Rather than becoming irritated by Radu's obstinacy, Jean-Pierre seemed amused by it. "That would create what one might call an ironic twist in this whole story," he commented.

"How so?"

"Because you'll be going into Romania to save your son, blow your cover for silly personal reasons and end up waiting the next ten years in some communist prison for Lucian to grow up and come to your rescue."

Chapter 24

Radu gazed out the car window, absorbed in his own thoughts. Sitting so close next to him in the back seat that their hips touched whenever the car took a sharp turn, Ioana stole occasional glances at him. Radu was dressed in a pinstripe black suit, white shirt, burgundy tie and shiny black shoes. He has probably never dressed so sharp in his life as now, when he was trying to pass for a *Securitate* officer, Ioana mused. I bet he never thought that he'd be driven around like the Boss himself in a black Mercedes! she told herself. The irony of the situation made her smile, despite her underlying anxiety.

"What are you thinking about, Comrade Troiescu?" she asked playfully, addressing Radu by his assumed identity.

"Nothing," he answered curtly, not reciprocating her flirtation. Since it was impossible to ignore each other under the circumstances, he resolved to remain as curt and professional as possible in his dealings with Ioana.

"It looks like a certain somebody's not in the best of moods," observed Jean-Pierre, who, dressed as a *Securitate* chauffeur right down to the cap, momentarily turned his head away from the road, craning his neck towards Radu. Quite predictably, nobody would give them any information about Lucian's whereabouts over the phone, so they decided that their best chance of finding the boy would be by visiting every major Secret Police run orphanage near Bucharest. Radu posed as a *Securitate* officer in charge of selecting the preadolescent boys who would be part of Petrescu's Special Brigade. Since such agents were sometimes accompanied by their mistresses or girlfriends, Ioana posed as his girlfriend while Jean-Pierre impersonated their chauffeur--and there was not much pretending there, since he was the one actually driving them around.

Despite having read CIA briefings on *Securitate* recruitment from Romanian orphanages, however, when confronted with their reality, Radu felt unsettled. What he had seen during the past few days stunned him. Children dressed in rags and walking barefoot, despite the low temperatures. Children who stared at him with large, vacant eyes. Children who were so thin that they resembled concentration camp victims. Starving, neglected children whom nobody wanted and nobody loved. He also found it disheartening to think that some of these orphans, whether they had been rejected by parents who didn't have the resources to take care of them or kidnapped by the authorities from loving parents, would become Petrescu's most loyal and ruthless defenders.

"Will this be the last orphanage we're visiting today, Jean-Pierre?" Ioana asked.

"Yes," Jean-Pierre confirmed.

"But there still are a few left, right?" Her voice had a nervous edge. She needed to hear that even if they couldn't find her son that day, or the next day, or the next, there would be other orphanages to visit and that, eventually, they'd find him.

"There seems to be an endless supply of orphanages since the dictator's ban on birth control," Jean-Pierre divined her wishes.

Radu, however, felt even less optimistic than Ioana. He lowered his eyes to examine once again the photographs of Lucian. In his hand, he held two pictures: the color photograph of the boy as he looked when he was three and a half years old, right before he was kidnapped, and a CIA computer sketch of what he might look like now, when he was almost ten years old. In the computer image, they had changed his baby teeth to larger ones and elongated his face to stipulate what he might look like without the baby fat. In both images, Lucian smiled. How soon that smile must have been effaced from his childlike lips; how soon those cheeks must have become sunken, Radu mused. "Even if he's still alive, which certainly isn't a given, what are the chances that we'll recognize him?" he commented out loud.

"I'll be able to recognize my little boy anywhere on this Earth!" Ioana declared, incensed by Radu's pessimism. "Besides, Lucian's a survivor. I'm sure he found a way to hold on. He probably never lost hope that one day I'll come and rescue him."

"We'll look for the birth mark you mentioned to us," Jean-Pierre commented more pragmatically.

"He may not be the only boy with a little beauty mark underneath his lower lip," Radu pointed out.

"I told you that he's got three little beauty marks on the left side of his face, forming a little triangle, like mine here," Ioana indicated with her index finger.

"They're unique. Why must you always be so negative about everything?" She resented Radu's defeatism.

Radu's immediate impulse was to defend himself by blaming his bad attitude on her past actions, as he usually did. But this time he restrained himself. He looked underneath Ioana's mouth and noticed for the first time three faint, brown dots like a minute constellation. The sight of the young woman's soft lips brought back memories he had tried so hard to forget. He looked into her eyes. She had the fervent gaze of a true believer, of a person who's willing, who absolutely needs, to take a leap of faith. Radu didn't have the heart to dash her hopes, a mother's hopes, any more. For the first time in so many years, he felt a hint of complicity, compassion and warmth towards her. He switched the photographs to his left hand and placed his right hand upon Ioana's. Their fingers intertwined. For that split second, they felt united in a personal mission that counted more than all of the political ones put together. The fight for the life of their son.

Chapter 25

Irina's throat felt constricted by pain; the tears flowed freely upon her cheeks. She followed by heart the familiar path she took several times a day when she shuttled back and forth from her dorm room to Paul's apartment. As she hurried along, the pavement, the buildings around her, even the barren trees reminded her of the dozens of times she had taken this familiar route, running with eagerness to be in her boyfriend's arms. Now she was running away from him.

This is the last time I'm taking this path, she thought. From the married student housing, where Paul had somehow managed to rent a studio even though he was single, she cut through the center of the campus, going past the Blair Arch, where they used to enjoy listening to the famous Princeton "Arch Sings" together, then a few steps to the right and she found herself at the door of her dorm room. The whole trip took at most five minutes.

They had had spats before. But this time she felt that she couldn't forgive him. Quite simply, Irina thought, Paul was too immature to be trusted as a boyfriend, let alone as a potential husband, as she had imagined in some moments of what she now took to be clinical insanity. He had basically told her that he considered her substitutable with another woman. That she wasn't special in his eyes, as he had been in hers from the very beginning. An idea crystallized in her mind and she couldn't let go of it: he takes me for granted. All of her sense of outrage came from this feeling of not being appreciated for everything she had to offer as a young woman in love. If a single conversation about reincarnation with a stranger could efface all of the intimate moments they had spent together, then Paul wasn't the man for her, she concluded.

With a trembling hand, she unlocked the door of her dorm suite, praying that her roommate wouldn't be home. If there was one thing she had no strength to endure at the moment, it was Lori's questioning. Fortunately, the suite was empty. Irina didn't turn on the light in the living room. She found some comfort in the semidarkness, which matched her melancholy mood. The red light of the answering machine flashed on and off. Maybe her parents had left her a message. She pressed "play," and regretted it as soon as she heard Paul's voice.

"I'm really sorry that I made you feel bad," he was saying. "I think we should discuss this matter calmly. I wanted to be perfectly honest with you, and instead I made a bigger deal of a small incident than I should have. But I swear the last thing on earth I ever want to do is hurt you. I love you very much." Beep.

Irina immediately erased the message. She didn't want to hear Paul's voice; she didn't want to listen to his facile apology. Her pride had been too wounded to reconcile with him. She wished, however, that she had a close friend, someone other than her boyfriend, to whom she could pour her heart out. Unfortunately, she only rarely kept in touch with Jean-Pierre nowadays, and, at any rate, he wouldn't be one to discuss with her feelings for another man. As for Lori, the two of them had drifted apart since becoming roommates. Irina realized with regret that her closest friend was, sadly enough, still Paul. With him she talked about everything: art, literature, politics, their families, their feelings. If she felt so shattered by his confession about the other woman it was not only because they were lovers. It was because, in her eyes at least, they were also best friends.

Irina shoved her coat, backpack and painting into the closet and dropped with fatigue unto the love seat where she used to occasionally make out with her boyfriend when Lori was away. Would she ever be friends with him again? she wondered. Probably not, she told herself. For instance, she wasn't that close to Jean-Pierre any more, even though they had parted on better terms than she and Paul just did. After reaching a high degree of intimacy, Irina thought, it was impossible to reverse everything and have just a friendship. You always remember and miss the intimacy. The problem remained, however, that she still needed her boyfriend. It may have been difficult to imagine staying friends with him, but having been so close, it was even harder to imagine life without him.

Irina's eyes burned. She went into the bathroom to wash away the makeup that had blended with the salty tears. Looking at herself in the mirror, she thought she looked like a mask. Mascara had formed dark, zigzag vertical streaks upon her cheeks; the peach blush had become clumpy and uneven. After washing thoroughly with soap, she splashed handfuls of cold water upon her face, attempting to find some relief in this cool cleansing ritual. She looked up at herself in the mirror again. Her appearance had improved, but the delicate skin around her eyes remained red and swollen. She patted her face with a towel, then went into the bedroom and lay down, fully clothed, on the lower bunk bed. The clock on the nightstand revealed it was only 7:00 p.m. Too early to go to bed. Irina shut her eyes and sought solace in this womb of solitude.

Despite the peaceful atmosphere, she couldn't rest. Pangs of emotion still moved her with a psychological pain that had surprisingly strong physical symptoms. Quite literally, her heart ached. Seeking relief, she let herself go, her hands upon her heaving chest, sobbing in spasms, her body trembling from head to toe. Fifteen whole minutes, which felt like an eternity, must have passed like this. Once the wave of emotion had run its course, Irina drifted into the light, troubled rest of half-dreams. She saw the image of her grandparents at the airport waving goodbye with tears in their eyes, right before her mother and she went through customs. She could hear their promises about how she'd see them again soon; how they'd visit her in America often. In the liminal space between dream and reality, she relived the pain of separating forever from those she loved most. A single tear rolling down her cheek was enough to fully awaken her. The two sources of pain, one from her distant past, the other from her recent break-up, blended together to form a single current of emotion.

Irina wished there was something she could do to accelerate the process of separation from Paul. She wanted to leave him without grieving the loss of their relationship. She thought about young men in her classes to see if she could imagine herself going out with any of them. But their images were unhelpfully vague. Since dating Paul, she hadn't paid that much attention to other men. Nor, truthfully, before meeting him either, since she was busy with Jean-Pierre. Perhaps she there was something she could do, something symbolic, that would help purge the traces of him from her mind, her room and eventually her life. After a few moments of brooding, she had an idea. She turned on the light and opened the upper right desk drawer. Inside, she found dozens of photographs of her boyfriend, invariably smirking since he didn't like having his picture taken, and a few of both of them, since, at Irina's insistence, they had asked nice passers-by to snap pictures of them together.

Methodically, she tore each photograph in half, then halved the halves, shredding the traces of their relationship into tiny little pieces which she then released from her open hand, like disoriented snowflakes, into the trash bin. She then proceeded to tear up his notes. The one telling her to meet him at the art library. The one asking where she wanted to go on a given weekend. The one announcing that he'd be a little late for dinner that evening. They were all signed, "Love, Paul." "What does he know about love? He just throws the word around and cheapens it," she told herself.

It then occurred to her that there was one more thing left to be destroyed. She went straight to the living room closet where she had placed the painting. She took it into the little bedroom with the same furtive movements with which a hungry animal drags its next victim into its lair. She examined it. In this image, they seemed to go so well together. To be so complementary, so united, so in love. She took out her brushes and oil colors from the bottom drawer of her desk. There was already a glass of water on her night stand. She dipped the brush into the glass, then smothered it in bright red paint and slashed with streaks of color the portrait of their love. But even this act of artistic violence didn't provide sufficient relief. She placed the portrait on the floor, dipped her brush in red, green, black, yellow and blue, mixed the colors together, then proceeded to flicker paint all over the canvas until the Modigliani-inspired image looked more like a Jackson Pollock action painting.

She heard her roommate come into their suite and rushed to clean up the area as best she could in ten seconds or less. When Lori stepped into the bedroom, her face reflected the shock of someone who stumbles upon the scene of a violent crime.

"My God! What have you done? I told you not to paint in here!" Lori shrieked, since specks of color had splattered unto the linoleum floor, the desk, even the white walls.

"I'll clean it all up, I promise," Irina suddenly felt ashamed about her behavior.

Lori looked down at the painting on the floor. It lay there defeated, completely covered by a hailstorm of splattered paint that, with its colors all mixed together into a dreary greenish gray, resembled a puddle of muck.

"Is this what your parents are spending their hard-earned money on?" Lori asked, not having too high of an opinion of the training offered by the Studio Art Department (otherwise known as S.A.D.).

"It's called Abstract Expressionism," Irina retorted, regaining her composure. If there's anything that was universally accepted, even revered, in the contemporary art world, it was hurling around, in the heat of one's passions, with all of one's energies focused upon each movement, powerful splotches of paint that had the power to blot out everything in their paths. Perhaps even love.

Part III

Chapter 1

After leaving three messages on her answering machine and slipping two handwritten notes under her door telling her he was sorry that she was overreacting, Paul began to get worried. Maybe something was wrong. Maybe Irina got sick, since she always went overboard in her emotions.

Each day he went to the spot at the library where they usually met at 5:30 in the afternoon, but Irina wasn't there. On the third day, Paul was concerned enough to check out the student cafeteria in Mathey Hall, where they usually ate together. He spotted her in the company of her roommate – a worrisome sign, since the two of them were no longer friends. He didn't approach her, just observed her from afar to make sure that she was okay. Irina was bent over an enormous salad, her favorite food along with chocolate, eating like a goat, with alfalfa beans sprouting from the corners of her mouth. Her table manners hadn't improved, but at least she seemed healthy and fine, Paul concluded with relief and left the dining hall.

The idea that his girlfriend might no longer wish to be with him any more occurred to him only on the fourth day of separation. Up to that point, he thought Irina was throwing one of her tantrums and it would be best to wait it out and let her calm down on her own. The whole episode resulted from a slight misunderstanding, which, from his perspective at least, could be easily clarified if they discussed the matter calmly.

After all, he asked himself purely rhetorically, what had he done? Nothing that's what. He had told his girlfriend that he was attracted to another woman and had spent the whole night talking to her. Big deal! If he had told her that he had spent the whole night fucking another woman, he would be slightly more sympathetic to Irina's reaction. But, as far as Paul was concerned, breaking up with someone over talking about reincarnation was completely absurd.

He reviewed the incriminating evidence from the point of view of an impartial observer. The episode was about as banal as it gets. At least 99% percent of men are attracted to other women even when they have a serious girlfriend or wife they truly love. Most of them would cheat on their girlfriend or wife if the opportunity presented itself, such as if the woman they're attracted to gave them the slightest sign of encouragement. If you believe *Playboy* and *Cosmo*, about 80 percent of men cheat on their girlfriends or wives. If you believe *Reader's Digest*, only 20 percent do. Either way, Paul concluded, he deserved to be congratulated. He was one of the good men who not only resists temptation—after all, he could have easily at least attempted to make moves on Shushma—but also is considerate enough to share this valuable piece of information with his girlfriend.

Seeing how Irina wasn't returning his phone calls and notes, however, Paul began to run out of patience. On the fifth day of separation, he became downright self-righteous. The characteristics which he had formerly considered to be Irina's qualities now turned into faults. Her passion, he thought, could be reduced to feelings of jealousy and possessiveness. Her sensuality, which had attracted him immensely, he dismissed as a common enjoyment of sex. Her strong-mindedness, which led to countless debates filled with erotic and psychological tension, now became nothing more than the stubbornness of a closed mind. Her artistic ambition, which he had for the most part admired, was mere illusion and reflected narcissistic tendencies. And her beauty, well, lots of young women are pretty. It was nothing special.

Despite this process of deidealization, things weren't as easy as they seemed. The idol may have fallen from her pedestal, but Paul still missed the woman he loved. Each place he went to was touched by Irina and their memories together. The library seemed strangely quiet without her loud whispering, giggling and their footsie matches under the table. It wasn't as much fun to wash alone; he missed the feel of Irina's delicate hands, the lightness of her kisses and their off-key duets in the shower. What was perhaps most difficult, however, was going to sleep. He recalled the warmth of her slim body in his arms; the way she'd curl up into the hollow of his stomach like a kitten; the pleasure bordering on rapture he experienced when they made love. Which is why when the feelings of anger subsided on the seventh day after their fight, Paul wanted his girlfriend back, flaws and all.

That Saturday he watched sports and read the newspaper, activities he usually did in Irina's company. He felt empty and alone. He recalled that when he watched football on weekends, she would nestle next to him with her homework, lavishing affectionate kisses and caresses on him during the commercials. I really blew it this time, he told himself. It almost didn't matter any more who was right and who was wrong—especially since he had already conclusively established that he was right. What counted was the consequences of their behavior, which, he was obliged to admit, had been somewhat negative. Once the football game was over, he turned off the T.V. and glanced over at the nightstand. A glossy object caught his attention. It was the animal-print bronze barrette he had bought for Irina at T. J. Maxx.

"I have to give this back to her," Paul decided, as if returning that piece of plastic were a moral duty of the highest order. Yet he was mildly aware of the fact that he faced one minor obstacle. It was clear from his girlfriend's behavior that, at least for the time being, she didn't want to see him any more. Though a very noble gesture, returning her barrette wouldn't be likely to change her mind and regain her trust. He needed to do something bolder, more magnanimous, to win her back. Irina wanted to be reassured that he was passionately in love with her, which he was, and that he was ready to commit, which he sort of was, especially now that he had lost her. What better way to express these feelings than by asking Irina to marry him? That was the only way to make his girlfriend understand that Shushma and other women meant nothing to him; they were passing infatuations which he wouldn't pursue. It was Irina he wanted to be with, to love and to cherish—and whatever other huge sacrifices the wedding vows unreasonably demanded of men.

He put on his shoes, grabbed his coat, checked to see if his wallet was still in his pocket and headed straight to the most expensive jewelry store he could find on Nassau Street, where he resolved to buy his girlfriend an impressive diamond engagement ring.

The man at the counter measured Paul up and down as he made his entrance into the jewelry store. Wearing his navy blue winter coat that resembled an old comforter, Paul didn't exactly strike the jeweler as Long's Jewels material.

"Hi, I would like to take a look at your collection of diamond engagement rings," Paul boldly declared.

"Sure." The salesman seemed pleasantly surprised, becoming more gracious all of a sudden. He pulled out a drawer from under the spotless glass counter and revealed two long rows of sparkling rings.

"Does your girlfriend prefer white, rose or yellow gold?" he asked.

Paul wasn't aware that gold came in several colors. He was under the impression that its color was... gold. Hence the name. "Yellow I guess," he answered with a shrug.

"What cut would she like?"

"Excuse me?"

"Princess, emerald, oval, marquise, trilliant or brilliant round?" the jeweler asked.

"Round," Paul replied after a moment's reflection. Once again, it was the only cut he knew about—not that he had ever lost sleep over the matter. Mary had picked out her own wedding ring and he couldn't even remember what it looked like.

"What price range did you have in mind?" the salesman asked.

This information Paul delivered with precision and confidence, being keenly aware of his meager savings, low salary and temporary employment situation: "About two or three hundred dollars," he announced.

The jeweler's face became long, just like the name of his store. "I'm afraid we don't sell engagement rings under the price of a thousand dollars. Our diamonds are of the highest quality: precision cut by the best jewelers, white in color, DI in clarity."

These impressive credentials were completely lost on Paul. "So then what do you have for about two hundred dollars?" he asked, giving up on the idea of a traditional engagement ring for the next dozen or so years. "And what's your return policy?" he followed up with another important question, since it also occurred to him that Irina might refuse his generous offer.

"We have a two week return policy," the salesman responded curtly, not seeming too pleased with Paul's line of inquiry. He carefully placed the expensive diamond ring collection back under the glass counter and, with gestures that indicated he was doing his customer a huge favor to even bother with him any more, went to another display and took out a tray of silver rings.

Most of the rings had beautiful golden amber stones, which reminded Paul of his travels to Eastern Europe and therefore of Irina herself. She'll love such a ring and not even notice it's not diamonds and gold, he naively told himself. In fact, I prefer jewelry like this, it's so much more tasteful and natural, he reassured himself further, peering down to see which ring had the smallest bug in the amber. He knew that Irina, who couldn't even tolerate a night of camping, would draw the line at the bugs--even if they did increase the value of the amber by almost twenty dollars.

Paul wisely selected the only ring which contained no insects. Held in the light, it glimmered with swirls of various shades of honey colors and even included a small portion of what might have been a prehistoric leaf. Who knows what reincarnations this little bit of amber has seen, Paul pondered. It might have even belonged to a Russian princess once. Heck, it might have even been a Russian princess once. And it would certainly be good enough for his princess, he decided, paying in cash the price of $189.97, which was only $169 dollars more than he would have paid for a similar ring at Kmart.

With the engagement ring safely enclosed in a fancy blue box in his pocket—the box explained the extra cost—he headed straight for the Mathey Hall cafeteria, where he felt confident he'd find Irina. He spotted her immediately, sitting by herself in the corner of a long table bent over the customary giant salad.

She seemed startled when he plopped down across from her with a silly smile on his face.

"Hi," he said, not really knowing how to begin the conversation.

"Hi," she responded, wavering between positive and negative emotions.

To his great relief, Paul observed that she had cooled off quite a bit since her explosion the previous week. "You forgot this in my apartment," he opened the conversation with his peace offering, extending her the bronze barrette.

"Thanks. I was wondering where it was," Irina replied, taking the barrette and quickly twisting her hair up in a chignon. Since she wasn't exactly awed by his gesture, however, Paul congratulated himself for having something a lot better up his sleeve—or rather in his pocket, in this case.

"So how have you been?" he asked.

"Terrible," she answered honestly.

"Why?" he asked.

"Because it rained yesterday. Why do you think?"

"I don't know, maybe your cat died," Paul engaged in his usual bantering.

Irina always took the bait, no matter how silly or transparent the provocation. "You know very well that I don't have a cat! We're not allowed pets in the dorms. And back home, my parents are even allergic to me, let alone other animals."

"Speaking of which, when are they coming?"

"Tomorrow," Irina answered morosely.

"Wow! So soon? I'm kind of nervous about meeting them."

Irina made an incredulous face: "Who says you're meeting them?"

"You did! Remember coaching me on how not to say anything?"

"That was before..."

"Before what?"

"Before we broke up. Duh..." Irina clarified.

"Then let's get back together," Paul proposed a solution. He preferred to avoid melodrama, if at all possible.

Which with Irina, it usually wasn't. Oh, oh, the serious conversation is starting, Paul thought, noticing her grave expression.

"I was so hurt by you," she said in a cracked emotional voice, not disappointing his expectations.

He was prepared with an answer: "What do you want me to say? I'm sorry. Millions of times, I'm sorry. I called you but you never returned my calls. I wrote you notes telling you how sorry I felt about hurting you. What more do you want from me?"

Unfortunately for Paul, Irina had had a full week to reflect upon this very question. "You want to know what I want from you?" she asked. "I want what every woman wants. I want to feel loved, desired and appreciated by you. I don't want to be placed in competition with other women. Even if those women may be more beautiful or smarter or more talented than I am. That shouldn't matter, just as it doesn't matter to me when I meet more handsome, more accomplished and smarter men than you."

"Whom have you run into this week?" Paul focused on the latter part of her statement.

"Nobody."

"Then no wonder I beat the competition!" he remarked.

"That's not the point. The point is that when we were together, I wasn't looking for other men. I didn't want them. I wanted you. You shouldn't make me feel like I'm easily substitutable with other women."

"Believe me, you're not," Paul reassured her. "You're a lot more high maintenance than any other woman I ever dated," he added, to appease her.

"Thanks."

"Besides, I didn't substitute you with Shushma. I just said I liked her too, that's all."

"And that's precisely the problem, can't you see?" Irina retorted. "Ever since we started dating and the whole waitress incident, I felt like you idealize perfect strangers while taking me for granted. It should be the other way around, don't you think?"

"Irina, you're so naive," Paul said with the smirk he had whenever he felt that he was not only older, but also infinitely wiser than his girlfriend. "The fact is that it's human nature to take those closest to us for granted. Who else are we going to take for granted if not them? Of course, ideally that shouldn't happen, but the fact is, it does. That's just life. And it's perfectly normal to be intrigued by someone you don't know. Everyone, including you, is excited by newness. That's how our own relationship began."

"And don't you think that our relationship's enough?"

"More than enough!" Paul readily conceded that point.

"Then why do you feel the need to start something with other women? Why do you flirt so much? Actually, what bothers me most about your behavior is not the fact you're attracted to other women, but that these attractions mean so much to you."

"They don't at all! You're the one who always makes a big deal out of them," Paul protested.

"Paul, the bottom line is that I want to be able to trust the man I love," Irina insisted. "I don't want to continue a relationship if I feel my boyfriend is very likely to hurt and betray me."

"I won't. The last thing in the world I'd ever want to do is to hurt you."

"But you already have."

"Well, I do my best," Paul fell back upon his favorite default statement. Irina's discouragement was contagious.

"Basically, I need to know: do you take our relationship seriously or are you just leading me on?" she asked him point blank.

Paul was surprised. "Irina, how can you even ask me such a question? Of course I'm serious about us. Or at least I was before you broke up with me. Didn't I spend all of my time with you these past two months? Didn't I help you with your homework and your art? Didn't I show how much I love you?"

"Sometimes you did. But at other times you acted like, in your heart of hearts, you didn't really want me," Irina replied.

"When did I ever act like I didn't want you? Aren't I always mushy?"

"I don't mean physically. I mean want me in your life, by your side."

"Well, the truth is, I was afraid because… just the opposite is the case."

"The opposite of what?"

"I was afraid of falling madly in love with you," he clarified.

"Did you succeed?" Irina was curious to know.

"Yes. That's part of the problem, in fact. I never felt like this before. It scared me a little bit."

"You know, most people would be pretty excited by love. Normal people, I mean."

"I was. But I was also trying to be more careful. I didn't want to jump into another relationship that failed."

"But you just said you never felt this way before."

"I didn't. Not so strongly. But come on, Irina, I wasn't born yesterday. I've fallen in love before. And it ended up, well, in divorce."

"Here we go again…"

"I've been doing a lot of thinking this week and… actually, I'm not that scared any more."

"Gee thanks. How flattering. You're going out of your way to be romantic."

"Hold on, it gets better. You remember that song by Meatloaf I sometimes sing to you in the shower?"

"The one where he says, 'Let me sleep on it?'" Irina asked, horrified.

"No, the other one. 'Two out of three ain't bad'".

"That's not much more reassuring either."

"Actually it is, because for me it's clearly three out of three ain't bad. I need you, I want you and I love you."

Irina couldn't help but smile. "That's not traditionally considered a romantic song, you know," she pointed out.

"Perhaps. But this is," he said, extending her the blue box. "Irina, what I'm trying to say is that you're the one for me. So…will you marry me?"

Irina was taken aback by Paul's recognizably awkward yet uncharacteristically romantic proposal. She took the jewelry box and opened it, fully expecting to see inside the brilliance of something huge in platinum and diamonds.

"A silver amber ring," she observed.

"You like it?"

"Sure," she said flatly.

"So you hate it?" Paul reformulated his question.

"No. It's just that you generally don't offer a woman jewelry in a blue box unless you want to create very high expectations."

Paul thought quickly on his feet: "Well, this isn't the real engagement ring, of course. That one's coming soon—I wanted us to select it together. This is only a promise ring," he emphasized. Fortunately, he recalled the term from reading the Ann Landers column back in the days when he was seeking advice on how to cope with his marital problems.

Irina was somewhat confused: "So what exactly are you promising me?" she asked.

"To love and to cherish you," Paul answered, recalling his old wedding vows.

"Faithfully?" Irina looked probingly into his eyes.

"Absolutely! I've learned my lesson."

"And what lesson is that?" Irina wanted to verify.

"Not to mention to you my crushes on other women ever again," Paul declared.

Irina's hand went to her forehead, a gesture she made when she wasn't happy with Paul's answers—which is to say, frequently. She couldn't believe this man. He couldn't even lie properly.

"And not to pursue them," Paul added, seeing how his first answer fell short.

Irina slipped on the amber ring, which slid off even her middle finger, since it was two sizes too big. "Listen Paul," she said, "let's just consider this a trial period and see how our relationship goes. Maybe you were right to be more cautious. You're my first real boyfriend. I fell so head over heels in love with you that I kind of rushed into everything. Living together, wanting commitment. Maybe I'm too young and inexperienced to handle such responsibility. And maybe moving so fast kind of scared you."

Paul nodded vehemently in agreement with all of her statements. "So, practically speaking, does this mean we're back together again?" he asked, eager to celebrate their reconciliation.

"Yes," Irina confirmed. "But you're on probation," she added.

"I'm on probation?" Paul objected to this one-sided formulation. "For what? You just admitted that you're the one who took things too fast."

"Yes, but I'm not the one who spent the night with another man."

"Me neither. Shushma's a woman," Paul smoothly exculpated himself. "Besides, for the millionth time, all we did was talk about reincarnation! What could be more pure and spiritual than that?"

"Especially when that's precisely the kind of thing that turns you on."

"You just blew the whole thing way out of proportion. You have the tendency to overreact."

"And you have the tendency to give me reasons to do so," she countered.

Things returned pretty much back to normal for the couple. This conversation led them back to her dorm room and then down the familiar path to Paul's studio, where he chivalrously carried all of Irina's stuff--her clothes, toiletries, shoes, hair accessories and school books—with the exception of the Modigliani-style painting. Paul wondered what had happened to it.

When they entered his studio, they stopped bickering. To Irina's surprise, Paul dropped all of her things in the middle of the living room, without even asking her to put them neatly away or showing any concern for the mess. He led her by the hand to the sofa, feeling that he had regained his girlfriend plus an entirely new woman, who, incidentally, wasn't Shushma. It was still Irina. Their brief breakup and the fear of losing each other had infused an exciting sense of freshness into their relationship.

Irina was also glad to be back in her boyfriend's life, in his arms. During the whole week they had been separated, she didn't believe that they'd ever be together again. And that had scared her. Tears of relief ran down her cheeks. He wrapped his arms around her; kissed her lips moistened by tears. He reassured her not with loving words, for which he was not exactly famous, but with his eloquent, gentle touch. He covered her with avid caresses that explored every part of her body, removing the barriers of cloth that barely separated them.

Still feeling mixed emotions, Irina yielded to him in body while resisting him with her words. "I hated you this whole week, Paul. I felt so jealous and really hated you," she whispered in his ear.

"I know. You've made that perfectly clear," Paul whispered back, kissing her forehead, her cheek, her lips. "And I hated you too for breaking up with me for such a flimsy reason," he felt compelled to return the compliment. Yet somehow, in the midst of their kisses and caresses, these mutual declarations of hate could be confused with vows of love. The heat of her breath juxtaposed with the coldness of her words; the softness of her body contradicted the harshness of her attitude, sending currents of desire throughout his whole being. Little waves of electricity that took unpredictable paths, from the neck to the hand and from the knee to the little toe. He cradled her light being in his arms, feeling like he had forgotten everything and yet at the same time like he had forgotten nothing. A whole human life, perhaps even happiness itself, could be concentrated into a single night of passionate reconciliation.

Chapter 2

Radu examined his felt-tip shoes. The polished black leather was splattered with mud freshly moistened by the melted snow. Specks of brown covered his gray suit. He felt awkward sporting the "gangster look," as he called *Securitate* outfits, when stepping into such impoverished surroundings. At least the mud is covering up some of this gloss, he thought, as if somehow that would make him fit in better with his environment. As he looked down, he couldn't help but notice that Ioana's black high heeled shoes were also covered with mud. His glance followed the arch of her lanky legs, up to her black shirt and white silk shirt, to the luminescent strand of pearls that surrounded her thin neck, to her delicate face. He was struck by her despondent expression.

"What's the matter?" he asked her.

The very question brought tears to her eyes, but she didn't respond. She picked up the pace and Radu fell slightly behind.

"What is it?" Radu repeated, taking two longer strides to catch up with her. They walked together side by side back to the car parked on the side of the dirt road, after yet another fruitless visit to an orphanage located on the outskirts of Bucharest. They had visited seven so far and still hadn't found Lucian. Ioana didn't want to lose hope. Yet at times like these she couldn't help but feel despondent.

"Nothing," she belatedly replied to Radu's question. "It's just so sad. I feel so sorry for Lucian."

"Don't worry. We'll find him," Radu attempted to comfort her, not knowing if he, himself believed what he was saying.

They slipped into the back seat of the car.

"Any luck?" Jean-Pierre asked them, even though the answer was obvious since they had, once again, returned alone.

"Not yet," Radu replied, not wishing to sound too negative, for Ioana's sake.

"I think we have time for one more visit today," Jean-Pierre announced, also attempting to elevate her spirits.

"Thanks," she replied, doing her best not to appear ungrateful to the two men, who, after all, were doing their best.

They drove down a winding road, bordered on both sides by beautiful, soaring evergreen trees. When one sees Romania's natural beauty, one almost forgets the misery of its people, Radu thought, gazing dreamily out the window.

After about twenty minutes, they stopped in front of an oversized wooden shed that might have been used to store cooperative farm equipment. A few emaciated children were playing outside. They wore no coats or hats, even though it was no more than thirty degrees Fahrenheit outside. Their feet, pink from the cold, were clad in rough, peasant clogs.

"You're it!" shouted a boy, who looked no older than five or six, as he tagged another boy about the same age. He then took off running, weaving his way among the trees.

"How can they let them play tag outside dressed like this?" Ioana objected.

"At least they play," Radu retorted. The most striking feature of the orphanages they had visited so far was the fact that children didn't laugh, didn't talk, didn't play. Usually they just huddled together in large, cold rooms staring in front of them with vacant eyes.

Radu knocked on the front door of the shed. Ioana stood right behind him. After the sixth knock, someone finally opened the door. A woman of indeterminate age peered at them without inviting them in. She wore a basma, or large colorful handkerchief, over her head and was dressed in an oversized skirt and ornate peasant blouse. To Radu, she looked like a grandmother yanked out of her little village and forced to tend to the misfortunate kids around her.

"We're from the *Securitate*," Radu informed her. The woman instinctively recoiled and crossed herself, as if he had just told her that he was the devil himself.

"We're here to recruit the best boys for the Comrade's Special Brigade," the young man added, to explain his purpose and simultaneously reassure her that they didn't come there to arrest anyone.

"We didn't get the winter supplies yet. They go hungry, poor souls," the peasant woman apologized in advance, waiving her hand vaguely towards the children. "Come on in, see for yourselves," she finally opened the door. As soon as the couple entered the room, a pungent odor of urine, defecation and vomit overpowered them, despite the fact that some of the shed's windows were cracked and cold air seeped in. Two holes in the ground, one on each of the far right and left corners of the room, served as toilets. Some of the younger kids had probably soiled themselves, Ioana surmised, and nobody seemed to have bothered to clean them or change their underclothes. If what she had observed at other orphanages held true for this one as well, they had no change of clothes and no hot water for baths. What made matters worse was the fact that even some of the older children were not yet potty trained and practically everyone suffered from chronic diarrhea due to malnutrition.

Ioana and Radu looked around. The large, sparsely furnished room was filled with kids of various ages, yet, perhaps due to their thinness and stunted growth, all of them appeared very young. Several children who looked about four or five years old huddled together on a cot, while a few toddlers lay down on the floor covered by a rough brown blanket that was spotted with a liquid, from the smell, was probably urine.

The peasant woman noticed that Ioana was looking with concern at the group of children and shook her head. "My heart goes out to them," she said, demonstratively putting her hand to her chest. "We have no heat, no hot water, no soap, no nothing. They don't give us anything. We've been waiting for the supplies since last summer. Poor souls," she repeated the expression she apparently used whenever referring to the orphans.

"We'll request that the supplies be sent," Ioana tried to reassure her.

"Eh...!" the peasant woman replied with a dismissive waive of the hand. She was no longer fooled by such empty promises.

Ioana continued her inspection of the room. She opened a door and stepped inside a smaller area that looked like a cross between a large closet and a bedroom. Radu followed her.

"The infants are sleeping!" the peasant woman said in a high pitched voice, attempting to prevent them from entering the room.

But it was too late. The couple stepped inside and were shocked by what they discovered there. Little kids, babies and toddlers, were tied to their beds with rope. Some of the babies had bottles of gruel propped into their mouths. Yet none of the children cried or showed emotion. Their eyes looked empty and unnaturally large, in the midst of their emaciated little faces. An older boy, who was perhaps three or four, sat on the floor with his arms wrapped around his bony knees and rocked back and forth, staring straight ahead.

"He's gone bonkers," the peasant woman said, twirling her finger around her ear. "He's almost seven and he still don't talk," she added.

"What's his name?" Ioana asked.

The woman shrugged. "Most of them have no names."

Ioana and Radu exchanged a meaningful glance.

Observing their disapproval, the peasant woman once again attempted to exculpate herself: "I am one woman with fifty kids. How can I do it all?" she opened her arms wide, as if to express her impotence and despair.

"Doesn't the government at least give you food and clothes for these poor children?" Ioana inquired.

Upon hearing the naiveté of this question, the peasant woman relaxed and exploded into hearty laughter, exposing her bad teeth. "You must be new," she said, feeling relieved that she didn't have to deal with one of the more seasoned agents. "They're supposed to give us food and other supplies every month. But it happens once in a blue moon. Maybe every six months—if we're lucky."

"So how do you even manage to survive?" Radu asked her.

"We live off the land and from whatever kind folks give us."

So these kids live off stealing and begging like the gypsies, Radu concluded. He made a signal with his head to Ioana, to indicate they should do one more tour of the place before leaving.

"What will you tell your bosses?" the peasant woman followed them around nervously. In her mind, there was very little difference between the inspectors and the *Securitate* agents. Both poked around, asked official questions and then left without doing anything to improve the children's lives.

By now, Ioana felt almost convinced that they wouldn't find Lucian there. The children seemed too young; none of them were even close to her son's age. Before leaving, however, she looked carefully at each child, her heart filled with sympathy, wishing she could have done something to alleviate their misery. She thought of all the possibilities, but none seemed promising. The CIA knew about what was going on in Romanian orphanages, of course, but wasn't interested in doing anything to remedy the situation. Human rights organizations got permission to inspect only select orphanages prepared just for them, which had been stocked in advance with supplies and filled with children who had loving parents. And the state inspections were not intended to improve the quality of life for the children, but rather to see if there were further ways to cut corners; to make sure that none of the scarce goods allotted to the orphanages were being wasted. As she was contemplating the hopelessness of the situation, Ioana heard the front door of the shed open.

In stepped a slightly older, lanky boy. He held under one arm a small pile of wood.

"This ought to warm us up for a bit, Grandma," he said to the peasant woman.

"Take it back! Didn't I tell you not to touch them things? They're state property!" the peasant woman objected, to save face in front of the visitors.

The boy seemed puzzled, his gaze shifting from the peasant woman to the guests.

"Let me help you with those," Ioana offered, taking some of the logs from the boy's arms and putting them in the ice cold fireplace.

Radu used one of his matches to light a fire.

The peasant woman remained guarded, not knowing how to react to this unusually nice behavior from state personnel. Meanwhile, Ioana gazed at the boy. He was slim and tall, yet, strangely enough for an orphanage, he looked healthy, or, at any rate, in better shape than the other kids.

"This is my grandson, Lucian," the peasant woman said, noticing Ioana's interest in the boy. "Lucian, these folks are from the *Securitate*," she said, making the proper introductions.

Lucian's deep brown eyes sparkled with distrust as he instinctively took a step back.

Ioana's heart beat uncontrollably. "Nice to meet you, Lucian," she said softly and approached the boy to shake his hand. That's when she finally saw the sign: three little dots below his chin; the constellation of life and hope that she had been seeking for so long.

Chapter 3

Ioana whispered something in Radu's ear. He, in turn, took the peasant woman aside. "I think we found the kind of young man we're looking for," he told her, pointing to Lucian. "We'd like to recruit this boy for training for the Comrade's special troops."

The peasant woman looked horrified: "Who? Lucian?" She couldn't believe her own bad luck.

"Yes," Radu confirmed. "He's the only one here who fits the profile." He hoped that he sounded sufficiently authoritative and official.

He must have, since the peasant woman broke down in tears: "Please don't take him away, Comrade. He's the only help I've got around here. He's like family to me!"

Lucian overheard the peasant woman's plaintive cries, walked straight to her, wrapped his arms around her waist and looked defiantly into Radu's eyes: "I'm not leaving Grandmother!" he announced.

"Wouldn't you be proud to help your country?" Radu attempted to use the stock argument under such circumstances, even though he felt it must have seemed rather weak in the face of the only person who had shown the little boy any affection since he was whisked away from his mother's love.

"I'm not leaving her," Lucian repeated.

"Please Comrade, let him stay here," she beseeched, putting her arms protectively around the boy's shoulders. "You can have any other kid you wish. There are other little boys who'll grow up to be strong and courageous lads. Why look, Mircea, over there," she pointed to a blond boy with freckles. "He's full of spirit. He'll grow up to be quite a soldier."

"Mircea looks a little too young," Radu came up with a counterargument on the spot, after giving the boy a cursory glance. "It's him we want."

"I'm not leaving you, Mama," Lucian looked up towards the peasant woman.

"You call her Mama?" Ioana asked, startled by the sound of the word she had longed to hear out of her son's mouth applied to a stranger.

"They say my real mom left me here. She didn't want me any more," Lucian replied. "She's the one who takes care of me, so that makes her my mom."

Ioana turned away for a moment, to avoid revealing her emotions. What hurt her most was not the fact that she had been replaced in her son's heart. She was glad that at least Lucian had had the benefit of a substitute, of some kind of human affection. She was nonetheless disturbed by the fact that he believed she didn't want him; that she had willingly abandoned him. The fact that he didn't recognize her troubled her as well. Had she changed that much? Had he blocked her from his memory as he had from his heart?

Radu was about to insist, but as soon as he opened his mouth Ioana gently placed her hand upon his, to stop him. She bent down to look the little boy in the eyes. Perhaps if he saw her face up-close, he might recognize her. But Lucian made no indication that he did. In fact, he gave his mother the same look of distrust that he directed towards Radu.

"We're not going to force you to do anything that you don't want to, Lucian," Ioana reassured the boy gently. His demeanor seemed to soften a little, but he didn't give up his tight grasp of the peasant woman's waist.

"We just wanted to take you to a better place," Ioana pursued. "Somewhere nice and warm, where you'll get more food and make new friends."

"I'm staying with her," Lucian stood his ground. "I already have friends here. All these kids are my friends," he made a sweeping gesture with one hand.

"You can stay here if you wish," Ioana replied. "But wouldn't you want to go for a little visit with us just to get some warm food in your stomach? Perhaps a little chicken soup? Some fresh-baked bread? And, for desert, a little bit of chocolate?"

Lucian's eyes sparkled with temptation.

"How about a hot bath?" Ioana continued. "It's so cold here. And, afterwards, we'll bring you right back to your grandmother if you wish. What do you say?" Ioana's voice was melodious, enticing, reminding Radu of the days when they were lovers.

The peasant woman smirked at the lure, but didn't go so far as to comment.

"Have you ever heard the tale of Mica Murdarica (the Little Dirty One)?" Ioana pursued. "She was a little girl who didn't like to bathe. All of her friends avoided her until she was all clean again," she alluded to her son's favorite bedtime story, this time almost whispering in the boy's ear.

"Nobody washes here," Lucian retorted. "We have no soap; nothing to wash with. So who cares about that!"

"Mica Murdarica, who didn't want to wash, took soap and water, lathered up, washed and combed her hair, and then she looked pretty and shiny and clean all over again," Ioana recited part of the story in a sing-song voice, the way she used to do when he was a little boy. But Lucian didn't respond.

Ioana stood up, feeling so discouraged that she seemed to Radu just about ready to collapse. Clearly, her son no longer recognized her. He had forgotten what she looked like, the sound of her voice, their rituals, his favorite bedtime story. He had blocked out everything about his past.

"Do you still have that book, Mama?" the boy asked quietly, almost in a whisper, this time looking not at the peasant woman, but at Ioana.

"Yes, I do. I keep it by my bedside at night," Ioana replied, her heart pounding with excitement.

The peasant woman looked quizzically from the boy to Ioana.

"Ioana, did you visit this orphanage before? You seem familiar with this boy," Radu intervened, afraid that this mutual recognition between mother and son would blow their cover and that the peasant woman would call the authorities.

"Yes, I believe I ran into him a few years ago," Ioana confirmed with a complicit smile, not taking her eyes off Lucian.

The boy just stood there, hesitant, suspended between contrary impulses. He was trying to decide if his instincts were right; if this woman really was the mother he vaguely remembered from what seemed to him as so long ago. At the same time, he didn't want to abandon his friends and his grandmother, the woman who had taken care of him all of these years. He settled for a compromise. Perhaps he could just go for a short visit with the blond lady and return to Grandmother with goodies for his friends, like fruit and bread and soap and chocolate. That way he'd "earn his keep" at the orphanage, as Grandma put it, and still get to find out if his hunch was right.

"I'd like to go just for a little visit with the lady, Grandma. I'll come right back and bring everyone food and presents," Lucian proposed out loud, looking up at the peasant woman. His gaze was tender and pleading, as if he were asking permission while an unconscious part of him was already anticipating regret, begging her pardon in advance. The peasant woman hesitated. She couldn't dissuade the boy openly, in front of the authorities. Yet, at the same time, she didn't remove her arms from his shoulders. She wasn't ready to let him go.

"Don't worry, we'll bring him back," Radu reinforced Lucian's message.

The peasant woman shook her head. She looked disconsolate. "I knew I should have never got attached to any of them kids," she said, reverting to a peasant accent and wiping her tears away with dingy, stubby fingers.

"Thank you," Ioana said warmly. The peasant woman gave her a look so filled with anger and pain, that, at that moment, she seemed a mirror image of her former self on the day she had discovered that her son had been kidnapped.

Chapter 4

"Sweet dreams, my love!" Ioana closed the storybook and leaned forward to kiss Lucian on the forehead. When she advanced towards him, the boy flinched as if her gesture of tenderness were a physical threat. His mother noticed that at times, particularly when he was sleepy or tired, Lucian confused affection with aggression, like a stray puppy who had been abused and hadn't quite gotten used to his new, kinder master. She persevered with the positive conditioning, however, stroking his cheek gently with the palm of her hand.

Feeling more alert, Lucian smiled faintly at her. "Goodnight…Mommy," he replied, hesitating for only a split second about what to call her. This too, took some adjustment. After a few weeks, the boy began to consider Ioana as his mother and referred to the peasant woman only as "Grandmother." He still talked from time to time about bringing goodies to her and to the other children at the orphanage, whenever he'd return there. When that day would come remained rather vague in his mind and Ioana wasn't about to raise the issue. She couldn't help but wonder, however, if her son had blocked her out of his mind as efficiently as he had his surrogate mother.

Ioana slept upon a blanket on the floor to leave her son the only bed in their hotel room. But she had trouble falling asleep. The floor was hard and what was even tougher was listening to the boy's whimpers and cries in the middle of the night. Lucian was frequently haunted by nightmares. He went with almost no transition from tranquil sleep, where anyone looking at him might have thought that he slept like an angel, to tumultuous, restless dreams.

"Lucian, tell Mommy, what's wrong?" Ioana would go to his bedside, pale with worry, when she heard him cry.

The boy's nearly translucent eyelids opened slowly, drowsily, as his large eyes adjusted to the darkness. "Nothing. I just had a bad dream," Lucian replied.

"What was it about?" Ioana asked him.

"The bad guy came to take me away."

"They don't know where you are, Lucinel," Ioana reassured her son, assuming that he was referring to the Secret Police. "I'm never going to let anyone take you away from me again," she promised him, with a voice filled with conviction.

"Then why do you let that mister live with us?" Lucian asked her.

"What mister?"

Lucian had employed term nenea, a word children use to say "gentleman" in Romanian.

"That nenea I saw you kiss the other day," Lucian answered, in a tone that resembled more of an accusation than a statement.

Ioana didn't know how to respond. She felt disappointed in, though not really surprised by Lucian's interaction with Radu. They obviously didn't take to one another. There was an instinctive distrust between them, as if Radu's ambivalence towards her translated into a psychological distance between him and their son. More straightforwardly, Lucian thought that Radu was from the Secret Police, as he was originally told. No matter how much his mother tried to dispel this negative image, the boy couldn't be dissuaded.

To make matters worse, she thought, Radu acted too harshly towards Lucian. Ioana regularly visited the Shops, or stores stocked especially for foreigners, to procure for her son special treats to his heart's delight. At supper, she watched Lucian shovel morsels of food into his mouth, often scooping up the globs of meat and sauce with chunks of baguette, barely chewing the food and sometimes even talking to her at the same time. When Radu witnessed this behavior, he became impatient.

"Please chew with your mouth closed!" he'd command. "And don't talk when you chew. It's not polite."

"He hasn't exactly been brought up with a silver spoon and trained at etiquette school!" Ioana came to her son's defense.

"That's right," Radu replied. "So now it's your job to educate him properly."

Ioana tried to hold her tongue, if only to spare her son's feelings. But she hardly thought that Radu, who didn't lift a finger for the boy, was in the position to give her unsolicited lessons on parenthood. "Lucinel, please chew your food well, my sweetie," she said in a tender voice, attempting to control her temper. She felt so much pity that her little boy had been deprived of so much in life, not least of all his childhood.

Although natural and untrained in his behavior, Lucian was at the same time mature beyond his years. He had an intelligent, cautious gaze with which he scrutinized everyone and everything. He was generally silent, except around her. He almost never laughed or even smiled. He didn't joke or play with the new toys his mother had bought him, the way a normal child would. When she asked him why he didn't, Lucian replied that he didn't know what to do with toys. At the orphanage they didn't have any. They played instead with twigs, rocks and--he opened his hands to expose red marks on his palms--dirty needles.

He didn't know how to read, but he loved being read to. Whenever she told him stories at night, Ioana felt like a trace of his childhood could be rediscovered in his usually much too serious expression. He seemed more engaged, exhibited curiosity, asked her questions, offered comments. "Why did Hansel and Gretel use bread crumbs? That's silly! Couldn't they have used rocks from the beginning? Then the birds wouldn't eat them." Good point, Ioana approved.

Watching the interaction between mother and child, Radu felt out of place, like an intruder. Am I really the father of this child? he wondered, and more than once when he, Ioana and Jean-Pierre got together to discuss their mission, he eyed his rival with a mixture of curiosity and suspicion. Ioana's maternal attitude towards her son made Radu feel closer to her. Yet he was touched by her love for the boy as a stranger might be, from a distance. He was a spectator to the rebirth of an almost forgotten sense of warmth and intimacy that he wished he could share.

During the day, Radu and Ioana worked together on their plans for the upcoming Petrescu demonstration. Sometimes, in the midst of a strategy session, he caught himself looking at her with reawakened desire. Occasionally, they made love. During such moments of intimacy, Radu was particularly struck by how different she was from the young woman he had known. Ioana's athletic, slim figure had become exceedingly willowy, frail. Her short hair gave her the waif look that was popular among teenage girls and fashion models. Because she had lost weight, she looked even younger than when they first met. Her blue eyes were stunning in an artificial sort of way. But what surprised him most was Ioana's reserve. She now spoke very little, only when necessary. And, like her son, she hardly smiled any more. Only in Lucian's company, Ioana became more animated, exuding a sense of wellbeing that Radu secretly envied.

He wished he could love her as before, with innocence, with trust. Although they were still drawn to each other, something felt irrevocably tainted about their contact, as if they'd spread a contagious disease even when, once Lucian fell asleep, they had the opportunity to make love. He would take her gently into his arms. Like the first time they met in her dorm room, their hands and lips did all the exploring while their clothes fell helplessly to the floor. He kissed her all over, refamiliarizing himself with her thin, wasted body, with her smell, with the sound of her voice when she whispered and moaned under his touch. Her whole body convulsed, as if intimacy itself had become unbearable, blurring the boundary between pleasure and pain. Radu himself felt drained. His physical desire was all he had left to offer her. Everything else, Ioana herself, the whole system of spying and betrayal, had destroyed long ago.

Chapter 5

"Hi, I'm Paul." When her boyfriend introduced himself to Irina's parents, Andrei mumbled "Nice to meet you" and Eva said "Enchantée," showing right off the bat that she spoke a word or two of French (quite literally).

After the introductions, Irina asked: "So where do you want to eat?"

"It doesn't matter. We're not picky," Eva replied, a comment which made Irina smile.

"How about the pancake house?" Paul proposed, since that was the most popular brunch place in town.

"Sure," "Fine with me," the Schwarzes agreed.

Once they were settled more or less comfortably on the wooden benches of The House of Pancakes—for which, incidentally, they had to wait 45 minutes outside in the cold, along with the rest of the undergraduate community—Eva initiated the proceedings. "Irina told us you're an artist," she began.

"No. I don't have the talent. I'm an art history professor," Paul said with characteristic honesty.

"That's much better," Andrei approved. "I've been telling Irina ever since she made the mistake to get into art that it's not a career. It's more like a lottery."

Irina rolled her eyes.

"I tell her the same thing. Very few artists actually become famous," Paul concurred.

"What famous?" Eva interjected. "We're not talking about fame here. We just don't want our daughter to starve to death."

"There's no such thing as starving artists anymore, Mom. That's just a stereotype from novels," Irina said.

"True. Nowadays they become waiters and waitresses," Paul chimed in to buttress her argument. Irina, however, didn't appreciate the help. She flashed him a glance of severe disapproval.

"So what do you do in your line of work?" Andrei inquired.

"Not much," Paul replied, since lately he was almost always on some kind of sabbatical.

Irina saw the necessity to intervene. "Paul's just being modest. Actually, he's an excellent scholar. He specializes on Impressionism."

"I love their art. Monet's my favorite," Eva approved.

"What kind of interpretations do you produce?" Andrei asked, interested in the scholarly angle.

Paul momentarily drew a blank, but Irina instantly came up with the answer: "He specializes in theories of the male gaze," she boasted.

"What's that?" Eva inquired, seeing a potential conflict between Paul's area of specialization and him dating her daughter.

"Oh, it's just a new feminist critique of how male painters represent female subjects," Paul explained matter-of-factly.

"'Female subjects' means 'women,'" Irina translated for her parents.

"You're a feminist?" Andrei asked with a note of surprise mixed with disapproval.

"Not at all," Paul reassured him. "I just pretend to be. You know, like everyone else."

Andrei begged to differ: "We haven't heard of feminism in math and physics. In fact, we've barely even heard of women," he declared, proud of the fact that at least some disciplines still maintained their high standards.

In the meantime, their breakfasts arrived. Irina ordered a plate of chocolate chip pancakes; Eva preferred hers with blueberries; Paul with apples, while Andrei, who was convinced that he had latent diabetes, ordered black coffee with plain toast.

"Irina told us you wish to visit Romania," Andrei pursued another fruitful thread of conversation.

"Yes, right after our trip to Czechoslovakia. Prague's one of my favorite cities."

While Paul was making this dangerous confession, Irina made silent pleas with her eyes expressively indicating, "No, no, please don't talk about this with my parents; are you totally insane?"

"Oh, so after your trip to Prague, you'll join Irina in Romania, is that it?" Eva reinterpreted his statement according to what she wanted to hear.

"Yes," Irina answered firmly on Paul's behalf. "That's nice. I can recommend a few decent affordable hotels in Bucharest. Unfortunately, my father's very ill and my brother has a very small flat. Otherwise we'd invite you to stay with our family," Eva graciously excused herself.

"I appreciate that, Mrs. Swartz, but lodging's not a problem," Paul answered. "Hotels in Eastern Europe are relatively cheap for Americans."

"Whatever you do, avoid Athenée Palace and Hotel International in Bucharest," Eva advised him. She leaned forward and whispered: "Those places are bugged and crawling with prostitute spies."

Paul thanked her and made a mental note to check out this promising recommendation.

After brunch, Paul and the Schwarz family parted ways since there was a football match that Paul absolutely couldn't miss. Later that afternoon, Irina gave her parents a brief tour of the campus. "This is Blair Arch, where they have the performances I told you about. You know, the ones where the cute boys sing nice love songs," she pointed out the archway closest to her dorm.

"Why can't you date one of those nice young men?" her mother took the opportunity to offer constructive advice.

Which led Irina to ask an important question: "So what did you think of Paul? By the way, this brownish gothic looking building here," she pointed straight ahead, "is Pyne Hall, where I have my comparative literature classes. In fact, it looks like there are a few study sessions going on right now. We're in the middle of midterms. Anyway, you and Paul seemed to get along pretty well together."

"Sure, we're nice, sociable people," Andrei modestly pointed out. "We get along with everybody. But he's not son-in-law material."

"You're too young for him," Eva responded. "Do you mind if we rest a little?" she asked, sitting down on a bench next to an open classroom window. Andrei and Irina took a seat on either side of her.

"Don't get me wrong, I have nothing against him," Andrei declared. "He seems to be a nice, honest guy. But he's certainly not for you. For one thing, he's got no ambition."

"So what? I have enough for both of us," Irina raised her voice, getting a bit defensive.

Andrei shook his head. "That never works in a couple. You need a man who can pull you up, just like I do your mother. He's too different from you."

His wife didn't seem too pleased with this explanation: "Excuse me? Since when do you pull me up? I always pull you up! You'd still be arguing with that traffic cop if I hadn't been there to save you," she objected.

"That's only because we complement each other so well, Papusica," Andrei hasted to rephrase his argument. "You have more practical sense; I have more theoretical sense. Irina and Paul are too similar."

"Didn't you just say that we were too different?" Irina reminded him.

"Yes. And I was correct." Being a physicist, Andrei had a talent for elucidating apparent paradoxes. "You see, on the one hand he's too old for you, he's not ambitious and he's not Jewish, so obviously you don't have enough in common. On the other hand, he studies art, which makes him too similar. What you need is a Jewish scientist," he elegantly returned full circle to his major premise.

At this point, a blond woman of uncertain age poked her head out of the classroom window adjacent to the bench where the Schwarzes were having these deliberations. "Do you mind? We're trying to have a study session in here," she informed them. "All we've been able to concentrate on for the past few minutes is your gibberish."

"You mean Romanian," Irina clarified, standing up. "I think we should move on," she suggested to her parents. "I'll show you the Woodrow Wilson School next. That's for the government classes. It's a modern looking building with a big fountain in the front."

That evening, after having spent the whole day with her parents, who refused to accept her fiancé or take their commitment seriously, Irina was a bundle of nerves. Paul had to give her several thorough massages to calm her down.

After they made love, she lay on his bed, staring at the ceiling. "I never learn my lesson. If there's one thing I should realize is that no matter how hard I try, I'll never get my parents' approval. They'll always find something negative to say about everything I do. Especially my dad, though Mom usually agrees with him."

"I thought you were very close to your father," Paul commented.

"I am. That's part of the problem! It's so unbelievably frustrating never to be able to please him. I mean, I'm sure he has good intentions. He wants the best boyfriend and the best career and the best of everything for me. But he can't understand that what he considers best isn't necessarily right for me. Which is why, no matter what boyfriend I'd pick, he'd still think that he's not good enough for me."

"So he told you he didn't like me?" Paul deduced.

"Before he even laid eyes on you."

"How about afterwards?"

"Then also. Nothing I choose will ever be good enough for him. Because whatever I choose won't be exactly the choice he'd make. I have different needs, a different personality, different talents. And he's only capable of judging me by his standards, not mine. "

"If you already know this, then why do you keep banging your head against the wall?" Paul asked. "Don't ask for your parents' blessing. Who cares about what they think?"

"Obviously I do," Irina declared morosely.

"Why?"

"Because they came to this country in large part to give me better opportunities. I wish so much that they could realize that their sacrifice, leaving our family and everything else behind in Romania, wasn't all for nothing. I wish they could see that I'm happy with my boyfriend, my aspirations in life, my identity. Basically, I want them to accept me for who I am. Is that too much to ask?"

"Apparently it is," Paul replied. "Irina, you can't depend on your parents, me or anyone else for your self-esteem," he continued, looking at his girlfriend tenderly and placing a wayward strand of hair behind her ear. "You need to feel confident enough to accept yourself. If your parents or I are approve of what you do or are proud of you, that's an added bonus. But it's what you want that counts. You need to feel comfortable in your own skin."

If only life were so simple, Irina thought. She decided, however, not to dwell on the negative, at least not at the moment. "You too. In mine, I mean," she clarified, in case there was any ambiguity.

"The thing I admire most about you is your subtlety," Paul replied, taking her cue and launching on a fresh wave of caresses.

Chapter 6

"This airport makes me dizzy," Irina announced, feeling overwhelmed by the fast-moving crowds of New York City's J. F. Kennedy International Airport.

"When are you not dizzy?" Paul asked, shuffling along with two duffle bags on his slim shoulders and dragging behind him two monstrously large and heavy suitcases.

"I'm hardly ever dizzy! I'm almost always ditzy," Irina refuted the unfair accusation.

"What I can't understand is why you need to bring along so much luggage. How many changes of clothes did you bring? No matter where I go and how long I plan to stay there, I only take one carry-on bag with me."

"That's not very wise if you're going to Romania," Irina retorted.

"Easy for you to say," Paul said. Then it occurred to him: "Hey, why don't you carry your own luggage?"

"I'm carrying as much as I can!" Irina pointed out, barely able to cope with one heavy duffle bag filled with smaller and more precious gifts for her family and one enormous suitcase chockfull of bigger and less important items, some of which, if absolutely necessary, could be stolen by the Romanian authorities at customs.

"You shouldn't travel with more than you, yourself can carry," Paul emphasized his rule of thumb.

"Paul, how many times do I need to tell you that 90 percent of the contents of those suitcases are gifts? You can't visit your family in a Second World country empty-handed. That's considered rude!"

"I just wish you had shipped it," Paul replied, squirming under the weight of one of the carry-ons, whose strap was biting into his shoulder.

"Then it would take a year for them to get about 25 percent of the contents. And it would cost a few hundred dollars, meaning more than the goods themselves, to mail and insure the packages. You obviously don't have relatives in Romania..."

"And I plan to keep it that way..."

"What's that supposed to mean?" Irina jumped.

"Nothing. I was just kidding."

After they checked in the luggage at the ticket counter, Paul and Irina felt momentarily relieved. At least they wouldn't have to worry about it again until they reached Ruzyne, Prague's international airport. By then, Irina postulated, if the Czechs were anything like the Romanians, the luggage might even be a lot lighter…

They took a seat at their gate and Paul began reading his *USA Today*. He might as well have waved a red flag before Irina's eyes, since whenever he picked up a newspaper and put it in front of his face, she took it as her cue to make conversation.

"So, are you excited about visiting Eastern Europe?"

"Yes," Paul replied succinctly, attempting to concentrate on the Sports section.

"Which city do you look forward to most? Prague, Timisoara or Bucharest?"

"Prague," Paul replied without any hesitation.

"Thanks a lot! I'll tell my relatives you look forward to seeing perfect strangers more than you do meeting them."

"You didn't ask me which relatives I prefer. You asked me about the cities. Prague is one of my favorites. It's got gorgeous women and beautiful architecture. What more could a man want?"

"Don't start with me on the women again!" Irina forewarned him.

"I won't if you let me read my newspaper," Paul offered a reasonable compromise.

Given such a powerful incentive, Irina managed to remain silent for a record time of about ten minutes. She focused on watching the people hurry by, evaluating which ones were the best dressed and which of their clothes her family would prefer most as gifts.

The airline stewardess interrupted her thoughts by announcing that first class and ambassador class passengers could board on the plane. I left the Second World only to become a second class citizen, Irina mentally bemoaned her fate. She had always wished that she could settle comfortably into one of those spacious, cushiony first class seats and wolf down the complimentary shrimp cocktail. Though very tempting, a few shrimp in red sauce weren't worth the extra thousand dollars, however.

Once their zone was announced, Irina and Paul gathered up their bags and walked to their seats.

"Do you prefer the middle or the aisle?" Paul asked his girlfriend.

"On planes, I get all jittery and have to go to the bathroom every few minutes," Irina informed him.

Paul promptly took the middle seat; Irina the aisle.

As soon as the plane started moving, Paul, who had finished reading the Sports section of his newspaper, began leafing through Skyshop, the magazine conveniently located in the seat pocket in front of him.

Irina, who got nauseous at takeoffs, leaned back in her seat and closed her eyes, hoping that after a little nap the discomfort would go away. She overheard

Paul chuckle. Curiosity overcame the nausea. "What's so funny?" she asked, opening her eyes and looking at the page that had amused her companion.

It featured a picture of a little white poodle with a pink bow around its neck who was climbing up a carpeted ramp unto a sofa. Irina did a double take to make sure that she was seeing correctly. The contraption costs $99.95, unless you wanted the deluxe version of the ramp for medium-sized dogs, which costs $50 extra.

Paul read the caption out loud: "Ideal for small breeds, this ramp system allows pets to climb unto furniture…"

"Why in the world would anybody need a staircase for a pet to get up on the furniture?" Irina interrupted. "Don't people generally work hard to train their pets to stay off the furniture?"

"It's so ridiculous," Paul concurred.

Then Irina began reading, backtracking slightly: "… this system allows pets to climb unto the furniture with ease (and you'll spare your back!)"

"I've never seen a cat or dog who can't climb on the sofa by themselves," Paul commented. "And for those who can't, you certainly don't need to buy an expensive thirty pound ladder, carry it over to the sofa, then train your pet to climb on it. You just pick up your ten pound dog and nicely place him on the sofa. Simple." Paul flipped the page to the health products section. Although the pet ramp may have seemed difficult to match in its futility, it faced some serious competition. "What's this?" Paul asked, pointing to a foot foam which cost about $100.

Having no obvious answer to this question, Irina read the caption: "For foot problems, doctors recommend custom-fit orthotics to provide foot support. Save time and money…."

"…By spending a hundred bucks on a foot insole?" Paul interjected.

"… and treat yourself to the same technology at home…"

"They call that technology?" he pursued.

"Hold on, they explain here," Irina continued reading, "You'll receive a foam box that takes an accurate impression of your foot. Send it along with a check of $99.99 to Footdoctor and prepaid postage of $29.99 for shipping and handling and in a mere five weeks you'll receive your own custom made foot support."

"Great. What a deal! You pay almost 150 bucks and wait over a month to get something you could run into the nearest pharmacy and buy for three dollars," Paul concluded.

"Haven't these people heard of Doctor Scholls?" Irina asked. Yet, to her dismay, she spotted an ad for an even more expensive pair of shoes. "Take a look at this one," she pointed with her finger at a picture featuring a pair of "hand-sewn slippers" that cost a mere $180. "It says here these slippers have "a special driving sole and heel pads for grip on pavement or pedals!"

"Don't all shoes have that?"

"Apparently these shoes have the additional advantage that they're not just for driving. You can also walk in them," Irina clarified. "You have to admit, that's quite an invention!"

"Why didn't other shoe companies think of that?" Paul added.

At this point in their joint mockery of the consumerist excesses of capitalist societies, Irina's attention was drawn to an Estée Lauder lipstick trio advertised on the next page of the magazine: it contained a bronze, peachy pink and rhubarb red lipstick, beautifully packaged in a complimentary silver purse. The whole thing cost a mere $59.99.

"Now here's something useful," she said, this time with no trace of irony in her voice whatsoever. "I think my aunts and cousins would like it."

With this comment, she instantly lost Paul's sympathy. He was considering more important matters. "Where exactly are we staying in Romania?" it occurred to him to ask, since Irina had made all the arrangements and he was still a little confused about the details.

"I already told you," she answered. "In Bucharest, we're staying at my grandparents' house, though most likely nobody will be there since my grandfather is in the hospital in Timisoara, where my uncle and his family can take care of him. And in Timisoara, which is where we're going first, we're staying with my uncle and cousins. They're very nice people; you'll love them. My cousins are both in med school, which is considered the most honorable profession in my country. You have no problem getting married if you're a doctor. In fact, their wives are also in med school. That's how they met."

"At least we'll have plenty of medical attention in case we get sick," Paul remarked.

"Let's try not to get sick, alright?" Irina proposed. "The mortality rate is worrisome in Romanian hospitals."

"Speaking of mortality rates, didn't you tell your parents that I'm staying at a hotel?"

"Yeah, so?"

"They might communicate with your family and find out I'm sleeping in the same bed as you at their house."

Irina made a dismissive gesture with her hand. "We've got nothing to worry about. My uncle's family is very hospitable. We'll just tell my parents that they insisted you stay with us. Which is what they'd probably do anyway."

"Shouldn't we wait for them to insist before showing up with ten suitcases at their doorstep?" Paul considered a more conventional approach.

"Absolutely not. They'd feel insulted. Nine of the suitcases are for them. Besides, why go through the expense and trouble of getting you a hotel room, only to immediately cancel the reservation?"

Paul was still a bit concerned about the lodging arrangements. "And where are we staying in Prague? Do you have family there also?"

Irina looked at her boyfriend with dismay. "No... You never listen to anything I say, do you? I have to repeat the same information at least three or four times before it finally registers."

"I think this is a classic case of the chicken or the egg," Paul remarked. "I'm not sure which came first. Your compulsive repetitions, which I do my best to block, or me blocking what you say until you repeat it enough times that I get it's important."

"Since my explanations are so redundant, then please tell me where we're staying in Prague," Irina assumed the tone of a school teacher examining her pupil.

"At someone's house. A family member or friend," Paul offered a vague yet educated guess.

"We're staying with the mother of Jean-Pierre's friend, Viktor," Irina informed him yet again.

Paul's eyes opened wide, since the name of Irina's ex-boyfriend never put him at ease: "Jean-Pierre's friend? Why?"

"Jean-Pierre gave me two free tickets to Prague and two return tickets from Bucharest, remember?"

"Yes, I'm not senile yet. But what does that have to do with us staying with his friend's mother or his mother's friend?"

"Obviously your self-diagnosis is a bit premature, since I already told you that Jean-Pierre also made lodging arrangements for our stay in Prague. Isn't that nice of him?"

Paul wasn't exactly thrilled by her ex-boyfriend's generosity: "Did you ever ask yourself why this guy, whom you broke up with, is doing you all these expensive favors?"

"Yes," Irina replied with confidence. "It's because he's a nice guy with plenty of money and connections. And he has other girlfriends, so he took our break up very well."

Paul wasn't convinced: "That may explain why he doesn't hate you. But it doesn't tell us anything about why he's giving you and the companion of your choice a free vacation in Eastern Europe."

"Well, he did mention doing him a little favor in return," Irina recalled.

"What favor? He wants to sleep with you again?" Paul asked, alarmed.

"Of course not! His friend is a Czech playwright whose plays are often performed at the Magic Lantern Theater in Prague. It's really famous, you know."

"Yes, I know. What about it?"

"Jean-Pierre wants us to meet with this friend of his, Viktor the playwright, and talk to him about what's going on politically in his country. Listen mostly, since presumably he knows more about Czech politics than we do. He also gave me the name of a few French and American journalists we're supposed to contact once we return to the States."

Paul looked even more concerned.

"And by we, I mean me, of course," Irina switched pronouns to put him at ease.

"In other words, you're supposed to spread anti-communist propaganda in exchange for airplane tickets and lodging in Prague for a week," Paul translated.

"I wouldn't call it propaganda," Irina objected.

"What would you call it then?" Paul launched headlong into one of his favorite diatribes. "Jean-Pierre works for Radio Freedom Europe, which has been sponsored by the CIA since 1971. You, yourself, told me that he's an agent for the organization and that he recruited your brother to work for them also. Now he's recruiting you and, against my better judgment and principles, I may also be entangled in this mess since I'm traveling with you at their expense. You're absolutely right about one thing though: I definitely should pay more attention to what you say! I could end up a political prisoner or a CIA agent if I don't. Geesh... This problem didn't come up when I was ignoring what my ex-wife was telling me."

"And you say I exaggerate..." Irina retorted. "From me telling you that Jean-Pierre was gracious enough to cover our travel and lodging expenses in Prague you automatically jump to the conclusion that we're on a spying mission for the CIA. Talk about being dramatic!"

"Irina, do you ever bother to read the international news?" Paul tried the Socratic approach.

"Sometimes."

"Did you happen to read that The Magic Lantern Theater is where a lot of the Charter 77 dissidents got together to plan seditious activities against the Czech communist government?" Paul quizzed his girlfriend.

"Of course I knew that! I've heard of Vaclav Havel, thank you very much. Come on, I'm not that ignorant!" Irina exhibited her political education. She also employed her sharp analytical skills: "But, first of all, not all of the playwrights working there are dissidents. Second, even if Jean-Pierre's friend is a dissident, I still don't understand how you can be against him. These dissidents are some of the most courageous artists and intellectuals in the world. They ran huge risks to speak against their totalitarian government and its abuses of human rights. Many of them lost their homes, their jobs and even their freedom."

"Irina, of course I'm sympathetic to the Charter 77 causes. I support the defense of human rights in Eastern Europe and throughout the world, for that matter. My point is that I don't want to be entangled in the CIA manipulation of these people and of the Western media. The CIA isn't helping out the Czech dissidents because it cares about Eastern European people and their rights. Remember that Roosevelt sold all of these countries out to Stalin."

"He basically had no choice."

"That's debatable. You know as well as I do that the CIA supports some of the most repressive governments on Earth, which show absolutely no respect for human or civil rights. The only thing this organization cares about is having friendly governments to the U.S., not the principles of democracy, freedom or human rights."

"Be that as it may, democratic countries are much more likely to be friendly to us and to respect the civil rights of their own people," Irina countered. "Besides, personally, I don't care what the CIA wants. I believe in the dissident cause and am willing to help out if I can," she declared heroically. "Especially once I'm out of the Eastern block and safely back in the United States," she toned down the heroism.

"You realize that you're also putting your life at risk in agreeing to this mission?"

"It's not a mission, for God's sake!" Irina objected.

"If you say so... I just wish to make it perfectly clear that I'm going to Prague to see the city and enjoy myself. For me, this will be a much-needed vacation. Nothing more."

"But you haven't done anything all semester except for working on one measly twenty-minute presentation on Monet," Irina pointed out.

"I need a rest from the emotional trauma of my recent divorce," Paul clarified. "In any case, I don't want in any way, shape or form to become involved with the CIA."

"You won't. We'll just visit the city, go to restaurants and museums, have fun and stay for free in a nice apartment in the old section of town. What could be more relaxing? I may have a few conversations with Jean-Pierre's friend, but so what? We've got to mingle with the locals, otherwise what's the point of traveling to other countries, right? As for the press, like I said, I'll talk to the journalists on my own once we're back in America. You've got absolutely nothing to worry about; everything will be as calm as a summer breeze, I promise," Irina reassured her boyfriend.

Chapter 7

The couple arrived at the Ruzyne Airport, located about 20 kilometers from downtown Prague, around 8:00 p.m. Several cabbies waited at the curb directly in front of the arrival hall. Paul, who was "a seasoned world traveler," as Irina put it, asked the taxi driver how much it would cost to reach their destination, which he read from a hand-written note from Jean-Pierre that Irina had given him. The driver, a young man with thinning hair and very light blue eyes, answered in English with a heavy Slavic accent: "Four hundred crowns." Paul thought it was ridiculous to spend that much money when the metro was practically free, but, after a brief debate, Irina's fatigue prevailed over his stinginess.

"Are you sure you know how to get to this address?" she asked the driver.

"Yes, yes. Near very famous tower," he assured her.

"Which one?"

"Powder Gate," the taxi driver answered, referring to the 65 meter tall tower in the historic part of town which was begun in 1475 by King Vladislav II and finished in 1886 by Josef Mocker. The tower was used in the 17th century to store gunpowder and had become one of the main attractions of what was called Old Prague.

The mention of one of Prague's most famous sites whetted Paul's appetite for exploring the city on foot. "Sleep well tonight because when I visit a city, I like to walk at least ten miles a day," he warned his girlfriend once they had settled in the taxi. "I hope you brought sensible shoes in one of your dozen suitcases."

"I did, but they're all for my relatives," she informed him.

"Wear them out walking in Prague first," Paul advised.

As they entered the city, spectacularly beautiful scenes whizzed by their eyes. Paul made mental notes, recognizing in the darkness illuminated by art deco lamps the most famous sites from his last visit to Prague. "What a pearl of a town!" he exclaimed.

The taxi driver, proud of his city, couldn't agree more: "The most beautiful city in the world," he modestly concurred.

In the middle of a busy intersection in the modern part of town, the taxi driver stopped briefly at a stoplight in front of the statue of King Wenceslas.

"This was a nice, very brave ruler," he offered a concise history lesson.

Irina and Paul looked at the famous statue. Wenceslas, the Duke of Bohemia, rode upon his horse holding the Czech flag proudly in one hand. He was surrounded by four saints, who ostensibly approved of the alliance he had forged between the Czechs and the Saxons, which brought the Czech people into the Holy Roman Empire during the tenth century.

"Wenceslas was an educated, benevolent ruler of the Czechs," Paul whispered to Irina, having read the history of the statue in a guidebook during his previous visit.

"Very nice to meet people here. Happens often," the driver added. "We say in Czech, 'See you under horse's tail.'"

"At least they don't say, see you under the horse's ass," Paul commented.

"Shh…" Irina said, worried that the taxi driver might take offense at Paul's wacky sense of humor.

After taking a few winding, cobblestone streets, they ended up in a picturesque neighborhood perched on a hill. Both sides of the streets were lined with beautiful old mansions and barren trees whose branches quivered in the cold November wind.

"It's where rich people live," the driver announced, his eyes glimmering in anticipation of a generous tip. Paul, however, thought that the extra 200 crowns he was kind enough to charge them just because they were Western tourists would more than suffice. The taxi driver looked a little miffed when Paul and Irina said "Thank you" and "Goodbye" without offering him as much as an extra crown. "Cheap stinky Americans," he muttered in Czech under his breath once they left.

The cheap Americans rang the door bell of a luxurious house which was surrounded by an ornate, wiry fence. A brick walkway divided the now dormant garden which, Irina surmised, would overflow with colorful flowers in the spring. A majestic doorway with a Roman arch greeted them. At the third ring, an elegantly dressed lady opened the door. Her hair was dyed an unnatural color of burgundy and permed into brittle curls. She wore a white silk blouse brightened by a long strand of garnet beads. Her lipstick matched the striking color of the beads; her skirt, however, was dark and stern. A colorful silk shawl covered her shoulders, giving her outfit a distinctly Eastern European flair.

"Dobry den, Jmenuji se Paul and Irina," Paul said hello and introduced himself and his girlfriend, practically exhausting his entire Czech vocabulary right off the bat. The other two useful words he knew were zeny, meaning "women," and Kde je vece?, "Where is the bathroom?" In Irina's company, Paul thought, it was safe to assume that he wouldn't ask about zeny that often. By way of contrast, he was quite confident he'd get a lot of practice with the inquiry regarding the location of the public toilets.

Fortunately, their hostess spoke comprehensible English--with a heavy Czech accent: "You must be the Americans. My son told me. I'm Mme Svoboda. Velcome to Praha. Please. Come in," she said, ushering them into a magnificent hallway with gorgeous parquet floors.

Irina looked around with curiosity, her gaze sweeping the art on the walls. In the hallway she recognized an original Chagall (or at least a damn good imitation of it) alongside what must have been local art which represented scenes from Prague in a postimpressionist style.

"What beautiful paintings you've got!" Irina articulated her thoughts out loud.

Mrs. Svoboda beamed with pride.

"My youngest daughter Zelenka painted these," the hostess indicated the city scenes. She's very good artist. Zelenka means 'little innocent' in our language."

"Does it mean she's got little innocence, or little innocent one?" Paul asked.

Mrs. Svoboda looked confused.

"Paul, don't start with your jokes," Irina warned him. "He likes puns," she explained to the hostess with an embarrassed, apologetic smile.

"And zevy," Paul added, not one to miss an opportunity to highlight that fact.

"Name Zelenka means little innocent one," Mrs. Svoboda clarified.

"All the better. That's the kind I prefer anyway," Paul approved while Irina squeezed his hand.

The hostess invited them to sit down on the plush living room sofa. The room was tastefully decorated with international folkloric motifs—some, such as the rugs on the walls, looked Eastern European, probably Czech; others, most notably the masks and statuettes, seemed to be imported from Africa. Someone in the family must have been allowed to travel outside of Eastern Europe, Irina speculated.

"Does your son go abroad often?" she asked.

Mrs. Svoboda measured Irina with her deep dark eyes. The question apparently made her uncomfortable.

"I see all these African statues," Irina added.

"Oh yes," Mrs. Svoboda answered. "My older son is doctor. He went on to Africa when he was in medicine school. Government send him on scholarship," she explained.

"What about Viktor?"

"Viktor is playwright," the hostess explained. "Very much respected in our country. His plays is show at Magic Lantern."

"I can't wait to meet him," Irina declared.

"He comes to show you around the city tomorrow. He's very happy with your visit to us," Mrs. Svoboda said.

All this hospitality bodes well, Irina thought. As usual, Paul had worried for nothing.

"You are so skinny," Mrs. Svoboda suddenly leaned forward from her chair and grabbed Irina's arm with a gesture ominously reminiscent of Grandma Sara, who used to feed her six big meals a day in a misguided effort to fatten her up as a child. "Vat you want to eat?" the hostess asked.

"We're fine," Paul replied with a smile. "We had dinner on the plane."

"Yes, please don't bother, Mrs. Svoboda. That's so nice of you, but we're not hungry."

"Nonsense!" Mrs. Svoboda exclaimed, and Irina felt at that moment that she had truly entered Eastern Europe, where a "no" was a "yes" when it came to anything concerning food. "I have hotova jidla ready for you!"

"What's jidla?" Paul asked, trying to pronounce the word.

"It's nothing," Ms. Svoboda informed him. "Simple food. Very light," the hostess explained. "Come vith me!" she commanded in a tone that offered no alternatives.

"My family will behave exactly like this, only worse," Irina forewarned her boyfriend in a whisper. "Whatever you do, don't pick at the food and don't refuse it. Even if it's meat. There's no greater insult to a homemaker than refusing her cooking," she explained the protocol.

"We'll see," Paul whispered back, not ready to abandon a life-long ethic of vegetarianism for a few moments of courtesy.

In a small kitchen that was much more modest than the rest of the house, Mrs. Svoboda had prepared a hot dish of what she presented in Czech as smazeny rizek s bramborem and translated as fried pork filled with potatoes, along with a huge bowl of Sopsky salat, filled with fresh diced tomatoes, cucumbers, peppers, onions and feta cheese bathed in a delicious vinegar and olive oil dressing. The wonderful smell of the dishes reminded Irina of her own grandmother's cooking. Paul, however, was not even remotely tempted by the dish.

Mrs. Svoboda dispensed generous portions on beautiful China plates with a delicate flower motif around the rim, which she used only on special occasions.

"I'm vegetarian," Paul announced despite his girlfriend's former warning.

"What it means? He vants more potatoes?" Mrs. Svoboda asked, looking at Irina.

"He's saying that he really enjoys your salad," Irina translated Paul's remark from impolite to polite English.

Ms. Svoboda piled on a second large helping of salad into Paul's bowl.

He smiled awkwardly in thanks.

"Tomorrow I vill make for you much more food," the gracious hostess promised.

"Thank goodness we'll be walking it off," Paul said, winking at Irina. "Otherwise, you'll be rotund by the time we leave Prague."

"Speak for yourself!" Irina countered, shoveling a mouthful of fried pork into her mouth.

Feeling tired and underslept, after the meal the couple refused the customary turecka kava—or cup of Turkish coffee with ground beans on the bottom that the Czechs usually drink after a meal. The last thing they needed that evening was caffeine. Mrs. Svoboda led them to a small bedroom decorated with paintings and statues similar in style to those in the living room. The couple changed into their pajamas and sank gratefully into a soft, embracing bed covered by clean white sheets and a warm, goose feather blanket. They fell asleep almost instantly, in preparation for the big day of touring that awaited them.

Chapter 8

At 6:07 a.m., partly because of jetlag, partly because of the excitement of being in a beautiful historic city with the man she loved, Irina got out of bed feeling wide awake. She went to the window, opened it, leaned forward and breathed in the crisp November air, letting the breeze flirt with her hair. The rising sun caressed the orange rooftops of orderly rows of gray stone houses with glimmers of rosy light. Since Mrs. Svoboda's house was situated on a hill,

Irina could see from above the winding cobblestone streets making their way all the way to the Powder Gate. The gate's intricate gothic architecture, seen from afar, reminded her of the sand castles she used to make with her father when they were on vacation in the sea resort town of Constanta. They would patiently drip wet sand into tall, ornate towers, in modest imitation of the Notre Dame Cathedral which she had seen as a little girl in pictures, paintings and postcards.

Irina felt a warm hand on her shoulder. Paul had quietly snuck up next to her.

"My little porcupine," she said and kissed the dark curls behind his ear.

"We've got a lot to do today; we're not going to start on that," Paul warned, though he was already warming up to her.

"Only a little bit," Irina whispered, slipping her hand under his pajama top and caressing his chest with a slow, soothing motion.

"Ten minutes tops!" Paul announced as if they were training for an important race and had to beat a rival's record. They kissed with soft little pecks, then more deeply, embracing in front of the window which revealed the beauty of Prague like a fresh, undiscovered treasure.

They quickly removed each other's clothes, slipped on the floor and continued planting hungry kisses all over each other's bodies.

"Good morning!" Paul said afterwards.

"What a nice way to wake up," Irina responded.

"Oh, it's our usual way," Paul answered, feigning nonchalance. But he was secretly thrilled to rediscover his girlfriend's soft, velvety body after having feared that he had blown his chances with her. "Here's what I propose," he laid out their schedule in his habitual organized fashion: "We take a shower, eat breakfast, then meet with your friend or visit the old part of town by ourselves. Tomorrow we can focus on the modern part of town, with Wenceslas Square and other interesting sites. What do you say?"

"I say yes to everything," Irina responded. A smile of contentment brightened up her features.

"But I hope not to everyone!" Paul could never resist a bad joke. "Let's hop into the shower!" he proposed.

That, however, turned out to be easier said than done. Mrs. Svoboda's house was equipped with two small bathrooms, one of which was adjacent to Paul and Irina's bedroom. Neither bathroom, however, had what could be considered a shower. The bathtub was a small oval, in which the couple barely fit sitting facing one another. There was no curtain, so taking their usual shower together was out of the question. In fact, the shower consisted of a hose connected to the faucet with a rusty head attached to it. The water pressure was so low that only a feeble stream trickled out.

They looked at each other and both had the same idea.

"Bath?" Irina asked.

"Bath," Paul concurred. "What's this? A rock?" he asked, picking up a tan, hard rounded object of indeterminate color.

Irina leaned over and examined it closely: "That's the soap," she clarified, then reached over to the other edge of the bathtub and picked up a gray, hard rounded object. "This is a rock."

Paul could barely see the difference. "If you say so. But why do they need rocks in a bathtub? Is this the Czech equivalent of a rubber duckie?" he asked, puzzled.

"No. The rock is for your feet."

"Instead of the soap?"

"What a question!" Irina exclaimed, feeling vastly more cosmopolitan than her well-traveled boyfriend. "It's a pummel stone to soften the soles of your feet." She reached down to feel Paul's. "Look how rough yours are! Like a peasant's. People who want smooth feet rub away the dead layers of skin with a rock. Like this," she attempted to demonstrate.

Paul immediately pulled his feet towards his torso, splashing some of the water out of the tiny tub. "No thanks! I like my feet rough, just the way they are. It's good for traction. That way I don't slip and fall in the shower."

"Are you that hopeless?"

The question answered itself. "Are sure the soap is not a rock also?" Paul asked, attempting in vain to produce some lather.

"No, it's just cheap glycerin soap. In fact, enjoy this bath as much as you can, since in Romania you might not even get one. There's no hot water most of the time." She leaned forward. "Here, let me wash you. I know how to make lather," she said, placing the soap in the palm of her hand and rubbing it circularly under the thin, lukewarm stream of water.

When they were all done, they dressed quickly—both in blue jeans, since, particularly in Paul's case, it was futile to try to hide the fact they were American—and went into the kitchen. Mrs. Svoboda had told them on the previous evening that they could help themselves to anything they wanted for breakfast, so Irina began heating water to make a pot of coffee with the instant mix she had brought along from the States.

"No, no, not this vay!" Mrs. Svoboda showed up in the kitchen, with a flowery apron already tied around her waist. "This is junk!" the hostess pointed out referring to the perfectly good container of Maxwell House. "I make real coffee for you," she announced, proceeding to heat up a pot of Turkish coffee.

Moving very quickly, she lay the table and placed on it fresh bread, homemade jam made from the rose leaves she had collected that summer from her own garden, prune marmalade, strawberry jam as well as honey and butter. Irina and Paul helped themselves to generous portions of bread, butter and jam while enjoying the aroma and potency of freshly brewed coffee.

"Thanks so much, Mrs. Svoboda, this is delicious. But you don't have to go to all this trouble for us," Irina said.

"You're so kind," Paul chimed in.

"It's nothing," Mrs. Svoboda said.

The breakfast made Irina feel nostalgic. It was exactly what her Grandma Marta used to make every morning for their family. No matter how scarce the food may have been in Romania, her grandmother somehow managed to stash away goods whenever they were available. She made several jars of jam during the summer and stored them for the harsher fall and winter days, when the food shortages were more severe.

"My son comes to see you this morning," Mrs. Svoboda announced. "He shows you around Praha."

"That's great!" Irina declared. "Please, come sit down and eat with us, Mrs. Svoboda," she suggested, seeing their hostess spin around like a top in the effort to please them but not tasting a bite herself.

"It's okay. I'm not hungry in the morning. Vhen you get old, you lose appetite," Mrs. Svoboda answered with a sigh.

"At least have some coffee," Irina persisted.

Mrs. Svoboda poured herself a cup of Turkish coffee, sat down at the table and smiled at Irina. They looked into each other's eyes and Irina thought she saw in her hostess' eyes the glimmer of intimacy and affection. "I tell Viktor to take you to Celetna Street. Very close and very nice. The Art Museum is there," Mrs. Svoboda said.

Irina nodded while Paul took out a pen and a little notebook from his shirt pocket and wrote down Mrs. Svoboda's suggestion.

"Have you lived here a long time? In this beautiful house, I mean?" Irina inquired.

"Very long time," Mrs. Svoboda answered, after taking a sip of her coffee. "This vas my grandmother's house, built before the communist days. My parents lived here. My husband and I also lived here. Now, since he passed, I'm all alone... I don't like it so much any more," she said with a sad smile.

"I'm sorry to hear that ..." Irina replied.

"It's nothing," Mrs. Svoboda answered, wiping away a tear from the corner of her eye with the back of her hand.

Irina once read in a Romanian writer's prison memoirs that in conversation people don't know how to react to other people's pain, so when a sad topic comes up, they usually change the subject to something more cheerful. And that, the writer said, only makes the situation worse, since sharing one's suffering can be cathartic. "When did your husband pass away?" Irina asked, making a conscious effort to stay on the subject.

"Two years ago," Mrs. Svoboda answered raising two fingers in the air. "He was a good man. And a good medical."

"He was a doctor?" Paul asked.

"Yes. Many important people in our government vent to see him," she declared proudly. "It's very lonely in this big house vithout him."

"Fortunately you have your children," Irina pointed out.

"Eh, children have own lives," Mrs. Svoboda answered. "They shouldn't vorry about an old voman like me."

"You're not old," Irina objected. Their hostess, she thought, was definitely what was known in her own country as a dama bine, meaning a lady who looks distinguished and dresses well.

"Eh! Vithout husband it doesn't matter," Mrs. Svoboda said.

"Would you like to join us in our tour of Prague today?" Irina offered, hoping to cheer her up a little.

Paul darted a disapproving glance at his girlfriend. "Irina, we've imposed enough on Mrs. Svoboda as it is," he said, since he planned to walk fast and see as much of the Old Town as possible.

Mrs. Svoboda didn't miss the subtle hint: "No, I von't go. You are young. You should go with my son. Viktor vill show you everything."

As if on cue, the door bell rang. Mrs. Svoboda wiped both hands on her apron, got up and walked quickly to open the door.

She returned to the kitchen with a smile on her face accompanied by a young looking man with prematurely white hair whom she introduced as "my son, Viktor."

"Nice to meet you," Viktor shook hands with his guests. "Jean-Pierre is a good friend of mine," he said, adding, "and his friends are my friends." Viktor's light blue eyes twinkled with warmth.

Paul couldn't help but notice that Viktor spoke perfect English with a subtle mixture of Slavic and British accents and dressed in the same manner as Western intellectuals, in what Paul referred to as "conference uniform." He wore a white shirt with a wool pullover on top of it and a gray blazer on top of that and a nice pair of twill gray pants to match. Irina, not accustomed to academic codes, was more positively impressed by Viktor. Above all, she enjoyed the fact that, so far, everyone in Czechoslovakia was treating them well. Apparently, it didn't hurt to keep on good terms with a famous artist like Jean-Pierre, she congratulated herself on her masterful diplomacy towards her ex-boyfriend.

"Have you been here long?" Viktor asked them.

"We arrived last night," Paul answered.

"Did you get a good rest?"

"Yes, we're grateful to you and your mother for your hospitality," Irina replied.

"It's our pleasure," Viktor said. "My mother told me this morning on the phone that you're interested in seeing the old city today. I took the day off work, so I'd be happy to be your tour guide. And tonight, if you haven't made other plans, my wife and I would like to invite you over to our house for dinner."

"That's so nice of you. We'd really appreciate that," Irina answered.

"I suggest that we start with Celetna Street, which goes from the Old Town Square all the way to the Powder Tower. We can see many beautiful historical houses en route and the Czech Museum of Fine Arts, which is world famous for its Cubism. Do you like Cubist art?" Viktor turned to Irina. "Jean-Pierre told me that you're studying to be an artist. He said you're very talented."

"Jean-Pierre told you I'm talented?" Irina asked, feeling very flattered.

"Yes, of course." Viktor confirmed with a smile.

"He was just being polite," Paul interjected.

Irina gave her boyfriend one of her lightning bolt looks: "I'm impressed to see that you know Jean-Pierre so well, especially since you've never met him." When she addressed their host, however, her voice became soft and sweet: "Well, like everyone else, I love Picasso," she answered Viktor's original question.

"We have very interesting Cubist painters also," Viktor replied. "It's quite chilly today. You might want to wear coats," he suggested, seeing that Paul and Irina were about to head out without jackets.

They walked side by side on Celetna Street, Irina and Paul holding hands; Viktor with his hands behind his back--the gait of an intellectual, Irina thought. Old Town Square was quite spectacular. The buildings around it congruously combined different architectural styles. One could see the imposing presence of the gray Gothic tower in the back; while the Romanesque buildings forming the square itself shone in the feeble November sun in warm hues of yellow, tan, light pink and orange.

"This part of town used to be our market. It was built a very long time ago, starting in the tenth century," Viktor explained. "I guess that's why they call it Old Town," he quipped. "Of course, everything is relative since the New Town isn't exactly a newborn either. It was built in the fourteenth-century."

"That's ancient by American standards," Irina commented. "In fact, that's part why I like Europe so much. You can really see its history."

"Well, not everything's great about Eastern Europe," Viktor commented.

They approached an impressive building that stood out like a diamond among pearls. Everything was beautiful in Prague; one didn't even know where to look first. Yet somehow this building, with its Neoclassical elegance, stole the show.

Viktor noticed the admiration in his guests' eyes. "This is the Estates Theater," he said. "It was built in the late eighteenth-century, after the French tradition. And it became one of the most famous theaters in Europe. Even the French actress Rachel played here during the nineteenth century. Would you like to step inside?"

Paul and Irina most certainly did.

With its rounded arches and gilded ceiling, the theater combined material opulence with the spiritual beauty that elevates the senses. It reminded Irina of the Roman basilicas she and her mother had seen during their brief stay in Italy before immigrating to America.

"Wow! This is awesome," Irina exclaimed, gazing at the magnificent golden ceiling, for the first time in her life using the expression "awesome" as an understatement, not a hyperbole.

Viktor smiled, flattered by his guests' appreciation of his native city.

Next they walked down Charles Street, where, Viktor informed them, the Jesuits used to live and study during the twelfth century. As they toured through the old city, the hours slipped by unnoticed. Although she didn't generally like walking as much as Paul did, Irina was so distracted by the history and beauty of Prague that she didn't feel discomfort or even the need to rest.

"This must be the most beautiful city in the world," she declared with the tone of someone converting to a new religion.

"Too bad the government destroys everything," Viktor said quietly under his breath. His attitude towards his country was clearly ambivalent, Paul noted. Viktor seemed very proud of Prague and his country's rich history, yet at the same time he dropped several not-so-subtle hints that he strongly disapproved of the current regime.

"Well, at least Jake's better than Petrescu," Irina gave her stock answer about any leader in Eastern Europe with the possible exception of Enver Hoxha.

"Yes, he's not quite as bad. But we're getting very tired of this," Viktor replied, his glance surveying the street. "People are not happy here."

Paul and Irina looked around. For the first time that day they focused their attention on the people inhabiting this beautiful city. They were struck by the contrast between their somber faces and the pastel cheerfulness of the architectural surroundings. Perhaps it was normal that people wore dark outfits in late fall, Irina thought, observing a marked preference for gray or black coats and fur hats. Yet what seemed a shade darker than the clothes was people's demeanor. They rushed by these historic sites looking serious, preoccupied, closed in on themselves. Even beautiful young women, Paul noticed, walked quickly and defensively, without as much as a friendly look or a smile.

Chapter 9

Viktor and Ekaterina Svoboda lived in a more modest apartment than Viktor's mother. They occupied a small two-bedroom in a modern section of Prague filled with rectangular cloned buildings.

Viktor introduced the American couple to his wife, a tall, slim blond with cool gray eyes and high cheekbones. "Pleased to meet you," Ekaterina said in a soft voice with a slight Slavic accent, limply shaking hands with her guests. Never failing to register first impressions no matter how wrong they proved to be, Irina decided that Ekaterina was chilly, perhaps even snobby. Paul, however, instinctively liked their hostess. For him personality in women, unless it was absolutely atrocious, didn't matter quite as much as looks, and he thought that Ekaterina looked pretty good.

In sharp contrast to his reticent wife, during the course of the day Viktor had warmed up to his guests and treated them like old friends. He ushered the couple into a living room furnished with a sofa, a dining room table surrounded by six upholstered chairs and a 1950's T.V. set which looked downright antique, reminding Irina of the black and white television set they had in Romania.

"We don't watch much T.V.," Viktor remarked, noticing Irina's interest. "There's nothing too see. Just government propaganda."

"Viktor..." Ekaterina cautioned, giving him a meaningful glance and pointing towards the radiators, which in Czechoslovakia, like in Romania, served the convenient double function of sometimes heating apartments and always monitoring conversations via hidden microphones.

Viktor, however, was undaunted: "Let them listen! What do I care?" he answered defiantly. "There's nothing they can do about it anyway. After what happened in Poland, Hungary and East Germany, everybody's talking. What are they going to do? Arrest the whole country?"

"These are uncertain times," his wife cautioned. "We don't know yet which way the wind will blow. We feel bold now, but tomorrow the winds may change, like they did before," she said, alluding to the Prague Spring. Ekaterina then turned to her guests: "How did you enjoy your tour of the city today?"

"We loved it," Irina answered.

"Prague is gorgeous," Paul seconded that opinion.

"Please, sit down," Ekaterina invited them to take a seat at the dinner table.

She asked many polite questions but didn't talk much herself and got up frequently to serve her guests. She had prepared a typical Czech dinner which, since it didn't include meat, everyone, including the finicky Paul, could enjoy. She served a fresh salad similar to the one they had the night before along with pstruh, or trout, and generous portions of french fries. For dessert, she offered them palacinka, or delicious crepes served with a fresh jam that, Irina suspected given its familiar taste, her mother-in-law had probably made. Although neither of the women drank alcohol and Paul had only a glass of red wine, Viktor seemed to take to the wine, emptying half the bottle and becoming increasingly talkative. His wife looked at him from time to time with apprehension, hopelessly trying to contain what she considered to be a potentially dangerous overflow of information. Most of the dinner conversation, to Ekaterina's obvious chagrin, centered around Czech politics.

"So what's Milo Jake like?" Paul asked, taking his host's lead and talking as freely as if he were in a Western country. "He presents himself as a reformer."

"Reformer?" Viktor snorted. "He's an illiterate peasant!"

"Viktor..." his wife intervened, gently placing her hand upon his.

"He talks about Gorbachev and perestroika while doing the same old communist shenanigans as Husak before him. He made many promises, but nothing's changed since he became General Secretary in '87. We haven't seen perestroika in Czechoslovakia since the Prague Spring," Viktor pursued.

"So Dubcek was a genuine reformer?" Irina wanted to confirm.

"Sure. That's why he got punished for it," Viktor answered, then paused to reflect further. "Look: none of these communist leaders are ideal. But at least Dubcek wanted a democratic communism, if that's not a contradiction in terms. And it might have worked if the Soviets hadn't invaded our country."

"Would you like more trout?" Ekaterina got up halfway from her seat eager to serve her guests more food, in the hope of changing the subject of conversation.

"No thank you," Irina answered.

"Only half of one, please. It's delicious," Paul complimented the hostess in his most gracious tone, which he reserved for attractive women. Ekaterina rewarded him with a partial smile and a whole fish.

"It's amazing you have the guts to call Jake a peasant. Petrescu is one too, quite literally in fact, but if anybody called the spade a spade in Romania," Irina said looking towards the heater, "they'd land directly in prison. ... And that's if they were lucky."

"That used to happen here as well," Viktor said. "Don't think we were that much freer. But now that other communist countries have shown some courage, it started a domino effect, at least in changing our attitude. It's like with the emperor's new clothes. Once one person dares to speak out and say that the emperor is naked, other people see the truth also. And eventually the whole sham's exposed." He paused to take another sip of wine. "Besides, Jake's a buffoon," he continued. "He makes a lot of public gaffes, like Khruschev used to. It's impossible not to laugh at him when he can't even speak his own language properly. For instance, he was talking about a Czech pop singer who earned a lot of money and said 'Nobody of us earns so much!' Even fellow communists make fun of him."

"Compared to Petrescu, he sounds like an intellectual," Irina observed.

"Well by Czech standards he's an oaf. And politically, if you compare him to someone like Gorbachev, he's a dinosaur."

"Then why don't the communists just resign and let the Czech people choose a democratic course, like they did in Poland?" Paul asked.

"What a naïve question, Paul!" Irina commented. "Only a Westerner could ask such a thing."

"It's a perfectly reasonable question," Paul defended himself.

"The thirst for power's universal," Viktor answered philosophically. "In Poland Solidarity struggled for ten years to democratize the country. Hungary never really wanted communism to begin with, so for them it was a lot easier to get rid of it. East Germany has always had West German support. The communists in Czechoslovakia aren't going to give up their hold unless we force them to."

"What do you mean we?" Paul inquired.

"We the intellectuals. We the students. We the artists. We the people. It takes guts, foresight and unity to overthrow communist regimes," Viktor declared.

"Either that or utter recklessness," Ekaterina added.

Viktor smiled indulgently at his wife, then turned towards his guests: "She's always on my case about the risks I take."

"Thanks to his courage, he was roughed up twice by Secret Police agents," Ekaterina informed Paul and Irina. "They took away our communist party membership and privileges. They forbid us to leave the country. They demoted us from our jobs. They've been following us for years. Hooligans destroyed our car. They bugged our apartment. They banned Viktor's plays. I'm tired of living like this, in constant fear. Let other people be heroes, not my husband."

"Spoken like a true martyr!" Viktor said jovially. "But a country where everyone expects others to be courageous is a country that will forever remain in shackles," he added.

"Very nice words. I promise to write them down for posterity when you're serving your life sentence," his wife retorted.

Viktor smiled. "Do you mind if I smoke?" he asked his guests, taking a lighter and a pack of Marlboro cigarettes from his pocket.

"Not at all," Irina said, resolving to offer him a few packs of cigarettes she had brought along as gifts for her family as a token of her appreciation for his hospitality.

Paul, who hated smoke, didn't reply.

"Viktor, you promised to quit," Ekaterina reminded her husband.

"I did!" her husband protested. "I used to smoke three packs a day and now I'm down to almost nothing--only two and a half."

"American research conclusively proves that smoking causes lung cancer," Paul chimed in with the medical report.

"That's okay. In Czechoslovakia men don't live long enough to die of lung cancer," Viktor countered, exhaling a puff of smoke through the side of his mouth.

Europeans smoke like chimneys, Paul observed, recalling seeing similar suicidal behavior during his previous trips. Well, nobody's perfect. "Is Adamec, the Prime Minister, any better than Jake?" he asked his host, returning to the subject of politics.

Viktor shook his head. "He's less of a clown than Jake and slightly better educated," Viktor replied between puffs. "But their policies are identical. They don't want anything to change. It's all rhetoric."

"Who do you think should lead Czechoslovakia?" Irina was curious to know.

Viktor chuckled. "Well, I may be a little biased, but I can't imagine anyone better for this country than my friend Vaclav Havel. The only problem is that he hates politics…"

"I read his *Largo Desolato* in one of my drama classes," Irina showed off her vast knowledge of culture.

"Did you like it?" Viktor asked.

"I don't remember," Irina admitted, sounding slightly less impressive to her hosts. "But I remember loving Ibsen," she attempted to correct the mistake of mentioning the only play she must have skipped in the drama course.

"Well, Vaclav's not only a great playwright," Viktor praised his friend and colleague, "but also someone with great vision. And integrity. I predict that, if the dinosaurs push him much further, he'll end up leading our country straight into democracy."

"And I predict that if you talk much more, you'll end up leading us straight into labor camp," Ekaterina offered what she considered to be an even more plausible hypothesis.

Far from feeling threatened, Viktor chuckled, amused by his wife's comment.

"If Havel doesn't want to do it, then how come you don't take political initiative?" Paul asked Viktor.

"I'm not a public figure," Viktor replied. "Besides, my wife won't let me," he added with a wink.

Ekaterina nodded. For once, she was in full agreement with her husband.

Chapter 10

"It looks like we're on our own today," Paul announced on Friday morning, after he and Irina had breakfast together and Mrs. Svoboda left for the market. Viktor had been kind enough to take the day off from work on Thursday to show them around the Old Town. Unfortunately, he couldn't take Friday off as well. He made it quite clear, however, that he had welcomed the break since he disliked his new job. During dinner the previous evening, Ekaterina had explained to her guests that as a result of his dissident activities, her husband had been demoted from a prestigious position as Professor of Drama at the Charles University in Prague to the post of Assistant Editor for a communist journal. Viktor called his new job a form of "psychological torture" and though he said it with a smile, he didn't seem to be joking.

Paul flipped to the page marked New Town in his old tour guide of Prague. "Today I want to show you the most interesting places I saw the last time I was here," he told Irina, who was applying the last touches of make-up in front of the dresser mirror. "Here they are," Paul indicated with his index finger. "Wenceslas

Square, the National Theater and New Town Hall, all clustered together. You haven't really seen Prague if you haven't visited these places."

"When was the last time you were here?" Irina asked, pressing her lips together to distribute the lipstick more evenly.

Paul looked up from his guide book, trying to remember: "It must have been in 1982. Geesh… Has it been that long?"

"Did you come here for a conference or on vacation?" Irina put her lipstick back into her purse and sat down next to her boyfriend on the edge of the bed.

"On my honeymoon," Paul replied.

His answer took Irina by surprise: "You mean you were here with Mary?"

"Who else? We stayed in a beautiful old hotel in Old Town called Hotel Central. It was very posh, but still, like everything else around here, very reasonably priced."

"So which do you like better?" Irina asked with a mysterious smile.

"To tell you the truth, personally I prefer to stay at a hotel, especially since they're so affordable in Eastern Europe. The Svoboda family is as nice as can be, but I don't like disturbing people. Plus I prefer to have the freedom to come and go as I please," Paul answered an altogether different question.

"No, I mean which trip do you prefer? The one with Mary or the one with me?" Irina reformulated her question.

"Of course I prefer the one with you!" Paul answered. "Mary and I divorced because we didn't get along." After a moment's reflection, however, he added: "Although the honeymoon part was pretty fun. We visited almost every capital in Eastern Europe. We went to Prague, Budapest, Warsaw, Belgrade and Sofia. But we didn't make it to Bucharest for some reason."

"What have you got against Romania?" Irina asked.

"I was saving it for you…." Paul answered diplomatically.

"Why do you think your marriage to Mary ended up so badly?" Irina returned to her original line of inquiry.

"I already told you why millions of times. We were never that compatible to begin with. Plus she was very young and wanted to explore life on her own. Too bad she realized that only after we got married. It would have saved us both a lot of trouble if we had known that from the very beginning."

"Did she love you?"

"Probably. At first. Who knows?" Paul became less and less confident of his answer.

"If she had truly loved you, it wouldn't matter that she was so young. My parents married when they were only twenty-one and they're still happy together."

Paul had his own opinions on the subject, however: "I don't think it's a good idea to marry too young. It's better to get a lot of dating experience to see what you want in life. That way you have no regrets later on about missing out on anything."

"Then why did you propose to me? I'm not even twenty yet," Irina asked him with apprehension in her eyes. "Or are you withdrawing the proposal?"

Paul smiled crookedly, like a man caught in a bind. "I thought your answer was that we should take it slower. You told me I'm on probation," he evaded her question.

Irina's eyes didn't leave his. "I know what I said. But what do you say?"

Paul looked at his girlfriend, with her delicate features, rosy lips and questioning gaze. Despite all of his theories about dating and marriage, he followed his instinct and stood by his words. "When I said people shouldn't marry young, I wasn't talking about you. You're the exception that confirms the rule," he replied. "Whenever you're ready, we'll get married."

"But aren't you scared we'll make the same mistakes that you did with Mary?" Irina pursued.

Having a case of Obsessive Compulsive Disorder whose main symptom was focusing upon negative possibilities, Paul preferred to avoid such anxiety-provoking inquiries—especially when on vacation. Nonetheless, he sensed that Irina needed his reassurance: "What do you want me to say? Sometimes I am. But I trust you more than I did Mary. And we're more compatible than I was with her. Nothing's certain in life. But I believe our love's real and strong. That's the best answer I can give you. You know I'm not the type to gush..."

"Paul, you're so sweet! That's all the gushing I need," Irina replied and gave him a hug. Something seemed to have changed for the better in his attitude, she thought. Before they had broken up, he had the tendency to do a kind of waltz, taking two steps forward and one backward in their relationship. To Irina, this was very unsettling. She wanted to be able to count on the man she loved, not dance around the issue of commitment, never knowing where he stood. But now they seemed to be on firmer ground.

The couple put on their coats and headed out the door to take the subway to New Town, which, as Viktor had told them and as the guide book confirmed, was founded in 1348 by Charles IV. Once they sat next to one another on the subway, Paul began to read the guide to Irina: " 'The New Town is laid out around three large market-places: the Hay Market (Senovazne Square), the Cattle Market (Charles Square) and the Horse Market (Wenceslas Square).' We've already seen the statue from the taxi on the way here, remember?" But it's definitely worth seeing it again up-close and personal," he added parenthetically, then continued reading: "During the nineteenth-century, much of the New Town was demolished and rebuilt, giving it the appearance it has today."

Once they reached their metro stop--the National Museum (Narodni Museum), Irina and Paul hopped out of the train and walked to the museum, which was housed in a large, neo-Renaissance building made of gray stone with a greenish roof.

"Do you want to step inside?" Paul turned to his girlfriend.

"Sure, why not? We've got time," Irina responded.

"This is kind of like the Czech version of the Smithsonian," Paul remarked, looking over the list of exhibits in the lobby. They walked hand in hand, pausing to examine the displays on the history of Bohemia, Moravia and Slovakia as well as at the zoological, anthropological and paleontological collections, the museum's main attractions.

"Do you think the dinosaurs will give up power, like Viktor predicts?" Irina asked, reminded of the subject by the paleontological collection.

"Just because they're dinosaurs, doesn't mean they'll go extinct," Paul replied.

"What about the domino effect theory?" Irina asked, feeling sympathetic to Viktor's hypothesis. "Now that some countries in Eastern Europe have overthrown communism, don't you think the others will follow?"

Paul considered the issue for a moment, then replied: "Maybe. But I don't think it's inevitable. I agree with Ekaterina."

"Only because she's pretty," Irina interjected, testing him.

"No, not just because of that. Although it always helps," Paul added with a wink. His girlfriend didn't seem amused. "Seriously, I don't believe that revolution is inevitable. And even if it happens, we can't be sure it will succeed. It may be violent and lead to political instability or to an even worse government. One can never tell. I'm not as optimistic as you and Viktor seem to be about the progress of democracy."

"If you had spent a few years under the Petrescu regime, you'd have more respect for democratic government, Irina countered."

Paul bristled at this charge: "That's your answer to everything. If there's one thing you anti-communists have in common with the communists it is a blind idealism. This irrational belief in the linear progress of humanity towards some utopic goal."

"This is not about utopic goals at all," Irina vehemently disagreed. "It's about making life better than it is. Other Eastern European countries gave the Czech people a spark. It's now up to them to start the fire."

"Fire burns," Paul concluded his side of the argument.

Next they visited the spectacular National Theater Opera, a beautiful nineteenth-century building that staged drama, opera and ballet performances. Irina was impressed by its ornate architecture and elegant rows of plush seats, which, through their beauty and majesty, carried you away to the bygone era of aristocratic balls, salons and opulent glamour.

Afterwards, Paul suggested that they take a peek at New Town Hall, a building which, with its triangular reddish-orange roofs, gothic halls, ribbed vaults and Renaissance tower, reminded them of a castle from Grimm's fairytales. By the time they had finished touring these landmarks, it was already two o'clock. Paul was hungry and Irina felt a little tired, so they decided to step into a little restaurant in Wenceslas Square to rest and have a light lunch. Both ordered a bowl of zelnacka polevka—a simple meal consisting of a tasty cabbage soup with dark peasant bread on the side. Paul drank two mugs of the famous Czech beer, while Irina enjoyed a glass of sparkling soda water.

"Who says there's no food around here?" Paul commented, feeling pleasantly full.

"Oh, come on! You can't be that naïve. You know very well that most of the locals can't afford these restaurants. They're mainly for party members and Western tourists. I'm willing to bet that this meal alone is worth a whole month's salary for most Czechs," Irina said.

"And do you think most Americans can afford fancy restaurants?" Paul retorted.

"This isn't a fancy restaurant. It's just got food, that's all."

The couple spent almost two hours at the restaurant, debating politics and society, eating, drinking, and going over the details of their upcoming trip to Romania.

Propelled by a surge of renewed energy, after the meal, Paul announced: "I saved the best for last: I propose that we go see the famous horseman statue." Irina agreed. When they stepped out of the restaurant, however, something was definitely amiss.

"What are all these people doing here?" Paul wondered, looking with amazement at thousands of people, most of them very young, about Irina's age, marching towards the center of Wenceslas Square. "Apparently we've chosen the wrong time to visit the horseman statue. Every tourist and his grandmother must have had the same idea."

"Paul, these aren't tourists! Can't you see we're in the middle of a revolution here?"

"Let's not exaggerate... It's just a little protest."

"You call this little? There must be literally tens of thousands of people gathered here!" Irina pointed out, gazing at the incoming stream of students pouring into the square.

Even Paul was obliged to admit that things looked pretty serious. "Maybe we should stay a little bit longer in the restaurant," he prudently suggested. "We can order some dessert. You know, just until the situation calms down."

Irina stared at her boyfriend as if he were from another planet: "Aren't you even a little curious to find out what's going on?"

"We can watch everything from the restaurant," Paul bravely suggested.

"You and I are not the same type of person," Irina said with disappointment.

Paul didn't respond to this provocation, however. His attention was now focused on the protest. He tried to make out what the students were saying. They were chanting not only in Czech, but also in English, most likely to attract the attention of the foreign media, in case any showed up. They yelled and put up signs saying, "Down with the dinosaurs!" "Communists get out!" and "Dinosaurs resign!"

Some of the restaurant staff had stepped out unto the front porch to observe the demonstration. Paul turned to one of the restaurant waiters standing next to him--a thin, middle-aged man with short, graying hair and glasses--and asked him in English: "Pardon me, do you know why all these students have gathered here?"

"They protest murder of Czech students by the Nazis," the waiter explained.

"Isn't it a little late for that?" Paul inquired.

"They vant to show the communists are as bad as the Nazis. They are really protesting against the Jake government," the waiter clarified. "These kids have lot of courage," he added admiringly, with a low whistle.

"Who are those military men?" Irina asked, pointing to a formation of white-helmeted and red-bereted soldiers that had surrounded a large group of students clustered around the statue.

"Oh, oh... this is very bad sign," the waiter said. "It is the communist police. Hooligans!" he shouted towards them.

"They look so young..." Irina couldn't help but comment, noticing that the police, especially those wearing white helmets, had youthful, innocent faces much like the student protesters.

There were a few heated exchanges between the students and the police. Since, apparently, the students still refused to disperse, the tension between the two groups mounted.

Paul noticed that the police began to strike the students with their white truncheons. They also handcuffed some of the protesters closest to the statue who refused to leave and kept on chanting.

"Why are they hitting the students?" Paul asked the waiter next to him, taken aback by the escalating violence. "Can't they see that this is a peaceful demonstration?" Some of students were attempting to give the soldiers flowers; others knelt on the ground with raised arms chanting in Czech. A group of students started singing louder.

"Our government doesn't vant any demonstrations," the waiter replied. "Except for phony ones they organize," he added in a tone filled with disgust.

"What are they saying?" Irina asked.

The waiter, who grew increasingly perturbed by the turn of events, translated: "They're singing 'We have bare hands' and the brutes are still hitting them! Vat monsters!" he said, then cupped his hands and bellowed something loudly in Czech. "They're butchers. Criminals. Jake's jackals," he subsequently translated the epithets into English for the benefit of the American couple.

Under the growing threat of violence, the large crowd of students began to disperse. People ran in all directions. Although the police had put an end to the demonstration, however, they couldn't dissipate the sense of anger and frustration that had provoked it. After the students had been forced to leave, people of all ages flocked back to the site of the protest. That evening, Paul and Irina watched mesmerized as parents, brothers, sisters, grandparents and children built shrines around Wenceslas Square, laying down candles that glowed in the twilight, to honor the students who been beaten, arrested, wounded and maybe even killed that afternoon. Some family members even left photographs of their loved ones to commemorate the tragedy, to reignite the hope. An elderly woman with a handkerchief tied around her head, who reminded Irina of a Romanian peasant, kneeled in silent prayer by a candle, the tears flowing down her cheeks. By nightfall, a large circle of candles illuminated the area around the statue of the brave King Wenceslas like a crown of light. That Friday, November 17th 1989, Prague itself seemed aglow in defiance of the government's brutality. Everything was fluid, filled with emotion. Even without understanding a word of Czech, you saw it in people's gestures, on their faces. Life just couldn't continue as it was.

Chapter 11

Two days after the student demonstration, Viktor showed up at his mother's house. Anticipating a larger wave of government violence, Paul and Irina had barely stepped outside. Mrs. Svoboda kept them abreast of the latest developments, however, at least as far as she could find out from neighbors or at the market. Rumors circulated that dozens of students had been killed, hundreds were wounded and dozens more were arrested during the Wenceslas Square protest. Viktor, however, had newer and more accurate information than his mother since he had just returned from a dissident meeting at the Magic Lantern Theater, where the main speaker had been his good friend and leader of the opposition, Vaclav Havel. As soon as he set foot in the apartment, Paul and Irina dispensed with formalities and asked him about the rumors they had heard from Mrs. Svoboda.

"It's not that bad in number, but it's much worse in fact," the playwright replied aphoristically.

"What do you mean?" Paul asked.

Viktor sat down on the sofa and crossed his legs. "As far as we know, one student was killed and dozens were wounded. Many were arrested overnight, but most were released the following morning. Still, if we don't respond to this brutality immediately to nip it in the bud, we can kiss the idea of freedom goodbye."

Irina nodded in agreement, but Paul wasn't persuaded: "I agree it's terrible that one student was killed and several were wounded, but this wasn't exactly a massacre like people believed."

Viktor looked at him with tired eyes: "So what? That's how it starts. If you don't do anything when the government takes one life, then it will take many more. They're seeing how we react; how much they can get away with. Like Stalin did at first."

"Let's not exaggerate! There's no comparison," Paul objected.

"Have you ever heard of Ryutin?" Viktor challenged him.

Paul hadn't, but Irina had: "I learned about him in a Soviet history class I took last year," she announced proudly. "Isn't he the one who had the courage to speak out against the communist regime even before Stalin started the mass purges?"

"That's right," Viktor confirmed. He then turned to Paul, directing the rest of his explanation to him: "In 1930, Ryutin was lucid enough to predict that Stalin would assume total power and launch on a path of destruction. He asked the communist party to remove Stalin from office. And at that point, if the Comitburo had been united, they probably could have. Especially the right wing, which was still strong--Bukharin, Rykov and others. But they didn't show enough backbone. Basically, all they did was oppose Stalin's proposal that Ryutin be executed, which amounted to doing nothing. And in 1934, after Kirov's murder, it was too late. By then, Stalin was unstoppable. His Secret Police, the *NKVD*, had infiltrated the whole fabric of Soviet society. That's how millions of people were sent to labor camps or murdered from '36 through '38."

By now, Paul felt comfortable enough with Viktor to indulge in his characteristic sarcasm: "Thanks for the history lesson, professor, but I'm still not persuaded that Jake is a Stalin."

"He's not yet and, who knows, may never become one. My point is that we must never give the government the chance to terrorize our people. As Stalin himself once said, 'The death of one person is a tragedy; the death of a million a mere statistic.' One student died on Friday and that's a tragedy. We must do everything we can to honor his life and show our government that we won't tolerate this; that they can't get away with murdering our kids."

"I totally agree," Irina interjected. "But what can you do? Do you have the power to overthrow the government?"

"I'm not sure. What I do know, however, is that it's worth trying. Now is as good a time as ever," Viktor responded, seeming very agitated. He lit a cigarette. Paul immediately got up and opened the window. "At least that's what Vaclav seems to think," he added more softly, as an afterthought.

"You talked to him about it?" Irina asked, impressed.

Viktor nodded. "We had a meeting at The Magic Lantern today. Basically, Vaclav feels that the students have shown us the way. Before the police started beating them up, we thought we should be cautious for the sake of our children. You know, to make sure they had a future, could go to the university, get a decent job. In a country where everything depends upon your communist dossier, people were afraid to put a stain on their children's record. But now that the government has shown us that it doesn't hesitate killing our children, we're sick and tired of being cautious."

"Your mother told us that even high school kids were protesting earlier today."

"That's right," Viktor confirmed. He laughed as one does at something absurd or unexpected. "That goes to show that kids are much more courageous than their parents. A large group of high school students gathered downtown and put up banners saying 'Parents come with us, we are your children!' How can we possibly refuse their call? As Vaclav said at the meeting, if we weren't strong enough to lead the way, the least we can do is follow our children's example."

"But what does that mean, practically speaking?" Paul was curious to know. "Will you organize an even bigger demonstration?"

"We've called for a nationwide strike starting tomorrow. A total work-stoppage. But even that won't be enough. Vaclav thinks we should engage in peaceful negotiations with the government, meaning of course, with Adamec. You can't really talk to Jake."

"And what do you think?" Irina asked, looking at Viktor straight in the eyes.

"Well, of course I go along with his decision. But, personally, I'm of the opinion that talking with the communists can't lead to democracy, which is our ultimate goal. Adamec will make some nice vague promises as he usually does and that's all. I'm for staging a coup d'etat. An all out, total revolution against the current regime. No dialogue, no compromises. After all, Czechoslovakia isn't Poland. We don't have ten years of Solidarity behind us. And there's nothing to negotiate anyway. We don't want communism in any shape or form. We want democracy."

Emboldened by Viktor's call for revolution, Paul and Irina crawled out of their shell. Instead of hiding in Mrs. Svoboda's house, they valiantly spent Monday afternoon walking around Prague. To be afraid, Viktor had told them, meant to give in; to accept defeat at the very moment when victory becomes possible. The couple followed their host's advice and returned to Wenceslas Square, where they witnessed an even bigger demonstration than two days ago.

They were surrounded by a sea of people; men, women and children of all ages and social backgrounds. Artists and professors chanted side by side with workers. Some grown men cried, their faces, distorted by strong emotions, resembling grimacing theater masks. Many carried high above their heads homemade posters declaring "Truth will prevail" and "Let the government resign!" On their way home, Paul and Irina passed smaller groups of people gathered around shop windows where televisions played over and over videos of the police attacking the peaceful student demonstrators, which incited expressions of outrage.

From their windows, some people waved the Czech flag—a blue triangle at the left and a band of red and white at the right—while singing patriotic songs. Cars honked in support of the strike. Even small children, no doubt prompted by their parents, yelled "Victory!" and made a V-sign with their little fingers. Later that evening, the Svoboda family was glued to the TV. Like everyone else, they were eager to see how the government would respond to the national strike. Would it escalate the violence to put a stop to the cry for democracy, or would it give in, at least partially, to popular demands?

Ladislav Adamec was featured on the national news. Although only a few weeks earlier he had dismissed Havel as "an absolute zero," now he had changed tactics and agreed to meet with him and other leaders of the Civic Forum. Irina was surprised to see that Adamec's voice was calm and that his speech, or at least the parts of it translated by Viktor, sounded reasonable, even conciliatory. The Prime Minister announced that he had ordered the withdrawal of troops from Wenceslas Square. He also promised there would be no martial law. In exchange for these concessions, he urged the Czech citizens to calm down, arguing that their protests were likely to escalate into meaningless violence; into a dangerous state of anarchy which would claim many more innocent lives. The Svobodas, however, weren't that interested in the Prime Minister's soothing rhetoric. They wanted to know what political actions he would take. In fact, they were much more concerned about Jake, the head of the Communist Party, rather than about the chameleon-like, more flexible Prime Minister.

In the middle of the broadcast negotiations between Adamec and Havel, a messenger arrived with a note from the Communist Central Committee. As Irina and Paul watched the Svoboda's silent tension in their little living room, they felt that the whole nation was holding its breath. The news sounded almost too good to be true. The messenger read that General Secretary Jake and the rest of the 13-member Politburo were stepping down. Karol Urbanek, a communist who wasn't generally known by the public, was named his successor.

"Fantastic!" Viktor burst out upon hearing this news, slapping his knee with excitement.

Right then and there, on national television, the Magic Lantern theater exploded in celebration. Havel was shown smiling for the camera and making a V sign for "victory." The members of the Civic Forum were besides themselves. Some cheered, others wept for joy. Champagne glasses were passed all around. Looking very Western in his white shirt and blue jeans, Havel made a toast to a free Czechoslovakia. "To our country and to democracy," he said, raising his glass. Standing next to him and looking distinguished in his gray suit, Alexander Dubcek, the hero of the Prague Spring twenty years before, smiled approvingly at this reincarnation of his political dreams.

When she was finally convinced by her son that she hadn't misheard, Mrs. Svoboda followed suit and took out her most expensive champagne bottle from the cabinet. Even Irina and Ekaterina, who didn't drink, made an exception for this special occasion. Viktor hugged his family and guests. "I've been waiting for this moment all my life," he declared, visibly moved.

"Let's not celebrate too soon," his cool-headed wife cautioned. "As they say in your country," she added, looking at Paul, "it's not over 'til it's over. Let's not forget that Adamec and Urbanek are still in power."

But Viktor was not alone in his hope. That evening, when Adamec met with Havel, the whole country rejoiced. In that historic meeting, many saw the beginning of the end.

Chapter 12

On their last full day in Czechoslovakia, Paul and Irina accompanied Viktor to Letna Field to see Havel and Adamec speak in person. Since the metro was filled to the brim, they took a bus to get there—which, as it turns out, was easier said than done since the busses were almost as crowded as the subway trains. They nonetheless managed to squeeze their way into the bus, standing packed together like sardines and holding on to the rail above them to avoid falling into strangers' laps during the bumpy ride. Irina wrapped her free arm around Paul and moved even closer to him, finding a sense of balance in their togetherness. They were so close that her lips brushed the nape of his neck. Taking advantage of this position, she began planting little kisses on his soft skin, cuddling next to his angular body.

"Watch your purse, okay? We don't want to lose our passports," he advised, attempting to distract himself from his girlfriend's proximity and affection with practical details. But it didn't work, at least not completely. He still felt tantalized by Irina's soft little body rocking into his to the uneven and not altogether unpleasant rhythm of the ride. He felt the warmth of her breath in her whisper: "Te iubesc."

"Really?" Paul asked, in mock disbelief. "You never told me that before..."

"It wouldn't kill you to say it to me once in awhile..." Irina retorted.

While the bus ride was hot, once they stepped outside they felt like they had entered a refrigerator. The stadium turned out to be so crowded that it made the bus ride seem spacious and comfortable by comparison. Viktor commented that about five hundred thousands people were expected at Letna Field that day. Apparently, these expectations were not disappointed.

By the time they arrived, Havel was already in the middle of his speech. The three friends were so far away that they could barely see him at the podium. However, with the aid of a microphone he was perfectly audible and, thanks to Viktor's periodic translations into English, also comprehensible. Apparently, the leader of the Civic Forum wasn't as enthusiastic as he had been the night before.

"My fellow citizens," Havel said in his calm and decidedly non-demagogic voice, "I urge you to continue putting pressure on the government. We can't drown in the last stretch. Democracy is within our grasp."

He was interrupted by loud cheering.

"Who is this Urbanek?" Havel asked rhetorically. Many booed when they heard the name of the new communist leader.

"He's a wildcard," Havel answered his own question. "We don't know anything about him except that he's a communist. And that's precisely why we're not satisfied!"

His words were supported by echoes of disapproval aimed at Urbanek.

"We need to pull together and let the government know: We are not satisfied!" Havel reiterated, this time much louder and enunciating each word.

The deafening applause and cheering were cut short by Adamec's arrival. Some people continued to applaud him also since, after all, he had been the only communist leader who had been willing to negotiate with the Civic Forum.

"My fellow comrades," Adamec began. Given the loud protest at the mention of the misfortunate word "comrades," this introduction didn't bode too well.

"We need to behave more responsibly toward our country if we don't want everything we built and worked for to fall apart," the resilient Prime Minister continued undaunted.

"Let it fall!" someone shouted.

"We need to show more discipline," Adamec urged. "Right now our country is in chaos. Czechoslovakia is being economically weakened by strikes and torn apart by violence. Riots are breaking out in all the major cities. For the sake of our nation, for the safety of our children, I urge you to be more reasonable and stop these senseless protests!"

A loud voice interrupted his speech.

"What did that man say?" Irina asked Viktor.

"He said, 'You didn't care about the welfare of our children when you ordered the police to strike at them.'"

"He's got a point," Paul commented.

"Resign! Resign!" many shouted from the audience.

Someone yelled: "Jingle your keys! Don't let him speak! Jingle your keys!"

Suddenly the whole stadium, about half a million people, began jingling their keys, orchestrating a cacophony which soon forced Adamec to leave the stage.

Havel took over the podium once again and, in defiance of Adamec's call for returning back to normal, enjoined people to continue their protest. "Let's not give up until we see the fruits of our labor in the triumph of democracy," he concluded his presentation to a roar of applause.

Once the rally was over, Irina, Paul and Viktor were propelled by a jet of human beings toward the exit. They almost didn't have to walk, there was such a powerful current pushing them forward from behind. Squeezed in and moved by the mass of people, Irina began to feel dizzy. Paul held on tightly to her hand, afraid they'd lose each other in the enormous, dispersing crowd. "Are you okay?" he asked, noticing her pallor.

"I'll be fine," Irina answered. "This is a little scary," she added, feeling disoriented.

A small being carried away by a mass of people, she sensed that even nonviolent revolutions had a menacing energy about them that made you feel that at any moment they could erupt in violence, or trample you unfeelingly to the ground with their sheer force, reducing the individual to nothingness. When they finally got back home, Irina practically collapsed on the sofa. Paul brought her a glass of water. She sat up to drink it quickly, then lay back down and closed her eyes. She was perspiring and pale. Their hosts hovered around her solicitously, asking her if she wanted anything. Mrs. Svoboda offered her a cold compress along with some anti-nausea medicine, but Irina refused. She just needed a little rest, she told them. Paul sat by her and began massaging her feet. He worried easily and was the first to panic whenever health problems arose. "I told you it wasn't a good idea to go get smooshed by half a million people," he said, trying to be helpful. Irina murmured something in reply.

"What did you say?" Paul asked.

"I said I didn't mind it. We lived through an important moment in history." Irina repeated.

"Well, if the feelings of nausea and suffocation appeal to you, then I'll take you to a big rock concert as soon as we get back to the States," Paul assumed a lighter tone, now that he was reassured that his girlfriend was feeling a little better. "Let's try to get a good night's sleep, okay? No more revolution; no more excitement. Tomorrow's a big day for you. How long has it been since you've seen your family?"

"Seven years," Irina replied, feeling suddenly apprehensive about her return. What would it be like to see her family after such a long separation? she wondered. And what would Romania itself mean to her without her loving grandparents there to nurture and protect her? She couldn't even imagine the answer to these questions. Because, in her mind, her country was synonymous with familial love. That was the only emotion that, after all these years, still bound her to that stretch of land where they had suffered and from which they had fled.

Chapter 13

Although Irina and Paul had planned to visit Budapest for a few days, they changed their plans and took the train from Prague through Bratislava, Budapest and then to Timisoara after Irina spoke on the phone to Uncle Mircea, her mother's brother. The news from home wasn't good. Her grandfather's health was rapidly deteriorating and the doctor's prognosis was grim.

"I won't forget to talk to the journalists as soon as we get back to the U.S.," Irina confirmed her initial promise to Viktor once they arrived at the train station, where he accompanied his guests.

"That may not be necessary any more," Viktor answered, alluding to the fact that Western journalists were now swarming into Czechoslovakia. "A lot has changed since you first got here."

Irina took out a little piece of paper from her purse and wrote down her uncle's address and phone number, where she and Paul would be staying in Romania, and handed it to Viktor. "Any time you and your family want to visit the United States or Romania, you're more than welcome to stay with us. Paul and I are so grateful for your family's hospitality. Please thank your mother once again on our behalf."

"I will," Viktor replied, taking the piece of paper and placing it in his shirt pocket. "But you better watch out! Ekaterina and I might take you up on your offer when we visit the United States. It's likely we'll go to New York City, and then we might drop by your place in New Jersey. But I think we're going to hold off on visiting Romania for now," he added with a smile.

"I wish I could say the same," Paul interjected.

Viktor laughed and said, "It was a pleasure meeting you both." The two men shook hands, after which Irina and Viktor hugged warmly.

"I'll really miss him," Irina said to Paul once they were settled in the train.

"You say that about everyone you meet," Paul pointed out.

"Yes, but in his case I actually mean it."

During the first stretch of their train ride through Czechoslovakia, the couple sat close together and gazed at the scenery, which gradually changed from plains to picturesque, gently rolling hills.

"This would have been even more beautiful in the summer or spring," Paul commented, looking out the window nostalgically at the vast stretches of barren land which he remembered as lush and green during the summer of his honeymoon trip to Eastern Europe.

Lulled by the gentle movement of the train, the couple took a nap. At the frontier with Hungary, the train stopped and an officer stepped in to verify everyone's passports. They fell back asleep and after a few hours, once they arrived in Budapest, the conductor woke them up once again to verify their tickets. They were soon joined in the train compartment by a peasant family with two little girls, around seven and nine years of age, who looked absolutely adorable and spent most of the ride playing with large cloth dolls. Across from them sat an elderly gentleman with dark brown eyes, dressed in a formal, professional looking navy blue suit. His most striking feature was a large square mustache which, by contrast to his gray hair, was still brown and reminded Irina of Bela Karoli, the gymnastics coach who had trained Nadia Comaneci.

Being extraverted, Irina attempted to engage in conversation the two little girls. She asked them in English what was the name of their dolls. The girls giggled into their palms and whispered something to one another. Their father answered on their behalf: "No speak English. We Magyar." Since Irina didn't speak Hungarian, that nipped the conversation in the bud.

The gentleman who resembled Bela Karoli, however, looked at Irina and asked her in her native language, Vorbiti Romineste? if she spoke Romanian. 'Da," Irina answered, surprised that the man could tell her nationality given that, on the train, she had spoken only in English without any trace of an accent. "How did you know?" she asked him in Romanian.

The man shrugged and smiled. "Lucky guess. The train is going to Timisoara and you don't look American, the way Domnul does," he said, indicating Paul with a movement of his head. Since the man had a Hungarian accent in Romanian and the conflict between native Romanians and ethnic Hungarians in Transylvania was escalating due to Petrescu's nationalist policies, Irina decided to set the record straight right off the bat: "My mother's Hungarian, born in Timisoara," she informed him. At least now he wouldn't take her for an enemy.

"I also have family in Timisoara," he said in a tone that revealed he wasn't too pleased with that fact. "I've been trying to buy exit visas for them to Hungary for the past two years now."

Irina was surprised. "When we were living in Romania that was relatively easy. Petrescu needed money to pay off his foreign debt so he was selling like hotcakes ethnic Hungarians to Hungary and Jews to Israel."

"When did you leave Romania?" the gentleman asked.

"About seven years ago."

"Eh! A lot has changed since then," he replied. "I only wish I had had the foresight to get my family out of Romania while it was still possible."

Irina was curious to find out more about the situation in her country, particularly in Transylvania, where all of her mother's side of the family now lived. Since Grandma Marta's death, her grandfather, who lived in a small flat in Bucharest, had also moved to Timisoara to be under the care of his son. Irina wanted to ask the Hungarian gentleman more questions, but it occurred to her that she didn't even know how to address him. "My name is Irina," she introduced herself.

"I'm Karol Kovacs," he replied.

"This is Paul, my fiancé," she said, not wishing to introduce Paul as only a friend or boyfriend, given that they were traveling together.

"Mr. Kovacs also has family in Timisoara," Irina began summarizing in English some of her conversation for Paul's benefit. "He told me that the situation has gotten a lot worse since we left. For one thing, there's a lot more tension between ethnic Hungarians and Romanians."

"Ask him why," Paul suggested.

"I already know a little bit about that from my family," Irina answered. "During the past few years, Petrescu has launched a nationalist policy against ethnic Hungarians and isn't allowing them to immigrate to Hungary any more. He's also forbidding teaching Magyar in their schools, which used to be permitted in the ethnically Hungarian parts of Transylvania."

"It looks like, with your perfect sense of timing, you've chosen the best moment for a vacation in Timisoara," Paul gathered from this information.

"I'm not going there on vacation! My grandfather's dying," Irina reminded her boyfriend with a reproachful look.

Paul felt intuitively apprehensive about their upcoming trip to Romania. The vacation in Czechoslovakia had been sufficiently eventful to give him enough excitement to last a lifetime. He now longed to return to the States and take a vacation from his vacation.

Suddenly the odor of onions overwhelmed the small compartment. It was almost noon and the peasant family was having lunch. The mother had laid out on a large napkin the food that she had kept in a covered woven basket under the seat. Their simple meal consisted of dark bread, goat cheese, tomatoes and onions. For dessert, they had grapes and strawberries. The two little girls didn't eat exactly gracefully, but they seemed to observe a systematic procedure nonetheless. They took a bite out of a pealed onion, which they held in one hand and a bite out of the cheese and bread sandwich, which they held in the other hand. Occasionally, when their eyes watered from the strength of the onion, they put it down on the napkin and traded it for the juicy tomato, which they bit into exactly as one does into an apple.

Even though the little girls didn't feel the need to use napkins and wiped the tomato seeds from their lips and chins with the back of their hands, Paul and Irina got hungry just watching them eat with such a healthy appetite. Mrs. Svoboda had made cheese and butter sandwiches for them also, which they began eating, but somehow their food seemed wilted by comparison to the mouth-watering meal of this Hungarian peasant family.

After lunch, Paul attempted to take a nap, propping his head against the windowpane, while Irina continued her conversation with Mr. Kovacs. There was something about the latter's appearance that intrigued her. In his impeccable navy suit and with his large, square mustache, he combined the air of bureaucratic refinement with the atavistic look of a nomadic conqueror. Looking at him more carefully, Irina noticed a large scar by the corner of his right eye.

In response to Irina's inquisitive glance, Mr. Kovacs pointed with his index finger to his scar: "I got this in prison."

"Prison?"

"Yes. Three years of it. It felt like an eternity. Of course, I should be grateful since compared to the others, I got off easy..." his voice trailed off.

Who was this man? Irina wondered. Was he a Hungarian Romanian dissident? Or a common criminal? "Were you imprisoned by Petrescu?" she asked him.

"No, by the Kadar regime. My parents and I left Romania when I was ten years old. Since then, we've lived in Hungary, though we still have family in Romania whom we visit from time to time. In fact, right now I'm going to my cousin's funeral."

"My condolences," Irina replied.

Mr. Kovacs sighed. "He was much younger than me. Died before his time..."

"Was he ill?"

"No. He was assassinated."

"By whom?"

"By some local Secret Police thugs in Timisoara. I plan to find out who they were and let them know exactly how I feel about what they did to my cousin," Mr. Kovacs said, with a fiery look in his dark eyes.

Noticing Mr. Kovacs' intense expression, despite her curiosity, Irina didn't dare ask him any more questions for the moment. One would have to be pretty courageous or pretty important to take on *Securitate* agents, she thought. After a few seconds of silence, however, Mr. Kovacs delivered the information himself.

"My cousin wasn't really a political person," he said. "He was just an architect doing his job. He worked on a church restoration project with the local pastor in Timisoara. That's why they had him killed."

"Has Petrescu turned that much against religion?" Irina asked. She knew that the dictator was never that friendly to religion, yet he had tolerated it if practiced privately back in the days when she and her family still lived in Romania.

"This assassination wasn't really about religion," Mr. Kovacs explained. "The priest in question was no ordinary pastor. His name is Laszlo Tokes, of the Reformed Church of Timisoara. Have you heard of him?" he asked, his tone indicating that she should have.

Irina shook her head. "They hardly give us any international news in the States. We hear mostly about President Bush," she attempted to justify her ignorance.

"Well, Pastor Tokes has become internationally famous, at least in Europe, since he's one of the very few men living in Romania who has the courage to speak out against Petrescu's human rights abuses against the ethnic Hungarians."

"But then why didn't Petrescu kill Pastor Tokes himself? Wouldn't that have been more logical than assassinating your cousin?"

"Not really. Laszlo Tokes has become too visible. They did harass him quite a bit, however. Anonymous callers threatened him on the phone; unmarked *Securitate* cars parked in front of his church and, when none of these intimidation tactics seemed to work, just a few days ago, four hooligans broke into his house, beat him up and cut his face with a knife. But they didn't dare kill him. If Petrescu had him assassinated, it would create an international scandal. Unfortunately, nobody outside the country knows about my poor cousin. Killing him accomplished the same goal—that of frightening those who were thinking about joining Tokes—only it did so much more quietly."

"How do you know that the *Securitate* killed your cousin? Couldn't it have been an ordinary crime?"

"No," Mr. Kovacs answered firmly. "When my cousin started rebuilding the church, he received threatening phone calls from the *Securitate* asking him in no uncertain terms to abandon his project. He refused to comply and within a few days he was found dead in a park. I don't believe that's a coincidence..."

Irina wondered if the town of Timisoara, one of the few places in Romania where ethnic Hungarians and native Romanians got along well, was by now smoldering with political tension beneath the calm surface. "Are the Romanians in Timisoara against Pastor Tokes also?" she asked.

Mr. Kovaks seemed surprised by her question. "Not at all! In fact, just the opposite's the case. Pastor Tokes has a growing following among ethnic Romanians. It doesn't matter to him if you're Hungarian or Romanian; you're still human and you should be treated with dignity. People admire his courage. Because deep in their hearts, Romanians hate the Petrescu regime also."

"What is he saying?" Paul asked Irina, becoming curious about her lengthy conversation in Romanian.

"He's telling me about this courageous Hungarian priest in Timisoara who is riling up people against the Petrescu regime. That's almost unheard of in Romania. I mean, some people, like my own brother, have had the courage—or the foolishness, depending upon how you look at it-- to criticize the government from abroad. But criticizing Petrescu from inside the country is like signing your own immediate death sentence. Unless the winds are changing..."

"Couldn't they stay still until we leave?" Paul inquired.

"As usual, I admire your heroism," Irina patted her boyfriend on the knee. Looking again at the Hungarian's weathered face, with deep wrinkles around the eyes and mouth, she couldn't help but wonder what he must have lived through. She guessed that he was only slightly younger than her own grandfather, perhaps in his late sixties or early seventies. Yet at the same time, Mr. Kovacs exuded such an aura of strength that he appeared ageless. Had he participated in the Hungarian revolution of '56 that her grandmother had told her about? Irina wondered. If so, on which side? Did he play any role in the more recent collapse of communism? Irina wondered.

"What are you thinking about?" Mr. Kovaks asked her with a strange smile, as if reading her mind.

"Pardon?"

"The way you were looking at me."

"Oh, I'm sorry. I was just thinking about… what you must have lived through."

"Well, when you get to be my age in Hungary, you've seen it all," Mr. Kovaks answered, his voice suddenly assuming the shaky frailty of that of an elderly man.

She would have liked to hear more about the days Grandma Marta, who traveled to Budapest once a year to visit her sister, had described to her. Whenever they went through particularly difficult times during their nearly three year ordeal of waiting for the official approval for immigration to America, her grandmother would tell her that they should have been smart and moved to Hungary. The Hungarians, she said, got to travel everywhere and put food on their tables because, when push came to shove, they had been more courageous than the Romanians. She told her granddaughter a little bit about Imre Nagy and the Hungarian revolution, which, though crushed by the Soviets, had nevertheless helped make Hungarian communism much milder than its Romanian counterpart. "When I visit Budapest," Grandma Marta used to say, "I can't afford to buy the clothes and the food. But at least I can look at them!" Which made the situation in Hungary enviable for most Romanians.

"What was it like in Hungary during the anti-communist revolution?" Irina couldn't resist asking her companion.

Paul couldn't understand what his girlfriend was saying since she was speaking only in Romanian, but he recognized her inquisitive tone enough to politely suggest: "Irina, why don't you leave the poor man alone? He's probably tired of answering all of your questions. Maybe he wants to take a nap or something."

"He's enjoying our conversation," Irina defended herself smiling graciously at Mr. Kovacs, who, out of politeness, smiled at her also. "See?" she turned to her boyfriend like a woman who has thoroughly proven her case.

As if on cue, Mr. Kovacs opened up further. "It was an exciting but very unstable time. Actually, at one time I was pretty good friends with Imre Nagy himself."

"What did he say? Did he tell you to be quiet?" Paul wished to confirm his initial hypothesis.

"No, he said he was friends with the Hungarian revolutionary hero, Imre Nagy!" Irina answered excitedly.

Mr. Kovacs must have understood the English word "hero," which was similar in Romanian (erou), since he shook his hand back and forth, as one does when saying "so-so." "In some ways a hero, in other ways a villain," he said. "It depends upon which Nagy we're talking about."

 Reincarnations of Love

"What do you mean? There was more than one?" Irina asked, confused. Her grandmother had only told her positive things about Imre Nagy. And in the West, Nagy was known as the martyr of the '56 anti-communist revolution. Even the Hungarian government had recently paid homage to him by reburying him with official pomp. It was all over the news last June.

"Well," Mr. Kovacs elaborated, "I knew Nagy back in the thirties. We were both working for the Comintern with Bela Kun in the Soviet Union. Then, in the forties, when the Comintern was purged, I left for Hungary and stayed out of politics for awhile, afraid that if I hung around in the Soviet Union any longer, I'd be disappeared like the rest of them. They used to say, you go to the U.S.S.R. of your own volition, but you leave only when they let you go or in a coffin. But somehow, even in the midst of the Great Terror, Nagy managed to thrive in the Soviet system by becoming an agent for Soviet security. Mind you, you couldn't keep your hands clean or be that heroic if you worked for Stalin. If you didn't do as you were told then you were terminated."

Irina had never heard such an ambivalent account of the Hungarian national hero. "So then how come he ended up leading the anti-communist revolution?" she asked.

Mr. Kovacs looked above, towards the roof of their train compartment. "God willed it. But there's no denying that Nagy was a clever man. Anybody who worked for Stalin and lived to tell about it had to be politically savvy. And very lucky."

Irina was still somewhat skeptical. "Are you saying that he didn't really believe in democracy?"

"No, I think he did," Mr. Kovacs replied.

"But how can you believe in both Stalinism and democracy?"

"When Stalin was alive, you couldn't believe in anything. Once Stalin died, you could believe in everything. Or at least so we thought… " Mr. Kovacs said with a chuckle. "Imre Nagy had both hindsight and foresight. He knew what Stalinism had done to the country; he could see that staying on that course would only continue the destruction."

Another doubt occurred to Irina. "If you were Nagy's friend, then why didn't Janos Kadar purge you and all of Nagy's other political allies?"

"Like I said, he threw me in prison for awhile. But you see, Kadar was a man who played the role of a hard-liner without really wanting to be one. He blew with the wind. When Nagy was strong in '53, he supported Nagy. When Nagy became unpopular with Khrushchev and the Soviets invaded our country, he hung him. And by the end of his life, his true nature showed."

"What do you mean?"

"All along, Kadar was only a shell of a man. Like an onion. You peal off the layers and never find the center," Mr. Kovacs answered, miming with his hands the act of pealing an onion.

"At least you never had it as bad in Hungary as Romanians did under Petrescu. Even under Kadar, you still had private businesses. And food. And beautiful quality clothes," Irina said, reliving the traces of envy she used to feel as a child whenever her grandmother would describe to her life in Hungary.

"Well, if Kadar had tried to return the country to full-fledged Stalinism it wouldn't have worked, despite the Soviet support. We had tasted a bit of freedom under Nagy and, even if bullied, we weren't about to give it all up."

Irina, however, saw the flip side of the coin. "Then don't you find it a bit strange that the Hungarian communists were ready to give up their power this year? When I was watching the whole thing on the news, it seemed like the communist party became democratic all of its own accord. It was a miracle."

Mr. Kovacs smiled. "A miracle whose magic took us decades to perfect. You see, for us becoming more democratic was a natural continuation of the way things had been progressing for many years. A few months ago, right after Nagy's state funeral, a lot of journalists tried to explain why the communists were willing to give democracy a try. The smartest among them gave the only plausible answer: because they couldn't think of one single good reason not to do it."

Somehow, Irina suspected, the Romanian government would come up with a few reasons why not to have democracy. The train stopped for another customs check at the border with Romania, where their passports were verified. Once it began moving again, Irina gazed out the window and recognized the geography of her own country. Even without customs check at the border, Irina would have been able to tell that they had entered the Romanian side of Transylvania. The huts were smaller and more rundown; the chicken, cows and other livestock scruffier and more emaciated and the people looked poorer and more weary than farmers in Czechoslovakia or Hungary. Dressed in their ragged, light-colored peasant outfits and dark wool coats with black boots, they resembled the pictures of nineteenth-century serfs she had seen as a child in books from her mother's library. With all its march towards collectivization, industry and progress, the Petrescu dynasty had somehow managed to keep Romania frozen in time. Not even his efforts to obliterate the country's picturesque villages by razing them to the ground and replacing them with cheap apartment buildings were able to efface the centuries of fatigue, hunger, war and hardship one could see on people's faces even from the distance and comfort of a train speeding quietly through the countryside.

Chapter 14

The train station in Timisoara reminded Irina of Monet's bleakest rendition of La Gare Saint-Lazare, except that the gray atmosphere of that painting was darkened further by the reality of people rushing back and forth, looking fatigued and disheartened in their somber winter clothes. Irina heard several languages around her, recognizing Hungarian, Romanian, German and Bulgarian. The city of Timisoara was Romania's melting pot, where different nationalities lived side by side and got along surprisingly well given the ethnic tensions in the rest of the country caused by hundreds of years of border struggles and intensified by Petrescu's policies.

"Are you sure that your uncle's supposed to meet us here?" Paul asked.

"Yes. He told me so on the phone and I gave him our ticket information," Irina confirmed. She looked around for a middle-aged man who was mostly bald with only a crown of hair close to the nape of his neck and large, warm brown eyes. Uncle Mircea was her favorite uncle. When he and his family visited them in Bucharest he always brought her presents—usually dolls or books. More importantly, he had the gentlest manner of anyone she had ever met. Irina recalled that when she was a little girl, she would sometimes get into fights with her two cousins, Gheorghe, who was a year younger, blond, blue-eyed and mild-mannered like his father, and Nicu, who was the same age as her, thin and unusually serious and taciturn for a child. Sometimes, when the three of them played a board game, Irina would get upset if she lost and vehemently challenge the outcome. If the boys stood their ground, sometimes a physical fight would ensue, often instigated by Irina. She would pull their hair, or even scratch them while they would run to their parents, having been taught by their parents never to hit a girl.

Little Gheorghe would complain loudly, in tears, to the adults: "Irina is beating us up again!"

Yet when the delicate little girl accused of ruthless physical violence would appear in the kitchen to face the parental verdict, she looked absolutely angelic.

"I don't believe it!" her uncle would automatically take her side. "Why don't the three of you play nicely, hmmm? You boys are too rough. You need to learn how to play with a young lady," he would suggest to the perplexed male victims. No matter what Irina did, her uncle, who had always wanted to have a little girl, came to her defense, giving her the benefit of the doubt.

Is that him? she wondered, seeing a man wearing a Russian fur hat over his head who seemed to have Uncle Mircea's stature and gentle eyes. The instant she recognized him, she felt like she had truly returned home, to her country.

"Uncle Mircea!" she screamed after him in Romanian, waving her hand.

"Irina!" he rushed quickly towards her. They barely had a chance to look at one another before they embraced and kissed each other on both cheeks.

"You have turned into such a beauty!" Uncle Mircea said, also in Romanian. "And this must be the happy fiancé," he shook hands with Paul, switching to English. "I speak English not so good," he said apologetically.

"He's too modest. He actually speaks pretty fluent English and has visited America several times," Irina boasted.

"I have been to Michigan," the uncle granted her that much. "Vork for the tire industria and visited Ford Motor Company," he elaborated. "Very enchanted to meet you."

"Nice to meet you too," Paul replied. "How come your family speaks English? I thought that French was the second language in Romania," he whispered to Irina.

"It is," she replied. "But since the sixties, the university students going into the sciences, especially physics, chemistry and engineering, were strongly encouraged to learn English. Then, during the seventies, Petrescu traded a lot with America after Romania got "most favored nation" status. And his policy became to get Romanians who went to scientific conferences to spy on Western technology. My uncle is the director of a tire factory in Timisoara. He was invited a few times to conferences in the U.S. My aunt is a pharmacist and she also speaks English."

"But I thought people in Romania weren't allowed to travel to the West," Paul answered, confused.

"Not so simple," Uncle Mircea, who overheard his comment, intervened. "At first he vanted us to go to many conferences in Vestern countries. Then, about twelve years ago, he changed. He vanted to make Romania independent from America and Vestern Europe. So everything got very bad, like in Albania."

They walked through the crowded train station to a side street where Uncle Mircea had parked his white '74 Trabant. Paul sat in the front, since the car was very small and he had long legs, while Irina sat by herself in the back.

"Vas your trip difficult?" Uncle Mircea asked Paul.

"Well, it was certainly eventful," Paul answered. "In just a few days we've witnessed a lot of changes in Czechoslovakia."

Uncle Mircea nodded while keeping his eyes on the road. "We hear about that. Listen to Radio Freedom Europe. Hope the same happen to in Romania."

"Do people here think it's likely to happen?" Irina chimed in from the back seat.

"Eh, who knows? Ve're not optimistic. Petrescu holds on as hard as he can, vith both hands," Uncle Mircea gripped the steering wheel more tightly, to demonstrate Petrescu's fierce hold on the country.

Irina looked around, recognizing familiar scenes from her family vacations. They passed by the City Center Square, whose gothic style buildings were vestiges from the time of the guilds. In the historic downtown area, they also saw the spectacular Romanian Catholic Cathedral glowing in the sun. Old Town Hall, built during the eighteenth-century in the Neoclassical style with bright red roofs, seemed to be a natural extension of the cathedral. The only modern building, other than the rows of rectangular apartment buildings dispersed everywhere throughout the town, was the Hotel Continental, which was reserved mostly for tourists and emulated a Marriot or a Hilton—one with poor management that had lost a star or two.

Suddenly, they were jolted by a huge pothole in the road, which the little Trabant barely had enough steam to escape. In fact, Irina and Paul couldn't help but notice that the whole ride home was exceedingly bumpy. To say that the roads needed repair would be a gross understatement.

"Geesh! That pothole was as big as a grave!" Irina exclaimed.

"I wouldn't be surprised if that's vat it vas," her uncle answered. "Petrescu started violence against us. It begins with a pastor here in Timisoara," he explained.

"Laszlo Tokes?" Irina inquired.

"Yes. How did you know?" Uncle Mircea turned his head back to look at her

"We met this Hungarian man on the train, Domnul Kovaks, who told us all about it," Irina explained.

"Is this pastor's protest really that big a deal?" Paul asked, still somewhat skeptical.

Uncle Mircea nodded, his eyes now back on the road: "So so. Not very big yet. But may become big, who knows?"

After a few more turns, Uncle Mircea parked the car in front of an apartment building with four floors. Irina noticed that the beige paint of the building, which, she recalled, used to be white, was now cracked and pealing off all over. Everything looked older, more worn-out than she remembered. But the neighborhood kids were still playing as before. A wave of childhood memories came back to her as she gazed upon these familiar sights. Somehow, she felt like an eternity had passed since being in Romania, yet at the same time it was as if she had been here only yesterday, playing with her cousins and friends during family vacations.

Even now, on this snow less, cold afternoon, kids swung on the rug beater behind the apartment building, pretending they were on the parallel bars (at least on one of them) in gym class. Irina recalled doing that with her friends as well as what seemed a much more dubious, but nonetheless highly entertaining, summer game. When it was warm, she and her friends would go hunting for "pets" in the flower beds around the apartment building. The "pets" consisted of bondari, or male bees, who, despite their supposed laziness, had a much tougher existence than their female counterparts, at least in that particular neighborhood. Kids would capture them upon a flower by cupping their hands quickly over the insects, then tie a string around one of their skinny legs, give them a name, and walk around the neighborhood with these unwilling pets until their fragile legs broke off and they finally escaped with their lives. No matter how much the neighborhood gardener would scream at them for trampling upon the flower beds, the kids would still persist in this benevolent hunt and torture of the hapless insects. Benevolent, because they actually became quite fond of their pets and felt sorry when all they had left of them was a tiny crooked leg on a string and their fond memories.

An odor of burnt onions and garlic greeted them in the hallway. They climbed up a staircase filled with litter to the third floor and rang the bell. A middle-aged woman with dark blond hair and blue eyes, wearing a print dress and a flowery apron on top of it, opened the door. Her aunt hadn't changed much, Irina observed, except perhaps for the fact that she had gained weight.

"Irinuca! It's so good to see you again," the sentimental Aunt Maria exclaimed in Romanian hugging Irina with tears in her eyes. "You've grown up! I can hardly recognize you," she added, taking a step back to take a look at her niece, who, in the blink of an eye it seemed, had left a girl and returned a woman.

The aunt then proceeded to greet Paul, who was considered by the whole family as Irina's fiancé, thus a priori, as one of their own. "Velcome, velcome," she said warmly in English.

"You must be starving," she said to Irina, switching back to Romanian.

"Actually, we're not that hungry since we ate a few sandwiches on the train," Irina answered.

"I'll make a little snack then," Aunt Maria compromised. No sooner had the couple sat down on the living room couch than she came back with a silver tray stacked with cups of strawberry preserves, spoons and glasses of cold water.

"This is what an afternoon snack consists of in Romania," Irina felt compelled to explain to her puzzled fiancé why he had in front of him half a jar of strawberry jam.

"You eat jam just by itself?" Paul asked his girlfriend in a whisper.

"Yes. It's considered a fancy dessert."

"If you say so…" Paul had his doubts, but smiled graciously at his hostess and, in the spirit of cultural relativism, accepted his bowl of preserves along with the glass of water.

"So tell me, how did you two meet?" Aunt Maria asked Irina in Romanian.

"Maria, let them rest before asking all your questions!" her husband advised.

"I haven't seen Irinuca in seven years! Of course I'm going to ask her questions," his wife replied.

"We met through a mutual artist friend," Irina said, not wishing to disclose the whole misunderstanding of their first meeting in Paul's apartment.

"Is Paul an artist?" her aunt asked.

"He's an art history professor."

Aunt Maria made a face, to indicate she was impressed. "Very nice," she approved. "You found someone important, like your father," she said. "Everybody in our family marries very young," she observed, still speaking in Romanian, then, addressing Paul, who was struggling to nibble some jam, she switched to English: "Ghiorhe and Nicu are engaged very young also. Is better that vay. You grow up together. Like brother and sister," she added and crossed her fingers to illustrate the familial closeness.

Paul wasn't exactly reassured by the comparison.

"I can't wait to see them again and meet their fiancées," Irina said.

"They coming here for dinner. Vant to see you and Paul."

Paul tried to wash down the excessively sweet jam with the glass of water, then put down his empty bowl on the tray, feeling that he had paid his dues to Romanian customs.

To his dismay, Aunt Maria immediately piled on six more spoonfuls of jam into his bowl. "Is very good, no?" she asked him, her eyes twinkling with satisfaction. "Grandpa Marta made it," she said, her mood suddenly changed. Then she addressed her niece in Romanian, since she found it difficult to express emotion in English. "Grandpa Mihai is devastated. The doctors can't even understand what's wrong with him. It's as if his whole body were shutting down. His heart, his liver, his kidneys, everything is failing. They can't find any medical explanation for it. We think he's dying of sorrow. He can't hold on without her."

Irina nodded. "We'll go to the hospital to see him first thing tomorrow morning, right?" she asked.

"Yes. First thing," Aunt Maria confirmed. Then, not wishing to begin crying again and make their family reunion an occasion for sadness, she tried to divert the conversation to a lighter topic. "Irina very funny girl," she said, forcing a smile to Paul. "Remember Mircea?" she asked her husband, who had kept quiet, giving his more loquacious wife the floor. "Remember Romeo and Jumulita?"

"Maybe she doesn't vant to talk about that," Uncle Mircea said tactfully.

But Irina smiled good-naturedly when she recalled that memory from her childhood. She was about ten years old, on summer vacation in Timisoara. She was playing outside this very apartment with her two cousins and a group of their friends and had made the fatal error of letting her older cousin, Nicu, know that she thought one of his friends, Lucian, was cute. The good news spread like wildfire among the kids. All of them started calling the lovebirds "Romeo and Jumulita," Jumulita being a distorted version of the name Juliet which meant, quite literally, "plucked feathers" in Romanian. Embarrassed, Irina had left the playground in tears, but when the cousins returned home that evening, it was their feathers which were in fact plucked by their parents. Irina recounted the incident to Paul, who commented: "Well, that goes to show you've always had spunk!"

By the time her aunt and uncle (mostly the aunt) went through all of Irina's embarrassing memories, it was already seven p.m.

"You know, I'm getting a little worried that Gheorghe and Nicu aren't here yet. They were supposed to come here for dinner," Aunt Maria said in Romanian, getting up to look out the window.

"Maybe tonight they're eating with their fiancées," Uncle Mircea proposed.

"What are you talking about, Mircea? They knew Irinica was coming tonight. It's a special occasion. I wonder what's holding them up," she sat back down and began nervously fiddling with her apron. As if to explain her behavior, she added in a whisper: "There's trouble here, in Timisoara."

"Maria, there's no point worrying the kids," Uncle Mircea said, though that wasn't his main concern. He preferred to avoid political discussions, knowing full well that ever since Andrei defected and Eva filed for immigration, he and his family were being closely monitored by the *Securitate.*

His wife wasn't easily intimidated, however. Besides, she assumed that if they spoke in a whisper the microphones in the radiators couldn't pick up their conversations.

"They've been persecuting our local pastor," she explained in a low voice in Romanian.

"You mean Pastor Tokes?" Irina asked also in a whisper.

Her aunt looked surprised. "Yes. How did you know?"

"We've heard about that from a Hungarian gentleman we met on the train who also has family in Timisoara. He was coming here for his cousin's funeral—an architect who was assassinated because he helped rebuild Pastor Tokes' church. Did you hear about that?" Irina asked.

Uncle Mircea seemed uncomfortable with the conversation. "Maria, don't you think it's time to start dinner? These kids must be starving by now," he said in Romanian.

To occupy herself and be gracious to her guests, Aunt Maria lay the table and heated up a pot roast (which was not vegetarian enough for Paul) along with a dish of steamy mashed potatoes.

"We kept meat in freezing for two months just for you," she announced proudly to Paul in English, happy to be able to put meat on the table. "You are a very special visit," she informed him. Although Paul expressed due gratitude, this information only augmented his fears regarding the freshness of their meal. Especially since Uncle Mircea had told them that the electricity didn't work half the time, which led him to rather disturbing speculations about what must have happened to the meat during those intervals.

"But why are you afraid Gheorghe and Nicu might have been involved in any of this story with Pastor Tokes?" Irina asked her aunt.

"She alvays vorries," Uncle Mircea answered on his wife's behalf.

"And for very good reason!" Maria defended herself, this time in English, for Paul's benefit. "Is dangerous here now. Last Sunday, the police vanted to throw out Pastor Tokes from his house. But many people helped him. They said this is wrong, and they vent to his house and made a ... how to say... margele around it, like a circle."

"You mean a human chain?" Irina translated.

"Yes, that's right. And this Monday there vas a lot of violence in Timisoara. Everywhere. Young people, Gheorghe and Nicu same age. They showed they are very angry vith Petrescu government for throwing priest out."

"And what did the government do?"

"A lot of screaming. Menace. But no shooting yet. Many students, friends with Gheorghe and Nicu, vere in this. But I say no. I told them to stay out of the trouble. Ve have enough probleme in life. But they never listen to vhat I say any more. They are big men. Ve'll call again," she decided, getting up and reaching for the telephone. She let it ring at least twelve times before hanging up.

Irina had a chilling flashback to her own parents' worries about Radu. She recalled the numerous nights when, pretending to be asleep, she could hear their anxious whispers in her room, which also doubled as her father's office, as they called her brother in Paris over and over again, to no avail.

Chapter 15

In the morning, Paul and Irina took a quick cold bath. The water looked a bit off-color, a pale reddish brown, as it trickled shyly from the rusty pipes.

That morning, they were going to visit Grandpa Mihai at the hospital. Uncle Mircea went to tend to his father twice a day, in the morning before work and then right afterwards, before supper.

"Does he still recognize you?" Irina asked her uncle in Romanian, as they were walking to the hospital, which wasn't far from their apartment.

"Yes. He's not senile, just very sick. He can barely walk any more," Uncle Mircea replied, also in Romanian.

"What do the doctors say?"

Uncle Mihai made a sign of discouragement with his hand. "Eh! The doctors! They don't know anything. And, worst of all, they don't care."

"What do you mean?"

"The conditions in hospitals here are inhuman," her uncle explained. "If I didn't go there to help him every day, he'd have already died from malnourishment or infections in a matter of days. You look around at the other patients and, quite honestly, you feel like bursting into tears."

This, as it turns out, wasn't an exaggeration. Irina always felt a little queasy in hospitals; they're not exactly cheerful places. But here it was not just the condition of the patients, but also that of the hospital itself that was depressing. They walked through corridors that, instead of being sparkling white and smelling of disinfectant like in the hospitals Irina had seen in the United States, had dingy grayish, blotchy walls with the paint peeling off, as if the building itself had developed some kind of rare skin disease. The hospital rooms reeked of an unpleasant mixture of sweat and some other indeterminate, acrid odor. The nurses and doctors rushing around the hallways looked tired and ill-disposed and the only people walking the patients in wheelchairs were dressed in regular clothes, which led Irina to deduce they were family members or friends, not hospital personnel.

Her heart beat rapidly as they approached her grandfather's room. They walked in and she saw him lying on the bed, a sheet and threadbare blanket covering him almost to the chin, his eyes closed, his hair still jet black and contrasting sharply with his pale skin. He shared the room with three other elderly patients, each of them resting in a similar bed. The urine smell in the room was overpowering.

"Mihai, your family has arrived!" an elderly woman with a handkerchief around her head announced with a tinge of jealousy in her voice. All of her best friends had died, her family lived in Bucharest and had problems of their own, so nobody ever came to visit her.

At first Grandpa Mihai didn't speak, just looked at his granddaughter, blinking several times in a row, as if not believing what he saw. Then Irina saw his thin mouth turn slowly into a smile and, for a moment, the sparkle came back into his eyes, which glimmered with tears.

"Irinuca," he finally said, lifting with difficulty his thin arms to embrace his granddaughter.

"It's so good to see you Grandpa," Irina answered and leaned over to hug him gently. A wave of pleasure mixed with sadness and regret passed through her. She kissed his cool, sunken cheeks over and over again.

Grandpa Mihai turned his gaze to Paul. Irina had written to him that she was engaged to a young professor, and Grandpa Mihai had been very supportive. Anything that made his granddaughter happy he approved a priori.

Her grandfather didn't speak a word of English. "Tell him that I'm so glad to meet him and wish you only happiness and good health," he said to Irina in Romanian. Irina did so and Paul thanked him in English and leaned over to give him a hug also. He was surprised by the frailty of the elderly man, whose arms were as skinny as twigs.

Irina noticed this also. "Why is he so thin? Don't they feed him in here?" she asked her uncle in English, not wishing to worry her grandfather about his own condition.

"I bring to him food two times a day," Uncle Mircea responded also in English. "But he is very sick. Everything wrong with him. His body doesn't vant the food."

"At least she went very fast. She didn't suffer much," Grandpa Mihai said to Irina in Romanian, referring to his wife, who was always on his mind.

"Now he only talks about her and the past," Uncle Mircea clarified in English.

"She was on a ladder, watering the hanging plants we have on the balcony. Then," Grandpa Mihai rolled his eyes, emulating someone who was fainting, "she fell just like that. I was in the kitchen when I heard a loud noise. I saw her on the floor, tried to help her, rushed to call the ambulance. She opened her eyes, I remember how they fluttered open when she looked at me and said, Mihai don't go. Don't leave me, Mihai. It's no use. I'm dying. A few seconds later she was gone. She didn't suffer much, she just left us like an angel..." Grandpa Mihai closed his eyes and looked like he, himself, had passed away.

Irina stroked her grandfather's jet black hair. "You have to try your best to get your strength back, my sweet little Grandpa," she said softly to him. "Please think of all of the happy times you had with her. And of all the happy times you can still have with us."

Grandpa Mihai summoned all his strength just to stubbornly shake his head. "No, Irinuca. My time has come also. I will join my wife very soon."

"You see? I told you so before. He doesn't vant to live any more," Uncle Mircea said in English.

"We brought you some breakfast," Irina said, trying to refute this loss of hope with actions if she couldn't do it with words.

She began unpacking the basket of fresh soft bread, with the crust removed, butter and soft goat cheese.

"Would you like me to feed you a little bit of this sandwich?" she asked her grandfather. "Aunt Maria made it just for you."

To please her, with Irina's help Grandpa Mihai propped himself up upon his elbows and took a few tiny, bird-like bites, moving the soft food around in the cave of his mouth. But after only a few seconds he gave up. "I'll eat it later," he lied, since he usually gave his food to his hungry roommates.

"I have a present for you from her," Grandpa Mihai said, feeling on his chest, underneath the pajama shirt, for a gold ring on a delicate chain. He removed the precious object and handed it with a trembling hand to his granddaughter: "This was her favorite ring. Ever since you left for America she talked about how much she wanted you to have it. She would have given it to you herself if you had come to see us during the summers. But you never came..."

Irina immediately recognized Grandma Marta's large aquamarine ring with an antique, vine design on a shank made of rose gold. She remembered telling her grandmother when she was a young girl that that was her favorite ring in the whole wide world. She slid it upon her finger and recalled her grandmother's hands, moving rapidly with dexterity when she was knitting sweaters for the family, her ring flashing with light blue, rose, even yellow tones. Everything about that scene, everything about her grandmother, had inspired a sense of comforting warmth which seemed magically encapsulated, as if frozen in time, by that lovely jewel.

"Thank you so much," she said, moved.

She then helped uncle Mircea, who proceeded to follow the morning routine before leaving for work. Together they gently massaged Grandpa Mihai's muscles, which had become much weaker since coming to the hospital a few weeks ago. Uncle Mircea propped his father up to a standing position and, after having pulled the curtains around the bed for privacy, helped him relieve himself into the bed pan, which he then emptied in the central bathroom down the hallway. There was only one toilet per fifty or more patients on each floor. Then the son washed his father's body with a wet cloth and helped him put on clean underwear and pajamas. Irina placed slippers upon her grandfather's feet, then helped him take his walk up and down the hallway, so that his muscles wouldn't completely atrophy.

As they hobbled along, Irina was struck by the sad irony of this situation. It seemed that only yesterday she was eight years old and couldn't walk away fast enough away from her grandfather, on the way to school with her best friend Sofia, trying to act all grown-up, like she didn't need her grandparents anymore. Now that she was all grown-up, she realized how much she needed them. With their warm personalities and their kind, indulgent manner, even when she could no longer have their love and long after they'd both be gone, alive only in her memories, she'd still need them. She'd need them always.

Chapter 16

By the time Irina and Paul headed home from the hospital, after Uncle Mircea left for work, the city of Timisoara erupted into total chaos. Thousands of people had organized a march, but this wasn't anything like the comparatively peaceful protests the couple had witnessed in Prague.

"They were waiting for us to arrive to start the revolution here also," Paul couldn't resist the comment.

Most of the protesters were young men. They shouted loudly, some in Hungarian, others in Romanian. Parents with children were running away from the scene, with their arms protectively wrapped around their kids. Irina slipped her own arm around Paul's, as if her slight, delicate boyfriend could provide any protection against this agitated mass.

An innocent-looking boy with blond hair and blue eyes, who couldn't have been older than sixteen, smashed a brick into a bookstore that displayed Petrescu's books in the window front. Other young men followed suit. Shattered glass rained like a hailstorm unto the street. Irina and Paul ran away from the scene before the violence got even worse. "Down with the tyrant! Down with Petrescu!" they heard loud shouts. When they looked behind them, the couple noticed that the young men had set fire to the bookstore. Another group of young men were turning upside down random cars parked on the side of the road, egged on by the wild cheers of onlookers hungry for the raw spectacle of violence.

When they finally returned home, Aunt Maria was waiting for them in an agitated state. "Everyone is saying that the revolution has begun," she said to Irina in Romanian, looking more frightened than happy about this moment she had prayed for most of her adult life. "I still haven't heard from Gheorghe and Nicu nor the girls," she added, referring to her son's fiancées. "And the girls' parents haven't either. I spoke to them on the phone this morning."

Hours later, after an unnerving wait, they heard the door bell ring. Aunt Maria thought it was her husband, coming home early from work. When she opened the door she nearly fainted with surprise and relief upon seeing her sons alive and well.

"Thank God! Where did you go?" she asked them, looking ready to hug them and then box their ears, as she did many years ago when they would disappear for hours without telling their parents where they went.

Gheorghe answered for both of them: "The students at the University of Timisoara organized a march against the Petrescu government. Didn't you hear about that, Mom? Every department participated, including the medical school."

"Why do you have to get involved in such dangerous things?" their mother chastised, not impressed by this explanation.

"It wasn't supposed to be violent," Nicu, the older brother, replied. "In fact, initially it was a peaceful protest organized by the Youth Union leaders. But then it got out of hand. First there was a lot of screaming and shouting, then some people started throwing Molotov cocktails into the soldiers who had been sent to monitor the situation. Then some of them started destroying stores, cars and pretty much everything in sight."

"Unfortunately, we ran into the riot on the way back from the hospital," Irina came into the hallway to greet her cousins, followed by her fiancé.

"Irina! It's so good to see you," Nicu exclaimed, while Gheorghe also came to embrace her.

"What a welcome we got!" Irina said. "Everywhere we go, we seem to start a revolution," she tried to joke, even though she was still shaken by the experience.

"How did you manage to escape the riot and make it back here? Were your fiancées involved in this?" Irina asked, still speaking in Romanian since her cousins didn't speak fluent English.

"No, they stayed at our place. They didn't even go home or to the university yesterday and today. We anticipated that it might get dangerous. But we thought it would be dangerous because of the Security Police forces shooting at us, not because our fellow students would go on a rampage. That was pretty unexpected."

"How did the Security Police respond to that?" Irina asked.

"At first, astonishingly enough, they did nothing," Gheorghe answered. "We were pretty surprised, since some of the students even threw Molotov cocktails at the town hall, right outside the Communist Party Headquarters.

Constantin Dascalescu, the Prime Minister, tried to calm down the situation. He and the mayor got up on a balcony and told people to stop the violence because the government will listen to them. He said we should all go back home peacefully and of our own accord."

"And did that end the rioting?" his mother wanted to know.

"On the contrary!" Nicu exclaimed. "As soon as the mayor, the Prime Minister and the Security Police left, the rioting began full force. People ran into the communist headquarters and tore down the portraits of Petrescu and his wife. Though we didn't go in, we saw their pictures hurled out the windows. The rioters must have broken into some kind of storage room, since they were also throwing salamis and huge wheels of cheese out into the courtyard, close to where we were standing. It was frightening yet also strangely comical, to see all these bags of that cheese and salamis flying out the window," Nicu said with a chuckle. "For the first time in Romanian history, it was raining food!"

"Well, I'm glad none of it landed on your heads," Aunt Maria commented. "When did you manage to get away from the bedlam?"

"When the Security Police returned with big guns and started shooting right and left into the student demonstrators. We took that as our cue to go home," Gheorghe answered.

"Do you know if any of the demonstrators were killed?" Aunt Maria asked, her eyes widening with curiosity mixed with trepidation.

"When we were leaving, things looked pretty bad," Nicu replied. At first, the Security Police came with this huge red fire truck to disperse the mob by spraying us down with the water hose. But a group of students set the fire truck on fire. That's when the *Securitate* started shooting at us with their machine guns. You couldn't tell who they were, except for the big guns—actually, that was a pretty good hint—because they were dressed just like us, in civilian clothes."

"Perhaps a little better than us," Gheorghe felt obliged to add, since *Securitate* agents, who had a much better standard of living than most people in Romania, were notoriously rich and elegant.

When Uncle Mircea came home that evening, he told them that the people, the buildings in Timisoara, looked like they had just been through a cataclysmic disaster. Rumors circulated that hundreds, if not thousands, of protesters had been massacred by the *Securitate* forces and that their bodies were thrown into mass graves. Not just civilians, but also young soldiers who refused to shoot down fellow citizens. For three days the fighting between the people and the government forces continued. All signs of normal life ceased. Schools and the university were shut down; people stopped going to work. Fed-up with communism, the citizens seemed to take inordinate risks to manifest their anger. The *Securitate* forces were equally determined to put down at all cost any sign of protest. But no matter how much blood they spilled, they still didn't succeed in killing the people's desire to overthrow the government. The city of

Timisoara was locked in a stalemate. But what would become of the rest of the country?

Chapter 17

On Thursday, December 21st, 1989, Radu and Ioana went to the convened place: the political rally orchestrated by Petrescu in the capital as a response to the Timisoara uprising. As usual, the demonstration was a highly organized event which included thousands of "volunteers," all members of the Romanian Communist Party, who were required to participate. As usual, the first four rows were occupied by *Securitate* Special Brigade agents dressed in civilian clothes. They were the ones who shouted the loudest "Petrescu PCR!" (Petrescu, Communist Party of Romania!) and "Ura, Petrescu!" (Hooray, Petrescu!), lifting the banners of the General Secretary's picture from about twenty years ago, when he was still young and vibrant.

Standing in the tenth row, Radu shouted these slogans along with everyone else. He was struck by the difference between the weathered old man regally greeting the crowd from the balcony of the Communist Party Headquarters and the youthful portrait of him displayed upon the banners. In this juxtaposition alone, he felt, the illusion of the dictator's strength was crumbling. Radu looked to the right, seeking Ioana. She stood, as planned, one row ahead, three people to the right, within his field of vision. She too was pretending to be an enthusiastic supporter of the Petrescu regime.

Following a long, resounding applause, Petrescu began his speech. His voice had a slight tremor, yet he retained his youthful mannerisms: instead of speaking, he shouted in a raspy voice and punctuated his statements with hammering gestures into the air with his fist. He said that the Timisoara uprising was instigated by a group of hooligans agitated by Hungarian fascists. Every single one of those criminals had been killed, Petrescu vowed. The government had put an end to the disorder. Behind him, his wife and the members of the Political Executive Committee applauded at this announcement. The front rows of demonstrators were especially vehement in their show of support.

Radu's heart beat rapidly. He knew the risk he was taking. If his ploy didn't work, or if Ioana didn't come to his aid effectively, he would be instantly shot by the police. Was it worth it? It was too late to wonder about that. If not now, at this crucial moment, then when? Radu gazed at the dictator's distorted features, repelled by his menacing gestures. He looked around at the mass of people faking enthusiasm and support. Would they have the courage to take their cue from other Eastern European nations, or had they been completely beaten into submission by twenty-five years of unrelenting tyranny? Everything hinged upon the unpredictable reaction of this mass indoctrinated by a lifetime of propaganda. Not just his life, but also the fate of the country.

Radu leaned for support against the lamp that his CIA contact had described to him in advance. He felt it wobble slightly under the weight of his shoulder. Radu pushed harder against the lamp, until it shook even more. Then, at a moment when the applause and cheering died down and Petrescu launched into a speech about how Romania would be protected from the horrible fate that befell Poland, Hungary, East Germany and most recently Czechoslovakia, Radu made his move.

He thrust his whole body into the lamp, which fell to the ground shattering with a loud crash. Ioana shrieked, theatrically raising her hand to her heart. Apparently some of the people around her assumed that she had been shot by the *Securitate* because they rushed around her, to offer help. Taking advantage of the commotion, Radu found the strength to shout, waving his fist into the air: "Timisoara! Timisoara massacre!" The ringing in his ears was the only noise that measured the deathly silence that followed. For a moment, which seemed to him like an eternity, nobody said anything. Time itself seemed to stand still. Out of the hundreds of demonstrations the government had organized in the capital during the past quarter of a century, none of them had ever deviated from the planned routine. Nobody knew how to react to something as extraordinary as a single voice raised in outspoken, public protest.

Then a few voices began to shout: "Rat! Rat!" and "Death!" This is it, Radu thought. The *Securitate* is asking for my head. He looked at Ioana, who had turned around and met his glance with trepidation. He noticed that she was very pale, her skin almost blending into the tones of her blond hair. She seemed more frightened than he was. Oh well, at least I'm dying for a good cause, Radu told himself. Yet, to his surprise, nothing happened. Not a single shot was fired.

Suddenly, dozens of voices erupted in protest: "Petrescu the Dictator!" "Down with Petrescu!" As if on cue, some students from the outer edges of the crowd unfurled homemade banners which they had hidden in their coats: "Down with Petrescu!" A moment ago Radu was all alone; now he felt like a single drop in an ocean of a long repressed and deeply felt political upheaval.

Never confronted with anything except adulation and obedience, Petrescu looked stunned. For once, the dictator infamous for shouting speeches was speechless. Perhaps he wasn't seeing correctly. Perhaps he hadn't heard right. Clearly something was wrong with the microphone since the crowd had reacted so strangely. He tapped into the microphone: "What? No… no.. Hello? Hello?"

His shrewd wife, however, immediately realized what was happening. She jabbed her husband in the ribs from behind. Petrescu recovered from his momentary confusion and continued his anti-democracy speech. But it was too late. The damage had already been done. His voice was drowned by the shouts of the crowd which had been assembled to adulate him. They had cheered enough. From the time they were young pioneers they had cheered, at times even believing in what they said like one does in an Orwellian double-think, to feel less misfortunate. Everywhere they lived in poverty, without adequate food, clothing, heat and running water, yet supposedly their country was flourishing. Everywhere they couldn't speak or even think for fear of persecution, yet supposedly they lived in freedom. Everywhere they saw the wealth of the ruling communist elite, yet supposedly they lived as equals.

One single voice which dared take the first step exposed one of these sets of statements as true and the other as false. Then everything else followed, as if 2+2 could equal 4 once again; as if facts, truth and reality were no longer mere figments of one's imagination. Their leader was not superhuman; he could no longer make the party lies magically become truth. People began throwing their shoes and potatoes at the balcony. In one split second, everything was turned upside-down. Unable to contain the situation, Petrescu, his wife and the Executive Committee retreated into the Communist Party Headquarters. They gave orders for the army to fire into the insurgent crowd, climbed on the roof and were whisked off by a helicopter. Maneanu, the Commander in Chief of the Army who had been courted by the CIA, finally chose his side. He refused to carry out Petrescu's command. Fate had it that he, rather than Radu, became the first martyr of the anti-communist revolution in Bucharest.

Chapter 18

Immediately after the Petrescu escape, the government-run television station was occupied by the army. As far as anybody could tell, the anchorwoman announced, the Petrescus were still at large and had left behind a force of about 15,000 highly trained *Securitate* officers, many of whom had been recruited from the infamous state-run orphanages, to wage a guerrilla warfare against the army and the Romanian people.

Watching the civil war on national television, however, the Lorenz family, like many Romanians, felt somewhat confused. It was hard to tell who was fighting for the fallen communist government and who was fighting for a new regime or even what form that regime would take. Many people wondered, was the Bucharest uprising a coup d'etat led by the military with foreign help or a revolution whose real impetus was the people's will? "It looks to me like a coup d'etat disguised as a revolution," Paul commented privately to Irina after watching the news clips. But most Romanians wanted to believe that their country had the courage to stage a popular revolution with military support. Only one thing was perfectly clear: every major city in the country—Bucharest, Timisoara, Brasov and Cluj-Napoca--had exploded into a bloody civil war.

Schools, offices, stores, industries, practically every institution was shut down. For Uncle Mircea, even something as simple as walking back and forth from his apartment to the hospital to visit his father each day had become a dangerous mission. Which is why he decided that, under the circumstances, it would be best to bring Grandpa Mihai home. The ill-equipped hospital staff was stretched to the limit with hundreds of incoming wounded and the doctors had already told the family that there was nothing they could do to save his life. The day Irina rode with Uncle Mircea in his car to help him bring her grandfather home, they both thought would be their last. Not only violence, but also confusion had overtaken Timisoara.

On television, the army was represented as being on democracy's side, or at least against the Petrescu dictatorship. Yet when you walked or drove down city streets, what you actually encountered was total chaos because the *Securitate* Special Brigade agents were often disguised as soldiers or civilians. From the car window, Irina saw men dressed in military outfits shooting at civilians and civilians shooting at other civilians. Snipers even shot at the ambulances that attempted to pick up the wounded.

In response to this confusion, some of the soldiers began to wear white armbands or place carnations in their rifles, to indicate their true identities. But the *Securitate* snipers soon mimicked those signs of peace as well. The most mysterious of all the fighters were the men dressed in Muslim outfits. Nobody knew who they were, where they came from or what they were doing in Romania. Even though they seemed to be fighting on the side of the Petrescu regime along with the *Securitate* forces, they still looked out of place, as if in the midst of an anti-communist revolution, they had arrived to fight for jihad.

The previous evening Irina and Paul had seen on the news a clip of a pregnant woman shot in the stomach, presumably by the *Securitate* agents. Her body was mutilated and her stomach torn open to expose the fetus. One could only assume, the anchorwoman had announced in a severe tone, that the government violence targeting women and children was cautionary in nature, to forewarn the Romanian citizens that any show of support for the insurgent military would lead to a violent death. But the military, who were in fact broadcasting these horrific scenes, were using these images to convey the opposite message: this is what Petrescu and his Security forces do to innocent citizens; this is the kind of government we're trying to eliminate. The news run by the army didn't show the charred and mutilated corpses of those suspected of being *Securitate* agents. Because in a guerilla warfare in which the enemy was often in disguise, nobody could tell who was what any more and there was no time to verify. You either shot or were shot.

Amidst all the death and destruction, however, one could also see on the news acts of heroism and generosity. A news clip covering the revolution in Bucharest showed women and children walking in the middle of the shooting and rubble to offer soldiers food and water. Another clip featured people rushing with brooms to sweep the debris from the streets, as if eliminating the signs of devastation could also somehow ease the suffering. And one news clip filmed in

Timisoara revealed the warmth of the Romanian Latin spirit: ordinary citizens were risking their lives to go up to soldiers and give them a few encouraging words and grateful hugs. Often when they saw journalists or photographers, people in the streets began cheering and making a "V" sign for "Victory" with their fingers. Hope rose from the bloodshed like dust from the rubble.

On the morning she drove with her uncle to pick up Grandpa Mihai from the hospital, Irina also witnessed with her own eyes the great risks Romanians were willing to take to get their first taste of freedom. In the midst of a vicious civil war, when each step you took in the city placed your life in danger, many waited in long lines to buy "Romania Libera," Free Romania, the nation's newspaper, which, for the first time in its history, was no longer controlled by the government. The front page displayed a picture from a demonstration in Bucharest, where tens of thousands of people had gathered for a rally in support of the anti-communist forces. The protesters wielded an immense flag with the national colors—red, yellow and blue—and the communist emblem ripped out from its center, leaving a giant hole in the flag.

"How appropriate!" Uncle Mircea exclaimed when, later that evening, the family watched together that very scene on the news. Because the question of what would be the country's new center, what kind of government would replace the communist one, was precisely the mystery that nobody could resolve. Were the insurgents truly pro-democracy? Who was this National Liberation Front and what kind of government did Ion Iliescu, their leader, propose?

Uncle Mircea hoped for the best but expected the worst: "Iliescu vas an old communist. Ve don't have non-communist leaders here. They all run avay or vere killed by the *Securitate*," he said to Paul.

"So then you don't think that if the National Salvation Front wins, anything will really change in Romania?" Paul asked him.

"Vell, even if ve get capitalism, capitalism is not magic vand. Many people vill be even vorse and more poor. In our country, ve have this saying: Marx vas wrong about everything he said about communism, but he vas right about vat he said about capitalism," Uncle Mircea declared in the aphoristic style many Romanians adopted when discussing politics. Yet despite his cynical words, his eyes were glued to the television screen, eagerly awaiting some encouraging news and quietly sparkling with hope.

Chapter 19

Many years ago, on Christmas morning, Irina used to tiptoe in the middle of the night to take a peek at the presents Mos Craciun had left under the tree. She would examine the colorful wrapping paper, sniff it to determine if there might be any chocolate inside, put it next to her ear and shake it up a little, since that usually yielded a few clues as well. Santa Claus, or Mos Craciun as he was called, apparently ignored the directives of the communist government to do away with religious holidays. Being as thin as the French Père Noël, he continued to slide down chimneys and leave kids presents under the tree. No matter how poor Romanian families may have been, parents and grandparents still scraped up their last bit of savings to see the delight in their children's' eyes when they hastily opened up their Christmas gifts. Grandma Marta and Grandpa Mihai would always be sure to wrap up honey drops and chocolates, a doll or two along with handmade sweaters for Irina as well as little toy cars and sweaters for Radu. The shiny ornaments on the tree didn't glow quite as much as their grandchildren's rosy, excited cheeks when they unwrapped their gifts.

That Christmas morning, however, there was no tree, no presents and no joyous celebration for their family. Grandpa Mihai had expired in the middle of the night. In the early morning, Uncle Mircea, who checked on him periodically, felt his forehead and neck and found his father cold, without a pulse. He woke up the whole family and called the ambulance. Aunt Maria verified if there might still be a chance she could save him by giving him C.P.R. She quickly determined that there wasn't. When she rearranged his head on the pillow, she discovered underneath it a little pile of old letters. They all began, "My dearest grandparents," and were written in Irina's round, childlike cursive. These letters had been the consolation of her grandfather's last days.

Uncle Mircea called his sister in America, to let her know the sad news. Eva decided to risk coming to Romania in the midst of the revolution to be there for her father's funeral. Andrei stayed behind in the United States, in case something would go wrong during the civil war. If, God forbid, Petrescu or others from the old communist guard reassumed power, he wanted to be able to fight from abroad to get his wife and daughter out of Romania once again.

By now, however, there were very slim chances that such a political reversal would take place. The Romanian news had broadcast all over the world that Petrescu's helicopter had landed near Tirgoviste, a town northwest of Bucharest. The dictator, his wife and their entourage had been found hiding in a seed distribution center in the area. The local police delivered them immediately into the hands of the army, which in turn took them to a barrack near Bucharest. Nicolae and Magdalena Petrescu were tried for genocide along with other "serious crimes against the people, which are incompatible with human dignity."

Everyone in the country who owned a television set must have kept it on at all hours of the day and night to find out the latest news about the coup. The dethroned dictators were the key defendants in a Stalinist show trial without the show, since the proceedings were closed to journalists and to the public. The couple remained united to the end, refusing to answer questions or admit any wrongdoing. An abundance of volunteers had lined up eager to serve on the firing squad. The Petrescus, who had always boasted of their heroism during the days of the communist revolution, now ran around the execution courtyard like headless chicken attempting in vain to avoid the flying bullets. Nicolae Petrescu was trapped in a corner and shot; his wife soon followed, shot in the back. Shortly afterwards, the national news televised a close up of their faces— Petrescu lying on his back, his eyes staring blankly--to assure the incredulous Romanian people that, after a twenty-five year reign, the tyrants really were dead. That was the first Christmas celebration the country had enjoyed in decades.

The Lorentz family was no exception, even though, at the moment, they were more devastated by their personal loss than happy about the revolution in their country. Uncle Mircea made all the funeral arrangements. Grandpa Mihai had asked to be buried next to his wife underneath a tombstone that was etched with roses, Grandma Marta's favorite flower. They had it built themselves fifteen years ago, not wishing to burden their children with the cost. In fact, Grandpa Mihai had left his son his last bit of savings, a little cash pile stashed away in a metal box which he had kept hidden under the hospital mattress, intended for the funeral expenses.

When they discovered her letters to her grandfather under his pillow, Irina burst into tears. "I wish I had visited them every summer, like I promised when I left," she said to Paul.

"But you, yourself told me it would have been dangerous to return to Romania while Petrescu was still in power," Paul tried to console her.

Irina wiped her eyes with her sleeve. "What did the government have against me? I hadn't done anything."

Paul didn't know what to say to alleviate her guilt. "It might still have been too risky..."

"No it wouldn't have!" Irina contradicted him. "I was just being selfish. I never wanted to feel the pain of separation from my grandparents ever again. But now I regret it and I always will. Didn't you see? My grandfather died with my letters under his pillow! The truth is that I abandoned my own grandparents, who loved and raised me."

Uncle Mircea went to his niece and gave her a hug. "Irinuca, don't be silly," he said to her in Romanian. "You were always Grandpa Mihai's good friend and your grandparents never felt abandoned by you. Please believe me. They knew you still loved them and understood that you had your own struggles in life."

Irina shook her head. "I could have done so much more to show them my love. Now it's too late. There's nothing I can do to turn back time."

"On the contrary, there's a lot you can do now and in the future," her uncle disagreed, still addressing her in Romanian. "Family has always been the most important thing for us. Now that Romania's likely to become a freer country, you can come visit us. We can become united and close once again. And..." here Uncle Mircea smiled and touched Paul's shoulder, switching to English for his benefit, "You can take care of this nice young man. And make each other very happy." Irina looked at Paul, who, as usual, had assumed a spaced-out expression around her family. He looks so clueless, she thought, almost admiringly. They sure would give happiness together their best shot, she told herself.

On the other side of Bucharest, Radu and Ioana had been summoned to the new Director of Relief's office. To win over the trust of the populace, Ion Iliescu, the leader of the National Salvation Front, a sixty-year old communist who had fallen out of favor with Petrescu in 1971 for "intellectualism," had just implemented emergency relief policies. Iliescu vouched on national television to turn on the heat and hot water in frigid apartments; to load the empty shelves of state-run grocery stores with food that Petrescu had used only for export, including rare treats such as chocolate, oranges and coffee; to abolish the death penalty (once the Petrescu couple was safely executed) and to release political prisoners. When they read the address they were given, Radu and Ioana were somewhat surprised to note that the Director of Relief for Bucharest resided precisely in the building where the Security Police had been stationed.

"Maybe they're trying to make a statement," Radu speculated, looking at Ioana as they walked briskly side by side through the crowd. "Kind of like the French revolutionaries taking over the Bastille."

"Honestly, I don't understand what's going on any more," Ioana replied flatly. She walked with her eyes fixed on the ground before her, as if she feared she might fall. She walks like an old lady, Radu observed, feeling strangely nostalgic for the vigorous and seductive young woman with whom he had fallen in love. They entered together the building that had formerly housed the Secret Police Agency and made their way down the hall to Room 224. A familiar voice answered, inviting them to "Come in!"

As soon as they stepped into the office, Ioana instantly recognized the slim, benevolent looking elderly man with silver-rimmed glasses. He looked slightly older, despite the fact that he had dyed his white hair dark brown.

"Please sit down, make yourselves at home," Comrade Stanescu encouraged them, pointing to the two empty chairs across from his mahogany desk. Radu and Ioana obeyed automatically. Even Radu knew of Stanescu from his earlier dealings with the *Securitate*. Was this a practical joke that the CIA was playing on them? he wondered. He quickly dismissed this hypothesis since members of the Agency generally lacked a sense of humor.

Ioana smiled faintly. "So you're the new Director of the Democratic Relief Agency?" she asked, not without a note of irony.

Stanescu looked into her eyes with a friendly gaze, as if he were rediscovering an old friend. "That's right! We get to work together again," he replied cheerfully. "Mr. Iliescu has asked me to organize the relief effort in Bucharest. Romanian citizens have been oppressed long enough. They need food and clothes; heat and hot water. Young people like yourselves are the heroes that will save the Romanian people from the misery and oppression of the Petrescu years." Ioana recognized in her boss's words the same rhetoric and sing-song intonation he had formerly used to incite them to fight against the "terrorist forces" which "sabotaged glorious Romania" and "our beloved leader" during the height of the Petrescu dictatorship.

Stanescu then proceeded to give the couple instructions about which managers to contact (namely, those who were formerly in charge of providing for the Communist nomenclatura) in order to jumpstart the redistribution of food to the city's empty stores. He then bid Radu goodbye after congratulating him once again on his patriotism and asked to have a moment alone with Ioana. Radu waited for his companion in the hallway. Five minutes later, the young woman stepped out of Stanescu's office.

"Why would the new supposedly pro-democratic government employ the old communist dogs?" Radu whispered to Ioana once they were safely back outside, walking in the street.

"Why would your CIA boss send you to help out the old communist *Securitate* Chief?" Ioana retorted. "Haven't you learned anything from all this? Nobody gives a damn about ideals or principles. Politics is all about power." As she expressed this cynical attitude, Radu thought that Ioana's face looked even thinner and sharper, almost angular. Yet in her worn-out features he thought he recognized the woman he had loved. He felt the impulse to take Ioana into his arms right then and there, in the middle of the sidewalk; to kiss her as avidly as before, when they had first met in Paris. He wished to disentangle himself from the web of politics and intrigue which had sapped his energies. Perhaps with a single courageous gesture, he could recapture their youth and hope by marrying Ioana, becoming a father to Lucian and creating a family out of the scattered pieces of their lives. He would finally get a normal job as a chemist, and stop leading this life of a tumbleweed, of an adventurer.

Radu cleared his throat, as one about to make an important announcement: "Ioana I wanted to ask you ...you know... perhaps we could," he ventured, struggling to express his desperate enthusiasm.

"You won't believe this," Ioana interrupted him, turning to him and placing her hand upon his arm to draw his attention. "Stanescu asked me if I wanted to be Assistant to the Deputy Director of the Relief Effort, the guy who works right under him," she said in a confidential whisper.

Radu looked at her with bewilderment.

"He recommended me for the job because he already knows me since I worked for him before. And to prove his good faith, he promised to cut some of the bureaucratic tape and release my parents from prison immediately," she added.

"Are you going to accept his offer?" Radu asked.

"Sure. Maybe my parents would be released anyways, but now they'll be more of a priority. Besides, if we stay in Romania, they can help me raise Lucian."

"Don't you want to return to the States?" Radu was surprised. Between a First World democracy that had economic and political stability and a Second World country in total disarray, to him, the choice was a no-brainer.

Ioana, however, begged to differ. "I feel more at home here. For some reason, I never felt at home in America." Then, as an afterthought, she added: "I'm sorry! I interrupted you. You were about to ask me something?"

Radu felt deflated. The mood had passed. "Oh, it was nothing in particular," he replied. "I think it's a good idea to stay here with your family. That way Lucian will get to know his grandparents."

Ioana thought that Radu was hinting that she was leaving his family out of the picture. "Do you want Lucian to meet your parents?" she offered.

"Sure," Radu replied. Which is the one thing he wasn't. "They'd be happy to meet him."

"I bet they won't be that thrilled about meeting his mother," Ioana commented.

But Radu felt that if they met Lucian, his parents might even give her a chance. He checked his watch. "I'm going to my grandfather's funeral in about three hours. Can you and Lucian please join me?"

"If you think that's a good idea," Ioana agreed, without much enthusiasm.

That afternoon, the three of them went to the cemetery together, arriving a little late, right after the funeral. Strangers watching them from afar might have mistaken them for a family. Lucian held his mother's hand, while Radu walked on the other side of him. He saw his mother crying silently by her father's grave, occasionally wiping her tears with a handkerchief. How she has aged, Radu thought. Eva had become smaller and rounder in form, with sloping back and shoulders, as if life's hardships had weighed her down. Irina seemed almost unrecognizable to him, since he had left her a little girl and now she was a full-grown woman. Despite her transformation, he recognized her instantly, however, by the manner in which she compulsively twirled a lock of hair when she was sad or nervous. The family members he had been less close to seemed to have changed the least. His uncle, aunts and cousins looked almost the same as when he left them, only older.

Radu walked next to his mother, close enough to overhear her whisper to her brother: "Now that I lost both of them, I feel so alone in this world. Nobody loves you like your parents."

"Mom?" Radu asked rather than said, as if he needed confirmation.

Eva abruptly turned around upon hearing that familiar yet estranged voice. Her eyes were red from crying. She stared at him in disbelief.

"Raducu!" she finally exclaimed and hugged him. "Oh, my God, I can't believe it's really you!"

He was instantly assailed by hugs and questions from the whole family. Where had he been? What had he done? Why was he hiding? How had he managed to escape? What was he doing with his life? Why didn't he visit his family?

He answered their questions briefly and evasively, then proceeded to focus on what struck him as more important. "Mom, I'd like you to meet someone," he said, turning his head and signaling to Ioana, who, along with Lucian, had kept a respectful distance, not wishing to intrude upon the mourning family. Upon seeing his gesture, Ioana stepped forward, holding her son's hand. Eva pursed her lips and looked at the young woman with distrust. But her eyes lingered with sympathy upon the lanky little boy who walked by her side.

"This is Lucian, my son," Radu said, resting his hands upon Lucian's shoulders. Ioana was startled by this introduction. Radu had never before referred to her boy as his child.

Eva looked at the little boy with warmth. His deep brown eyes reminded her of Radu's, the son she had lost for so long, the son she had even mourned during all those years when they could not find him.

"Hello Lucian," Eva addressed the boy warmly. She struck up a conversation with him, asking him about what he liked to eat, his favorite color, his favorite stories. She avoided asking Lucian about his past. However, once she got the opportunity, she took her own son aside to ask him many poignant questions about his future. What were his plans? Did he intend to marry Ioana? How did he intend to take care of Lucian?

"We haven't worked it all out yet, Mom," Radu replied. "Ioana wants to stay with Lucian in Romania. Her parents might help her take care of him. But we haven't decided anything for sure."

Eva didn't seem too pleased with her son's noncommittal replies. "You have parents too, you know," she remarked. "And when you have a child, you better know how you're going to take care of him. There's no room for doubt."

"Don't you need to have a wife you love first?" Radu whispered, hoping that Ioana wouldn't overhear him.

Eva raised one eyebrow, as she did when she was delivering a lecture or being sarcastic. "You should have asked yourself that question ten years ago. Now it's too late. But it's not too late to ask yourself how you can be a responsible and loving father to your child."

"You mean her child?" Radu retorted, still in a whisper. As soon as he said this, however, he felt ashamed of his own cowardice. The life of flight, of constantly being pursued by spies and of spying, had shaped him into an emotional nomad, rooted nowhere and bound to no one. Which was something that his loyal, loving mother could not understand.

"Don't worry. We'll take care of Lucian somehow. Everything will be alright, Mom," he tried to comfort her vaguely. But Eva wasn't reassured. When will the shattered pieces of this family spread all over the world be made whole again? she wondered, her gaze surveying her family. When will her children learn a sense of responsibility and commitment to their loved ones? At that moment, she caught sight of Paul holding Irina tenderly, his arms wrapped around her shoulders, attempting to comfort her grief. No matter what Andrei might say, Eva thought, they seemed happy and in love. And wasn't that what mattered most?

Two days later, when the political unrest in the country had subsided and Irina and Paul were safely on a plane about to leave for New York City, Irina glanced at her grandmother's ring upon her finger.

"We'll return to Romania often," Paul reassured his fiancée, noticing her sadness. Irina recalled how she had heard that promise before, only now there were no more loving grandparents to visit and everything would change rapidly, perhaps even beyond recognition, in the country of her childhood. The communist pioneers; the discipline and the fear; the food lines and the countless daily struggles; the secrecy and the spying, might all soon become the stuff that history books and novels are made of. No doubt, she thought, the Romanian people would undergo radical transformations and face new struggles, finding unforeseen sources of suffering and hope in their efforts to give birth to a new democracy out of the ashes of totalitarianism.

Inspired by these thoughts, Irina turned to Paul and spoke with conviction: "I want our children to remember what it was like for tens of millions of people to live under communism. I don't want them to learn about life in Eastern Europe just from history books. For our family, it wasn't history or an abstraction. It was our daily life."

Never one to handle well heroism, sentimentality or inflated rhetoric—and, somehow, Irina had managed to successfully intertwine all three in her discourse--Paul replied rather casually to his girlfriend's prophetic announcement: "What children? You mean we're getting married? Since when?"

Irina fell from her soapbox: "Since you proposed to me!" she reminded him.

"Oh, I forgot," Paul quipped.

"Do you even have a clue what the wedding vows mean?" she quizzed him.

"Of course! I've been down the aisle before," he announced proudly.

"Are you ready to commit?" Irina double-checked.

"I told you I was."

"So then you're ready to love and respect me, through good times and through bad..." Irina recited, to jog his memory.

"I prefer the good times," Paul replied.

"For better or for worse..." she pursued.

"For better," he affirmed.

"In sickness and in health..."

"In health."

"As long as we both shall live, 'till death do us part," Irina concluded.

"Let's not exaggerate," Paul said, since talk of eternal commitment made him feel queasy, especially during take offs and landings.

As they embarked on their new life together in America, Irina no longer felt torn between her old life and the new one, between East and West, as she had when she left Romania as a child. This time she was carrying her past with her, in her memories and in her heart, hoping that some day she'd be able to convey to her children, and to her children's children, the lost traces of an era in which ordinary people were forced to lead extraordinary lives.

About the Author

Claudia Moscovici is the author of seven scholarly books on political philosophy and the Romantic movement, which include *Romanticism and Postromanticism* (Rowman and Littlefield, 2007), *Gender and Citizenship* (Rowman and Littlefield, 2000) and *Double Dialectics* (Rowman and Littlefield, 2002). She co-founded the international art movement called *postromanticism* with the Mexican sculptor Leonardo Pereznieto (postromanticism.com). She taught philosophy, literature and arts and ideas at Boston University and at the University of Michigan. She has also published poetry, short stories and essays in several literary magazines, including *Portland Magazine, Enigma Magazine, The Palo Alto Review, The Fairfield Review, WINGS, Outsider Ink, Nanny Fay Poetry Magazine, The Poetic Matrix, Three Cup Morning, Soul Fountain, Slate and Style* and *Möbius*. The painting featured on the cover is *Red*, by the postromantic artist Edson Campos.

www.ingramcontent.com/pod-product-compliance
Lightning Source LLC
Chambersburg PA
CBHW050612110726
47899CB00001B/73